TERMINAL
&
THE
SISTERHOOD

Colin Forbes writes a novel every year. For the past twenty-seven years he has earned his living solely as a full-time writer.

Forbes visits all the locations which will appear in a new novel. He says, 'It is essential for me to see for myself where the book will take place. Only in this way can I conjure up the unique atmosphere of the chosen locales.'

He has explored most of Western Europe, the east and west coasts of America, and has made excursions to Africa and Asia. Each new book appears on all major bestsellers lists. He is translated into thirty languages.

Surveys have shown his readership is divided equally between women and men.

COLIN FORBES

TERMINAL
&
THE
SISTERHOOD

PAN BOOKS

Terminal first published 1984 by William Collins.
First published by Pan Books 1985
The Sisterhood first published 1988 by Macmillan.
First published by Pan Books 1998

This omnibus edition published 2005 by Pan Books
an imprint of Pan Macmillan Ltd
Pan Macmillan, 20 New Wharf Road, London N1 9RR
Basingstoke and Oxford
Associated companies throughout the world
www.panmacmillan.com

ISBN 0 330 44094 2

1 3 5 7 9 8 6 4 2

A CIP catalogue record for this book is available from
the British Library.

Printed and bound in Great Britain by
Mackays of Chatham plc, Chatham, Kent

TERMINAL

For Jane –
who holds the fort

Author's Note

Swiss clinics are among the finest and most advanced medical establishments in the world. They provide a standard of care without equal. The Berne Clinic, which plays a prominent part in this novel, does not exist. All characters are creatures of the author's imagination.

terminal – most concise form of an expression; fatal illness; point of connexion in electric circuit; railway or airway terminus . . .

The Concise Oxford Dictionary

Prologue

No night should have been as cold as this one. No woman should have to endure what Hannah Stuart endured. She ran screaming down the snowbound slope – screaming when she wasn't choking and coughing her lungs out. Behind her she heard the snarling and barking of the ferocious Doberman dogs coming closer.

Wearing only a nightdress, over which she had thrown her fur coat, her feet shod in rubber-heeled sensible shoes which gripped the treacherous ground, she stumbled on towards the wire fence surrounding the place. As she ran, she tore the 'thing' off her face and head, dropping it as she took in great gulps of icy air.

The night was dark but the whiteness of the snow showed her where she was going. Another few hundred yards and she would reach the fence which bordered the highway, the outside world – freedom. Now she could breathe the night air she wondered if it were even worse than the 'thing' she had discarded. With the temperature below zero it was like breathing in liquid ice.

'Oh, my God, no!' she gasped.

Something had landed just ahead of her, a shell-like projectile which quietly burst with a hissing sound. Desperately she tried to hold her breath while she ran through what billowed ahead. It was impossible. She absorbed more lungfuls of the filthy stuff and started choking again.

Behind the dogs they had released ran men in military-style uniforms, their heads and faces hideously disfigured by weird apparatus. Hannah Stuart didn't look back, didn't see them – she just knew they were coming for her.

At the point she was heading for a large wire gate bisected the fence. It was closed but she knew that under her feet lay the snow-covered road leading to that gate. It made her progress faster – such as it was. Still choking, she reached the gate, her hands clawing at the wire as she struggled to haul it open.

If only a car would come up the highway, if only the driver saw her. If only she could get this god-damned gate to open she might even survive. So many 'if's . . .' The panic she fought to hold in check was welling up. Frantically, she stared up and down the deserted road for sight of a pair of headlights. In the dark nothing moved. Except the dogs which were nearly on top of her and the men who, fanned out in an arc military fashion, came up behind the animals.

She gave one last choking gulp. Her hands, bleeding now as she went on clawing at the gate, lost their grip. Smears of red blood coated the ice-encrusted gate as she slipped down, and then fell the last few feet. The iron-hard ground smashed her face a savage blow.

She was dead when they reached her, eyes sightless, her complexion already showing signs of cyanosis poisoning. Two men with a stretcher took her back up the slope. The dogs were leashed. One man took out a piece of surgical gauze to remove all traces of blood from the gate, then followed his companions.

This was in Switzerland in the year 1984. On the gate a metal plate carried an engraved legend. *KLINIK BERN. Wachthund!* BERNE CLINIC. Guard Dog!

Chapter One

Tucson, Arizona. 10 February 1984. 75°

A sizzling tremor of heat haze. In the shimmer the harsh, jagged Tucson Mountains seemed to vibrate. Behind the wheel of her Jaguar, newly imported from England, Dr Nancy Kennedy let her frustration rip, ramming down on the accelerator.

Expertly, she corrected a rear wheel skid as she swung off Interstate Highway 10 and headed up the hairpin bends towards Gates Pass. Her passenger alongside her, Bob Newman, did not appreciate the experience. Clouds of dust from the road enveloped them and he began choking. He felt like yelling – even screaming.

'Do you have to drive your latest toy as though you're racing at Brands Hatch?' he enquired.

'Typical British understatement?' she asked.

'Typical American way of handling a new car. You're supposed to run it in,' he commented.

'That's what I'm doing . . .'

'What you're doing is ripping the guts out of it. Just because you're worried about your grandfather in that Swiss clinic you don't have to kill us . . .'

'I sometimes wonder why I got engaged to an Englishman,' Nancy snapped.

'You couldn't resist me. Christ, it's hot . . .'

Newman, forty years old, had thick, sandy-coloured hair, cynical blue eyes of a man who has seen too much of the seamy side of the world, a strong nose and jaw and a firm mouth with a droll, humorous expression. He knew it was 75°: he had seen the temperature register on a digital sign outside a bank as they left Tucson. He wore fawn slacks, an open-necked white shirt and his jacket with a small check design was folded in his lap. He was already sweating profusely. The dust was adhering to the sweat. It was eleven o'clock in the morning and they had just finished one row. Maybe it was time for another. He risked it.

'Nancy, if you want to check on why your grandfather was rushed off by air to that place in Switzerland you're going the wrong way. This road does *not* lead to the Berne Clinic . . .'

'Oh, shit!'

She rammed her foot on the brake and he would have gone through the windscreen but for the fact they both wore safety belts. A second earlier she had swung off the road into a lay-by. Flinging open the door, she stormed out of the car and stood with her back to him, arms folded, standing by a low wall.

He sighed. She had, of course, left the engine running. Turning off the ignition, he pocketed the keys and joined her, his jacket over one arm. He studied her out of the corner of his eye.

Twenty-nine years old, Nancy Kennedy was at her most attractive in a rage. Her smooth skin was flushed, her raven hair falling to her shoulders. He loved exploring that dense mane of hair, soothing the back of her neck, and then nothing could stop them.

Five feet eight, four inches shorter than Newman, she had legs your fingers itched to stroke and a figure which caused all men's eyes to stare when they walked into a restaurant. Angry, she tilted her head, emphasizing her superb bone structure, high cheekbones and pointed chin expressing self-will.

It constantly amazed him. He had seen her in a white coat practising her profession, supremely competent and self-controlled – but in her private life Nancy had the temper of a she-devil. Often he suspected it was the contrast which attracted him – apart from her physical assets.

'What does the famous foreign correspondent have in mind?' she enquired bitingly.

'Looking for facts – evidence – instead of flying off into the wild blue yonder . . .' He looked at the staggering view and corrected his description. 'The dirty grey yonder . . .'

Beyond the wall the road began to descend again in an even more terrifying series of twists and bends. Beyond that it looked like the mountains of Hell – a pile of gigantic cinder cones without a trace of green vegetation on the scarred rock faces.

'We were going to have a lovely day at the Desert Museum,' she pouted. 'They have a beaver lodge

7

underground. You can go down a staircase and see the beavers nestled in the lodge . . .'

'And all the time you'll be worrying and talking about Jesse Kennedy . . .'

'He raised me after my mother and father were killed in a car crash. I don't like the way Linda secretly had him moved to Switzerland while I was at St Thomas's in London. There's an odd smell about the whole business . . .'

'I don't like Linda,' he remarked.

'You like her legs – you never stop looking at them . . .'

'I'm a connoisseur of good legs. Yours are almost as good . . .'

She thumped him, turned round and leaned against the wall, her expression serious. 'Bob, I really am worried. Linda could have phoned me when they diagnosed leukaemia. She had my number. I'm not happy at all. She may be my older sister but she's no right to take the law into her own hands. Then there's her husband, Harvey . . .'

'Don't like Harvey either,' he said easily, twirling an unlit cigarette in his mouth. 'You realize the only way to check this? Not that I think for a moment there's anything wrong – but you won't settle until I convince you . . .'

'So, convince me, Mr World Foreign Correspondent who speaks five languages fluently.'

'We proceed systematically as though I was checking out a big story. You're a doctor and a close relative of the man we're enquiring about – so the right people will have to talk to me as long as you're present. The family doctor is on my list – but first we interview the specialist who took the blood tests that showed it was leukaemia. Where do we find him?'

'A man called Buhler at Tucson Medical Center. It's in the city. I insisted on Linda telling me all the details – I say *insisted* because I had to drag the information out of her . . .'

'Doesn't prove a thing,' Newman commented. 'Knowing you're a doctor she might have been worried she hadn't done it your way. She might also have resented your questioning . . .'

'We seem to be doing it backwards,' she objected. 'I can't see why you don't talk to Linda first, then our doctor, then the specialist at the Center . . .'

'Deliberately backwards. That way we get testimony and check what the others say later. It's the only technique which will show up any discrepancies. I still think it's a wild-goose chase but . . .' He spread his hands. '. . . I just want to settle your mind and then we can get on with living.'

'It's queer – Linda not phoning me while I was doing my post-graduate work at St Thomas's . . .'

'You said that before. Let's get some action. Specifically, let's get to the Center before Buhler goes to lunch. And no argument – I'm driving. Hop in the passenger seat . . .'

*

'Didn't you know, Nancy? No, of course not – you were away in London when Buhler was killed . . .'

They were at the Center talking to a slim man of fifty wearing a sweat shirt and slacks. Dr Rosen had taken them to his private office and Newman sat watching him and drinking coffee. Rosen had an alert, professional manner and was clearly glad to help Nancy in any way he could.

'How was he killed?' Newman asked casually.

'*Killed* was perhaps the wrong word . . .'

'But it was the word you used,' Newman pointed out. 'Maybe you could fill us in on the details. I'm sure Nancy would appreciate that . . .'

Dr Rosen hesitated. He stroked his thinning hair with his right hand as though searching for the right words to express himself. Newman frowned at Nancy who was about to say something and she remained silent.

'It was *very* tragic. He went off the road near Gates Pass in his new Mercedes. He was DOA when we got him back here . . .'

'He must have earned a lot of money to afford a Mercedes,' Newman remarked.

'He told me he got lucky during the one trip he made to Vegas. He was that kind of man, Mr Newman – if he made a killing . . . I'm using that word again – don't read any significance into it. What I'm saying is, if Buhler came into a lot of money he would hang on to it.'

'You said "very tragic" and I noticed you emphasized the first word. He had a family?'

Rosen swivelled in his chair, gazed out of the
window and then turned back to face Newman who
had the impression Rosen was uncomfortable about
the subject of their conversation. Clasping his hands,
he leaned forward across his desk and looked at both
his visitors.

'Buhler went off that road at speed because he was
drunk. It was a shock to all of us because we'd never
suspected he was an alcoholic . . .'

'Driving off a road when you've had one too many
doesn't make you an alcoholic,' Newman pressed.
'Why not complete the story?'

'Buhler had no family, wasn't married – except to
his job. He had no relatives we were able to trace.
When the police checked his home they found
cupboards stacked with empty bottles of whisky. The
evidence was conclusive – he'd been a secret drinker.
That's why I said very tragic . . .'

'And he *was* the specialist who checked my grandfather's blood sample and diagnosed leukaemia?'
Nancy interjected.

'That's correct. Young Dr Chase brought them in
himself for Buhler to check. Unfortunately, there was
no doubt about it – if that's what you're wondering,
Nancy.'

'I wasn't wondering that – why this Dr Chase? For
years our doctor has been Bellman . . .'

'All this has to be in confidence, Nancy. Some of it I'm only telling you because of our long acquaintance – and to put your mind at rest about Jesse being sent to that clinic in Switzerland. Mrs Wayne changed your doctor – she never liked Bellman. Said she preferred someone younger . . .'

'Linda chose this Dr Chase!' Nancy's tone expressed near amazement. 'Someone entirely new – and young – advised her to shuttle Jesse off to Europe?'

'Well . . .' Rosen hesitated again, glancing at Newman, who gazed back with no particular expression. 'Frank Chase has gone up like a rocket – he's very popular. My guess is he'll soon have a string of wealthy patients. He has a way with . . . people.'

'The records,' Nancy persisted, 'the blood samples Buhler took to check my grandfather. They're here at the hospital?'

'They were destroyed . . .'

'That's not right,' Nancy protested.

'Wait a minute. Please!' Rosen held up a placating hand. 'Let me finish. Buhler was an eccentric. As I told you, he lived for his work. He had a habit of carrying his files round with him so he could study them whenever he felt like it. They were inside the car when he went over the edge. There was a partial fire – all his records were incinerated . . .'

'How young is this Dr Frank Chase?' Newman enquired.

'Thirty-two. He still has a long way to go to get to

the top of the tree, if that's what you were wondering. But he's climbing.'

'Could we have Dr Chase's address?' Newman asked.

'Sure. He's out on Sabino Canyon Road.'

'Very nice, too,' Nancy commented. 'Skyline Country Club territory. Linda is practically his neighbour if he's far enough out.'

Rosen said nothing as he took a pad and wrote carefully in a fine Italian script. Newman read the address upside down and for a member of the medical profession it was surprisingly legible. Something in Rosen's attitude puzzled him: the doctor had given Newman several close scrutinies as though trying to make up his mind about something, an aspect which was bothering him. He tore off the sheet, folded it neatly and handed it to Newman – which caused Nancy to raise her eyebrows.

He stood up and came round his desk to shake hands and escort them to the door, opening it to let Nancy leave first. His handclasp was warm and reassuring.

'I really don't think you have anything to worry about,' he told her. 'The Swiss are very good . . .'

He waited until Newman was half way along the corridor leading to the exit before he called him back. Newman told Nancy he would be with her in a minute and to wait in the car. Rosen closed the door once the Englishman was inside his office. He handed him a visiting card.

'That has my phone number here and at home. Could I meet with you this evening? Just the two of us over a drink for half an hour? Do you know the Tack Room?'

'Nancy took me there.' He slipped the card inside his wallet. 'It's a nice place . . .'

'MOBIL give it a five-star rating. Seven o'clock? Good. Maybe considerate not to mention this to Nancy. A few weeks before Jesse was shunted out of Tucson, we had an eminent Swiss medical personality here on a tour of the States. Linda, Nancy's sister, attended one of his lectures.'

'Any significance in that?'

'He happens to be head of the Berne Clinic . . .'

Chapter Two

'Where the hell have you been, Nancy?' Newman demanded. 'I've sat here roasting in your Jag. for exactly forty-three minutes. At least I've got the smell of that place out of my system . . .'

'And how long were *you* with Rosen?' she flared. 'I might have sat here waiting forty-three minutes for you . . .'

'Three minutes,' snapped Newman.

'Well, how was I to know? I popped into another department to see an old friend and she had a lot to tell me. I've been away at St Thomas's for a year in case you've forgotten. And do you mind getting out of the driving seat?'

'I'm driving . . .'

He inserted the ignition keys and switched on the engine. She said something under her breath and her classic, pleated skirt swept high up her long legs as she sat in the passenger seat and slammed the door. She asked the question as he drove smoothly out of the Medical Center.

'What smell were you referring to – the one you got out of your system?'

'Disinfectant. Hospital disinfectant . . .'

'You hate anything medical, don't you? I can't imagine what you ever saw in me the night we first met in that place in Walton Street. Bewick's, wasn't it?'

'My favourite London restaurant. And I saw your lovely legs. You display them frequently . . .'

'*Bastard!*' She thumped his shoulder. 'What did Rosen want to tell you that was too spicy for my delicate ears?'

'With my not being a doctor, being British, he wanted to emphasize the conversation had been strictly confidential. He's a careful type, very ethical and all that. Now, guide me to the mansion of Dr Frank Chase . . .'

Holding the slip of paper Rosen had given Newman in her hands and staring straight ahead, Nancy spoke only to give directions. Sabino Canyon Road starts in a well-populated area on the north-east outskirts of Tucson heading for the Catalina Mountains. It starts as a district for the well-off and progresses up the canyon into an oasis for the wealthy.

Newman noted the houses were getting bigger, the grounds more extensive, and again ahead the mountains danced in the heat dazzle. But the Tucson range was like a series of gigantic, broken-backed dinosaurs turned into rock. Like the Skyline Country Club, the Catalinas were opulent, welcoming and had vegetation.

He accelerated past the Wayne property in case Linda happened to be looking out of a window. Nancy glanced at him with a hint of amusement.

'Why the sudden burst of enthusiasm?'

'So Linda can't phone Chase and warn him we're coming.'

'Robert, you never miss a trick,' she needled him.

She always called him Robert when she was either annoyed or wanted to get under his skin, knowing he disliked his Christian name. He parried the thrust by grinning and not replying. The Jag. went on climbing and behind them the city of Tucson spread out in the bowl formed by three separate mountain ranges.

'Slow down, Bob,' she warned, 'we're close now. That place on the left must be Chase . . .'

A split rail fence enclosed the property, a large, L-shaped house with two storeys and a green pantile roof. Newman drove through the open gateway and along the drive which divided – one arm leading to the front porch, the second to the double garage at the side of the house. The wheels crunched as they pulled up.

In front of the house the 'garden' was a generous stretch of gravel out of which grew evil-looking saguaro cacti. Shaped like trees, they had a main trunk from which sprouted prickly branches stretching up towards the sky as though trying to claw it down. A man standing by the double garage pressed a button and Newman, who had switched off the engine, heard the purr of power-operated doors closing over the garage. In the wing mirror he watched the man approaching with a wary tread.

Thirty-two, Rosen had said. The man wore tight blue jeans and an open-necked shirt with a large check design. His face was bony, the skin tanned under a mop of thick brown hair. Seeing only that much in the mirror, Newman took an instant dislike to him. He looked up as the man put a long-fingered hand on the door top. Manicured nails and a strong whiff of after-shave lotion.

'Dr Frank Chase?'

'Yes.'

The word hung in the hot air like a challenge and the brown eyes which stared down at Newman measured him for the operating table. Newman smiled amiably and said the one thing which he thought would throw Chase off balance.

'I don't think you've met Dr Nancy Kennedy. Sister of Linda Wayne. Grand-daughter of Jesse Kennedy. She's about to launch an investigation into why her grandfather was hustled off five-and-a-half thousand miles away without consulting her. This is a lovely place you've got here, Dr Chase.'

'Miss Kennedy, I'm afraid there was no question your grandfather was suffering from leukaemia ...' Dr Chase laid a thin, bony hand on the arm of the reclining chair Nancy sat in at the rear of the house by the side of the oyster-shell-shaped swimming pool. His smile was sympathetic but Newman observed the smile did not reach the brown eyes which studied her. 'You see,' Chase continued, 'we had the top specialist in the state examine him. Dr Buhler . . .'

'Who conveniently died in a car accident,' Nancy interrupted him coldly. 'And even more conveniently had the records of those tests with him so they now no longer exist. The only real evidence, when you get to the bottom line, that he has this disease.'

'*Conveniently*?' Chase's smile became a little tight. 'I don't quite follow.' His hand clasped Nancy's gently. Here we go with the famous bedside manner, Newman thought as he stretched in his own chair and sipped his glass of bourbon. 'Dr Kennedy,' Chase continued more formally, 'I do realize you must be overwrought. You were fond of your grandfather . . .'

'I *am* fond of my grandfather . . .'

She pulled her hand free and swallowed a large gulp of her own drink. Newman stood up and eased his shoulders as though stiff from sitting. He grinned as Chase glanced up at him sharply.

'Mind if I just wander round your place?' he suggested. 'I'll leave you and Nancy to talk this thing out alone.'

'That might be a very good idea,' Chase agreed. 'Feel free . . .'

The obligatory swimming pool and its surrounding patio were tiled with marble. The walls of the house were plaster painted a dark sludge green. The picture windows looking down on Tucson were huge and triple plate glass doors slid open on to the patio. As he wandered towards the side of the house Newman peered inside.

The largest hi-fi system he had ever seen occupied the end wall of the sitting-room. The rest of the furniture reeked of money. He looked back before he disappeared round the garage end of the house and Chase had his back to him, crouched forward as he spoke earnestly to Nancy, whose expression was blank as she listened.

It intrigued Newman that Chase's first action on seeing them arrive had been to close the garage. He may well have recognized Nancy – the Wayne house was full of photographs of her with Linda. His shirt stuck to his back as he shuffled quietly over the gravel which had a gritty feel that seemed to compound the heat.

Holding his glass in one hand, he lifted the lid of the control box attached to the wall. Two buttons, one green, one red. He pressed green. The same purring sound of highly efficient – and expensive – hydraulics as the doors elevated. He stood staring at the occupants. One red Ferrari. One red Maserati. Blood-red. Very new. A small fortune on eight wheels.

'You're interested in cars, Mr Newman?'

'I'm a car buff, Chase. So, apparently, are you,' Newman said easily.

The doctor had come after him silent as a cat. Even the sneakers he wore should have made some sound on the gravel. He stood looking at Newman and the smile was gone. His right hand held a refilled glass of bourbon. He swallowed half the contents in one gulp and wiped his mouth with the back of his other hand.

'You usually go creeping round people's homes, prying? That's the foreign correspondent coming out, I guess. Incidentally, I understood you and Nancy were engaged – but I notice no ring on the third finger of her left hand . . .'

Newman grinned amiably. He made a throwaway gesture with his hand. Chase did not respond. His mouth twisted in a faint sneer, he waited, his head tilted forward. Newman put a cigarette in his mouth before replying.

'Let's take that lot in sequence, shall we? You have something to hide because you can afford a couple of brand new sports jobs?'

'I don't like your tone . . .'

'I'm not crazy about yours, but as long as enough rich patients continue to love you what does it matter? As to Nancy, we have a trial engagement . . .'

'I'd just as soon you didn't light that cigarette, Newman. You should read the statistics . . .'

'You think I'll pollute the atmosphere out here?' Newman lit the cigarette. 'Did you know that in Britain a lot of doctors have given up smoking and preach the gospel? Did you also know that the graph showing the degree of alcoholism among British doctors shows a steady climb.' Newman glanced at Chase's glass. 'You should read the statistics.'

'I've heard of trial marriages . . .' Chase's sneer became more pronounced. 'But a trial engagement is a new sexual exercise . . .'

'So, I've broadened your experience. Hello, Nancy. I think we ought to leave now – unless you have more questions for your friendly family doctor . . .'

Tight-lipped, Nancy waited until they were driving back along Sabino Canyon Road before she spoke. Extracting the cigarette from Newman's mouth, she took a few puffs and handed it back to him. He knew then she was in a towering rage.

'The condescending bastard! God knows what Linda sees in a man like that. Our previous doctor, Bellman, is a nice man.'

'I've nothing against Frank Chase,' Newman remarked airily as he swung round a bend. 'He's a hyena – scooping up red meat wherever he can find it, holding rich old ladies by the hand as they tell him about their imaginary ailments. That doesn't make him a conspirator. Your sister's place next? I'd like to talk to her on her home ground rather than at the Smugglers Inn. In people's homes you see them as they really are. The other night when she brought Harvey over for dinner at my hotel she put on an act. Her public image.'

'Do you know the one thing Chase didn't suggest when we were out by the pool – the one thing he should have suggested if he had really wanted me reassured about Jesse?'

'Oddly enough, as I wasn't there all the time, I don't know.'

'He never suggested that we visit the Berne Clinic so I could see Jesse for myself. And yes, I think you should talk to Linda. I'll leave you alone. Mind she doesn't seduce you . . .'

'It all started when Jesse – we all called him that – had a bad fall from his horse, Bob . . .' The large dark eyes stared at Newman, the long lashes half-closed demurely over them. 'You do prefer to be called Bob, don't you? Nancy calls you Robert when she wants to make you mad. My kid sister is full of little tricks like that. Is that the way you like your tea? Have I got it right?'

Linda Wayne sat beside Newman on the couch, her long legs sheathed in the sheerest black nylon and crossed with her skirt just above her shapely knees. She wore a high-necked cashmere sweater which emphasized her full figure . When she had shown him into the vast living-room her right breast had briefly touched his forearm. He had felt the firmness under the cashmere, a material quite unsuited to the temperature outside but perfect for the stark coolness of the air-conditioning.

Her hair was jet black, thick and shoulder-length like Nancy's. Thick, dark eyebrows made her slow-moving eyes seem even larger. Her voice was husky and she exuded sexuality like a heavy perfume. Newman stopped himself gazing at the sweep of her legs and tried to recall what she had just said.

'Your tea,' she repeated, 'is it the right colour?'

'Perfect . . .'

'It's Earl Grey. I bought it in San Francisco. I just love your English teas. We drink a lot of tea in the States now . . .'

'But you don't ride horses much down here any more.' He swallowed a gulp of the tea quickly. He hated Earl Grey. 'So what was Jesse doing on a horse?'

'He rode every day like they used to years ago, Bob. We put him to bed upstairs and called the doctor . . .'

'Frank Chase?'

'That's right . . .' She had paused briefly before she replied. She began talking more quickly. 'Bellman, our previous doctor, was getting out of touch with modern developments. I thought a younger man would be more likely to move with the times. It's a good job I took that decision – he gave Jesse a thorough examination, including blood tests. That's how we found out Jesse was suffering from leuk-aemia. You can imagine the shock . . .' She moved closer to him and clasped his free hand. She looked very soulful.

'It was a very big jump,' he said.

She looked puzzled, wary. 'Bob, I'm not following you . . .'

'From Tucson, Arizona to Berne, Switzerland.'

'Oh, I see what you mean.' She relaxed, gave him a warm smile. 'Jesse was a mountaineer. He liked Switzerland. He discussed it with Frank – Dr Chase. He simply acceded to my grandfather's expressed wish, bearing in mind the patient's best interests . . .'

'Come again? No, forget it. No thanks, no more tea.'

He simply acceded to my grandfather's expressed wish, bearing in mind the patient's best interests.

Linda's dialogue had suddenly gone wrong – she would normally never talk like that. But Frank Chase would. It confirmed what Newman had expected to happen. During the time between driving away from Chase's place down Sabino Canyon Road to Linda's home the hyena had called Linda to report their visit – to instruct her.

She squeezed his hand gently to get his full attention and began talking again in her soft, soothing voice. 'Bob, I'd like you to do everything you can to settle my kid sister's mind. There's nothing she can do about Jesse except worry . . .'

'The kid sister can fly to Berne to find out what the hell is really going on . . .' Nancy stood in the open doorway, her manner curt, her tone biting. 'And when you've finished with it you might give Bob back his hand – he's only got two of them . . .'

'Nancy, there's simply nothing to go on,' Newman said emphatically. 'As a professional newspaper man

I look for *facts* when I'm after a story – *evidence*! There isn't any showing something's wrong . . .'

It was mid-afternoon and they were eating a late lunch at the Smugglers Inn where he had insisted on staying. It gave him independence and kept Linda Wayne at arm's length. Nancy slammed down her fork beside her half-eaten steak.

'Fact One. Nobody asked for a second opinion . . .'

'Buhler, who did the blood tests, was tops according to Rosen. I gather you respect Rosen?'

'Yes, I do. Let that one slide, for the moment. Fact Two. I never heard Jesse say a word about he wished he could live in Switzerland. Visit it, yes! But God, he was always so glad to get back home.'

'When a man is ill, he dreams, to blot out reality . . .'

'Fact Three!' Nancy drummed on. 'At the very moment Jesse is ill because he falls off his horse Linda calls in an entirely new doctor. Fact Four! The only man who can confirm this diagnosis of leukaemia, Buhler, is dead. And his records go up in smoke with him! So everything rests on Dr Chase's word, a man you called a hyena . . .'

'I didn't like him. That doesn't make him Genghis Khan. Look, I'm seeing Rosen this evening. If nothing comes of that, can we drop the subject? I have to decide whether to accept this pretty lucrative offer from CBS to act as their European correspondent. They won't wait forever for a decision . . .'

'You want the job?' she interjected.

'It's the only way we can get married – unless you agree that we both live in London or somewhere in Europe . . .'

'I've given up years of my life to practise medicine and I want to live in the States. I'd feel lost and marooned anywhere else. And, Bob, I *am* going to Berne. The question is – are you coming with me? There might even be a big story in it . . .'

'Look, Nancy, I write about espionage, foreign affairs. Where in God's name is there that kind of story in this Berne business?'

'You've been there. You've done your job there. You speak all the languages – French, German, Italian, plus Spanish. You told me you have friends there. The bottom line is, are you going to help me?'

'I'll decide after I've seen Rosen . . .'

'Bob, what does a woman take off first? Her earrings, isn't it?' She divested herself of each gold earring slowly, watching him with a certain expression. 'Let's go to your room . . .'

'I haven't finished my steak.' He pushed his plate away and grinned. 'It's underdone, anyway. I've just lost my appetite.'

'You ordered your steak rare. The experience I'm offering is rare too . . .'

Chapter Three

The slim, attractive Swissair stewardess in her pale blue uniform noticed this passenger the moment he came aboard Flight SR 111, bound for Geneva and Zurich. She escorted the man, over six feet tall and heavily-built, to his reserved first-class window seat and tried to help him take off his shaggy sheepskin jacket.

'I can do it myself . . .'

His voice was gravelly, the tone curt. He handed her the jacket, settled himself in his seat and fastened the belt. He inserted a cigarette between his wide, thick lips and stared out into the darkness. The flight was due to depart at 18.55.

As the stewardess arranged his jacket carefully on a hanger she studied him. In his early fifties, she estimated. A dense thatch of white hair streaked with black, heavy, dark eyebrows and a craggy face. Clean-shaven, his complexion was flushed with the bitter wind which sheared the streets of New York. His large, left hand clutched a brief-case perched on the adjoining seat. She straightened her trim jacket before approaching him.

'I'm very sorry, sir, but no smoking is permitted . . .'

'I haven't lit the damned thing, have I! I am very familiar with the regulations. No smoking before the words up there say so . . .'

'I'm sorry, sir . . .'

She retreated, carrying on with her duties automatically as the Jumbo 747 took off and headed out across the Atlantic, her mind full of the tall American passenger. It was the blue eyes which worried her, she decided. They reminded her of that very special glacial blue you only saw in mountain lakes.

'Thinking about your boy friend?' one of her companion stewardesses enquired while they sorted out the drink orders.

'The passenger in Seat Five. He fascinates me. Have you noticed his eyes? They're chilling . . .'

The white-haired man was sipping bitter lemon, staring out of the porthole window, when a hand lifted the brief-case off the seat next to him and dumped it in his lap. He glanced sideways as a small, bird-like man with restless eyes settled into the seat and began talking chirpily, keeping his voice low.

'Well, if it isn't my old pal, Lee Foley. Off to Zurich on more Company business?'

'Ed Schulz, go back to your own seat.'

'It's a free country, a free aircraft – just so long

as you've paid. And I've paid. You didn't answer my question. The senior roving foreign affairs correspondent for *Time* magazine always gets answers to his questions. You should know that by now, Lee . . .'

'I quit the CIA and you know it. I'm with one of the top international detective agencies in New York. You know that, too. End of conversation.'

'Let's develop this thing a bit . . .'

'Let's not. ' Foley leaned across Schulz. 'Stewardess, could I have a word?' He produced two airline tickets from his breast pocket as the girl bent forward attentively. 'I've reserved both these seats. These tickets say so. Could you kindly have this intruder removed? He's trying to sell me something.'

He settled back in his seat, slipped the tickets she had looked at into his pocket and resumed his gaze out into the night. His whole manner indicated *the matter is settled, no more to say.*

'I'm afraid this seat is reserved,' the girl told Schulz. 'If you could return to your own seat maybe I could bring you something more to drink?'

'Another large whisky.' Schulz, his normal chirpiness deserting him, stood up and glanced at the back of Foley's head. 'See you in Zurich. *Pal!*' He walked off down the gangway.

'I hope that man didn't disturb you, sir,' the stewardess who had originally shown him to his seat said to Foley.

'You did the job,' he said without looking at her.

Shaken, Schulz sagged into his aisle seat and realized he was sweating. Ice-cold bastard! He mopped his damp forehead, adjusted his tie and glanced at the blonde creature alongside him. She gave him the same warm, welcoming smile he had experienced when he first sat down.

Forty years old, he guessed. Wedding ring on her finger. The right age – Schulz was forty-five. Once they got away from their husbands they were ready for a little dalliance. He hoped she was going all the way to Zurich. He hoped she'd go all the way with him! The unspoken joke felt a little sour. It was the encounter with Foley. He thanked the stewardess for the fresh drink and memories drifted through his mind.

Lee Foley. Executioner for the CIA. They shied away from that word. Special operative was the euphemism. The rumoured body count down to Foley's expertise was as high as twenty-five men – and women. Now the story was he had quit the CIA and was working for CIDA – the Continental International Detective Agency. Schulz thought he might radio a cryptic signal to the Zurich office to have a man waiting to follow Foley. He'd think about it when his nerves settled. He turned to the blonde woman.

'Going on to Zurich, I hope? I'm Ed Schulz of *Time* magazine. I know a nice little restaurant in Zurich, the Veltliner Keller . . .'

*

No memories drifted through the mind of Lee Foley. He refused dinner and ordered more bitter lemon. Not from virtue, he seldom touched alcohol – it clouded the mind, slowed down the reflexes. How many people who used it as a pick-me-up realized it was a depressant? Cigarettes and the occasional woman were his relaxations. They had to be classy women and definitely not professionals. This thought triggered off another one.

'When I have to buy it I'll hang up my boots . . .'

Some Brit. had used that phrase when they were passing a brothel on the Reeperbahn in Hamburg. Bob Newman, foreign correspondent. The guy who had recently broken the Kruger case in Germany and earned himself another cluster of laurels. Now Ed Schulz could never have come within a mile of cracking that espionage classic. He wondered where Newman was tonight – and immediately pushed the irrelevant thought out of his head.

'Maximize your concentration,' was one of Foley's favourite phrases. 'And *wait* – forever if need be – until the conditions are right . . .'

Foley was waiting now, eyes half-closed in an apparent doze as he observed the progress of dinner round Ed Schulz's seat. The conditions were right now he decided as coffee was served. He felt inside the little pocket he had unzipped earlier and squeezed a single soluble capsule from the polythene envelope.

Standing up, he strolled along the corridor to where two stewards cluttered the aisle next to Schulz whose head was turned away as he talked to his travelling companion. He held a balloon glass of Rémy Martin in the accepted manner, fingers splayed, and in front of him was a cup of black coffee which had just been poured.

Foley nudged the nearest steward's elbow with his left hand. As the man turned Foley flicked the capsule neatly into Schulz's cup. Alcoholic fumes drifted in the air, no one noticed a thing. Foley shook his head apologetically at the steward and went back to his seat.

He checked his watch. Another six hours to Geneva. After he'd drunk his coffee laced with the special barbiturate Schulz would sleep for eight hours. He'd stagger off the plane at its ultimate destination, Zurich. He wouldn't even notice an unfamiliar taste. And many times in his apartment Foley had practised the quick flip with his thumbnail, spinning capsule into empty cup.

Foley had bamboozled Schulz earlier when he had displayed two tickets for Zurich in front of him to the stewardess. At the check-in counter he'd told the girl to put Geneva tickets on his baggage. Whenever he was travelling, Foley always booked ahead of his real destination – or followed a devious route, changing aircraft. He glanced round before extracting the documents from his brief-case. He wouldn't be disturbed again tonight.

The night flight had reached the stage he knew so well. All the passengers were sleepy – or asleep, lulled by the monotonous and steady vibrations of the machine's great engines. He refused a pillow offered by a stewardess and opened the brief-case.

In the last few hours since the surprise phone call to CIDA his feet had hardly touched the ground. He had the typed record of his long phone conversation with Fordham at the American Embassy in Berne. It was headed, *Case of Hannah Stuart, deceased, patient at Berne Clinic, Thun.*

Nothing in the typed record indicated that Fordham was military attaché at the American Embassy. His eyes dropped to the comment at the end of the record.

We are extremely worried about the possible implications on the international situation about rumoured events and situation at this medical establishment.

Foley opened a large-scale map of Switzerland and concentrated on the Berne canton. His finger traced the motorway from the city of Berne running southeast to the town of Thun. In either Geneva or Berne he'd have to hire a car. He was certain he was going to need wheels for this job.

Chapter Four

Gmund, Austria. 10 February 1984. 1°

For Manfred Seidler, thousands of miles east of
Tucson and New York, the day dawned far more
grimly. The Renault station wagon was still inside
Czechoslovakia as it moved swiftly towards the lonely
frontier crossing point into Austria at Gmund – now
less than two kilometres ahead. He glanced at the
driver beside him, sixty-year-old Franz Oswald who,
with his lined, leathery face and bushy moustache,
looked seventy.

Seidler checked his watch. 6.25 a.m. Outside it was
night and the deserted, snowbound fields stretched
away into nothing. Despite the car heater it was cold
but Seidler was used to cold. It was Oswald's nerve
which bothered him.

'Slow down,' he snapped, 'we're nearly there. We
don't want them to think we're trying to crash the
border – to wake them up . . .'

'We mustn't be late.' Oswald reduced speed and
then confirmed Seidler's anxiety. 'Let's pull up for a
second. I could do with a nip of Schnapps from my
flask to get us through . . .'

'No! They mustn't smell drink on your breath. Any

little delay and they may make a thorough search.
And leave all the talking to me . . .'

'Supposing they have changed the guard earlier,
Seidler? If fresh men are on duty . . .'

'They never change their routine.'

He replied curtly, forced himself to sound confident. He glanced again at Old Franz – he always
thought of him as old. Oswald's chin was grizzled
and unshaven. But Seidler needed him on these trips
because Oswald carried frequent *legal* supplies over
the border. To the men at the frontier post he was
familiar. Just as the vehicle was a familiar sight. Now
they could see the distant guard-post.

'Headlights full on,' Seidler ordered. The old boy
was losing his grip – he had forgotten the signal to
Jan. 'Dip them,' he snapped.

The stench of fear polluted the chilly atmosphere
inside the Renault. Seidler could smell the driver's
armpit sweat, a sour odour. Beads of perspiration
began to form on the old man's forehead. Seidler
wished to God Franz hadn't made that remark that
they might have changed the guard earlier.

If the car was searched he could end up in Siberia.
No! It wouldn't be Siberia. If he were tortured he
knew he would tell them about the previous consignments. They would be crazy with rage. He'd face a
firing squad. It was at that moment that Manfred
Seidler decided that – if they got through this time –
this would be the last run. God knew he had enough
money in his Swiss numbered bank account.

Taking out a silk handkerchief, he told Franz to sit still and he gently mopped the moisture from the old man's brow. The car stopped. By the light shining through the open door of the guard hut Seidler saw the heavy swing-pole which was lowered and barred their way into Austria.

'Stop!' he hissed. The old fool had nearly switched off the engine. Leaving the motor running was *familiar*, creating in the minds of the guards a reflex feeling that after a perfunctory check they would raise the barrier and wave the Renault on. A uniformed figure with an automatic rifle looped over his shoulder approached Seidler's side of the car.

Seidler tried to open the door and found the damned thing had frozen. Quickly, he wound down the window. Icy air flooded in, freezing the exposed skin on his face above the heavy scarf. The soldier bent down and peered inside. It was Jan.

'Sorry,' apologized Seidler, 'the handle's frozen.' He spoke in fluent Czech. 'I should check the wooden crate in the back. The *wooden crate*,' he emphasized. 'I'm not sure I'm permitted to take the contents out. Just take it and dump it if it's not allowed . . .'

Jan nodded understandingly and his boots crunched in the crusted snow as he walked with painful slowness to the rear of the hatchback. Seidler lit a cigarette to quiet his nerves. They were so close to safety he dared not glance at Franz. He knew he had committed a psychological error in emphasizing the *wooden crate*. But as on earlier trips he was taking a gigantic risk on the assumption that people are never suspicious of something under their noses. It was the much larger *cardboard* container alongside the crate Jan must not investigate.

Compelling himself not to look back, forgetting that his window was still open, he took a deep drag on his cigarette as he heard Jan turn the handle and raise the hatchback. Thank God that handle wasn't frozen! There was a scrape as Jan hauled out the crate – followed by the divine sound of the hatchback being closed.

A light flashed to his left through the open window. Someone with a torch must have emerged from the guard hut. He continued staring steadily ahead. The only sounds in the early morning dark were the ticking over of the motor, the swish of the windscreen wipers maintaining two fan-shapes of clear glass in the gently falling snow.

A returning crunch of boots breaking the hard snow. At the window Jan, his high cheekbones burnished by the wind, reappeared. The rifle still looped on one shoulder, the crate expertly balanced on the other. His expression was blank as he bent down and spoke.

'Until next time . . .'

'The same arrangement,' replied Seidler and smiled, stubbing out his cigarette in the ash-tray. A small gesture to indicate that this transaction was completed.

Jan vanished inside the hut as Seidler wound up

the window – God, he was frozen stiff. With the feeble heater he'd be lucky to thaw out by the time they reached Vienna. The barrier pole remained obstinately lowered across their path. Franz reached for the brake and Seidler stopped him.

'For Christ's sake, wait! No sign of impatience . . .'

'It's not going as it usually does. We'd be away by now. I can feel it – something's wrong . . .'

'Shut up! Didn't you see Jan yawn? They're half-asleep at this hour. They've been on duty all night. Nothing ever happens at this Godforsaken spot. They're bored stiff. They've slipped into a state of permanent inertia . . .'

Seidler realized he was talking too much. He began to wonder whether he was trying to convince himself. He stared hypnotized by the horizontal pole. It began to wobble. Christ! The tension was beginning to get to him.

The pole wasn't wobbling. It was *ascending*. Franz released the brake. The Renault slid forward. They were across! They paused briefly again while an Austrian official glanced without interest at Seidler's German passport, and then they were driving through the streets of the small town of Gmund.

'You realize you were photographed back at the frontier post?' Franz remarked as he accelerated along the highway beyond Gmund towards distant Vienna.

'What the hell are you talking about?'

'You were photographed by a man in civilian clothes. Didn't you see the flash-bulb go off? He had a funny camera with a big lens . . .'

'A civilian?' Seidler was startled. 'Are you sure? Someone with a torch came out of the guard hut . . .'

'No torch. A flash-bulb. I watched him out of the corner of my eye. You were looking straight ahead.'

Seidler, a man in his late forties with a thatch of dark brown hair, slimly built, a bony face, a long, inquisitive nose and wary eyes, thought about it. It was the reference to a civilian which worried him. Always before there had been no one there except uniformed guards. Yes, this was definitely the last run. He had just relaxed with this comforting thought when Franz said something else which disturbed him.

'I'm not helping you again,' the old man rasped.

Suits me to the ground, Seidler thought, and then glanced to his left sharply. Franz was staring straight ahead but there was a smug, conniving look in his expression. Seidler knew that look: Franz was congratulating himself on some trick he was going to pull.

'I'm sorry to hear that,' Seidler replied.

'That business back at the frontier post,' Franz went on. 'I felt certain they'd changed the guard. It's only a matter of time before they *do* change the guard. Jan won't be there to collect his Schnapps and wave you through. They'll search the car . . .'

He was repeating himself, talking too much, over-emphasizing the reasons for his decision. That plus the satisfied smirk. Seidler's devious and shrewd mind began searching for the real reason. His right hand thrust deep inside his coat pocket for warmth felt the flick knife he always carried in the special compartment he had had sewn into the pocket.

Money! Franz worshipped the stuff. But from what source could he obtain more money than the generous amount Seidler had always paid? The road to Vienna passes through some of the loneliest and bleakest countryside west of Siberia. Flat as a billiard table – a monotonous snow-covered billiard table – the bare fields stretched away on both sides, treeless.

It was still dark when they drove through one of the few inhabited places between Gmund and the Austrian capital. Horn is a single street walled by ancient, solid farmhouse-like buildings. Giant wooden double doors seal off entrances to courtyards beyond, entrances large enough to admit wagons piled high with hay and drawn by oxen.

What the devil could Franz be up to? Seidler, an opportunist par excellence, a man whose background and character dictated that he would always live by his wits, probed the problem from every angle. A *Mittel-European*, his father had been a Sudeten German in Czechoslovakia before the war, his mother a Czech.

Seidler spoke five languages – Czech, German, English, French, Italian. The Czechs – and Seidler was mostly Czech – have a gift for languages. It was this facility, plus the network of contacts he had built up across Europe – allied with a natural Czech talent for unscrupulousness – which had enabled him to make a good living.

Six feet tall, he sported a small moustache and had the gift of the gab in all five languages. As they approached Vienna he was still wrestling with the problem of Franz. He also had another problem: he had a tight schedule for the consignment inside the cardboard container resting at the tail of the Renault. The aircraft waiting for him at Schwechat Airport. His employers were sticklers for promptness. Should he risk a little time checking out Franz when they reached Vienna?

The first streaks of a mournful, pallid daylight filtered from the heavy overcast down on Vienna as Franz stopped the Renault in front of the Westbahnhof, the main station to the West. Here Seidler always transferred to his own car parked waiting for him. It wouldn't do to let Franz drive him to the airport – the less he knew about the consignment's ultimate destination the better.

'Here's your money. Don't waste it on drink and wild, wild women,' Seidler said with deliberate flippancy.

The remark was really very funny – the idea of Franz Oswald spending good money on girls instead of at the tavern. The old man took the fat envelope and shoved it into his inside pocket. His hands tapped the wheel impatiently, a gesture out of character Seidler noted as he went to the rear of the car, lifted the hatchback and grasped the large cardboard container by the strong rope handle. Slamming down the hatchback, he walked back to the front passenger window and spoke.

'I may have a different sort of job. No risk involved. A job inside Austria,' he lied. 'I'll get in touch . . .'

'You are the boss.' Franz released the brake without looking at his employer and the car slid past. Seidler only saw it by pure chance. On the rear seat a rumpled, plaid travelling rug had slipped half on to the floor, exposing what it had hidden. Seidler froze. Franz had stolen one of the samples from the consignment.

Early morning workers trailed out of the station exits below the huge glass end wall and down the steps as Seidler moved very fast. There was a jam-up of traffic just at the point where you drove out of the concourse and Franz's Renault was trapped.

Running to his parked Opel, Seidler unlocked the car, thrust the cardboard container onto the rear seat and settled himself behind the wheel. He was careful not to panic. He inserted the ignition keys first time, switched on the motor and pulled out at the moment Franz left the concourse, turning on to Mariahilfer-strasse. Dreary grey buildings loomed in the semi-dark as Seidler followed. It looked as though Franz was heading into the centre of the city – away from his home.

Seidler was in a state of cold fury and, driving with one hand, he felt again the flick knife in the secret pocket. The smirk on Franz's face was now explained. He was selling one of the samples. The only question in Seidler's mind now was who could be the buyer?

Stunned, Seidler sat in his parked Opel while he absorbed what he had just observed. A spare, brisk-looking man with a military-style moustache had been waiting for Franz. Outside the British Embassy!

Seidler had watched while Franz got out of his Renault, carrying the small cardboard container as he joined the Englishman. The latter had taken Franz by the arm, hustling him inside the building. Now it was Seidler who tapped his fingers on the wheel, checking his watch, thinking of the aircraft waiting at Schwechat, knowing he had to wait for Franz to emerge.

Ten minutes later Franz did emerge – without the container. He climbed in behind the wheel of the Renault without a glance in the direction of Seidler who sat slumped behind his own wheel, wearing a black beret Franz had never seen. Something in the way he had walked suggested to Seidler Franz was very satisfied with his visit to the British Embassy. The Renault moved off.

Seidler made his move when Franz turned down a narrow, deserted side street lined with tall old apartment buildings. Flights of steps led down to basement areas. Checking his rear view mirror, Seidler speeded up, squeezed past the slow-moving Renault and swung diagonally into the kerb. Franz jammed on his brakes and stopped within inches of the Opel. Jumping out of his car, he ran along the pavement in the opposite direction with a shuffling trot.

Seidler caught up with him in less than a hundred metres opposite a flight of steps leading into one of the basement areas. His left hand grasped Franz by the shoulder and spun him round. He smiled and spoke rapidly.

'There's nothing to be frightened about ... All I want to know is who you gave the box to ... Then you can go to hell as far as I'm concerned ... Remember, I said this was the last run ...'

He was talking when he rammed the knife blade upwards into Franz's chest with all his strength. He was surprised at the ease with which the knife entered a man's body. Franz gulped, coughed once, his eyes rolled and he began to sag. Seidler gave him a savage push with his gloved hand and Franz, the hilt of the knife protruding from his chest, fell backwards down the stone steps. Seidler was surprised also at the lack of noise: the loudest sound was when Franz, half-way down the steps, cracked the back of his skull on the stonework. He ended up on his back on the basement paving stones.

Seidler glanced round, ran swiftly down the steps and felt inside Franz's jacket, extracting his wallet which bulged, although the envelope of Austrian banknotes Seidler had passed to him was still inside the same pocket. He pulled out a folded wad of Swiss banknotes – five-hundred-franc denomination. At a guess there were twenty. Ten thousand Swiss francs. A large fortune for Franz.

The distant approach of a car's engine warned Seidler it was time to go. His gloved hand thrust the notes in his pocket and he ran back up the steps to his car. He was just driving away when he saw the sidelights of the approaching car in his wing mirror. He accelerated round a curve and forgot about the car, all his thoughts now concentrated on reaching Schwechat Airport.

Captain 'Tommy' Mason, officially designated as military attaché to the British Embassy in Vienna, frowned as he saw the driverless Renault parked at an angle to the kerb, the gaping entrance to the basement area. He was just able to drive past the vehicle, then he stopped and switched off his own engine.

The sound of the Renault's motor ticking over came to him in the otherwise silent street. With considerable agility he nipped out of his Ford Escort, ran to peer down into the basement, ran back to the Ford, started up the motor again and drove off at speed.

He was just in time to see the rear lights of the Opel turn on to a main highway. He caught up with it quickly and then settled down to follow at a decent interval. No point in alarming the other party. First thing in the morning and all that.

Mason had first noticed the Opel parked outside the Embassy when he was interviewing Franz Oswald. Peering casually from behind the curtains of the second floor window he had seen the car, the slumped driver wearing one of those funny, Frog-style berets. At least, the Frogs had favoured them at one time. Didn't see them much these days.

He had seen no reason to alarm his visitor who, much to his surprise, had actually kept their appointment. More surprising still – even a trifle alarming – had been the contents of the cardboard box. When his visitor had left Mason had thought there might be no harm in following the chap – especially since Black Beret appeared also to be in the following business. You could never tell where these things might lead. Tweed, back in London, had said something to this effect once. Odd how things Tweed said, remarks casually tossed off, stuck in the mind.

Mason, thirty-three, five feet ten, sleepy-eyed, trimly-moustached, drawly-voiced, crisply-spoken, using as few words as possible, was a near-walking caricature of his official position. At a party shortly after his arrival in Waltz City, the Ambassador had indulged in his dry humour at the new arrival's expense.

'You know, Mason, if I was asked to show someone a picture of the typical British military attaché I'd take a photo of you . . .'

'Sir,' Mason had replied.

Mason was soon pretty sure that the Opel chap was

heading for the airport – unless he continued on to the Czech border and Bratislava, God forbid! But any man who left bodies in basements at this hour was worth a little attention. A quarter of an hour later he knew his first guess had been spot on. Curiouser and curiouser. What flight could he be catching before most people had downed their breakfast?

Seidler drove beyond the speed limit, checking his watch at frequent intervals. Franz Oswald was only the second man he had ever killed – the first had been an accident – and the reaction was setting in. He was shaken, his mind taken up with one thing. Getting safely aboard the aircraft.

Customs would be no problem. Here again, timing was vital – the chief officer on duty had already been paid a substantial sum. When it came to essentials his employer, so careful with money, never hesitated to produce the requisite funds. Turning into the airport, he drove past the main buildings and continued towards the tarmac. Josef, who didn't know anything, was waiting to take the hired car back to Vienna.

Seidler jumped out of the car, nodded to Josef, lifted the large container from the back of the Opel and walked rapidly towards the waiting executive jet. The ladder was already in position. A man he had never seen stood by the ladder, asking the question in French.

'Classification of the consignment?'

'Terminal.'

Chapter Five

London 10 February 1984. 8°

Tweed, short and plump-faced, middle-aged, was gazing out of the window of his office at SIS headquarters in Park Crescent when Mason called from Vienna.

Through his horn-rimmed glasses he looked out towards Regent's Park across the Crescent gardens. Small clusters of gold sprouted amid the green in the watery morning sunlight. Early spring crocuses. It was something – promising the ultimate end of winter. The phone on his desk rang.

'Long distance from Vienna,' the internal switchboard operator informed him. Tweed wondered when Vienna was a short distance. He told her to put the call through and settled himself in his swivel chair. They exchanged the normal preliminaries identifying each other. Mason sounded rushed, which was unusual.

'I've got something for you. Won't specify on the phone . . .'

'Mason, where are you speaking from?' Tweed asked sharply.

'A booth in the General Post Office, middle of

Vienna. The Embassy phone goes through the switchboard. I've just hurtled back from Schwechat Airport – that's . . .'

'I know where it is. Get to the point . . .'

Tweed was uncharacteristically sharp again. But he sensed a terrible urgency in his caller's voice. Mason was the SIS man in Vienna under the cloak of military attaché. The British were at last learning from their Soviet colleagues – who were never who they seemed at embassies.

'I've got something for you, something rather frightening. I won't specify over this line – I'll bring it with me when I come to London. Main thing is a Lear jet with Swiss markings left Schwechat half an hour ago. Destination Switzerland is my educated guess . . .'

Tweed listened without interrupting. Mason was his normal concise self now. Short, terse sentences. Not a wasted word. As he listened Tweed made no notes on the pad lying in front of him. When Mason had finished Tweed asked him just one question before breaking the connection.

'What is the flight time Vienna to Switzerland?'

'One hour and ten minutes. So you have less than forty minutes if I've guessed right. Oh, there's a body involved . . .'

'See you in London.'

Tweed waited a moment after replacing the receiver and then he lifted it again and asked for an open line. He dialled 010 41, the code for Switzerland, followed by 31, the code for Berne, followed by six more digits. He got through to Wiley, commercial attaché at the British Embassy in Berne, in less than a minute. He spoke rapidly, explaining what he wanted.

'. . . so alert our man in Geneva and the chap in Zurich . . .'

'The time element is against anyone getting to the airports to set up surveillance,' Wiley protested.

'No, it isn't. Cointrin is ten minutes from the centre of Geneva. Twenty minutes in a fast car gets you from Zurich to Kloten now they've finished the new road. And *you* can check Belp . . .'

'I'll have to put my skates on . . .'

'Do that,' Tweed told him and broke the connection again.

Sighing, he got up and walked over to the wall-map of Western Europe. Mason could run rings round Wiley. Maybe he ought to switch them when Mason arrived home. Vienna was a backwater – but Berne was beginning to smoulder. And why did everyone forget Belp? Even Howard probably had no idea Berne had its own airport fifteen minutes down the four-lane motorway to Thun and Lucerne. Plus a thrice-weekly service from Belp to Gatwick. He was studying the map when his chief, Howard, burst into the office. Without knocking, of course.

'Anything interesting cooking?' he asked breezily.

Howard had all the right connections, had gone to all the useful schools and university, which completed the circle, giving him all the right connections. An able admin. man, he was short on imagination and not a risk-taker. Tweed had been known – in a bad mood – to refer to him privately as Woodentop.

'Possibly Berne,' Tweed replied and left it at that.

'Berne?' Howard perked up. 'That's the *Terminal* thing you latched on to. What the hell does the word mean – if anything?'

'No idea – that it means anything, Just that we keep getting rumours from a variety of sources.' He decided not to mention to Howard the reference Mason had made to 'a body involved'. It was too early to excite Howard.

'I hope you're not employing too much manpower on this,' Howard commented. '*Terminal*,' he repeated. 'Might be an idea to watch the airports. That would link up – airport, terminal . . .'

'I've just done that.'

'Good man. Keep me informed . . .'

Wiley phoned Park Crescent at exactly 4 p.m. He apologized for not calling earlier. The lines from the Embassy had been jammed up most of the day. Tweed guessed he had really waited until nearly everyone – including the Ambassador – had gone home. It was now 5 p.m. in Berne since Switzerland was one hour ahead of London in time.

'I got lucky,' he informed Tweed. 'At least I think so. If this was the plane you're interested in . . .' He described the machine and Tweed grunted and told him to go on. 'A passenger disembarked and carried a large cardboard container to a waiting truck. A canvas-covered job. Stencilled on the side were the words *Chemiekonzern Grange AG* . . .'

'Let me write that down. Now, go on . . .'

'It's a weird story. I followed the truck – the passenger travelled in the cab beside the driver – back along the motorway towards Berne. It turned off on to a road I knew was a cul-de-sac, so I waited. Pretended my car had broken down and stood in the freezing cold with my head under the bonnet. God, it was cold . . .'

Mason would have left that bit out. Patiently this time, Tweed waited. At four in the afternoon he had the lights on. It was near-darkness outside and cars passing along the main road had their lights on also. Tweed felt a little disappointed in the report so far. He couldn't have said why.

'About a quarter of an hour later a small van appeared down the same side road. I nearly missed it – then I spotted the same passenger sitting beside the van driver. I followed the van which headed towards the city. Lost it in the traffic on the outskirts. Funny thing is, I could have sworn it passed me later driving down the opposite lane – *away* from the city . . .'

'So, that's that?'

'Hold on a minute. I did notice the name painted on the side of the van. I'm damned sure it was the same one both times . . .'

Tweed was writing down the name when Howard

came into the office, again without knocking. Tweed scribbled out the second name as Howard came round the desk to peer over his shoulder, another irritating habit. He thanked Wiley and put the phone down.

Tweed had no doubt Howard had paid one of his frequent visits to the switchboard room – to see if anything was going on. He also knew that Howard often stayed back late at night so he could poke around his staff's offices after they had gone home. Which was why Tweed locked away anything of interest and only left trivia on his desk.

'Any developments?' Howard enquired.

'I'm not sure. I haven't decided yet but I may have to go to Berne myself. As you know, we're fully stretched. Keith Martel is away on a job and it's all hands to the pumps . . .'

'Any excuse,' Howard commented drily and rattled loose change in his pocket. 'You like Berne. Any developments?' he repeated.

'This morning Mason reported he had something for me – *something rather frightening* were the exact words he used. I think it was delivered to him at the Embassy. He's bringing it to us within a few days, so it has to be serious – maybe very serious . . .'

'Oh, Christ! You're building up another crisis.'

'Crises build themselves up,' Tweed pointed out. 'And that was Wiley on the phone . . .' As if you didn't know, he thought. 'From Vienna Mason reported to me this morning he followed a man – who may be an assassin – to Schwechat Airport outside the city. He saw this man board a private Swiss jet. I put tags on three Swiss airports – although there are plenty of others. Wiley has just told me a similar aircraft landed at Belp . . .'

'Belp? Where the hell is Belp? Funny name . . .'

'Look at the pin sticking in the wall map. It's the airport for Berne.'

'Didn't know there was one.' Tweed said nothing but peered over his glasses as Howard scrutinized the map. 'So it was an airport,' Howard said with satisfaction. 'A terminal! This is getting interesting . . .'

With Howard it always helped to get him on your side – or at best in a neutral status – if he thought he had contributed an idea himself. Tweed continued talking in his level tone.

'Wiley saw the aircraft disembark one passenger carrying a large container. Eventually he was driven away in a small van. Wiley noted the name on the side of the van. At the moment I have several disconnected pieces which may eventually build into a pattern.'

'Or a crisis . . .' It was the nearest Howard ever came to cracking a joke. He swung round on one heel, flicked an imaginary speck of dust off his regulation pin-striped suit. Howard was a trendy dresser; always wore a camel overcoat of the length which was the latest vogue. 'Well, what was the name on the van?' he asked.

'Klinik Bern . . .'

55

Chapter Six

Tucson, Arizona. 10 February 1984. 55°

The sun had sunk behind the mountains and Tucson was bathed in the purple glow of dusk as the temperature also sank. Newman raised his glass to Dr Rosen in the Tack Room, probably the most luxurious eating establishment in the state. The tables were illuminated by candlelight.

'Cheers!' said Newman. 'I've seen Frank Chase, I've talked with Linda Wayne – and got nowhere. No evidence of anything odd about Jesse Kennedy being sent to the Berne Clinic . . .'

'You know Jesse was flown direct to Berne by executive jet?'

'Linda didn't say that . . .'

'Have you ever heard of Professor Armand Grange, eminent Swiss specialist?'

'No. Should I?'

'Surprising Linda didn't mention him. Grange was on a lecture tour of the States – drumming up business was my impression. And from the moment Linda met him she treated him as her *guru*.'

'*Guru?*' Newman looked at the kindly but shrewd face of Rosen. 'I thought you used that word for some

Indian fakir who offers salvation – provided you obey the gospel . . .'

'That's right,' agreed Rosen. 'Grange is into cellular rejuvenation – something the Swiss have practised for years. We're still not convinced. Maybe we're old-fashioned. But Grange certainly gathered in some disciples on that tour – always rich, of course.'

Newman turned sideways to study his guest. 'I'm sorry, I'm not sure I'm following this. You're trying to tell me something, is that it?'

'I suppose so.' Rosen accepted a refill. He seemed to mellow outside the Medical Center. Maybe it was the relaxing atmosphere of the Tack Room, Newman thought. Rosen went on. 'Some of what I'm saying may not be strictly ethical – could even be taken for criticism of a professional colleague – but we are talking about a foreigner. I suspect Grange's clinic is full of wealthy patients he attracted during his tour. Two carrots – one for relatives, one for the seriously ill patient. ' He smiled ruefully. 'You know something, Newman? I think I'm talking too much . . .'

'I'm still listening. Sometimes it's good to get things off your chest.'

Newman watched Rosen with an attentive expression. It was part of his stock-in-trade as foreign correspondent – people often opened out to him when they wouldn't say the same things to their wives or colleagues – especially their wives.

'Linda Wayne,' Rosen continued, 'went overboard with Professor Grange the way a drowning woman grasps at a floating spar. He was the answer to her prayer – to get Jesse Kennedy far away, as far away as possible. The carrot Grange offers is to take sick relatives off the hands of their nearest and dearest. The price is high, but like I said, he deals only with the very wealthy. The carrot to the sick patient is the hope of cellular rejuvenation, a new chance at life. I suppose it's a brilliant formula.'

'The carrot worked with a man like Jesse Kennedy?'

'There you put your finger on the key, what's worrying me.' Rosen sipped at his drink and Newman carefully remained silent. 'If Jesse had leukaemia he'd face up to it – but no way would he be into cellular rejuvenation. Did you know he once did a job for the CIA? It was over ten years ago when we had German pilots being trained by our people at a secret air base out in the desert. A very tough CIA operative came down to cooperate with Jesse. Can't recall his name. Linda Wayne fooled around with him. Now I *am* talking too much . . .'

'What exactly did Jesse do?'

'He used to ride his horse for miles by himself in the desert every day. They gave him a camera. One morning he spotted a German pilot handing an envelope to a stranger who stopped his car on 1 10 – Interstate Highway 10 which runs all the way from LA to Florida. The stranger came after Jesse with a gun . . .' Rosen smiled, a dreamy look on his face. 'That was very foolish of him. Jesse rode him down with his horse, the CIA man turned up and one German pilot disappeared for ever. The CIA man shot the stranger. Jesse told me about it years later . . .'

'You said "If Jesse had leukaemia . . ."'

'Slip of the tongue. You think a man like Jesse would crawl off to Switzerland when he loved the desert? A man who started from nothing and parleyed a bank loan into twelve million dollars?'

'Just *how* did he do it?'

'Vision. He was a crystal ball gazer – he looked into the future. When he came to Tucson from Texas over twenty years ago he guessed Tucson would expand one day. He bought options on land outside the city limits – and when that increased in value he used the extra collateral to buy more and more land further and further out . . .'

'So,' Newman commented, 'Linda is worth eight million dollars when Jesse goes and Nancy gets four million?'

'His will is common knowledge. He made no secret of it. And if anything happened to Nancy first, then Linda collects the whole twelve million. Maybe you see why it worries me – that kind of money at stake.' Rosen played with his empty glass. 'No thanks. Two is my limit. You know, Newman, I thought you'd be just the man to check out this mystery. You cracked the Kruger espionage case in Germany – I read the book you wrote afterwards. That must have made you a pile . . .'

'Not four million dollars,' Newman said shortly.

'Oh! Now I get it – I sensed you couldn't make up your mind about marrying Nancy. The money worries you, which is to your credit. I still think you ought to go to Berne . . .'

'Now you sound like Nancy. She never stops . . .'

'Argue against her and it will just make her more determined.' Rosen smiled again. 'Or maybe you've found that out?'

'We've had our moments. Jesus, look what just walked in . . .'

'Harvey Wayne, Linda's husband. He's into electronics, as you doubtless know. He's another one greedy for a dollar . . .'

Rosen stopped talking as a fat, pasty-faced man in his early forties came over to them. He was wearing a cream-coloured dinner jacket, dark trousers and the oily smile Newman found so distasteful. He put an arm round the Englishman's shoulder.

'Hi, pal! Hear you and that cute sister-in-law of mine will soon be in Berne. Give my regards to that old coot, Jesse . . .'

'You heard what?'

Newman's tone was cold. He glanced at his shoulder and Harvey reluctantly moved his hand. He gave Rosen a throwaway gesture of resignation with his hand, then shrugged.

'Did I say something I ought not to have?'

'You haven't answered my question,' Newman replied.

'You're not rousting Dr Rosen the way you did

Frank Chase, I hope.' Harvey looked towards the entrance and smiled again. 'We have company. You have the opportunity of getting a direct answer to your question . . .'

Linda, wearing an off-the-shoulder cocktail dress and a come-hither smile, had entered the Tack Room and was heading towards them, her innocent eyes staring straight at Newman. Beside her walked Nancy, a few inches shorter, dressed in a cream blouse and a midnight blue skirt. Heads turned as the two women progressed across the room. Newman stood up, his expression bleak.

'Let's go somewhere quiet,' he said to Nancy. 'We have to talk and I do mean now . . .'

The blazing row took place in the lobby, carried on in low tones so the receptionist couldn't hear them. Newman opened the conversation, treading warily at first.

'I'm sure that creep, Harvey, has got it wrong. He's just told me we're going to Berne . . .'

'I have the tickets, Bob.' Nancy produced two folders from her handbag and handed them to him. 'It's a very direct route. An American Airlines 727 from Tucson to Dallas. One hour stopover in Dallas. Then an eight-hour flight – again American Airlines – to Gatwick in England from Dallas. The last lap is by Dan-Air from Gatwick to Belp. That's the airport just outside Berne . . .'

'I have actually heard of Belp,' Newman replied with deceptive calm.

'We take off on tomorrow's flight . . .'

'I can actually read an airline ticket . . .'

'Somebody had to take a decision.' She looked pleased with herself. 'And I've just got out of Linda that Jesse didn't go that route. He was flown to Belp by private jet . . .'

'So?'

'Jesse was careful with money. If he'd agreed to go he'd have travelled in a wheelchair on a scheduled flight rather than hire a jet. Don't you think I've done rather well?'

'You'd have done a bloody sight better to consult me first. How do you think I felt when your louse of a brother-in-law comes up to me in front of Rosen to give me this news?'

'Really? Linda must have phoned him at the office. He was working late. She's planned a farewell dinner for us here . . .'

'Count me out . . .'

'Robert! It's all fixed.' Her temper began to flare. 'I'm all packed. You said you could pack anytime in ten minutes even to go to Tokyo . . .'

'That's when *I* want to go to Tokyo. Look, Nancy – and don't interrupt. There's not a shred of evidence that there's anything wrong about Jesse being flown to the Berne Clinic. I've talked to Dr Chase. I've had two conversations with Rosen. I've stared at Linda's legs while she talked to me . . .'

'Is that what you're so anxious not to leave – Linda's legs?'

'Now you're getting nasty. Nancy, you can't just push me around like this. It's no basis for any kind of relationship – let alone marriage.'

'Oh, shit, Bob . . .'

'Look, Nancy, this argument has been going on practically since we first met in London three months ago . . .'

'That was when I tried to phone Jesse and heard from Linda that he'd been sent to Switzerland. I really do feel something's very wrong. Remember, I am a doctor . . .'

'And I'm a foreign correspondent who looks for evidence. I haven't found anything to justify your anxiety. Now you present me with this *fait accompli*, this package deal all wrapped up in pink ribbon.'

He waved the ticket folders under her shapely nose. She took both his wrists in her hands, leaned up to him and nestled her face alongside his, whispering in his ear.

'Bob, would you please come with me to Berne to quiet my fears. For my sake?'

'That's a better approach . . .'

'It's the approach I should have used first. You're right – I should never have bought those tickets without consulting you. I'm sorry. Truly.'

He freed one hand and reached under her hair to stroke her neck. The receptionist was putting on quite a performance at not noticing them. She nestled her head against his chest and purred contentedly. He freed his other hand, grasped her chin and lifted it up to kiss her full on the lips.

'Nancy, I have to go back to Dr Rosen to ask him one more question. We leave for Berne tomorrow . . .'

Harvey Wayne had just left Rosen when Newman sat down opposite the doctor. Rosen nodded towards Harvey's retreating back with a grimace.

'He's been pumping me, trying to find out what we were talking about. How did the argument go?'

'The way I expected it to.' Newman's manner had changed. He was crisp, decisive. 'Have you any idea where the majority of patients in the Berne Clinic come from?'

'My impression – it was no more than that – was they mostly come from the States. Plus a few from South America where they can still afford the fees. Is it significant?'

'It could be the key to the whole operation.'

Chapter Seven

11 February 1984

The DC10 flew at 35,000 feet above the invisible Atlantic as the machine proceeded at 500 mph in a north-easterly direction for Europe. In her first-class seat Nancy was fast asleep, her head flopped on Newman's shoulder. He moved her carefully so he could leave his seat. No risk she would wake up: when Nancy fell asleep she went out cold.

Taking a pad from his pocket, Newman wrote the signal in capital letters so there could be no error in transmission. Standing up, he summoned a steward-ess, put a finger to his lips and nodded towards Nancy. Taking the girl by the arm he guided her towards the pilot's cabin and spoke only when they were inside the galley.

'I'd like this message radioed immediately to London. Find out the cost while I wait here . . .'

The stewardess returned in less than a minute. An attractive girl, she studied Newman frankly. You weren't supposed to fraternize with passengers but . . . She found Newman's droll, easy manner irresistible. And her flat wasn't far from Gatwick. And he was English. *And* the female passenger he was travelling with wore no ring. A girl had to make the most of her opportunities. She told him the cost of the message and he took his time paying her in dollars.

'The radio operator is already transmitting, Mr Newman . . .'

'You're a helpful girl to have around . . .'

'I have two days off at Gatwick . . .'

'Give me the phone number?'

'I'm not supposed to . . .'

'But you will . . .'

He loaned her his pad and ballpoint pen, tucked a cigarette in the corner of his mouth, and watched her while she wrote the figures on the pad. She added a name and upside down he read *Susan*. He took the pad off her and slipped out of sight as the curtain moved and a steward appeared. He gave her a little salute.

'Thank you for dealing with that for me,' he said for the benefit of the steward who was unnecessarily polishing glasses. 'When should it reach London?'

'Within a matter of minutes, sir . . .'

'Thank you again.'

He winked at her, pushed aside the curtain and went back to his seat. Nancy was awake, stretching her arms, thrusting out her well-rounded breasts against her tight cashmere sweater. He gave her a look of amiable resignation as he settled himself beside her.

'You're a dog,' she said. 'You've been chatting up

that stewardess.' She wrapped a proprietary arm round his. 'You know, sometimes I think I should grab you for good while I can. You're not safe to leave roaming around loose.'

'What stewardess?'

'The one with the superb legs who showed us to our seats, the one you couldn't take your eyes off, the one whose eyes ate you up. Discreetly, of course . . .'

'Change of plan,' he said abruptly.

'Which means?'

'You'd better have some coffee to get you properly awake before I tell you.' He summoned the steward who had finished polishing glasses and gave the order. Then he relapsed into silence until she had drunk half the cup.

'I've been a good girl,' she said. 'What change of plan?'

'We don't take the Dan-Air flight from Gatwick to Belp. We take the bus from Gatwick to Heathrow. Then we catch a Swissair flight to Geneva. Going in via Geneva disguises our real destination.'

'Bob!' She straightened up so abruptly she almost spilt her coffee. 'You're taking this thing seriously. You do think there's something peculiar going on. God, you're a dark horse. Sometimes I feel I'll never really know you. Your whole manner has changed . . .'

'If we have to do the job we might as well do it professionally . . .'

'That isn't the reason,' she pounced. 'Rosen told

you something which changed your whole attitude. So why the hell did we have to have that embarrassing row in the lobby of the Tack Room?'

'Rosen told me nothing. We're just doing it my way. You might call it a *fait accompli*,' he replied airily.

'I asked for that one,' she conceded. 'And I still don't believe you. Well, isn't that nice?'

She looked at him and Newman's head was rested against the back of the seat. His eyes were closed and he had apparently fallen into a catnap, something he was able to do anywhere at any time.

In the pilot's cabin the radio operator crumpled up the note from Newman's pad he had transmitted. The signal seemed innocuous enough and he didn't give it a second thought. Addressed to Riverdale Trust Ltd with a PO Box number in London it was brief and to the point.

Aboard American Airlines Flight ... ETA Gatwick ... Proceeding to Heathrow to board Swissair flight to Geneva, repeat Geneva. Newman.

Manfred Seidler was running for his life. He used every devious means to throw a smokescreen in the eyes of those who would try to track him. Using a fake set of identity papers, he hired a car from the Hertz agency next door to the Bellevue Palace in Berne.

He drove only as far as Solothurn where he handed in the car. From the station he caught a train to Basle.

If anyone *did* manage to trace him so far they would – with luck – think he had gone on to Zurich. He fostered this fiction by buying two separate one-way tickets – to Zurich and to Basle. He bought them at ten-minute intervals, using two different ticket windows. As the express slowed down and slid into the main station at Basle he was standing by the exit door, clutching his suitcase.

He phoned Erika Stahel from a booth in the huge station. He found himself staring at every passenger who lingered anywhere near the booth. He knew his nerves were in a bad way. Which was when a man made mistakes. Christ! Would the cow never answer? Her voice came on the line as if in response to his plea.

'It's Manfred . . .'

'Well, well, stranger. Isn't life full of surprises?'

Erika didn't sound welcoming, certainly not enthusiastic, he thought savagely. Women needed careful handling. He forced himself to sound confident, pleasant, firm. Any trace of the jitters and she wouldn't cooperate. She knew a little of what he did for a living.

'I need a place to rest, to relax . . .'

'In bed? Of course?'

Her melodious voice sounded sarcastic. He wondered if she had a man with her. That would be a disaster area. It was a few months since he'd last contacted her.

'I *need* you,' he said. 'As company. Forget bed . . .'

'This *is* Manfred Seidler I'm talking to?' But her voice had softened. 'Where have you come from?'

'Zurich,' he lied easily.

'And where are you now?'

'Tired and hungry – inside a phone booth at the Hauptbahnhof. You don't have to cook. I'll take you out. Best place in town.'

'You counted on me being here – just waiting for your call?'

'Erika,' he said firmly, 'this is Saturday. I know you don't work Saturdays. I just hoped . . .'

'Better come on over, Manfred . . .'

Erika Stahel lived in a small, second-storey apartment near the Munsterplatz. Seidler lugged his suitcase through the falling snow, ignoring the cab rank outside the station. He could easily have afforded transport but cab-drivers had good memories. And often they were the first source the Swiss police approached for information.

It was ten o'clock in the morning when he pressed the bell alongside the name *E. Stahel*. Her voice, oddly recognizable despite the distortion of the speakphone, answered as though she had been waiting.

'Who is it?'

'Manfred. I'm freezing . . .'

'Come!'

The buzzer zizzed, indicating she had released the front door which he pressed open as he glanced up and down the street. Inside he climbed the steps, ignoring the lift. You could get trapped inside a lift if someone was waiting for you. Seidler had reached that state of acute nervousness and alertness when he trusted no one.

Her apartment door was open a few inches and he had reached out to push it when he paused, wondering what might be on the far side. The door opened inward and she stood looking at him without any particular expression. Only five feet four tall, she was a trim brunette of twenty-eight with a high forehead and large, black steady eyes.

'What are you waiting for? You look cold and frightened – and hungry. Breakfast is on the table. A jug of steaming coffee. Give me your case and eat . . .'

She said it all in her calm, competent voice as she closed the door and held out her hand for the case. He shook his head, decided he was being too curt and smiled, conscious of a sense of relief. He was under cover.

'I'll put the case in the bedroom if you don't mind. A couple of minutes and I'll be myself . . .'

'You know where the bedroom is. You should by now.' Her manner was matter-of-fact but she watched him closely.

Inside the bedroom with the door closed, he dropped the case on one of the two single beds and looked round quickly. He needed a hiding-place and only had minutes to find a safe one.

Moving a chair quietly against a tall cupboard, he

stood on it and ran a finger along the top. His fingers came away with a thin film of dust. The rest of the place was spotless – but small women often over-looked the tops of tall cupboards. He stepped down and opened his suitcase.

The smaller, slim executive case was concealed beneath his shirts. He raised the catches quietly and took out several envelopes. All of them contained large sums of money – he had emptied his bank account in Berne on Friday just before the bank closed. Another envelope held the twenty five-hundred-franc notes he had extracted from the dead Franz Oswald's wallet in the Vienna basement.

Clutching the envelopes, he climbed back on the chair and distributed them across the top of the cupboard which was recessed. His final touch was to put two shirts into the executive case – to explain its presence – and then he closed the larger case, locked it and shoved it under the bed nearest the window.

'One ravenous lodger gasping for that steaming coffee and your lovely croissants,' he told Erika cheer-fully as he emerged into the comfortably and well-furnished living-room which served also for a dining-room.

'My!' Her dark eyes searched his. 'Aren't we sud-denly the bright, suave man-about-town. Good to get off the streets, Manfred?'

He swallowed the cup of coffee she poured even though it almost scalded him. Then he sat down and devoured three croissants while she sat facing him, studying him. Like Seidler, her parents were dead and she had no close relatives. Erika had worked her way up to the post of personal assistant to the chief executive of the bank she worked for. And her background was modest. Probably only in Switzerland could she have risen so high on sheer hard work and application.

'I'm quite happy on my own,' she had once confided to a girl friend. 'I have a good job I like, a lover' (she meant Manfred, although she didn't identify him). 'So what more do I need? I can certainly do without being tied down at home, touring the supermarkets with some yelling brat – and a husband who, after three years, starts noticing the attractive secretaries in his office . . .'

'You were glad to get in off the streets, Manfred?' she repeated.

'Look outside the window! It's snowing cats and dogs. And I have been working very hard. I feel like holing up – some place no one knows where I am. Where the telephone won't ring,' he added quickly.

For once Seidler was telling the truth. He had cleverly chosen Basle to go to ground; Basle where three frontiers meet – Swiss, French and German. In case of emergency, the need for swift flight, he only had to board a train at the main station and the next stop – minutes away – was in Germany. Or, from the same station he could walk through a barrier to the other section and he was already on *French* soil. Yes, Basle was a good place to wait until he decided on his next move – until something turned up. Because for Manfred Seidler something always did turn up.

Then there was Erika. Seidler, a man who spent most of his time making money engaging in illegal, near-criminal activity – and who was now a murderer – appreciated that Erika was a *nice* girl. It was such a pleasant change to have her for company. He woke up from his reverie, aware she had said something.

'Sorry, I was dreaming . . .'

'Since you were last here I've been promoted . . .'

'Higher still? You were already PA to a director . . .'

'Now I'm PA to the president of the bank.' She leaned across the table and he stared at the inviting twin bulges against her flowered blouse. 'Manfred,' she went on, 'have you – you get around a lot, I know – have you ever heard anyone refer to the word *terminal*?'

Seidler's sense of well-being – brought on by a full stomach, the apartment's warmth (Erika could afford to turn up the central heating) and the proximity of Erika – vanished. One word and the nightmare was back on his doorstep. He struggled to hide the shock she had given him.

'I might have,' he teased her, 'if you tell me where you heard it.'

She hesitated, her curiosity fighting her integrity. Curiosity won. She took a deep breath and stretched out her small hand to grasp his.

'I was taking coffee in to a board meeting. My boss said to the others, "Has anyone found out any more

74

about this *terminal* business, what it means, or is it just another rumour about the Gold Club?"'

'Gold Club? What's that?'

'Well, it doesn't really exist officially. I gather that it comprises a group of bankers who have certain views on national policy. The group is known as the Gold Club . . .'

'And your boss belongs to it?'

'On the contrary. He doesn't agree with their views, whatever they may be. The Gold Club is based in Zurich . . .'

'Zurich? Not Berne?' he probed.

'Definitely Zurich . . .'

'Who is your boss?' he enquired casually.

'I'm talking too much about my job . . .'

'I could find out so easily,' he pointed out. 'I'd only have to phone you at work and you'd say, "Office of . . ." There are other ways. You know that.'

'I suppose you're right,' she agreed. 'In any case, it really doesn't matter. I work for Dr Max Nagel. Now, does *terminal* mean a railway station? That's the current thinking . . .'

'They got it right first time. More than that I don't know.'

'A railway station – not an *airport*?' she persisted. 'We do have an airport at Basle.'

'Positively nothing to do with airports,' he assured her.

He stood up and wiped his mouth with his napkin. He offered to clear the table but she shook her head and stood close to him, coiling her hands round his neck. As they kissed he wrapped his arms round her body and felt the buttons down the back of her blouse.

'That Gold Club,' he whispered. 'Something to do with gold bullion?'

'No. I told you. It's just a name. You know how wealthy the Zurich bankers are. It's a good name for them . . .'

He unfastened the top two buttons and slipped his hand inside, searching for the splayed strap. His exploring fingers found nothing. He undid two more buttons and realized that beneath the blouse she was naked. She had stripped herself down while he trudged through the snow from the station.

He enjoyed himself in the bedroom but when the aftermath came he began to worry like mad about what she'd said. Was Basle the worst place in the world he could have come to escape? Had he wandered into the lion's pit? He'd have to keep under cover. He'd also watch the newspapers – especially those from Geneva, Berne and Zurich, plus the locals. Something might show up in them, something which would show him the way – the way to escape the horror.

Chapter Eight

London, 13 February 1984. 6°

The atmosphere inside Tweed's office at 10 a.m. was one of appalled mystification. Besides Tweed, the other people gathered in the office included Howard, who had just returned from a weekend in the country, Monica, the middle-aged spinster of uncertain age Tweed called his 'right arm', and Mason, summoned urgently from Vienna on an apparent whim of Tweed's.

The 'object' Mason had brought with him and which he had purchased from Franz Oswald, was now locked away in Tweed's steel filing cabinet. No one had wanted to continue staring at *that* for long.

Howard, wearing the small check suit he kept for the country, was furious. He was convinced Tweed had exploited his absence to set all sorts of dangerous wheels in motion. To add insult to injury, Tweed had just returned from Downing Street where he had remained closeted with the Prime Minister for over an hour.

'Did you ask her for that document?' he enquired coldly.

Tweed glanced at the letter headed *10 Downing*

Street which he had deliberately left on his desk. It gave him full powers to conduct the investigation personally. There was even a codicil promising him immediate access to her presence at any time there were developments.

'No,' replied Tweed, standing like the rest and polishing his glasses with a shabby silk handkerchief. 'It was her idea. I didn't argue, naturally . . .'

'Naturally,' Howard repeated sarcastically. 'So, now you've got the whole place in an uproar what's the next move?'

'I need outside help on this one.' Tweed looped his glasses over his ears and blinked at Howard. 'As you know, we're fully stretched. We have to get help where we can . . .'

'A name – or names – would be reassuring . . .'

'I'm not sure that's wise. Reliable help will only cooperate on a basis of total secrecy. If I'm the only person who knows their identity they know who to point the finger at if things go wrong. I take full responsibility . . .'

'You've hired an outsider already,' Howard accused.

Tweed shrugged and glanced at the letter on his desk. Howard could have killed him. It was an uncharacteristic action on the part of Tweed, but he would go to any length to protect a source. He decided he had treated Howard rather badly – especially in front of the others.

'There's already been a body,' he informed his

chief. 'A man was murdered in Vienna. Mason can tell you about it . . .'

'God Almighty!' Howard exploded. 'What are you letting us in for?'

'Permission to explain, sir?' the trim, erect Mason interjected. Taking Howard's curt nod for an affirmative he described in concise detail his experience with Franz Oswald. Howard listened in silence, his pursed lips expressing disapproval – and anxiety, a reaction Tweed sympathized with. He wasn't at all happy about the way the situation was developing himself.

'And did he tell you – while he was alive – how he obtained the *thing*?'

Howard nodded again, this time towards the locked drawer in the filing cabinet. He had calmed down while listening to Mason, a man he disliked but respected – they came from the same background. The trouble was he was Tweed's man. Like that bloody old spinster, Monica, who hadn't spoken a word – but Howard knew that later she could repeat the entire conversation back verbatim from memory.

'No, sir, he didn't,' Mason answered. 'I did ask but he refused point-blank to go into details. I have, however, got a photograph of the man who boarded the plane at Schwechat – that new camera is a wizard and I always carry it with me. It was a long shot, telephoto lens, but it's come out rather well.'

'Show it to me. You have got it on you?'

Mason glanced quickly at Tweed, which infuriated Howard once more. Tweed nodded acquiescence and wished Mason hadn't asked his permission. Still, Mason was being ultra-careful with this one. He watched Howard studying the photograph Mason handed to him.

'Any idea who he is?' Howard demanded.

'He's familiar,' Tweed replied. 'It will come back to me . . .'

'Put it through Records,' Howard suggested. 'Now, Mason, I'm going to say a word and I want you to react instantly. Give me the first association that comes into your head. Don't think about it. Ready? *Terminal* . . .'

'An electrical circuit,' Mason responded promptly.

'That's interesting.' Howard turned to Tweed. 'The Swiss are transforming their whole economy to run on electric power. New houses are heated by electricity – to avoid dependence on oil. Did you know that?'

'Yes, I knew that. You might have a shrewd point there,' he agreed.

'Supposing this whole business hinges on a massive sabotage operation?' Howard warmed to his theme. 'The enemy is planning to hit all the key points in the Swiss power system when the moment comes for them to make their move.'

'You could be right. We'll know when we find out what really is going on inside Switzerland. I need to send in someone the Swiss police and military intelligence don't know. Mason would fit the bill. And the

Ambassador in Vienna agreed to bring forward his leave – three weeks . . .'

'Good idea,' agreed Howard. He felt a little better about the whole thing now he was *contributing*. Time to show a modicum of goodwill. He nodded towards the letter on Tweed's desk. 'With her backing we have an open-ended call on resources. But this business still worries me. Who would imagine the Swiss getting mixed up in a situation of such international dimensions? Yes, Mason, was there something?'

'Permission to find some breakfast – if you're finished with me, sir? Airline meals turn my stomach. I haven't eaten since last night.'

'Fuel up!' Howard said breezily, still buoyant. 'That is, if Tweed has nothing more?'

'I'll be organizing your flight to Zurich,' Tweed told Mason. 'Get a train from there to Berne – it's only ninety minutes. Breakfast first though. And thank you, Mason. I'm not certain what you've triggered off yet, but it's something very big. I feel it in my arthritic bones . . .'

'Howard is a pain in the proverbial,' Monica remarked to Tweed when they were alone. 'Up and down like a bloody yo-yo . . .'

'It's his wife, Eve,' Tweed said, slumping back in his swivel chair. 'I only met her once. Very County, very superior. She went out of her way to make me feel uncomfortable . . .'

'That's because she fears you,' Monica commented shrewdly.

'And that's ridiculous,' Tweed protested.

'She's ambitious, the driving force behind Howard. When he tells her the Prime Minister has given you *carte blanche* she'll really hit the roof. I know the type. On top of that she has money – a large block of ICI shares she inherited. That gives a woman a sense of power.'

'Poor Howard,' said Tweed and his sympathy was genuine. He looked at Monica, a comfortable woman whose deep loyalty to him he sometimes found worrying. Under other circumstances he might have considered marrying her, but that, of course, was quite impossible. 'I have an appointment,' he said, standing up. 'Expect me when you see me . . .'

'No way of getting in touching?' she enquired mischievously.

'Not this time.' He paused near the door and she was careful not to help him on with his coat. Tweed hated fuss. 'Monica, when Mason gets back, ask him to wait for me. Tell him one job will be to compile a file on Professor Armand Grange, head of the Berne Clinic . . .'

It was 12.30 p.m. when Tweed returned to hung up his coat by the loop and settled himself behind his desk. Monica, checking a file with Mason.

Lee Foley walked along Piccadilly, his expression bleak, hands thrust inside the pockets of his duffel coat. Christ, it was cold in London, a raw, damp cold. No wonder the Brits. had once conquered the world. If you could stand this climate you could stand anywhere across the face of the earth.

He checked his watch. The timing of the call was important. The contact would be expecting him at the appointed number. He glanced round casually before descending into Piccadilly underground station. No reason why anyone should be following him – which was the moment to check.

Inside the phone booth he checked his watch again, waited until his watch registered precisely 11 a.m., then dialled the London number, waited for the bleeps, inserted a tenpenny coin and heard the familiar voice. He identified himself and then listened before answering.

'Now let me do the talking. I'll catch an early flight to Geneva today. I'll wait at the Hotel des Bergues. When the time comes I'll proceed to Berne. I'll reserve a room at a hotel called the Savoy near the station – you can get the number from the Berne directory. We'll keep in close touch as the situation develops. You must keep me informed. Signing off . . .'

It was 12.30 p.m. when Tweed returned to his office, hung up his coat by the loop and settled himself behind his desk. Monica, checking a file with Mason, frowned. He should have put the coat on a hanger – no wonder he always had such a rumpled look. She carefully refrained from so doing. Tweed had been away for over two hours.

'I've booked Mason on Swissair Flight SR 805. Departs Heathrow fourteen forty-five, arrives Zurich seventeen twenty, local time . . .'

'He'll catch it easily,' Tweed agreed with an absent-minded expression. 'What are you two up to?'

'Looking through hundreds of photos. We've found the man he saw boarding that Swiss jet at Schwechat Airport. Manfred Seidler . . .'

'You're sure?'

'Positive,' Mason replied. 'Look for yourself.'

He handed across the desk the photo he had taken and which the photographic section in the basement of Park Crescent had developed and printed. Monica pushed Seidler's file across the desk open at the third page to which another photo was pasted.

'Poor old Manfred,' Tweed said half to himself. 'It looks as though this time he's mixed up in something he may not be able to handle.'

'You know him?' Mason queried.

'*Knew* him. When I was on the continent. He's on what we used to call the circuit . . .'

'Not an *electric* circuit?' Monica pounced. 'Remember Howard asking Mason what *Terminal* suggested to him?'

Tweed stared at her through his glasses. Monica didn't miss a trick: he would never have thought of that himself. He considered the idea. 'There could be a connection,' he conceded eventually. 'I'm not sure. Seidler is a collector – and seller – of unconsidered trifles. Sometimes not so trifling. Lives off his network of contacts. Just occasionally he comes up with the jackpot. I've no idea where he is now. Something for you to enquire about, Mason.'

'I'm going to be busy. Searching for Manfred Seidler building up a file on this Professor Grange. We've nothing on him here.'

'The computer came up with zero,' Monica added.

'Computer?' An odd expression flickered behind Tweed's glasses and was then gone. He relaxed again. 'Mason, from the moment you leave this building I want you to watch your back. Especially when you've arrived in Switzerland.'

'Anything particular in mind?'

'We've already had one murder – Franz Oswald. People will kill for what I've got in that locked drawer . . .' He looked at Monica. 'Or has the courier from the Ministry of Defence collected it?'

'Not so far . . .'

'They must be mad.' Tweed drummed his thick fingers on the desk. 'The sooner their experts examine it . . .'

'Charlton is a careful type,' Monica reminded him. 'He's very conscious of security. My bet is the courier will arrive as soon as night has fallen.'

'You're probably right. I shan't leave my office until the thing is off our hands. Now, Mason,' he resumed, 'another unknown factor is the attitude of the Swiss authorities – the Federal police and their Military Intelligence. They could prove hostile . . .'

'What on earth for?' Monica protested.

'It worries me – that Lear executive jet Mason watched leaving Schwechat. The fact that it bore a flag on its side with a white cross on a red ground, the Swiss flag. Don't accept anyone as a friend. Oh, one more thing. We've reserved a room at the Belle-vue Palace in Berne.'

Mason whistled. 'Very nice. VIP treatment. Howard will do his nut when he finds out . . .'

'It's convenient,' Tweed said shortly. 'I may join you later.'

Monica had trouble keeping her face expression-less. She knew that Tweed had his own reservation at the Bellevue Palace a few days hence: she had booked the room herself. Tweed, naturally secretive, was playing this one closer to the chest than ever before. He wasn't even letting his own operative know about his movements. For God's sake, he couldn't suspect Mason?

'Why convenient?' enquired Mason.

'It's central,' Tweed said shortly and left it at that. 'We're getting things moving,' he went on with that distant look in his eyes, 'placing the pieces on the board. One thing I'd dearly like to know – where is Manfred Seidler now?'

*

Basle, 13 February 1984. 0°

Seidler still felt hunted. He had spent the whole weekend inside Erika Stahel's apartment and the walls were starting to close in on him. He heard a key being inserted in the outer door and grabbed for his 9-mm. Luger, a weapon he had concealed from Erika.

When she walked in, carrying a bag of groceries, the Luger was out of sight under a cushion. She closed the door with her foot and surveyed the newspapers spread out over the table. She had dashed out first thing to get them for him. Now she had dashed back from the office – only one hour for lunch – to prepare him some food.

'Anything in the papers?' she called out from the tiny kitchen.

'Nothing. Yet. You don't have to make me a meal . . .'

'Won't take any time at all. We can talk while we eat . . .'

He looked at the newspapers on the table. The *Berner Zeitung*, the main Zurich morning, the *Journal de Genève* and the Basle locals. He lifted one of them and underneath lay the executive case. He'd made up his mind.

Since he was a youth Seidler had involved himself in unsavoury activities – always to make money. Brought up by an aunt in Vienna – his mother had been killed by the Russians, his father had died on the

Eastern Front – Seidler had been one of the world's wanderers. Now, when he had the money, when he felt like settling down, the whole system was trying to locate him.

He felt a great affection for Erika because she was such a *decent* girl. He laid the table, listened to her chatting with animation while they ate, and only brought up the subject over coffee.

'Erika, if anything happens to me I want you to have this . . .'

He opened the executive case, revealing the neatly stacked Swiss banknotes inside. Her face, which always showed the pink flush Seidler had observed when women were pregnant, went blank as she stood up. Her deft fingers rifled through several of the stacks at random and replaced them. She stared at him.

'Manfred, there has to be half a million francs here . . .'

'Very close. Take them and put them into a safety deposit – not at the bank where you work. Call a cab. Don't walk through the streets with that – not even in Basle . . .'

'I can't take this.' She grasped his hand and he saw she was close to tears. 'I'm not interested – you're the only one I'm interested in.'

'So, bank it for both of us. Under your own name. Under no circumstances under my name,' he warned.

'Manfred . . .' She eased herself into his lap. 'Who are you frightened of? Did you steal this money?'

'No!' He became vehement to convince her. 'It

was given to me for services rendered. Now they no longer need me. They may regard me as a menace because of what I know. I shouldn't stay here much longer . . .'

'Stay as long as you like. Who are these people?'

'One person in particular. Someone who wields enormous power. Someone who may be able to use even the police to do his bidding.'

'The Swiss police?' Her tone was incredulous. 'You look so tired, so worn. You're over-estimating this person's power. If it will make you feel any better I will put that case in a safety deposit – providing you keep the key . . .'

'All right.' He knew it was the only condition under which she'd agree to do what he asked. They'd find some place inside the apartment to hide the key. 'You'd better hurry. You'll be late for work,' he told her.

She hugged him as though she'd never let go. He almost had tears in his own eyes. So decent, so nice. If only he'd met her years ago . . .

Inside their bedroom at the Penta Hotel, situated amid the vast enclave of Heathrow Airport, Newman checked his watch again. Nancy had gone out hours ago on her own – she knew how he hated shopping expeditions. They still had plenty of time to catch Swissair Flight SR 837 which departed 19.00 hours and reached Geneva 21.30 hours local time. The door opened and she caught him looking at his watch.

'I've been hours, I know,' she said cheerfully. 'Think we were going to miss our flight? Have I enjoyed myself . . .'

'You've probably bought up half Fortnum's . . .'

'Just about. It's a marvellous shop – and they'll post off purchases anywhere in the world.' She looked at him coyly as she hung up her sheepskin in the wardrobe. 'I'm not showing you the bills. God, I love London . . .'

'Then why don't we settle down here?'

'Robert, don't start that again. And you've been out. Your coat is on a different hanger . . .'

'For a breath of fresh air. Tinged with petrol fumes. You're cut out to be a detective.'

'Doctors have to be observant, darling.' She looked at the bed. 'Do we eat now – or later?'

'Later. We have things to do.' He wrapped his arms round her slim waist. 'Afterwards we'll just have a drink. Dinner on the plane. Swissair food is highly edible . . .'

Belted in his seat aboard an earlier Swissair flight, Lee Foley glanced out of the window as the aircraft left Heathrow behind and broke through the overcast into a sunlit world. He was sitting at the rear of the first-class section.

Foley had reserved this particular seat because it was a good viewing point to observe his fellow-passengers. Unlike them, he had refused any food or drink when the steward came to put a cloth on his fold-out table.

'Nothing,' he said abruptly.

'We have a very nice meal as you can see from the menu, sir.'

'Take the menu; keep the meal . . .'

'Something to drink then, sir?'

'I said nothing.'

It was still daylight when the aircraft made its descent over the Jura Mountains, heading for Cointrin Airport. Foley watched the view as the plane banked and noted Lac de Joux, nestled inside the Juras, was frozen solid. At least, he assumed this must be the case – the lake was mantled in snow, as were the mountains. He was the first passenger to leave the plane after it landed and he carried his only luggage.

Foley always travelled light. Hanging around a carousel, waiting for your bag to appear on the moving belt, gave watchers the opportunity to observe your arrival. Foley always regarded terminals as dangerous points of entry. He showed his passport to the Swiss official seated inside his glass box, watching him out of the corner of his eye. The passport was returned and, so far as Foley could tell, no interest had been aroused.

He walked through the green Customs exit into the public concourse beyond. For strangers there was a clear sign pointing to *TAXIS*, but Foley automatically turned in the right direction. He was familiar with Cointrin.

The chill air had hit him like a knife thrust when he came down the mobile staircase from the aircraft. It hit him again when he emerged from the building and walked to the first cab. He waited until he was settled in the rear seat with the door closed before he gave the instruction to the driver.

'Hotel des Bergues . . .'

Foley's wariness about terminals was closer to the mark than he realized when he walked swiftly across the concourse without turning his head. Looking back drew attention to yourself – betrayed nervousness. So he had not seen a small, gnome-like figure huddled against a wall with an unlit cigarette between his thin lips.

Julius Nagy had straightened briefly when he saw Foley, then he took out a bookmatch and pretended to light the cigarette without doing so – Nagy didn't smoke. His tiny, bird-like eyes sparkled with satisfaction as he watched the American pass beyond the automatic exit doors. His neat feet trotted inside the nearest phone box and closed the door.

Nagy, who had escaped from Hungary in 1956 when Soviet troops invaded his country, was fifty-two years old. Streaks of dark-oily hair peeped from under the Tyrolean-style hat he wore well pulled down. His skin was wrinkled like a walnut, his long nose pinched at the nostrils.

He dialled the number he knew by heart. Nagy had a phenomenal memory for three things – people's faces, their names, and phone numbers. When the police headquarters operator answered he gave his name, asked to be put through immediately, please, to Chief Inspector Tripet. Yes, he was well-known to Tripet and he was in a hurry.

'Tripet speaking. Who is this?'

The voice, remote, careful, had spoken in French. Nagy could picture the Sûreté man sitting in his second-floor office inside the seven-storey building facing the Public Library at 24 Boulevard Carl-Vogt, at the foot of the Old City.

'Nagy here. Didn't they tell you?'

'Christian name?'

'Oh, for God's sake. Julius. Julius Nagy. I've got some information. It's worth a hundred francs . . .'

'Perhaps . . .'

'Someone who just came in from London off the flight at Cointrin. A hundred francs I want – or I'll dry up . . .'

'And who is this expensive someone?' asked Tripet in a bored tone of voice.

'Lee Foley, CIA man . . .'

'I'll meet you at the usual place. Exactly one hour from now. Eighteen hundred hours. I want to talk to you about this – see your face when I do. If it isn't genuine you're off the payroll for all time . . .'

Nagy heard the click and realized Tripet had broken the connection. He was puzzled. Had he asked too little? Was the information pure gold? On the other hand Tripet had sounded as though he were rebuking the little man. Nagy shrugged, left the booth, saw the airport bus for town was about to leave and started running.

At 24 Boulevard Carl-Vogt, Tripet, a thin-faced, serious-looking man in his late thirties, a man who had risen quickly in his chosen profession, hoped he had bluffed Nagy as his agile fingers dialled the Berne number.

'Arthur Beck, please, Assistant to the Chief of Federal Police,' he requested crisply when the operator at the Taubenhalde came on the line. 'This is Chief Inspector Tripet, Sûreté, Geneva . . .'

'One moment, sir . . .'

Beck came to the phone quickly after first dismissing from his tenth-floor office his secretary, a fifty-five-year-old spinster not unlike Tweed's Monica. Settling himself comfortably in his chair, Beck spoke with calm amiability.

'Well, Leon, and how are things in Geneva? Snowing?'

'Not quite. Arthur, you asked me to report if any odd people turned up on my patch. Would Lee Foley, CIA operative, qualify?'

'Yes.' Beck gripped the receiver a shade more firmly. 'Tell me about it.' He reached for pad and pencil.

'He may have just come in on a Swissair flight from London. I have a report from Cointrin . . .'

'A report from who?' The pencil poised.

'A small-time informer we call The Mongrel, sometimes The Scrounger. He'll burrow in any filthy trashcan to make himself a few francs. But he's very reliable. If Foley interests you I'm meeting Julius Nagy, The Mongrel, shortly outside. Can you give me a description of Foley so I can test Nagy's story?'

'Foley is a man you can't miss . . .' Beck gave from memory a detailed description of the American, including the fact that he spoke in a gravelly voice. 'That should be enough, Leon, you would agree? Good. When you've seen The Mongrel, I would appreciate another call from you. I'll wait in my office . . .'

Tripet went off the line quickly, an action Beck, who couldn't stand people who wasted time, appreciated. Then he sat in his chair, twiddling the pencil while he thought.

They were beginning to come in, as he had anticipated. The crisis was growing. There would be others on the way, he suspected. He had been warned about the rumours circulating among various foreign embassies. Beck, forty years old in May, was a stockily-built man with a thick head of unruly brown hair and a small brown moustache. His grey eyes had a glint of humour, a trait which often saved his sanity when the pressure was on.

He reflected that he had never known greater pressure. Thank God his chief had given him extraordinary powers to take any action he thought fit. If what he suspected was true – and he hoped with all his Catholic soul he was wrong – then he was going to need those powers. Sometimes when he thought of what he might be up against he winced. Beck, however, was a loner. *If necessary I'll bullfight the whole bloody system,* he said to himself. He would not be defeated by Operation Terminal.

Unlocking a drawer while he waited for Tripet to call him back, he took out a file with the tab, *Classification One,* on the front of the folder. He turned to the first page inside and looked at the heading typed at the head of the script. *Case of Hannah Stuart, American citizen. Klinik Bern.*

Chapter Nine

Geneva, 13 February 1984. −3°

'On duty' again at Cointrin, Julius Nagy could hardly believe his eyes. This was Jackpot Day. After meeting Chief Inspector Tripet, who had asked for a detailed description of Lee Foley, who had been sufficiently satisfied with the information to pay him his one hundred francs, Nagy had returned to meet the last flights into the airport despite the bitter cold.

Flight SR 837 – again from London – had disgorged its passengers when Nagy spotted a famous face emerging from the Customs exit. Robert Newman had a woman with him and this time Nagy followed his quarry outside. He was just behind the Englishman when he heard him instructing the driver of the cab.

'Please take us to the Hotel des Bergues,' Newman had said in French.

Nagy had decided to invest twenty or so of the francs received from Tripet to check Newman's real destination. They were tricky, these foreign correspondents. He wouldn't put it past Newman to change the destination once they were clear of the airport. As he summoned the next cab Nagy glanced over his shoulder and saw Newman, on the verge of stepping inside the rear of his cab, staring hard at him. He swore inwardly and dived inside the back of his own cab.

'Follow my friend in that cab ahead,' he told the driver.

'If you say so . . .'

His driver showed a little discretion, keeping another vehicle between himself and Newman's. It was only a ten-minute ride – including the final three-sided tour round the hotel to reach the main entrance because of the one-way system.

He watched the porter from the Hotel des Bergues taking their luggage and told his driver to move on and drop him round the corner. Paying off the cabbie, he hurried to the nearest phone box, frozen by the bitter wind blowing along the lake and the Rhône which the des Bergues overlooked. He called Pierre Jaccard, senior reporter on the *Journal de Genève*. His initial reception was even more hostile than had been Tripet's.

'What are you trying to peddle this time, Nagy?'

'There are plenty of people in the market for this one,' Nagy said aggressively, deliberately adopting a different approach. You had to know your potential clients. 'You have, I presume, heard of the Kruger Affair – the German traitor who extracted information from the giant computer at Dusseldorf?'

'Yes, of course I have. But that's last year's news . . .'

Nagy immediately detected the change in tone

from contempt to cautious interest – concealing avid interest. He played his fish.

'Two hundred francs and I'm not arguing about the price. It's entirely non-negotiable. You could still catch tomorrow's edition. And I can tell you how to check out what I may tell you – with one phone call.'

'Tell me a little more . . .'

'Either another Kruger case, this time nearer home, or something equally big. That's all you get until you agree terms. Is it a deal? Yes or no. And I'm putting down this phone in thirty seconds. Counting now . . .'

'Hold it! If you're conning me . . .'

'Goodbye, Jaccard . . .'

'Deal! Two hundred francs. God, the gambles I take. Give.'

'Robert Newman – you *have* heard of Robert Newman? I thought you probably had. He's just come in on Flight SR 837 from London. You think he arrives late in the evening anywhere without a purpose? And he looked to be in one hell of a hurry . . .'

'You said I could check this out,' Jaccard reminded him.

'He's staying at the Hotel des Bergues. Call the place – ask to speak to him, give a false name. Christ, Jaccard, you do know your job?'

'I know my job,' Jaccard said quietly. 'Come over to my office now and the money will be waiting . . .'

*

Arthur Beck sat behind his desk, a forgotten cup of cold coffee to his left, studying the fat file on Lee Foley. A good selection of photos – all taken without the subject's knowledge. A long note recording that he had resigned from the CIA, that he was now senior partner in the New York outfit, CIDA, the Continental International Detective Agency. 'I wonder . . .' Beck said aloud and the phone rang.

'I'm so sorry I didn't phone earlier . . .' Tripet in Geneva was full of apologies. 'An emergency was waiting for me when I got back to the office . . . a reported kidnapping at Cologny . . . it turned out to be a false alarm, thank God . . .'

'Not to worry. I have plenty to occupy myself with. Now, any developments?'

'The Mongrel – Julius Nagy – confirmed exactly your description of Foley. He is somewhere in Geneva – or he was when he left Cointrin at seventeen hundred hours . . .'

'Do something for me, will you? Check all the hotels – find out where he's staying, if he's still there. Let me give you a tip. Start with the cheaper places – two- and three-star. Foley maintains a low profile.'

'A pleasure. I'll get the machinery moving immediately . . .'

Beck replaced the receiver. He rarely made a mistake, but on this occasion he had badly misjudged his quarry.

*

Foley, who had dined elsewhere, approached the entrance to the Hotel des Bergues cautiously. He peered through the revolving doors into the reception hall beyond. The doorman was talking to the night concierge. No one else about.

He pushed the door and walked inside. Checking his watch, he turned left and wandered up to the door leading into one of the hotel's two restaurants, the Pavillon which overlooks the Rhône. At a banquette window table he saw Newman and Nancy Kennedy who had reached the coffee stage.

Newman had his back to the door which had a glass panel in the upper half. Foley had a three-quarter view of Nancy. Newman suddenly looked over his shoulder, Foley moved away quickly, collected his key and headed for the elevator.

The Pavillon, a restaurant favoured by the locals as well as hotel guests, was half-empty. Newman stared out of the window as several couples hurried past, heads down against the bitter wind, the women wearing furs – sable, lynx, mink – while their men were clad mostly in sheepskins.

'There's a lot of money in this town,' Nancy observed, following his gaze. 'And Bob, that was a superb meal. The chicken was the best I've ever eaten. As good as Bewick's in Walton Street,' she teased him. 'What are you thinking about?'

'That we have to decide our next move – which doesn't mean we necessarily rush on to Berne yet . . .'

'Why not? I thought we were leaving tomorrow . . .'

'Maybe, maybe not.' Newman's tone was firm. 'When we've finished do you mind if I take a walk along the lake. Alone. I have some thinking to do.'

'You have an appointment? You've checked your watch three times since the main course . . .'

'I said a walk.' He grinned to soften his reply. 'Did you know that Geneva is one of the great European centres of espionage? It crawls with agents. The trouble is all the various UN outfits which are here. Half the people of this city are foreigners. The Genevoises get a bit fed up. The foreigners push up the price of apartments – unless you're very wealthy. Like you are . . .'

'Don't let's spoil a lovely evening.' She checked her own watch. 'You go and have your walk – I'll unpack. Whether we're leaving tomorrow or not I don't want my dresses creased.' Her chin tilted at the determined angle he knew so well. 'Go on – have your walk. Don't spend all night with her . . .'

'Depends on the mood she's in.' He grinned again.

Newman, his sheepskin turned up at the collar, pushed through the revolving doors and the temperature plummeted. A raw wind slashed at his face. Across the road, beyond iron railings, the Rhône chopped and surged; by daylight he guessed it would have that special greenish colour of water which was melted snow from peaks in the distant Valais.

By night the water looked black. Neon lights from

buildings on the opposite shore reflected in the dark flow. Oddly British-sounding signs. The green neon of the British Bank of the Middle East. The blue neon of Kleinwort Benson. The red neon of the Hongkong Bank. Street lamps were a zigzag reflection in the ice-cold water. Thrusting both hands inside his coat pockets he began walking east towards the Hilton.

Behind him Julius Nagy emerged, frozen stiff, from a doorway. The gnome-like figure was careful to keep a couple between himself and Newman. At least his long wait had produced some result. Where the hell could the Englishman be going at this hour, in this weather?

Sitting in Pierre Jaccard's cubby-hole office at the *Journal de Genève*, Nagy had received a pleasant shock. Jaccard had first pushed an envelope across his crowded desk and then watched as Nagy opened it. Thirty-year-old Jaccard, already senior reporter on the paper, had come a long way by taking chances, backing his intuition. Thin-faced with watchful eyes which never smiled even when his mouth registered amiability, he drank coffee from a cardboard cup.

'Count it, Nagy. It's all there. Two hundred. Like to make some more?'

'Doing what?' Nagy enquired with calculated indifference.

'You hang on to Newman's tail for dear life. You report back to me where he is, where he goes, whom he meets. I want to know everything about him – down to the colour of the pyjamas he's wearing . . .'

'An assignment like that costs money,' Nagy said promptly.

It was one of the favourite words in Nagy's vocabulary. He never referred to a job – he was always on an *assignment*. It was the little man's way of conferring some dignity on his way of life. A man needed to feel he had some importance in the world. Jaccard was too young to grasp the significance of the word, too cynical. Had he understood, he could have bought Nagy for less.

'There's another two hundred in this envelope,' Jaccard said, pushing it across the desk. 'A hundred for your fee, a hundred for expenses. And I'll need a receipted bill for every franc of expenses . . .'

Nagy shook his head, made no effort to touch the second envelope. Despite Jaccard's expression of boredom he sensed under the surface something big, maybe very big. He clasped his small hands in his lap, pursed his lips.

'Newman could take off for anywhere – Zurich, Basle, Lugano. I need the funds to follow him if I'm to carry out the assignment satisfactorily . . .'

'How much? And think before you reply . . .'

'Five hundred. Two for myself for the moment. Three for expenses. You'll get your bills. Not a franc less.'

Jaccard had sighed, reached for his wallet and counted five one-hundred franc notes. Which cleaned him out. Tomorrow he'd been on his way to Munich – but he was gambling again, gambling on Newman who had cracked the Kruger case. Christ, if he could only get on to something like that he'd be made for life.

Which was how Nagy, shivering in his shabby overcoat and Tyrolean hat, came to be following Newman who had now reached the lakeside. Earlier, just before crossing the rue du Mont Blanc, the Englishman had glanced back and Nagy thought he'd been spotted. But now Newman continued trudging along the promenade, his head bent against the wind.

As he approached the Hilton, which faces the lake, the street was so deserted that Newman heard another sound above the whine of the wind. The creaking groan of a paddle steamer moored to one of the landing stages, the noise of the hull grinding against the wood of the mooring posts. A single-funnel paddle steamer going no place: it was still out of season. Waiting for spring. Like the whole of the northern hemisphere. No more neon signs across the broadening expanse of the lake. Only cold, twinkling lights along some distant street. He stopped by the outside lift and pressed the button.

A small version of the external elevators which slide vertiginously up the sides of many American hotels, the lift arrived and Newman stepped inside, pressing another button. It occurred to him how exposed he was as the small cage ascended – the door was of glass, the lift was lit inside, a perfect target for any marksman.

Nagy timed it carefully, running up the staircase to

the first floor so he saw Newman vanishing inside the restaurant. He waited, then followed. Before entering the restaurant, Nagy removed his shabby coat, stuffed his Tyrolean hat inside a pocket, smoothed his ruffled hair and walked inside. A wave of heat beat at his bloodless face.

The restaurant is a large rectangle with the long side parallel to the lake. Newman was sitting down at a window table at the far end, a table for two. The other chair was already occupied by a girl who made Nagy stare.

The little man sat at a table near the exit, ordered coffee from the English waitress who appeared promptly – the waitresses here are of various nationalities. He studied Newman's companion surreptitiously. Some people had all the luck he thought without envy.

The girl was in her late twenties, Nagy decided, memorizing her appearance for Jaccard. Thick, titian-(Nagy called it red) coloured hair with a centre parting, a fawn cashmere (at a guess) sweater which showed off her ample figure and tight black leather pants encasing her superb legs from crotch to ankle as though painted on her. Gleaming leather. The new 'wet' look. Very good bone structure – high cheekbones.

A stunner. At first Nagy thought she was a tart, then decided he was wrong. This girl had class, something the little man respected. Exceptionally animated, their conversation gradually developed so she listened intently while Newman talked, drinking his cup of coffee at occasional intervals.

At one stage she reached across to straighten his tie, a gesture Nagy duly noted. It suggested a degree of intimacy. Something else for Jaccard. Nagy had the impression Newman was instructing her, that she asked a question only to clarify a point.

When Newman paid the bill and left she remained at the table. Nagy had a moment of indecision – who to watch now? But only a moment. Newman walked towards Nagy – and the exit, putting on his sheepskin as he walked past the little man without even a glance in his direction. Nagy, who had paid his own bill as soon as his coffee had arrived, followed.

This time Newman jibbed at the exposed elevator. He ran down the staircase and walked back briskly along the Siberian promenade. He *dived* inside the revolving doors of the Hotel des Bergues and went straight up to Room 406. Nancy, wearing a transparent nightdress, opened the door a few inches, then let him inside.

'Was she good?' was her first question.

'You think I'm some kind of stud?' he replied genially.

'I'll tell you something – when we arrived and you had to register, I was like a jelly inside with embarrassment. Mr and Mrs R. Newman . . .'

'The Swiss are discreet. I told you . . .' He had

already taken off his tie. '. . . they only want to see the man's passport. And it's bloody freezing outside. I walked miles.'

'Come to any decisions?'

'Always sleep on decisions. See how they look in the morning.'

It was in the morning that the world blew up in Newman's face.

108

Chapter Ten

Geneva, 14 February 1984. −2°

The concierge called out to Newman as they made their way to the Pavillon for breakfast. Nancy had tried to persuade him to use Room Service and he had refused point-blank.

'You Americans can't think of any other ways of living except Room Service ...'

He excused himself, stopping at the concierge's desk. With a broad smile the concierge spread out the front page of the *Journal de Genève*. Newman's photograph stared back at him inside a box headed *Sommaire*. The text was brief, not a wasted word.

M. Robert Newman, famous foreign correspondent (author of the bestseller KRUGER: THE COMPUTER THAT FAILED) has arrived in Geneva. He is staying at the Hotel des Bergues. We have no information as to his ultimate destination or the new story he is now working on.

'It is good to be famous, yes, no?' the concierge remarked.

'Yes, no,' Newman replied and gave him a franc for the paper.

His face was grim as he pushed open the door into the restaurant. Nancy had chosen the same window table, sitting in the banquette. Newman sat in the chair opposite and stared out of the window. At eight in the morning Geneva was hurrying to work, men and girls heavily muffled against the chilling breeze.

'I've ordered coffee,' Nancy said, breaking a croissant as she studied him. 'Bob, what's wrong?'

He passed the newspaper across without a word, steepled his fingers and went on staring at the swollen Rhône. She read the news item and glowed, waiting until the waitress had arranged their coffee pots.

'I'm going to marry a real celebrity, aren't I? Where did they get the photo? I rather like it . . .'

'From their files. It's appeared often enough before, God knows. This changes everything, Nancy. It could be dangerous. I think I'd better leave you here for a few days. Go on to Berne alone. I'll call you daily . . .'

'Like hell you will! I've come to see Jesse and I won't be left behind. Why dangerous?'

'Sixth sense . . .'

He paused as a small man in a shabby coat and a Tyrolean hat walked past, glancing briefly inside the restaurant and away as he caught Newman looking at him. A titian-haired girl strolled past in the same direction. She wore a short fur coat, the collar pulled up at the neck, and clean blue jeans tucked inside her leather boots. Newman winked at her and she turned her head to stare ahead.

'You're starting early today,' Nancy observed. 'I saw that . . .'

'Did you see the little man who was walking ahead of her?'

'No. Why?'

'Julius Nagy, a piece of Europe's drifting flotsam.'

'Flotsam?' Nancy looked puzzled.

'One of the many losers who live on their wits, by their contacts, peddling information. He was at the airport last night. He followed us here in a cab. He could be responsible for that piece of dynamite . . .'

His finger tapped the *Sommaire* box and then he poured coffee and broke a hard roll, covering a piece with butter and marmalade. Nancy, her mind in a whirl, kept quiet for a few minutes, knowing he was always in a better mood when he'd had his breakfast.

'You're not going off on your own,' she told him eventually. 'So, what are *we* going to do *together*?'

'Finish our breakfast. Then I'll decide . . .'

But by the time he'd swallowed his fourth cup of coffee, his orange juice and consumed two rolls, the decision was taken out of his hands.

Berne

Inside a large mansion in Elfenau, the district where the wealthy live, Bruno spread out the front page of the *Journal de Genève* on an antique drum table. He studied the picture of Newman carefully.

'So they have arrived,' he said in French.

'We knew they were on the way, Bruno. The question is, will they pose a problem? If so, they will have to be dealt with – you will have to deal with them.'

The large man with tinted spectacles who stood in the shadows spoke with a soft, persuasive voice. The huge living-room was dark even in the morning. Partly due to the overcast sky – and partly because heavy net curtains killed what pallid illumination filtered from the outside world.

Bruno Kobler, a hard-looking man of forty, five feet ten tall, heavily built and in the peak of physical condition, glanced towards the massive silhouette. Light from the desk lamp glinted on the dark glasses. He was trying to gauge exactly what his employer had in mind. The man in the shadows continued speaking.

'I recall so well, Bruno, that when I was building up my chemical works it looked as though a rival might upset my calculations. I didn't wait to see what he would do. I acted first. We are on the eve of a total breakthrough with Terminal: I will allow nothing to stand in my way. Remember, we now have the support of the Gold Club.'

'So, I set up close surveillance on Newman and his woman?'

'You always come to the correct conclusion, Bruno. That is why I pay you so well . . .'

*

Arthur Beck of the Federal Police sat with the receiver to his ear, waiting while the operator at Geneva police headquarters put him on to Tripet. A copy of the *Journal de Genève* lay in front of him. As he had anticipated, the momentum was accelerating. They were coming in. First Lee Foley, alleged detective with the CIDA, now Newman. Beck didn't believe in coincidences – not when events were moving towards a crisis. And this morning his chief had warned him.

'Beck, I'm not sure how much longer I'm going to be able to give you *carte blanche*. Very powerful interests are at work – trying to get me to take you off the case . . .'

'I'm getting to the bottom of this thing whatever happens,' Beck had replied.

'You can't fight the system . . .'

'You want to bet? Sir?'

Tripet came on the line and they exchanged brief courtesies. Beck then told the Geneva chief inspector what he wanted, how to handle it with *finesse*. As the conversation proceeded he detected a note of worry in Tripet's manner. He's unsure of his position, Beck judged.

'Between you and me, Tripet, this comes right from the top. And that's just between you and me. I just hope you can pick him up before he leaves town. You know where he's staying. Call him, send over a car right away if you'd sooner handle it that way. I leave it to you, but do it, Tripet . . .'

Beck replaced the receiver and picked up the paper,

studying the photograph. He was going to need all the help he could muster – even unorthodox help. If it came to the crunch the press was one thing they couldn't muzzle. Yes, he needed allies. His face tightened. Christ! He wasn't going to let the bastards get away with it just because they had half the money in the western world.

Basle

Erika Stahel closed her apartment door and leaned her back against it for a moment, clutching the armful of newspapers. Seidler guessed she had been running as he looked up from the table. Her face was flushed an even higher colour than usual.

'We've time for another cup of coffee before I go to work,' she told him.

'That would be nice . . .'

She placed the papers in a neat pile on the table. She was such a tidy, orderly girl, he reflected. It would be marvellous to settle down with her for ever. She danced off into the kitchen, expressing her joy that he was back. He could hear her humming a small tune while she prepared the coffee. He opened the first paper.

'You cleared the table for me,' she called out. 'Thank you, Manfred. You're getting quite domesticated. Do you mind?'

'It could become a habit . . .'

'Why not?' she responded gaily.

The moment she returned to the living-room she sensed a major change in the atmosphere. Sitting in his shirt-sleeves, Seidler was staring at the front page of the *Journal de Genève*. She placed his cup of black coffee within reach – he never took sugar or milk and drank litres of the stuff, another indication that he was living on his nerves. She stood close to his shoulder, peering over it.

'Something wrong?'

'My lifeline. Maybe . . .'

He took the gold, felt-tipped pen she had given him and used it to circle the box headed *Sommaire*. She was so generous – God knew how much of her month's salary she had squandered on the pen. He'd have liked to go out and buy her something. He had the money. But it meant *going out* . . .

'Robert Newman,' she read out and sipped coffee. 'The Kruger case. Newman was the reporter who tracked his bank account to Basle. We still don't know how he managed that. Why is he so important?'

'Because, Erika . . .' He wrapped an arm round her slim waist, 'he's such an independent bastard. No vested interest in the world can buy him once he gets his teeth into a story. No one can stop him.'

'You know this Newman?'

'Unfortunately, no. But I can reach him. You see it even says where he's staying. I'd better call him – but I'll use that public phone box just down the street . . .'

'You didn't want to be seen outside . . .'

'It's worth the risk. I have to do something. Newman might even be working on the Gold Club story. Terminal . . .'

'Manfred!' There was surprise, a hint of hurt in her voice. 'When I told you about that you gave me the impression you'd never heard of either the Gold Club or Terminal.'

He looked uncomfortable. Taking the cup of coffee out of her hand he hauled her on to his lap. She really weighed nothing at all. He stared straight at her. He was about to break the habit of a lifetime – to *trust* another human being.

'It was for your own protection. That's God's truth. Don't ask me any more – knowledge can kill you when such ruthless and powerful forces are involved. Whatever happens, say nothing to Nagel, your boss . . .'

'I wouldn't dream of it. Can't you go to the police?' she asked for the third time, then desisted as she caught his look of fear, near-desperation. She saw the time by his watch and eased herself off his lap. 'I simply have to go, Manfred. My job . . .'

'Don't forget to deposit that case. In your own name . . .'

'Only if you sign this card. I collected it yesterday. No argument, Manfred – or I won't take the case . . .'

'What is it?'

'A deposit receipt for a safety box. We both have to

be able to get access to it. Those are the only terms on which I'll take that case.'

He sighed, signed it with his illegible but distinctive signature and gave back the card. When she had left the apartment he sat there for some time, amazed at his action. A year ago he'd have laughed in the face of anyone who told him that one day he would entrust half a million francs to a young girl. The nice thing was he felt quite contented now he had taken the plunge.

The real effort, he knew, would be to phone Newman.

They were waiting for him when Newman followed Nancy out of the Pavillon. Two men in plain clothes seated in the reception hall who stood up and walked straight over to him. A tall man with a long face, a shorter man, chubby and amiable.

'M. Newman?' the tall man enquired. 'Could you please accompany us.' It was a statement not a question. 'We are police officers . . .'

'Nancy, go up to our room while I sort this out,' Newman said briskly. He stared at the tall man. 'Accompany you where – and why?'

'To police headquarters . . .'

'Address,' Newman snapped.

'Twenty-four Boulevard Carl-Vogt . . .'

'Show me some identification, for Christ's sake.'

'Certainly, sir.' Ostrich, as Newman had already nicknamed the tall one, produced a folder which Newman examined carefully before handing it back. As far as he could tell it was kosher.

'You've told me where – now tell me why . . .'

'That will be explained by someone at head-quarters . . .' Ostrich became a little less formal. 'Frankly, sir, I don't know the answer to that question. No, a coat isn't necessary. We have a heated car outside . . .'

'I'm going up to my room. I have to tell my wife where I'm going . . .'

He found Nancy waiting at the elevator, making no attempt to get inside. With his back to the two men, who had followed him to where they could watch from the end of the corridor, he took out his scratch pad, wrote down the address of police head-quarters, and gave it to her.

'If I'm not back in an hour, call this number and set Geneva alight. That number under the address is the registration of the car they've got parked outside.'

'What is it all about, Bob? Are you worried? I am . . .'

'Don't be. And no, I'm not worried. I'm blazing mad. I'll tear somebody's guts out for this . . .'

Hidden inside the alcove of the doorway, Julius Nagy watched as Newman climbed inside the back of the waiting car with one of the men while the shorter man took the wheel. He hurried to a waiting cab and climbed inside.

'That black Saab,' he told the driver. 'I want to know where they're taking my friend . . .'

Newman thought Chief Inspector Leon Tripet, as he introduced himself, was young for the job. He sat down as requested, lit a cigarette without asking permission, and looked round the room, his manner expressing a mixture of irritation and impatience. He carefully said nothing.

Tripet's second-floor office, overlooking the Boulevard Carl-Vogt, was the usual dreary rabbit hutch. Walls painted a pale green, illuminated by a harsh overhead neon rectangular tube. Very homely.

'I must apologize for any inconvenience we may be causing you,' Tripet began, sitting very erect in his chair. 'But it is a very serious matter we are concerned with . . .'

'*You* are concerned with. Not *me*,' Newman said aggressively.

'We all admired your handling of the Kruger case. I have met German colleagues who are full of praise for the way you trapped Kruger and exposed his links with the DDR . . .'

'You mean Soviet-occupied East Germany,' Newman commented. 'Also known as The Zone. What has this to do with my summons here?'

'Coffee, Mr Newman?' Tripet looked at the girl

who had come in with a tray of cardboard cups. 'How do you like it?'

'I don't – not out of a cardboard cup. I can get that at British Rail buffets, which I don't patronize.'

'I read your book,' Tripet continued after dismissing the girl who left him one of the cardboard cups. 'One thing which really fascinated me was the way you were able to tap in to the *terminal* keyboard . . .'

He paused to drink some coffee and Newman had the oddest feeling Tripet was watching him with all his concentration for some reaction. Reaction to what? He remained silent.

'I refer to the keyboard at Dusseldorf where the Germans house their giant computer which has so helped them track down hostile agents. You have come to Switzerland on holiday, Mr Newman?' he added casually.

Newman stubbed out his half-smoked cigarette in the clean ashtray, watching Tripet with a bleak look as he did so. He stood up, walked over to the window behind the Swiss policeman and stared down into the street. Tripet asked was there something wrong?

Newman didn't reply. He continued staring down, being careful not to disturb the heavy net curtain. Julius Nagy was standing in the entrance to the building opposite which Newman had observed when he had arrived. *Bibliothèque Municipale*. Public Library.

'Tripet,' he said, 'could you join me for a moment, please?'

'Something is bothering you,' Tripet commented as he stood beside the Englishman.

'That man in the doorway over there. Julius Nagy. He's been following me since we arrived at Cointrin. A friend of yours?'

'I'll have him checked out,' Tripet said promptly and headed for the door out of his office. 'Give me a minute . . .'

'There's a phone on your desk,' Newman pointed out.

But Tripet was gone, closing the door behind him. Newman lit a fresh cigarette and waited while the comedy was played out. Within a short time he saw two policemen in their pale grey uniforms, automatic pistols sheathed in holsters on their right hips, walk briskly across the road.

There appeared to be a brief altercation, Nagy protesting as the policemen each took an arm and escorted him across the road out of sight into the building below. Newman grinned to himself and was seated in his chair when Tripet returned.

'We are questioning him,' he informed Newman. 'I have told them to concentrate on learning the identity of his employer.'

'Who do you think you're fooling?'

'Pardon?'

'Look here,' Newman rasped, leaning across the desk, 'this charade has gone on long enough . . .'

'Charade?'

'*Charade,* Tripet! There was a time not long ago when I was welcome in Switzerland. I helped over a certain matter which has not a damn thing to do with you. Ever since I came in this time I've been watched and harassed . . .'

'Harassed, Mr Newman?'

'Kindly listen and don't interrupt! I said harassed – and I meant harassed. You drag me over here for a meaningless conversation. You send two of your menials to pick me up publicly at the Hotel des Bergues like a common criminal. You don't even have the decency to phone me first . . .'

'We were not sure you would come . . .'

Newman rode over him. 'Don't interrupt, I said! Then you pretend you don't know Nagy. You go out of the room to give an order instead of using the phone in front of you – so I won't hear the order you give. "Bring in Nagy. Make it look good – he's watching from my office window." Something like that, yes, no? Well, I've had it up to here. I'm communicating with Beck of the Federal Police in Berne. Arthur Beck, Assistant to the Chief of the Federal Police . . .'

'It was Beck who asked me to bring you here,' Tripet informed him quietly.

Newman insisted on returning to the Hotel des Bergues in a cab despite Tripet's efforts to provide an unmarked police car. On the way back across the river he sat thinking, his mind tangled with contradictory ideas. There was no peace for him when he'd paid off the cab and went upstairs to his room. Nancy opened the door and he knew something had happened. She grasped his arm and wrapped it round her waist.

'Bob, I thought you'd never come. Are you all right? What did they want? While you were out I had the weirdest phone call. Are you all right?' she repeated. 'Shall I get coffee? Room Service does have its uses.' All in a rush of words.

'Order three litres. No, sit down, I'll order it myself – and I'm fine. Tell me about the phone call when I've organized coffee.' He grinned. 'We have to get our priorities right . . .'

He refused to let her talk until the coffee had arrived. He gave her an edited version of his visit to police headquarters, conveying the impression they were intrigued by the newspaper article and wanted to know what story he was working on. And he reflected, that might just be the real motive behind his interview with Tripet.

'Now,' he began after she had swallowed half a cup, 'tell me in your own words about this phone call.' He grinned. 'I'm not sure, of course, who else's words you would use . . .'

'Stop kidding. I was jumpy at the time, but I'm better now. Anyone ever tell you you're a good psychologist?'

'Nancy, do get to the point,' he urged gently.

'The phone rang and a man's voice asked to speak

to you. He spoke in English but I know he wasn't English – or American. He had a thick, Middle-European accent . . .'

'Whatever that might be.'

'Bob! We *do* have a mixture of nationalities in the States. And I'm not bad on accents. Can I go on? Good. I told him that you weren't here, that you'd be back sometime, but I didn't know when. He was persistent. Did I have a number where he could reach you? It was urgent . . .'

'Urgent to him,' Newman interjected cynically.

'He *sounded* urgent,' she insisted. 'Almost close to panic. I asked him for a number where you could call him back, but he wouldn't play it that way. Eventually he said he'd call you later, but he asked me to give you a strange message, made me repeat it to make sure I'd got it . . .'

'What message?'

'He gave his name, too. Reluctantly and only when I said I was going to put down the receiver, that I didn't take messages from anonymous callers. A Manfred Seidler. I made him spell it. The message was that for a generous consideration he could tell you all about terminal . . .'

'He said what?'

'Not *a* terminal. I checked that. Just terminal . . .'

Newman sat staring into space. He was alone in the bedroom. Nancy had gone shopping to buy a stronger pair of boots. She'd observed that the smart girls in Geneva had a snappy line in boots, Newman suspected. She was not going to be left behind by the competition.

Terminal.

Newman was beginning to wonder whether his conversation with Chief Inspector Tripet had been as meaningless as he'd thought at the time. Correction. Beck's conversation with him by proxy via Tripet. What was it he'd said?

One thing which really fascinated me was the way you were able to tap into the terminal keyboard. And Tripet had emphasized the word *terminal* – and had watched Newman intently as he spoke.

Now this weirdo, Manfred Seidler, was offering to tell him all about – terminal. What the hell did the word signify? Tripet – Beck – had linked it to the operation of a highly sophisticated computer. Could there be any connection with the Kruger affair?

Kruger was serving a thirty-year sentence in Stuttgart for passing classified information to the East Germans. The Kruger case was over, fading into history. What signal was Beck sending him? Was he sending him any signal? More likely he was checking to see whether Newman's trip to Switzerland had anything to do with – terminal. Well, it hadn't. But maybe when he arrived in Berne he'd better contact his old friend, Arthur Beck, and tell him he was barking up the wrong tree. He had just reached that conclusion when the phone rang. He picked it up without thinking, assuming it was Nancy telling him she would be later than she'd expected.

'Mr Robert Newman? At last. Manfred Seidler speaking . . .'

Chapter Eleven

Bruno Kobler came into Geneva from Berne by express train. He paused in the booking hall, an impressive-looking man who wore an expensive dark business suit and a camel-hair overcoat. Hatless, his brown hair was streaked with grey. Clean-shaven, he had a strong nose, cold blue eyes which Lee Foley would have recognized immediately. A killer.

His right hand gripped a brief-case and he waited patiently for the two men who had travelled separately on the train from Berne. Hugo Munz, a lean man of thirty-two wearing jeans and a windcheater, approached him first.

'Hugo,' said Kobler, 'you take Cointrin. Go there at once and watch out for Newman. You've studied the newspaper photo so you will spot him easily. I doubt if he's flying anywhere but if he is, follow. Report back to Thun.' He looked directly at Munz. 'Don't lose him. Please.'

He watched Hugo walking briskly towards where the cabs parked. A moment later the second man, Emil Graf, wandered casually up to him. Graf was a very different type from Munz. Thirty-eight years old, small and stockily-built, he wore a sheepskin. A slouch hat covered most of his blond hair. Thin-lipped, he spoke on equal terms to Kobler.

'We've arrived. What do I do?'

'You wait here,' Kobler told him pleasantly. 'You also watch out for Newman. If he leaves Geneva, my guess is he'll go by train. In case I miss him, hang on to his tail. When you have news, report back to Thun.'

He watched Graf wander back inside the station, his right hand holding the carry-all bag which contained a Swiss Army repeater rifle. Kobler had made his dispositions carefully. Graf was more reliable, less impetuous than Munz. Typically, Kobler had saved for himself the most tricky assignment. He walked out of the station, got inside the back of a cab and spoke in his brisk, confident voice to the driver.

'Hotel des Bergues . . .'

Inside the cab as it proceeded on the short journey to the hotel Kobler dismissed both men from his mind. A first-rate business executive, he was now concentrating on what lay ahead. Kobler had come a long way. The only man his chief trusted implicitly, millions of francs passed through Kobler's hands in the course of a year.

A commanding personality, a man attractive to women of all ages who sensed his dynamic energy, he could walk into the Clinic, the laboratory and the chemical works on the shores of Lake Zurich and issue any instruction. He would be obeyed as though the order had been transmitted by his chief. He was paid four hundred thousand Swiss francs a year.

Unmarried, he dedicated his life to his work. He had a string of girl friends in different cities – chosen for two qualities. Their ability to feed him confidential information about the companies they worked for – and their skill in bed. Life was good. He wouldn't have exchanged his position for that of any other man he had ever met.

He had served his obligatory military service with the Army. He was an expert marksman and was classified to act as a sniper when they came from the north-east. Not if. *When* the Red Army moved. Still, very soon they would be ready for them – really ready. He jerked his mind into total awareness of his immediate surroundings as the cab pulled up outside the Hotel des Bergues.

'I don't know any Manfred Seidler – just assuming that's your real name,' Newman snapped back on the phone. He was sliding automatically into his role of foreign correspondent. Always put an unknown quantity on the defensive.

'Seidler is my real name,' the voice continued in German, 'and if you want to know about a very special consignment brought over an eastern border for KB then we should arrange a meeting. The information will cost a lot of money . . .'

'I don't deal in riddles, Seidler. Be more specific . . .'

'I'm talking about *Terminal* . . .'

The word hung in the air. Alone in the bedroom, Newman was aware of a feeling of constriction in his stomach. This had to be handled carefully.

'How much is a lot?' he asked in a bored tone.

'Ten thousand francs . . .'

'You're joking, of course. I don't pay out sums like that . . .'

'People are dying, Newman,' Seidler continued more vehemently, 'dying in Switzerland. Men – and women. Don't you care any more? This thing is horrific.'

'Where are you speaking from?' Newman enquired after a pause.

'We're not playing it that way, Newman . . .'

'Well, tell me, are you inside Switzerland? I'm not crossing any frontiers. And I'm short of time.'

'Inside Switzerland. The price is negotiable. It's urgent that we meet quickly. I decide the place . . .'

Newman had made up his mind, thinking swiftly while he asked questions. He was now convinced that Seidler, for some reason, was desperately anxious to meet him. He broke a golden rule – never give advance notice of future movements.

'Seidler, I'm just about to leave for Berne. I'll be staying at the Bellevue Palace. Phone me there and we'll talk some more.'

'To give you time to check me out? Come off it . . .'

'I'm impressed with what you've said.' Newman's

voice was tight and he let the irritation show. 'The Bellevue Palace or nothing. Unless you will give me a phone number?'

'The Bellevue Palace then . . .'

Seidler broke the connection and Newman slowly replaced the receiver. His caller had managed to disturb him on two counts. The 'eastern border' reference. Which eastern border? Newman didn't think he'd been talking about the Swiss frontier. That conferred on *Terminal* potential international dangers.

And then there had been the mention of 'KB', which Newman had deliberately not queried over the phone. KB. Klinik Bern? The talk about people dying he had dismissed as window-dressing to arouse his curiosity. Strangely enough, as he walked round the bedroom, smoking a cigarette, the words began to bother him more and more.

When the conversation opened, Newman had put Seidler in the category of a peddler of information – reporters were always being approached by these types – but later he had detected fear in Seidler's attitude, stark fear. There had been a hint of a terrible urgency – a man on the run.

'What have I walked into?' he wondered aloud.

'Tell me. Do . . .'

He swung round and Nancy was leaning with her back against the door she had opened and closed with extraordinary lack of noise. She moved like a cat – he'd found that out on more than one occasion.

'Seidler phoned while you were out,' he said.

'And he's worried you. What is going on, Bob?'

'He was trying to sell me a pup. Happens all the time.' He spoke in a light-hearted, dismissive tone. 'I'm glad you're back – we're catching the eleven fifty-six train to Berne. An express – non-stop . . .'

'I must dash out again.' She checked her watch. 'I saw some perfume. I'm packed. I have time. Be back in ten minutes . . .'

'You'll have to move. You're like a bloody grass-hopper. In and out. Nancy, I don't want to miss that train . . .'

'So you can use the time settling up the bill. See you . . .'

'M. Kobler,' the concierge greeted the man who had just walked into the Hotel des Bergues. 'Good to see you again, sir.'

'You haven't seen me. Robert Newman is staying here.'

'He's upstairs in his room. You wish me to call him?'

'Not at the moment . . .'

Kobler glanced quickly inside the Pavillon before walking into the restaurant. He chose a table which gave him a good view through the glass-panelled door of the reception hall, ordered a pot of coffee, paid for it, and settled down to wait.

The cab he had travelled in from the station was parked outside. He had paid the driver a generous tip with instructions to wait for him. A titian-haired beauty wearing a short fur over her jeans tucked inside knee-length boots walked in and he stared at her.

Their eyes met and a flicker of interest showed in hers as she passed his table and chose a seat facing the reception hall. It was nice, Kobler reflected, to know that you hadn't lost your touch. She had, of course, in that long glance assessed his income group. Not a pro. Just a woman.

Half an hour later he saw a porter carrying luggage out of the reception hall, followed by an attractive woman, followed by Newman. He stood up, put on his coat and walked out of the revolving doors in time to see Newman's back disappearing inside the rear of a cab. He glanced along the pavement to his left and stiffened. Kobler missed one development as he climbed inside his own cab and told the driver to follow the cab ahead.

The titian-haired girl he had admired came out of the door leading direct on to the street. Running round the corner, she climbed on to the scooter she had left parked there, kicked the starter and followed Kobler's taxi.

Cornavin Gare, Geneva's main station, was quiet on a Tuesday in mid-February near lunchtime. Kobler paid off his cab and followed Newman and the expensively-dressed woman with him into the concourse.

Standing to one side, he watched Emil Graf go into action, joining the ticket queue behind Newman. Only two people were ahead of the Englishman, so Emil, after purchasing his own tickets, soon came over to Kobler.

'He bought a one-way ticket to Berne, two tickets actually. I've bought tickets for both of us – in case you wish . . .'

'I do wish. Tickets to where?'

'Zurich. The eleven fifty-six goes through, of course.'

Kobler congratulated himself on his choice of Graf for the station. He took the ticket Graf handed him and put it inside his crocodile wallet.

'Why to Zurich, Emil – when Newman booked seats for Berne?'

'These foreign correspondents are tricky. His real destination could be Zurich . . .'

'Excellent, Emil. You see that little man with the absurd Tyrolean hat, the one buying his own ticket? That's Nagy. He is scum. The police once threw him out of Berne. He followed Newman in a cab from the hotel.' Kobler checked his watch. 'Your next job is Julius Nagy. Hang on to his tail. Wait your opportunity. Get him in the train lavatory – or some alley when he gets off. Find out who he is working for. Break a few arms, legs, if necessary. Scare the hell out of him. Then put him on our payroll. Tell him to continue following Newman, to report all his movements and contacts to you.'

'It's done.'

Kobler picked up his brief-case and watched Graf trotting away with his holdall. The contents might come in useful to persuade Nagy where survival lay. Kobler checked the departure board and headed for the platform where the Zurich Express was due to leave in five minutes.

In the far corner of the station Lee Foley watched all these developments with interest from behind the newspaper he held in front of his face. He had left the Hotel des Bergues only five minutes ahead of Newman and Nancy, anticipating this would give him a ringside seat. After buying a one-way first-class ticket to Berne he had taken up his discreet viewing point where he could watch all the ticket windows. As Kobler disappeared he folded the paper, tucked it inside the pocket of his coat, picked up his bag and made his own way towards the same platform.

The passenger everyone – including Foley – missed noticing was a titian-haired girl. A porter carried her scooter inside the luggage van. She boarded the next coach and the express bound for Berne and Zurich glided out of the station.

Chapter Twelve

Berne! A city unique not only in Switzerland but also in the whole of Western Europe. Its topography alone is weird. Wrapped inside a serpentine bend of the river Aare, it extends eastward as a long peninsula – its length stretching from the main station and the University to the distant Nydeggbrucke, the bridge where it finally crosses the Aare.

Its width is a quarter of its length. At many points you can walk across the peninsula, leaving the river behind, only to find in less than ten minutes, the far bend of the river barring your way.

Berne is a fortress. Built on a gigantic escarpment, it rears above the surrounding countryside. Below the *Terrasse* behind the Parliament building, the ground slopes steeply away. Below the *Plattform* at the side of the Munster the massive wall ramparts drop like a precipice one hundred and fifty feet to the Badgasse. Beyond, the noose of the Aare flows past from distant Lake Thun.

The escarpment is at its peak near Parliament and the station. As the parallel streets wind their way east they descend towards the Nydeggbrucke.

Berne is old, very old. The Munster goes back to 1421. And because it is centuries since it endured the curse of war, it has remained old. It is a city for human moles. The streets are lined with a labyrinth of huddled arcades like burrows. People can walk through these arcades in the worst of weathers, secure from snow and rain.

When night falls – even during heavily overcast days – there is a sinister aspect to the city. Few walk down the stone arcades of the Munstergasse, which continues east as the Junkerngasse until it reaches the Nydeggbrucke. All streets end at the bridge.

Backwards and forwards across its waist, a network of narrow alleys thread their way, alleys where you rarely meet another human being. And when the mist rolls in across the Aare, smoky coils drift down the arcades, increasing the atmosphere of menace.

Yet here in Berne are located – principally in buildings close to the Bellevue Palace – centres of power which do not always see eye to eye with the bankers. Swiss Military Intelligence, the Federal Police of which Arthur Beck is a key figure – are housed either next door to or within minutes' walk of one of the greatest hotels in Europe.

At the station a keen observer sees that Berne is where German Switzerland meets its French counterpart. The station is *Bahnhof/Gare*. At the foot of the steps leading to pairs of platforms the left-hand platform is *Voie*, the right-hand *Gleis*. The express from Geneva arrived on time at precisely 1.58 p.m.

During the journey from Geneva Newman, facing Nancy in her own window seat, had not moved. Gazing out of the window while the express sped from Geneva towards Lausanne he watched the fields covered in snow. The sun shone and frequently he had to turn away from the harshness of the sun glare.

'It's not non-stop as I thought,' he told Nancy. 'Lausanne, Fribourg and then Berne . . .'

'You look very serious, very concentrated. Too many things happened in Geneva?'

'Keep your voice down.' He leaned forward. 'Police headquarters for a start, then our friend on the phone. A lot to open the day . . .'

He was careful not to tell her he had seen Julius Nagy board the second-class coach immediately behind them. Who was Nagy really working for? The problem bothered him. At least they were heading for Berne. At the first opportunity he would go and talk to Arthur Beck. If anyone could – would – tell him what was going on, that man was Beck.

Several seats behind him Bruno Kobler sat facing Nancy, his brief-case perched on the seat beside him to keep it unoccupied. Kobler had also observed Nagy boarding the express. He hoped that Graf had accomplished his mission of persuading – forcing – the little creep to switch his allegiance.

Kobler was dressed so perfectly as the Swiss businessman that neither Newman nor Nancy had noticed him. But someone else had observed Kobler's interest in them, someone Kobler himself had overlooked.

Lee Foley had taken a seat in the non-smoking section of the coach, a section separated from the smokers by a door with a glass panel in the upper half. Twice, on the way to Lausanne, Foley had stood up and taken time extracting a magazine from the suitcase he had perched on the rack.

Foley was the only man who saw it all. Through the panel he observed Newman's grim expression as he stared out at the countryside. He also caught the fleeting glances of the Swiss business type behind the correspondent – glances always at Newman and the woman seated opposite. He would remember that hard face.

He observed more. At the far end of the smoking section Nagy appeared and looked inside. Only for a moment. A small, stocky man appeared beside him. Foley saw Nagy's startled expression. Both men disappeared inside the lavatory. Foley reacted at once.

Walking into the smoking section, staring straight ahead, he slid aside the end door, waited for it to shut automatically, and listened outside the lavatory. He heard choking noises. He reached out a hand to rattle the handle and then withdrew it. He could not afford to advertise his presence on the express. He went back to his own seat.

Inside the lavatory Graf had one hand round Nagy's throat as he extracted the Army rifle from the holdall with the other hand. Bending the little man back over the wash-basin, he put the rifle muzzle

139

under his chin. Nagy's eyes nearly popped out of their sockets with stark terror.

'Now,' said Graf, 'you can end up being tossed off this train. People do fall off expresses. Or you can tell me – first time please, there will be no second chance – who you are working for. We know you're following Newman . . .'

'You can't get away with this,' Nagy gasped.

'I said first time . . .'

Nagy heard a click, guessed it was the safety catch coming off. He nearly filled his pants. The remote, glassy look on his attacker's face was almost more frightening than the rifle.

'Can't speak . . .' The vicious grip of the hand on his throat relaxed. A little. 'Tripet,' he said. 'I am following Newman. For Tripet . . .'

'Who the hell is Tripet?' Graf asked quietly, his eyes never leaving Nagy's.

'Chief Inspector Tripet. Sûreté. Geneva. I've worked for him before. I'm his snout . . .'

Nagy, almost universally despised, a man you used, had guts. He was determined not to give away Pierre Jaccard of the *Journal de Genève*. There was more money there. And Jaccard had always kept his word. In Nagy's world trust was credit beyond price.

'So,' Graf told him, 'you forget this Tripet. From now on you work for me. No, shut up and listen. You carry on doing what you're doing – following Newman. You call me at this number . . .' Graf tucked a folded piece of paper inside Nagy's coat pocket.

'Whoever answers, give your name immediately, tell them about Newman's movements, who he meets, where he goes. You will be paid . . .' He tucked several folded banknotes in the same pocket. 'First, wherever Newman gets off, find out where he's staying, get a place to stay yourself. Report to the number at once where you're staying and the phone number . . .'

'Understood . . .' Nagy replied hoarsely, feeling his damaged throat when Graf removed the hand and the rifle, still aiming the muzzle point-blank. 'I'll do what you say . . .'

'You might be tempted to change your mind – when you think things over,' Graf went on in the same casual tone which Nagy found so disturbing. Christ! The swine had almost murdered him. 'Don't,' Graf warned. 'One of my associates will always be close to you. You won't see him. He'll simply be there. He's impetuous. Very rough. Any hint you're going independent and he'll chop you. You do understand, Nagy, I hope?'

'I understand . . .'

It was the contemptuous affront to his *dignity* which roused Nagy. He had been savagely assaulted in a lavatory. Graf, who would never have understood his victim's reaction, had added one further insult to intimidate the little man. Prior to leaving him in the lavatory he had stuffed a tablet of toilet soap inside Nagy's mouth.

Seated inside the second-class coach as the express left Lausanne and swung north away from the lake towards Fribourg, Nagy could still taste the soap. He was going to pay back these new employers, whoever they might be. Obstinately, he was determined about that.

The snow lay deeper on the fields – the express was climbing as it sped north. Newman was still silent, deep in thought as the train stopped at Fribourg and then proceeded on the last lap to Berne. When he stood up to lift their bags down from the rack as they pulled into Berne station Kobler had already left the coach and was waiting by the exit door. He was almost the first passenger to step down off the express.

One coach behind, Julius Nagy hurried off the train, his hat crumpled inside his coat, the coat folded over his arm. He was no longer immediately recognizable. His eyes gleamed with deep resentment as he followed Emil Graf along the platform. In his right hand he held the small Voigtlander camera he always carried.

Ahead of Graf walked Kobler, very erect and brisk, briefcase in right hand. He ran down the steps with Graf trotting behind. Outside the station where a 450 SEL Mercedes was waiting for him with a chauffeur he paused, turning up his collar against the cold. Graf caught up with him and looked around as though searching for a taxi.

'He's tamed,' he reported to Kobler. 'He's ours . . .'

'You're sure?'

'Certain. Scared shitless . . .'

Only one person noticed the brief exchange. Nagy raised his small camera and clicked it once as Kobler turned his head to catch what Graf said. Kobler walked to the Mercedes where the chauffeur held the rear door open. Nagy's camera clicked again. He then used the piece of paper Graf had stuffed in his pocket to write down the registration number. He had faded back inside the station when Graf turned round and the Mercedes was driven off.

The two plain clothes men watching the platform exit for the Zurich express missed spotting Lee Foley. The American walked past them wearing a very British-looking check overcoat he had bought in London. His distinctive white hair was concealed beneath a peaked golfing cap pulled well down. The horn-rimmed glasses he wore (with plain glass lenses) gave him a professorial appearance.

Foley walked out of the station among a crowd of passengers who had come off the same train. Ignoring the taxi rank, his case in his left hand, he continued walking down the narrow Neuengasse. Pausing to glance into a shop window in an arcade, he used the plate glass as a mirror to check the street.

Satisfied that no one was following, he resumed the short walk to the Savoy Hotel and turned inside the entrance quickly. The lobby and a sitting area were all of a piece. The girl at the reception counter looked up and Foley was already filling in the obligatory registration form in triplicate – one copy for the police who would collect it later.

'You have a room. I reserved it by phone from Geneva.'

'Room 230. It's a double . . .'

The girl looked round for a companion. Foley showed his passport and then pocketed it. He picked up his bag.

'I'll get a porter . . .'

'Don't bother. That's the elevator?' He went up inside the cage, found his room, dumped his bag on the bed and sat by the phone, waiting for the call.

Arthur Beck sat behind his desk eating the last of the English-style ham sandwiches his secretary had prepared for him. As far as Beck was concerned, the Earl of Sandwich was one of the great historical figures Britain had produced. He had acquired this liking during a stint spent with Scotland Yard in London. He was drinking coffee when the phone rang. His caller spoke in German.

'Leupin here, sir. Reporting from the station. Newman came in on the thirteen fifty-eight express from Geneva. He was accompanied by a woman. American I would guess from her clothes. Marbot tailed them to the Bellevue Palace where they booked in ten minutes ago.'

'What about Lee Foley?'

'No sign of anyone answering his description. We both watched the passengers arriving off the train . . .'

'Thank you, Leupin. Continue watching all trains from Geneva.'

'Marbot is on his way back here . . .'

Beck put down the receiver and ate the last sandwich while he thought. He had been right about one thing – that Newman would turn up in Berne. What bothered him was the earlier call from Chief Inspector Tripet. Newman, apparently, had shown no reaction to the casual reference to *Terminal*. Was it possible that the Englishman was working on an entirely different story?

Of one thing Beck was convinced – knowing Newman the way he did. The foreign correspondent wasn't visiting Berne just for a holiday. Newman was a workaholic: he never stopped looking for a fresh story.

But what really worried Beck was the non-appearance of Foley. Or should he say *disappearance*? If Lee Foley had slipped past the net Beck had a dangerous wolf stalking the streets of his city. He decided to call New York.

Lee Foley picked up the receiver on the second ring. Holding the phone to his ear he waited. The voice which spoke at the other end sounded impatient.

'Is that Mr Lee Foley?'

'Speaking. I'm in position. Listen, the first move is yours. You need to visit the place in question. Find out what the situation is. Could you please report back to me as soon as you can? No, please listen. Check out the security at the place in question. Any small item may be vital. When I'm armed with facts I can go into action. If it comes to it, I'll raise hell. I do have a talent for that, as you well know . . .'

Foley broke the connection and wandered over to the window of his bedroom which looked down a small alley. That was the place an experienced watcher would choose to observe the Savoy. The alley was empty.

Newman put down the phone as Nancy came into the small hallway, shut the door and entered the bedroom. She had a pensive look.

'Bob, who were you calling?'

'Your beloved Room Service for a large bottle of mineral water. You know my thirst, especially at night. They must be busy – I'll call again in a minute. Incidentally, you never showed me that Gucci perfume you rushed out to buy just before we left the Hotel des Bergues.'

'*Voilà!*' She produced the bottle from her handbag. 'You should have noticed I was wearing it on the express. Isn't this a lovely room?'

They had been allocated Room 428. A bathroom led off the entrance hall. There was a separate toilet.

But the room itself was the cherry on the cake. Very large with a couple of comfortable armchairs, a desk in front of the spacious windows where Newman could work. Two generous single beds had been placed alongside each other to form a double. Nancy bounced her backside on one of the beds.

'Bob, this is marvellous. We could live here for weeks . . .'

'Maybe we will. Come and look at the view. The porter made a big fuss about it and rightly so.'

They stood with his arm wrapped round her and she made cooing noises of sheer delight. Newman opened the first set of windows and then the outer ones a foot beyond. Chill air floated into the room which had the temperature of a sauna bath.

'That hill beyond the river with the snow is the Bantiger,' he explained. 'If this overcast clears over there to the left you'll get the most fantastic panorama of the Bernese Oberland range. Now,' he became businesslike, 'this afternoon I'm hiring a car from Hertz next door. We're driving to the Berne Clinic at Thun . . .'

'Just like that?' Her professional instincts surfaced. 'We should phone for an appointment to see Jesse . . .'

'We do nothing of the sort. We arrive unannounced. You're not only a relative, you're a doctor. With me accompanying you we can bulldoze our way in, maybe catch them on the hop . . .'

'You really think that's a good idea?'

'It's what we're going to do. After a quick lunch . . .'

'Bob, they have *three* separate restaurants. One gorgeous room overlooking the terrace down there. The Grill Room. And the coffee shop . . .'

'The coffee shop. It will be quick. We have to move before our arrival is reported. Don't forget that bloody newspaper article.'

'Let me just fix myself.' She left him and sat down in front of the dressing table. 'Did you notice that Englishman who was registering while you waited? I was sitting on a sofa and I saw him look back and stare at you.'

'He'd probably seen my picture in that paper . . .'

Newman spoke in an off-hand manner, dismissing the incident from her mind. But he knew the guest she was talking about. He even knew the man's name, but he had detected no significance in the guest until Nancy's remark.

He had waited patiently while the other Englishman filled in the registration form, ignoring the receptionist's attempt to do the job for him. A slim, erect man with a trim moustache, he wore a short camel-hair coat and would be in his early thirties.

'The porter will take your bag to your room, Mr Mason,' the receptionist had informed him, returning his passport.

'Thank you,' Mason had replied, accepting the small hotel booklet with his passport and turning away to where the porter waited.

Now he remembered Mason had glanced over his shoulder at Newman before leaving the counter. A swift, appraising glance. He frowned to himself and Nancy watched him as she combed her hair.

'That man at the reception desk. You know him?'

'Never seen him before in my life. Are you ready? It will have to be a very quick meal. I have to hire the car and it's a half hour's drive to Thun along the motorway.'

'How did you locate it so quickly?'

'By asking the concierge when you wandered off into that huge reception hall. They have a fashion show this afternoon . . .'

'And a medical congress reception in a few days' time . . .'

'So what?' he asked, catching a certain inflection in her tone.

'Nothing,' she answered. 'Let's go eat . . .'

Mason sat on the bed in his room, dialling the number which would put him straight through to Tweed's extension. He never ceased to be impressed with how swiftly the continental phone system worked – providing you were in Sweden, Germany or Switzerland.

'Yes,' said Tweed's voice. 'Who is it?'

'Mason. How is the weather there? We have eight degrees here . . .'

'Nine in London . . .' That established not only their identities, but also told Mason that Tweed was alone in his office – that Howard wasn't leaning over his shoulder, listening in.

'I've just booked in at the Bellevue Palace,' Mason said crisply. 'I stopped over in Zurich to gather a little information. Grange.' He said the name quickly.

'Do use the Queen's English,' Tweed complained. 'You *stayed on* in Zurich. Continue . . .'

'I've built up a dossier on the subject in question. Not easy. Swiss doctors close down like a shutter falling when you mention his name. I found an American doctor working in Zurich who opened up. God, the subject carries some clout. He's a real power in the land. Right at the top of the tree. You'd like a quick run-down?'

'Not over the phone,' Tweed said quickly, aware the call had to be passing through the hotel switchboard. 'I'm coming out there soon myself. Keep making discreet enquiries. Don't go near the British Embassy . . .'

'One more thing,' Mason added. 'Don't imagine it means anything. Robert Newman, the foreign correspondent, booked in here after me. He had his wife with him. I didn't know he was married . . .'

'He probably isn't. You know the bohemian life those correspondents lead . . .' Tweed sounded dreamy. 'Keep digging. And stay in Berne . . .'

Tweed put down the phone and looked at Monica who was sorting files. 'That was Mason calling from the Bellevue Palace. He has data on Professor Armand Grange of the Berne Clinic. Anything on the computer? Just supposing the damned thing is working . . .'

'It is working. I did check. Not a thing. I tried Medical and came up with zero. So then I tried Industrialists – because of his chemical works. Zero again. I even tried Bankers. Zero. The man is a shadow. I even wondered whether he really exists.'

'Well, at least that has decided me.' Tweed was polishing his glasses again on the worn silk handkerchief. Monica watched him. He was always fingering the lenses. 'I'm going to Berne,' Tweed told her. 'It's just a question of timing. Book me on Swissair flights for Zurich non-stop. As I miss one flight, book me on the next one. When I do leave it will be at a moment's notice.'

'What are you waiting for?' Monica asked.

'A development. A blunder on the part of the opposition. It has to come. No one is foolproof. Not even a shadow . . .'

Chapter Thirteen

The coffee shop at the Bellevue Palace is a large glass box-like restaurant perched above the pavement on the side overlooking the Hertz car hire office. Newman gobbled down his steak as Nancy ate her grilled sole. Swallowing his coffee in two gulps, Newman wiped his mouth with a napkin and signed the bill.

'You're going to hire the car now?' Nancy asked. 'I'll dash up to the room and get my gloves. Meet you over there?'

'Do that.'

Newman waited at the exit until she had disappeared and then retraced his steps to one of the phone booths near the *garderobe*, the cloakroom where guests left their coats. It took him one minute to make the call and then he ran back to the exit, along the pavement and into the Hertz office. Slamming down his driving licence and passport he told the girl what he wanted.

'They have a Citroen. Automatic,' he told Nancy when she came inside. 'This chap is going to take us to the car. It's on Level Three . . .'

In less than five minutes he was driving the car round the sharp curves up to street level. Nancy put on her wool-lined leather gloves, fastened her seat belt and relaxed. An expert driver, she still preferred to travel as a passenger.

The sky was a heavy pall hovering close to the city as they crossed one of the bridges and within a short time Newman was on the four-lane motorway which runs all the way to Lucerne via Thun. Inside forty minutes they should have arrived at the Berne Clinic.

Lee Foley paid a very generous sum in Swiss francs to borrow the red Porsche from his Berne contact. He needed a fast car although normally its conspicuousness would have worried him. But this was an emergency.

He drove just inside the speed limit through the suburbs of Berne, but as soon as he turned on to the motorway he pushed his foot down. The highway was quiet, very little other traffic in mid-afternoon. His cold blue eyes flickered from side to side as he increased speed.

'Watch it on that motorway,' his contact had informed him as he handed over the Porsche which he had brought to the Savoy. 'It's a favourite place for the police to set up speedtraps . . .'

Foley had driven away from the Savoy so fixed on getting to his destination in time that he for once omitted to check that no one was following him. So he completely missed noticing the helmeted figure who jumped on a scooter parked further along the pavement. The scooter was still with him, little more than a dot behind the Porsche, when he spotted the Citroen ahead.

He kept up his speed, pulling closer to the Citroen until he had a good view of the two occupants. Newman behind the wheel, his woman seated alongside him. Foley breathed a sigh of relief and reduced speed, widening the distance between the two vehicles. Behind him the scooter rider – going flat-out – also slowed down.

Foley drove under a large destination indicator board, one of several at regular intervals. The board carried the legend THUN – NORD.

Inside the Citroen the warmth from the heater had dispelled the bitter cold and Nancy removed her gloves. Her right hand played with the fingers of one glove in her lap. The motorway was in superb condition, its surface clear of snow. But as they left Berne behind, passed the turn-off to Belp, the snow in the fields on both sides lay deeper. Here and there an occasional naked tree stretched gnarled branches towards the dark grey pall overhead. The atmosphere was sullen, unwelcoming. Newman glanced at her restless hand.

'Nervous? Now we're so close?'

'Yes, I am, Bob. I keep thinking about Jesse. And

I'm not at all sure they're going to let us in, just dropping on them like this . . .'

'Leave me to do the talking when we arrive. You're a close relative. I'm a foreign correspondent. A lethal combination for a clinic which wants to preserve its reputation. There's no publicity like bad publicity . . .'

'What are you going to do?' She sounded worried.

'I'm going to get inside that clinic. Now, have one of your rare cigarettes, stop fiddling with that glove, here's the pack.'

They passed under a fresh sign which indicated two different destinations. THUN – SUD, THUN – NORD. Newman signalled to the huge trailer truck coming up behind him and swung up the turn-off to Thun–Nord. Nancy lit a cigarette and took a deep drag. Now they were crossing the motorway which was below them and from this extra elevation she had a view of grim, saw-toothed mountains to the south, mountains only dimly seen in a veil of mist so for a moment she wasn't sure whether she was watching a mirage.

'Those must be pretty high,' she observed.

'They rise to the far side of Thun, to the south and the east. One of them is the Stockhorn. Probably that big brute towering above the rest . . .'

They were climbing a gradual but continually ascending slope up a hillside between more fields. An isolated farm here and there, a glimpse of neatly stacked and huge bales of hay inside barns with steep roofs. The lowering sky created an ominous sense of desolation. Over to the east a great castle perched on a hilltop with turrets capped with what looked like witches' hats.

'That's the famous Thun Schloss,' Newman remarked. 'The town is below it, out of sight . . .'

'You do know the way?'

'We turn off this road somewhere higher up according to that helpful concierge at the Bellevue. Check it on the map I put in the glove compartment if you like – he marked the route . . .'

'It's creepy up here, Bob . . .'

'It's just a lousy afternoon.'

But there was something in her remark. They were very close to the snow-line. Earlier sun had melted the snow blanket on the lower fields facing south. Beyond the snow line houses were dotted at intervals towards Thun. Near the top of the ridge a dense forest of dark firs huddled like an army waiting to march. Then they reached the snow-line and here no ploughs had cleared the road. Newman reduced speed, slowed even more as he saw a sign-post. The sign read *Klinik Bern*. He swung right on to a narrower road, corrected a rear-wheel skid, drove on.

'Do you think that's it?' Nancy asked.

'I imagine so . . .'

A large, two-storey mansion with a verandah running round the ground floor was perched in an isolated position on the wide plateau which extended to the group of private houses several kilometres to the east. The grounds, which looked extensive, were surrounded by a wire fence and ahead Newman saw a gatehouse. Close behind the mansion the forest stood, a solid wall of firs mantled with snow. He pulled up in front of the stone, single-storey gatehouse beside double wire gates which were closed. Before he could alight from the car large, black dogs appeared and came leaping towards the gate.

'Dobermans,' Newman commented. 'Charming . . .'

A heavy wooden door leading from the gatehouse direct on to the road opened. A lean man in his early thirties, wearing jeans and a windcheater, walked out towards the Citroen. Glancing over his shoulder he called out a curt order in German. The dogs stopped barking, backed away reluctantly and disappeared.

'This is private property,' the lean man began in German.

'Not where I'm standing, it isn't,' Newman snapped back. 'This is the public highway. My passenger is Nancy Kennedy. She's here to visit her grandfather, Jesse Kennedy . . .'

'You have an appointment?'

'She has flown from America for the precise purpose of visiting her grandfather . . .'

'No admittance without an appointment . . .'

'You're the boss here?' Newman's tone dripped sarcasm. 'You look like paid help to me. Get on the phone and tell the Clinic we're here. And tell them I'm a newspaper man – it would make a very good story, don't you think? Granddaughter flies all the way from America and is refused admission to see her sick grandfather. What are you running here – a concentration camp? That's the impression I'm getting – a wire fence and Dobermans . . .'

'And you are?'

'Robert Newman. I'm getting pretty chilled standing here yacking to you. I'll give you two minutes – then we'll drive back to Berne and I'll file my story . . .'

'Wait!'

'For two minutes . . .'

Newman made an elaborate pantomime of looking at his watch and went back to the car. The lean man disappeared inside the gatehouse while Newman settled behind the wheel and lit a cigarette. Nancy took the pack and lit one for herself.

'It might have been better to make an appointment,' she said.

'Now I've seen the set-up I think not. This place smells very peculiar. While I was talking to Lanky I saw another man peer through that open doorway, a man wearing a uniform which looked very much like the Swiss Army . . .'

'Bob, that's crazy! You must have been mistaken . . .'

'I'm only telling you what I saw. The whole goddamned place is laid out like a military encampment. Surprise, surprise – here comes Lanky, looking even more sour than before . . .'

'You may go up to the Clinic. Someone will meet you there . . .'

The lean man spoke curtly, then walked away before there was time for a reply. Newman guessed that someone inside the gatehouse had pressed a button – the double gates opened inward automatically. Remembering the dogs, he closed his window before he drove forward and up the long curving drive to the distant building. No sign of a Doberman. They had been locked inside the gatehouse until the Citroen was clear.

He drove slowly, taking in the wintry landscape, and realized the grounds were even more vast than he had first thought. The wire fence at the front ran away across the white world, disappearing down a dip in the hillside. As he approached the Clinic the whole place seemed deserted. He could now see the verandah was glassed in and six steps led up to the entrance door.

Parking the car facing the exit drive, he locked it when Nancy had alighted and they went up the steps together. Grasping the handle of the door, he opened it and they went inside on to the verandah. It stretched away in both directions, the floor tiled and spotless, a few pots with plants at intervals. The inner door led into a large tiled lobby. The smell of antiseptic hit Newman and he wrinkled his nostrils. Nancy noticed his reaction and her lips tightened.

At the back of the large lobby was a heavy, highly-polished wooden counter and behind this, sitting on a high stool with an adjustable back, was a large, fat middle-aged woman, dark hair tied at the back in a

bun and with small, darting eyes. She put down the
pencil she had been writing with on a printed form,
clasped her pudgy hands and stared at them.

'You know who we are,' Newman said in German,
'and I want to see the man in charge of this place . . .'

'Please to fill in the forms,' she replied in English,
her tone of voice flat as she pushed a pad across the
counter.

'Maybe, after I've seen your superior. We've come
to see Jesse Kennedy. You know that already from the
lackey on the gate . . .'

'I am very much afraid that without an appointment that will not be possible . . .' The man who had
appeared from a side door spoke quietly but firmly in
excellent English. Something in the tone of voice made
Newman turn quickly to study the speaker. He had
an impression of authority, supreme self-confidence,
a human dynamo. 'We have to consider the patient,'
the voice continued. 'I also should tell you that at the
moment Mr Kennedy is under sedation.'

A man almost his own height, Newman estimated.
More heavily-built. A man of about forty with dark
brown hair streaked with grey shafts. The eyes stared
at Newman and expressed force of character. Eyes
which assessed his visitor, weighing up a possible
opponent. A very self-controlled, formidable man.

'I am Dr Bruno Kobler,' he added.

'And I am *Dr* Nancy Kennedy,' Nancy interjected.
'The fact that my grandfather is sedated makes no
difference. I wish to see him immediately.'

'Without a doctor in attendance that would be irregular . . .'

'You're a doctor,' Newman snapped. 'You just told us . . .'

'I am the chief administrator. I have no medical qualification.'

'You're telling us,' Newman persisted, 'that at this moment you have no medical practitioner available on the premises? Is that the way you run this clinic?'

'I didn't say that.' There was an edge to Kobler's voice. 'I indicated no one was available to accompany you . . .'

'Then we'll drive straight back to the American Embassy,' Newman decided. 'Dr Kennedy is an American citizen. So is Jesse Kennedy. Kobler, we're going to raise hell . . .'

'There is no need to get excited. Bearing in mind that your companion is a doctor, I think we might make an exception. We may be able to call on Dr Novak – he is the physician in charge of Jesse Kennedy . . .'

He turned to the woman behind the counter and clicked his fingers as though summoning a waiter. 'See if you can locate Dr Novak, Astrid. Ask him to come here at once.'

'How is my grandfather?' Nancy enquired.

Kobler turned to her, spread his hands and gave her his whole attention, staring straight into her eyes. His manner became conciliatory but for at least half a minute he delayed his reply. She had the impression he was looking inside her. She remained silent, sensing he was hoping to make her say more.

'I am afraid I cannot answer your question, Dr Kennedy. Unlike yourself, I am not a medical doctor. My job is to administer the Clinic. I would prefer that you ask Dr Novak. I think you will find him sympathetic. You see, he is one of your countrymen.'

'Dr Novak is an American?'

'Indeed he is. A very clever man, which is why he was asked to come here. The Clinic, as you doubtless know, has a world-wide reputation . . .'

'I'd also like to see Professor Armand Grange.'

Kobler shook his head regretfully. 'That, I regret to say, will not be possible. He only sees visitors strictly by appointment.'

'He's on the premises at this moment?' Nancy demanded.

'I really have no idea . . .'

Kobler glanced over his shoulder, his attention caught by the sound of the front door opening. Newman had stepped out on to the verandah. Closing the door he walked along to his left past chairs of basketwork with cushions; presumably when the weather was good patients sat here. It was very quiet, the central heating was turned up so the enclosed corridor had the atmosphere of a hothouse.

Alongside the inner wall he passed windows at intervals, all of them with frosted glass so he could not see into the rooms beyond. At the end of the corridor he tried the door on the inner wall and found it locked. He stood gazing across the ground to the east. In a bowl stood a modern complex of single-storey buildings with tall, slim windows. The place reminded him of a chemical laboratory. A covered way, windowless, extended from the direction of the Clinic to the complex. He returned to the reception hall as Nancy was being introduced by Kobler to a tall, fair-haired man in his early thirties. He wore a white coat and a stethoscope dangled from his left hand. Kobler turned to Newman.

'This is Dr Novak, Mr Newman. I expect you will not mind sitting in the waiting room while Dr Kennedy sees her . . .'

'Bob is coming with me,' Nancy interrupted brusquely. 'He's my fiancé . . .'

Novak glanced at Kobler, as though waiting for his reaction. Kobler bent his head towards Nancy and smiled. 'Who am I to dispute the wishes of a beautiful woman? Of course Mr Newman may accompany you.'

'Waldo Novak,' the American said and held out his hand to shake Newman's. 'I've heard a lot about you. The Kruger case man. Boy, did you do a job in Germany . . .'

'Just a story.' Newman turned to Kobler as he shook hands with Novak. 'Why the Dobermans?' he asked abruptly. 'Plus uniformed guards and the fence. This place is like Dartmoor.'

Kobler's head, turned to one side, swivelled to Newman and his smile remained fixed. Again he took his time about replying while he studied Newman.

Like Nancy, Newman said nothing, gazing back at Kobler.

'Vandals,' Kobler replied eventually. 'Even in Switzerland we have young people who have too much energy, too little respect for private property. One of my duties is to ensure that the patients endure no disturbance from the outside world. And now, if you will excuse me, I will leave you in Dr Novak's capable hands.' He spoke to Novak in a brief aside. 'I have explained the patient is under sedation. Goodbye, Mr Newman. I'm sure we shall meet again . . .'

'You can count on it.'

'Dr Kennedy . . .' Kobler bowed and left them, disappearing behind the side door he had used earlier. Newman heard the click of an automatic lock. Novak produced a computer card and ushered Nancy towards a door at the rear of the reception hall. He inserted the card in a slot and the door slid open. Newman estimated it was one-inch thick steel. The door closed behind them as the fat woman, Astrid, brought up the rear.

'You speak German fluently, Mr Newman?' Astrid enquired in a thick, throaty voice.

'No, I don't,' he lied. 'When they start to talk fast I lose it . . .'

He left it at that as he followed Nancy and Novak along a wide corridor which was spotless and deserted. They passed closed doors with porthole windows. Again the glass was frosted so it was impossible to see inside. He noticed that near the end

164

of the corridor the smooth surface began to slope downwards, then vanished round a corner. The same smell of disinfectant he associated with hospitals and so disliked pervaded the place. Novak stopped outside a door in the right-hand wall, another door with a frosted glass porthole. He had extracted another computer card from his coat pocket.

'Dr Kennedy,' he said, 'you're accustomed to seeing patients, of course. But in my experience it's different when the patient is a relative. He won't be able to talk with you . . .'

'I understand.'

Inserting the card inside the slot, Novak waited while the door slid open and gestured for them to walk inside. Newman followed Nancy who stopped suddenly as Novak and Astrid joined them and the door slid shut. He took her by the arm.

'Easy does it, old girl . . .'

'It's not that,' she whispered. 'He's *awake!*'

In a single bed centred with its head against the far wall lay a gaunt-faced man with a hooked nose, wispy white hair, a high forehead, a firm mouth and a prominent jaw. His complexion was ruddy. For a brief moment his eyes had flickered open as Nancy walked in, then closed again like a shutter closing over a lens. Newman doubted whether either Novak or Astrid had seen the eyes open – they had been masked by his own bulk.

'You see,' Novak said gently, 'he sleeps well. He is a very strong man, a tough constitution. I was going to add, for his age – but he's one of nature's survivors . . .'

'You think he will survive then?' Nancy asked quietly.

'He is very sick man,' Astrid broke in. 'Very, very sick man.'

Newman stood back from the rest of them, hands in his pockets as he watched. He had the distinct impression Novak was glad to see the two visitors. Glad? No, *relieved*. And not because one of his own kind – Nancy – had arrived. Astrid stood with tight lips and looked at her watch.

'Five minutes. Your visit. No more . . .'

Newman turned on her, raising his voice. 'Dr Novak, I want this woman out of the room. Who the hell is she to dictate the length of our stay? You're in charge of Jesse Kennedy's case – Dr Kobler said so in front of me. Kindly assert your authority.'

'You will see that the visit is five minutes and not one second more . . .' Astrid was speaking German like a machine-gun. 'I will report this outrage to Professor Grange unless you do as I say . . .'

'Tell her to fuck off,' Newman snapped. 'Or has this fat old bag got you by the short and curlies? Novak! Are you – or are you not – the physician in charge here?'

Waldo Novak flushed. He spoke to Astrid over his shoulder, also in rapid German. 'I suspect that the last thing Grange would be pleased to hear is that you were responsible for a scene. If these people storm out of the Clinic have you any idea of the potential consequences? Newman is a foreign correspondent of international repute, for God's sake. Kindly leave us alone . . .'

She was mouthing protests as he extracted the computer card key and inserted it in the slot. The door slid open. She bit her lip and shuffled out into the corridor. The closing door shut out her enraged face. Novak looked at Newman and Nancy apologetically.

'Every institution has one of them. The faithful servant who is tolerated because she has been on the staff since the dinosaurs.'

'She's a bit of an old dinosaur herself,' Nancy commented.

She had her handbag open and was using a handkerchief to dab at her eyes. Newman noticed that Jesse's gnarled hand was now lying outside the sheet. When they had entered it had been underneath. His eyes were still closed. Nancy pulled up a chair close to the bed, sat down and took his hand in hers.

'He doesn't know you're here,' Novak told her.

'What sedative are you using, Dr Novak?' she asked.

He hesitated. 'It's not normal to discuss treatment . . .' he began and then stopped speaking. Newman noticed he had glanced towards a porthole-shaped mirror let into the side wall. Above it was a coat-hook. Of course! The window in the door was of frosted glass. Every hospital or clinic had some technique for observing seriously ill patients.

I bet that next room is empty, he said to himself. And I bet that corpulent old pig is standing on the other side of that fake mirror. That is what is worrying Novak. He took off his jacket, walked over to the mirror and hung the jacket over it.

'Dr Novak ...!' Nancy's tone was sharp-edged.

'Keep your voice down, Nancy,' Newman whispered. 'All the time.'

He looked round the room carefully, searching for a hidden microphone. Then he took a chair and placed it alongside Nancy's and gestured to Novak to sit down. The American sank into the chair and stared at Nancy who started speaking again, this time very quietly.

'I'm a doctor. I'm entitled to know the treatment ...'

'Sodium amytal,' Novak said promptly. 'He's a very vigorous man and must be kept in bed.'

He looked up over his shoulder at Newman who had rested a hand on the shoulder. Jesse's eyes flickered open, stared straight at Newman and frowned, his head jerked in a brief gesture. *Get Novak away from me and Nancy.*

'Novak,' said Newman, 'let's leave her with him. He is her grandfather. Come over with me by the window ...' He waited until Novak joined him. The window, which presumably looked on the outside world from the daylight showing through, was also frosted. Which was another peculiarity of the Clinic.

'What is it?' Novak enquired, his back to the bed.

'You and I have to meet outside. Very fast. You live on the premises?'

'Yes, I do. Why?'

'I guessed as much. This place smells of a closed community – a community locked away from the normal world. I suppose they do let you out,' he continued with a trace of sarcasm.

'During my off-duty hours I do what I like . . .'

'Don't sound indignant. But so far we haven't exactly felt welcome inside this place. I repeat. I insist on meeting you – so suggest somewhere. Thun would be closest?'

'I suppose it would be.' Novak sounded dubious. 'I don't see why I have to meet you anywhere . . .'

'Don't you?' Newman, observing what was happening behind Novak's back, kept talking fast. 'You're not compelled to, I agree. But then I could start writing articles about this place – naming you as my informant . . .'

'For Christ's sake, no . . .'

'No smart lawyer will get me for libel. I'm an expert at hinting at things and I know just how far I can go. Be honest with yourself, Novak – you're desperate to talk to someone. I sensed it within minutes of meeting you . . .'

'The Hotel Freienhof . . .' The words tumbled out. '. . . in Thun on the Freienhofgasse . . . it overlooks the

Inner Aare ... a stretch of the river flowing in from the lake ... the cheaper restaurant ... do you know the place?'

'I'll find it. Tomorrow suit you?'

'Day after tomorrow. Thursday. Seven in the evening. It will be dark then ...'

While Newman distracted Novak's attention Nancy had been talking to her grandfather, who suddenly woke up, his eyes fierce and alert. She leaned close to him so they could whisper and he spoke without any trace of being drugged.

'What are they doing to you here, Jesse?'

'It's what they're doing to the others. I never wanted to come to this place. That bastard Dr Chase shot me full of some drug in Tucson after I fell off the horse. I was hustled aboard a Lear jet and flown here ...'

'What do you mean – what they're doing to the others?'

'The patients. It's got to be stopped. They're carrying out some kind of experiments. I keep my ears open and they talk when they think I'm doped out of my mind. The patients don't survive the experiments. A lot of them are dying anyway – but that's no reason for murdering them ...'

'Are you sure, Jesse? How are you feeling?'

'I'm OK. As long as I'm inside here you've got a pipeline into this place. Don't worry about me ...'

'I do,' she whispered.

'Nancy.' Newman had left the window and was walking round the bed. 'Maybe it would be better if we came back another day when your grandfather isn't sedated . . .'

She looked up at him and saw him stop suddenly. Her expression was a mixture of pathos, anxiety and puzzlement. Newman put a finger to his lips to hush both Novak and Nancy. Jesse lay inert in the bed, his eyes closed. Newman bent down close to the head of the bed and listened. No, he had not been mistaken. He had caught the sound of a whirring noise, of machinery working.

Lee Foley had followed Newman at a discreet distance until he rounded a bend on the snowbound hillside in time to see Newman turn off along the narrow road leading to the Berne Clinic. He drove the Porsche straight past the turn-off and continued up the slope towards the fir forest.

As he ascended higher and higher he looked down on the buildings of the Clinic. He continued climbing until he reached the forest where he swung off the road, wheels skidding dangerously, heading for a narrow opening between the towering black firs. Always take the high ground.

Turning the Porsche through a hundred and eighty degrees – ready for a quick departure – he switched off the engine. On the floor of the empty seat behind him lay a pair of powerful binoculars in a leather case. He extracted them from the case, climbed out of the car and stood half-behind the erect trunk of an immensely tall tree.

Lifting the binoculars he adjusted the focus and slowly swept the lenses across the view far below. Within half an hour he had memorized the entire layout of the Clinic, the weird covered tunnel connecting it to the laboratory complex, and the laboratory itself. Then, ignoring the bitter east wind which scoured his craggy face, he settled down to wait, taking a nip of whisky from his hip flask.

Lee Foley was not the only watcher who took an interest in the Berne Clinic that wintry afternoon in mid-February. The rider on the scooter who had – by driving the machine to the limit – kept up with Foley, took a different route.

The scooter proceeded up the hillside to the point where the sign indicated the turn-off to the Clinic. Here it swung right, following the road taken earlier by Newman. Instead of stopping at the gatehouse, it went on past full tilt, so fast that the Dobermans, again released, had no time to reach the gate.

The rider headed towards Thun, then turned off along a side track leading up the far side of the plateau. The surface of the track was diabolical but the rider continued upwards with great skill until a snow-covered knoll to the left and close to the track obscured the grounds of the Clinic. The rider stopped, perched the machine against a pile of logs and used both hands to remove the helmet.

A cascade of titian hair fell down her back in a waterfall, was caught in the wind and streamed behind her. The girl opened the carrying satchel and took out a camera with a telescopic lens. She strode up the side of the knoll, her black leather pants sheathing her long, agile legs. At the summit she peered over. The entire, huge estate comprising the grounds and the buildings of the Berne Clinic spread out below.

Crouching down, she raised the view-finder to her eyes, scanning the laboratory complex, the igloo-like tunnel linking it to the side of the Clinic, the main building of the Clinic itself. Deftly, she began taking pictures, swivelling the lens, clicking almost continuously.

Inside Jesse Kennedy's room Newman, who had acute hearing, remained stooped as he searched for the source of the continuous whirring sound. Then he saw the metal, louvred grille set low down in the wall. It looked like an air-conditioning grille.

He knelt on the floor, pressing his ear against the louvres. The sound was much louder – a whirring noise with an occasional click at regular intervals. Putting a finger to his lips again to keep them quiet, he stood up. Facing Nancy and Novak, he gestured towards the grille and mouthed the words. *Tape recorder.*

Walking a few feet away from the grille, he started talking, raising his voice. His manner was aggressive, his target Novak.

'Now listen to me, Dr Novak – and listen well. We're leaving total responsibility for Jesse Kennedy's welfare in the hands of the Berne Clinic. You understand that clearly? Answer me!'

'That has always been the situation,' Novak replied, playing along with Newman. 'Nothing will be changed by your visit – and you can rest assured Mr Kennedy will continue to receive every care and attention . . .'

'He'd better.' Newman stabbed a finger into Novak's chest. 'I don't know whether you're aware of the fact, but in a few days' time a major international medical congress is being held – including a reception at the Bellevue Palace. If anything happened to Jesse I'll shout my head off at that reception. We haven't exactly had the red carpet rolled out for us since we arrived at this place . . .'

'I do assure you . . .' Novak began.

'You'd better talk to Kobler and Grange and get their assurances, too. I blew the Kruger case wide open and I'm a man who can make a lot of noise. We're leaving now. Nancy . . .'

'Dr Novak, we'll be back – and very soon,' Nancy said firmly as Novak produced his key card.

Newman was close to the door when it slid back

and he was looking beyond it. Two men in white coats walked past the opening, pushing a long trolley. Something lay on the trolley, something covered with a sheet which protruded upwards at the rear end – at the end where a patient's head would be. The silhouette was very large and shaped like a cage. From underneath the sheet a hand projected, a hand which moved in a grasping movement.

'Excuse me . . .'

Newman pushed in front of Nancy and Novak and turned right, away from the exit. The man behind the trolley glanced over his shoulder and the trolley began to move faster on its well-oiled wheels. Newman quickened his pace. As he had passed the door leading into the room with the mirror in the wall the door opened and behind him he heard Astrid call out. He ignored her and quickened his pace further. The two men with the trolley were almost running and had reached the point where the corridor became a downward sloping ramp. The trolley increased its momentum and Newman started running.

Reaching the corner where the corridor curved he saw ahead a steel door lifting. The trolley passed under it and the door began to descend. He arrived just as the steel plate closed with a hydraulic purr. Beyond he had caught a glimpse of the ramp descending steeply into the distance. To his right, set into the wall, was another of those infernal computer-operated slots. He heard a shuffling tread and turned to face Astrid.

'You have no business here, Mr Newman. I shall have to report this act of trespass . . .'

'Do that. What are you trying to hide? Report that remark too . . .'

He walked past her and retraced his steps rapidly along the corridor to where Nancy and Novak stood waiting for him. The American looked worried and took a step forward to speak in a whisper before Astrid reached them.

'I should leave here quickly if I were you . . .'

'It will be a pleasure . . .'

'First,' Astrid demanded, 'you must fill in the visiting forms at reception. It is the regulation . . .'

'It will be a pleasure,' Newman repeated.

The chill air of darkening night swept across the exposed plateau as they stood at the top of the steps outside the glassed-in verandah. But it was still daylight as Newman pulled on his gloves and Nancy shivered beside him. Novak had not come out to see them off, presumably to avoid any impression of intimacy.

'Cold?' Newman asked.

'This place gives me the creeps. My first impression – as soon as I saw the place – was right. There's something abnormal about the Clinic, Bob . . .'

'We'll talk about it in the car. With a bit of luck we should be back in Berne just before night . . .'

He drove down the curving drive slowly, again

looking round to check the layout. A pallid light glowed over the stark and grim mountains on the far side of Thun. Nancy huddled herself inside her coat and turned up the heater. She looked out on both sides and then back through the rear window.

'There never seems to be anyone about – and yet I get the uncanny feeling unseen eyes are watching our every move. I'm not usually like this. Look – that's the sort of thing I mean . . .'

As they approached the gatehouse there were no signs of life but the gates opened. Newman drove between them, turned right and headed down the narrow road to the wider road where they had placed the sign to the Berne Clinic. She glanced at his profile.

'You've changed recently,' she remarked. 'I date it from when we'd been a few hours in Geneva.'

'Changed? In what way?'

'You used to be so light-hearted, always smiling and cracking jokes. You look so terribly serious and determined. And why did you go running after that trolley when we left Jesse's room? Novak thought you'd taken leave of your senses.'

'What do you think was lying under that sheet?'

'Some unfortunate soul who'd just passed away . . .'

'Do corpses normally waggle their hand? Whatever was under that sheet did just that.'

'Oh, my God. The sheet was pulled right over the body . . .'

'And that's only done when the patient is dead.

That one was very much alive. My guess is that whoever was spread out under the sheet heard us and was trying to signal. Now you know why I ran after them. They beat me to a door which closed in my face – an automatic door, of course. That damned place is more like a giant computer than a clinic.'

'You mean they were running from you? I thought the trolley's brakes weren't working – that the momentum was carrying it down that ramp. Where does that corridor lead to?'

'A good question. There's a complex of new buildings further down the slope. I think they have a covered tunnel leading there. The corridor runs into the tunnel.'

'What kind of complex?'

'That, my dear Nancy, is one of the things I plan to ask our friend Dr Novak when I meet him in Thun on Thursday night . . .'

'He agreed to meet you! That's strange. Where are you seeing him? I can come, can't I?'

'The rendezvous is immaterial. It is strange that he agreed. And no, you can't come . . .'

'Bastard! Why do you think he did agree?' she asked as they came close to the bridge over the motorway and the slip road leading down on to the highway.

'I got the impression he's scared witless about something. I also think he's been waiting for the chance to contact someone outside that claustrophobic prison he can trust, he can confide in. And why are you so bothered about the Berne Clinic?'

'Did you notice the absence of something from Jesse's room?'

'I don't think so. I was too busy talking to Novak – to cover the fact you were talking to Jesse. What did I miss?'

'I'll tell you later,' she said, 'when we're back at the hotel. Do you think Jesse is safe in that place?'

'For the next few days, yes. Didn't you get the point of my shouting the odds about the medical reception at the Bellevue? They have a tape recorder behind that grille . . .'

'It really is creepy . . .'

'My strategy,' he continued, 'was to frighten them to ensure they don't harm him. They'll be very careful with Jesse until that medical congress is over. By then we may know what's going on at the Berne Clinic. I was buying time . . .'

They had turned down the slip road and were now speeding along the deserted motorway back towards Berne. It was so overcast Newman had his lights on and they were approaching the point where another slip road entered the motorway beyond a bridge. In his rear view mirror Newman saw a black Mercedes coming fast behind him. It signalled and swung out into the fast lane prior to overtaking. Then all hell broke loose on the motorway.

A helmeted figure appeared behind Newman on a

scooter, sounding the horn in urgent, non-stop blasts. The Mercedes had not yet drawn alongside. Newman frowned, his eyes moving from side to side. At the exit to the slip road ahead a giant orange-coloured snowplough was moving slowly forward, its huge blade raised to its highest arc. The scooter horn continued its blasting sound.

'What's the matter with that man?' Nancy asked.

She was speaking when Newman signalled – signalled that he was turning out into the fast lane ahead of the oncoming Mercedes. The snowplough emerged from the slip road like some monstrous robot, moving straight into the path of the slow lane. Newman rammed his foot down, swinging to his left. The Mercedes began sounding its own horn. He ignored it. 'Hang on!' he warned Nancy. 'Oh, Christ!' she muttered. The snowplough was almost on top of them. Like a guillotine the massive steel blade descended. Nancy saw it coming down. She froze with horror. It was going to slice them in two. The Citroen was now moving at manic speed, way above the limit. The blade flashed past Nancy's window, missed hitting the Citroen by inches. She flinched. The Mercedes jammed on its brakes to avoid the coming collision. In the fast lane Newman accelerated. The scooter passed the Mercedes, still speeding in the slow lane, weaving past the now stationary snowplough.

Behind the wheel of the Mercedes Hugo Munz swore foully to his passenger, Emil Graf. He reduced speed, checking in his mirror for any sign of a police patrol car. The motorway was still deserted.

'You should have hit him,' said Graf.

'You're crazy! I could have bounced off, hit the steel barrier and we both end up dead. That scooter warned him . . .'

'So,' Graf replied in his toneless voice, 'he's better organized than we gave him credit for. We'll have to try something else.'

Chapter Fourteen

Blanche Signer sat waiting at a corner table in the bar of the Bellevue Palace while Newman fetched the drinks. She had paid a brief visit to the cloakroom to comb her titian hair, to get her centre parting straight, to freshen up generally for the Englishman after her dangerous ride back along the motorway on the scooter.

Thirty years old, the daughter of a colonel in the Swiss Army, she ran the most efficient service for tracing missing persons in Western Europe. She was the girl who had secretly helped Newman to trace Kruger when the German had gone underground. She was determined to take Newman away from Nancy Kennedy.

'A double Scotch,' Newman said as he placed the glass before her and sat down alongside her on the banquette. There was not a lot of space and his legs touched hers. 'You've earned this. Cheers!'

'You know, Blanche,' he went on after swallowing half his drink, 'you took one hell of a risk back there on the motorway. I was scared stiff for you . . .'

'That's nice of you, Bob. Any risk of Nancy finding us here?'

'She's taking a bath. If she walks in you tried to pick me up. I think we have half an hour. What happened?'

'I waited at the Savoy as arranged. Lee Foley did follow you to the Clinic, then drove on past the turn-off and went on higher up the hill. I suspect he was doing what I did – checking out the layout of that place. It's peculiar. I've got a host of photos for you . . .' She squeezed her handbag. 'The film is in here. I can get it developed and printed overnight. I know someone who will do that for me. I'll get them to you tomorrow somehow . . .'

'Leave them in a sealed envelope addressed to me with the concierge. Now, what *did* happen? You probably saved my life.'

'It was simple, really, Bob. I took the photos, got on the scooter and started back to a place where I could wait to pick up Foley if he followed you back. I saw this car leaving the Clinic and decided to follow that. Pure hunch. The driver, a nasty-looking piece of work, knew what he was doing. He drove to where a snow-plough was clearing a slip road. He got out, walked up to the snowplough operator and pointed something in his face. I'm sure it was a hair spray. The man grabbed for his eyes and Nasty hit him. It was pretty brutal. The poor devil's head came into contact with a steel bar – my guess is his skull is cracked. The driver from the Clinic then put on the snowplough man's overalls and guided the machine down to the end of the slip road – just before it turns on to the motorway.'

'Waiting for me,' Newman commented. 'It was a fair assumption that when we left the Clinic I'd drive back the way I came from Berne. I blundered. I thought someone inside that place was at risk. Instead they decided to wipe me out first. But they have blundered too. Now I know something is wrong with that place. I'm not sure you ought to help me any more on this one . . .'

'Bob . . .' She took his hand and squeezed it affectionately. 'We make a good team. We did before. Remember. You don't get rid of me as easily as that. When are you coming to see me at my apartment? It's only a five-minute walk from here along the Munstergasse and into the Junkerngasse . . .'

'I'm involved with Nancy . . .'

'Officially?' she pressed.

'Well, no, not yet . . .'

'So you come and see me . . .'

'You're blackmailing my emotions . . .'

'And I'll go on doing it,' she assured him in her soft, appealing voice.

He studied her while he finished his drink. Her blue eyes stared back at him steadily. She had beautiful bone structure, Newman reflected. A lot of character – you could see that in her chin and high cheekbones. To say nothing of her figure which was something to knock any man out.

'What do I do next for you?' she asked.

'Go home. Relax . . .' He saw the look in her eyes. 'Oh, hell, Blanche, all right. You still go home and rest. Get some warmer clothes and maintain the watch on Lee Foley.' He leaned forward and grasped her upper arm. 'But you be very careful. Foley is dangerous.'

'I can handle him. Incidentally, when he's lying low at the Savoy he eats at a Hungarian place a few doors down the Neuengasse. The street is arcaded – so I can keep under cover. And it's perfect for parking the scooter. Anything else?'

She made it sound so everyday, Newman marvelled. Blanche was always very cool. She watched him over the rim of her glass; she couldn't take her eyes off him.

'There might be something else,' he decided. 'You've built up that register of people with unusual occupations. Check it and see if you have anything on a Manfred Seidler . . .'

'Will do. Maybe I'd better go before your pseudofiancée turns up. If I get something on this Seidler I'll type out a report and include it in the envelope with the photos. I'll head it MS. If there's an emergency I'll call your room number, let the phone ring three times, then disconnect. You call me back when you can. OK, Mr Newman?'

'OK, Miss Signer . . .'

She leaned forward, kissed him full on the mouth, stood up and walked away, her handbag looped over her shoulder. The bar at the Bellevue Palace is dimly lit, very much like many American bars. But as she walked erectly across the room men's heads turned to

185

watch her. She stared straight ahead, apparently unaware of the impression she was creating. At the exit she passed Nancy Kennedy who was just entering.

Newman had moved Blanche's lipsticked glass on to the next table as she left. He stood up to greet Nancy. As she came closer he saw by her expression that something had disturbed her.

'That man phoned again,' she said as she sat down on the banquette. 'The same one I took the call from in Geneva. Seidler? Wasn't that his name? I told him you'd be back much later in the evening. He sounded very agitated. He put the phone down on me when I tried to get a message.'

'That's my strategy now, Nancy. Agitation. All round. By the time I talk to him he'll be going up the wall, which will make him more pliable. Same thing with the Berne Clinic. Agitation. Although there,' he said ruefully, 'it seems to have acted with a vengeance. They tried to kill us on that motorway . . .'

'*Us?*'

'You as well as me is my guess.' Newman's manner was forbidding. 'I'm giving it to you straight so you'll take care. You make no trips to Thun without me. Now, in the car you mentioned something missing from Jesse's room. What was it?'

'You have a good memory . . .'

'It's my main asset. Answer the bloody question.'

'You are in a mood. Something to tell the time by. No clock on his bedside table. No wristwatch. Jesse has no way of keeping track of the time. It's a disorientation technique. I know that from my psychiatric studies.'

'Trick-cyclists drive me round the bend . . .'

'You're hostile to everything medical,' she flared. 'When we were at the Clinic I saw you wrinkling your nose at the smell. They do have to keep those places hygienic. To do that they use disinfectant . . .'

'OK,' he said irritably. 'No clock. I've got the point. I agree it's odd.'

'And Novak told the truth when he said they used sodium amytal to sedate Jesse.' She reached into her handbag, produced a blue capsule from a zipped pocket and handed it to him. 'You can't see in here but it's a sixty-milligram dose coded F23. Jesse slipped it to me while you were talking to Novak. That's why Jesse was still awake.'

'Maybe I'm dim, but I don't follow what you've just said.'

'Jesse has become expert at palming a capsule when he's given one to swallow. He pretends to swallow it and hides it in the palm of his hand.'

'How does he get rid of it?'

'He drops it inside that metal grille where they've hidden the tape recorder . . .'

'That's a laugh,' Newman commented. 'It's also clever. It doesn't suggest a sick man who's lost most of his marbles. And one absent thing I did notice.

There wasn't a single mention of the fact that Jesse is supposed to be suffering from leukaemia.'

'Soon you'll be as good as me,' she said smugly. Then her expression drooped. 'But they are sedating him heavily. He showed me the fleshy part of his arm – it's riddled with punctures. The sods are pumping him full of the stuff with a hypodermic. We were just lucky it was capsule day. Can't you find out what's really going on when you meet Novak in Thun on Thursday night?'

'I intend to. If he turns up. He's getting very shaky about the situation there, so let's hope Kobler and Co. don't notice. I want you to stay inside this hotel the whole time I'm away at Thun. If you get any calls saying I've had an accident, ignore them. Anything that tempts you out of the Bellevue. You'll do that, won't you?'

'You have changed. You're getting very bossy . . .'

'I'm not asking you. I'm telling you.' His tone was bleak. 'I can no longer keep wondering what you're doing, looking over my shoulder.'

'You could ask me more nicely . . .'

She broke off as a waiter came to their table. He handed to Newman a folded sheet of paper. Inside was a sealed envelope. Taking the envelope, Newman looked at the waiter.

'Who gave you this?'

'A rather shabbily dressed individual, sir. He pointed you out and said would I be sure to hand this to you personally. I have never seen him before .'

'Thanks . . .'

Newman tore open the envelope and extracted a second, smaller sheet of folded paper which bore no clue as to its origins. The message was brief.

Can you come to see me at seven o'clock this evening. A crisis situation. Beck.

Newman checked his watch. 6.15 p.m. He put the folded sheet back inside the envelope and slipped the envelope inside his wallet. Nancy stirred restlessly.

'What is it?'

'Things are hotting up. I have to go out. Expect me when you see me. If you're hungry start dinner without me. Choose whichever restaurant you fancy.'

'Is that all?'

'Yes. It is. Remember – stay inside this hotel . . .'

As he walked through the night Berne was deserted. The workers had gone home, the bright sparks hadn't come in for an evening on the town yet. He crossed over by the Casino and walked into the right-hand arcade of the Munstergasse, an arched stone tunnel with a paved walk, shop windows lit up and closed.

Newman wondered why he had been so abrupt with Nancy. A man has a habit of comparing one woman with another. Had the fact that he had been talking with Blanche so amiably before Nancy arrived influenced his attitude? Not a pleasant conclusion. But Beck's summons had decided him. With half his mind he heard the footsteps behind which synchronized with his own. He crossed the lonely street into the opposite arcade without looking back.

Yes, he had made up his mind. Before he saw Beck he was going to see Blanche – to tell her she was out of the whole business. *Crisis* was the word Beck had used. Beck didn't use words like that lightly. He was going to pull Blanche out of the firing line.

The footsteps synchronized with his own, the click-clack of a second pair of feet on the stones had followed him across the street. They were now following him down the same arcade. He didn't look back. It was an old trick – to mask your own footfall by pacing it with the man you were following.

He was nearly half-way towards the Munsterplatz when he passed a narrow alley leading through to the street beyond. The *Finstergasschen*. A spooky alley with only a single lamp which emphasized the shadows of the narrow walk. He continued towards the Munster, his right hand stiffened for a chopping blow.

'Newman! Come back here! Quick . . .!'

A hoarse, whispering call. He swung round on his heel. Two figures were struggling at the entrance to the *Finstergasschen*. One tall, heavily-built, wearing a cap. The second much smaller. He walked back quickly as they vanished inside the alley, slowed down near its entrance, peered round the corner.

Lee Foley had his arm round the neck of the smaller man. The American was dressed in an English check suit, a checked cap. A walking stick held in his free hand completed the outer trappings of an Englishman. The small man he held in a vice-like grip was Julius Nagy.

'This little creep has been tracking you all over town,' Foley said. 'Time we found out who his employer is, wouldn't you agree?'

Before Newman could react Foley thrust Nagy inside the alcove formed by a doorway. Shoving him back against the heavy wooden door, he suddenly lifted the stick, held it horizontally and pressed it against Nagy's throat. The little man's eyes bulged out of his head. He was terrified.

'Who is your paymaster?' rasped Foley.

'Tripet . . .' Nagy gasped as Foley relaxed the stick slightly.

'Who?' Foley rasped again.

'Chief Inspector Tripet. Sûreté. Geneva . . .'

'That came too easily,' Foley growled. 'Geneva? This happens to be Berne. You're lying. One more chance. After a little more persuasion . . .'

'Watch it,' Newman warned. 'You'll crush his Adam's apple.'

'That is exactly what I'm going to do if he doesn't come across.'

Nagy made a horrible choking sound. He beat his small, clenched fists against Foley's body. He might as well have hammered at the hide of an elephant. Newman glanced down the alley. Still empty. By the glow of the lamp he saw Nagy was turning purple. Foley pressed the stick harder. Feebly, Nagy's heels pattered against the base of the wooden door, making no more noise than the scutter of a mouse. Newman began to feel sick.

Foley eased the pressure of the stick. He pushed his cold face within inches of Nagy's ashen skin, his ice-blue eyes watching the little man's without pity, without any particular expression. He waited as Nagy sucked in great draughts of cold night air. It was the only sound in the stillness of the night.

'Let's start all over,' Foley suggested. 'One more chance – I simply don't have the time for lies. Who is your employer?'

'Coat pocket . . . phone number . . . car registration . . . Bahnhof . . .'

'What the hell is the jerk talking about?' Foley asked in a remote voice as though thinking aloud.

'Wait! Wait!' Newman urged.

He plunged a hand inside Nagy's shabby coat pocket, scrabbled around. His fingers felt a piece of paper. He pulled it out urgently – Foley was not a man who bluffed. He stepped back a few paces and examined the paper under the lamp.

'There is a phone number,' he told Foley. 'And what looks like a car registration number. It is a car registration . . .' Newman had recognized the car registration. The figures were engraved on his memory. The letters too. 'Let him talk,' he told Foley. 'Ease up on him. What was that reference he made to the Bahnhof?'

'Your employer,' Foley said to Nagy. 'This time we

want the truth – not some crap about the Geneva police . . .'

'The other coat pocket . . .' Nagy was looking at Newman. 'Inside it you'll find a camera. I took a shot of a man getting into that Mercedes – outside the Bahnhof. He came in off the one fifty-eight p.m. express from Geneva . . .'

Foley held the walking stick an inch from the little man's throat while Newman scrabbled around inside the other pocket. His hand came out holding a small, slim camera. A Voigtlander. Three shots had been taken. He looked up and caught Nagy's expression as the little man stared straight at him over the bar of the walking stick.

'I only took two shots,' Nagy croaked. 'The man getting into the car – and the Mercedes itself.' He switched his gaze to Foley. 'I think that man is the boss, my employer – and somebody important. There was a chauffeur with the car.'

'Mind if I take out the film?' Newman asked. 'I'll pay for it . . .'

'Jesus Christ!' Foley exploded. 'Take the film. Why pay this shit?'

Newman broke open the camera after winding the film through. Extracting the film, he dropped it inside his coat pocket, shut the camera, took a banknote from his wallet and replaced camera with banknote inside Nagy's pocket.

'I'll get it developed and printed,' he told Foley. 'Now let our friend go . . .'

193

'Break an arm – just to teach him not to follow people . . .'

'No!' Newman's tone was tough and he took a step towards the American. 'He was following me, so I decide. I said let him go . . .'

With a grimace of disgust the American released Nagy who felt his injured throat, swallowed and then straightened his rumpled tie. He seemed oddly reluctant to leave and kept eyeing Newman as though trying to transmit some message. Foley gave him a shove and he shuffled off down the alley, glancing back once and again it was Newman he stared at.

'You and I have to talk,' Foley said. It was a statement. 'I want to know what's on that film – and on that piece of paper . . .'

'Not now. I'm late for an appointment. Thanks for spotting my shadow, but you play pretty rough. Sometimes you get more if you coax . . .'

'I coax with the barrel of a gun, Newman. I'll call you at the Bellevue. Then we meet. Inside twenty-four hours. You owe me.'

'Agreed . . .'

Newman walked rapidly away down the Munstergasse and continued along the Junkerngasse, which is also arcaded, but without shops. Crossing the cobbled street which was now running downhill, he looked back. No sign of Foley, but that didn't surprise him. The American was too fly to follow him. He reached the closed door with three bell-pushes, a recently-installed speakphone, a name alongside each bell-push. He pressed the one lettered *B. Signer*.

Blanche had taken his advice or, woman-like, she had hoped – expected – he would turn up. Her quiet voice came to him through the speakphone grille clearly when he announced himself.

'I thought it was you, Bob. Push the door when the buzzer buzzes . . .'

Beyond the heavy wooden door, which closed automatically behind him on the powerful sprung-hinge, a dim light showed him the way up a flight of ancient stone steps, well-worn in the middle. On the first floor landing he noticed another new addition in the door to her apartment. A fish-eye spyhole. The door opened inward and Blanche stood there, wearing only a white bathrobe.

He sensed she had nothing on underneath as she stood aside and the bathrobe, loosely corded round her waist, parted to expose a bare, slim leg to her thigh. She closed the door, fixed the special security lock and put on the thick chain.

'Blanche, I have another film for you to develop and print.' He handed the spool to her. 'Only three shots – the third one intrigues me. The party who gave it to me said there were only two . . .'

'Because someone else was present? Tomorrow you have prints and negatives along with my own contri-bution. No, don't sit there. In here . . .'

Here was a tidily-furnished bedroom with one large single bed. He paused and swung round to face her. She had closed the door and stood facing him, brushing the cascade of titian hair slowly, her face expressionless.

'No, Blanche,' he said. 'I've come to tell you to forget all about the Berne Clinic. Too many pretty tough characters keep turning up. You could get hurt – that I won't risk . . .'

'You'll hurt me if you don't . . .'

She pushed him suddenly, a hard shove. The edge of the bed acted as a fulcrum against the back of his legs and he sprawled on the white duvet. She flicked the cord round her waist free, dropped the bathrobe and he had guessed right about her lack of attire. She was on top of him before he could move.

'I'm engaged,' Newman protested as she spread herself.

'Of course you are – engaged in battle . . .'

She giggled as her slim hands industriously burrowed, whipping open the buttons of his coat, the buttons of his jacket underneath, unfastening his tie, his shirt buttons. He had never known a woman's hand operate with such skill and agility. He sighed. When it's inevitable . . . relax . . . enjoy . . .

Julius Nagy was livid with rage and resentment. He shuffled back along the deserted *Finstergasschen*. They never expected you to come back the same way. This was twice he had been subjected to violent abuse. First the obscene experience with that thug in the lavatory aboard the express to Zurich. Now the same thing had happened again at the end of this alley.

The injury to Nagy's dignity hurt him even more than the injury to his throat. Only the Englishman, Newman, had treated him like a fellow human being. Well, he would get his revenge. He emerged from the end of the alley and peered cautiously both ways along the Munstergasse. No one in sight anywhere. Pulling up the collar of his shabby coat against the bitter cold, he turned left towards the Munster.

'Make a sound and I'll blow your spine in half . . .'

The violent threat, spoken in German, was accompanied by the equally violent ramming of something hard against his back. A gun barrel. Nagy froze with sheer fright, standing quite still.

'Keep walking,' the voice ordered. 'Don't look round. That would be the last mistake you'd made. Cross the street. Head for the Munsterplatz . . .'

There was still no one else about. It was still the interval between the workers going home and the night revellers appearing. Nagy crossed the street, the gun muzzle glued against his back, and walked down under the other arcade, praying a patrol car would drive down the street.

'Now walk round the Munsterplatz – on the pavement . . .'

The gunman knew what he was doing, Nagy realized with growing terror. Following this route they stayed within the dark shadows. On the far side of the square the huge bulk of the front façade of the Munster sheered up. The great tower was enclosed inside a series of builder's boards – like tiers in a theatre. Above that speared the immense spire, all knobbly and spiky.

Nagy began to suspect what was their ultimate destination – the Plattform. The large garden square alongside the Munster which overlooked the river Aare. He was pushed and prodded through the gateway and guided across the square towards the far wall. The naked trees in the garden were vague skeletal silhouettes, the only sound the crunch of two pairs of feet on the gravel. Nagy, sweat streaming down his face despite the cold, was trying to look ahead to predict the next move. His mind wouldn't function.

'I need information,' the voice growled. 'Here we can talk undisturbed . . .'

So that was it. The raw wind beat across the exposed heights of the Plattform, sliced at his face. No one would come out here on such a night. His attacker had worked it out well. And this was the third time! A hint of fury welled up, faded into fear again. His feet walked with leaden step. Then they reached the wall near the corner furthest from the lift which descended to the Badgasse. Nagy was pressed against the wall.

'Now I will tell you what we want to know. Then you will tell me the answers to the questions I put to you . . .'

Nagy stared out beyond the wall which was thigh-high, stared out at the lights of houses twinkling in the chilling night on the Bantiger, the hill which rises from the far bank of the Aare. The gun had been removed from his back. Suddenly Nagy felt two hands like steel handcuffs grasp his ankles. He was elevated bodily and projected forward over the wall. He screamed. His hands thrust out into space. The earth, one hundred and fifty feet below, rushed up to meet him. The scream faded into a wail. Then it ceased. There was a distant thud. Steps retraced their path across the gravel.

Chapter Fifteen

Newman took the devious route to the Taubenhalde (the Pigeon Hill) which houses Federal Police Headquarters in Berne.

He was becoming almost neurotically wary of shadows – and not only the shadows which cloaked the arcades. He had heard Nagy's footsteps but he had missed Lee Foley's cat-like tread. So, when he walked back up the Munstergasse from Blanche's apartment, made his way back past the Casino and crossed to the Kochergasse, he quickened his pace.

He proceeded on past the entrance to the Bellevue Palace, stopped to light a cigarette while he glanced back, checked the far pavement, and disappeared down an alley leading to the *Terrasse* in front of the Parliament. At that hour the elevated walk was deserted. Beyond the walk the ground fell away, sloping steeply towards the Aare. Ahead he saw the funicular – the Marzilibahn – which travels down the slope almost to river level. The small red car had just reached the top of the slanting rails. He broke into a run.

Sixty centimes bought him a ticket from the attendant inside the small building at the top of the funicular. The car, very new and toy-like, was empty and the door slid shut as soon as he stepped inside. It began its steeply-angled descent down a pair of ruler-straight rails.

Newman stood at the front, surrounded by windows, his hands on a rail. In the dark the lights across the river were sharp as diamonds. The descent continued and Newman felt exposed inside the illuminated car. He realized his hands were gripping the rail tightly.

The lower station came up to meet him. The car slowed, slipped inside, stopped. The moment the door opened he stepped out and left the cover of the base station. The wind blasted along the river and hit him in the face. He kept walking as he turned up his coat collar. There appeared to be no one about.

He passed one of the original wooden cars, preserved as a monument and perched on a tiny hill. The Taubenhalde was still some distance when he entered a modern building and presented his passport to the receptionist.

'I have an appointment with Arthur Beck,' he said. 'Seven o'clock . . .'

Seated behind his counter, the receptionist examined the passport, stared at Newman and then at the photo. He opened a file and took out a glossy print which Newman recognized as a photograph of himself taken the previous year during the Kruger affair. They were careful inside this place.

'You know the way to the Taubenhalde, M. Newman?' the receptionist asked as he returned the passport. 'It is a little complex . . .'

'I know the way. I've been here before . . .'

From this building a long subterranean passage leads to Pigeon Building. Newman walked along it while behind him the receptionist picked up the phone and spoke rapidly. At the end of the passage a travelator – an 80-metre-long moving staircase – ascends to the main entrance hall to the Taubenhalde. Newman stood quite still, working out what he would tell Beck, as the travelator carried him upwards.

He had come a long way round to reach this entrance hall – by doing so he avoided being recognized by any watcher checking who entered the building through the main doors. The moment Newman entered the hall he knew something was wrong. Arthur Beck was waiting for him by the reception counter where normally all visitors filled in a detailed form.

'I will deal with the formalities,' Beck told the receptionist curtly and pocketed a pad of forms. He walked to the lift without even greeting Newman. Inside the lift the policeman pressed the button for Floor 10 and stood in silence as the lift ascended. Reaching 10, the lift door remained closed until Beck inserted a key into a slot and turned it. The security inside the place, Newman recalled, was formidable.

Beck still said nothing as he unlocked the door of his office and stood aside for Newman to enter. It was unnerving – especially the business downstairs about not filling in any form. Beck explained that as he went round to the far side of his desk, sat down, and gestured for Newman to occupy the chair opposite.

'Officially, you may never have been here. We shall see . . .'

Beck was plump-cheeked, his most arresting feature was his alert grey eyes under thick brows. His manner was normally recessive, observant. He moved his hands and feet quickly and his complexion was ruddy. He was one of the cleverest policemen in Western Europe.

Dressed in a navy blue business suit, blue-striped shirt, a blue tie which carried a kingfisher emblem woven into the fabric, he fiddled with a pencil, watching Newman. No welcoming words, nothing to indicate that they were old friends. Suddenly he threw down the pencil. His voice was abrupt.

'Can you tell me where you were this evening between six fifteen and seven o'clock?'

'Why?' Newman demanded.

'I'm asking you if you have an alibi for those forty-five minutes?'

'*Alibi?*' Newman's tone expressed astonishment, irritation. 'What the hell are you talking about?'

'You haven't answered the question.'

'Is this something to do with the crisis you mentioned in your note dragging me over here?' Newman realized his mistake. 'It can't be – I got that note earlier . . .'

'It is my duty to put the question to you once more formally. Think before you reply . . .'

Newman was thinking. There was no way he could tell Beck where he had been. That would mean dragging in Blanche. He wasn't going to do that. Not because of the possible publicity. Not because of Nancy. Because of Blanche. He was surprised by the strength of his own decision.

'I'm not prepared to answer the question until I know exactly what this is all about.'

'Very well.' Beck stood up stiffly. 'I will show you what it is all about. I think you had better wear some different clothes – to avoid the chance of recognition . . .'

Newman carefully said nothing as Beck opened a cupboard, took out a dark blue overcoat and handed it to Newman. 'Put that on. Leave your sheepskin here. We shall be coming back afterwards.'

'After what?' Newman enquired. 'And this coat is pretty floppy. You're fatter than I am . . .'

'It will do. You look fine. Now try on this hat . . .'

Beck slipped on a fawn raincoat he took from the cupboard as Newman put on the hat. The police chief slammed the cupboard door shut, picked up the phone and spoke rapidly.

'Be sure the car is ready. We're coming down now . . .'

'The hat is too big,' Newman commented. 'Your head is fatter than mine . . .'

'You look fine. Put on these dark glasses. Please do

not argue. It is very important that you are not recognized – and God knows there will be enough people hanging around . . .'

'Hanging around where? I want to know where you're taking me before I move from this office.'

'Not far, Bob. This is just as unpleasant and unsettling for me as well as for you. It blew up in my face very recently. I ask you to say nothing, to talk to no one but me. If you don't do as I request you may well regret it . . .'

'*Request* – that's a bit more like it. Try and push me around and we won't be cooperating on anything ever again. You do know that, I hope, Beck?'

'I know that. Time is precious. The car is waiting. We have only a very short distance to go. Not five minutes' walk from the Bellevue Palace. Something terrible has happened . . .'

Seated in the back of an unmarked police car neither Beck nor Newman said a single word during the short journey. Newman peered out of the window and realized they were driving along the Aarstrasse in the direction of the Nydeggbrucke. In the darkness lights across the river reflected in the water.

A tram was crossing the Kirchenfeld bridge high above them just before they passed under its span. Very little traffic at that hour. Then, ahead, he saw a line of parked police cars, their blue lamps flashing on the roofs. The car slowed down at a barrier which had been erected at the entrance to the Badgasse, the street which runs immediately below the Munster Plattform.

Beck opened the window as a uniformed policeman approached and showed his identity card without saying a word. The barrier was raised and they passed up a narrow street into the ancient Badgasse. Here there was frenetic activity.

More police cars, more winking blue lamps. Flash-bulbs lighting the street in brief blazes of brilliance. Newman was reminded of the strobe lights in a disco. They drove slowly to a point near the far end of the Plattform wall on their right which faced old houses on their left. A high canvas screen had been erected around something. The car stopped. Beck grasped the door handle.

'This is pretty nasty,' he warned.

Newman stepped out of the warmth of the car into the raw chill of the night. He felt slightly ridiculous in Beck's blue overcoat and the ill-fitting hat. Fortunately the glasses he wore were only lightly tinted. Police milled around. A grim-faced man in plain clothes pushed his way through to Beck.

'This is Chief Inspector Pauli of Homicide, Cantonal Police,' Beck remarked without introducing Newman. 'Pauli, would you kindly repeat the message you received over the phone?'

'The caller was anonymous,' Pauli reported in a clipped voice. 'He said we'd find a body in the Badgasse. He also said that a Robert Newman had been seen arguing with the deceased earlier this evening in the Munstergasse . . .'

'Pauli is from Hauptwache – police headquarters on the Waisenhausplatz,' Beck commented. 'He came at once and this is what he found . . .'

Behind the canvas shield a Ford station wagon was parked at a right angle to the base of the wall, facing outwards ready to be driven away. The hideous mess which was the remains of Julius Nagy lay spread all over the roof, his head twisted at an impossible angle, one eye staring at Newman like the eye of a dead fish in the beam of a searchlight mounted on top of a police car.

Newman recognized the mangled corpse as Nagy by the Tyrolean hat rammed slantwise across the crushed skull, a hat with a tiny blood-red feather. But it was not really the colour of blood – the real colour, much darker and coagulated, smeared the Ford's windscreen in snake-like streaks.

A man in civilian clothes, carrying a black bag, climbed down a ladder which had been perched against the far side of the car. Removing a pair of rubber gloves, he shook his head as he gazed at Beck.

'Dr Moser,' Beck said briefly. 'Cantonal police pathologist.'

'I'd say every other bone in his body is broken,' Moser commented. 'I can tell you more later – or will you be taking over?'

'I will be taking over,' Beck informed him.

'In that case, it's a pleasant night's work for Dr

Kleist – and better her than me. I'll send over my written report . . .'

'Any suggestion – an educated guess – as to how it happened?' Beck enquired.

'I never guess.' Moser stared upwards at the wall towering above them. 'Of course, he'd hit the car like a cannon-ball from that height. Obviously it was either murder, suicide or an accident.' Moser paused. 'There are pleasanter ways of ending it all. And I managed to extract this envelope he had in his overcoat pocket.' He handed a crumpled envelope to Beck and glanced at Newman. 'I'll be off to start work on my report. Another late night – and my wife is already beginning to wonder why I get home so late . . .'

Beck produced a cellophane packet, held the envelope by one corner and slipped it inside the packet. 'Probably useless for fingerprints but one goes through the motions. What idea are you playing with now in that fertile brain of yours, Newman?'

The Englishman was staring up into the night where the massive wall sheered up. At intervals huge flying buttresses projected. It was vertiginous – even gazing up the terrifying drop. He looked at Beck as they stood alone with the pathetic and horrifying crumpled form which had once been a living, breathing man. At that moment Moser returned briefly.

'One suggestion, Beck. I'd cover the top of the Ford with a waterproof sheet and have it driven slowly to the morgue. Kleist will find she has to scrape some of the remains clear of the car. He's practically glued to the roof. Enjoy yourself . . .'

'I think,' Newman said after Moser had gone, 'it might be an idea to go up to the Plattform by the lift at the corner. If I remember rightly it doesn't stop working until eight thirty p.m.'

'You have a remarkable memory for details about the Plattform.'

'It's up to you . . .'

'I'll get the car to drive round and meet us at the exit . . .'

'No. Near the top of the Munstergasse . . .'

'If you say so . . .'

They emerged from the canvas shelter into hectic activity in the Badgasse. Uniformed police in leather greatcoats, 7.65-mm. automatics holstered on their right hips, walking up and down to no apparent purpose that Newman could see. Beck spoke briefly to his car driver and followed Newman who was striding to the distant corner of the wall.

The ancient lift is a small cage which ascends vertically inside an open metal shaft to the top of the Plattform. Newman had bought two 60-rappen tickets from the old boy who attended the lift when Beck arrived. They stood in silence as it made its slow ascent.

On a seat was perched a piece of newspaper with the remains of a sandwich and the interior of the lift smelt of salami. The old boy had moved from the entrance door to the exit door at the opposite end of the cage. Beck watched Newman as he stared out of the window overlooking the Aare, then switched his gaze to the facing window where he could see the slope terraced into kitchen gardens, the continuous walls of houses along the Munstergasse running into the Junkerngasse. In one of those houses Blanche would be in her apartment, probably phoning the man who would develop and print the films. At all costs he had to keep her name out of this horror.

The lift door was opened by the attendant after it reached the tiny shed at the corner of the Plattform. Newman did not make any move to get out. He spoke casually.

'You won't have many passengers at this time of night. Can you recall anyone who used the lift at about six thirty p.m.? Maybe six forty-five?'

'For sixty rappen you want me to answer foolish questions?'

Beck said nothing. He produced his identity folder and showed it to the attendant, his face expressionless. Returning it to his pocket he stared out of the open doorway.

'I am sorry . . .' The attendant seemed confused. 'I did not know. That awful business of the man who fell . . .'

'That's what I'm talking about,' Newman said amiably. 'We think he may have had a friend – or friends – who could identify him. Someone who was so shaken they took your lift down after the tragedy. Take your time. Think . . .'

'There was a big man by himself.' The attendant screwed up his face in his effort to concentrate. 'I didn't take all that notice of him. He carried a walking stick . . .'

'How was he dressed?' Beck interjected.

'I was eating my supper. I can't remember. A lot of people use this lift . . .'

'Not at this time of night,' Newman pointed out gently. 'I imagine you can remember the time?'

'Seven o'clock I would say. No earlier. The lift was at the bottom – he called it up – and I heard a clock chime . . .'

Beck walked out of the cage and Newman followed. In the distance, almost at the end of the thigh-high stone wall protecting them from the drop, uniformed policemen with torches searched the ground. A section was cordoned off by means of poles with ropes. The point, Newman guessed, where Nagy had gone over.

'Nothing, sir – at least as yet,' one of the policemen reported to Beck who shrugged.

'They're looking for signs of a struggle,' Beck remarked. 'God, the wind cuts you in two up here. And it wasn't an accident,' he continued. 'There's no ice on the stones he could have slipped on . . .'

Newman placed both hands on the top of the wall close to the roped-off section and peered over. Vertigo.

The great wall fell into the abyss. He studied the area, looking along the wall in both directions. His hands were frozen.

'Interesting,' he commented.

'What is?' Beck asked sharply.

'Look for yourself. This is the one place where there are no buttresses to break his fall. He'd still have been seriously injured – but he might just have survived. He went over at the very place where it was certain he'd be killed . . .'

He looked round the great Plattform which was divided up into four large grassy beds. Stark, closely trimmed trees reared up in the night which was now lit by the moon. Behind them the huge menacing spire of the Munster stabbed at the sky. Newman thrust his hands into his pockets and began walking towards the exit he knew led into the Munsterplatz. Beck followed without comment.

Emerging from the gateway, Newman stood for a moment, staring round the cobbled square and across at the Munstergasse. The arcade on the far side was a deserted tunnel of light and shadow. He walked diagonally across the square and inside the arcade. He continued walking until he reached the *Finstergasschen*, the narrow alley leading towards the Marktgasse, one of the main streets of Berne. He checked his watch. Five minutes. That was the time it had taken for him to walk from the place where Nagy had died to the *Finstergasschen*.

The patrol car Beck had sent on ahead was parked

by the kerb. Newman climbed into the rear seat without a word as Beck settled himself beside him. He gave the driver a brief instruction.

'Not the front entrance. We'll take the long way round to my office.'

'Why?' asked Newman when the policeman had closed the partition dividing them from the driver.

'Because the front entrance may well be watched. I rushed you into the car on the way out but I don't want anyone to see you come back – even in those togs . . .'

Togs. Newman smiled to himself. During his stint in London Beck had picked up a number of English colloquialisms. He left the talking to Beck who continued immediately.

'Do you know that pathetic crumpled wreck back there?'

'Julius Nagy,' Newman replied promptly. 'The Tyrolean hat. He was wearing it when he followed me about in Geneva . . .'

He had to admit that much. He had no doubt Beck had contacted Chief Inspector Tripet of the Sûreté in Geneva. Beck turned to face the Englishman.

'But how did you identify him in Geneva?'

'Because when I was last here I used him. He deserved a better death than that. He was born to a poor family, he hadn't enough brains to get far, but he was persistent and he earned his living supplying people like me with information. He had underworld contacts.'

'Here in Berne, you mean?'

'Yes. That was why I was surprised he had moved his sphere of operations to Geneva . . .'

'That was me,' Beck replied. 'I had him thrown out of the Berne canton as a public nuisance, an undesirable. I too felt sorry for him. Why did he risk coming back is what I would like to know . . .'

Again Newman refused to be drawn into conversation. They were approaching the building close to the base of the Marzilibahn when Beck made the remark, still watching Newman.

'I am probably one of the very few people in Switzerland who knows that what you have just seen is the second murder in the past few weeks.'

'Who else knows?'

'The murderers . . .'

The atmosphere changed the moment they entered Beck's office from the hostility which had lingered in the air during Newman's earlier visit. A small, wiry woman whose age Newman guessed as fifty-five, a spinster from her lack of rings, followed them inside with a tray. A percolator of coffee, two Meissen cups and saucers, two balloon-shaped glasses and a bottle of Rémy Martin.

'This is Gisela, my assistant,' Beck introduced. 'Also she is my closest confidante. In my absence you can pass any message to her safe in the knowledge it will reach my ears only.'

'You're looking after us well,' Newman said in German and shook hands as soon as she had placed the tray on the desk.

'It is my pleasure, Mr Newman. I will be in my office if you need me,' she told Beck.

'She works all hours,' Beck commented as he poured the coffee. 'Black, if I recall? And it is a swine of a night – on more accounts than one. So, we will treat ourselves to some cognac. I welcome you to Berne and drink your health, my friend. You must excuse my earlier reception.'

'Which was about what?'

'That bloody anonymous phone call to Pauli reporting you were seen in the vicinity. Someone wants you off the streets. We have procedures – and my immediate purpose was to close off the cantonal police. I can now tell Pauli I cross-examined you and am fully satisfied you had nothing to do with the death of our late lamented Julius Nagy. He minutes the file – sends it over to me and I lock it away for good.'

He wheeled his swivel chair round the desk to sit alongside Newman. They drank coffee and sipped their cognac in silence until Beck started talking, the words pouring out in a Niagara.

'Bob, in the last twelve hours there have been no less than five incidents all of which worry me greatly. They form no clear pattern but I am convinced all these incidents are linked. First, a mortar was stolen from the military base at Lerchenfeld near Thun-Sud. The second mortar stolen within a month . . .'

'Did they take any ammo. – any bombs?'

'No, which in itself is peculiar. Just the weapon. The second incident also concerns the theft of a weapon. You know that all Swiss have to serve military service up to the age of forty-five, that each man keeps at his home an Army rifle and twenty-four rounds of ammunition. A house was broken into while the owner was at work and his wife was out shopping. A rifle – plus the twenty-four rounds – has disappeared. Also the sniperscope. He was a marksman . . .'

'Which area? Or can I guess?'

'Thun-Sud. Late this afternoon the third incident occurred on a motorway. The driver of a snowplough was viciously attacked and his machine later found on the motorway. You want to guess the area?'

'Somewhere near Thun?'

'Precisely. Always Thun! The fourth incident you know about. The murder of Julius Nagy . . .'

'And Number Five?'

'Lee Foley, alleged ex-CIA man, has disappeared today from the hotel we traced him to. The Savoy in the Neuengasse. Bob, this American is one of the most dangerous men in the west. I rang a friend in Washington – woke him up, but he's done the same to me. I wanted to know whether Foley really has left the CIA and he said he had. I'm still not totally convinced. If the job was big enough Foley could get cover right to the top. He's a member – a senior partner – in the

Continental International Detective Agency in New York, so I'm told . . .'

'For argument's sake,' Newman suggested, 'let's suppose for a moment that is true. What then?'

'It does nothing to ease my anxiety. Foley is a skilled and highly-trained killer. That poses two questions. Who has the money to pay a man like that?'

'The Americans . . .'

'Or the Swiss,' Beck said quietly.

'What are you hinting at?'

Beck glanced at Newman and said nothing. He took out of his jacket pocket a short pipe with a thick stem and a large bowl. Newman recognized the pipe and watched as the police chief extracted tobacco from a packet labelled *Amphora*. He began packing tobacco into the bowl.

'Still wedded to the same old pipe,' Newman remarked.

'You are very observant, my friend. It's made by Cogolet, a firm near St Tropez. And the tobacco is the same – *red* Amphora. The second question Foley's presence poses is *Who is the target?* Identify his paymaster and that may point to who he has come to kill . . .'

'You're convinced that is why he is really here?'

'It is his trade,' Beck observed. 'Why have you come to Berne?'

So typical of Beck. To throw the loaded question just when you least expected it. He had his pipe alight and sat puffing at it while he watched Newman with a quizzical expression. The Englishman, who knew Beck well, realized the Swiss was in a mood he had never seen him display before. A state of fearful indecision.

'I'm here with my fiancée, Nancy Kennedy, who wanted to visit her grandfather.' Newman paused, staring straight at Beck behind the blue haze of smoke. 'He's in the Berne Clinic.'

'Ah! The Berne Clinic!' Beck sat up erect in his chair. His eyes became animated and Newman sensed a release of tension in the Swiss. 'Now everything begins to come together. You are the ally I have been seeking . . .'

Beck had poured more coffee, had freshened up their glasses of cognac. All traces of irresolution had vanished: he was the old, energetic, determined Beck Newman remembered from his last visit to Berne.

'I noticed something strange when we were at the Clinic this afternoon,' Newman said. 'Is that place by any chance guarded by Swiss troops?'

The atmosphere inside the bare, green-walled office illuminated by overhead neon strips changed again. Beck gazed at his cognac, swirling the liquid gently. He took a sip without looking at his guest.

'Why do you say that?' he asked eventually.

'Because I saw a man inside the gatehouse wearing the uniform of a Swiss soldier.'

'You had better address that question to Military Intelligence. You know where to go . . .'

Beck had withdrawn into his shell again. Newman was aware of a sense of rising frustration. What the hell was wrong with Beck? He allowed his irritation to show.

'If you want my cooperation – you mentioned the word "ally" – I need to know what I'm getting into. And how much freedom to act has the Chief of Federal Police given you? Refuse to answer that question and I'm walking away from the whole damned business.'

'Plenipotentiary power,' Beck replied promptly. 'Incorporated in a signed directive in that locked cabinet.'

'Then what are you worrying about?'

'The Gold Club . . .'

Newman drank the rest of his cognac slowly to hide the shock Beck had given him. He placed the empty glass carefully back on the desk top and dabbed his lips with a handkerchief.

'You have heard of the Gold Club? Not many have . . .' commented Beck.

'A group of top bankers headed by the Zurcher Kredit Bank. Its base is in Zurich. The only other group capable of standing up to them are the Basle bankers. Where does the Gold Club fit in with the Berne Clinic?'

'A director on the board of the Zurcher Kredit Bank is Professor Armand Grange who, as you doubtless know, controls the Berne Clinic. He also has a chemical works on the shores of Lake Zurich near Horgen. I am under extreme pressure to drop my investigation of a project code-named *Terminal . . .'*

'Which is?'

'I have no idea,' Beck admitted. 'But there are rumours—unpleasant rumours which have even reached the ears of certain foreign embassies. Incidentally, a fellow-countryman of yours who is also staying at the Bellevue Palace is making enquiries about Professor Grange. A dangerous pastime – especially as news of his activities has already started circulating. Switzerland is a small country . . .'

'This fellow-countryman of mine – he has a name?'

'A Mr Mason. He flew in via Zurich. That is where he started his investigation – and that is where news of what he was doing leaked out. Now, as I have told you, he is here in Berne.'

'Anything else I should know?'

'Have you ever heard of a man called Manfred Seidler?'

'No, I haven't,' Newman lied. 'Where does he fit into the picture?'

Beck's pipe made bubbling noises. He was a wet smoker. He stirred in his chair restlessly as though bracing himself for a major decision.

'Everything about our conversation is confidential, classified. Now we are coming to the guts of the whole crisis. I have been asked by Military Intelligence to put out a dragnet for Manfred Seidler. They *say* he stole something vital from the chemical works at Horgen. Once I find him I am supposed to hand him over to Military Intelligence. Immediately! No questioning.'

'You don't like it?'

'I am *not* going to put up with it. I shall grill Seidler when we find him until I find out what is going on. There is a split between two power blocs on military policy. One group, the Gold Club, believe we should adopt more extreme measures to protect the country against the menace from the East. They even suggest we should organize guerrilla forces – that teams specially trained in sabotage should be positioned *outside* our borders. Specifically in Bavaria. That is a complete reversal of our policy of neutrality.'

'Beck, I'm not following this. Why should a group of bankers concern themselves with military strategy?'

'Because, my friend, a number of those bank directors are also officers in the Swiss Army. Not regulars. Captains, colonels. They carry a lot of clout inside the Army where the policy dispute is raging. The Gold Club, which advocates total ruthlessness, is beginning to get the upper hand. The whole thing scares me stiff. And these are the people who are trying to stop my investigation into the Berne Clinic . . .'

'You said the killing of Nagy was the second murder. What was the first?'

Beck walked round his desk, unlocked a drawer and brought out a file. He handed it to Newman. The file had been stamped *Classification One* on the cover. Newman opened it and read the heading at the top of the first typed page. *Case of Hannah Stuart, American citizen. Klinik Bern.*

'Who is Hannah Stuart?'

'She was an American patient at the Berne Clinic. She died at the end of last month – as you will see recorded in the file. I have a witness, a farm worker who was cycling home late near the grounds of the Clinic. He states he saw a woman running towards the fence surrounding the grounds, a woman screaming, a woman pursued by dogs . . .'

'They do have Dobermans prowling the place . . .'

'I know. That was the night Hannah Stuart died . . .'

'Haven't you confronted the people at the Clinic with your witness?' Newman asked.

'It would be useless – and would show my hand. The witness has a history of mental instability.' Beck leaned forward and spoke vehemently. 'But he is completely recovered. I personally interviewed him and I am convinced he is telling the truth. He had the sense to come to police headquarters in Berne with his story. Pauli phoned me and I took over the case. That woman was murdered in some way.'

'It says here she died of a heart attack. The death certificate is signed by Dr Waldo Novak . . .'

'Who is also American. A curious coincidence . . .'

'What about getting an order for an autopsy?' Newman suggested.

'The body was cremated. And that is where the trouble really started. I had an official from the American Embassy here who complained. Apparently

Hannah Stuart was very wealthy – from Philadelphia. Her heirs, a son and his wife, were furious. In her original will she had made the inheritance conditional on her body being buried in Philadelphia . . .'

'Then how the devil was the Clinic able to get away with cremation?'

'Dr Bruno Kobler, the chief administrator, produced a document signed by Hannah Stuart stating she wished to be cremated. You'll find a photocopy at the end of the file. I had the signature checked by hand-writing experts and they say it's genuine.'

'Which blocked you off. Neat, very neat . . .'

He broke off as someone knocked on the door. Beck called out come in, a small, myopic-looking man wearing thick glasses and a civilian suit entered. He was carrying a cellophane envelope.

'We have obtained some fingerprints,' the man informed Beck. 'All of them the same person. Probably the deceased's – but we shall only know that when the pathologist has released the body.'

'Thank you, Erich . . .' Beck waited until the man had gone and then handed the envelope to Newman. 'Inside is the envelope – still sealed – which Moser found inside Nagy's coat pocket . . .'

Newman extracted the crumpled, cheap white envelope and saw it carried a few words. *For M. Robert Newman, Bellevue Palace.* He opened it and inside there was a scrap of paper torn from a pad and a key. In the same semi-literate script as the wording on the envelope were written the words *M. Newman –*

Bahnhof. He replaced the contents inside the envelope and slipped it into his wallet.

'It was addressed to you,' Beck said, 'so I gave strict orders it was not to be opened. Don't I get to see it?'

'No. Not until you tell me what you want me to do – and maybe not then.'

'I need someone I can fully trust who has access to the Berne Clinic. I have no reason to go there myself – and I don't want to tip my hand. I have not a shred of evidence – even in the case of Hannah Stuart. Only the gravest suspicions. I need to know exactly what is going on inside that place . . .'

'I would have thought it was the chemical works at Horgen you needed to investigate. Especially in view of this story about tracing this Seidler . . .'

'Hannah Stuart died at Thun,' Beck replied sombrely. 'Now, that envelope . . .'

'I work on my own or not at all. I'll keep the envelope for the moment . . .'

'I have to warn you you are up against men with unlimited power. One more thing. I have found out that the Gold Club people have secretly allocated the enormous sum of two hundred million Swiss francs for *Terminal*.' He held up a hand. 'Don't ask me how I discovered that fact, but the Americans are not the only ones who go in for what they call creative book-keeping.'

'Who controls that money?' Newman asked.

'Professor Armand Grange. Every franc of it . . .'

'And Grange is also a part-time member of the Swiss Army – another of those officers you mentioned?'

'At one time, yes. Not any more. You must take great care, Bob. I know you are a lone wolf, but on this one you may need help.'

'Is there anyone powerful enough, any *individual*, who can stand up to Grange and his fellow-bankers?'

'Only one man I know of. Dr Max Nagel, the Basle banker. He is also on the board of the Bank for International Settlements, so he has world-wide connections. Nagel is the main opponent of the Gold Club . . .'

'This Manfred Seidler – you are really looking for him?'

'I am trying to find him before the counter-espionage lot get to him. All the cantonal police forces have been alerted. I think that man could be in great danger . . .'

'From counter-espionage?' There was incredulity in Newman's tone. 'You really mean that?'

'I didn't say exactly that aloud . . .'

'And this Englishman, Mason, who is checking on Grange. Where does he come in?'

'Frankly I have no idea who he is working for. I am not sure yet *who* is working for *who*. But I also believe Mason could be at risk. Remember, we have lost track of Lee Foley, and he is a killer. Never forget, you are walking in a minefield . . .'

*

It was nine o'clock at night when Newman reached the luggage locker section at the Bahnhof. He had walked through the silent city from the Taubenhalde, doubling back through the network of arcades until he was certain no one was following him. As he had guessed, the key from Nagy's envelope fitted the numbered locker which corresponded to the number engraved on the key.

Unlocking the compartment, he stooped to see what was inside. Another envelope. Again addressed to himself at the Bellevue Palace in the scrawly hand-writing which was becoming familiar. Pocketing the envelope, he walked to the station self-service buffet. He was thirsty and famished.

He chose a corner table in the large eating place and sat with his back to the wall. As he devoured the two rolls and swallowed coffee, he watched the passengers who came in through the entrance. No one took any notice of him. He took out the envelope and opened it.

M. Newman. I don't know I can last much longer. The first two photos I took outside the Bahnhof. Chief Inspector Tripet (Geneva) told me follow you. That was when I came off the Zurich train. I was beat up inside a lavatory on the train. The thug gave me money and told me follow you. The phone number on the bit of paper you took off me in the alley is the number I had to call to tell them what you was doing. The car number was a

Mercedes waiting outside the Bahnhof. The man I think is the thug's boss got into the car. That's the first two photos. The third photo is the same man who got into the Mercedes. I saw him back here in Berne just before dark. Don't know the man he's talking to. I saw the first man by chance near the Bellevue Palace. Which is why I took the photo. These are very tough people M. Newman.

He felt slightly sick. He had a vivid memory flash of Julius Nagy being pinned against the wooden door by Foley's walking stick. The reaction was swiftly replaced by an emotion of cold fury. He sat working out what must have been the sequence of events after Nagy had walked away down the *Finstergasschen*.

The little man must have caught a tram – maybe even splashed out on a cab fare – to the Bahnhof. Quite possibly he had scribbled his message – Newman had had difficulty deciphering some of the words – in this very buffet. He must have then hurried to the luggage lockers, slipped the envelope inside, put the key into the second envelope with the shorter note also scribbled in the buffet – or wherever – and shoved it inside his coat pocket. The mystery was why Nagy had then hurried back to the Munstergasse.

Newman calculated the little man could have carried out these actions by 6.30 p.m. if he had hustled. By the time he arrived back at the Munstergasse someone had been waiting for him. Who lived in that

227

district? The only person he could think of was Blanche Signer – which reminded him it might be worthwhile calling her.

He was inside one of the station phone booths when it occurred to him maybe he should first call Nancy. He dialled the Bellevue Palace with a certain reluctance. He had to wait several minutes before they located her. It was not a pleasant conversation.

'It's a bloody good job I didn't wait for you for dinner,' she greeted him. 'Where are you, for Christ's sake?'

'In a phone booth . . .'

'I suppose you expect me to believe that . . .'

'Nancy . . .' His tone changed. '. . . I came to Berne to help you find out what was happening to Jesse. The whole evening has been spent with that very objective. I have not enjoyed it overmuch.'

'Well, that makes two of us. I waited so long for dinner I was beyond enjoying it when I eventually decided I'd better eat something. May I expect to see you sometime tonight? Or will your investigations keep you out till morning?'

'Expect me when you see me . . .'

He put down the phone and dialled Blanche's number. She answered almost at once. When she heard his voice she sounded excited.

'Bob! I'm so glad you phoned – I've got those photos for you. My friend stayed late to develop and print them. Considering the poor light they've come out very well. All three of them. Are you coming over?'

'I'll be there in ten minutes . . .'

On his second visit to the apartment in the Junkerngasse she showed him straight into the sitting room, a small, comfortably-furnished place lit only by table lamps. On a low table by a large sofa two glasses stood on place mats.

Blanche was dressed in a pleated skirt and a black cashmere sweater which showed her figure without making her look tarty. It had a cowl neck, which she knew he liked. Her long mane of titian hair glistened in the half-light.

'I may have traced Manfred Seidler,' she announced, 'but more of that later. Have you eaten? I'll get the Montrachet from the fridge . . .'

'No food, thank you. I can't stay long . . .'

She vanished into the kitchen. Newman wandered over to look at a silver-framed photograph of a serious-faced officer in Swiss Army uniform. He was staring at it when she returned and filled their glasses from an opened bottle.

'Your stepfather?'

'Yes. I hardly ever see him. We're simply not on the same waveband. Cheers!'

She sat alongside him on the sofa, crossing her long shapely legs encased in sheer black nylon. Clasped under one arm was a large, cardboard-backed envelope she tucked between herself and a cushion. Newman reflected that this was only the second time in the whole ferocious day he had felt relaxed. On the first occasion they had been in another room in this same apartment.

'Manfred Seidler may be in Basle,' she said, putting down her glass on the table. 'I've been on the phone almost the whole time since you left – except for rushing out to get the photos. I'd almost given up when I phoned a girl friend in Basle who is in banking. There's a girl called Erika Stahel who works in the same bank. Erika has let drop occasional rueful hints that she only sees her boy friend, Manfred, when he's in town, which isn't often. This Manfred moves about a lot . . .'

'Manfred is a fairly common name . . .'

'He's quite a bit older than Erika. Recently he brought her back a present from Vienna. An owl in silver crystal. That's how my girl friend heard of the trip. She showed the owl to her friend she was so pleased with it. Erika has a very good job,' Blanche remarked.

'What's a good job?'

'Personal assistant to Dr Max Nagel. He's chairman of the bank.'

Newman had trouble holding his glass steady. He hastily had another drink. Blanche was watching him. She tucked her legs underneath herself like a contented cat. Reaching for the envelope, she spoke again.

'It's probably the wrong Manfred. But apparently Erika is very careful not to mention his second name. Mind you, that could simply mean he's married. That could be the reason this Erika is so mysterious about his background and his job. I've got Erika Stahel's phone number if you want it.'

'How did you get that?'

'I asked my friend to look it up in the directory while we were talking, of course. Here it is on this piece of paper, plus her address. She has an apartment near the Munsterplatz. I must have phoned thirty people before I came across anyone who knew someone with the name Manfred. Want to see the pics?'

'Blanche, you have done so well. I'm very grateful. God, you move . . .'

'You have to if you're operating a tracing service. People like quick results. They recommend you to other clients – which is the way to build up any business. The pics . . .'

Newman looked at the first glossy print. The rear of a Mercedes, the registration number clearly visible. The number of the car which had almost driven them under the blade of the snowplough on the motorway. Poor little Nagy might yet pay back his killers from the grave. He kept his face expressionless as he looked at the second print. Bruno Kobler. No doubt about it.

'These prints are invaluable,' he told her.

'Service with a smile – of all kinds,' she said mischievously. 'The third one any good?'

Newman felt as though he had just been hit in the solar plexus. He gazed at the last print with a funny feeling at the pit of his stomach. He recognized the building in the background. Bruno Kobler had again proved very photogenic. It was the man he was talking to who shook Newman and made his brain spin, made him start looking at everything from a new, brutally disturbing angle. The man was Arthur Beck.

Chapter Sixteen

Newman met – collided with – 'Tommy' Mason when he entered the bar at the Bellevue Palace on his way back from Blanche. It was precisely 10 p.m. Mason turned away from the bar holding a tumbler of whisky which he spilt down Newman's jacket. Newman grinned and shrugged.

'I say, I'm frightfully sorry. Waiter, a damp cloth. Quick!'

'I wouldn't lose any sleep over it . . .'

'Jolly careless of me. Look, the least I can do is buy you a drink. Double Scotch – or whatever . . .'

'You called it . . .'

Newman took his glass and led the way to the same corner table where he had talked with Blanche. The place was crowded. He sat with his back to the wall, raised his glass and drank as his companion eased his way on to the banquette.

'Captain Tommy Mason,' he introduced himself. 'The "Tommy" is purely honorary. They tacked it on when I was in the Army and the damn name stuck . . .'

'Bob Newman. No honorary titles . . .'

'I say, not the Robert Newman? The Kruger case and all that? I thought I recognized you. I'm market research. I've nearly completed my present assignment.' Mason smiled. 'Really I'm not hurrying the job – I like this place. Marvellous hotel.'

Newman nodded agreement while he studied Mason. A military type. Early thirties. Trim moustache. Held his slim build erect. Shrewd eyes which didn't go with his general air of a man who would rise to captain and then that would be his ceiling. Mason continued chattering.

'They're all talking about some poor sod who took a dive from that square by the Castle – no, Cathedral – earlier this evening. Ended up like mashed potato on top of a car, I gather . . .'

'Who says he took a dive?'

Mason lowered his voice. 'You mean the old saw – did he fall or was he pushed?'

'Something like that . . .'

'Well, that's a turn-up for the book. I was trotting round that square earlier today myself. Peered over the wall and nearly had a fit. Like a bloody precipice. In Berne too, of all places . . .'

'Berne is getting as dangerous as Beirut,' Newman remarked and drank the rest of his whisky. 'Thanks. It tastes better going down the gullet . . .'

'Berne you said was getting dangerous? Watch your back and all that? Don't walk down dark alleys at night. Place is full of dark alleys.'

'Something like that. A research trip, you said?' Newman probed.

'Yes. Medical. Standards of and practice in their private clinics. They rate high, the Swiss do. Their security is pretty formidable too. Here on a story?'

'Holiday. I think I'd better go. My fiancée will be going up the wall. I've been out all evening . . .'

'Nice of you to join me in a drink – especially considering the first one I gave you. But don't let me keep you. May see you at breakfast. Avoid the dark alleys . . .'

As Newman threaded his way among the packed tables Mason sat quite still, watching the Englishman until he had vanished out of the bar. Then he stood up and strolled out, his eyes flickering over the other drinkers.

'Who is this stranger I see?' Nancy enquired when Newman came into the bedroom. She raised a hand as though to shield her eyes. The gesture irritated Newman intensely. He took off his jacket and threw it on the bed along with the folded coat he had carried over his arm.

'You should keep the bedroom door locked,' he told her.

'Criticism the moment he does eventually decide to come back.'

'Look, Nancy, this is a busy hotel. If I wanted to get

at you I wouldn't use the main entrance – the concierge might see me. I'd come in by the coffee shop entrance and up those stairs from the basement. The lift is then waiting for me. I'm simply thinking of your safety . . .'

'Have a good evening? Your jacket stinks of alcohol. Did she spill her drink in her excitement?'

'A man in the bar bumped into me. He bought me a drink to say sorry. So, before you comment on it, I also have alcohol on my breath. I've had a swine of an evening . . .'

'Dear me,' she said sarcastically, 'was it very rough?'

'A man who was following me earlier, a man I've used in the past for the same purpose, a nice little man, ended up spread like a goulash over the top of a car. He went over the wall behind the Munster. He was probably pushed. That sheer drop must be a hundred and fifty feet . . .'

'God, I've just had a very large dinner. You do have a way of putting things . . .'

'A large dinner. Lucky you. I've got by on a couple of bread rolls . . .'

'Room Service . . .!'

They both said it at the same time. Newman couldn't help recalling how Blanche had asked whether he had eaten. He undid his tie and loosened his collar, made no attempt to phone down for a meal. He was beyond it. She didn't press him.

'Who was killed tonight then?' she asked.

'The little man you said you didn't see passing the

window of the Pavillon in Geneva when we were having breakfast . . .'

'Oh, I remember.' She was losing interest. 'Flotsam, you called him. One of life's losers . . .'

'Sympathetically I said it. You know, you should hail from New York. They divide the world there into winners and losers. He was a refugee who fled from Hungary in fifty-six. He made his living any way he could. He deserved a better epitaph.'

'I had company at dinner,' she told him, changing the subject. 'Another Englishman. Beautiful manners. I think he had been in the Army. We got on very well together . . .'

'Some crusty old colonel of about eighty?' he asked with deliberate indifference.

'No! He's very good-looking. About thirty. Very neat and with a moustache. Talks with a plum in his mouth. I found him very amusing. What time do we meet Dr Novak on Thursday?'

'*We* don't. I go alone. He won't open up in the same way if you're present. And Thun is getting a dangerous place to visit. Or have you forgotten what nearly happened to us on the motorway?'

'No, I haven't!' she burst out. 'Which is why I think you might have made more of an effort to get back earlier – to have dinner with me. I needed company. Well,' she ended savagely, 'I got company . . .'

The phone started ringing. Newman glanced at Nancy who shrugged her shoulders. He suddenly realized she was wearing a dress he hadn't seen before. Another black mark, he supposed. No comment. The bell went on ringing and ringing. He picked up the receiver.

'A M. Manfred Seidler to speak to you,' the operator informed him.

'Newman, we must meet tomorrow night. I will phone details for the rendezvous late tomorrow afternoon . . .'

Truculent. Hectoring. Was there also a hint of desperation in Seidler's tone? Newman cradled the phone on his shoulder while he lit a cigarette.

'Newman? Are you still there?'

'Yes. I'm still here,' Newman replied quietly. 'Tomorrow is out of the question . . .'

'Then we do not meet at all! You hear me? Other people will pay a fortune for the information I have . . .'

'Sell it to the other people then . . .'

'Newman, people are *dying*! I told you that before. Don't you even care?'

'Now you listen to me, Seidler. I can probably meet you three days from now. That's my best offer. And I need to know in advance the rendezvous . . .'

'You have a car?'

'I could get hold of one.' Never give out even the smallest item of information to someone who is a completely unknown quantity. 'And if you don't come to the point I'm going to put down the phone . . .'

'Don't do that. Please! For God's sake! Newman, I will call you again tomorrow at five o'clock. No, not tomorrow. Five o'clock on the day we meet. You must have a car. And, believe me, it is too dangerous over an open line to give you details of the rendezvous. Dangerous to you – as well as to me . . .'

'Five o'clock the day we meet. Good night . . .'

Newman replaced the phone before his caller could say one word more. He lit a cigarette and sat down on the edge of the bed, smiling at Nancy who sat watching him intently.

'You were pretty tough with him,' she said.

'In a two-way pull situation like that one partici- pant comes out on top – dominates the other. When we do meet I'll get a lot more out of him if he's at the end of his tether. I think he's pretty near that point now. For some reason I'm his last hope. I want to keep it that way.'

'And the day after tomorrow you see Dr Novak in Thun?'

'Yes. I'm banking a lot on that meeting. I suspect we may have a similar case with Novak to the Seidler situation. Both men living on their nerves, scared witless about something. I just wonder if it's the same thing . . .'

'Bob, there's something I didn't tell you. But first you've got to eat. An omelette? Very digestible. Fol- lowed by fruit?'

He nodded and sat smoking while she called Room Service. The atmosphere between them had changed, had turned some kind of corner. They'd needed that phone interruption to quench their irritation with each other. Seidler had done them a favour. He waited patiently until she'd given the food order, asking also for a bottle of dry white wine and plenty of coffee. She then sat on the bed beside him.

'Bob, what do we do next? I don't know.'

For Nancy Kennedy it was a remarkable comment. She sounded bewildered, as though it was all happening too fast and she couldn't take it in. He put it down to her American background. Europe functioned differently, was infinitely complex.

'First, as I said, I see Novak. Find out what is really happening inside the Berne Clinic. That's why we are here. I'll have to find some way of putting the pressure on him, break him down. That's Item One. Next, the following day, we meet Seidler, find out what he knows. I have a feeling it's all beginning to come together. Fast. What was it you'd omitted to tell me?'

'When I was talking to Jesse at the Clinic while you occupied Novak's attention he told me they were conducting some kind of experiments . . .'

'*Experiments*? You're certain he used that word?'

'Quite certain. He didn't elaborate. I think he was worried Novak would hear us talking . . .' There was a knock on the outer door. 'I think this is your food. Eat, drink and then bed . . .'

Half an hour later they had undressed, turned out the lights and Newman knew from Nancy's shallow breathing that she was fast asleep. Exhausted by the day's events. He lay awake for a long time, trying to see a pattern to what he had learned.

The weird business of the rapid incidents which Beck couldn't understand. The theft of an Army mortar. The theft of one Army rifle plus twenty-four rounds of ammo. The snowplough incident he had good reason to understand, Newman thought grimly.

Then the murder – it had been murder, he was convinced – of Julius Nagy. The disappearance of Lee Foley. And Blanche had told him Foley had been in the vicinity of the Berne Clinic at the time of his visit with Nancy. So everything – excluding the Nagy killing – was happening in the Thun district.

The Gold Club business which seemed to bother Beck so much. And Seidler's reference in his Geneva phone call to bringing in a consignment across an eastern border. A consignment of what? Across which border? Newman felt certain that if only he could arrange these different factors in the right sequence a pattern would emerge.

He fell asleep with a disturbing thought. The photo showing Bruno Kobler, administrator of the Berne Clinic – again Thun – in conversation in front of the Taubenhalde with – Arthur Beck.

Chapter Seventeen

Wednesday, 15 February

Lee Foley had been sitting in the cinema for an hour when he checked his watch. He had spent most of the day inside different cinemas – there are over half-a-dozen in Berne. It had been a more restful activity compared with the previous day's expedition to spy out the lie of the land round the Berne Clinic.

He had used this technique before when he went under cover, when an operation reached the stage of a loaded pause. After leaving the Savoy Hotel, he had parked the Porsche at different zones. He bought food he could take away and eat while he sat inside a cinema. He slept while inside a cinema. He emerged into the outside world well after dark.

Leaving the cinema, he took a roundabout route to where the car was parked. Satisfied that no one was following him, he headed straight for the Porsche. He approached the car with caution to be certain no one was watching it. He strolled past it along the deserted arcade, then swung on his heel, the ignition key in his hand. In less than thirty seconds he was behind the wheel, had started the engine and was driving away.

Tommy Mason had finished writing his report for Tweed which included details of his brief trips to Zurich by train. He was stiff from sitting in one position in his bedroom for so long and he wanted to think. Mason thought best while he was walking and wanted to ease the stiffness out of his limbs before he went to bed.

He walked out of the main entrance to the Bellevue Palace. At that time of night the huge hall and the reception area beyond – the area which within days would be used for the Medical Congress reception – were empty. The night concierge looked up from behind his counter, nodded to Mason and went back to checking his schedule for early morning calls.

Mason, protected against the freezing cold of the night with his British warm, woollen scarf and a slouch hat, made his way down to the river. He had taken the same walk the night before. It crossed his mind he was breaking a cardinal rule. Never keep to a routine. Vary your habits – daily. Worse still, he had left the Bellevue about the same time the night before. He had become so absorbed by his report he had not realized what he was doing.

Still, it was only the second night. He damned well had to get some exercise or he wouldn't sleep. His mind was active. Mason guessed that he was close to promotion. The fact that Tweed had pulled him out of Vienna and stationed him temporarily in Berne indicated that.

The wind caught him as he reached the Aarstrasse. He stepped it out, heading for the Dalmazibrucke, a much lower bridge than the Kirchenfeldbrucke he would eventually use to cross back over the river to reach the Bellevue.

Absorbed as he was by his thoughts – the report for Tweed, his coming promotion – Mason continued to look round for any sign of life. No traffic. No other pedestrians. To his left, in the dark his eyes were now accustomed to, the ancient escarpment on which Berne is built rose sheer in the night. He continued walking.

He reached the Dalmazi bridge, and still the whole city seemed to have gone to bed. The Swiss started their day early so they were rarely up late. Below him the dark, swollen flow of the water headed for the curious canal-like stretch below the Munster. At this point the Aare empties itself through a number of sluices to a lower level before continuing its curve round the medieval capital. He heard the car driving slowly behind him. It stopped. He turned round.

At the same moment the driver switched his headlights on full power. Mason was temporarily blinded. Bloody nincompoop. The headlights dipped and the car remained stationary. A courting couple, Mason guessed, oblivious to the cold of the night inside their heated love nest. The driver had probably intended to turn them off and had operated the switch the wrong way, his mind on more enticing prospects.

He was in the middle of the bridge when he resumed his walk. The lead-weighted walking stick – the most innocuous of weapons – struck him with tremendous force on the back of his skull. He was sagging to the pavement when powerful arms grasped him, hoisted him and in one swift, final movement propelled him over the rail of the bridge.

Unconscious, Mason hit the ice-cold water with a dull splash. Less than half a minute later a car's engine fired at the entrance to the bridge and was driven away. In that half-minute Mason's body had been carried close to the Kirchenfeldbrucke. Passing under the high, vaulted arch supporting the bridge, the body was suddenly swept to the right as the flow of the Aare increased in power and speed.

Caught up in a frothing whirlpool, Mason's skull hammered with brutal force against the sluice where it lay trapped. Time and again the river hurled the body into the sluice with the action of a sledgehammer. The slouch hat had gone its own way, bobbing along the surface until it, too, was swept sideways through a more distant sluice. It passed through effortlessly, soggy now with water. Somewhere before the next bend in the Aare it sank out of sight. Bernard 'Tommy' Mason would never see his cherished promotion.

*

245

Gisela, assistant to Arthur Beck, looked up from her desk as her chief came into the office, took off his overcoat and hung it by the loop. He sat down behind his own desk, unlocked a drawer and took out the file on Julius Nagy.

'It's terribly late,' Gisela chided. 'I thought you'd gone home. Where have you been?'

'Walking the arcades, trying to make some sort of sense out of this apparently disconnected series of events. One stolen mortar, one stolen rifle with its ammunition, the disappearance of Lee Foley. No news about him yet, I suppose?'

'None at all. Would you like some coffee?'

'That would be nice. Then, talking about going home, you push off to your apartment. As you said, it's very late . . .'

When she had left the room Beck pushed the file away. Sitting gazing blankly into the distance, he began drumming the fingers of his right hand on the desk.

Behind the wheel of the Porsche Lee Foley was careful to keep inside the speed limit as he drove along N6, even though the motorway from Berne to Thun was deserted. He had divested himself of his English outfit and now wore jeans and a windcheater. Pulled well down over his thick thatch of white hair he wore a peaked sailor-style cap of the type favoured by Germans.

He would spend the night at a small *gasthof* outside Thun. By the time the registration form reached the local police in the morning – or maybe even twenty-four hours later as he would be registering so late – he planned to be away from Thun.

When he got up in the morning he would use a public booth to make the agreed phone call at the agreed hour. This, Foley was convinced, could be the first decisive day. And very shortly he would surface, come out into the open again. It was all a question of getting the timing right. Foley was very good at sensing timing: he had established the right contacts.

He drove on, his profile like that of a man carved in stone. Taken all round, it had been a strange day. He dismissed it from his mind. Always tomorrow – the next move – was what counted.

In Basle it was well past midnight as Seidler paced back and forth across the sitting room. On a sofa Erika Stahel stifled a yawn. She made one more effort.

'Manfred, let's go to bed. I have been working all day . . .'

'That bastard Newman!' Seidler burst out. 'He's playing me like a fish. People don't do that to me. If he knew what I've got in that suitcase he'd have seen me when I first called him in Geneva . . .'

'That *locked* suitcase. Why won't you let me see what you have got inside it?'

'It's a sample, a specimen . . .'

'A sample of what?'

'Something horrific. Best you don't know about it. And it's the key to *Terminal*. It's worth a fortune,' he ranted on, 'and I'll end up giving it to Newman for a pittance, if I'm not dead before then. A pittance,' he repeated, 'just to gain his protection . . .'

'I've banked a fortune for you in that safety deposit,' she reminded him. 'Surely you don't need any more. And when you talk about it being horrific you frighten me. What have you got yourself involved in?'

'It will soon be over. Newman said he'd meet me. The rendezvous will have to be a remote spot. I think I know just the place . . .'

Erika realized he could go on like this for hours. He was nervy, strung up, maybe even close to a breakdown. She stood up, walked into the kitchen and came back with a glass of water and a bottle of tablets.

'A sleeping tablet for you tonight. You'll need to be fresh for your meeting, all your wits about you. We're going to bed now. To *sleep* . . .'

Ten minutes later Seidler was sprawled beside her in a deep sleep. It was Erika who stared at the ceiling where the neon advertising sign perched on the building opposite flashed on and off despite the drawn curtains. *Horrific*. Dear God – what could the suitcase contain?

*

The same atmosphere of restlessness, of moody irritability which infected Basle was also apparent all day in Berne. Gisela had noticed it in her chief, Arthur Beck, and both Newman and Nancy had found the day a trial. They had felt lethargic and everything seemed such an effort they passed the whole day trying not to get on each other's nerves. Before going to bed, Newman went out for a long walk by himself.

Returning, he tapped on their bedroom door and heard Nancy unlock it. She was wearing her bathrobe. The second thing Newman noticed as he walked into the bedroom and threw his coat on the bed was a fresh pot of coffee, two cups and a jug of cream on a tray.

'I've had a bath,' Nancy said as she lit a cigarette. 'Did you enjoy your walk? You've been out ages . . .'

'Not especially. Enjoy your bath?'

'Not especially. Trying to bathe myself was one hell of an effort. Like paddling through treacle. What's wrong with us?'

'Two things. The concierge explained one cause – the *fohn* wind is blowing. You get edgy and tired. Yes, I know – you don't feel any sense of a wind but it drives people round the bend. And the suicide rate goes up . . .'

'Charming. And the other thing?'

'I sense this whole business about the Berne Clinic is moving towards a climax. That's what is getting to us . . .'

*

249

The unmarked police car with the two plain clothes Federal policemen drove slowly along the Aarstrasse towards the lofty span of the Kirchenfeld bridge. The river was on the far side of the road to their left. Leupin sat behind the wheel with his partner, Marbot, alongside him. They were the two men Beck had earlier in the week sent to the Bahnhof to watch for Lee Foley. It was Marbot who saw the sluice.

In the middle of the night it was freezingly cold. Because they had the heater on full blast the windscreen kept misting up with condensation. Leupin cleared it with the windscreen wipers while Marbot lowered the side window at intervals to give him a clear view.

'Slow down, Jean,' Marbot said suddenly. 'There's something odd over there by that sluice . . .'

'I can't see anything,' Leupin replied but he stopped the car.

'Give me the night-glasses a sec . . .'

Shivering, rubbing his hands as the night air flooded in through the open window, Leupin waited patiently. Marbot lowered the binoculars and turned to look at his companion.

'I think we'd better drive over there – where we can get on to the walkway to the sluices . . .'

As the car was driven away to cross the Aare, Mason's battered, waterlogged body continued to be churned against the sluice, a sodden wreck of a man with the head lacerated in a score of places.

Chapter Eighteen

Thursday, 16 February

The headquarters of Army Intelligence in Berne is located in the large square stone building next to the Bellevue Palace if you turn left on emerging from the hotel. This is Bundeshaus Ost.

Newman entered the large reception hall beyond glass doors, walked up to the receptionist and placed his passport on the counter. His manner was brisk, confident and he spoke while his passport was being examined.

'Please inform Captain Lachenal I have arrived. He knows me well. I am also rather short of time . . .'

'You are expected, M. Newman. The attendant will escort you to Captain Lachenal's office . . .'

Newman gave no indication of his astonishment. He followed the attendant up a large marble staircase. He was escorted to Lachenal's old office on the second floor, an office at the rear of the building with windows overlooking the Aare and the Bantiger rising beyond on the far bank of the river.

'Welcome to Berne again, Bob. You come at an interesting time – which no doubt is why you are here . . .'

Lachenal, thirty-five years old, tall and thin-faced
with thick black hair brushed over the top of his head,
exposing an impressive forehead, came round his
desk to shake hands. The Swiss was an intellectual
and in some ways – with his long nose, his commanding bearing, his considerable height and his aloof
manner – he reminded Newman of de Gaulle. He was
one of the world's greatest authorities on the Soviet
Red Army.

'You expected me,' Newman remarked. 'Why,
René?'

'The same old Bob – always straight to the point.
Sit down and I will help you as far as I can. As to
expecting you, we knew you had arrived in Berne,
that you are staying at the Bellevue Palace. What
could be more natural than to expect a visit from you?
Does that answer your question?'

'No. I have come here with my fiancée whose
grandfather is a patient in the Berne Clinic. Why
should that involve a visit to you?'

'Ah! The Berne Clinic . . .'

Seated in a chair facing the Swiss, Newman studied
his friend. Dressed in mufti, he wore a smart, blue,
pin-striped business suit, a blue-striped shirt and a
plain blue tie. Newman shifted his gaze to the uniform
hanging on a side wall. The jacket carried three yellow
bars on shoulder epaulettes, bars repeated round the
peaked cap – indicating Lachenal's rank of captain.

But what interested Newman were the trousers.
Down each side was a broad black strip. Lachenal was

more than a captain – he was now an officer on the General Staff. The Swiss followed his gaze.

'Yes, a little promotion since last we met . . .'

'And you report to?'

'Again the direct question! To the chief of UNA which, as you know, is the Sub-Department Information chief and a certain two-star general. I have direct access to him at all times . . .'

'So you are working on a special project?'

'You will not expect me to reveal information which is not only confidential but also classified,' Lachenal replied drily.

'Why have I come at an interesting time?'

'Oh, that is simple . . .' Lachenal spread his long, slim-fingered hands. 'Certain military manoeuvres are taking place.'

'Military manoeuvres are always taking place,' Newman countered. 'And why did you perk up when I mentioned the Berne Clinic? Incidentally, is that place being guarded by Swiss troops?'

Lachenal shook his head, more in sorrow than anger. 'Now you know I can neither confirm nor deny what establishments in this country come under military protection. Bob, what a question!'

'It's a damned good question,' Newman persisted aggressively. 'I actually spotted a man wearing Swiss Army uniform *inside* the place . . .'

He watched Lachenal's dark, steady eyes for any sign of anxiety. You might just as well hope for de Gaulle himself to reveal his real feelings. There was only one tiny out of character reaction. Lachenal took a king-size cigarette from a pack on the desk and lit it, then remembered his manners.

'Sorry.' He offered the pack and lit Newman's cigarette. 'Can I talk about something for a few minutes?' he began, sitting very erect in his chair. 'As you know, we are preparing for military conflict. All able-bodied men serve specific periods annually in the forces until they are forty-five. When the war will come from the East we shall be ready to defend ourselves. What we are worried about is the enemy's massive use of helicopters. Still, that problem may soon be solved. At this very moment we are testing certain missiles in the Bernina Pass area – because in that zone we have deep snow and it is very cold. War in low temperatures, Bob . . .'

Newman was puzzled. At first he had thought Lachenal was skilfully guiding the conversation away from the subject of the Berne Clinic. Now he sensed the General Staff officer was telling him something quite different, something he wished to get across by subtle means.

'I do know the general attitude of the Swiss,' Newman remarked. 'I wish to God our War Office would send a team here so it could study your techniques for use in Britain . . .'

'Please!' Lachenal held up a slim hand. 'Let me continue so you get the complete picture. Then ask questions.' He puffed at his cigarette and continued. 'What I am about to tell you is highly confidential –

on no account to be reported. You see, we have two competing military philosophies, two schools of thought, if you like. One is held by the majority – at the moment – of the regular Swiss Army. They believe we should continue to stick to orthodox strategy. But there is a second school, mostly made up of officers who spend most of the year working at their civilian jobs. Like the regulars they also subscribe to the theory of defence *tous azimuts* . . .'

They were conversing in French. Lachenal had an excellent command of English but when he was absorbed in what he was saying he preferred to use his own language. Newman was familiar with the phrase *tous azimuts*. It expressed all-round defence – fighting to hold back the enemy on every Swiss frontier regardless of geography.

Lachenal had paused to stub out his cigarette and light a fresh one. Newman had the impression the pause was really intended to emphasize the phrase just used – as though in some way this was the key to the conversation.

'But,' Lachenal went on, 'unlike the regulars this faction, which is very influential, takes an even more ruthless view. After all, we are a small nation – but we are determined to do everything in our power to protect the few millions who make up our population. The civilian school takes *tous azimuts* very seriously. That is why I said you come at a very interesting time.'

'The civilian officers . . .' Newman threw the

question at him. '... they are controlled largely by bankers?'

Lachenal froze. Outwardly his expression hadn't changed – it was the sudden total lack of expression. He leaned back in his chair, speaking with the cigarette in the corner of his mouth.

'What makes you say that?'

'I also have my sources. Inside and *outside* Switzerland.'

Newman emphasized the word to throw Lachenal off the track. It might be important to protect Arthur Beck. Something very strange was happening inside Switzerland.

'I can't imagine why you say that,' Lachenal commented eventually.

'It's obvious,' Newman rapped back quickly. 'You referred to the civilian group being very influential – your own words. Influence suggests power, power suggests money, money suggests bankers.'

'Theories are abstract, abstractions are misleading,' Lachenal said brusquely.

Newman stood up to leave and slipped on his coat. He chose the moment deliberately. Lachenal was a brave, very able man but he was also sensitive. He had just spoken almost rudely and Newman knew he would regret it. Lachenal followed his visitor as the latter put his hand on the door handle.

'You must realize, Bob, that none of us really believe you are here on holiday. You have to be working on a story ...'

'I am here with my fiancée for the reason I gave,' Newman said coldly. 'Check up on me, if you wish to . . .'

'Instead of that, let us have dinner together one evening. I am truly glad to see you again. But you must admit that your reason for being here would make an excellent cover story . . .'

Newman paused in the act of turning the handle, looking back at Lachenal. The Swiss was one of the shrewdest, most intuitive men he knew. He took the hand Lachenal had extended and shook it.

'I accept your invitation with pleasure. René, take care of yourself . . .'

Tous azimuts. That had been the key phrase, Newman felt sure as he descended the marble steps and walked out of Bundeshaus Ost. And Lachenal was genuinely deeply worried about something. Newman had the strongest hunch that if he knew what that worry concerned it might unlock the whole strange business.

Nancy came running towards him as he pushed his way through the revolving doors inside the Bellevue Palace. She had been sitting where she could watch the entrance. Looping an arm through his, she guided him quickly to an obscure corner table.

'Now we have the Swiss Army on our backs,' he told her. 'I don't like the way things are developing . . .'

'I've got something to tell you, but what are you talking about. Who have you seen?'

257

'A high-ranking Swiss Army officer, an old friend. We had coffee at that restaurant across the street. Don't ask me his name. I think he was warning me off the Berne Clinic . . .'

'You said an old friend. If he's that he should know the one way to encourage you to go on is to threaten you . . .'

'That occurred to me. Curious, isn't it? Now, I can see you're agog to tell me some news . . .'

'There's been a phone call from a man called Beck. He says will you go and see him at once. He said it was very urgent.'

Chapter Nineteen

'Newman, do you know this man?'

Beck was hostile again. His manner was stiff. His voice was flat, toneless. His official voice. Three people stood in the morgue. The room was cold. The floor and walls were tiled. The place had all the comfort and cheerful atmosphere of a public lavatory, a spotless public lavatory.

The third person was Dr Anna Kleist, Federal Police pathologist. A tall, dark-haired woman in her late thirties, she wore a white gown and watched Newman through tinted glasses with interest and a sympathetic expression. He had felt she liked him from the moment they had been introduced.

Newman gazed down at the body lying on the huge metal drawer Dr Kleist had hauled out for his inspection. The sheet covering the corpse had been partly pulled back to expose the head and shoulders. The head was horribly battered but still recognizable – mainly from the sodden moustache. Newman suddenly felt very angry. He turned on Beck.

'Am I the first person you have asked to identify him?'

'Yes . . .'

'Well, Beck, you had better know I am getting fed up. Why choose me? This is the second time you've dragged me to view the wreck of a corpse . . .'

'Just answer the question. Do you know this man?'

'He told me his name was Tommy Mason. That he was engaged on market research. Medical. Something to do with clinics – Swiss clinics . . .'

'You do know this man then? You were using him as a contact?'

'For Christ's sake, Beck, shove it. I was brought here without a hint as to what was waiting for me. I've answered your question. If you want to ask me anything else we'll go straight back to the Taubenhalde . . .'

'As you wish . . .'

Beck turned away to leave the room but Newman lingered. Dr Kleist had considerately closed the drawer. A tag was attached to the handle by a piece of string, a tag bearing a number. Tommy Mason was no longer a person, only a number.

'Dr Kleist,' Newman requested in a normal voice, 'have you any idea how he died – or is it too early?'

'He was found floating . . .'

'Anna!' Beck broke in. 'No information . . .'

'And why not, Arthur?' She removed her glasses and Newman saw she had large pale blue eyes with a hint of humour. 'Mr Newman has answered your question. And remember, I am in control here. I intend to answer Mr Newman . . .'

'You have the independence of the devil,' Beck grumbled.

'Which is why you had me appointed to this position.' She turned her attention to Newman. 'The body was found in the river. His injuries are due in part to the fact that for some time before he was found he was caught in one of the sluices below the Munster.'

'Thank you, Dr Kleist.'

As he left the room Newman hoped she would get married and leave this place before her emotions became as dead as the body she had just shown him.

He said nothing to Beck during the drive back to the Taubenhalde. Inside the building the same routine. The ascent to the tenth floor. Beck producing the key which unlocked the lift. Outside Newman gestured towards a punch-time clock on the wall.

'Do you still clock in and out morning and night? The Assistant to the Chief of Police?'

'Every time. It is the regulation. I am not exempt . . .'

Beck was still stiff and unbending but once inside the office he did ask Gisela to make them coffee and then please leave them on their own. Newman, his mind still focused on his interview with Captain Lachenal, made a great effort to push that into the past. He needed all his concentration on this new development. Beck stared out of the window, hands clasped behind his back, until Gisela brought the coffee on a tray and left the office.

'I'm sorry, Bob,' he said, walking wearily round his desk and sagging into his chair before attending to the coffee. 'You see, this is the second body you have been directly linked with. First, Julius Nagy . . .'

'You said that was an anonymous phone call to Pauli . . .'

'This was an anonymous phone call to Gisela. A man. Someone who spoke in broken German – or pretended to. Last night you were seen with Bernard Mason, or so the caller alleged . . .'

'*Bernard?*'

'Yes, I noticed you called him Tommy in the morgue. When we fished him out we found he carried his passport in a cellophane folder which protected it to some extent against the water. He is – was – Bernard Mason. How did you come to know him, Bob?'

'In the bar at the Bellevue Palace. I went in for a drink and he turned round with his glass in his hand and bumped into me. The contents of the glass spilt over my jacket and he insisted on buying me one to compensate. We sat talking for maybe five minutes. That's how I know him. It's also how I know the data I gave you on him back at the morgue. He told me. A chance acquaintance . . .'

'I wonder . . .'

'And what do you mean by that?'

'Could he have spilt his drink over you deliberately – to contrive this chance acquaintance? Chance always worries me.'

'How could he have contrived anything?' Newman demanded. 'I only decided to pop in there for a drink at the last moment. Any more questions?'

'I'm only doing my job, Bob. And I'm getting a lot of flak from the British Embassy. A chap called Wiley. He's a British citizen and was apparently an influential businessman. First, this Wiley wants to know exactly how he died . . .'

'How did he die?'

'I think it was murder. I called the Embassy to see if they had any information on him. Wiley asks a lot of questions – then he puts in an urgent request for the minimum of publicity. So who was Mason is what I keep asking myself. And, like it or not, two men have now died in peculiar circumstances – both less than a kilometre from the Bellevue Palace, both who had links, however tenuous, with you . . .'

Newman emptied his coffee cup and stood up. Beck watched while he slipped on his coat, buttoned it up. The Swiss also stood up.

'You haven't asked me why I think this Mason was murdered.'

'That's your job . . .'

'He's number two. Julius Nagy ends up at the bottom of the Plattform wall, which faces the sluice where Mason was found floating. Mason was thirty-three – I got that from the passport. He ends up in the river. You think he stumbled into the Aare? Two very convenient accidents. Were you outside the Bellevue late last night?'

'Yes, as a matter of fact I was. I went for a walk along the arcades. I couldn't sleep. And no one saw me. May I go now?'

'Gisela, what is it?' Beck asked his assistant who had opened the door to the connecting office where she worked most of the day.

'He's on the phone. Would you like to take it in here?'

Newman waited while Beck disappeared into the next room. *He* would be the Chief of Police, he imagined. Gisela asked if he would like more coffee but he refused and asked her a question, keeping his voice low.

'Mr Beck tells me you took that mysterious call reporting that I knew Mason, the man they dragged out of the river. I gather the caller spoke in broken German?'

'Yes, I had only just arrived. I ran to the phone, expecting it to stop ringing before I got there. The voice sounded muffled – like someone talking through a handkerchief. I had to make him repeat what he said, then he rang off. I've just realized something – I think I detected a trace of an American accent.'

'I should tell your boss that,' Newman suggested. 'Had Beck arrived in the building when the call came through?'

'No. He came in about a quarter of an hour later . . .'

'Thanks. Don't forget that bit about an American accent. I was leaving – tell Beck I couldn't wait any longer. I'm in a rush . . .'

Lee Foley was humming Glenn Miller's *In the Mood* as he drove the Porsche back along the motorway towards Berne. He had spent the night in a *gasthof*, had breakfasted in Thun, made the agreed call to Berne, and now he was coming into the open.

Despite his almost infinite capacity for patience, he found it highly stimulating that the time for action had arrived. He had most of the data he needed, the equipment, he thought he knew at long last what was going on. The moment had come to stir things up, to raise a little hell. He pushed his foot down on the accelerator and let the Porsche rip.

'Who was that on the phone?' Newman asked as he came into the bedroom. 'And you left the door unlocked again . . .'

'A wrong number.' Nancy had replaced the receiver. She came towards him with an anxious expression. 'Forget about the door – I've been worried sick. What did the police want?'

'Pour some of that coffee. Sit down. And *listen!*'

'Something is wrong,' she said as she handed him his cup and sat down, crossing her legs.

'Everything is wrong,' he told her. 'On no account are you to take the car and visit the Berne Clinic on your own . . .'

'I'll do so if I want to. And I do want to see Jesse today. You have your date with Dr Novak tonight in Thun. You won't want two trips . . .'

'Nancy, listen, for God's sake. There's been another killing. At least, that's the theory the police are working on. This time some Englishman – and he was staying at this hotel. They hauled his drowned body out of the river in the middle of the night. A man called Mason. There's something odd about him – the British Embassy is making too much fuss.'

'That's dreadful. But that is a problem for the police . . .'

'Nancy! We can no longer trust the Swiss police. I have also visited an old friend in Swiss Army Intelligence – counterespionage – it comes to the same thing. We can no longer trust Army Intelligence. They're both trying to manipulate me. I'm almost certain they're using me as a stalking horse – and that is very dangerous. For you as well as for me.'

'A stalking horse?' She wrinkled her smooth brow. Nancy really did have a superb complexion Newman thought. He had a vivid recall of the state of Tommy Mason's complexion in the morgue. 'I don't understand,' Nancy said.

'Then I'll try and explain it, so you'll understand, so maybe just for once you'll listen to me. And – no maybe – do as I tell you . . .'

'Give me one good reason.'

She annoyed him by standing up and walking over to gaze out of the window. It was another overcast day. A cloud bank like a grey sea pressed down on Berne. A white mist drifted closer along the river, heading in towards the city off the Bantiger.

'There's some kind of conspiracy,' Newman began. 'It's very widespread. I'm still vague on the details but I sense that it affects the whole of Switzerland – what you'd call in America the industrial-military complex. The police – the Federal lot – may be mixed up in it. Do you realize what that means?'

'I'm sure you're going to tell me . . .'

'I'm sure as hell going to do just that. You didn't understand my reference to a stalking horse. I happen to be a well-known foreign correspondent. I can't convince anyone I'm not here after another big story. The Kruger thing has caused them to think like that. So if we make one wrong move, take one step that disturbs them, the whole Military Intelligence and police machine will crash down on our heads. Are you with me so far?'

'I think so. The weather is beginning to look fantastic . . .'

'Bugger the weather. There appear to be two rival power groups fighting each other for supremacy. One group may be trying to use me to break the other – by exploding the whole conspiracy in a sensational exposé story in *Der Spiegel*. The group working underground is very powerful – I think it may have millions

of Swiss francs at its disposal. Money means power –
power to infiltrate the security organs of the state . . .'

Newman stopped in mid-sentence. When she
turned round he was staring at the bottom of his cup.
She went to him and placed her arm round his neck.

'What is it, Bob?'

'I may have missed something. What if we are
dealing with patriots? Not villains in the normal sense
of the word – men who sincerely believe they are
protecting their country, who will go to any lengths
to achieve their purpose?'

'And if that is the case?'

'It makes things far worse, more dangerous.'
Newman put the cup on the tray and started pacing
the room, hands clasped behind his back. 'I'm right,
Nancy. There is no one we can trust. We're on our
own. There are only two men who could crack this
thing wide open . . .'

'Waldo Novak?'

'Yes. And Manfred Seidler. The police have put out
a dragnet for Seidler. I have to reach him first. You
make no trips to the Berne Clinic on your own. A
certain Army officer went cold on me when I mentioned the place. So, we only visit the Clinic together.
And when I'm out on my own – as I will be tonight
when I see Novak – you stay in this hotel. Preferably
in one of the public rooms . . .'

'You make me feel like a prisoner,' she objected.

He grabbed her by both arms and pulled her close

to him. She stood quite still when she saw his expression.

'One more thing you'd better prepare yourself for. We might have to make a run for the border. I know places where it's possible to slip across quietly . . .'

'I won't go without Jesse . . .'

'Then we may have to take him with us. I don't like that remark he made to you about "experiments". God knows what is happening inside that place. Swiss Army guards. Dobermans. It's abnormal.'

'Bob, listen to me. In two days' time they're holding a reception here for that medical congress. I made some enquiries on my own from the concierge. He has a list of guests expected. One of them is Professor Armand Grange. Why don't we wait for him to come to us?'

He released his grip and she rubbed her upper arm. He had held her so tightly she felt bruised. She had never known him so alarmed and yet so determined at the same time. He went to the window. She had been right about the view. It was fantastic. The drifting wall of white mist now blotted out the lower slopes of the Bantiger so the flat summit appeared to be an island floating on a white sea.

'You could have an idea there,' he said slowly. 'So tonight it's Novak. Seidler as soon as we can arrange a rendezvous. Then I believe we shall know . . .'

*

269

A heavy grey overcast also shrouded lunchtime London, but here there was no mist creeping in. Inside the Park Crescent office Monica inserted the documents into the folder and handed it to Tweed who was checking the small suitcase he always kept packed ready for instant departure.

'Here are your air tickets for Geneva,' she said. 'A return flight booked for tomorrow. If anybody is checking at Cointrin they'll assume it's an overnight visit. You have that note with the train times to Berne?'

'In my wallet . . .'

Tweed looked up as Howard strolled into the office, again without knocking on the door first. He snapped the catches on his case shut and dumped it on the floor. Howard stared at it as Tweed, taking no notice of him, put a file in a drawer and locked it.

'I've just heard the appalling news,' Howard said gravely. 'Are you off somewhere?'

'Berne, of course.'

'Because of Mason? The decoded telex from the Embassy refers to an accident . . .'

'Accident my foot!' Tweed allowed the contempt he felt to show in his tone. 'I talked to Wiley on the phone. Mason goes for a walk late at night, then falls into the river. Does it sound likely? Look at his age, his track record. Mason was murdered and I'm going to find out who did it.'

'Isn't that a job for the Swiss police?'

Howard brushed an imaginary speck from his

sleeve, shot his cuffs and strolled round the office, glancing at the papers on Tweed's desk. Tweed sat in his chair and adjusted his glasses. He said nothing, waiting for Howard to go.

'The Swiss police,' Howard repeated somewhat peevishly.

'Have you forgotten what Mason brought back from Vienna? I gather you read the Ministry of Defence report on the object. I find the implications quite terrifying. I think that is why they killed Mason.'

'And who might be "they",' Howard enquired with characteristic pedantry.

'I have no idea,' Tweed confessed.

'You're going alone? No back-up?'

'I told you earlier I might have to call in outside help – that we're fully stretched with Martel being away. I've had someone out there for some time.'

'Who?' Howard pounced.

'The helper's safety – survival – may depend on secrecy, total secrecy. The person concerned knows Switzerland well.'

'You're being very coy about their sex,' Howard observed.

Coy. Tweed winced inwardly at the use of the word. Taking off his glasses, he polished them with his handkerchief until Monica gave him a paper tissue. Howard stared at Monica.

'Does she know?' he snapped.

'She does not. You can leave the whole matter in my hands.'

'I don't seem to have much choice. When do you leave?'

'This evening . . .' Tweed decided he had been very cavalier with Howard. 'I'm catching the nineteen hundred hours flight to Geneva. It arrives twenty-one thirty local time. Then the express on to Berne. At that hour anyone watching the airport is likely to be less alert.'

'You'll contact Beck, I suppose?'

'Frankly, I have no idea what I'm going to do.'

Howard gave it up as a bad job. He walked stiffly to the door and then paused. It occurred to him that if Mason had been murdered this could be a dangerous one. If anything did happen to Tweed he'd regret an abrupt departure.

'I suppose I'd better wish you luck.'

'Thank you,' Tweed replied politely. 'I think I'm going to need a lot of that commodity . . .'

On the first floor of the Berne Clinic Dr Bruno Kobler had finished checking the medical files when the door to his office opened. A large shadow entered the room which was lit only by the desk lamp despite the darkness of the afternoon. Kobler immediately rose to his feet.

'Everything is ready for tonight,' he informed his visitor.

'We are nearly there,' the huge man wearing tinted glasses commented in his soft, soothing voice. 'One more experiment tonight and then we shall be sure. Any other problems?'

'There may be several. Newman for one . . .'

'We can deal with extraneous matters after the medical congress and the reception at the Bellevue Palace,' the large man remarked as though referring to a minor administrative detail.

His bulk seemed to fill the room. His head was large. He was plump-faced and had a powerful jaw. His complexion was pallid, bloodless. He stood with his long arms close to his sides. He created the impression of a human Buddha. He had a capacity for total immobility.

He wore a dark business suit which merged with the shadows. The huge picture windows were smoked plate glass, which deepened the gloom. He wore tinted glasses because strong light bothered his eyes. He was a man who would dominate every room he entered without speaking a word. And his powers of concentration were phenomenal.

'Once the medical reception at the Bellevue is over they will all go home,' he observed to Kobler. 'Then will be the time to clear up loose ends. Then we shall present *Terminal* as a fait accompli. *Tous azimuts,*' he concluded. 'The dream of a generation of the General Staff will be reality.'

He stared out of the window at the distant mountains. The massive butte, rugged and brutal, rearing above the low cloud bank. The Stockhorn. There was a similarity between the rock which had dominated

Thun for eons and the man who stood, still quite immobile, staring at it.

'This is the subject I have chosen for tonight's experiment,' Kobler said, walking round his desk to show the open file, the photo of the patient attached to the first page. 'You approve, Professor?'

Chapter Twenty

For the rest of the day Newman encouraged Nancy to explore Berne with him. Anything to get her outside the hotel. He had not forgotten her remark, *You make me feel like a prisoner.* He expected to be away for a long time in the evening, interviewing Dr Novak in Thun. He wanted to be sure she did stay inside the Bellevue Palace.

Their exploration was also therapy for himself. He needed to clear his mind of two tense interviews which had already taken place. The trip to the morgue with Arthur Beck, followed by their conversation in his office. And his encounter – it had seemed like that – with René Lachenal kept running through his mind. Why was the normally cool Lachenal worried? Something, Newman was convinced, was preying on the Intelligence man's mind.

It was bitterly cold as they wandered along the arcades, stopping while Nancy gazed in shop windows. He took her the full length of the main street, the cobbled Marktgasse with an ancient tower at either end, continued along the Kramgasse and the Gerechtigkeitsgasse.

They were walking down the centre of the peninsula towards its tip at the Nydegg bridge where the Aare swings in a huge hairpin bend and sweeps on parallel with its earlier course on the other side of the city. Gradually the streets began descending until the arcaded walks were elevated above the street below. Slim, pointy-nosed green trams rumbled past but otherwise there was little traffic.

They reached the approach to the Nydeggbrucke and Newman peered over a wall down at a huddle of weird old houses that fronted on a street at a lower level. Nancy stared down with him.

'They must have been here for centuries . . .'

'It's the Matte district. No wars, you see. So the past is preserved. Let's hope to God it continues that way – it would be a crime for this lovely old city to be touched . . .'

He vetoed her suggestion that they should visit Jesse. She didn't argue the point when he explained.

'It could scare off Novak from coming to meet me this evening. I sensed he was nervous enough about the whole idea as it is . . .'

'I wonder why?'

'I think he's a frightened man. Frightened but at the same time desperate to talk to someone he can trust.'

'There seem to be a lot of frightened men. Manfred Seidler is another. What do I do if he calls while you're out?'

'Tell him I'm sticking to the arrangement we

made. If he'll call me tomorrow, I'll meet him tomorrow . . .'

They had lunch at the Restaurant Zum Ausseren Stand inside the heated Zeughauspassage off the Marktgasse. First, they walked through the snack place which was full of people eating and watching the Winter Olympics at Sarajevo on a colour television set.

The restaurant was comfortably furnished with heavily-upholstered green armchairs, the walls covered with posters of Yugoslavia. Again, Sarajevo. They had an excellent soup, a plate of superbly-cooked chicken and finished the meal with ice cream which Nancy pronounced 'Gorgeous. And even the coffee is first-rate.'

'It has to be good, if an American approves . . .'

He watched her glowing eyes and didn't want the evening to come. For almost the first time since they had landed in Geneva there was a carefree atmosphere. Cynically, he hoped it wasn't the prelude to something quite different.

Newman timed it so they arrived back at the Bellevue Palace at 6.15 p.m. Dusk had crept in over the city. The lights had come on in the streets and on the bridges. He wanted her to be alone for the shortest possible period. Following her into the entrance hall where people were circulating back and forth, he paused.

'I'm off to Thun,' he told her. 'I suggest a leisurely dinner, a good bottle of wine. Expect me when you see me – I've no idea how long this will take. The longer I'm away the more information I'll be getting . . .'

He stopped speaking, staring over her shoulder. Lee Foley had just stepped out of the lift. The American appeared not to have seen him, turning right and disappearing down the staircase in the direction of the bar. Nancy also had turned to see what he was looking at.

'Is something wrong, Bob?'

'No. I was just making up my mind about something. You'd better know now I'm meeting Novak at a hotel called the Freienhof in Thun . . .' He spelt it out for her. 'The phone number will be in the directory. Just in case you have to reach me urgently. I'm off now . . .'

'Take care . . .'

The tall thin man hurried across the Kochergasse to one of the phone booths near the Hertz car hire offices. He had been waiting inside the café opposite the Bellevue for ages, pretending to read the *Berner Zeitung*, ordering three separate pots of coffee and making each last while he watched both the main entrance and the way in to the coffee shop. He dialled a number and spoke rapidly when he heard the voice at the other end.

'Newman has just got back. He's gone inside the hotel with a woman. About two minutes ago. Hold on. I think he's come out again. By himself? Yes. He's walking towards me. Now he's crossed the street. He's heading for a silver Citroen parked by a meter. He's opening the door. I can't do a thing about it. He's driving off any second . . .'

'I can,' the voice replied. 'We have cars waiting for just such a development. I must go. And thank you . . .'

Driving down the N6 motorway to Thun, Newman felt tired. It had been a full day and it was only just starting. A lot of enjoyable walking round Berne, but still tiring.

He switched off the heater, lowered his window. Icy night air flooded in. He welcomed it. He had to be alert when he met Novak. The four-lane highway – two lanes in either direction separated by a central island – swept towards him in the beams of his headlights. He immediately began to feel better, sharper.

The red Porsche appeared from a slip road, headlights dipped as it followed him at a proper distance. He idly noticed it in his wing mirror. No attempt to overtake. Newman was driving close to the limit. The Porsche was behaving itself.

Bridge spans flashed past overhead. Occasional twin eyes of other headlights came towards him in the lanes heading back towards Berne. He checked his watch. As planned, he should arrive at the Freienhof before 7 p.m. Ahead of Waldo Novak. He drove on. He would know about the Porsche when he reached Thun. If it was still with him . . .

Behind the wheel of the Porsche, Lee Foley had two problems to concentrate on. The Citroen ahead. The black Audi behind his car. He had first noticed the Audi as two specks of light a long way back. It attracted his attention because the two specks swiftly became large headlamps. It was coming up like a bat out of hell.

Then it lost a lot of speed, began to cruise, keeping an interval of about a hundred yards between itself and his tail-lights. Foley swivelled his eyes alternately between the Citroen and the Audi in his rear-view mirror.

Why break all records – and the speed limit – and then go quiet? He came to a point where the normally level motorway reached a gentle ascent at the very point where it curved. A car heading for Berne beyond the central island came over the brow of the rise. Headlights full on.

Foley blinked, looked quickly again in the rear-view mirror as the other vehicle's undipped lamps hit the Audi like a searchlight. Two men in the front. He thought there were two more in the back. Full house.

Turning off the motorway, Foley came into Thun

behind the Citroen along the Bernstrasse, then turned down the Grabenstrasse as Newman continued along the Hauptgasse. He pulled in to a parking slot almost at once, switched off his motor and watched his rear-view mirror.

The Audi paused at the corner turn, as though its driver was unsure of his bearings. Two men got out of the rear of the car which then drove on quickly along the Hauptgasse, the route the Citroen had taken. Foley still waited, hands on the wheel.

One of the men – something about his manner, a man in his forties with a moustache, suggested he was in charge – let an object slip from his right hand. His reflexes were very good. He caught the object in mid-air before it hit the cobbles. An object which looked exactly like a walkie-talkie.

Foley smiled to himself as he climbed out of his car and locked it. He thought he knew their profession.

Unlike Berne, the town of Thun is as Germanic as it sounds. The river Aare, flowing in from Thunersee – Lake Thun, too far from the town to be seen – bisects it. The river also isolates the central section on an island linked to both banks by a series of bridges.

Arriving in Thun, as with Berne, is an excursion back to the Middle Ages. Ancient buildings hover at the water's edge. Old covered bridges, roofed with wood, span stretches of the Aare which, leaving Thun behind, flows on to distant Berne.

Driving along the Hauptgasse, Newman saw the red Porsche as it turned down the Grabenstrasse and decided his suspicions were groundless. He drove on, turned right on to the island over the Sinnebrucke and parked the Citroen in the Balliz. He then walked back through the quiet of the dark streets to the Freienhof Hotel which overlooks a stretch of the Aare. The first surprise was Waldo Novak had got there before him.

Taking off his coat and hanging it on a hook in the lobby, he studied the American who sat at a corner table in the public restaurant. Two empty glasses on the table told Newman that Novak had arrived early to tank up, to brace himself to face the Englishman, which suited Newman very nicely.

'Another Canadian Club,' Novak ordered from the waiter and then saw Newman.

'I'll have the same . . .'

'Don't forget – doubles,' Novak called out to the waiter's back. 'Okay, Newman, so you made it. Where do we go from here?'

'Why did you take that job at the Berne Clinic?' Newman enquired casually.

He sat waiting while Novak downed half his fresh glass and sipped at his own. The American wore a loud check sports jacket and grey flannel slacks. His face was flushed and he fiddled with the glass he had banged down on the table.

'For money. Why does anyone take any job?' he demanded.

'Sometimes because they're ... dedicated is the word I'm seeking, I think.'

'Well, you found it – the word! Found anything else recently I should know about?'

'A couple of bodies.'

Novak stiffened. The high colour left his young-looking face. He gripped his glass so tightly, the knuckles whitened, that Newman thought he was going to crush it. Although the tables close to them were unoccupied he stared round the restaurant like a hunted man.

'What bodies?' he said eventually.

'First a little man called Julius Nagy. There's an ironclad link between him and Dr Kobler. Someone shoved Nagy off the Munster Plattform in Berne the other night. It's a drop of at least a hundred feet, probably more. He ended up on top of a car. Mashed potato.'

'You trying to frighten me?'

'Just keeping you informed of developments. Don't you want to know about the second body?'

'Go ahead, Newman. You're not scaring me . . .'

'An Englishman called Bernard Mason. He had been investigating Swiss clinics – which I'm sure we'll find was a cover for checking on the Berne Clinic. He ended up in the river – his body pounded to pulp by a sluice. It doesn't seem to be too healthy an occupation – taking an interest in the Berne Clinic. Waiter, another two doubles. We like reserves . . .'

'I don't think I want to talk to you, Newman.'

'You have someone else you can trust? What makes it worth your while to work for Professor Armand Grange?'

'Two hundred thousand bucks a year . . .'

He said it with an air of drunken bravado, to show Newman he counted for something, that even at his comparatively early age he was a winner. Newman discounted the enormous salary – Novak had to be exaggerating. Wildly. He paid the waiter for the fresh round of drinks and Novak grabbed for his glass, almost spilling it in the process.

'What kind of a boss is Grange to work for?' Newman enquired.

'I've come to a decision, Newman.' He made it sound like Napoleon about to issue orders for the battle of Austerlitz. 'I'm not talking to you any more. So why don't you just piss off?'

That was the moment Newman knew he had lost him. It was also the moment Lee Foley chose to walk in and sit down in the chair facing Novak.

'I'm Lee Foley. You are Dr Waldo Novak of New York. You are at present assigned to the Berne Clinic. Correct?'

Bare-headed, Foley wore slacks and a windcheater. His blue eyes stared fixedly at the doctor. He had not even glanced in Newman's direction. There was something about Foley's manner which caused Novak to make a tremendous effort to sober up.

'So what if I am?' he asked with an attempt at truculence.

'We are worried about you, Novak.' Foley spoke in a calm, flat tone but his voice still had a gravelly timbre. 'The fact is, we are growing more worried about you day by day,' he added.

'Who the hell is "we"? Who the hell are you?'

'CIA . . .'

Foley flipped open a folder and pushed it across the table. Novak put down his glass without drinking. He picked up the folder and stared at it, looked at Foley, then back at the folder. Foley reached across and wrenched it out of his hand, slipped it back inside his breast pocket and the blue eyes held Novak's as he went on talking quietly.

'I'll tell you what you're going to do. You're going to give Newman answers to any and all questions he may ask. Do I make myself clear?'

'And if I don't?'

'Nothing to drink, thank you,' Foley said, refusing Newman's offer, his eyes still holding Novak's. 'If you don't, I think you should know we are already considering withdrawing your passport. And I understand the Justice Department has gone further. Discussions are under way on the possibility of revoking your American citizenship . . .'

Foley still spoke in a cool, offhand manner. He

glanced at Newman and said yes, he would have a drink, just some Perrier water. His throat was rather dry. It must be the low temperatures. He checked his watch.

'I'm short of time, Novak. And don't approach the American Embassy in Berne. That will only make matters worse for you. This comes direct from Washington. Make up your mind. Are you – or are you not – going to cooperate with Newman?'

'I'd like a little time to consider . . .'

'No time! Now! Yes. Or no.'

Foley drank his Perrier and stared away from Novak, gazing out of the window. Beyond a narrow road was an arm of the river. Beyond that old buildings whose lights reflected in the dark water. He finished his Perrier, checked his watch again and looked direct at Novak.

'And you haven't met me. I don't exist. That is, if you value your health. Now, which is it to be?'

'I'll cooperate. This will be kept confidential, I hope?'

Foley stood up without replying, a very big man, nodded to Newman and walked out into the night. Novak gestured to the waiter who brought two more glasses. Newman waited until he had downed more Canadian Club and left his own glass on the table.

'What do you want to know?' Novak asked in a tone of resignation.

'What is the nationality of the patients in the Berne Clinic? Mixed?'

'It's odd. No Swiss. They're all American – with a few from South America when they can afford it. Grange charges enormous fees. Most of them come to him as a result of his lecture tours in the States. He's into cellular rejuvenation in a big way. So, it's a two-way pull.'

'What does that mean?'

'Look, Newman . . .' Novak, ashen-faced from his encounter with Foley, turned to look at the Englishman. '. . . this isn't an ideal world we live in. There are a lot of American families reeking with money, often new money. Oil tycoons in Texas, men who have made millions in Silicon Valley out of the electronics boom. Others, too. Grange has a sharp eye for a set-up where the money is controlled by some elderly man or woman whose nearest and dearest are panting to take that control away. They send the head of the family to the Berne Clinic for this so-called cellular rejuvenation. That gets them out of the way. They apply for a court order to administer the estate. You get the picture?'

'Go on . . .'

Novak's voice changed and he mimicked a man making out a case to a judge. 'Your Honour, the business is in danger of going bankrupt unless we have the power to keep things running. The owner is in a Swiss Clinic. I don't like to use the word "senile" but . . .' He swallowed more of his drink. 'Now do you get the picture? Grange offers the patient, who is seriously ill, the hope of a new lease of life. He offers the dependants the chance to get their hands on a fortune. At a price. It's a brilliant formula based on a need. Professor Grange is a brilliant man. Has a hypnotic effect on people, especially women.'

'In what way – hypnotic?'

'He makes the relatives feel what they want to feel – that they're doing the right thing in exiling to Switzerland the man or woman who stands in their way. Loving care and the best attention.' Novak's voice changed. 'When all the bastards want to do is to get their hands on the money. Grange has worked out a perfect formula based on human nature.'

'There's nothing specifically criminal so far,' Newman commented.

'*Criminal?*'

Novak spilt some of his drink on the table. The watchful waiter, ready for a fresh order, appeared with a cloth and wiped the table. Novak, shaken, waited until they were alone.

'Who said anything about criminal activities?'

'Why is the Swiss Army guarding the Clinic?' Newman threw at him.

'That's a peculiar business I don't want to know about. I do my job and don't ask questions. This is Switzerland. The whole place is an armed camp. Did you know there is a military training base at Lerchenfeld? That's at the other side of the town. In Thun-Sud . . .'

'But you have seen men in Swiss Army uniform

inside the Berne Clinic?' Newman persisted. 'Don't forget what Foley said.'

'I've been here a year. In all that time I've only seen men in some kind of uniform. Once inside the main gatehouse, once patrolling the grounds near the laboratory . . .'

'Ah, the laboratory. What goes on inside that place?'

'I have no idea. I've never been allowed there. But I have heard that's where the experiments with cellular rejuvenation are carried out. I gather the Swiss are very advanced with the technique of halting the onset of age.' Novak warmed to his theme, relaxing for the first time. 'The technique goes back before the war. In nineteen-thirty-eight Somerset Maugham, the writer, first underwent treatment. He was attended by the famous Dr Niehans who injected him with cells scraped from the foetus of unborn lambs. Timing was all-important. No more than an hour had to elapse between the slaughter of the pregnant ewe and the injection of the cells into the human patient. Niehans first ground up the cells obtained from the foetus and made them soluble in a saline solution. The solution was then injected into the patient's buttocks . . .'

'It all sounds a bit macabre,' Newman remarked.

'Somerset Maugham lived to be ninety-one . . .'

'And Grange has a similar successful track record?'

'That is Grange's secret. His technique, apparently, is a great advance on Niehans'. I do know he keeps a variety of animals in that laboratory – but what I don't know. There's also another clinic which goes in for the same sort of treatment near Montreux. They call it *Cellvital.*'

Newman quietly refilled his glass with Perrier from the bottle Foley had left. He found the information Novak had just given him interesting. It could explain Jesse Kennedy's reference to 'experiments' – an activity no more sinister than the fact that it was not yet accepted by the medical profession everywhere.

'You've told me the nationality of the patients,' he said after a short pause. 'You're American. What about the other doctors?'

'They're Swiss. Grange asked me to come during one of his American tours . . .'

'And you came for a very normal reason – the money?'

'Like I told you, two hundred thousand dollars a year. I make a fortune – at my age . . .'

So, Novak hadn't been clutching a figure out of the air to impress him, Newman reflected. He felt he still wasn't asking the right questions. He flicked Novak on the raw to get a reaction, posing the query casually.

'What do you do for that? Sign a few dummy death certificates?'

'You go to hell!'

'I get the impression there may be some kind of hell up at that Clinic – and that you suspect more than you're telling. You live on the premises?'

'Yes.' Novak had gone sullen. 'That was part of my contract.'

'And the Swiss doctors?'

'They go home. Look, Newman, I work very long hours for my money. I'm on call most of the year . . .'

'Calm down. Have another drink. What about the staff – the guards, cleaners, receptionists. Where do they come from?'

'That's a bit odd,' Novak admitted. 'Grange won't employ anyone local – who lives in Thun. They also live on the premises. Most of them are from other parts of Switzerland. All except Willy Schaub. He goes to his home in Matte – that's a district of Berne near the Nydeggbrucke. Goes home every night.'

'What job has he got?' Newman asked, taking out his notebook.

'Head porter. He's been there forever, I gather. The odd job man. Turns his hand to anything. Very reliable . . .'

'I'll take his address . . .'

Novak hesitated until Newman simply said, 'Foley,' then he changed his mind. 'I do happen to know where he lives. Once I needed some drugs urgently and since I was in Berne I picked them up from his house. Funny old shanty. Gerberngasse 498. It's practically under the bridge. There's a covered staircase runs down from the end of the bridge into the Gerberngasse. He probably knows as much about the Clinic as anyone – except for Grange and Kobler . . .'

'Thank you, Novak, you've been very accommodating. One more thing before I go. I'll need to see you again. Will you be attending the medical reception at the Bellevue Palace?'

'The Professor has asked me to be there. Most unusual . . .'

'Why unusual?'

'It will be the first public function I've been to since I came out here.'

'So you'll be able to slip away for a short time. Then we can talk in my bedroom. I may have thought of some other questions. Why are you looking so dubious? Does Grange keep you on a collar and chain?'

'Of course not. I don't think we ought to be seen together much longer . . .'

'You could have been followed?' Newman asked quickly.

He looked round the restaurant which was filling up. They appeared, from snatches of conversation, to be farmers and local businessmen. The farmers were complaining about the bad weather, as though this was unique in history.

'No,' Novak replied. 'I took precautions. Drove around a bit before I parked my car. Then I walked the rest of the way here. Is that all?'

'That laboratory you've never been inside. It has a covered passage leading to it from the Clinic. You must have heard some gossip about the place.'

'Only about the *atombunker*. You probably know

that the Swiss now have a regulation that any new building erected, including private houses, has to incorporate an *atombunker*. Well, the one under the laboratory is enormous, I gather. A huge door made of solid steel and six inches thick – the way it was described to me made it sound like the entrance to a bank vault in Zurich. It has to accommodate all the patients and the staff in case of emergency . . .'

So that could explain something else innocently which Newman had thought sinister – the covered passage to the laboratory also led to the *atombunker*. Despite all his questions, there was still nothing positively wrong on the surface about the Berne Clinic. It was an afterthought: he asked the question as he was slipping on his coat.

'You thought then that you might have been followed?'

'Not really. Kobler said he had been going to suggest I took the evening off. He urged me to spend the night out if I felt like it . . .' Novak paused and Newman waited, guessing that the American had made a mental connection. 'Funny thing,' Novak said slowly, 'but the last time he did that was the night when Hannah Stuart died . . .'

Chapter Twenty-One

Newman walked into a silent, freezing cold night. Deserted streets. He waited until his eyes became accustomed to the dark. He was about to light a cigarette when he changed his mind. Nothing pinpoints a target more clearly than the flare of a lighter. And he had not forgotten that one of the weapons Beck had reported stolen was a sniperscope Army rifle – from the Thun district.

Checking for watchers, he strolled to the Sinnebrucke. He was still not convinced that Novak had told him everything. The American could have been sent by Kobler – to lure Newman to Thun. Later, after too much drinking, Novak might have decided to take out insurance by talking to him. Newman was convinced of one fact – he could trust no one.

Water coming in from the lake lapped against the wall below the bridge. Then he heard the sound of an approaching outboard motor chugging slowly. The small craft was flat-bottomed. As it passed under a street lamp he saw it was powered by a Yamaha outboard. One man crouched by the stern.

Newman stepped back into the shadows, unsure

whether he had been seen. The man lifted a slim, box-like object to his mouth. A walkie-talkie. They had been watching him from the one area he had over-looked – the river. It would have been easy to observe Newman and Novak sitting at the window table inside the illuminated restaurant. Was he reporting that Newman had just left the restaurant?

Berne is like a colossal ocean liner built of rock and stone, rearing up above the surrounding countryside. Thun's centre lies on the island in a basin. Newman glanced up at the northern bank where the forested hillside climbed steeply, a hillside where the lights of houses glittered like jewels. He left the bridge, crossed the street in the shelter of one of the numerous smaller arcades – smaller than Berne's.

He followed a roundabout route to where he had left his car parked in the Balliz. He was looking for a red Porsche, any sign of Lee Foley, any sign of more watchers. With its network of waterways Thun is like a tiny Venice or Stockholm.

Looking south, at the end of a street he saw the vague outline of a monster mountain, its upper slopes white with snow. He continued walking slowly, lis-tening. He passed one of the old covered bridges on his right and had a view to the north. On the highest point immediately above the town reared the great walls and turrets of the ages-old Schloss, a sinister, half-seen silhouette in the starlit night. The only sound was the slosh and gush of the river flow. He made up his mind.

Newman had not only been checking for watchers: he had taken his lonely stroll while he wrestled with a decision. He could not get out of his mind something Novak had said. *Kobler said he had been going to suggest I took the evening off . . . the last time he did that was the night when Hannah Stuart died.*

He walked swiftly back to where the Citroen was parked, got behind the wheel, fired the motor and drove off through the empty streets uphill towards Thun-Nord, towards the Berne Clinic.

The horrific scene jumped towards Newman's head-lights as he came over the brow of a hill. He had followed a route which would take him to the main gatehouse of the Berne Clinic – coming in from the north-west. To his right alongside the narrow road was the wire fence guarding the Clinic's extensive grounds which, at this point, included some rough country. He had crossed the snow-line some time earlier and he knew the laboratory was beyond the fence, hidden by a fold in the landscape.

In his headlights he saw a gate in the wire fence wide open. Two police cars, the blue lights on their roofs flashing and revolving, were parked in the road by the gateway. A woman inside the grounds was running up the rocky slope towards the gateway, a woman wearing some kind of robe. Behind her in the gloom a vague shape bounded after her. One of the bloody Dobermans. The woman ran on, a stumbling run. In front of one of the police car's lights stood two people. Beck and, Oh, Christ! Nancy . . .

The Doberman was going to get her, the running woman. She was just too far from the open gateway. Jesus! It was a nightmare. Newman pulled up near the gateway as Beck raised both hands and stood very still. He was gripping a gun. Behind him a third car appeared. Not a police car. It braked savagely and someone jumped out. That was the moment when Beck fired. The dog leapt vertically into the night, seemed to stay there in suspension, then flopped to the ground. So much was happening it was difficult to take it all in.

Newman left his car. The man who had just arrived was Captain René Lachenal. In full uniform. The running woman staggered through the gateway and collapsed on the road. Her robe fell open and Newman saw she was wearing pyjamas underneath a thick dressing gown and sensible shoes caked with snow.

Nancy was already bending over the inert form. Beck was using his walkie-talkie. Newman counted six uniformed policemen, all wearing leather overcoats and automatics holstered on their right hips. Beck slipped his weapon into his pocket and put on gloves. He closed the gate and stooped over it, fiddling with something. Newman couldn't see what he was doing.

'You are trespassing inside a military zone,' Lachenal called out angrily. 'We will look after this woman . . .'

'Military zone?' Beck straightened up and walked away from the gate which Newman saw was now padlocked. 'What the hell are you talking about? And I have summoned an ambulance for this woman. It will be here very shortly . . .'

'We are conducting military manoeuvres,' Lachenal insisted. 'There was a barrier at the entrance to this road . . .'

His tall, gaunt-faced figure towered over Beck who was staring in the direction of Berne where an approaching siren could be heard, growing louder every second.

'Yes, we saw the barrier,' Beck told him. 'We drove through it. And, it appears, a good job we did. In any case, there was no formal notification beforehand of any manoeuvres. And, we have saved this woman. You saw that dog . . .'

Newman had a series of vivid impressions he recalled later like pictures taken by flash-bulbs. An armoured personnel carrier pulling up behind Lachenal's car. Troops jumping out clad in battle gear – helmets, camouflage jackets and trousers and carrying automatic weapons – who spread out in a circle. Lachenal lifting a pair of field glasses looped round his neck and briefly scanning the grounds beyond the wire fence, lowering them with a grave expression. Nancy, who was close to Newman, standing up slowly and whispering to Beck so the only other person who heard her was Newman.

'We haven't saved her, I'm afraid. She's dead. I don't like the look of her. I can't be sure, of course, but all the signs are she died of asphyxiation. More serious still, I detect distinct signs of some form of poisoning. If you asked me to guess – it could be no more than that – I diagnose cyanosis . . .'

'Say no more,' Beck suggested. 'I have all I need.'

The ambulance had arrived. The determined driver eased his vehicle past the personnel carrier and Lachenal's car, drove on until his bonnet almost touched Newman's Citroen, backed into the gateway area, turned so the ambulance faced back towards Berne, and stopped it alongside the woman's body in the road. The rear doors opened, two men in white emerged carrying a stretcher, and this was the moment when Lachenal intervened.

'What are you doing?' he demanded. 'I can have her taken for immediate attention to a military hospital . . .'

'She's dead, Lachenal,' Beck told him in a cold voice.

It was extraordinary. The lofty figure of the Intelligence captain, a member of the General Staff, was dominated by the much smaller figure of Beck by sheer force of personality. The policeman took out his automatic again and held it so the muzzle pointed at the ground.

'We can still take her,' Lachenal said after an

interval. 'This may be a matter for counter-espionage . . .'

'Forget it, Lachenal. I'm taking over jurisdiction. And I am treating this as a case of suspected homicide. It is a matter entirely for the Federal Police. Incidentally, if you do not immediately order your men to lower their weapons I'll bring a charge against you for obstructing the course of justice the moment I arrive back in Berne . . .'

'They are not threatening anyone . . .'

'I am waiting.'

Lachenal gave a quick order to the officer in charge of the detachment. The troops boarded the personnel carrier which was then, with some difficulty, reversed before it was driven off towards Berne. Beck watched these proceedings with an icy expression, the gun still by his side. Lachenal turned and stared down at him.

'Homicide? I don't understand . . .'

'Neither shall I – until after the autopsy has been performed. One more thing, I have a fully-qualified doctor here who has examined the body. She states the dead woman shows clear signs of having died from cyanosis or some other form of poisoning. Just in case you have second thoughts. You have your own walkie-talkie, I imagine, to keep in touch with these manoeuvres which sprung up so suddenly? Good. Let us synchronize wavebands. I wish to keep in direct touch with you until we reach Berne safely. Perhaps you would be so good as to follow in your car?'

'I find the implications behind that request outrageous . . .'

'But you will comply,' Beck told him grimly. 'Homicide was the word I used. That takes precedence over everything with the sole exception of a state of war. Agreed?'

'I will accompany you in my car to the outskirts of Berne. Perhaps you would like to drive off first, then the ambulance, and I bring up the rear?'

Beck nodded, still in full psychological command of the situation. The bearers had carried the woman's body inside the ambulance and closed the doors. At Newman's request Beck had agreed one of his own men should drive the Citroen back to the Bellevue so Newman could travel in Beck's car with Nancy.

Before leaving, Beck gave the remaining policemen orders to pile into the other car and patrol the entire perimeter of the Berne Clinic. Passing the ambulance, he clapped a gloved hand on to the edge of the driver's window to indicate he should follow him. As they left, he exchanged not one more word with Lachenal, maintaining his total control of the situation to the last.

He opened the rear door of his car, ushered Nancy inside and introduced her to his subordinate, Leupin, who joined her on the other side. He made the remark as he climbed behind the wheel and Newman settled himself alongside.

'I'm not too happy yet about Lachenal. He seems to have so many troops at the snap of a finger. You do realize that he must have called up that armoured personnel carrier when he'd arrived but *before* he got out of his car?'

Beck had started driving when Newman pointed to the walkie-talkie lying in Beck's lap. The communication switch was turned to *off*.

'You can keep tabs on him with that, can't you?' Newman observed.

'But who is he calling at this moment – on a different waveband? I simply don't know. Certainly, Lachenal looked very worried and uncertain about the whole business. He's a very complex character, our René Lachenal – but basically a man of integrity. His one concern is Switzerland's security . . .'

'And how far would he go to protect that? The military do live in a world all their own.'

'A great deal may depend on how he reacts during the next few minutes – before we reach the motorway to Berne . . . My God! I think he's gone over the top. Look at that . . .'

Ahead of them as they went downhill, blocking the road like a wall, was a gigantic tank with a gun barrel like a telegraph pole. Newman went cold. It was a German Leopard 11.

The tracked monster was stationary. Except for one moving part. The immense gun barrel, with a massive bulge of a nozzle at its tip, was elevated at a high angle. Slowly it began to drop. In the rear of the car

Nancy, stiffened with fear, bit her knuckles, unable to take her eyes off the muzzle which was being lowered. Soon it would be aimed at them point-blank.

Beck had stopped the car. Newman had an awful premonition. He knew the capacity of the Leopard. One shell could blow them into fragments. The car would disappear. The ambulance on their tail would disintegrate. They would have to scrape the remnants of the two vehicles – and their occupants – off the road. The elevation continued to fall.

'They must have gone mad,' Beck said hoarsely.

He reached for the walkie-talkie to contact Lachenal, then dropped the instrument back in his lap. Newman shook his head in agreement. There simply wasn't time to reach Lachenal. Always supposing the officer was tuned in to the agreed waveband.

'No time for Lachenal,' Newman warned.

'I know . . .'

The gun barrel seemed to move in slow motion, remorselessly. Originally it had pointed at the sky. Now it had lost half that elevation. Now it only had a few more degrees to lose before they would be staring straight at that diabolical nozzle.

Nancy glanced at Leupin, a tall, thin-faced man. His face was moist with sweat. He seemed hypnotized by the inevitable descent of the huge tube. Still gazing ahead, he reached out his left hand and grasped her arm, an attempt to bring her a little comfort.

'Hold on tight!' Beck shouted suddenly.

He released the brake and rammed down his foot

on the accelerator. The Audi shot forward down the icy road, skidded, recovered its equilibrium under Beck's iron control as they went on speeding towards the tank which was growing enormously in size as it rushed towards them through the windscreen. The gun tip was almost facing them. Newman had a horrible preview of the huge shell hitting. A fraction of a second and the explosion would be ripping through metal, tearing apart flesh, incinerating it in one horrendous inferno under the hammerblow force of the detonation.

Beck, facial muscles tensed, drove on – passed *underneath* the gun barrel extending far beyond the tank's chassis. He jammed on the brakes. Although braced, everyone inside the car jerked forward. Beck had stopped within inches of the massive caterpillar tracks. It was no longer possible to fire the cannon. He snatched up the walkie-talkie.

'Lachenal! Are you there? Good. What the fucking hell are you trying to do? There's a bloody great tank which aimed its gun at us. I'm in direct radio communication with Berne. They've heard it all. Get this piece of scrap metal out of my way. Tell it to back off, clear the road . . . Do you read me . . .?'

'I've been trying to call you . . .' The strain in Lachenal's voice came clearly over the walkie-talkie. 'You kept talking. It's all a mistake. Kobler is waiting in a car to speak to you. The tank was to stop you driving past him. He caught me at the main exit from the Clinic . . .'

'Tell Kobler to go jump off a cliff,' Beck rapped back as he reversed the car a few inches, using one hand to drive. 'I'm telling you just once more. Tell that tank commander to back off. There will be an enquiry . . .'

'I've already given the order,' Lachenal reported when he came back on the walkie-talkie. 'You must understand there are manoeuvres . . .'

'Dr Bruno Kobler's manoeuvres?'

That silenced Lachenal. They sat without speaking as the Leopard began its reverse movement, its tracks grinding ponderously as the commander backed it and turned it up a fork road just behind him. Beck glanced in the rear-view mirror and briefly saluted the driver of the ambulance to show him the crisis was over. As soon as the road was open he shot forward, turning left away from the Leopard and downhill on the road which led to the motorway.

Chapter Twenty-Two

'I think, Bob, I should explain Dr Kennedy's presence,'
Beck said as he drove along the motorway. 'One of
my men – Leupin, in fact, who is sitting behind me –
was watching the Bellevue Palace when he saw her
leaving. He asked her to wait and called me. It is only
two minutes by car from my office – using the siren,'
he added with a ghost of a smile.

'I told you on no account to go anywhere,
Nancy . . .' Newman began.

'Please!' Beck interjected. 'Let me finish. Her help
back there at the gateway was invaluable. She told me
she had received an urgent phone call from the Berne
Clinic. Her grandfather had taken a turn for the worse.
I persuaded her to come back with me to the hotel
and I called Dr Kobler. He said they had made no
such call, that Jesse Kennedy was fast asleep. We still
don't know who tried to lure her out. I was on the
way to the Clinic myself and she agreed to come with
me in the police car. I thought it best to keep an eye
on her . . .'

'What took you to the Clinic tonight of all nights?'

'I have someone inside,' Beck replied cryptically.

'Who?'

'You, as a foreign correspondent, are in the habit of revealing your sources?' Beck enquired in a mocking tone. 'We drove past the main gateway to that second gate . . .'

'Which was open,' Newman commented.

'I opened it myself. In the boot is a pair of strong wire-clippers I used on the padlock chain. Quite illegal, of course, but we could see that poor woman fleeing for the gate. Afterwards, I locked it again with an identical padlock I had taken the precaution of bringing with me.'

'You seem amazingly well-organized,' Newman remarked. 'I know the file on Hannah Stuart backwards. I told you of a certain witness I can't use. Afterwards, I paid a visit to that gate from the laboratory and noticed the type of padlock used. I was banking on a second opportunity – although I did not foresee the consequences would be so tragic.'

'What are you going to do?'

'First, you must realize everything I have told you has to be in the strictest confidence. I am walking a tight-rope – I explained that to you also. Now, we are proceeding with the ambulance to the morgue. I have already alerted poor Anna Kleist who will lose yet another night's sleep. But I wish her to hear Dr Kennedy's diagnosis. And you should be thanking her for being there – not chastising her!'

'You are grateful for her help?'

'Yes!' Beck settled himself more comfortably

behind the wheel. They had passed the turn-off to Belp and would soon be approaching the outskirts of Berne. He glanced in his rear-view mirror before continuing. 'Dr Kennedy completely neutralized any authority Lachenal might have asserted by her diagnosis of asphyxiation and possible cyanosis. That made it potential homicide. That put it in my court. That check-mated Lachenal . . .'

'There is some borderline between yourself and Military Intelligence, I gather?'

'Yes. Tricky on occasion. Officially we always co-operate. We are both concerned with the security of the state. A very flexible phrase. If Lachenal could have made out a case that it concerned counter-espionage the dead woman would have been his. Once it became homicide, even suspected, I had him.'

'I suppose as regards Nancy I should really thank you . . .'

'You really should!'

Newman glanced in his own wing mirror and then turned as though to speak to Nancy. The ambulance had dropped back to give reasonable clearance. Some distance behind it was a red streak, a Porsche. He wondered whether Beck had seen it.

'I hate the stink of these places,' Newman remarked without thinking as they sat round a table drinking coffee. 'And an empty stomach doesn't help . . .'

'There you go again!' Nancy flared in a sudden rage. 'Anything to do with a medical atmosphere and you're off – and maybe that includes doctors, too?' she ended savagely.

'We are all tired,' Beck intervened. He clasped Nancy's hand affectionately. 'And we have all had a series of most unnerving shocks.' He glanced at Newman. 'Maybe the best solution would be not to take him with you when you visit patients,' he suggested humorously.

They were sitting in the ante-room of the morgue and they had been quarantined there for a long time. At least, that was how Newman termed it to himself. There was the usual smell of strong disinfectant. The walls, painted white, were bare. There was the minimum of furniture. The single window was frosted glass so there was nothing to look out at in the street beyond.

'Anna does a thorough job,' Beck remarked to break the new silence which had descended on their conversation. 'I am sure she will be here soon . . .'

Dr Anna Kleist, the pathologist, had been waiting to examine the body of the unknown woman as soon as they arrived. Beck had made brief introductions between Nancy and Kleist, who had asked no questions before she disappeared. Newman had just stood up to stretch his legs when the door opened and Anna Kleist appeared. She addressed herself to Nancy.

'I'm so sorry to keep you waiting so long. I think I

am now in a position to have a preliminary discussion as to how this unfortunate woman died . . .'

Tweed came into Geneva on Flight SR 837 which landed him at Cointrin at 21.30 hours. He moved swiftly through Passport Control and Customs, ran across the reception hall, clutching his small suitcase, and hailed a cab. He gave the driver a good tip and he was lucky. Green lights all the way along empty streets to Cornavin Gare.

He caught the 21.45 express by the skin of his teeth, panting as he sank into his first-class seat and the train glided out of the station. His short legs were not built for such sprints. Reaching Bern Bahnhof – or Berne Gare – at 23.34, he took another cab to the Bellevue Palace and registered.

'Take my bag up to the room for me,' he told the porter and turned back to the receptionist, speaking in French. 'I am the executor of the estate of the late M. Bernard Mason who, you doubtless know, was drowned in the Aare. My London office phoned you about this . . .'

'Yes, sir, we have a note . . .'

'Thank God for that.' He paused. 'M. Mason was also one of my closest friends. Can I see any papers he left in the safety deposit? I don't want to take them away – you can watch me while I scan them briefly. Something to do with his estate . . .'

'M. Mason did not have a safety deposit box . . .'

'I see.' Tweed looked nonplussed. 'Could I make a rather unusual request? I would like to look at the room he occupied. That is, if it is still vacant . . .'

'I do understand, sir. And it will be quite possible.' The receptionist produced a key. 'The room has been cleaned and all his personal effects impounded by the Federal Police . . .'

'Naturally. May I go up alone? Just to look . . .'

'Certainly, sir. The lift . . .'

'I know where the lift is. I have stayed here before on several occasions.'

Tweed took the lift to the fourth floor and stepped out. The mention of the Federal Police worried Tweed as he inserted the key, opened the bedroom door, went inside and closed and locked the door. That suggested Arthur Beck. Still, they had no reason to suspect Mason had been anything but the market researcher he had registered as under the heading *Occupation*.

He stood for a moment just beyond the threshold, a mark of respect, and then the inhuman emptiness of the room hit him and he muttered, 'Sentimental old fool . . .' The thing now was where would Mason have hidden his report?

Tweed had no doubt Mason had compiled a written report on Professor Armand Grange – for just the appalling eventuality which had overtaken him. Mason was a professional to his fingertips. *Had been*, Tweed corrected his mental comment.

First, he checked the bathroom and the separate

lavatory – without much hope. Chambermaids, especially Swiss chambermaids, were notoriously proficient in their cleanliness. He found nothing in either place.

So, that left the bedroom – and very little scope. Which was the same problem Mason must have faced. How had he solved it? Tweed climbed on a chair and searched behind the curtains at the top near the runners for an envelope attached with adhesive surgical tape. Nothing. Wardrobe empty.

He peered underneath two tables, getting down on his hands and knees. Standing up, he stood with his back to a wall and coolly surveyed the room. The only thing left was a small chest of drawers. He opened the top one. Lined with paper, it was impeccably clean – and empty. He ran his hand along the inner surface of the drawer. Zilch – awful word – as the Americans would say.

The notebook was attached with surgical tape to the lower surface of the third drawer down at the back. He found it when he was checking the bottom drawer. Even Swiss chambermaids could hardly be expected to dust this area.

It was a cheap, lined notebook measuring approximately three-and-a-half inches wide by five-and-a-half inches deep. Comparatively cheap. On the cover it still carried the tiny white sticker which gave the price. 2.20 francs. Also the shop where it had been purchased. *Paputik*. Am Waisenhausplatz Bern. Near

Cantonal police headquarters. Which told Tweed
nothing.

The neat script – a fine Italianate hand – inside the
notebook, which was so familiar it gave him a pang,
told him a great deal. The first page began, *Professor
Armand Grange, age: sixty* ... Standing by the chest of
drawers, Tweed rapidly read everything in the notebook and then placed it in an inside pocket.

Tweed had exceptional powers of concentration –
and total recall. In future, if it should be necessary, he
would be able to recite Mason's last will and testa-
ment – because for Tweed that was what it amounted
to – word for word.

He left the bedroom, locked the door and went
down in the lift to the ground floor. He handed back
the key and pushed his way through the revolving
doors. He hardly noticed the cold night air as he
turned right, hands thrust inside the pockets of his
worn, patched sheepskin.

He covered the ground at surprising speed, his legs
moving like stubby pistons. Crossing the road in front
of the Casino, he walked on down the right-hand
arcade of the Munstergasse, deep in thought. Another
part of his brain kept an eye on the tunnel of the
arcade ahead, the arcade across the street.

Reaching the large square in front of the Munster,
he walked round rather than across it. A car could
drive you down crossing wide open spaces. He
entered the Plattform through the open gateway and

between the bare trees the wind scoured his face as his feet crunched gravel.

He walked on to the low wall and stopped, staring down at the Aare far below. Tweed didn't realize at the time, but he was standing at almost the exact point where Julius Nagy had been tipped into the depths. Nor was he making a pilgrimage to look down where Mason had died. Such an idea would have made the dead man snort.

Tweed was trying to work out how they had killed him. It was the work of a professional, of course. A trained assassin, a commando-type soldier – or a policeman. No one else could have got close enough to Mason to do the job. His eyes scanned the river from the Dalmazi bridge to the Kirchenfeld.

Wiley, 'commercial attaché' at the British Embassy, had given him sufficient details when he phoned him in London for Tweed to work it out. He started from the premise as to how he would have planned the killing.

Dropping the body into the river so it would be battered by one of the sluices had been deliberate, he felt sure. It was a brutal warning, an intended deterrent. No good pushing Mason over the railings lining the Aarstrasse below – the body might easily have simply drifted into the backwater near the Primarschule in the Matte district.

The Kirchenfeld bridge was out – too great a danger of traffic. No, it must have been the small and much lower Dalmazi bridge he decided. A body – Mason must have been unconscious because he was a strong swimmer – dropped from the centre of that bridge would inevitably be carried by the river's natural flow until it was hurled against one of the sluices.

Satisfied that he knew now how it had been done, Tweed walked back to the exit from the Plattform and continued along the Munstergasse. It was very quiet. No sound except his own footsteps. He walked on into the Junkerngasse and the pavement was sloping downwards now. He paused just before he reached his destination, listening. He was very concerned to protect her.

He resumed his walk a short distance and stopped outside a doorway with three bell-pushes. He approved the sight of the newly-installed speakphone. He pressed the bell-push alongside the name, *B. Signer*.

'Who is it?' Blanche's voice twanged through the metal grille.

'Tweed . . .'

'Come on up . . .'

Chapter Twenty-Three

Anna Kleist pulled up a chair to the table and sat down facing Nancy. The two doctors, Newman had already noticed, were on the same wave band. Kleist removed her tinted spectacles, clasped her hands on the table and began speaking.

'Now, this could be important to me, Dr Kennedy. I was told by Mr Beck you were the first person to examine the body of the unfortunate woman who was brought here. You may like to know I have phoned Dr Kobler of the Berne Clinic. He informs me the patient was called Holly Laird from Houston, Texas. According to his version she was suffering from a state of mental imbalance. She overpowered one of the staff, a woman called Astrid, stole her keys to their poisons cupboard and made off with a quantity of potassium cyanide. Although outwardly calm, I detected in Kobler a state of agitation. He qualified every statement he made. "Subject to further verification", was the phrase he used. Could you please tell me your impression after you examined Mrs Laird?'

'It was not a proper diagnosis, of course,' Nancy

replied promptly. 'It was carried out under the least ideal conditions. I was surrounded with not only policemen but also armed soldiers. It was dark. I used a torch borrowed from one of the police. You understand?'

'Perfectly . . .'

'One factor I had to take into consideration was exposure. It was a bitterly cold night. The temperature was sub-zero. Mrs Laird was wearing only a pair of pyjamas and a thick dressing-gown. She may have run quite some distance before she reached the road.'

'Death due to exposure?' Kleist asked. 'That was what you concluded?'

'No!' Nancy began talking more rapidly. 'I had the strong impression she died from some form of asphyxiation. And the complexion of the face showed distinct traces of cyanosis. Her mouth was twisted in the most horrible grimace – a grimace consistent with cyanosis.'

'May I ask, Anna,' Beck intervened, 'what is your reaction to Dr Kennedy's on the spot conclusions?'

When she sat at the table Kleist had taken a scratch pad from a pocket of her pale green gown and she now produced a ball-point pen and began doodling on the pad. Newman guessed it helped to concentrate her thinking. She continued her doodling as she replied in her soft voice.

'My examination so far confirms precisely Dr Kennedy's impression. We have taken blood samples and they, in time, may tell us more . . .'

'How much time?' Newman demanded. 'That may be a commodity we are very short of – time.'

'A week. Possibly only a few days. Another pathologist is dealing with that aspect. I have requested that he give the matter the most urgent priority . . .'

'So we just have to wait,' Newman commented.

'I did find something else, something which puzzles me greatly,' Kleist went on. 'There are unexplained lacerations round the neck and over the crown of the skull . . .'

'You mean she could have been strangled?' Beck probed.

'Nothing like that. It is almost as though her neck and head had been bound in cloth straps . . .' She was still drawing something on her notepad. 'One explanation – although it seems bizarre to say the least – is that shortly before she died she was wearing some kind of headgear . . .'

'Some kind of mask?' Beck queried.

'Possibly,' she agreed, with no certainty in her tone. 'I can only be positive at this stage about the asphyxiation . . .'

'An oxygen mask?' Beck persisted. 'That would fit in with the equipment you'd expect to be available in a clinic. Maybe the oxygen supply was turned off, causing asphyxiation?'

Kleist shook her head. 'No. You have forgotten – she was seen running some considerable distance according to what you told me. It is the *agent* which caused death we have to isolate and identify. There we have to wait for the results of the blood tests.' She frowned. 'It is those lacerations which I find so strange. Still, I am probably saying far too much at this early stage. After all, I have not yet completed the examination.'

'You said she was a Mrs Holly Laird from Houston,' Newman remarked. 'Did you get any further information from Kobler about this woman's background? How old was she, by the way?'

'Fifty-five. And yes, I did press Kobler for more details. He was reluctant to say much but also, I sensed, wary of not appearing to cooperate fully. Mrs Laird is the nominal head of a very large oil combine. She was brought to the Berne Clinic by her step-daughter in one of the company's executive jets . . .'

'Any information on her husband?' Newman said quickly.

'He's dead. I couldn't obtain any further details.' She glanced at Beck. 'I had to use your name to get that much out of him . . .'

'Another similar case,' Newman commented.

'And what might that mean?' Beck enquired.

'I'll tell you later.' Newman stood up. 'And now I think we have taken up more than enough of Dr Kleist's time. I appreciate her frankness at this early stage . . .'

'My pleasure . . .' Kleist hesitated, staring at Newman. 'It is just possible I may be able to tell you more by morning.'

'You're working through the night?' Newman asked with a note of incredulity.

'This man . . .' Kleist also stood up and linked her arm in Beck's, '. . . is the most unfeeling taskmaster in Switzerland. You do realize that, Arthur?' she added mischievously.

Beck shrugged and smiled. 'You would do the job, anyway, but I appreciate your dedication. And I have the same premonition as Newman – time is what we don't have . . .'

'Dr Kleist,' Newman said as they were about to leave, 'I wonder if you would mind if I took your doodle? I collect them . . .'

'Of course.'

She tore off the sheet, folded it and handed it to him. He slipped it inside his wallet and she watched him with a quirkish smile.

Beck drove them back to the Bellevue Palace in a police car and in silence. Nancy had the impression the experiences of the night had exhausted everyone. She waited until they were inside their bedroom before she asked the question.

'What is on that sheet of paper you took off her?'

'Exhibit A. When they doodle, clever people sometimes reveal what is in their subconscious. Prepare yourself for a shock. The Kleist is very clever. Here you are . . .'

'Oh, my God!'

Nancy sank on to the bed as she stared at the doodle the Swiss pathologist had drawn while she talked. It showed a picture of a sinister-looking gas-mask.

Chapter Twenty-Four

Tweed sat down on the sofa and Blanche Signer arranged a cushion behind him, treating him like a favourite uncle. She was very fond of Tweed. He was a nice man, a kindly man. He watched her as she disappeared inside the kitchen, walking with agile grace.

Settling himself against the cushion, he looked round the sitting-room to see if anything had changed since his previous visit. Then he spotted the silver-framed portrait of a late middle-aged man in the uniform of a colonel in the Swiss Army. He blinked, got up and moved swiftly across to examine it more closely.

'That's my stepfather,' Blanche called out as she returned and flourished a bottle behind his back. 'He adopted me when my mother – who died recently – remarried.'

'I don't think I've ever seen him before,' Tweed remarked slowly. 'He's a handsome-looking man.' He made a great effort to speak casually.

'Look!' she said exuberantly. 'Montrachet. Especially for you, this one. See!' She held out the bottle for his inspection, so he could note the year. He felt it and the bottle was as chilled as the waters of the Aare.

'I was going to ask for coffee . . .'

'No,' she told him firmly, 'you've had a beastly journey. All the way from Geneva – from London, in fact. And it's well after midnight. You need something relaxing.'

'I'm sorry to be so late . . .'

'But you phoned me first . . .' She was pouring wine into the two elegant glasses already waiting on a low table. '. . . and like you, I'm an owl, a creature who prefers the night, who perches on branches and hoots a mournful sound!'

'I think I'd have trouble getting up a tree these days,' he observed. 'Cheers! And this *is* very welcome. Do you see your stepfather often?'

'Hardly ever. We don't see eye to eye on anything. He goes his way, I go mine. He doesn't even know what I do to earn my living – at least I don't think so. He is the sort of man who seems to know about almost everything that's happening in Switzerland. He's not regular Army.'

'I see,' said Tweed, and left it at that. 'I imagine it's far too early for you to have found out anything about the man whose name I gave you?'

Shoeless, she was wearing her black leather pants with a white blouse which, even in the dim light of shaded table lamps, displayed in all its glory her cascade of titian hair. She had perched herself next to him on the arm of the sofa, her long legs crossed. He suspected she was capable of teasing him and for a moment wished he had such a daughter, a lively, mischievous girl you could carry on an intelligent conversation with for hours.

'I do already have some possible information about Manfred Seidler,' she said. 'The trouble is ethics are involved – and you were cryptic on the phone. Could I trace a man who had flown in from Vienna very recently on a private Swiss jet. And could I also get any info. on this Seidler type. Are they the same person?'

'Frankly, I don't know,' Tweed replied evasively. 'The man who flew in from Vienna is important. Seidler is purely an inspired guess on my part. I know a lot about him and his activities. Always close to the borderline of legality and, sometimes, probably over the edge.' He drank more of his wine and she refilled his glass. 'This is really excellent. What's your problem about ethics? Not another client?'

'You cunning old serpent . . .' She ruffled his hair. He couldn't remember when he had last let a woman do that to him but Blanche made it seem the most natural, affectionate gesture in the world. 'Yes, another client,' she said.

'It's important – to my country,' he said, gazing at the photo. 'So probably to yours. We're all in the same boat.'

'You know, I'd hate to be interrogated by you. You're too damned persuasive by half.'

He waited, sipping his wine. She had dropped her hand so it rested on his shoulder. He glanced up from behind his glasses and she was staring into space. He still kept quiet.

'All right,' she said. 'It means breaking a confidence with a client for the first time, but I'm assuming you wouldn't let me do that unless it was something very serious. I'm placing all my integrity in your hands. For me,' she continued on a lighter note, 'that's equivalent to entrusting you with my one-time virginity . . .'

'That's safe enough with me,' he said drily.

'Bob Newman, foreign correspondent. He asked me only this week to trace a Manfred Seidler. I may have got lucky – but I'm not sure. I have an address – and a phone number – for a Manfred. No guarantees issued that he's Seidler, but he does sound like him . . .'

'Address, phone number . . .'

Tweed had his small notebook on his lap, his old-fashioned fountain pen in his hand. She gave him both items of information out of her head. He knew that both would be correct. Like himself she only had to see a face once, hear a name, read an address or phone number, and it was registered on her brain for ever.

'What I've given you,' she went on, 'are the details of a girl called Erika Stahel. She may be Seidler's girl friend. Incidentally, Stahel is spelt . . .'

'It sounds as though he may be holed up in Basle,' Tweed suggested. 'If it is Seidler . . .'

'I've no idea. I have an idea I'm going to regret giving you this information.'

'You expect to see this foreign correspondent, Newman, again soon?'

'Why?' she asked sharply.

'Just that I wondered whether you had any idea what story he is working on . . .'

'You're going too far!' The annoyance showed in her tone and she didn't care. She stood up from the sofa arm, walked across to a chair and sat facing him, crossing her legs again. He gazed into her startling blue eyes and thought how many men would be clay in her slim hands, clay to mould into any shape she wished. She spoke angrily.

'Again you ask me to betray a confidence. Are you really working for the Ministry of Defence in London? I keep your secrets. If I give away other people's, you should cease trusting *me*!'

'I spend most of my life in a thoroughly boring way – reading files . . .'

'Files on people I have helped you track across Europe . . .'

'Files on people who are dangerous to the West. Switzerland is now part of the West in a way it never has been before. No longer is neutrality enough . . .'

He took off his glasses and started polishing them on his pocket handkerchief. Blanche reacted instantly, tossing her mane of hair as she clicked her fingers. He paused, holding the glasses in his lap.

'You're up to something!' she told him. 'I always

can tell when you're plotting some devious ploy. You take off those glasses and start cleaning them!'

He blinked, thrown off balance for a moment. She was getting to know him too well. He put away the handkerchief and looped the glasses behind his ears, sighing deeply.

'Is Newman interested in the Berne Clinic at Thun?' he asked quietly.

'Supposing he was?' she challenged him.

'I might be able to help him.' He reached inside his pocket, brought out Mason's notebook and handed it to her. 'In there is information he might find invaluable. You type, of course? I suggest you type out every word inside that notebook. He must not see the notebook itself. Give him your typed report without revealing your source. Make up some plausible story – you are perfectly capable of doing that, I know. I'll collect the notebook when next I see you.'

'Tweed, what exactly are you up to? I need to know before I agree. I like Newman . . .'

'The data from that notebook will keep him running.'

'Oh, I see.' She ran a hand through her hair. 'You're using him. You use people, don't you?'

'Yes.' He thought it best not to hesitate. 'Isn't it always the way,' he commented sadly. 'We use people. We all use each other.'

Reaching inside his breast pocket he brought out an envelope containing Swiss banknotes. He was careful to hand it to her with formal courtesy. She took it and dropped it on the floor beside her chair, a sign that she was still annoyed.

'I expect it's too much for what I've done,' she remarked. Her mood changed as the blue eyes watched him. Uncrossing her legs, she pressed her knees together, clasped her hands so the fingers pointed at him and leaned forward. 'What is it? Something is worrying you.'

'Blanche, I want you to take great care during the next week or two. There have been two killings, probably three. What I am going to say is in the greatest confidence. I think someone may be eliminating anyone who knows what is going on inside the Berne Clinic . . .'

'Will Newman know?' she asked quickly.

'He is one of the world's top foreign correspondents. He will know. Providing him with that typed report may well be a form of protection. What I am getting at is this – no one must connect you even remotely with that Clinic. I am staying at the Bellevue Palace. Room 312. Do not hesitate to call me if anything happens that worries you. And use the name Rosa – not your own.'

She was astonished and perturbed. It was out of character for Tweed to reveal his whereabouts, let alone to suggest that she could call him. Always before he had called her. She gave a little shiver as he stood up to go and then ran to help him on with his coat.

'It's time you bought yourself a new sheepskin. I know a shop . . .'

'Thank you, but this is like an old friend. I hate breaking in new things – coats, shoes. I will be in touch. Don't you forget to call me. Anything unusual. An odd phone call. Anything. If I'm out leave a message. "Rosa called . . ."'

'And you take care, too.' She kissed him on the cheek and he squeezed her forearm. He was glad to see that before opening the door she peered through the fish-eye spyglass. 'All clear,' she announced briskly.

As he trudged homeward up the Junkerngasse through the silent tunnel Tweed's mind was a kaleidoscope of conflicting and disturbing impressions. Berne was like a rabbit warren, a warren of stone.

As the raw wind fleeced the back of his head exposed above his woollen scarf he remembered standing by the Plattform wall, staring down at the frothing sluices where poor Mason had been found. Mason had done his job so well – the notebook was a mine of suggestive information.

But the image which kept thrusting into his mind was that silver-framed portrait of Colonel Signer in Blanche's sitting-room. That had been the greatest shock of all. Victor Signer who was now president of the Zurcher Kredit Bank, the driving force behind the Gold Club.

Chapter Twenty-Five

Friday, 17 February

Kobler stood behind the desk in his first floor office at the Berne Clinic, his back to the huge smoked glass picture window overlooking the mountains beyond Thun. It was ten o'clock in the morning and he was staring at the large man with the tinted glasses who again remained in the shadows. The soft voice spoke with a hint of venom.

'Bruno, you do realize that last night's experiment was a disaster.' It was a statement, not a question. 'How could the Laird woman possibly have left the grounds? Now we have no way of knowing whether the experiment succeeded or not . . .'

Kobler never ceased to be astounded by the Professor's colossal self-confidence, by the way he could focus his mind like a burning-glass on a single objective. Wasn't it Einstein who had said, 'Clear your mind of all thoughts except the problem you are working on' – or something like that? And Einstein had been another genius.

Kobler's mind was full of the problem of the police holding the Laird woman's body and the dangerous developments that could lead to. All of this seemed to pass the Professor by. As though reading his thoughts, the soft voice continued.

'I leave to you, Bruno, of course, the measures which may be necessary to deal with those tiresome people who had the impertinence to interfere last night.'

'It will be attended to,' Kobler assured him. 'I may have more positive news – about Manfred Seidler . . .'

'Well, go on. God knows you've been searching for him for long enough. Another tiresome distraction.'

'I concentrated men in Zurich, Geneva – and Basle,' Kobler explained. 'Knowing Seidler, I felt sure he would hide himself in a large city – one not too far from the border. The most likely, I decided, was Basle. Not Zurich – because of the works at nearby Horgen he is too well-known there. Not Geneva because the place crawls with agents of all kinds who spend their lives looking for people. So, the largest number of men I put on the ground in Basle – and it paid off . . .'

'Do tell me how.'

The flat, bored tone warned Kobler he was talking too much. The events of the previous night had imposed an enormous strain on him. He came to the point.

'We got lucky. One of our people spotted Seidler walking into the rail terminal. He bought a return ticket to Le Pont up in the Jura mountains. It's a nowhere place, a dot on the map. The interesting thing is he didn't use the ticket right away. He just bought his ticket and left the station. We are covering that station with a blanket. When he does use that ticket we'll be right behind him. I'm flying Graf and Munz to Basle Airport from the airstrip at Lerchenfeld . . .'

'They leave when?'

'They are on their way now.' Kobler checked his watch. 'I expect them to be at Basle Hauptbahnhof within the hour. And Le Pont would be an excellent place to deal with the final solution to the Seidler problem. Everything is under control,' he ended crisply.

'Not everything,' the voice corrected him. 'My intuition tells me the main danger is Robert Newman. You will yourself delete that debit item from the ledger . . .'

Having gone to bed in the middle of the night, Newman and Nancy slept until the middle of the following morning. Newman, for once, agreed without protest to the suggestion that they use Room Service for a late breakfast.

They ate in exhausted silence after dressing. The weather had not improved: another pall of dense cloud pressed down on the city. Nancy was in the bathroom when the phone rang and Newman answered it.

'Who was that?' she asked when she came back into the bedroom.

'It was for you.' Newman grinned. 'Another wrong number . . .'

'That's supposed to be funny?'

'It's the best I can do just after breakfast. And I'm going out to see someone about what happened last night. Don't ask me who. The less you know the better the way things are turning out . . .'

'Give her my love . . .'

Which, Newman reflected, as he walked down the Munstergasse, had been a shrewder thrust than Nancy probably realized. The brief call had been from Blanche Signer. The photographs she had taken of the Berne Clinic from the snow-covered knoll were developed and printed. The surprise, when he arrived at her apartment, was that she was not alone. Carefully not revealing his name, she introduced a studious-looking girl who wore glasses and would be, Newman judged, in her late twenties.

'This is Lisbeth Dubach,' Blanche explained. 'She's an expert on interpreting photographs – normally aerial photos. I've shown her those I took of the Fribourg complex. She's found something very odd . . .'

The Fribourg complex. Blanche, Newman realized, was showing great discretion. First, no mention of his name. Now she was disguising the fact that the photos were taken at the Berne Clinic. On a corner table where a lamp was switched on stood an instrument Newman recognized in the middle of a collection of glossy prints.

The instrument was a stereoscope used for viewing a pair of photographs taken of the same object at slightly different angles. The overall effect obtained by looking through the lenses of the instrument conjured up a three-dimensional image. Newman recalled reading somewhere that during World War Two a certain Flight Officer Babington-Smith had – by using a similar device – detected from aerial photos the first solid evidence that the Nazis had created successfully their secret weapon, the flying bomb. Now another woman, Lisbeth Dubach, years later, was going to show him she had discovered what? As he approached the table he was aware of a tingling sensation at the base of his neck.

'This building,' Dubach began, 'is very strange. I have only once before seen anything similar. Take a look through the lenses, please . . .'

The laboratory! The building jumped up at Newman in all its three-dimensional solidity as though he were staring down at it from a very low-flying aircraft. He studied the photos and then stood upright and shook his head.

'I'm sorry, I don't see what you're driving at . . .'

'Look again, please! Those chimneys – their tips. You see the weird bulges perched on top – almost like huge hats perched on top?'

'Yes, I see them now . . .' Newman was stooped again gazing through the lenses, trying to guess what he was looking at could mean. Once again he gave it up and shook his head.

'I must be thick,' he decided. 'I do now see what you've spotted but I can't detect anything sinister . . .'

'Once while visiting England,' Dubach explained, 'I made a trip to your nuclear plant at Windscale, the plant where Sir John Cockcroft insisted during its design that they had to install special filters on the chimneys . . .'

'Oh, Christ!' Newman muttered to himself.

'There was a near-disaster at Windscale later,' Dubach continued. 'Only the filters stopped a vast radiation cloud escaping. The filters you are looking at now at the Fribourg complex are very similar . . .'

'But one thing we can tell you,' Newman objected, 'is that this building has nothing whatever to do with nuclear power.'

'There is something there they are making which needs the protection of similar filters,' Dubach asserted.

Newman, still absorbing the appalling implications of what Lisbeth Dubach had detected in the photos, now found himself subjected to a fresh shock.

As soon as they were alone, Blanche produced a sheaf of papers from an envelope and placed them on the sofa between them. They were, Newman observed, photocopies of typed originals. He had no suspicion that – by making photocopies of the sheets she had typed from the notebook – Blanche was protecting her source, Tweed.

She had gone to the length of typing them single-spaced, whereas her normal typing method was double-spacing, as Newman was well aware. She was careful with her explanation.

'Bob, I can't possibly tell you the identity of the client concerned. I'm breaking my iron-clad rule as it is – never to show information obtained for one client to another . . .'

'Why?' Newman demanded. 'Why are you doing it now?'

'Bob, *don't push me*! The only reason I'm showing you this data is because I happen to be very fond of you. I know you are investigating the Berne Clinic. What worries me is you may not realize what – who – you are up against. If you read these photocopies it might put you more on your guard. The power wielded by this man is quite terrifying . . .'

'So I read these and give them back to you?'

'No, you can take them with you. But for God's sake, you don't know where they came from. They were delivered to you at the Bellevue Palace. See, I've typed an envelope addressed to you at the Bellevue Palace. They were left with the concierge at the hotel . . .'

'If that's the way you want to play it . . .'

'I'll make you coffee while you're reading them. I could do with some myself. What Lisbeth Dubach told us has scared the wits out of me. What have we got into?'

Newman didn't reply as he picked up the photocopies and started reading. The report on Professor Armand Grange had, he realized quickly, been pre- pared by an experienced investigator who wasted no words. There were also signs that he – or she – had been working under pressure.

SUBJECT: Professor Armand Grange. Born 1924 at Laupen, near Berne. Family wealthy – owners of watchmaking works. Subject educated University of Lausanne. Brief period military service with Swiss Army near end World War Two.

Rumoured to be member of specialist team sent secretly into Germany to obtain quantity of the nerve gas, TABUN, ahead of advancing Red Army. Note: Repeat, rumour – not confirmed.

After war trained as doctor at Lausanne Medical School, followed by post-graduate work at Guy's Hospital, London, and Johns Hopkins Memorial Hospital, Baltimore, Maryland, USA. Brilliant stu- dent, always top of his class.

Military service not continued due to eye defect. After qualifying as lung consultant, trained as accountant. He proved to be as brilliant in this field as in the medical.

1954. Due to financial flair became director of Zurcher Kredit Bank at early age of 30. 1955. Founded Chemiekonzern Grange AG with factory at Horgen on shores of Lake Zurich. Chemiekon- zern manufactures commercial gases, including oxygen, nitrous oxide, carbon dioxide and cyclo-

propane, a gas used in medical practice. Rumoured
finance for foundation of Chemiekonzern provided
by Zurcher Kredit Bank. Note: Repeat, rumour –
not confirmed.

1964. Subject bought controlling interest in Berne
Clinic. This establishment reported engaged in
practice of cellular rejuvenation since subject took
over.

General comment: subject speaks fluent German,
French, English and Spanish. Has made frequent
visits to USA and South America. Believed to be
millionaire. I was told by reliable contact no
decision affecting Swiss military policy taken without reference to subject. One of the most influential
voices in Swiss industrial-military complex. This
comprises preliminary report based on sources in
Zurich and Berne.

Newman read through the report twice and his
expression was grim as he inserted the sheets inside
the addressed envelope. Recent incidents flashed into
his mind, triggered off by the report.

The doodle he had been given by Anna Kleist, a
doodle of a gas-mask. Arthur Beck's comment about
Hannah Stuart. 'The body was cremated . . .' The
photograph Julius Nagy had taken of Beck outside the
Taubenhalde – talking to Dr Bruno Kobler, chief
administrator of the Berne Clinic.

Captain Lachenal's reference to *tous azimuts* – all-
round defence of Switzerland. And, most recent of all,

Lisbeth Dubach's interpretation of the photos Blanche had taken of the laboratory at the Berne Clinic – '. . . something there they are making which needs the protection of similar filters.'

Another aspect of the report intrigued Newman: it bore all the hallmarks of a military appreciation with its terse, precise phraseology. That took his mind back to his meeting in the bar at the Bellevue Palace with Captain Tommy Mason. What was it the Englishman had said during their conversation when Newman had queried his research trip?

'Yes. Medical. Standards of and practice in their private clinics . . .'

Newman had little doubt he had just read a report drawn up by Mason – Mason who had 'accidentally' bumped into him in that bar, who was now dead. He asked Blanche the question, feeling pretty sure he already knew the answer.

'At the end of the report the word "preliminary" is used. That suggests more to come. Did you get the impression from your other client this would be the case?'

'No, I didn't.' Blanche paused. 'Nothing was said about any further data coming from the same source.' She perched on the arm of the sofa next to him. 'Bob, that report is frightening. Where is all this leading to? There is a mention of the Zurcher Kredit Bank – my stepfather is president of that bank . . .'

'There really isn't a close relationship between you two?'

'If you don't do exactly what my stepfather wants you to – and I didn't – he just forgets all about you. He's very much the military man. Obey orders – or else . . .'

'Blanche . . .' He took her hand. '. . . this whole business is beginning to look far more dangerous than I ever suspected. Is there any way your father could know that we are friends?'

'Our lives have gone separate ways. He doesn't know who my friends are – and doesn't want to know. And he *is* my stepfather. My mother divorced my real father who is now dead. You see now why we're so far apart . . .'

'I'd like you to keep it that way.' Newman kissed her and walked across the room to collect his coat. 'I'm off now – and thanks for this report . . .'

'Take care, Bob. Please. Where are you going now?'

'To blow someone up with verbal gelignite . . .'

Lachenal agreed to see Newman as soon as he arrived. It is only a ten-minute walk from the upper Junkerngasse to the Bundeshaus Ost. On that morning it had been a freezingly cold walk through the warren-like arcades and on the way Newman had taken the precaution of slipping into the Bellevue Palace to leave the report on Grange in a safety deposit box at the hotel.

Coming out of the safety-deposit room, he bumped into a small, plump-faced man who had turned away from the reception counter, a man who blinked at him through his glasses before he spoke.

'I'm sorry,' Tweed said. 'I didn't see you coming . . .'

'No harm done,' Newman assured him.

'I haven't been here long,' Tweed rambled on as though pleased to encounter a fellow-countryman. 'Has the weather been as beastly as this recently?'

'For days – and I think we're due for snow. Best thing is to stay indoors if you can. The wind out there cuts you in two . . .'

'I think I'll take your advice. This is a marvellous hotel to take refuge in . . .'

Tweed wandered off across the inner reception hall and Newman paused by the door, taking his time putting on his gloves. Sitting in a corner with her back to him was Nancy and the plump Englishman was heading straight towards her table followed by a waiter carrying a tray of coffee – coffee for two.

Newman waited just long enough to see the Englishman sit down opposite her while the waiter served them with coffee. They were talking together when Newman walked out and turned left to the Bundeshaus Ost.

'Lachenal,' Newman began savagely in the Intelligence chief's office as he sat facing the Swiss across his desk, 'what was all that bloody nonsense out at the Berne Clinic? I'm referring to that Leopard tank –

for a moment it looked as though it was going to blow us to kingdom come. My fiancée nearly had a fit. I didn't enjoy the experience too much myself. And what is a German Leopard 11 tank doing in Switzerland? If I don't get some answers I'm going to file a story . . .'

'Permission to reply?' Lachenal's tone was cold, hostile. Even seated he seemed a very tall man, his back erect, his expression mournful. He's not a very happy man, Newman was thinking as he remained silent and the Swiss continued.

'First, I must apologize for the most unfortunate incident due entirely to a brief lack of communication. It was a simple but unforgivable misunderstanding. The people responsible have been severely reprimanded . . .'

'What's a Leopard 11, the new German tank, maybe the most advanced tank in the world, doing in Switzerland . . .'

'Please! Do let me continue. That is not classified. As you know, we manufacture certain military equipment but we buy a lot abroad – including tanks. We are in the process of re-equipping our armoured divisions. We have just decided to buy the Leopard 11 after thorough testing at Lerchenfeld. It is no secret . . .'

'Tabun. Is that a secret? The special team sent into Germany near the end of the war to bring back Tabun gas. Is that a secret?' Newman enquired more calmly.

'No comment!'

Lachenal stood up abruptly and went over to the window where he stood gazing at the view. Even dressed in mufti, as he was that morning, Lachenal reminded Newman of de Gaulle more than ever. The same distant aloofness at a moment of crisis.

'You know the *fohn* wind has been blowing,' Lachenal remarked after a pause. 'That probably contributed to the incident outside the Berne Clinic. It plays on the nerves, it affects men's judgement. It is no longer blowing. Soon we shall have snow. Always after the *fohn* . . .'

'I didn't come here for a weather forecast,' Newman interjected sarcastically.

'I can tell you this,' Lachenal went on, thrusting his hands into his pockets and turning to face Newman, 'it is true that the Germans had a large quantity of Tabun, the nerve gas, near the end of the war. Twelve thousand tons of the stuff, for God's sake. They thought the Soviets were going to resort to chemical warfare. The Red Army captured most of it. They've now drawn level with the West in a more sinister area – in the development of organo-phosphorous compounds. They have perfected their toxicity . . .'

'I do know that, René,' Newman said quietly.

'But do you also know the Soviets have perfected far more deadly toxic gases – especially those highly lethal irritants which they have adapted for use by their chemical battalions? I am referring, Bob, specifically, to hydrogen cyanide . . .'

Hydrogen cyanide . . .

The two words rang through Newman's head like the

clang of a giant hammer hitting a mighty anvil. Lachenal continued talking in a level voice devoid of emotion.

'This substance is regarded in the West as being too volatile. Not so by the Soviets. They have equipped their special chemical warfare sections with frog rockets and stud missiles. Artillery shells filled with this diabolical agent are also part of their armoury. Did you say something, Bob?'

'No. Maybe I grunted. Please go on . . .'

'The Soviets have further equipped aircraft with sophisticated spray tanks containing this advanced form of hydrogen cyanide gas. We have calculated that a single shell fired through the vehicle of a missile, an artillery shell or from a spray tank – aimed by a low-flying aircraft – would destroy all life over an area of one square kilometre. Just a single shell,' Lachenal repeated.

Newman heard him but he also heard Nancy's diagnosis of how Mrs Holly Laird had died. *And the complexion of the face showed distinct traces of cyanosis.* What was it Anna Kleist had replied? *My examination so far confirms precisely Dr Kennedy's impression* . . .

Lachenal walked back from the window and again sat behind his desk, clasping his hands as he stared at his visitor who sat motionless. Newman shook his head slightly, brought himself back into the present. He had the distinct conviction that the Swiss was labouring under enormous tension, that he was concealing that tension with a tremendous effort of will.

'And so,' Lachenal concluded, 'all that started with

Tabun. Which was what you came here to talk about – not the Leopard.'

'If you say so, René.' Newman heaved himself to his feet and reached for his coat. 'I'd better be going now . . .'

'One more thing, Bob.' Lachenal had stood up and he spoke with great earnestness. 'We all have to be the final judge of our own conduct in this world. No hiding behind the order of a so-called superior . . .'

'I would say you're right there,' Newman replied slowly.

It was this conversation which decided Newman as he left the Bundeshaus Ost – decided him that at the very first opportunity he would get Nancy out of Switzerland – even if it meant he had to crash the border.

Chapter Twenty-Six

'I'm going to visit Jesse – with or without you,' Nancy announced when Newman returned to their bedroom. 'They're holding that Medical Congress reception here tomorrow evening. Are you, or are you not, coming with me?'

'I agree – and I'm coming with you.'

Newman dragged a chair over to the window and sank into it, staring at the view. The dark grey sea of cloud was lower than ever. He thought Lachenal had been right: they would have snow in Berne within the next twenty-four hours. Nancy came up behind him and wrapped her arms round his neck.

'I expected an argument. You're looking terribly serious. God, you've changed since we started out on this trip. Has something upset you?'

'Nancy, I want you to listen to me carefully. Most people think of Switzerland as a country of cuckoo clocks, Suchard chocolate and skiing. In one of his novels a famous writer made a wisecrack about the cuckoo clocks. There's another side to Switzerland most tourists never even dream exists.'

'Go on. I'm listening . . .'

'That makes a change. The Swiss are probably the toughest, most sturdy nation in Western Europe. They are ruthless realists – in a way I sometimes wish we were in Britain. They'll go a long way to ensure their survival. You know about their military service. This country has been on a wartime footing ever since nineteen thirty-nine. They still are. From now on we have to move like people walking through a minefield – because that's what lies in our path. A minefield . . .'

'Bob, you've found out something new since you left the hotel. Where have you been? And why the sudden turnabout as regards visiting the Berne Clinic?'

Newman stood up and began pacing the large room while he lit a cigarette and talked. He punctuated each remark with a chopping gesture of his left hand.

'We started out with four people who might have told us what is really going on. Julius Nagy, Mason – the Englishman I met briefly in the bar – together with Dr Waldo Novak and Manfred Seidler. The first two have been murdered – the police are convinced of that although they can't prove a thing. That leaves us Novak and Seidler . . .'

'You want to see Novak again? That's why you agreed to go back to the Berne Clinic?'

'One reason. If I can get Novak on his own for a short time I think he will tell me more – especially after that appalling episode over the death of Mrs Laird. He's very close to cracking, I'm convinced. Incidentally, you mentioned the Medical Congress reception. Why do you want to see Jesse before that takes place?'

'To get more information from him, if I can. To find out again if I can, what his real condition is. Then at that reception I'm going to confront Professor Grange. We know he's going to be there. Don't try and stop me, Bob – I've made up my mind. Now,' she continued briskly, 'what about Seidler?'

'He could be the key to the whole labyrinthine business. He's phoning me here at five and we'll meet him this evening. Better pack a small case for both of us – essentials for an overnight stay . . .'

'Why?' she asked suspiciously.

'Seidler sounds even more trigger-happy than Novak. My guess is he'll fix a rendezvous point a long way off – some place we can just reach in time after his call by driving like hell. That way he'll hope we won't have time to alert anyone else. He smells like a man who trusts no one.'

'Oh, by the way, Bob,' she said casually, 'Novak knows I'm visiting the Clinic today. I phoned him while you were out. I got lucky. That creepy old bitch, Astrid, must be off duty. A man answered the phone and put me straight through to Novak. And he told me Kobler is away some place.'

'Kobler's not at the Clinic?' Newman asked quickly.

'That's right. Neither is Grange. Novak did ask me if you would be coming. He sounded anxious that you would be. Can we leave soon?'

'After I've kept a brief appointment with someone in the bar. I met him on my way in. One of your own countrymen – a Lee Foley . . .'

'And who might he be?'

'A killer . . .'

He left her on that note, driving home again that she had better watch her step if she wanted to live.

The tall American with the thatch of white hair stood up courteously as Newman came across to his table inside the bar. He already had a drink in a tall glass crammed with ice. Newman said he would have a large Scotch and sat down on the banquette alongside Lee Foley who wore an expensive blue business suit, a cream shirt and a smart blue tie with small white checks. Gold links dangled from his cuffs.

'You're staying at the Bellevue, Lee?' Newman enquired.

'For the moment, yes. Unfinished business.' He raised his glass. 'Cheers! I've just had a visit from that bastard Federal policeman, Beck. I could feel sorry for the gentleman – he can't find a reason to throw me out of the country . . .'

'Not yet . . .'

'By then I'll be gone . . .'

'You still keep up your flying – piloting a plane?'

'Just light aircraft. Pipers, stuff like that . . .'

'What about a Lear executive jet?' Newman suggested.

'Now you're reaching.' Foley smiled his dry smile which was not reflected in the ice-blue eyes. 'Beck,' he continued, 'is concerned with the way the body count is rising. Two so far. The little man you and I talked with – and now some Englishman . . .'

'*Three*,' Newman amended. 'An American woman has just died outside the Berne Clinic . . . .'

'I know. Just goes on climbing, doesn't it?'

'I get the impression,' Newman ruminated, 'that Clinic is a place needing a lot of protection. They could afford someone expensive . . .'

'You'd better apply for the job . . .'

'More your line of country, I'd have thought . . .'

Foley put down his glass and stared at it. 'Remember that night we took the town apart on the Reeperbahn in Hamburg? You're the only man who ever drank me under the table . . .'

'The night *you* took the town apart,' Newman amended. 'Do you still speak good German?'

'I get by. You know something, Bob? The West is getting too civilized. There was a time when the Brits stopped at nothing when survival was at stake. I'm thinking of Churchill ordering the sinking of the whole goddamned French fleet at Oran – to stop the Nazis getting their hands on some real sea-power. Ruthless. He was right, of course . . .'

'You're trying to tell me something, Lee?'

'Just having a drink with an old friend, making a few random observations . . .'

'You never made one of those in your life. I have to go now. See you around, Lee . . .'

Newman let Nancy take the wheel of the Citroen for the drive to the Clinic. She handled the car with the confident ease of an expert driver along the motorway. In his wing mirror Newman kept an eye on the black Audi behind them which maintained its distance. Beck's minions were on the job.

'We're approaching the turn-off,' he warned.

'And who is driving this goddamn car?'

'You are, I hope – otherwise we're in trouble . . .'

'How did you get on with that man you went to meet in the bar? What was his name?'

'Lee Foley. I'm still trying to work out why he wanted to see me. He's a cold-blooded sod. As much a killing machine as that Leopard 11 we met. What I can't yet decide is who he is working for. If I knew that I might have the final piece of this enormous jigsaw in my hand.'

'We're both meeting some interesting people,' she observed as she turned off the motorway. He checked the mirror. Yes, the Audi kept on coming. 'This morning while you were out doing God knows what,' Nancy went on, 'I was having coffee in the reception hall with an intriguing little man, another English-man. He seemed so mild and yet I sensed, under the surface, a very determined personality. Tweed, his name is.'

'What did you talk about?'

'I told him about the Berne Clinic . . .' There was a touch of defiance in her tone, challenging him to criticize her indiscretion. He said nothing as she chattered on. 'He's a very sympathetic type – easy to talk with. He advised me to be very careful . . .'

'He did what!'

'I've just told you. He explained that as I was a foreigner I ought to tread carefully . . .' She glanced at Newman. '. . . that I should stick close to you from now on . . .'

'And just how did the Berne Clinic subject crop up?'

'No need to get piqued. He's a claims investigator for a big insurance company. It's weird, Bob – last month another American woman, a Hannah Stuart, died under similar circumstances to Mrs Laird. Why always women?'

'I've wondered that myself. Too many unanswered questions. And here we are. Brace yourself . . .'

They had arrived at the gatehouse to the Berne Clinic. But this time their reception was in surprising contrast to their previous visit. A man they had never seen before came out of the gatehouse, checked their passports, gestured towards the gatehouse and the automatic gates opened.

No sign of a guard, a Doberman, as they proceeded up the drive across the bleak plateau. It always seemed more overcast, more oppressive at Thun than in Berne. Newman thought it could have something to do with the big mountains holding the cloud bank.

'Novak told me to park the car in the lot at the side of the main building,' Nancy remarked. 'And I don't get the same feeling of being watched this time . . .'

'Maybe with both Grange and Kobler being away the hired help has gone slack. Or maybe they just want to give us that impression. Nancy, park the car in fresh snow . . .'

'Anything you say. I'm only the bloody chauffeur . . .'

'And when you get out disturb the snow as little as possible.'

'Christ! Any more instructions?'

'I'll let you know when I think of some . . .'

Waldo Novak, his fair hair blowing in the wind, came out of the glassed-in verandah entrance and down the six steps to meet them. Alone. No sign of the come-hither Astrid.

'I'll take you straight in to see him,' Novak told Nancy as he shook her hand. He stepped back alongside Newman to let her go first and dropped his voice to a whisper. 'Newman, on your way out, ask Mrs Kennedy to go to the powder room. That will give me the chance to tell you something.'

There was a male receptionist behind the counter, a man who took no interest in them. No nonsense about filling in visitors' forms. The same business with Novak's computer card keys to let them into the corridor and then inside the room where Jesse Kennedy sat propped up in bed against several pillows.

'Hold everything a minute,' Newman warned.

Taking off his coat he hung it from the hook, sealing off the mirror window. From his jacket pocket he extracted a compact transistor radio he had purchased for the purpose. He switched it on low power to some music, bent down and placed it next to the wall grille. That neutralized the hidden tape-recorder. He straightened up.

'Go ahead . . .'

'I have not followed my instructions,' Novak informed them. 'Mr Kennedy is not sedated – but to cover me I'd appreciate it if he'd take this capsule just before you leave . . .'

'We do understand – and thank you,' replied Nancy before she pulled up a chair and sat close to her grandfather. 'How are they treating you, Jesse?' She hugged him warmly, kissed him on both cheeks. 'Now tell me, do you really have leukaemia?'

'So they keep telling me. Including Novak here. Jesus H. Christ! I don't believe a word of it. You know some other poor woman was killed the other night? The cellular rejuvenation treatment didn't work is the story. She'd have died anyway they say. Poppycock! But I'm going to get to the guts of what's going on here – just like I did with that spy in Arizona ten years ago.' He chuckled. 'That CIA operative sure cleaned up that mess of . . .'

'You mean you want to stay here awhile longer?' Nancy asked.

'Sure do. Didn't want to come in the first place – but now I'm here I'm going to clean up *this* mess. Just see if I don't. No need to worry about Novak. He's feeding everyone information so fast he's practically running his own wire service. Ain't that the truth, Novak? See, he's shy – don't like talking in front of strangers . . .'

It went on for another fifteen minutes. Nancy trying to persuade him to leave the Clinic. Jesse insisting he had to stay on to clean up the mess. Novak, clad in his uniform of white coat with stethoscope dangling from one hand, and Newman, listening in silence.

Suddenly Jesse, tired out by his unaccustomed burst of conversation, said he'd like to get some sleep. He took his capsule of sodium amytal, swallowed, opened his hand to show it was empty, winked at Newman and fell fast asleep.

Novak stood outside the Clinic in the snow, alone with Newman. Nancy had agreed to Newman's suggestion without a word of protest, asking the receptionist to show her the way to the powder room.

'Now,' Newman said, 'what is it you wanted to tell me? We'd better be quick – we may not have much time . . .'

'Willy Schaub, the head porter I told you about back in Thun. He's agreed to talk with you. I gave you his address in the Matte district. He'll see you at three in the afternoon tomorrow. He's got the day off and he knows more about this place than anyone . . .'

'Why has he agreed?'

'Money. Two thousand francs should turn the trick. Maybe a little less. He'll want cash – cheques can be traced through a bank. It's up to you, Newman. I've done my best. And I am leaving when I can. What do I tell Schaub?'

'That I'll meet him. One more question before Nancy arrives. All the patients in this place – just how ill are they?'

'We've got leukaemia, multiple sclerosis. You name it, we've got it. All the patients are – terminal . . .'

Chapter Twenty-Seven

Basle

About the same time when Newman and Nancy ended their second visit to the Berne Clinic, Bruno Kobler was sitting in his bedroom at the Hotel Terminus which faces the Hauptbahnhof at Basle. Kobler had flown to Basle and this hotel had been chosen because of its strategic position.

Manfred Seidler had been seen purchasing a ticket to Le Pont, the tiny town close to the edge of Lac de Joux in the Jura Mountains. Since then they had lost track of Seidler, which was unfortunate, but Kobler possessed almost the calm patience of Lee Foley when it came to waiting. He spoke to the short, stocky Emil Graf who stood by the window, waiting for a signal from Hugo Munz who was in charge of the team inside the Hauptbahnhof.

'Seidler has to show,' Kobler observed. 'I'm sure he has a rendezvous with someone at Le Pont. And we have more men waiting at the Hotel de la Truite . . .'

'I don't know Le Pont,' Graf replied. 'From the map it looks a godforsaken place . . .'

'It is – just the remote spot where Seidler will feel safe to meet whoever he's going to sell the sample he stole from us. And the Hotel de la Truite is near the station . . .'

'He must have arrived! Munz has just signalled . . .'

Kobler was already opening the bedroom door, slipping into his astrakhan coat. He gestured towards the holdall bag on the bed to remind Graf not to forget it. Kobler had no intention of carrying the holdall, considering what it contained. Hired lackeys were paid to take such risks. Kobler would only lay his hands on the weapon when the time came to use it. He might not even have to use it at all – not when he had hired backup.

'He's boarded the two o'clock train,' Munz informed them as they hurried inside the huge station. 'Here are your tickets – and you'd better move . . .'

'It's Lausanne first,' Kobler guessed as he settled himself in his first-class seat alongside Munz. Graf had boarded the coach where Seidler was seated.

Kobler studied the rail timetable he had brought with him. He nodded his head as the train glided out of the station, turning the pages as he checked connections, then he glanced at Munz who sat in a rigid posture.

'Relax. We have to wait until we get him on his own. It may be hours yet. We're doing a simple job – like cleaning up some garbage . . .'

He looked out of the window as the train picked up speed, moving through the suburbs. He was not sorry to leave – the city of Basle was hostile territory, the home base of Dr Max Nagel, the main opponent

357

of the Gold Club. Kobler need not have worried. At that moment Nagel was aboard another train – bound for Berne.

Five coaches ahead Manfred Seidler was a bundle of nerves. He broke open a fresh pack, lit his forty-first cigarette of the day as he thought of the scene back in the flat before he had left.

Erika had rushed back from the office to make him a meal during her lunchtime break. It was during the meal that he had told her he was leaving. She had looked appalled.

'Do you have to? I could take a long lunch hour. Nagel has gone to Berne . . .'

'What for?' Not that he was really interested.

'It's queer. I had to make him a reservation at the Bellevue Palace. He's attending some Medical Congress reception. He's not even a doctor. And I've never seen him look grimmer – he's up to something . . .'

'Probably to tie up some deal which will net him another million or two. Erika, I may not be back till tomorrow – so don't start worrying . . .'

'You know I will – until I see you safe and sound again. Where are you going? What is it all about? I'm entitled to know something, surely?'

'Where doesn't matter,' he had told her. 'I'm going to meet – that British foreign correspondent, Robert Newman. He can give me protection – by blowing

Terminal wide open. No, don't ask me any more. And thanks for the meal . . .'

Seated in the train he wished he had said more. He looked up at the rack where he had stored his two suitcases. One contained some of the newspapers Erika had brought him, the other the sample. It would be difficult for anyone to snatch *two* suitcases off him when he was walking along a platform. And they wouldn't know which case contained the sample. You had to think of little things like that.

Seidler stirred restlessly and took a deep drag on the cigarette. They had turned up the heating and he would dearly have liked to take off his jacket. But that was impossible. He was too aware of the 9-mm. Luger inside the spring-loaded holster under his left armpit.

Berne. Beck sat behind his desk in his office and looked at Gisela who had just taken the call. She put down the receiver and turned to speak to her chief.

'That was Leupin. Newman and Dr Kennedy are just leaving the Berne Clinic. He spotted them through his binoculars and radioed in the information . . .'

'Thank you. Gisela, I want you to make reservations at the Bellevue Palace for three of our men. I want them there during that Medical Congress reception tomorrow. Professor Grange will be there. I may put in an appearance myself.'

'Things are coming to a head, aren't they?'

'Your instincts are usually good, Gisela. The one

piece still missing is Manfred Seidler. The fox has gone to cover, but he has to surface. When he does I want to be there – before the military get him. Send out a fresh alert. Seidler must be found at all costs . . .'

Newman infuriated Nancy when they had left Novak and were approaching the parked Citroen. She just wanted to get away from the place – she was so depressed by Jesse's attitude.

'Let me check the car,' Newman warned. 'Wait here . . .'

'Why in God's name!'

'To make sure no one has tampered with it.'

He looked for fresh footprints, for any sign that someone had been clever, using their own footprints still sculpted in the hard snow. He checked the bonnet where he had pressed a small amount of snow on arrival, snow which had frozen immediately at the point where the bonnet lifted. The snow was undisturbed. He unlocked the car and waved to Nancy to get into the passenger seat.

'I'm driving this time,' he informed her as he got behind the wheel and she flopped beside him.

'You don't like my driving?' she flared.

'Remember last time – the snowplough?'

'Maybe you're right. Why all the fuss about someone tampering with it?'

'In case they'd placed a bomb,' he told her brutally as he continued his policy of unnerving her.

'Jesus! You want a nervous wreck on your hands?'

They said nothing more to each other during the drive back to Berne which was uneventful. At the Bellevue Palace they had a late lunch in the coffee shop which was quiet so it was safe to talk freely. Nancy brought up the subject over their coffee.

'The next thing is Seidler?'

'That's right. Don't forget to pack the two overnight cases. I have an idea we're going to need them . . .'

'Which was the first thing I was going to do. At least this time I'm permitted to accompany you . . .'

'Nancy, do shut up . . .'

They spent the whole of the rest of the afternoon inside the bedroom in case Seidler phoned early. Newman had purchased a road map the previous day and he studied this while Nancy kicked off her shoes, lay on the bed and tried to sleep. She was certain she'd stay awake and the ringing of the phone jerked her back into consciousness with a start. Newman grabbed for the instrument, the map spread out on the other bed.

'Newman speaking . . .'

'This is Manfred Seidler. I am only going to say this one time . . .'

'You'll repeat it if I don't get it. Go on . . .'

'Le Pont, in the Juras, near Lac de Joux. You know it?'

'Yes . . .'

'We rendezvous at exactly nineteen twenty-eight

hours. At the station. I will be on the train which arrives at nineteen twenty-eight . . .'

'For Christ's sake, I'll never make it. Don't you realize it's five o'clock now?'

'If you are interested in the information I can provide – no details over the phone – bring two thousand Swiss francs in cash. Park your car a very short distance from the station – but out of sight. I shall be carrying two suitcases.'

'I need more time. There's snow in the Juras. The roads will be hell . . .'

'Nineteen twenty-eight hours. And I won't wait. Are you coming or not?'

'I'm coming . . .'

There was a click at the other end of the line. Seidler had broken the connection. Newman replaced the receiver and checked his watch again. He examined the map quickly while Nancy leaned over his shoulder.

'Can we make it?' she asked.

'If we go this way we just might. He's cutting it bloody fine . . .'

His finger traced a route from Berne along motorway N12 down to Lake Geneva. The finger turned on to motorway N9 – roughly running parallel westward to the lake until it joined the third motorway, N1. At a place called Rolle, between Lausanne and Geneva, on the shore of the lake, Newman traced a route along a road winding up over the Juras and stopped at Le Pont.

'That's a long way round,' Nancy objected. 'It's two sides of a triangle . . .'

'It's also the only way we'll get there in time – by using the motorways. And I've driven up the section from Rolle, so I know the road. It will be diabolical when we get above the snow line. Come on, girl. I'll take the cases. Thank God I had the tank refilled on the way back from Thun . . .'

They were waiting for the lift when Nancy told Newman to go ahead to the car and she'd follow. 'I've forgotten my purse,' she explained as the lift arrived and Newman, swearing, stepped inside.

Lausanne Gare

Seidler lugged the two suitcases out of the phone booth back on to the platform. He felt a sense of relief: Newman was coming. He hurriedly made his way to the restaurant where there would be plenty of people while he waited for his next train.

He was deliberately taking a roundabout route – to make sure he was not being followed. Now he had to wait for the *Cisalpin*, the Paris express which travelled non-stop to the frontier station at Vallorbe. From there he would back-track on the small local leaving Vallorbe at 19.09 and reaching Le Pont at 19.28.

*

Berne

'Leupin calling, Chief. Newman has just left the hotel carrying two cases. He's putting them in the back of his car, the Citroen. Hold on, his fiancée has dashed out to join him . . .'

'It's all right, Leupin,' Beck reassured his subordinate. 'I have allocated another six men to the job – as a contingency measure. Six men with three more cars. They can leapfrog to make sure he doesn't know what we're doing. You and Marbot tail him for the first lap. Good luck . . .'

Beck put down the phone and sighed as he looked across at Gisela. She brought over the fresh cup of coffee she had poured for him. It looked as though it was going to be quite a night: Beck was in his shirtsleeves, the sure sign of a long siege.

'Newman and his girl just left the Bellevue with two cases,' he told her. 'They're getting into that hired car . . .'

'They're trying to leave the country?'

'That would be out of character for Newman at this stage of the game. You have laid on that other facility I requested?'

'The machine is already standing by . . .'

It was very dark that night. It was very cold. Newman almost made the Citroen fly, moving well over the limit when he felt he could risk it on the motorways. At that, they were overtaken several times, twin headlights turned full on, flashing past them at God knew what speed.

'That couldn't be the police, could it?' Nancy wondered aloud when the second car sped past.

'Hardly. The first was a Saab, that was a Volvo . . .'

'I keep thinking about Jesse. I don't see what we can do about him.'

'Nothing. I can see where you get your stubborn streak from.'

'We can't just do nothing . . .'

'Leave him to me . . .'

'And what does that mean?' she asked.

'I'll think of something . . .'

He slowed down on the way to Geneva. A few minutes later the route sign appeared indicating a turn-off. *Rolle VD* – Rolle, Canton of the Vaud. Newman swung away from the lake, away from the N1 on to the side road north which immediately began to climb. In the distance the Juras loomed like a giant white tidal wave arrested in mid-motion. Then they were above the snow line.

In their headlights the narrow road ahead was like a mirror, a mirror of ice. The road turned and twisted, climbing steeper and steeper. The danger signs began to appear, signs with a sinister zigzag. *Risque de Verglas*. Skid. Ice. Now the road really began the ascent. Newman's arms ached with the strain of holding the wheel, keeping the car on the road. Nancy glanced at him. His lips were compressed, eyes narrowed. She lit a cigarette, glanced in the wing mirror. The lights of the black Audi were still there. A long way back on an unusually straight section. First the Saab, then the Volvo, now the Audi. She looked ahead and stiffened.

'Oh, Christ!'

The wave of the Juras hung above them. *Verglas.* The zigzags were incredible. Newman was constantly turning the wheel. And now they had entered a narrow gulch. Snow banked high on both sides. Beyond reared dark walls of dense fir forest, the branches of trees sagging under the weight of the snow. She reached to turn up the heater and found it already full on. They went on climbing, twisting inside the gulch. The clock on the dashboard registered 19.20 hours. Eight minutes to rendezvous time. They'd never make it.

They went over the top without warning. Swinging round a particularly suicidal bend, the road suddenly levelled out. They started to descend. Lights appeared in the distance.

'Le Pont,' Newman said.

A cluster of houses, steep-roofed, spilling down a hillside. The roofs heavy with snow. Wooden balconies at first-floor level. Hardly more than a hamlet. Newman nudged the car past a hotel ablaze with lights. Hotel de la Truite.

'Look!'

Newman pointed up at the hotel. Under the eaves shards of ice a foot long projected downwards. A palisade of icicles. Inverted. The station was little more than a one-storey hut, an isolated building with no one about. The dashboard clock registered 19.26 hours. Newman parked the car beside the building, out of sight of the exit. First, he had swung it through one hundred and eighty degrees – involving a major rear-wheel skid which made Nancy clench her hands. Ready for a swift departure. He left the engine ticking over.

'I want you to take over the wheel,' he told Nancy. 'I'm going to stand near the exit when the train comes in. This could be a trap. If I come running move like a bird when I dive inside – back the way we came. I'm leaving you now – look, the train is coming . . .'

The train, three small coaches, an abbreviated caterpillar of lights, stopped behind the station – no more than a wayside halt. Newman heard the distinctive sound of a door slamming. A gaunt-faced man, hatless, carrying two suitcases, appeared under the pallid light over the exit. He had a haunted look, calling out in German.

'Newman! Where is the car . . . I am being followed . . .'

Two men appeared behind him in the exit. A car driven at high speed came up the road from the direction of Neuchatel – and Berne. Its headlamps swept like searchlights – over the station exit.

367

Newman caught a flash of red – red like the Porsche he had seen on the Thun motorway. There was a scream of brakes applied savagely. The barrel of a rifle projected from the driver's window. At the same moment Nancy drove the Citroen round from the side of the station, pulled up, threw open the doors.

'Inside the car, Seidler!' Newman yelled.

He grabbed one suitcase, hurled it on the rear seat, shoved Seidler after it, shut the door and dived into the front passenger seat. The other car was still moving, slithering in a skid on ice as the rifle barrel moved further out of the window. One of the two men following Seidler was pulling something out from inside his coat.

'Move!' Newman shouted at Nancy. 'Back the way we came . . .'

The rifle was fired, a detonating report above the sounds of both cars' engines. The man hauling something out from inside his coat pocket was thrown backwards as though kicked by an elephant. The rifle spoke a second time. The other man performed a weird pirouette, clutching his chest, then sagging into the snow.

It was incredible marksmanship. Two bullets fired by a man who had to be driving with one hand, operating the rifle with the other, all while his car was recovering from a skid. Two men died. Newman had no doubt that neither had survived the impact of what had sounded like a high-velocity rifle.

Nancy was driving the Citroen across the beam of

the other vehicle's headlights, speeding beyond them as she pressed her foot down regardless of the treachery of the ground beneath their wheels. Then the station was behind them and they were going back over their previous route.

'That man behind him pulled out a gun,' Seidler croaked hoarsely.

'I saw it,' Newman replied tersely.

They were approaching the Hotel de la Truite when a black Mercedes swung out from the drive straight across the path of the Citroen. Nancy jammed on the brakes, the car slithered, then stopped. The Mercedes drove on past towards the station.

'Bastard!' Nancy snapped between clenched teeth.

'Maybe he's on his way to meet two bodies,' Newman speculated.

Nancy glared at him and started the car moving again. Outside the hotel a pair of skis had been rammed vertically into the ground. During their brief stop Newman had heard singing with a drunken cadence coming from inside the hotel. Death at the station, revelry at the inn. *Après-ski* in full swing.

Seidler leaned forward, grasping the backs of their seats. He stared through the windscreen as though getting his bearings. He spoke suddenly, this time in English for Nancy's benefit.

'Not the left turn to Rolle! Bear right. Take the lakeside road . . .'

'Do as he says,' Newman said quietly. 'Why, Seidler? I'd have thought this was a good place to leave fast . . .'

'There is a house on the left-hand side of this road at the foot of the mountain. We talk there . . . *Mein Gott*, what was that?'

'It's that helicopter again,' Nancy said, glancing out of her side window. 'If it is the same one. I first heard it when we turned off at Rolle . . .'

'So did I,' agreed Newman. 'It followed us up the mountain. There are a lot of military choppers floating around . . .'

'*Military?*' Seidler sounded alarmed. 'You were followed?'

'Shut up!' Newman told him. 'Just warn us before we reach this house . . .'

'Keep to the road round the lake before I tell you to stop. Keep the very fast speed . . .'

'I need directions as to the route, not how to drive,' Nancy replied coldly.

At about three thousand feet the Vallée de Joux nestles inside folds of the Jura Mountains. To their right the lake was a bed of solid ice covered with a counterpane of snow. To the left the mountain slopes were scarred with the graffiti of daytime skiers propelling themselves across the snow. Here and there loomed the silhouettes of two-storey houses constructed of shiny new wood. As a winter ski resort Le Pont was prospering.

'This is it,' Seidler called out, 'just before we arrive in the L'Abbaye village . . .' He leaned forward again. 'Place the car in the garage . . .'

'Don't,' Newman interjected. 'Drive it under that

copse of firs. Back it in if you can – facing the way we're going now.'

'You know something? I might just manage that, Robert . . .'

Newman's mind was galloping. He had just seen his opportunity. L'Abbaye. Beyond the far end of the lake was Le Brassus. Only a few kilometres beyond Le Brassus was a tiny *Douane*, a Customs post, thinly manned. And beyond that the road passed into *France*. The road continued over French soil for another twenty kilometres or so to La Cure. He could even remember the Hotel Franco-Suisse where he had once stayed the night – the strange hotel where you went through the front door still in France and out of the back door into Switzerland! At La Cure they could turn north, continuing into France. That was how he was going to get Nancy out of Switzerland – to safety – tonight.

'Why not the garage?' Seidler complained.

'With the car left outside we can escape quickly – or have you not noticed that chopper is still with us?'

'You have brought the two thousand Swiss francs?' demanded Seidler.

'No. You just put that in because people don't value something they can get for nothing.' Newman turned to face Seidler. 'If you don't want to talk we'll drop you here and drive away. Make up your mind . . .'

'We go into the house . . .'

Seidler looked to be near the end of his tether.

Haunted eyes, deep in their sockets, stared back at Newman as Nancy skilfully backed the Citroen off the road a short distance up the slope under the firs. She switched off the engine and Newman got out of the car, standing for a moment to stretch his aching limbs.

The two-storey house stood a few yards back from the road on the lower slope. It was old, decrepit and a verandah ran the full length of the ground floor. A short flight of wooden steps led up to the front door and there were balconies in front of the shuttered windows on the first floor. The downstairs windows were also shuttered. Nancy thought it was a grim, eerie-looking place.

The beat of the chopper's motor was louder now the Citroen was silent. Newman craned his neck but it was somewhere behind the copse and going away from them. He slapped his gloved hands round his forearms.

'God, it's freezing,' commented Nancy.

At that height it was arctic. No wind. Just a sub-zero temperature which was already penetrating Newman's shoes and gloves. Another row of stiletto-like icicles was suspended from the house's gutter. Newman made no effort to help with the two suitcases Seidler carried up the steps.

'Whose place is this?' he asked as Seidler took a key out of his pocket.

'A friend's. He dwells here only in the summertime . . .'

'Sensible chap . . .'

To Newman's surprise, the key turned in the lock first time. They entered a huge room which seemed to occupy most of the ground floor. At the far end on the left-hand side a wooden staircase led up to a minstrel's gallery overlooking the room below.

The floor, made of wooden planks, was varnished and decorated with worn rugs scattered at intervals. The furniture was heavy and traditional; old chairs, tables, sideboards and bookcases. Nancy noticed a film of dust lay over everything.

Along the right-hand wall was the only modern innovation – a kitchen galley with formica worktops. She ran a finger along them and it came away black with dust. Opening a cupboard she found it well-stocked with canned food and jars of coffee.

'I will demonstrate at once what this is all about,' Seidler informed Newman in German. 'Please wait here . . .'

He disappeared through a doorway in the rear wall, dumping one suitcase on the floor and carrying the other. Newman turned to Nancy and shrugged. She asked him what Seidler had said and he told her. Even inside the house with the front door closed it was icy – and they could still hear the chopper in the distance as though it were circling. Nancy opened her mouth and screamed at the top of her voice. Newman swung round and stared at the back of the room.

A hideous apparition had appeared in the doorway through which Seidler had disappeared. Newman understood the scream as he gazed at the man with no head standing there, the man with the blank goggle-eyes of an octopus. Seidler was wearing a gas mask, a mask with strange letters stencilled above the frightening goggle-eyes. *CCCP.* USSR.

Chapter Twenty-Eight

'I brought half-a-dozen consignments of these gas masks over the border ... smuggled them across the Austrian frontier from the Soviet depot inside Czechoslovakia ... I speak Czech fluently which helped ...'

The words tumbled out of Seidler – like a man who has carried too much locked away in his mind for too long. After the macabre demonstration he had removed the mask and Nancy was now making coffee. She had broken the seal on one of the jars of instant coffee, found a saucepan inside a cupboard and had boiled a pan of water on the electric cooker. Pouring the water into each of three chunky mugs containing some of the coffee, she stirred and then handed them round.

'We need some internal central heating in this icebox,' she observed. 'And I do wish that bloody chopper would go away ...'

Newman heard a car approaching along the icy lakeside road from the direction of Le Pont. The shuttered windows made it impossible to see outside. He ran to the front door and heaved it open – just in time to see the tail-lights of the car vanishing towards

Le Brassus. A red car. It was moving like a bat out of hell despite the icy surface. He closed the door again.

'Who employed you for this job, Seidler?'

'You'll write a big story – get it in the international press, expose them . . . otherwise I'm finished . . . I'm giving you the scoop of a lifetime . . .'

Seidler was badly rattled, self-control gone, almost on the verge of hysteria as he rambled on in German. He wore an expensive camel-hair coat, a silk scarf, hand-made shoes. Newman drank some of the scalding coffee before he replied.

'Answer my question – I'll decide how to handle it later. Keep to the point. I think we have very little time left,' he warned in English for Nancy's benefit.

'That car which shot past worries you?' she asked.

'Everything worries me. That car, yes. Plus the Audi, the Saab and the Volvo which kept passing us on our way up here. And that military chopper up there. Add the carnage back at the station and we all have a great deal to worry about. So, Seidler, who employed you? One question at a time . . .'

'The Berne Clinic. Professor Grange – although mostly I dealt with that brute, Kobler. Grange used me because of my connections inside Czechoslovakia . . .'

'And how did you obtain these consignments? You can't just walk in and out of a Soviet military depot.'

For the first time a bleak smile appeared on Seidler's cadaverous face. He sat down gingerly on the arm of a large chair as though it might blow up under him. He gulped down some of his coffee, wiped his mouth with the back of his hand.

'You've heard of the honey-traps the Russian secret police use? They get a girl to compromise someone, take photos . . .'

'I know all about honey-traps. I told you to keep to the point! Any moment now this house may become one of the most dangerous places in Switzerland . . .'

'This honey-trap worked in reverse. By pure chance. The brilliant Czech they use to operate the computer for stock control at the depot met an Austrian girl on holiday while he was in Prague. He's crazy over her. She's waiting for him in Munich – waiting for him to get out. For that you need money, a lot of it. I provided that money. He provided the gas masks and fiddled the computer . . .'

'Why does Grange want this supply of Soviet gas masks?'

'To defend Switzerland, of course – and to make another fortune. Seventy per cent of the Swiss population have *atombunkers* they can go to in case of nuclear war. Imagine how many gas masks it would take to equip the same number of people to protect them against Soviet chemical warfare.'

'But why have them delivered to the Berne Clinic? The place isn't a factory. I still don't get it . . .'

'He *tests* the gas masks there . . .'

'He does what!'

'Bob,' Nancy interrupted, 'do we have to talk to him here? There's something about this place I don't like . . .'

The wind had started to rise in the Juras. The timbers of the ancient house began to creak and groan. The place seemed to *tremble* like a ship in a choppy sea. Newman guessed it was the low temperature – the wood was contracting. During their brief drive from Le Pont he had noticed in the glare of the headlights places on the verge of the road where the snow had melted. The sun must have shone down on the Vallée de Joux; hence the criss-cross of ski-tracks on the slopes. It was the extreme change in temperature which was affecting the old building – plus the onset of the wind.

'We have to talk here,' he said rapidly in English, hoping Seidler would miss his meaning. 'I told you, I think we have very little time. God knows what's waiting for us outside when we do leave . . .'

'Thank you. You are *so* reassuring . . .'

Newman's callousness was deliberate. He was preparing Nancy psychologically for the dash to the French frontier. He continued questioning Seidler.

'How does Grange test the gas masks?'

'He started using animals. I once saw an obscene sight – a chimpanzee escaped. It was wearing a gas mask, clawing at it to try and get it off its head . . .'

'And then?'

'He decided he had to progress to testing the masks

on human beings. He uses the patients – they're terminal, anyway. I arrived late in the Lear jet from Vienna a few weeks ago with the previous consignment. A cock-up at Schwechat Airport outside Vienna. The driver of the van waiting for me at Belp was ill – food-poisoning, he said. I had to take over the wheel and drive to the Clinic well after dark. I saw a woman – one of the patients she must have been – running in the grounds wearing a gas mask and a bathrobe. She was trying to tear off the mask while she ran. They were firing canisters from something at her – the canisters burst in front of her . . .'

'So where do they get the gas from?' Newman demanded.

'How the hell do I know? I certainly never brought any gas out of Czechoslovakia. Luckily they didn't see the van – so I turned it round and arrived at the Clinic later. The Swiss Army is guarding that place . . .'

'How do you know that?'

'I've caught glimpses of men in Swiss uniform – inside that gatehouse and patrolling the grounds at a distance. We're in real trouble, Newman, the worst kind . . .'

'What goes on inside that laboratory – and inside the *atombunker*?'

'No idea. I've never been there . . .'

'I'm still not convinced. Give me your full name . . .'

'Gustav Manfred Seidler . . .'

'And you brought these gas masks on the orders of Dr Bruno Kobler of the Berne Clinic?'

'I told you that. Yes. He takes his orders from Grange . . .'

'Seidler, why did you do this?'

'For money, a lot of money. One other thing, I have a girl friend in . . .'

'That's enough!' Newman rapped out.

He walked over to a large armchair which stood with its tall back to Seidler who suddenly frowned and crossed the room to stare at the miniature tape-recorder Newman had placed there and turned on during Seidler's brief absence when they first arrived. The German grabbed for it but Newman grasped his arm and shoved him away. Seidler's expression was livid.

'You bastard!' Seidler exploded.

'Part of any self-respecting newspaper man's equipment,' Newman lied as he pressed a button and ran the tape to the end. 'Some take notes, but I thought that might inhibit you . . .'

'So that was what you bought today in that shop in the Marktgasse,' Nancy commented as she peered over the back of the armchair.

'I want you to find somewhere to hide this, Nancy . . .'

Newman had extracted the small tape and he handed her the machine. He next took the gas mask Seidler had left on a table and placed it on the working top in the kitchen under the glare of the spotlights which illuminated the galley. Standing back a few feet, he took from his pocket Nagy's small Voigtlander *Vitoret 110* camera and attached one of the flash-bulbs he had purchased from the same shop. He took four pictures of the mask with flashes and then excused himself, asking Seidler to guide him to the lavatory.

'Through that door where I went when we arrived,' Seidler told him sullenly. 'You'll find it on your right when you get inside . . .'

Hidden in the lavatory, Newman pulled up his trouser legs and concealed the miniature tape inside the thick sock on his left foot. The film from the camera he shoved down inside his other sock. When he came out Seidler was putting the gas mask into one of the suitcases and snapping the catches shut.

'I'll keep this if you don't mind . . .'

'It's your property. Why the sudden desire for cleanliness, Nancy? We've got to get out of here fast before something unfortunate happens.'

She was crouched by the huge open fireplace filled with logs, using a dustpan and brush to sweep up the hearth. She stood up, put the pan and brush back inside a cupboard and rubbed her hands clean of dust.

'You wanted the tape-recorder hidden. It's underneath the logs,' she snapped.

'That's a good place. Thanks, Nancy.' Newman turned towards Seidler. 'You were saying something about a girl friend – I didn't think you'd want her details on record . . .'

'I am grateful . . .' Seidler swallowed and showed signs of emotion. 'If anything happens to me I would like her to know. She had nothing to do with Terminal. Will you take down her address and phone number? Erika Stahel . . .'

Newman wrote the details in his notebook with a wooden expression as though he had never heard of her. He went on writing and then froze for a second at Seidler's next words.

'She works for Dr Max Nagel, the big Basle banker. Nagel is the only man powerful enough to oppose Grange. He has just left Basle for Berne to attend some medical reception at the Bellevue Palace . . .'

'The reception tomorrow?' Nancy asked sharply.

'I don't know when. Hadn't we better leave this place?'

'Immediately,' responded Newman. 'And prepare yourself for a rough ride. I'm driving like hell along the road to Le Brassus . . .'

'Why Le Brassus?' Seidler queried, picking up the suitcase containing the gas mask.

'Because we want to avoid Le Pont – after what happened at the station. God knows what could be waiting for us there.'

Nancy had washed up the pan, their mugs and replaced them where she had found them. She was carrying the opened jar of coffee which she said ought to be taken away. No trace of their visit remained when Seidler, still nervy and anxious to leave, opened the front door. There was a score of questions

Newman would have liked to ask him but the priority was to move, to get over the border into France. Newman held the front door key Seidler had handed him. The first shot was fired as Newman locked the door while Seidler and Nancy were heading for the Citroen parked under the trees. In the cold silence of the night the report was a loud *Crack!*

'Run!' Newman yelled. 'Crouch down! Get into the car for Christ's sake!'

The second shot – Newman now realized it was a rifle – was fired in rapid succession. Stumbling down the icy steps, holding the second suitcase Seidler had left behind in his left hand, Newman saw the case Seidler had taken jerk out of his hand. The shot had passed through the case. Seidler picked it up and continued his shambling trot towards the car which Nancy had already reached, unlocked and opened the doors.

A third shot was fired, a fourth – neither came anywhere near them. That was when Newman realized there was a second rifleman – firing at the first. The night reverberated with a fusillade of shots.

The wind blew and there was a strange weather phenomenon Newman had never seen before. A wave of snow dust, as fine as salt particles, cruised a foot high across the lower slopes, swirling round his ankles as he reached the car. Seidler had dived into the rear seat, Nancy was in the front passenger seat. She had inserted one of the keys Newman had given her on their arrival while he studied the old house, in the ignition. He slid in behind the wheel, slammed the door, drove out from under the trees and a rifle shot grazed the bonnet.

'Oh, Jesus!' said Nancy. 'What's happening?'

'It's weird – there are two of them. One firing at us, the other firing at the first marksman. Christ, how many people know we're up here?'

The sound of the shots faded as he drove as fast as he dare. In their headlights the road was gleaming like a skating rink. He passed through the main street of L'Abbaye and the village seemed deserted. Now for Le Brassus – and the French border. That was when he heard again the sound of the chopper coming closer.

Le Brassus VD – the road sign said – was a village of ancient villas, stark trees and gardens fronted with beech hedges half-buried under a coating of snow. Again deserted. They had left the lake behind. Newman pulled out of a skid and drove on.

'The second case I threw in the back,' he called out. 'It contains what, Seidler?'

'Old newspapers. Where are you taking me?'

'To safety. The French frontier is just ahead. If I have to, I'll crash the border to get through . . .'

'We're leaving Switzerland?' Nancy asked.

'You'll be safer in France, so will Seidler. And I may be able to operate more freely outside Switzerland. I plan to phone Beck, tell him we have Seidler's evidence, see if he'll raid the Berne Clinic . . .'

The sign came up in their headlights. *Zoll – Douane. 2 km.* They were within a couple of kilometres of escape. Newman pressed his foot down, at times gliding over the ice shining threateningly in the beams. He glanced at Nancy and she nodded her approval of the course he was taking. She had been badly shaken by the violence at Le Pont station, by the shooting outside the old house.

'Oh, God! No!' she exclaimed.

Something else was showing up in the headlights and Newman slowed down. The black Audi had been positioned at right-angles, acting as a road-block. To one side a second car, a Saab, was parked on the verge. Uniformed policemen stood waving torches frantically. Newman stopped the car, sagged behind the wheel. They were trapped.

The first sound he heard as he stepped out on to the slippery road was the roar of the chopper's rotors as it landed, a large, dark silhouette, in a nearby field. He told Nancy and Seidler to stay in the car and went to meet the nearest policeman.

'What the devil do you think you're doing?' he asked in French.

'Instructions, sir. Someone is coming . . .'

The policeman gestured towards the field where

the chopper had landed. A compact figure came out of the darkness, hatless and wearing an overcoat. Arthur Beck. Of course. The Federal police chief trod his way carefully across the road and peered inside the Citroen.

'You've no reason to stop us,' Newman snapped.

'You were thinking of leaving the country?' Beck enquired.

'What concern is it of yours?'

'Every concern, my friend. You are a material witness in my investigation into the deaths of Julius Nagy and Bernard Mason . . .'

Another man had emerged from the helicopter and was walking towards Beck. A man of medium height, well-built, who walked with a deliberate tread. As he passed in front of the headlights of the Citroen Newman saw he was dressed in the uniform of a colonel in the Swiss Army. Under his peaked cap, beneath his thick eyebrows, motionless eyes stared at Newman. Clean-shaven, he had a strong nose, a thin-lipped mouth and he carried himself with an air of confidence verging on arrogance. Newman recognized him before Beck made his introduction.

'This is Colonel Victor Signer, president of the Zurcher Kredit Bank. He called on me just before I was leaving – he expressed a wish to accompany me. This is Robert Newman . . .'

No handshake. Signer half-smiled, not pleasantly, dipped his head in acknowledgement. The blank eyes, still studying Newman, reminded him of films he had seen of sharks, which was fanciful, he told himself. Of one thing he was sure. God had just arrived.

'I hear you have been causing us some trouble, Newman,' Signer remarked.

He spoke through his nose, like a man with adenoids and he looked at the ground as though addressing a subordinate.

'You are speaking personally?' Newman suggested.

'I didn't come here to fence with you . . .'

'Why did you come here, Signer?'

The eyes snapped up and there was a brief flicker of fury. He would be a bastard to serve under. Autocratic, callous, sarcastic. The original martinet. Newman understood now why Blanche disliked her stepfather so much. The colonel clasped his hands which, despite the cold, were clad in fine suede gloves. A very tough baby, Victor Signer. Beck intervened, as though afraid things were getting out of control.

'Newman, I have to ask you to return with me to Berne – together with your two companions . . .'

Signer walked slowly round the Citroen and peered in at the rear seat. Seidler shrank back from his gaze, clutching his suitcase.

'Not Dr Kennedy,' Newman said firmly. 'You have no grounds for detaining her . . .'

'She witnessed the death of Mrs Laird. Until that case is resolved I must insist that she remains on Swiss territory . . .'

'You bastard,' Newman whispered.

'And the man in the rear of the car. He wouldn't by chance be Manfred Seidler?' Beck opened the rear door. 'Please step out, Mr Seidler – we have been searching everywhere for you.'

'Grab his case,' Newman whispered again. 'Don't open it – and don't let Signer get his hands on it . . .'

Seidler emerged shakily from the car, releasing the suitcase Beck reached for without protest. Signer wandered round the Citroen to join them, flexing his gloved hands. Then he stood waiting. He would be about five feet ten tall, Newman guessed, but the controlled force of his personality made him seem taller. This was a man who dealt in millions at his bank.

'I would like to see the contents of that suitcase,' he remarked.

'No! Colonel,' Beck replied, 'I am investigating three potential homicides, two positive ones. Not an hour ago a couple of men arriving at Le Pont station were murdered. This case may well contain evidence. It goes straight to our forensic people unopened. It is not a matter I care to debate . . .'

'As you wish . . .'

Signer half-smiled again and walked across to stand in front of the headlight beams of the Saab parked on the verge. He removed his left glove and clenched his hand. Beck, still holding on to the suitcase, gestured for Seidler to follow him. Newman sensed that something was wrong but couldn't immediately put his finger on it. Signer had given up too easily . . .

'Seidler! Get away from those headlights!' he shouted.

Following Beck, Seidler was illuminated by the headlamps of the Citroen – illuminated like a target on a firing range at night. There was a loud report and Seidler leapt forward, vaulted clear off the ground and sprawled over the bonnet of the Audi. A second rifle report shattered the night. The sprawled body coughed, a convulsive movement, then flopped back over the bonnet. In the headlights a patch of dampness – blood – began to spread midway down the centre of Seidler's back. The second shot had fractured his spine. He was dead twice over.

Chapter Twenty-Nine

Chaos. Beck shouting, 'Douse those bloody lights . . .' An order hardly necessary – the drivers inside the Audi and the Saab turned them off while he was shouting the order. No one wanted to be a target for the marksman. Policemen running all over the place. Newman had turned off his own lights.

It was Beck who regained control of the situation, issuing terse commands through his walkie-talkie. Policemen crouched under cover of the vehicles. Nancy was crouched over Seidler's spread-eagled body, checking his pulse. She turned to Beck who gently pressed her down by the car as Newman joined them.

'He's dead,' Nancy told them. 'Half his head was shot away by the first bullet . . .'

'My commiserations, madame,' said Beck.

'Why?'

'For your most unfortunate experiences in my country. This is the second time this week you have been present to confirm a violent death. If I may offer my services? We can fly you back to Berne in the helicopter. A policeman can drive your Citroen back to the Bellevue Palace.' He looked up. 'There is something wrong, Newman?'

'Signer. Look at him. He's the only man who didn't move . . .'

The colonel was still standing motionless in front of the Saab where he, also, had been silhouetted in the glare of the beams of headlights. He stood with his hands clasped over his lower abdomen. Newman noticed he had now replaced the suede glove on his left hand.

'He is a soldier,' Beck commented, 'a man accustomed to the experience of being under fire. Here he comes . . .'

Signer walked slowly towards the crouched trio and remained standing as he stared down at them. His tone was remote and calm when he spoke.

'He missed me. You realize I was the target?'

Newman stood up slowly. He shook his head, staring direct at the colonel. Signer made an irritable gesture with one hand. When he spoke his tone suggested he was addressing a corporal he had decided to demote.

'Why are you shaking your head? Of course I was the target. I was standing still. Doubtless one of these crazy terrorists.'

'The killer was a marksman,' Newman replied. 'Maybe if there had been only one bullet the target would have been disputable. There was a second – which also hit Seidler straight on. That means a marksman. How many marksmen do you have under your command, Signer?'

'You are implying . . . what?'

'Gentlemen!' Beck had also stood up, retaining his hand on Nancy's shoulder to keep her under cover. 'Gentlemen,' he repeated, 'we have another murder on our hands. Many here are still in a state of shock. No arguments, no quarrels. That is final. Colonel, you wish to accompany us back to Berne in the helicopter?'

'Give me a car, a driver. I will go on to Geneva now we are so close. And I understood Military Intelligence wished to interview this man Seidler . . .'

'They might have some difficulty doing that now,' Beck observed. 'I will deal with the body – and you may have both a car and a driver to take you to Geneva. The Saab, I suggest. If you could leave at once, Colonel, it will help me to go about my duties.'

It was a dismissal and Signer knew it. He didn't like it. He turned on his heel witnout a word of thanks and climbed inside the rear of the Saab. Within a minute the tail-lights of the Saab were vanishing towards the French frontier.

'I thought that was the way to France,' Nancy said to Beck.

'Madame, it is a most curious road. You cross the border into France, drive fifteen to twenty kilometres over French soil to La Cure, and there the road forks. One way north to the French hinterland, the other way down a devilish road to Geneva – after re-crossing the border into Switzerland.' He glanced towards Seidler's crumpled form. 'And now some unknown marksman has eliminated our only surviving witness.'

'There may be someone still left,' Newman replied.

'The name, please,' Beck demanded.

'I think the person I'm thinking of may be safer if for the moment I keep that information to myself. Incidentally, Beck, I noticed you led Seidler in front of those headlights.'

'I have never claimed papal infallibility,' Beck responded stiffly. 'Shall we all board the helicopter and return to Berne . . .' He reached inside the rear of the Citroen. 'And I think we will take this second suitcase with us . . .'

'Beck, I'm asking you one more time. Let Dr Kennedy go. She can drive this car into France . . .'

'Out of the question. It is regrettable, madame, but you are a vital witness . . .'

'Then you'll get the minimum of cooperation from me,' Newman told him.

'Again regrettably, if necessary I shall have to soldier on by myself. May we now depart? I insist . . .'

'What about that poor sod's body?'

'I have already summoned an ambulance to take him to the morgue in Berne. More work for the unfortunate Dr Kleist. And there are two more bodies at Le Pont station. Which route did you take to arrive here? And where did you pick up Manfred Seidler?'

Newman spoke quickly before Nancy could say anything. 'I drove up from Rolle. Seidler had phoned me earlier this evening to make the arrangement. He was waiting for us outside the Hotel de la Truite. I turned the car round and we drove for the French border. Seidler wanted to get out of Switzerland before he'd talk . . .'

'You did not go on to the station? Are you certain?'

'I was driving the bloody car. When we'd collected Seidler the job was done. The next objective was the French border. How many times do I have to tell you? And these bodies at the station. Whose bodies?'

'That we do not know. One of my patrol cars – I have them covering the whole Jura – reported finding the corpses over the radio. A message reached me aboard the helicopter. Two men – carrying no means of identification. Both armed with 9-mm. Lugers. One man was clasping his weapon when they discovered them.' He turned to Nancy. 'Tomorrow there is to be a large medical reception held at the Bellevue. Will you be attending that?'

'Yes. Since we have to go back I'll take the opportunity to talk with Professor Grange. There are a few questions I want to ask him . . .'

'That reception may be an explosive affair,' Beck commented. 'Before I flew here I heard that Dr Max Nagel had just arrived from Basle – Professor Grange's most bitter enemy. There may be more than one confrontation. Something tells me this affair is coming to a head . . .'

'I'm frozen,' Nancy protested. 'Can we get moving . . .'

'Of course. My apologies. Let me lead the way. It is a large machine so you should have a comfortable flight . . .'

'Don't expect much conversation,' Newman rapped back.

The helicopter was a French Alouette. As it lifted off and gained height Newman looked down on the white wasteland below, the graveyard of three men in one night. There were two incidents during the flight to Belp.

Beck opened each suitcase, raising the lids so no one else could see the contents. Newman saw him freeze for a moment when he saw the gas mask. Beck leaned over in his seat and he spoke with his mouth close to Newman's ear.

'Did you have a chance to open these cases?'

Newman shook his head, making no verbal response above the roar of the rotors. A short while later Beck received a message over the radio. He made no reference to it as the chopper flew on to Belp.

Another black Audi was waiting for them when they landed at Belp. Beck took the wheel after placing both suitcases in the boot, inviting Nancy to sit in the back while Newman sat alongside him. They drove in silence along the motorway to Berne. Newman was determined to give the police chief no conversational opening. His only comment was to insist that Beck drove them to the Bellevue Palace. No more interviews at the Taubenhalde: Nancy was exhausted with her ordeal and he was pretty tired himself.

'That radio message I received aboard the Alouette,' Beck began as they approached the outskirts of Berne. 'One of the patrols stopped a red Mercedes for checking near Neuchatel, a car driven by a chauffeur with one passenger in the back.'

'That concerns me?'

'It might concern us both. The passenger was Dr Bruno Kobler. He said he was on his way to Geneva from Berne. A curious route to take. He brushed aside any suggestion he had been anywhere in the vicinity of the Juras. One of the patrol car men noticed the car's tyres had faint traces of snow crust embedded in the treads. There is no snow at that level . . .'

'I see. Why didn't they search the car?'

'On what grounds? And I have to be careful. Very powerful men are waiting for me to make one false move – so I can be removed from the case. I found his destination interesting – recalling that Colonel Signer said he also was heading for Geneva.'

'You did say a *red* Mercedes?' Newman enquired. He said no more when Beck confirmed the colour of the car.

'God! I feel *trapped*, Bob,' Nancy said as they settled down in their bedroom. She kept walking about restlessly. 'One part of me wants to stay – to be near Jesse, to try and haul him out of that place. Another part wants to get away – yet I like Berne, I like the people. Do I have to go to Beck's office with you in the morning?'

'Stop pacing round like a tigress. Sit down and have something to drink. It will relax you . . .'

They had used Room Service to send up plates of smoked salmon and a bottle of Yvorne, a dry Swiss white wine. Newman filled their glasses and sipped at the wine as Nancy flopped in a chair beside him.

'Beck needs affidavits from both of us. We witnessed the murder of Seidler . . .'

'We witnessed two more murders. You were quick with your reply when he asked you about the station at Le Pont. Can we get away with that? Is it wise?'

'It's self-preservation. Beck has enough ammunition to hold us here already. Why give him more? Aren't you curious as to who the marksman was?'

'I'm more concerned about challenging Grange face to face at the reception – now we have to stay. What are you going to do about all this, Bob? You said there was another witness. Who is it?'

Newman shook his head and drank more wine before he replied. 'I'm meeting the witness tomorrow afternoon. Better you don't know who or where. And don't forget we still have Novak. He is coming to that reception. Explosive was the word which Beck used. I think he could be right – especially if Nagel from Basle turns up. Beck is stage-managing something, I'm sure. The trouble is, I'm not sure about Beck.'

'We can't trust anyone then?'

'I've tried to hammer that into you. It was a natural route towards the chopper when Beck led Seidler past those headlights but, as I said, I wonder. Then Signer cleverly placed himself in front of the Saab's head-lights. I suspect he signalled to the marksman . . .'

'That I *could* believe. He's a creepy, cold-blooded swine. But how did he do it?'

'You didn't notice? He took off one of his suede gloves and clenched his fist. *Kill him!* I think that was the way it was done.'

'You mean Beck and Signer worked as a team?'

'Nancy! I don't *know* yet!'

'Is that why you didn't give Beck that tape of your conversation with Seidler in the house – or the photo-graphs you took of that hideous gas mask? That's vital evidence . . .'

'It is, but Beck gets it only when I decide I can fully trust him – if ever. That would be the time for another sworn affidavit from you – that you witnessed the recorded conversation.'

'I'm flaked out.' She drank her glass of wine, slipped off her skirt and sprawled on the bed, her raven hair spread out on the pillow. 'So what do you plan on doing next?' she asked sleepily.

'First, see my final witness tomorrow. He may just blow the whole thing wide open. Second, accompany you to the reception so I can get a good look at Grange, maybe Max Nagel, too – the leaders of the two opposing power blocs. Third, if nothing else has worked, I'm going to try and break in to the Berne

Clinic – with Novak's help. I want to see inside the laboratory – and their *atombunker* . . .'

He stopped speaking. Nancy had fallen fast asleep, leaving her smoked salmon untouched. Newman swallowed his own food, drank some more of the wine, put on his coat and slipped out of the bedroom, locking the door behind him. As soon as he had left the room Nancy opened her eyes, sat up and reached for the phone.

Newman stepped inside the lift and pressed the button for the lowest level, the floor below the main entrance hall. Using this route he hoped to leave the hotel unseen. When the doors opened he turned right past the *garderobe* which was now closed. It was 10 p.m.

Climbing a flight of steps into the deserted hall below the coffee shop, he walked out into the street, pausing to turn up his collar and glance in both directions. Then he walked rapidly to the public phone box, glancing all round again before he went inside. He dialled the number from memory. The familiar voice answered immediately.

Inside Room 214 at the Bellevue Palace, seated on the bed, Lee Foley picked up the phone on the second ring. He had been expecting the call for the past half hour. He listened for several minutes, then interrupted his caller and spoke rapidly.

'I know about Le Pont. I think from now on you're going to have to let me operate on my own. God-dammit, we do have enough information at this stage in the game to guess at what is going on. It's going to get pretty tough. Playing tough games is what I'm trained for. Just go on keeping me informed . . .'

Inside Room 312 at the Bellevue Tweed perched on a chair, crouched forward, his expression intent as he held the phone to his ear. When the conversation ended he replaced the receiver and walked over to his bed where he had spread out two maps.

One map, large-scale, showed the Canton of Berne. The second was a road and rail map of the whole of Switzerland. Polishing his glasses on the silk handker-chief, he looped the handles over his ears and stopped to examine closely the map of Berne.

Reaching for a ruler lying on the bed, he measured roughly the distance between Berne and Thun along the motorway. He'd have to hire a car in the morning – although he knew Blanche would have been happy to act as *chauffeuse*. Tweed hated driving; perhaps he should have asked Blanche who, he knew, had a car as well as her scooter. He decided he would sleep on the decision. Tomorrow promised to be D-Day.

'And who was that calling at this hour?' asked Gisela. 'It is after ten o'clock. Time you went home . . .'

'An informant,' Beck replied. He felt depressed. On his desk lay the new file Gisela had opened. *Case of Manfred Seidler*. He turned to the first page she had typed from his dictation and his eyes wandered to the neat stack of other files to his right. Hannah Stuart, Julius Nagy, Bernard Mason. To say nothing of the files which would need to be opened on the two bodies found at Le Pont station as soon as some sort of identification had been established. It was becoming a massacre.

'Things will look better in the morning,' Gisela said gently. 'You're tired and in a black mood . . .'

'Not really. All the players in this terrible drama have – or soon will be – assembled under one roof. The Bellevue Palace. Tweed, Newman, Dr Kennedy, Lee Foley. Tomorrow we'll have under that same roof Armand Grange – doubtless accompanied by his hatchetman, Bruno Kobler. Also Dr Max Nagel is there already. Very satisfactory that to a policeman – to know the location of all concerned. Our people are already inside the Bellevue, I take it? With my trip to the Juras I've not been in touch . . .'

'Three of our men – all unknown to the Bellevue staff – booked in at the hotel at different times. Their names are on the pad by your left elbow.'

'So, as the august Colonel Signer would say, we have made our dispositions. The Bellevue will be our battlefield . . .'

*

401

It was close to midnight when Bruno Kobler arrived back at the Berne Clinic and hurried inside to his office on the first floor while his chauffeur parked the red Mercedes in the garage. His employer was waiting for him.

Huge curtains were drawn over the smoked glass picture window. The office was illuminated by shaded lamps which threw dark shadows. The Professor stood listening while Kobler reported on the evening's events in terse sentences.

'Very good, Bruno,' he commented, 'that solves one outstanding problem very satisfactorily. All other discordant elements can be dealt with after the dispersal of the doctors attending the Congress. I have decided to bring forward our final experiment. Once that is confirmed as successful, *Terminal* becomes a *fait accompli*.'

'Bring it forward?' Kobler sounded puzzled. 'To when?'

'Tomorrow evening.'

'While the reception is taking place at the Bellevue Palace?'

'Exactly.' There was a note of contentment in the soft voice. 'It occurred to me the opportunity was too good to overlook. You see, Bruno, everyone will have their eyes focused on the reception. It has become known that I shall put in an appearance.'

'But you will not be present to witness the results . . .'

'You are perfectly capable of supervising the experiment. As to the results, I can examine the body when I return from the reception. We chose female patients for the previous trials because – as you know – they are biologically stronger than men. This time, as I mentioned earlier, we will use a male patient.'

'I may have the perfect subject, Professor. Also, we know now this patient has been playing tricks on us. We moved him to another room for a few hours to clean out his permanent quarters. While removing the grille to feed a fresh reel on to the tape-recorder we discovered a quantity of sodium amytal capsules. This patient has not been sedated when it was assumed he was. He may have overheard anything.'

Kobler took a file from his drawer, opened it to the first page, which carried a photo and the name of the patient, and placed it under his desk-lamp for the Professor's inspection.

'Excellent, I agree.'

The photograph showed a man with strongly defined features and a hooked nose. The name at the top of the page typed in red and underlined was Jesse Kennedy.

Chapter Thirty

Saturday, 18 February

Newman himself used Room Service to order breakfast – the complete works. He did this from sympathy with Nancy's ordeal the previous day; also because he wanted to talk in privacy. And this was Confrontation Day.

Nancy climbed out of bed and pulled back the curtains. She stared at the view, slipping on her dressing-gown. Standing there, she crossed her arms, deep in thought as he came up behind her and grasped her round the waist.

'Look at it, Bob. Not a good omen?'

The mist had returned, a sea of dirty cottonwood blotting out the Bantiger and rolling slowly along the straight stretch of the Aare to envelop the city. Soon it would be drifting into the arcades, creating an eerie silence.

'Come and have breakfast, an American breakfast,' Newman said, pulling her away from the window. 'Bacon, eggs, croissants, rolls – the lot. How did you sleep?' he asked as they faced each other across the table.

'I didn't – but I'm ravenous . . .'

'You ate nothing last night. What especially kept you awake?'

'Your conversation with Seidler inside that house. You translated some of it – but considerately not all. What you didn't realize was I know German rather well. It was my second language at high school. Then, a few weeks before I left St Thomas's – when we first met at Bewick's – I'd come back from Germany where I spent time with a German medical family. Do you really think they're using patients at the Clinic to test those gas masks, Bob?'

'I'm convinced we still don't know the whole story. I'm not sure Grange's ultimate purpose ends with the testing of those Soviet masks.' He continued quickly. 'Let's not talk about it until I've seen Grange, had a chance to weigh him up. Maybe we ought to take Jesse out of that place today. We could drive there immediately after breakfast if you agree . . .'

'I don't think it will do any good. Jesse will refuse – and without his consent we've no authority to force the issue. I want to talk to Grange myself first. And I'm sure Grange will play it cool until the reception is over . . .'

'It's your decision. I'm not too happy about it,' Newman said and drank more coffee. 'You seem very confident about this reception. You wouldn't know something you haven't told me?'

'And what might that be, I'd like to know? You always want to do things your way,' she bridled.

'You're tired. Forget it!'

*

405

Tweed was on the warpath. After an early breakfast in the dining-room – he couldn't be fussed with Room Service – he left the hotel without delay to keep his appointment with Arthur Beck. He walked into the main entrance of the Taubenhalde, placed his passport on the receptionist's counter. At that moment Beck emerged from the lift.

'Let's go straight up,' he invited Tweed. 'Don't fill in a form . . .'

Anyone who knew Tweed well would have recognized the danger signs. There was an intent expression in the eyes behind his spectacles. He crossed the hall to the lift with a brisk stride and the look on his face was forbidding as he stared at Beck.

They travelled up to the tenth floor in silence, Beck unlocked the door with his key. In the hall beyond he took out a card and inserted it in the time clock before opening the door to his office. Tweed took off his coat and sat facing Beck across his desk.

'Welcome to Berne once more,' Beck began.

'I hope you will still think me welcome when we have ended this conversation,' Tweed warned. 'I have come here because we are very worried about the Berne Clinic – and the experiments which are being carried out there, possibly under military supervision . . .'

'I don't like your tone,' Beck replied stiffly.

'I don't like the reason for my visit . . .'

'You are talking nonsense. Where have you picked up this nonsense about a Swiss clinic?'

'From various sources.' Tweed dropped his bomb. 'We know about Manfred Seidler. We have in London one of the gas masks he has supplied to the Berne Clinic. Our Ministry of Defence experts have examined it and confirmed it is the sophisticated type now issued to the Soviet chemical battalions . . .'

Beck stood up, his expression frozen. He stood behind the desk, his hands thrust inside his jacket pockets, studying his visitor who gazed back at him.

'Just supposing I found there was even one iota of truth in this extraordinary story, how would it concern you?'

'It concerns the President of the United States, the Prime Minister of Britain – both of whom are fighting to conclude a new treaty with Moscow, a treaty effectively banning the use of chemical warfare in Europe. You read the papers, don't you? Can you imagine the propaganda advantage Moscow would have if they could point to one single country in Western Europe – a country outside NATO at that – which was equipping its forces with chemical warfare units? It would give them just the excuse they need to continue building up their own resources in this diabolical field. That, Beck, is why I am here. That is why it concerns London. That is why I take such an interest in the Berne Clinic.'

'Quite a speech,' Beck commented. He sat down again. 'I take your point. May we speak in confidence? Good. Manfred Seidler was murdered last night in the Juras . . .'

'My God! He was a vital witness . . .'

'Agreed. It doesn't make my job any easier, Tweed. Can I ask you how you know so much?'

'An associate of Seidler's sold one of the gas masks from the latest consignment to someone at the British Embassy. Our agent followed Seidler to the airport outside Vienna – and saw him board a Swiss jet. I alerted our people here to watch your airports. We had a piece of luck at Belp. My man saw the consignment from Vienna being taken away in a van – that van carried the legend *Klinik Bern* on the outside. The van proceeded in the direction of the Clinic after leaving the airport at Belp . . .'

'You have been very busy in our country.' Beck smiled, a smile of resignation. 'Under other circumstances I might be angry.' He pressed the switch on his intercom. 'Gisela, coffee for two, please. Black without sugar for my guest . . . just a moment.' He looked at his visitor. 'A little cognac in your coffee?'

'Not at this hour, thank you.'

'That is all, Gisela.' He switched off. 'Anything else you know, my friend?'

'We know,' Tweed continued in the same flat tone, 'you are under great pressure to drop your investigation – pressure from the Gold Club. I come here to help you resist the pressure at all costs. You are at full liberty to disclose what I have said – what I am going to say. As a last resort – I emphasize that – we might feel compelled to leak the news of what we believe is going on at the Berne Clinic . . .'

'To some foreign correspondent like Robert Newman?'

Tweed looked surprised. 'He is investigating the same subject?'

'I don't know,' Beck admitted. 'He is here with his fiancée, an American. Her grandfather is a patient in the Clinic.'

'May I suggest how we should proceed?' Tweed requested with a hint of urgency.

'I am open to any suggestion. You seem to have established a network inside Switzerland. You may know more than me.'

'We put the Berne Clinic under total surveillance – round the clock. Specifically, smuggle a film unit into the area, choosing a strategic position where you can survey and photograph not only the Clinic but also the laboratory and their very extensive grounds. There is a dense forest behind the Clinic on high ground . . .'

'You have been out there?'

'I have studied a map.'

'I know the forest you mean and it would be the best point of vantage. The film unit will be inside a plain van with porthole windows which open – but I cannot send it to take up position until well after dark, late tonight. Otherwise it would be spotted . . .'

'By Military Intelligence?' Tweed interjected.

'You *have* been busy . . .'

Beck paused at a knock on the door, called out to Gisela to come in and played with a pencil while she served coffee. When she had gone Tweed leant forward to emphasize his words.

'Please use one of your sophisticated, infra-red cine cameras. The danger – the evidence to be obtained – probably is during the night. Hannah Stuart died after dark. So did Mrs Holly Laird . . .'

'I have kept all reference to Mrs Laird out of the papers,' Beck said sharply.

'Certain individuals inside Military Intelligence are as uneasy about this business as we are,' Tweed observed and sat back to drink his coffee.

'Who are you going to see?' Nancy asked as Newman put down the phone inside their bedroom. 'You didn't mention a name.'

'I'm stirring the pot to boiling point before that reception tonight – hoping to break someone's nerve. Then they may make a mistake. I'm on my way now to start the process. You wait here till I get back . . .'

Two minutes later he walked out of the main entrance of the Bellevue. There was the smell of fog in the heavy air. The clammy damp of mist caressed his cheeks. He went straight inside the Bundeshaus Ost and was taken to Captain Lachenal's second-floor office. When the attendant closed the door and Lachenal, dark circles under his eyes, rose from behind his desk, Newman unbuttoned his coat but made no attempt to take it off.

'Manfred Seidler is dead,' was his opening shot.

'My God! I didn't know, I swear to you . . .'

'He was murdered up in the Juras. You were looking for him. I was there when a marksman blew off half his head – and so was Colonel Signer. Do you take orders from Signer?'

'Have you gone crazy? Of course not . . .'

'Maybe indirectly – through a complex chain of command whose ultimate origin even you don't know . . .'

'That's impossible. Bob, you don't know what you're saying . . .'

'That rifle with a sniperscope that was stolen from the Thun district was probably the murder weapon. Who are the marksmen in Thun? There can't be too many of them – and you hold a record of such things. Care to let me look at that record? Or are you going to try and cover up? We are talking about cold-blooded murder, Lachenal.'

'Two such rifles have been stolen – both from the Thun district,' Lachenal said quietly. 'We tried to keep the second theft quiet. It reflects on the Swiss Army . . .'

'So you will have consulted that record of marksmen very recently – probably still have it in this office,' Newman pounded on. 'May I see it? I might believe in you if you show it to me.'

'You are telling me the truth about Seidler?'

'You really didn't know? There's the phone. Call Beck and ask him . . .'

'There is a temporary hitch in liaison.'

Which, Newman thought, was a neat way of saying they were no longer speaking to each other. Lachenal looked worried sick, close to the end of his tether. Without another word he went over to a steel filing cabinet, produced a ring of keys, unlocked the cabinet, took out a red file and brought it back to his desk.

'This is classified information . . .'

'Since when did brutal assassination become classified?'

Lachenal rifled through the typed sheets inside the file. He stopped at a page near the end and Newman guessed it was arranged alphabetically by district. 'T' for 'Thun'.

The Intelligence chief gestured for Newman to join him on his side of the desk. He used the flat of both hands to prevent Newman flipping over to another page. There were five marksmen in Thun, a high proportion, Newman guessed. Alongside one was an asterisk. He pointed to this name. Bruno Kobler.

'What's the asterisk for? Or is that top secret?'

'Expert with both rifle and handgun. A crack shot . . .'

'Get the link?' Newman queried. 'Kobler, deputy to Professor Grange. And Grange's closest financial supporter is Victor Signer – present at the execution of Manfred Seidler . . .'

'Execution?' Lachenal was shocked.

'By a one-man firing squad, a marksman. And Signer may have given the order. Think about it, check it, Lachenal. And I'm leaving now . . .'

'There are questions I would like to ask . . .'

Newman shook his head. He buttoned up his coat. He had turned the handle of the door when he fired his closing shot over his shoulder.

'And at long last I know what Terminal means – yesterday in conversation with someone they told me by chance.'

Chapter Thirty-One

'I'll be there if I'm needed,' Lee Foley said, gripping the phone with his left hand while he reached for the lighted cigarette with his other hand. 'All those people at that reception means something's going to break. I'll be there like I said – to watch it happen . . .'

Inside Room 214 the American replaced the receiver, checked his watch and stretched out on the bed. 11.30 a.m. Today he was staying in the bedroom which had already been cleaned. On the outside door handle a notice hung. *Please Do Not Disturb.*

He had used Room Service to order lunch. The fox was in its hole – and would remain there until the moment came to act. Closing his eyes, he fell fast asleep.

Newman walked out of the phone booth and headed along the familiar route to the Junkerngasse. Blanche was waiting for him, clad in a beige sweater and her wet-look black pants, the outfit she wore when she thought she might need to ride her scooter.

'I have a big favour to ask,' Newman told her, 'and very little time to spare. Would you be willing to evacuate your flat for a day or two – I've provisionally booked you a room at the Bellevue. I may need a hideaway – this would be ideal geographically . . .'

'Of course you can have it . . .'

'Not for myself. If you agree, lock up any valuables or confidential papers. Your temporary lodger might be nosy. I just don't know . . .'

'When do I move to the Bellevue? And here is a spare key.'

'By one o'clock. About clothes, pack what you're wearing. And something dressy – for a reception. This has two plusses for me. I have what the pros call a safe house. And I have you where I can keep an eye on you. People are getting killed. A lot of people.'

Inside the Bellevue Tweed knocked gently on the door after first making sure the corridor was deserted. The door to the suite was opened by a small, very broad-shouldered man with a large head, thick black hair and a wide, firm mouth. He was smoking a Havana cigar and he wore an expensive and conservative dark grey business suit.

'Come in, Tweed,' said Dr Max Nagel. 'On time to the minute, as always.'

'We may be getting somewhere,' Tweed replied as Nagel shut the door and ushered him to a deep arm-chair which enveloped the small Englishman.

'Tell me,' Nagel continued in English, drawing up a similar chair to join his guest. 'You saved me a lot of embarrassment over that Kruger affair when you traced the funds he'd embezzled to my bank.'

'That was only achieved by keeping track of that newspaperman, Newman's, activities. I've manoeuvred all the pieces on the *Terminal* board as best I could. Now we hope and we pray . . .'

'Maybe not.' Nagel, who spoke in a hoarse growl, reached for his brief-case, unlocked it and handed a file to Tweed. 'Those are photocopies of highly intricate banking transactions covering the movement of no less than two hundred million Swiss francs. At one stage they went out of the country to a company in Liechtenstein – then, hey presto! they come back again and end up, guess where?'

'In a bank account accessible to Professor Armand Grange?'

'Where else? You can keep that set of accounts. What is your strategy? When you phoned me before you left London telling me you were coming here you didn't say too much . . .'

'Not over an open line . . .'

Tweed then told Nagel all he had discovered – including the gas mask 'an emissary' had brought from Vienna and Manfred Seidler's involvement. Nagel listened in silence, smoking his cigar. His appearance reminded Tweed of a gorilla in repose, an amiable, determined and highly intelligent gorilla. Great force of character emanated from the man and his energy was proverbial.

'So,' he declared when Tweed had finished, 'I repeat, what is your strategy?'

'To squeeze Grange from every possible quarter – to exert such psychological pressure he miscalculates. I don't think we have much time left, Max. And have you another spare set of those accounts?'

'Certainly. Here you are. May I ask who they are for?'

'Newman, the foreign correspondent – passed to him through an intermediary so he doesn't know their source. I can't believe he's here simply to pay a visit with his American fiancée who, incidentally, has a grandfather as a patient at the Berne Clinic. Max, as the Americans say, we may have to go public as a final resort.'

'That I'd like to avoid. This Newman, can you trust him?'

'When these documents are handed over it will be conditional on his not publishing them. Yes, he lives on trust. But if Grange knows he's got them it will unnerve him . . .'

'I hope so.' There was a hint of doubt in Nagel's voice. 'Grange is a fanatic – you do know that? He'll go to any length to achieve his objective – which is to change the whole military policy of this country. Tread carefully – Grange is a very dangerous and unpredictable man. Like a cobra he strikes when you least expect it . . .'

*

417

Half an hour later Newman, who had phoned from Blanche's flat, walked into Beck's office. The police chief began to feel he was under bombardment when Newman started speaking.

'I don't see any reason why you shouldn't take a full team including Forensic to the Berne Clinic today with a warrant to examine not only the Clinic but also the laboratory . . .'

'You are trying to rush me? On what grounds could I furnish myself with a warrant?'

'On the basis of the findings of Dr Kleist concerning the death of their patient, Mrs Holly Laird. Cyanosis poisoning was the diagnosis, for God's sake . . .'

'Please!' Beck held up a defensive hand. 'And won't you sit down. All right, stay on your feet! Dr Kleist has not yet produced her final report. There are aspects about Mrs Laird's demise which still puzzle her. Until I do receive her report I cannot – will not – obtain a warrant. Haven't I already explained I have to move cautiously – that there are powerful forces trying to have me taken off the case?'

'Then I'll give you my affidavit about the events in the Juras last night and go . . .'

'I also need a statement from Dr Kennedy . . .'

'She is waiting downstairs. I insist on being present when you take her statement . . .'

'That I cannot permit . . .'

'Then you only get her statement in the presence of the most high-powered lawyer in Berne. Take your choice . . .'

418

'You give me one?' Beck spread his hands. 'You are in a ferocious mood, Bob. I will ask them to send Dr Kennedy up now and we will take both statements and get the damned paperwork out of the way. What frightens me is that you are going to do something independent – and highly dangerous . . .'

Their statements had been taken, signed and witnessed by Gisela. Beck had courteously asked Nancy whether he could have a few words in private with Newman and she had been taken to another room. It was Beck's turn to startle Newman. Opening a drawer he brought out a shoulder holster, a 7.65-mm. police automatic and six magazines which he pushed across the desk.

'Bob, I am not convinced Seidler was the target last night. I also believe you were earlier at Le Pont station when two hired gunmen were killed. No, please don't interrupt. I think you were the target. I recall you are familiar with the use of firearms?'

'What are you proposing?'

'Take this automatic for your protection . . .'

'So you can have me picked up, searched and found to be in possession of a deadly weapon? No thanks. I happen to know the Swiss penalties for carrying firearms . . .'

'Then for the protection of Dr Kennedy . . .'

Beck produced from the same drawer a permit to carry the weapon which he again pushed across the desk. Newman read the document upside down without touching it.

'I will sign the permit personally,' Beck continued, 'and Gisela – or a policeman chosen at random – will witness my signature. I am pleading with you. For old times' sake . . .'

Newman agreed to take the weapon.

The day was moving fast. It was 1 p.m. when Tweed, seated in a chair in the reception hall, saw Blanche Signer arrive with a case. He waited until she had registered, then stood up and strolled over to join her by the lift. He spoke only when the lift doors had closed, holding his brief-case in his left hand.

'Come to my room, Blanche. We have to talk . . .'

She slipped inside his room unseen by anyone and dropped her case on the floor. In her concise manner she explained why she had booked in at the hotel – that Newman needed her flat for a purpose unknown to her.

Tweed listened and nodded his head in approval. He should have thought of this precaution himself – Blanche would be safer inside the Bellevue until they had brought this matter to a successful conclusion – if that were possible. Taking a set of the accounts he had received from Dr Nagel and which he had put inside a sealed envelope, he handed the envelope to her.

'Can you get this into Newman's hands very urgently? And he must have no inkling as to where you obtained it . . .'

'I'm sure I can manage that. I'm just not sure when. He may be staying here but I don't want his fiancée to see me.'

Tweed smiled sympathetically. 'I understand. But as soon as possible. Any moment now everything may blow up in our faces . . .'

Newman had strapped on the shoulder holster, slipped the automatic inside it and dropped the magazines inside his coat pocket before he joined Nancy and they left the building. He made no mention of the weapon to her.

He insisted that they had a leisurely lunch in the Grill Room and, because he sensed she was jumpy, steered the conversation away from recent events. Occasionally he checked his watch.

'You're going to meet that last witness this afternoon,' she observed quietly, watching him over the rim of her glass. 'Isn't that why you keep checking your watch?'

'I looked at it twice . . .'

'Three times . . .'

Oh, Jesus! he thought. He smiled. 'Yes, I am. It may take me a couple of hours – I can't tell. I'd appreciate it if you would stay inside the hotel . . .'

'After last night wild horses wouldn't drag me out . . .'

'You wanted to see me, Bruno?'

Kobler stood up behind his desk and closed the file he had been checking, the file on Jesse Kennedy. He walked round the desk and hesitated, unsure of his employer's reaction.

'If something is worrying you, Bruno, tell me. So far I have found your instinct for problems infallible. Do we have a problem?'

'It's Willy Schaub, the head porter. I saw him carrying on a long conversation with Dr Novak before he went off duty. And Schaub is greedy for money,' added Kobler who was paid an enormous salary.

'So?'

'It's Schaub's day off. He lives in the Matte district in Berne. I really think it might be worth checking him out.'

'Do it,' said the Professor.

Lee Foley's plans for a quiet afternoon inside the hotel were changed by the phone call. Wasting no time, he put on his jeans and windcheater and left the hotel, carrying the holdall in his right hand.

Like Newman, he had also realized that the way to leave unseen was by descending in the lift to the lowest level, walking past the *garderobe* and emerging by the exit from the coffee shop. He crossed the road, went inside the café facing the Bellevue and ordered coffee. He was careful to pay as soon as the beverage was served. The Porsche was parked round the corner so there was nothing more he could do. Except to sip at his coffee and wait – and watch.

Newman drove a long way round to reach Gerberngasse 498, the home of Willy Schaub. Novak had made the appointment for three in the afternoon so he left the Bellevue in the Citroen half an hour earlier.

One of the great advantages of Berne, he reflected, was that it was not too difficult to throw off a tail. The place was such an intricate network of streets – and with a little audacious driving the trams could be exploited.

At 2.50 p.m. he was driving along the Aarstrasse with the river on his right. He drove on past the sluices into the Schifflaube which brought him deep into Matte where everything was centuries-old. Continuing on into the Gerberngasse, he slowed down as he approached the Nydegg bridge and slid into an empty parking slot.

On both sides of the street ancient houses formed a continuous wall, a huddle of misshapen edifices – several storeys high – which protruded at intervals. The street was deserted in mid-afternoon and the mist, which had withdrawn earlier, was coming back. It was very silent in the canyon and Willy Schaub's place was on the left, overshadowed by the bridge high up. 2.55 p.m. Newman peered up a covered wooden flight of steps which ran up to the bridge alongside it and went back to Schaub's house. He pressed the bell alongside Schaub's name and wriggled his shoulders. He was still very much aware of the automatic nestling inside the holster under his left armpit.

A short barrel-shaped man, late middle-aged and holding a bottle of beer in his left hand which, Newman reflected, explained his large belly, opened the creaking door and stared suspiciously at his visitor. Wisps of white hair stuck out from his turnip-like head and his only small feature was the wary eyes peering at Newman.

'Willy Schaub?'

'Who wants to know?' the man asked truculently in German.

'Robert Newman. You're expecting me. Three o'clock . . .'

'Got some identification?'

Newman sighed audibly. 'It might not be too bright keeping me out here on view, you know.' He produced his passport opening it at the page which showed his photograph, closing it again and holding up the cover which bore his name.

'You'd better come inside, I suppose.'

The interior was gloomy and strangely constructed, stepped up on different levels because it climbed the steep hillside on which it was built. Newman followed the wheezing barrel up three twisting staircases and the place had a musty smell. He wondered whether Schaub lived on his own and they entered a weird, box-like room with the far wall occupied almost entirely by a grimy window broken up into large panes of glass. A decrepit roller blind ran across the top of the window.

'We'll sit here and talk,' Schaub announced. 'Beer?'

'Not just now, thank you,' Newman replied, noticing the grubby glass on the table.

It was only when he walked over to the window and gazed up the slope of terraced garden that he realized he was inside one of the old houses he had looked down on with Nancy the previous Thursday when he had walked her to the Nydegg bridge and told her this was the Matte district. When he turned round Schaub was seated at the table in the middle of the room, guzzling beer from the upturned bottle. He reached up and pulled the roller blind down to cover the upper half of the window.

'What you do that for?' Schaub demanded. 'I like to look at the view . . .'

'This room is very exposed.' Newman took a folded five-hundred-franc note from his pocket and placed it on the table. 'That's for answering questions about the Berne Clinic. You've worked there long enough – you have to know just about everything that goes on there . . .'

'Novak said you'd pay more . . .'

Newman produced a second five-hundred-franc

note and sat down alongside Schaub, facing the window. The porter was wearing a baggy pair of stained corduroy trousers, an open-necked shirt and shoes which hadn't seen polish in months. He shook his head at the second note.

'More . . .'

'This is the lot. No more haggling . . .' Newman produced a third note and placed it with the others. 'What goes on inside that laboratory for starters . . .'

'More . . .'

'Forget it!' Newman reached slowly for the notes but Schaub beat him to it, grabbing all three in one scoop and thrusting them inside his trouser pocket. 'All right, answer the question . . .'

'Never been inside the lab . . .'

The bullet shattered a pane in the window and blew the beer bottle Schaub had left on the table into small pieces. Newman put his hand against Schaub's shoulder and shoved the porter's considerable weight off the chair, toppling him onto the wooden planks of the uneven floor.

'Keep down, you fat slob, or they'll kill you!' he yelled.

Newman had dropped to the floor as he shouted. His shout synchronized with the second bullet which shattered two more panes and thudded into the rear wall. Newman could never recall how the automatic found its way into his right hand but he realized he was holding it as he scrambled low down across the floor to the window – just in time to see the muzzle of a rifle disappearing over the top of the wall on the street leading to the bridge.

'Get behind that cupboard! Stay behind it! I'll be back in a minute . . .'

He rushed, stumbled, half-fell down the bloody staircases, threw open the front door, the automatic inside his pocket now. Running along the empty street, he turned up the covered steps leading to the bridge. There were a hell of a lot of steps, treads worn in the centre by the feet of ages. Why do people always walk straight up the middle? The useless question flashed through his mind as, panting, he reached the top and came out on to the street.

He glanced in both directions. Nothing. Not even a pedestrian. He walked a few paces towards the centre of Berne, then scooped up off the pavement an ejected cartridge which he pocketed. No sign of the other one. The killer must have collected one and departed in a hurry.

Newman leaned over the wall at the point where the cartridge had fallen and stared down direct into Schaub's living-room. If he hadn't lowered the blind the porter would now be a bloated corpse. He looked towards the city centre again and saw a man standing outside a shop who was watching him.

'Thought I heard something,' Newman remarked in German as he joined the portly man who wore no overcoat.

'Sounded like a shot, two shots . . .'

'Or a couple of backfires.' Newman smiled. 'I

427

arranged to meet a girl at the top of the staircase. A brunette – a slim girl in a pant suit, maybe wearing a windcheater. I wondered whether you'd seen her?'

'That description fits half the girls in Berne. I only came out to check this window I'm dressing. No, I haven't seen your girl. All I saw after the backfires was the red car . . .'

'Red? What make? A Porsche? A Mercedes?'

'Couldn't say – I just saw the flash of red as it roared out of sight across the bridge. Exceeding the speed limit, too . . .'

Returning to the house, Newman found Schaub still crouched behind the cupboard, a shivering jelly of a man. He looked up, his beady little eyes terrified.

'Have they gone?'

'Yes. I'll give you two minutes to pack a small bag – just your pyjamas and shaving kit. I'm taking you where no one will dream of looking for you. Hurry it up . . .'

'But my job at the Clinic . . .'

Newman looked at him with a stare of sheer amazement. 'I thought you'd have grasped it by now. The people at your Clinic are out to kill you . . .'

Newman drove the Citroen up to Schaub's front door and the porter did what he had been told to do. Running in a crouch, he dived inside the rear of the car through the door Newman had opened, hauled the door shut and pressed his bulk close to the floor.

To all outward appearances the Citroen was occupied only by the driver.

In the centre of Berne Leupin, behind the wheel of a Fiat, a car Newman had not seen in the Juras, followed one car behind the Citroen. Marbot sat alongside him.

'I wish we could have got closer to that house in Gerberngasse,' Leupin remarked.

'Then he would have spotted us. We'll have to find out who lives there,' Marbot replied. 'Beck will want to know that – but first let's find out where Newman is going. He seems to be leading us round the houses . . .'

'My thought, too . . .'

Newman glanced in his rear-view mirror again. The Fiat was still there. He timed it carefully, slowing down as he came up to the intersection. The tram which had stopped in the main street to his right began to move forward again. Newman accelerated, sweeping forward and missing the nose of the on-coming tram by inches. The tram made a rude noise. Behind him Leupin jammed on the brakes.

'The clever bastard! We've lost him . . .'

Five minutes later Newman led Schaub inside Blanche's flat and showed him how to operate the special security lock. He also gave the porter a lecture on keeping the place clean, although to be fair, despite his clothes, Schaub had the appearance of a man who bathed regularly and his jowly chin was well-shaven.

'Now,' Newman said, 'you stay here until I come

for you. No answering the door or the phone. No calls to anyone – it could be the last call you ever made. There's food in the fridge – to go on living, stay here. And I have fifteen minutes before I must go. For starters, what goes on inside that laboratory? Talk . . .'

Schaub talked.

Chapter Thirty-Two

Nancy took trouble over her battle gear for the Medical Congress reception. Coming out of the bathroom, swearing at having to wear a dinner jacket, Newman stopped and stared. She was clad in a long, form-fitting dress of red taffeta. Round her slim neck glittered a pearl choker.

'Well, will I do?' she enquired. 'I'm out to kill the competition . . .'

'You'll slay them. You look terrific. And isn't that the outfit you were wearing that first night we met in London – when by chance I was also at Bewick's?'

'By chance?' She was amused. 'Half London knew you took your latest fling to that place. It's seven – shouldn't we be getting downstairs? I *am* completely ready and rearin' to go.'

'Give me a minute to fix this bloody tie. You're nervous, aren't you? I can tell.'

'So are a lot of doctors before a tricky case – if they're not they're probably no good. But I can tell you one thing, Bob. When I walk into that reception I'll go cold as ice. I don't care how much clout Grange carries – he's going to hear from me . . .'

431

'Pioneer stock,' Newman joked as he finished fixing the tie. 'There's still some of it left in Arizona. I'm ready. Are you?'

She thumped his arm and they made their way to the bank of lifts. The celebration was being held in the large reception room between the lobby and the terrace restaurant. The floor was covered with priceless carpets, including one huge Persian hunting carpet. A large buffet table had been furnished with champagne glasses and a selection of food. There were a lot of people there already. Newman held Nancy back by the arm.

'Let's just see who is here and where they are. Tonight could be very decisive . . .'

Blanche Signer was talking to Beck. She wore an emerald green dress with a mandarin collar which showed off her superb figure to full advantage. Her small feet were sheathed in gold shoes.

'Your next conquest?' Nancy enquired.

'I was wondering what Beck is doing here . . .'

In a chair offside with his back to the wall sat Lee Foley, holding his glass as his cold eyes studied each person in the room. Tweed, looking uncomfortable in his dinner jacket, sat near Foley, watching the room with no particular expression.

'I think that must be Grange over there, holding court,' Nancy whispered.

At the back of the room, surrounded by half-a-dozen men, a tall, very heavily-built man wearing tinted glasses was talking while others listened. His left hand was close to his side, the fingers stretched downwards while his right hand held a glass. There was a gap in the crowd and Newman had a good view of him. A large head, his complexion pale, his lips appeared hardly to move as he spoke. The feature about him which intrigued Newman was his sheer immobility.

'Is that Professor Grange over there in the corner?' Nancy asked a passing waiter with a tray of glasses.

'Yes, it is, madame. May I offer you champagne?'

They both took a glass for appearance's sake. Newman sipped at his champagne, listening to the babble of voices, the clink of glasses. Another large man brushed past him without apology and made his way, very erect and confident, over to join Grange's group. Victor Signer had arrived.

'I can't see Kobler,' Newman whispered. 'That worries me . . .'

'Someone has to mind the store back at the Clinic, I suppose . . .'

'You're probably right. Let's circulate – horrible word. When are you going to challenge Grange . . .'

'Bob!' She grabbed his arm. 'Wait! Look at that . . .'

Newman was looking at the weird incident. Grange had just greeted Signer when a waiter tipped a full glass of champagne off his tray. The liquid spilt down the lower half of Grange's dinner jacket and the upper half of his trousers. The waiter, obviously appalled, took the napkin folded over his sleeve, ran to the buffet, dipped it in a jug of water, returned to Grange and began to sponge the damp material.

The uncanny aspect of the incident was that as the waiter sponged and dabbed at the damp cloth Grange remained totally motionless, his left arm still close to his side, his large figure more Buddha-like than ever as he listened to Signer, ignoring the waiter as though nothing had happened. It was abnormal, unnatural. Newman stared incredulously as Nancy spoke in a low, tense tone.

'My God! No sane man has that amount of self-control. I think he's unbalanced – and I've had psychiatric training . . .'

It was the first doubt raised in Newman's mind as to Professor Grange's *sanity*.

Chapter Thirty-Three

Jesse Kennedy opened his eyes and blinked. What the hell was going on? He was lying full-length on a trolley which was being wheeled somewhere. He couldn't see properly – a mask of some sort had been placed over his head and face. He was gazing through eyepieces up at a white sheet pulled over the mask thing. The trolley was moving downhill now.

He tried to move his hands and realized both were strapped down by the wrists. He attempted to shift the position of his legs and found they too were strapped down round the ankles. He was completely immobilized. What was happening to him?

Then he recalled his last memory. They had injected him with a sedative. Not Novak. That bitch, Astrid, had done the job. He fought down a feeling of panic, of claustrophobia, and began to flex his fingers to get some strength back into them. The same with his feet – but cautiously. He sensed that the orderlies pushing the trolley, which was now tilted at an angle as it moved down a steep slope, must not know he was preparing himself for escape.

The sound of hydraulically-operated doors closing.

The angle of the decline increased. He blinked again. It was more difficult to see even the sheet: the eye-pieces were steaming up. He was suddenly wide awake and became aware of other sensations and sounds. The squeak of the trolley's wheels, the dryness in his throat, the circulation returning to his arms and legs. Another door opened and they moved on to a level surface. Weird, animal-like sounds – was he going out of his mind? He closed his eyes when the trolley stopped moving.

The sheet was whipped off him. There should be voices, the voices of the orderlies. Why weren't they talking to each other? The absence of voices got on his nerves, was frightening – together with the continuous animal-like gibbering. It recalled monkeys chattering inside cages in a zoo. Ridiculous . . .

They were removing the straps now. One near the head of the trolley taking off the straps binding his wrists, the other unfastening the ankle straps. Then he was free. He remained inert, eyes closed. Hands grasped both his forearms, jerked him upright. In a sitting position he was swivelled round until his legs dangled over the edge of the trolley. He let his head flop, still keeping his eyes shut. Holding him by both arms, they hauled him off the trolley and held him upright. They shook him roughly. He opened his eyes and gasped in horror.

He was wearing a heavy dressing gown over his pyjamas, the cord round his waist tied firmly. He was inside the laboratory, he was convinced of it. It was colder. The steam cleared completely from the eye-pieces. Plastic green curtains were closed over long narrow windows. The huge room was filled with large benches. The tops of the benches were crowded with cages – wire cages. Inside the cages, which varied in size, were the animals he had heard. It was a nightmare.

The two orderlies wore gas masks. Soulless eyes stared at him. From their height, their build, he guessed they were the two men he had heard called Graf and Munz. A third man stood further back, also wearing a mask, pacing among the cages. His way of moving told Jesse this was Bruno Kobler. Jesse pretended to sway unsteadily on his feet as Munz and Graf approached him.

A variety of animals occupied the cages: mice, rats and a lot of chimpanzees which chattered incessantly, their faces grinning hideously at him seen through the Plexiglas of the eyepieces. This section of the laboratory was dimly lit by low-power neon strips which cast an eerie light over the horrific scene.

Still swaying, stooping, Jesse noticed a giant door which was open, the door to the *atombunker*. A fourth man appeared from inside, a man carrying a metal cylinder in each hand, cylinders which reminded Jesse of mortar bombs he had once seen in a war film. Graf took hold of the side of Jesse's mask and eased it upwards so he could speak.

'This is the final stage of treatment, a revolutionary technique invented by Professor Grange. It may cure you – but you must follow instructions. When we take you outside you run *down* the slope – *down*. I will point the way . . .'

Could the chimpanzees sense that something evil was about to be perpetrated, Jesse wondered. They were going wild, their chattering increasing in volume as they scrambled up and down inside their cages, clutching at the wires, staring at Jesse as the two men grasped him firmly by both arms and led him to a door Kobler had opened. Icy cold night air flooded into the laboratory and Jesse shivered. They had slipped walking shoes on to his feet, his own shoes, while he had lain unconscious.

He dragged his feet, slumped, a dead weight between the two masked men. They went outside into the bitter night. Jesse shook his head slowly, glancing all round. On top of a small rocky hill men in uniform crouched round a squat barrel like a piece of sawn-off drainpipe, a barrel aimed at a trajectory across a declining slope. A mortar. Jesse again recognized the weapon from a war film. And Christ! It was manned by men in uniform, army uniform. Grange was a puppet of the Swiss Army . . .

'You run *down* that slope,' Munz yelled in his ear. 'Go!'

They released his arms and Jesse stood swaying. Beside the mortar was a neat pile of bombs, bombs like those carried by the man who had emerged from the *atombunker*. Behind the mortar a windsock billowed from a small mast, a windsock like those seen on small airstrips. The windsock was whipping parallel to the ground showing the direction the wind was blowing. Down the slope. *Away from* the mortar position.

Jesse staggered towards the edge of the slope. Masked figures like robots watched him. One man held a bomb over the mouth of the mortar. Ready to open fire as the target moved on to the range. The target. Himself . . .

Bastards! The adrenalin was flowing fast through Jesse. He paused at the edge of the slope and stared down it to check for obstacles, to accustom his eyes to the darkness. The slope was blind territory, could not be seen from the road, was concealed under a fold in the ground. They were waiting for him now. He thought he heard Munz shout again. He took a step forward, stumbled like a man on the verge of collapse. They couldn't fire their infernal machine yet. Suddenly he took off, running like mad.

He caught them off balance. As he ran with long strides, stretching his legs, increasing speed, he heard the thump of a bomb exploding *behind* him. A long way off the clouds parted briefly and he caught a glimpse of a huge mountain, a flat-topped butte, like the buttes of Utah. He was heading for the distant road. That butte was the Stockhorn. He had watched it when they had let him sit for brief periods inside the enclosed verandah.

Despite his age he was a virile man, strong from so many hours of riding in the saddle. His legs were gaining power, flexibility. He paced himself like a professional runner, knowing he would cover the ground faster that way. He wished Nancy could see him – he was giving the swine one hell of a surprise. He heard a thud. The ground quavered under his feet. Closer, that one.

He made no attempt to tear off the mask. He could feel the tightness of the straps round his neck, over his head. Stopping to attempt that would be fatal. And they had made another mistake. By tying the cord tightly round his waist they had obviated the danger that he might be slowed down by the flapping of the dressing gown. He ran on.

The bomb landed ten feet in front of him. It burst. A cloud of mist-like vapour drifted across his face as he ran through it. Too late to run round it. He began coughing, choking. Another bomb landed ahead of him, another cloud spread. He was choking horribly, his eyes trying to force themselves through the Plexiglas. He reached out with both hands and crashed to the ground. His gnarled hands scrabbled, twitched once more and then he lay still.

Five minutes later the stretcher bearers took him away.

Chapter Thirty-Four

By 7.30 p.m. there was a mellow, relaxed atmosphere at the reception. Over a hundred people were present and the room was crowded, shoulder to shoulder. With Newman following her, Nancy threaded her way through the mob to where Professor Grange stood in deep conversation with Victor Signer. She walked straight up to Grange.

'I'm Dr Nancy Kennedy. My grandfather is a patient at the Berne Clinic . . .'

'If you care to make an appointment, my dear,' the soft voice intoned. Blank eyes stared down at her from behind the tinted glasses. 'This is hardly the moment . . .'

'And this is an intrusion on a private conversation,' Victor Signer informed her in a tone which suggested women were an inferior species.

'Really?' Nancy turned on him, raising her voice so that people nearby stopped talking to listen, which made their conversation carry an even greater distance. 'Maybe you would like to talk about the convenient execution of Manfred Seidler up in the Juras last night? After all, Colonel, you were there.

Alternatively, perhaps you could kindly shut up while I talk to Professor Grange . . .'

'Gross impertinence . . .' Signer began.

'Watch it,' Newman warned. 'Remember me? Let her talk.'

'Your suggested appointment is not helpful,' Nancy continued in the same clear, carrying voice, staring straight at the tinted glasses. 'You hide behind Bruno Kobler at the Clinic. You are never available. Just exactly what is it you fear, Professor?'

An expression of fury flickered behind the glasses. The hand holding the champagne glass shook. Grange tightened his pouched lips, struggling for control while Nancy waited. The silence was spreading right across the room as people realized something unusual was happening: a woman was confronting the eminent Professor Armand Grange.

'I fear nothing,' he said eventually. 'What exactly is it you want, Dr Kennedy?'

'Since I have no confidence in your Clinic and the secretive way it is run, I wish to transfer my grandfather, Jesse, to a clinic near Montreux. I wish to arrange this transfer within the next twenty-four hours. That is what I want, what I am going to get. You have no objection, I assume?'

'You question my competence?'

Nancy sidestepped the trap. 'Who was mentioning your competence – except yourself?' Nancy's voice rose and now every person in the room could hear her loud and clear. 'Are you saying it is against the law – or even medical etiquette – in this country to ask for a second opinion?'

Possibly for the first time in his life – and in public – the head of the Berne Clinic was checkmated. Newman could see it in the rigid way he held himself. There were even beads of moisture on his high-domed forehead and the tinted glasses stared round at the silent assembly which stood gazing at him.

'Of course,' Grange replied eventually, 'I agree to your request. May I, with the greatest possible courtesy, remind you that we are here to enjoy ourselves tonight?'

'Then start enjoying yourself, Professor . . .'

On this exit line Nancy turned and made her way between the crowd which parted to let her through. Watched by Grange and Signer she went straight up to Beck and started talking to the police chief, giving the impression she was seeking further backing for the decision she had prised out of the Professor. Newman seized his opportunity, guessing that Grange would not welcome a fresh public row.

'I'm glad to meet you at last.' He smiled amiably without offering to shake hands. 'I'm writing a series of articles on Swiss industry and I understand you have at Horgen one of the most advanced factories in the world for the production of commercial gases?'

'That is so, Mr Newman . . .' Grange seemed relieved at the change of subject, by the prospect of

443

conversing with someone in normal tones. 'Horgen is totally automated, the only type of plant in that field in the whole world . . .'

'Except that, naturally, the containers are supplied from outside . . .'

'But they are not, Mr Newman. We manufacture our own cylinders.'

'Some photographs would help . . .'

'I will send some to you here by special courier. It will be a pleasure . . .'

'Thank you so much. And now I had better . . . circulate.'

Newman smiled and withdrew. He joined Nancy who was still chatting with Beck. The police chief looked quizzically at Newman and then glanced across the room to where Signer was talking rapidly to Grange.

'You had a pleasant conversation?' he enquired.

'Grange just made one of his rare – and possibly fatal – mistakes. He gave me the last piece of information I was seeking . . .'

'You know Dr Novak has arrived?' Nancy said to Newman as soon as they were alone. 'I think he tanked up in the bar before he decided to join us . . .'

She stopped speaking as a hush fell on the guests. The silence was so pronounced that Newman turned towards the entrance to see what had caused every head to turn in that direction. A short man with a large head and a wide mouth, smoking a cigar, stood surveying the assembly.

'My God!' he heard someone behind him say in French. 'Dr Max Nagel has arrived. Now we'll see some real fireworks.'

Nagel, whose dinner jacket emphasized the great width of his shoulders, carried two large envelopes tucked under his arm. He dipped his head, acknowledging a waiter and taking a glass of champagne from the proffered tray, then walked across the room slowly, his mouth tightly clamped on the cigar.

There was a feeling of tension, hardly anyone was talking as Grange and Signer watched him coming. Nagel paused, thanked another waiter who held a tray with an ash-tray for him. He carefully dropped the ash from his cigar, increasing the tension. The man was a superb actor, Newman reflected. He held the entire gathering in the palm of his large hand.

'Good evening, Grange. Colonel Signer. I have something for you both . . .'

'This is a medical reception,' Grange said coldly. 'I was not aware you had joined the profession . . .'

'Signer is a doctor?' Nagel's voice was a rumbling growl.

Newman glanced over his shoulder. Signer had switched his gaze to someone behind him. Blanche was watching the scene with a frown. Not Blanche. Lee Foley, one of the few men present not in evening dress, who was wearing a dark blue business suit with matching tie, a cream shirt and gold links fastening his cuffs, was now standing, staring at Signer. Close to him stood the small Englishman, Tweed, who was gazing intently through his spectacles. Newman had the impression of a stage manager studying the actors performing in a play he had rehearsed. Newman heard the growl continuing and faced the other way.

'I think we're near the end of the line,' Nagel pronounced. 'It has taken two months for the most brilliant accountants to trace the movement of two hundred million francs to its ultimate destination. A copy of the report for you, Professor Grange, one for you, Colonel Signer. *Terminal* is terminated . . .'

'What is this to do with me?' Signer asked with a sneer as he took the sheaf of stapled papers from the envelope and gave them a mere glance.

'They are photocopies,' Nagel rumbled on, 'the original is in my vault. And I expect you're capable of recognizing your own signature, Colonel. It appears three times on those documents. And you might care to know, Grange, I have called a meeting of bankers to take place in Zurich. We will travel to meet you from Basle. The main item on the agenda? Those complex transactions. I bid you good night. Enjoy your medical ruminations, gentlemen . . .'

Newman turned round again as the banker left, smoking his cigar. He saw Dr Novak leaning up against a wall, holding a glass at a precarious angle. Novak was watching the drama like a man hypnotized. It seemed a good moment to persuade the

American to fall in with his plans. He excused himself and the buzz of many voices talking started up as Nagel let himself out through the revolving doors and climbed into the rear of a waiting limousine.

'Novak,' Newman said, 'they're all watching Grange and Signer. Go to the lift – I'll join you there in a second. We have to talk. Don't argue – the whole thing is collapsing and they'll be looking for scapegoats. You could fit the part beautifully. And dump that glass on the table . . .'

He walked out into the main hall, asked the concierge to have two pots of black coffee sent up to his room, and went along to the lift where Novak was waiting.

'Novak, tomorrow night I'm going to break in to the Berne Clinic and you're going to help me . . .'

'You crazy, Newman?'

The American was sagged on the bed in Room 428, his shirt collar open at the neck, his tie loose. He also wore a business suit and Newman had emptied one jug of black coffee inside him. Novak was sober, reasonably so.

'You saw Lee Foley tonight at the reception?' Newman asked. 'One word from me and he'll put in motion the revoking of your passport. You have access to those computer key cards which open the outer doors. I'm going inside that laboratory . . .'

'Those keys I don't have . . .'

'But I do. I got them off Willy Schaub this afternoon – they're so important he carries them with him everywhere. He talked, Novak. And he won't be coming back to the Clinic. I imagine Sunday is quiet at the Clinic?'

'Yes, it is. The only day both Grange and Kobler are away from the place. Grange spends the night at his large house in Elfenau – that's a suburb of Berne. Kobler spends the night with a girl somewhere. But there are a whole posse of guards left . . .'

'So I'll have to evade them. We meet after dark. The only problem I haven't solved is the Dobermans . . .'

'They're keeping them indoors. They don't patrol at the moment – not since that business with Mrs Laird. Grange has said he wants the place to look normal. I go off duty myself Sunday night at nine in the evening.'

'I'll be there before then. About eight o'clock. Just be waiting for me inside that lobby. And Novak, I'd pack a bag and clear out yourself. I've booked a room for you here at the Bellevue. Stay inside it. Use Room Service for food until I arrive back. You'll do what I'm telling you?'

'I want out. I'll do it. It sounded downstairs like Nagel is going to blow the whole thing wide open . . .'

Newman escorted him to the door. 'If you think of changing your mind, just say two words to yourself. Lee Foley.'

He was closing the door when someone pushed

against it from the outside. He eased it open a few inches, then opened it wide. Blanche walked into the room carrying an envelope similar to those Nagel had handed to Grange and Signer. She pirouetted in the middle of the bedroom.

'Like my dress, Bob? If you come closer you'll be able to appreciate my perfume . . .'

'You've the nerve of the devil. Nancy could arrive at any moment . . .'

'When I slipped up to my room and then along here she was deeply involved in conversation with a doctor from Phoenix . . .'

'Blanche, I think your dress is out of this world, to say nothing of what's inside it. By the way, how did you manage to arrive just after Novak left?'

'By waiting on one of those seats in the corridor. Bob, I don't like the look in your eye, the set of your mouth. You aren't planning on doing something foolish, I hope? Watch your answer – I know you . . .'

'I have no intention of bedding you here . . .'

'That's not what I meant.' She held out the envelope. 'I was asked to give this to you by Mr X. No probing trying to get his identity out of me. Maybe I had letter leave now.'

Newman slipped the envelope inside a drawer. 'Your stepfather is at the reception. Have you talked to him?'

'You must be joking. He walked straight past me as though I didn't exist. I was rather glad. I took a good long look at him and I didn't like what I saw.

He's grown even harder. I'll go now. ' She kissed him full on the mouth, then gave him a tissue from her handbag. 'You're wearing the wrong shade of lipstick. Bob, for God's sake don't do anything I would worry about. Promise?'

'I'll bear your affectionate request in mind . . .'

It was midnight when the unmarked van carrying Beck's film unit arrived at the forest above the Berne Clinic. Leupin was behind the wheel with Marbot alongside him. In the back of the van was the cine camera technician, Rolf Fischer, and his equipment.

Leupin stopped the van and then backed it off the snowbound road into a clearing under the trees. He had no way of knowing he was choosing the same vantage point Lee Foley had selected to observe the Clinic on the previous Tuesday. Leupin, having tested the firmness of the ground, now swung the vehicle through a hundred and eighty degrees so the rear of the van faced the panoramic view of the Clinic and its grounds.

In each rear door of the van was a round window of frosted glass, a hinged window which could be opened so Fischer's telephoto lens could be aimed at any required area of the Clinic, a lens which could see what was happening as clearly in the darkness as in broad daylight. Leupin got out, treading carefully in the snow, and made his way to the back where Fischer had already opened one of the windows.

'This suit you?' Leupin called out.

'Perfect. I can see everything – the Clinic, the laboratory, the grounds, even that deep slope near the lab.'

'And they won't see us in the daytime – not a white van against the snow. Just a moment, something's moving beyond the Clinic . . .'

Leupin raised the night-glasses looped round his neck and focused them on the drive curving down to the gatehouse. A black, six-seater Mercedes was driving away from the Clinic. Leupin lowered his glasses, calling out again to Fischer.

'That's funny. I'm sure that car is Grange's. He's not supposed to be here tonight . . .'

It was Beck who had vetoed the suggestion that they should arrive earlier. He was determined the van should not be spotted. And, as he had remarked, nothing would happen that evening with Grange at the reception and later spending the night at Elfenau.

Chapter Thirty-Five

Sunday, 19 February

The call came late in the morning just after Newman and Nancy had got out of bed. They had slept in late and Nancy drew back the curtains as Newman reached for his wristwatch on the bedside table. 11.45 a.m. He threw back the bed-clothes and hoped no one would make a loud noise.

'Bob! Just come and look at this . . .'

He blinked at the unusually strong light. The sun was shining brilliantly. Slipping into his dressing-gown, he yawned and joined Nancy at the window. No more mist. No traffic on the Sunday roads. Nancy gripped him by the arm and pointed to the left.

'Isn't it just magnificent? And we might never have seen it if the weather hadn't cleared.'

In the near distance – or so it seemed – they were gazing at the vast panorama of the Bernese Oberland range, a wall of mighty snowbound peaks silhouetted against a background of an azure sky. Newman wrapped an arm round her waist, squeezing her. The long night's sleep, the dream-like view, had relaxed her.

'I think that big job is the Jungfrau,' he commented. 'It's the right shape . . .'

'Isn't it just wonderful? We can have breakfast up here, can't we?'

'Probably the only way we'll get some at this hour . . .'

That was when the phone started ringing. Nancy danced to the phone, picked up the receiver and announced herself in a lilting tone.

Newman realized something was very wrong from the change in her expression, in her tone of voice, in the way the conversation turned. She was standing very erect now, her complexion drained of all its natural colour and she began to argue, her voice harsh and aggressive.

'You can't do that! I forbid it! You bastard! I'll call you a bastard any time I want to – because that's what you are . . . I don't believe any of it . . . I'm going to raise bloody hell! Don't interrupt . . . You murdering swine . . .' Her voice suddenly went strangely quiet. 'You'll pay for this – that I promise you . . .'

'Get them to hold on,' Newman called out. 'Tell me what it's about. I'll talk to them . . .'

She had slammed down the receiver. She turned to look at Newman and he stared back at her. Her face had closed up. She began to walk slowly round the room, sucking her thumb, which Newman guessed was reversion to a childhood habit.

'Tell me,' he said quietly.

She went into the bathroom and closed the door.

He tore off his night clothes, slipped into vest and pants and pulled on a pair of slacks, his shirt and shoes. At that stage she emerged from the bathroom where he had heard the tap running. She had washed and applied her makeup. She moved like a sleepwalker.

'Do as I tell you,' he snapped. 'Sit down in that chair. Talk.'

'They've killed Jesse . . .' She spoke in a flat monotone. 'That was Kobler. He said Jesse had had a heart attack – that he died almost immediately. They've already cremated him . . .'

'They can't do that. Who signed the death certificate? Did Kobler say?'

'Yes, he said that Grange signed the certificate. He said they have a sworn document signed by Jesse requesting cremation . . .'

'They can't get away with that. It's too quick. Christ, this is Sunday . . .'

'They covered themselves on that one, too. Kobler said Grange found Jesse was infected with cholera. That could justify immediate cremation. I think it could. I'm not familiar with Swiss law . . .'

She was talking like the playback of a slow-running tape-recorder. She sat quite still, her hands slack in her lap as she looked up and Newman was startled by the coldness in her eyes.

'We'll get them to send up some coffee . . .'

'That would be nice. Just coffee, no food. You order for yourself. You must be hungry . . .' She waited while he gave Room Service the order and then asked the question. 'Bob – can you tell me something? Is Signer really mixed up in this Terminal thing Dr Nagel mentioned last night?'

'Yes, I'm sure now. I'll show you something while we're waiting for the coffee.' He was glad to get her mind moving on another track – any other track. He produced the report Blanche had brought him. She remarked wasn't that what he had been reading when she'd fallen asleep? He said it was and showed her three pages where he had turned down the corners.

'His signature confirming the transfer of these huge sums of money is clear enough. Victor Signer. He's president of the Zurcher Kredit Bank, the outfit which dominates the Gold Club which backs Grange. After breakfast,' he went on, 'I suggest we go and see Beck if he's in his office – which I'm sure he will be. He's practically sleeping on the job . . .'

'So,' she said, ignoring his last suggestion, 'Grange and Signer and Kobler are the mainspring behind the Terminal thing?'

'It's beginning to look very much like that. Did you hear what I said about Beck? That we go and see him after we've eaten?'

'I think I'd like that . . .'

Beck, clean-shaven and spruce, sat behind his desk listening while Nancy repeated the gist of her phone call from Kobler. As she talked he glanced at Newman once or twice, raising an eyebrow to indicate he was disturbed by the calm, detached way she spoke. At the end of her story he used the intercom to call in Gisela and was waiting by the door when she came in.

'Stay with Dr Kennedy until we come back,' he whispered. 'On no account leave her alone – not for a moment. I think she is in a state of severe shock.' He raised his voice. 'Bob, could you come with me, please? There's someone you will want to meet.'

When they were outside in the corridor he closed the door and folded his arms. He pursed his lips as though uncertain how to phrase what he was going to say.

'Ever since you arrived I have sensed you found it difficult to trust anyone – probably for very good reasons. That included myself. We are now going to the radio room. You have met Leupin, you know his voice. Since about midnight I have had a film unit van in position watching the Berne Clinic from the edge of the forest above it. When we reach the radio room you can ask Leupin any question you like – bearing in mind security – including checking his position. Now, let's get this poison of mistrust out of your system. I need all the help I can get . . .'

It took less than five minutes inside the radio room and Newman immediately recognized Leupin's voice. The policeman confirmed that they were in position 'by the forest'. He further mentioned that they had watched 'a certain eminent personage's well-known car leave the place in question about midnight . . .'

And that, thought Newman, unfortunately would fit in with the story that Grange had diagnosed cholera, had signed the death certificate, had been present at the Clinic after leaving the Bellevue reception to carry out these actions. He asked Beck if they could have a few minutes alone where they could talk privately. Beck led him inside an interrogation room and closed the door.

'This tape,' said Newman, placing the spool on a table, 'is the recorded interview I had with Manfred Seidler when he admitted bringing in Soviet gas masks on the instructions of Professor Grange. Nancy will give you a sworn statement confirming she witnessed the interview – but not today, if you don't mind. And this is the film of several shots I took of the gas mask Seidler handed to you when you grabbed his suitcase . . .'

'I am grateful,' Beck replied.

'And this cartridge is from a rifle fired at a certain member of Grange's staff at the Clinic. I'm talking about Willy Schaub, head porter. You'll find him at this address. When you pick him up include a man who speaks good English. Tell him to knock on the door of the first-class flat and call out, "Newman here". He'll tell you a lot. Keep him in a safe – very safe – place. Don't be worried by the name alongside the bell-push, B. Signer. She's Victor Signer's daughter and I don't want her bothered. Signer has no time for her. May I rely on you?'

'For every request, yes.'

'You can bring in Grange now?' Newman asked.

'Not yet. That cholera nonsense is clever. He will have put the Clinic in a state of quarantine . . .'

'So we still haven't got him?'

'Not yet. He is very powerful.'

It was 6 p.m. Soon it would be dark. Blanche sat at a window table in the Bellevue coffee shop, eating a leisurely meal which she had paid for in advance. Earlier, she had watched Newman's parked Citroen from her bedroom window at this side of the hotel. Now she watched it from the table. Her scooter was parked against the wall of the Hertz offices and she was dressed in her riding gear. The wet-look pants, a thick woollen sweater – and her windcheater was thrown over the back of her chair.

Pausing before dessert, she glanced round the empty room and opened her handbag. The hand grenade she had brought from her flat bulged in the side compartment. Strange how she had acquired it – going back to the days when her stepfather had tried to mould her to his will.

He had taken her with him to a grenade practice range and, she had suspected, only his rank had permitted her to accompany him. He had thrown several grenades himself, then asked her to follow his example, watching her for any sign of nerves. That was when she had pocketed this grenade while he watched the previous one explode behind the concrete barrier. She had already escaped being raped in a dark alley by producing the egg-shaped weapon and threatening to blow herself and her attacker to pieces. She zipped up the compartment, looked out at the Citroen again and continued her meal. She was convinced Newman was going to make some reckless move before the evening was out. And to reach the Berne Clinic he had to use that Citroen.

Chapter Thirty-Six

It was that intense dark which only comes on a cold, starlit night when Newman parked the Citroen within inches of the wire fence surrounding the Clinic. Switching off the motor, he got out and his feet ground into crusted snow. This part of the fence was a long way from the gatehouse.

He climbed on to the bonnet, heaved himself up on to the roof of the car, and he was within six inches of the top of the fence. He flexed his legs, crouched down and jumped up and over. He landed the way he had seen paratroopers land, rolling over, and when he stood up his only memento of the leap was a bruised shoulder. He walked briskly across hard snow towards the Clinic entrance at a diagonal angle, his ears attuned for the slightest warning that Dobermans were on the prowl despite Novak's assurance to the contrary.

He reached the entrance without seeing anyone, frozen by the wind blowing from the north. Without hesitation he mounted the steps, opened the first door, strode across the deserted verandah, threw open the inner door and two people turned to stare at him.

Astrid was seated behind the counter. Novak, wearing a business suit ready for departure, was checking a file which lay open on the counter-top. Astrid stood up, astounded, then she recovered her poise and grabbed for the phone. Newman leaned over the counter and smashed his fist against her full, fleshy chin. She reeled over backwards, caught her head against the rear wall and sagged out of sight.

'My God! You could have killed her . . .'

'No such luck. Let's move, Novak. Open that door into the corridor. Come on! Is that your car outside?'

'Yes, I . . .'

'When you've opened the door, get behind the wheel and pretend it's Indianapolis . . .'

Novak produced his card, inserted it inside the slot and the door slid back. Newman snatched the key card out of Novak's hand and walked into the deserted corridor. The door closed behind him. He was wearing a dark padded windcheater and a pair of jeans – clothes he rarely used – and his tough walking shoes were rubber-soled.

The only sound in the eerily silent corridor was the muted hum of the air-conditioning. He walked on rapidly, moving down the slope now. He paused where the corridor turned and the angle of descent increased, peering round the corner. A further stretch of empty corridor illuminated by overhead neon strips until it reached the hydraulically-operated steel door which was closed.

As he walked up to the door he extracted from his

pocket the six key cards Willy Schaub had handed to him. The first three cards he tried didn't work. He inserted the fourth card and there was a sound of whirring machinery as the steel slab elevated. He walked through quickly and again heard the door closing behind him.

This section was different. At intervals in the green walls on both sides were windows. He paused to glance through one and there was something about the surface of the glass which suggested this was one-way glass – you could see outside but no one would be able to look inside from the grounds.

He guessed he was very close to the laboratory – it was probably behind the closed door at the end of the passage. He was looking uphill towards the wall of dark fir forest which overlooked the Clinic. On top of a small mound uniformed figures moved slowly round some device perched on top of the mound. He couldn't see too clearly.

By the side of the door at the end of this passage was a box with a slot exactly like the previous lock. The first card he chose operated the door which slid up, revealing what lay beyond. A dimly-lit chamber, very large and crammed with tables which supported wire cages. Inside these cages were housed animals. The chimpanzees turned round to stare silently at the intruder.

The room was not only occupied by animals. At the rear of the chamber behind the cages stood Professor Armand Grange. Two figures wearing the weird gas masks stepped forward, grabbed Newman by the arms as the door closed. A fourth man stood near Grange. Bruno Kobler. Newman ground his shoe down on the instep of the man on his left who grunted in pain but retained his grip. Kobler walked over, staring at the prisoner, not hurrying, and while the two men held Newman he searched him, running his hands over his padded windcheater, under his armpits and down the sides of his arms and legs.

'He is carrying no weapon,' he reported.

'But why should he carry a weapon, Bruno?' Grange asked as he padded closer. The poor lighting had the effect of blanking out the tinted glasses so he seemed eyeless. 'He is a reporter,' Grange continued. 'He works on the basis that the pen – the typewriter – is mightier than the sword. This may be an occasion when the old adage is proved wrong . . .'

'How the hell did you know I was coming?' Newman enquired. His tone expressed disgust, his expression showed a hint of fear.

'Through the medium of radar, of course! Also we have concealed television cameras sweeping the approaches. The security here has been brought to a fine art, Mr Newman . . .'

'Along with gassing people to test those Soviet masks . . .'

'A well-informed reporter, Bruno,' Grange commented, his tone mocking.

'Except that isn't the real object – it's the *gas* which you're testing, the gas you manufacture at Horgen.

You made a slip when you told me you manufacture your own cylinders at Horgen – you have the facilities to make the bombs which contain the gas you test here. *Tous azimuts*. All-round defence of Switzerland, isn't that it, Professor?'

'Oh dear, he is *too* well-informed, Bruno . . .'

'You *have* developed a new gas, haven't you?' Newman persisted. 'A gas which will penetrate the latest Soviet masks. Hence *tous azimuts*, the new strategy. If the Red Army does come you plan to encircle the whole of Switzerland with this wall of gas they will never get through – alive. But you had to be sure the latest Soviet masks were useless against it – so you used patients to test it . . .'

'But, Mr Newman, these patients are terminal . . .'

'Hence the name of the operation which has puzzled so many people – because the word has different meanings. What kind of gas, Grange? Something developed from Tabun, the gas you grabbed out of Germany when you were a member of the special team sent in at the end of the war?'

'Worse and worse, Bruno. So *very* well-informed. I repeat, the patients are terminal, so what difference does it make? We have a population of millions to defend. It is a question of numbers, Mr Newman. As to the gas, we have come a long way from Tabun. We now have the most advanced form of hydrogen cyanide in the world – and we have found a way to control its volatility. We can distribute belts of the gas as we wish – in the face of an advancing armoured division. They will be dead within thirty seconds, their tanks useless scrap metal. But the gas, Mr Newman, disperses very quickly – swiftly loses its toxicity . . .'

'You think you'll get away with murder?'

'We have triumphed . . .' Grange's voice rose to a pitch of ecstasy. Newman realized finally he was faced by a megalomaniac – Grange was a madman. He went on in the same tone of exhilaration. 'Signer has called a meeting of the General Staff for Wednesday night. The new policy will be adopted – with the aid of what we call the irregulars – those officers who support our determination to defend our country at all costs . . .'

'And Nagel's conference of the bankers?'

'It is scheduled for Thursday morning. The meeting will be cancelled. A matter of military security. And now, since you know it all, we will convince you I am right. You will be our final experiment – a more virile specimen than those who went before you. Bruno! Proceed . . .!'

'You dare not let me see inside the *atombunker* then?'

'Of course you may see. Bring him inside . . .'

Grange led the way, a massive figure in the gloom. Newman estimated the half-open door to the *atombunker* was at least six inches of solid steel. They paused as a man wearing one of the masks emerged. He carried in each hand a small blue cylinder with a flow meter attached to its head. Stencilled along each cylinder were the words *Achtung! Giftgas!* Beware! Poison gas!

Inside the vast windowless bunker piles of the blue cylinders were stacked against a wall. The man who had walked out wore a uniform which Newman briefly mistook for a Swiss Army uniform. Then he realized it was *similar* in appearance – but not the same. It was the outfit of a security unit designed to look superficially like the military version. The Swiss Army was *not* guarding the Clinic. Grange had been diabolically clever – he had given the impression he was being protected by the military.

'The filters on top of the chimneys,' Newman asked Grange as they stood staring round the place. 'Why do you need them?'

'He knows everything, Bruno. The filters, Mr Newman, were designed by my top chemist at Horgen in case of an accident here – in case the gas escaped. It would not do to exterminate a dozen patients wandering round the grounds in summer. Those filters render the gas harmless. On the basis of that design we shall develop a mask to protect ourselves against a change in wind direction in wartime. But the gas comes first. Now, Bruno, time for Mr Newman to leave us . . .'

Bruno Kobler supervised the operation. They held his arms by his sides and Kobler himself fastened the mask over Newman's head and face. He struggled but they held him firmly. Through the Plexiglass eyepieces he saw the tinted glasses of Professor Grange staring at him with no expression at all. It was a scientific experiment he was engaged on.

Kobler led the way out of the *atombunker* across the laboratory chamber to a door one of the other masked figures had opened. Icy air crawled over Newman's hands. The straps round his neck chafed the skin. Kobler paused at the doorway, lifted the mask over one ear and gave instructions.

'You run *down* the slope. It is your only chance of survival. Who knows? You are a fit man – you might just make it to the road. Not that anyone will believe what you have seen here. I will point the way you go . . .'

The two men held Newman in a vice-like grip as Kobler slipped on an overcoat. Then they led him into the night. He looked round quickly through the eyepieces, checking where everyone was positioned. The nearby mound overlooking the downward slope, the mound where the mortar was mounted, a stock of bombs by its side. The men grouped round it – one holding a bomb near the mouth of the barrel. The slope behind them, climbing up towards the forest.

Hannah Stuart and Holly Laird had died running *down* that slope, doubtless hoping to reach the road they would have seen earlier while sitting inside the enclosed verandah – Mrs Laird had even reached the road, but had then died.

Kobler was pointing down the slope. On top of the mound a few yards away half-a-dozen masked figures watched him, watched their target. The two men on either side released him. Kobler gestured impatiently down the slope. Newman flexed his stiff arms, nodded his head to show he understood and walked slowly forward to the edge of where the slope started downhill. Kobler, wearing no mask, retreated inside the laboratory.

Newman flexed each leg, easing the stiffness, then bent down to rub his left ankle. He jerked upright, the automatic Beck had given him, the weapon he had concealed behind his sock, gripped in his right hand. He aimed it at the men grouped round the mortar, firing over their heads.

They scattered, abandoned the mound as Newman ran straight for it, kicking over the mortar barrel, running on *uphill*. The wind blew in his face. He knew they dare not fire the mortar even if they remounted it successfully. The gas would blow back in *their* faces. They could only pursue him up the steep incline on foot. He doubted they would risk the sound of any more shots. But he was handicapped by the bloody mask which was constricting his neck. No time to stop and try to tear it off – they'd be on top of him. God, the ascent was steep, the forest seemed so very far away.

*

Blanche stood on the knoll above the Clinic, the knoll she had used when she had photographed the Clinic and its grounds. She had followed Newman's Citroen on her scooter along the motorway. She had watched through her pair of night-glasses from a distance when he vaulted the fence. She had ridden on to the knoll, the only point from where she might see what was happening.

She had the night-glasses pressed to her eyes now, watching in horror as Newman kicked over something after scattering the men in Swiss uniform. She knew the running figure was Newman – his movements were familiar enough for her to be quite certain.

The swine had recovered from their surprise, men who wore horror film masks, and they were running after Newman, gaining on him as, bunched together, they took the same route up a gulch below where she stood. Her mouth was tight as she bent down to pick up her helmet. Her hair was blowing in her face, confusing her vision. She rammed the helmet over her head. Reaching into her pocket, she brought out an egg-shaped object. The hand grenade.

Blanche removed the glove from her right hand. At the Gstaad finishing school she had been a top-flight player of tennis with a vicious backhand. She hesitated, gauging the distance between Newman, who was slowing down, and his pursuers. Newman reached a point where the defile turned at an angle. He ran round the corner. She took out the pin and counted, her hand held behind her. It was ironic that Victor Signer had furnished her with the opportunity to obtain the grenade.

Her hand came up in a powerful, controlled swing. She lobbed the grenade and held her breath. It landed a few feet in front of the group of men hurrying up the defile, detonated. The lead pursuer threw up both arms in a wild gesture and fell. The men behind sagged to the ground, some of them crawling on all fours before they, too, collapsed.

Newman heard the explosion. It gave him the strength for one final burst up to the end of the defile – he thought they were using grenades to stop him. He came out on top of the hill and the wire fence – with the road beyond in front of the forest – was a few yards away.

To his right there was a gate in the fence. He found it was padlocked when he reached it. Hauling out the automatic from his pocket, he shot off the padlock, pulled the gate open and staggered along the road. He was still wearing the gas mask when Leupin came to meet him.

Chapter Thirty-Seven

Monday, 20 February

Snow came to Berne in the middle of the night. Newman, who had spent half that night with Beck at the Taubenhalde, dragged himself out of bed, grabbed his wristwatch and went over to the window to pull back the curtains. 7.30 a.m. He looked over his shoulder at Nancy who was lying on her back with her eyes open.

'Come and look at this,' he said.

Without a word she got out of bed and joined him, pulling on her dressing gown. For the first time since their arrival it was a white world. Rooftops heavy with snow across the river. The twin headlights of cars crawled along the snowbound Aarstrasse. A tram, its lights blurred, crept over the Kirchenfeldbrucke. Large snowflakes drifted down past their window.

'What will happen to Grange and Signer and Kobler?' she asked. 'You flopped out when you got back from seeing Beck. I guess that experience at the Clinic must have been pretty horrible. I appreciate your calling in here first . . .'

'Beck was vague. They have the film they took

from the van they'd parked in the forest of my being chased. They have the gas mask I was wearing. They have my statement – but I'll be required to stay on for the inquiry . . .'

'Inquiry?'

'The Swiss don't like washing dirty linen in public. What country does? And there's military security involved. They also have the sworn statement of Willy Schaub, the head porter who knows a lot . . .'

'They haven't arrested Grange yet?'

'They have to handle it carefully. They won't want the fact that the most deadly poison gas in the world was being made and tested to hit the world's press if they can avoid it . . .'

'But if Grange is still at the Clinic won't he destroy the evidence – those cylinders you saw in that *atombunker*?'

'Oddly enough, no. He's arrogant enough – mad enough – to feel confident he can bluff his way through. He's proud of the fact that he's produced that gas. These men think they are patriots. And it's complicated by Grange's tactic saying Jesse had suspected cholera. Note the word "suspected". He can always say it was a wrong diagnosis later – meantime he has the place under quarantine. It's a kind of stalemate . . .'

'Jesse raised me.' Her voice was suddenly harsh. 'He was the only father I ever had.' He glanced at her. Her posture was rigid and she stared at the drifting snowflakes as though looking at something way beyond them. 'He deserved a better way to go,' she continued in the same disturbing tone of voice.

'I'm sure they'll eventually get the lot,' he said.

'I'm going to bathe. Order me a full breakfast . . .'

He dressed quickly in a troubled frame of mind. He had a feeling this thing wasn't over yet. When she emerged from the bathroom she was wearing a cashmere sweater and slacks tucked inside short leather boots, the kind of outfit she wore in Arizona. Over breakfast he realized her mood had changed. Her speech was brisk, her chin tilted at an aggressive angle.

'I'm leaving for Tucson on Wednesday,' she announced. 'I shall catch the three o'clock Dan-Air flight to Gatwick, then on to Dallas by American Airlines . . .'

'I told you, I have to stay on for the inquiry . . .'

'I don't like being used, Bob. You've used me from that very first evening we met in London. You needed someone who could get you inside the Berne Clinic. I fitted the role perfectly. My birthday party at Bewick's that night was well-advertised in advance. Enough people knew about it at St Thomas's. And there was that patient they kept under armed guard – men in civilian clothes everyone knew were Secret Service. One of those guards tipped you off about my party. You turn up at the table next to mine. Really it was very neat. I first began to wonder about you in Geneva. You changed, you turned into a hunter. Since then there have been a whole series of odd incidents.

Phone calls you said were wrong numbers. Trips off without me to see people you never told me about when you got back. I don't know who you're working for, but by Christ, I know you've used me. I am right, aren't I?'

'Up to a point, yes . . .'

'Jesus! Why qualify it?'

'Because later I became genuinely very fond of you . . .'

'Shit!'

'If you say so . . .'

'And now I'd like the room to myself for awhile. I have to call Tucson to warn Linda I'm coming home . . .'

'She'll be asleep,' Newman pointed out. 'They're eight hours behind us in Arizona . . .'

'Linda is never in bed before two in the morning – and it's only midnight now in Tucson. So, maybe you could go downstairs and read a paper – or find a girl to screw . . .'

Lee Foley called the Berne Clinic from his room and asked to speak to Dr Bruno Kobler. When Kobler came on the line Foley continued speaking in German, giving his name as Lou Schwarz and explaining that his wife was seriously ill. He asked for details of fees and carried on a conversation for five minutes, studying Kobler's voice, before ending the call.

He then went down to reception for his case, which

he had kept packed – as always – ready for a speedy departure. He paid his bill after questioning the amount they were charging for phone calls, which involved a lengthy conversation. As he left the hotel Leupin, who had been sitting nearby, pretending to read a newspaper, stood up and walked to the Taubenhalde to report on this development to Beck.

Foley next drove the Porsche to the friend he had hired it from and gave him precise instructions. Foley was keeping the Porsche a little longer. At one o'clock the following day the friend must phone the cantonal police headquarters in Berne to report the theft of the Porsche.

He further arranged for the friend to have ready for him a Volvo – any colour except red. He would collect the Volvo the following morning. He paid over a large sum of money in Swiss banknotes and asked permission to use the phone in privacy. As soon as he was alone in the office he called a private airfield near Paris and gave further instructions. He thanked his friend and left.

Climbing behind the wheel of the Porsche, he drove out of Berne and took the motorway north. He was careful to keep inside the speed limit. His next destination was Zurich.

Epitaph

Tuesday, 21 February

At 1 p.m. Victor Signer, wearing his uniform, sat in the back of the Mercedes while his chauffeur drove up to the entrance of the Berne Clinic. He was puzzled by the urgent summons but assumed some crisis had arisen.

Bruno Kobler had phoned him at his office inside the Zurcher Kredit Bank in Zurich. Kobler had sounded agitated. A fresh development had taken place at the Clinic. No, it was not something he could discuss over the phone. Professor Grange wished to see him urgently.

The car swung in a half-circle as it reached the entrance to the Clinic and pulled up. Signer did not bother to wait for the chauffeur to open the door. He was an impatient man who did not stand on ceremony except for the purposes of intimidating someone.

He stood for a moment in the sunshine, straightening his tunic. The first bullet slammed square into the centre of his broad chest. He stood quite still for a fraction of a second as the red patch spread, staining his immaculate uniform. The second bullet whipped his cap off, skimming the top of his head away. He

476

sagged to the ground. The third bullet hammered into his abdomen.

Armand Grange, who had been talking to Astrid, her chin bandaged where Newman had hit her, heard the shots and came out to the top of the steps. He stared at the crumpled form of Signer like a man who cannot credit what lies before him.

The fourth bullet penetrated his neck. As he staggered under the impact blood gushed from an artery. The fifth bullet slammed into the huge body as it sprawled at the foot of the steps. Grange jerked convulsively and then he also lay still.

Bruno Kobler reacted with greater decision. Looking out of his office window at the scene beyond the verandah, he ran to a cupboard, opened it, grabbed his repeater rifle and ran downstairs. Both doors were open and his military training asserted itself. He looked for cover. The parked Mercedes, inside which the chauffeur was crouched behind the wheel, terrified.

Kobler went out through both doors at a rush and dived behind the car. A bullet ricocheted close to his right heel as he crouched at the rear of the vehicle. He peered through the rear window and caught a brief movement at the top of the knoll perched near the forest. The marksman was up there.

As he ducked his head a bullet smashed through the rear window. Kobler recognized this was first-rate shooting. A professional marksman. He poked the barrel of the rifle round the right-hand side of the car and loosed off a shot. There was a puff of dust at the top of the knoll. He had the range.

Put yourself in the other bastard's shoes. He would expect Kobler to appear next on the *left*-hand side of the car. Kobler thrust the barrel close to the right-hand side, moved out to get a clear shot and an express train crashed into his chest, throwing him clear of the car and into the open. The next shot smashed his throat, the final shot shattered what was left of his chest. He lay in a spreading pool of blood and it was very silent in the sunlight.

'Grange, Kobler and Victor Signer were shot dead this morning at the Clinic,' Newman said as he shut the bedroom door and came into the room. 'It's in the stop press in the *Berner Zeitung* . . .'

'I know,' said Nancy, staring out of the window without turning round.

'You can't know – it's not in the paper. Too early. I've just heard from Beck. So how do you know? You had advance knowledge – that's how you know . . .'

'What do you mean?' She had swung round and her expression was bleak. She wore the same outfit as the previous day, her Arizona outfit. Newman recalled some remark he had made that she was the last of the pioneer stock.

'Yesterday you lashed me for using *you*,' he said, walking towards her. 'You omitted to say *you used me* . . .'

'Just what the hell are you talking about?'

'You felt you needed back-up when you came to Switzerland – someone who spoke the languages, who knew people in high places. I qualified. In the beginning you got to know me, used your feminine wiles so I'd make the trip with you . . .'

'I'm glad you said "in the beginning",' she replied quietly. 'Yes, I did feel I needed someone. Then gradually I became very fond of you . . .'

'If that was all, I might accept it. But it wasn't all . . .'

'I don't know what you're talking about,' she flared.

'I'm talking about Lee Foley. You're ruthless. Maybe it's that pioneer stock. You could be right, but I can't take being tricked *twice* over. That first night we had dinner in Geneva I spotted Foley outside the Pavillon. I spotted him again in the next coach on the train from Geneva to Berne. Then I met him in the bar downstairs one evening and he made a rare slip. I referred to the death of Mrs Laird – Foley replied "I know." But Beck kept the news out of the papers. The only people who witnessed Mrs Laird's death were Beck, myself, Lachenal, Dr Kleist later – and *you*. The only possible candidate for passing that information to Foley is yourself . . .'

'You're crazy . . .'

'There's a whole lot more. Foley kept following us – in a red Porsche, for God's sake. He'd never normally use such an easily recognizable car – he used it

479

so you would know he was on the job, to reassure you . . .'

'What job?' she demanded.

'First, you hired him as extra – and very tough – back-up to supplement me. Remember over ten years ago in Tucson they sent a CIA operative to cooperate with Jesse? I think we'll find that operative was Lee Foley. You'd be about seventeen or eighteen then. That was when you first met Foley . . .'

'You're reaching . . .'

'We wondered about Foley for quite awhile – was he ex-CIA, a real detective? I'm sure now he was. I think you phoned him in New York from Tucson – when we decided to come to Berne – and hired him. You phoned him again while we waited at Heathrow – when you went into the West End to shop at Fortnums. How else would he know we'd be at the Hotel des Bergues? Before we left Geneva you rushed out to get some Gucci perfume, and to phone the news to Foley we were leaving. How else would he know we'd be aboard that express?'

'You're even brighter than I thought . . .'

'It doesn't end there. He became protection. He shot those gunmen at Le Pont station. Only someone with Foley's skill with a rifle could gun down both men from a moving car . . .'

'Have you finished?' She was tense. 'I've had enough . . .'

'No! Beck and I puzzled quite a bit over who could afford to hire Foley . . .'

'I could afford him?'

'You could borrow whatever it took from any USA bank on the basis of your four million dollar expectations from Jesse's will. Everyone knew about it. You must have paid him a packet for his final mission . . .'

'Final mission?'

'For shooting down Grange, Signer and Kobler. And Kobler was a marksman – it would take a Foley to pull that off. I gather Beck has a dragnet out for him now . . .'

The phone rang. Nancy moved to reach it but Newman grabbed the instrument first. It was Beck. The time was 5 p.m.

'We've traced his Porsche,' Beck said. 'Left in the car park at Kloten, the airport for Zurich, as you know. He has a first-class reservation on Flight SR 808 out of Zurich for London. I've flooded Kloten with men. Wish me luck . . .'

'Good luck . . .'

And you're going to need it, he thought as he replaced the receiver. He told Nancy who had called, the gist of their brief conversation. Then the phone rang a second time. Newman lifted the receiver, asked who it was and a familiar gravelly voice replied.

'Thought I'd just say goodbye for now, Newman,' Foley opened. 'Save Beck a little time. He found the Porsche? Good. Did he find the Volvo I stole and left at Belp? I had a Cessna waiting for me there. I warned you the body count would go on rising. The finish reminded me of *Hamlet*'s ending – a stage strewn with corpses. Oh, by the way, they're calling my flight for New York. I'm at Paris, Orly. See you around . . .'

The connection broke and Newman replaced the receiver slowly. He looked at Nancy and she stared back at him defiantly, then asked him who had called. He shook his head. 'If I were you, I'd make sure you catch that three o'clock flight from Belp for Gatwick tomorrow. Beck is no fool – but I think he'll hold off for twenty-four hours. I'm going to see him now . . .'

'You blame me, Bob? You'll tell him?'

'I neither condemn nor condone it. I haven't made up my mind. And no, I won't tell Beck. I've had my things moved to another room. Goodbye, Nancy.'

'René Lachenal has shot himself. Placed the barrel of a gun in his mouth and pulled the trigger. He left this note addressed to you, Bob,' said Beck and handed him a sealed envelope. In another chair Tweed sat polishing his glasses.

'Oh, God, no!' Newman sank into a chair alongside Tweed and opened the envelope. The letter was handwritten, concise as you would expect from a man who had written so many military appreciations. 'I really liked René,' Newman said and read.

My dear Robert, I would like you to know I had no inkling of what they were doing at the Berne Clinic. My orders – verbal – were to give the impression the place was under military protection, to conduct frequent manoeuvres in the vicinity. That night the unfortunate Mrs Laird died I saw through my binoculars figures moving inside the grounds – but I could not be certain whether they wore uniforms or not. A ghastly error of judgement was committed for which I hold myself solely responsible. Adieu, my friend.

Newman passed the letter to Beck. He turned to Tweed who now wore his glasses and gazed back at him unhappily.

'How did it go with Dr Kennedy?' Tweed enquired.

'Badly, but that was always inevitable, wasn't it? After all, I did trick her. It was a nasty business . . .'

'I'm sorry,' Tweed replied, 'really sorry. But we needed the help of someone totally unconnected with our organization. Thank you for all you did.' He paused. 'If ever you notice something you think I should know about . . .'

'I'll look the other way.'

'If I were in your position I'd do the same thing,' Tweed agreed. He had no intention of letting Newman know anything about Blanche: you kept your helpers in separate cells.

'We have gone into the Berne Clinic in force,' Beck continued. 'We found the gas intact. It will be destroyed. And Leupin,' he said, looking out of the window, 'reported that he saw a girl throw that grenade. All the casualties are recovering – the grenade was defective, must have been hanging about for a long time. We shan't try to trace her – we have enough on our plates, including searching Grange's factory at Horgen.'

'I do have several unanswered questions,' Newman remarked. 'I have a photograph of you talking to Bruno Kobler outside the Taubenhalde, which worried me a lot. Also, who was your contact inside the Clinic? Then I'm curious as to who killed Nagy, Mason and Seidler – and tried to kill Willy Schaub, the porter.'

Beck smiled. 'Kobler called to see me and I said I'd meet him outside the building – a calculated insult. He tried to pressure me into dropping the investigation, so I told him to shove off or I'd have him for attempting to suborn a policeman. My contact at the Clinic? Dr Waldo Novak, of course! He was scared I'd find a way of deporting him. My guess about Nagy and Mason is they were killed by Kobler – or his thugs. Seidler and Schaub we can be positive about. One of the stolen rifles was the gun lying next to Kobler's dead body outside the Clinic. Ballistics have just confirmed he killed Seidler – and tried to kill Schaub. They dug the bullets out of Schaub's sitting room wall. All satisfactory, Bob?'

'That isn't the word I'd have chosen, but there we are.' Newman stood up wearily. 'If you don't mind, I'll go. I feel like a long walk to clear my mind . . .'

*

They had found the other stolen Army rifle on top of the knoll from where the marksman had killed three men in thirty seconds, Beck had reported earlier in the conversation. And Ballistics had confirmed this was the same weapon which had eliminated two men at Le Pont station.

It was close to dusk as Newman wandered through the arcades, the only sign of life a single tram rumbling past in the slushy snow. It would take years to explore every arcade and alley, he thought. He really liked Berne. It had a unique quality he had never encountered in any other city during his worldwide travels.

He had one more job to do. Someone had to tell Blanche her stepfather was dead. He had no idea what her reaction would be – but the job had to be done. His footsteps trailed in the relics of slush other feet had brought inside the arcade. He stopped outside the door with the bell-push and a name alongside it. *B. Signer*. He pressed the bell and braced himself.

'Who is it?' her voice called through the speakphone.

'Bob. Blanche, I have a single, one-way ticket for a flight to London . . .'

'I see . . .'

'I thought you'd like to watch me tear the ticket into a thousand pieces . . .'

THE
SISTERHOOD

For my daughter,
JANET

Prologue

Darkness was her friend – and her enemy.

Paula Grey arrived at the address in Vienna in Annagasse after night had fallen. The side street was deserted. On both sides ancient buildings rose up like the walls of a canyon. The deep silence was unsettling and her rubber-soled shoes made no noise on the cobbles. She opened the small door set into one of two huge wooden gates. In past times the gates had been opened to allow horses to haul large carriages into the spacious courtyard beyond.

Closing the door behind her quietly she paused to gaze round, to listen. More oppressive silence. On three sides of the courtyard apertures in the old grey stone led to staircases giving access to different apartments. Paula looked up and saw lights in Norbert Engel's apartment behind closed curtains. Tweed had sent her to warn the only statesman who could save Germany from chaos in an emergency that his life was in danger.

Paula checked the time by the illuminated hands of her watch as she stood in the shadows. Eleven o'clock. Deliberately she had arrived early for the appointment she had made over the phone. Glancing up again she saw a curtain pulled aside high up. The unmistakable head and shoulders of Engel peered down, then vanished as the curtain closed again. It was as though the German was expecting someone else before she arrived.

That was the moment when she heard the outer door from the street opening. She slipped inside an alcove, waited, then stared in disbelief.

The figure of a woman passed under a lantern. She was clad from head to foot in a black robe, her face and head masked by a black veil. Paula stood stock-still, watching the veiled woman enter the staircase leading to Engel's apartment on the fourth floor, then vanish. Was the widowed Engel keeping a secret assignment with a woman friend? Maybe with a married woman – hence the strange garb she wore. Paula waited, conscious of the creepy silence of the courtyard shut away from the world of bustling Vienna. In June there were many tourists in the city.

Five minutes later the veiled woman reappeared, paused before entering the courtyard, then hurried to the door and vanished into the street beyond. Paula glanced up again at the window of Engel's apartment. The curtain was still closed, the light behind it still on. Why was she filled with a sense of deep anxiety? The veiled woman could have called on another occupant in a different apartment – except that the only light showing was in Engel's window.

She checked her watch, made up her mind. She would still be early for her appointment but she strode across the courtyard, entered the same staircase the veiled woman had used. The stone steps were ancient, worn in the middle where people over the centuries had walked. The silence of the building was nerve-racking – as though Engel was the only person to be in his apartment. But this was the holiday season. The locals would be liable to go away to escape the crowds of tourists visiting the city.

The staircase was circular, winding its way up between old stone walls. She paused on the first landing, heard nothing and continued upwards. The building was lit by dim wall lanterns, giving very little illumination, casting unsettling shadows. She reached the fourth floor.

Earlier in the day Paula had paid a brief visit to locate Engel's apartment, to check on potential hiding places in case she was followed. She stopped suddenly, gazing at the heavily studded wooden door leading to the apartment. The door was ajar.

Opened only a few inches, but wide enough to allow a streak of light to spear across the dark shadows. Instinctively she slipped her hand into the special pocket inside her shoulder bag, the pocket designed to enable her to haul out swiftly her loaded Browning .32 automatic.

Gripping the butt, she moved closer to the partly open door. She had the impression someone had left quickly. Her eyes dropped to a small piece of black material attached to the rough stonework framing the doorway. Using her left hand, she gently detached the cloth, thrust it into her pocket. She listened for any sign of life inside the apartment. Silence.

Again using her left hand, she pushed the door open wider, slowly in case it creaked. Silence again. The hinges were well oiled. She continued pushing the door until she felt it touch the wall behind it. Gazing beyond the doorway she was looking into a large stone-walled living-cum-dining room. A heavy Jacobean table was the centrepiece with six wooden chairs round it. Beyond was a tall round ceramic stove, the source of heating for old Viennese apartments in winter. The stone-flagged floor was partly covered with a Persian rug. She walked softly over the stone flags, reached the rug and eased her way round the table.

In the right-hand wall a single arched wooden door was half open. She paused, listened for the faintest sound of life. There was none. Holding the Browning in front of her, gripped in both hands, she approached the

3

door, alert for any kind of sound. Nothing. As though no one lived here. Arriving at the door, she glanced back, checking to make sure no one was behind her. Then, peering through the open doorway, she froze.

Norbert Engel was seated behind a large antique desk and the bookcase-lined walls suggested this was his office when he visited Vienna. Ice-cold, her nerves under perfect control, Paula looked behind the half-open door to check no one was waiting for her hidden behind the solid slab. No one. She advanced slowly towards the desk, her eyes everywhere, but they kept staring back at the German.

Engel's chair was a leather-covered swivel type. His body was slumped forward over the desk, one large hand close to a Luger, a 7.65 mm pistol. The back of his head was blown off, spattered over the desk, a grisly mix of bone and blood.

Paula walked round the back of him, saw his stocky legs sprawled under the desk because the chair was so close to it. He wore a dark-blue business suit, a white shirt, soiled at the front with more blood. Attached to the muzzle of the Luger was a very modern silencer. Which explained why, waiting in the yard below, she had not heard the shot.

Pointless to check his pulse. Returning her Browning to its pocket in her shoulder bag, she took out a small camera and took four flash shots from different angles. After returning the camera to her shoulder bag she put on a pair of surgical gloves she always carried. Protruding from the top drawer to the right of Engel's slumped body the end of a sheet of paper was just visible. Opening the drawer a short distance, she extracted the sheet. It was headed *Institut de la Défense*. She read a list of names. Seven were crossed out with a single ink line. All had been assassinated. One name startled her, the name Tweed, her boss at SIS headquarters in Park

4

Crescent. She looked for the last time at Engel, touched his left hand with her own gloved hand. Rigor mortis had not yet started. She mouthed the words soundlessly.

'Poor devil. You're number eight. Suicide my foot . . .'

Before leaving the apartment, the sheet of paper folded, inserted inside her shoulder bag, she used a silk handkerchief to wipe the outer door where she had touched it, removing all trace of her fingerprints. Then she began the nerve-racking descent of the weird staircase.

The building seemed to close round her as she moved from one landing down to the next. Still no sign that anyone else was inside the place. Creepy. Like a mausoleum. She held the Browning in her hand, stopped frequently to listen and heard only the eerie silence of the grave.

Reaching the courtyard, she paused for the last time. Then she headed swiftly for the small door which led into the side street. She had removed her gloves earlier and made no attempt to remove fingerprints from that door – she was too anxious to find herself in a street with people.

The night had become very hot and humid. Anna-gasse appeared deserted. So why were her nerves beginning to tingle? Halfway to Kärntnerstrasse, the main shopping street, she glanced back – just in time to see a man vanish into the courtyard she had left. Something moved in the shadows. Careful not to break into a run, she walked more swiftly. At the exit to the main street she turned briefly, looked back. A short, heavily built man clad in a windcheater, a beret on his head, was hurrying towards her.

She entered Kärntnerstrasse, breathed a premature sigh of relief. Had she gone straight back to the Hotel Sacher they would have known where she was staying.

5

Instead she turned right, strode down the middle of the pedestrian street – no traffic allowed. There were far fewer people about than she would have wished for. As she progressed towards the far end she glanced to either side, as though scanning the windows of the expensive shops, many of them illuminated although closed. To her right the stocky man, now minus beret, was talking into a mobile phone, keeping close to the shops. To her left a tall thin man with a hooked nose, a slight stoop, kept pace with her. She was caught in a pincer movement. What were they planning now? The kidnap attempt came at the end of Kärntnerstrasse where traffic flowed.

Paula was distracted by catching sight of a woman walking ahead of her. Her hair was auburn, thick, trimmed just above her shoulders. She wore a sleeveless white cotton blouse, a navy blue short straight skirt, and carried a Chanel carrier bag. She would be in her thirties, Paula estimated. When she glanced back Paula saw she was very beautiful, walking with elegance. But it was the body language which hypnotized Paula. Twice she had seen the veiled woman, who had entered and left the staircase to Engel's apartment. Could it possibly be the same woman?

The more she watched the woman, who had only glanced back once, the more certain she was it *was* the same woman. What had happened to the black robe and the veil? Paula began to think she must be wrong, then she looked again at the Chanel carrier and knew she was right. At that moment the stocky man approached her.

'Excuse me, you ha-a-ve dropped something.'

East European accent. Paula kept walking as she replied, 'Go and pick it up, then . . .'

He sidled away from her, continued his patrol close

6

to the shops. Paula looked ahead. The auburn-haired woman had disappeared. Nowhere to be seen. Her attention had been diverted so Auburn-Hair could vanish. She reached the end of Kärntnerstrasse and a large black stretch limousine had cruised to a stop close to her. The driver leaned over, threw open the rear door. Paula stopped. A sweaty hand closed over her mouth from behind, began to push her into the car.

Paula knew that the only chance of escaping being kidnapped is at the moment when the onslaught begins. Her body twisted like a snake's until she was facing the stocky assaillant. She raised her leg, pressed the sole of her shoe against his shin, scraped it down with all her strength. He grunted with pain. She jerked up her right knee and hit him in the groin. As he doubled over, groaning horribly, she saw the thin man with the hooked nose coming for her with a rope between his hands. She was reaching for her Browning when a third man, a huge apelike figure, appeared to her left. A hand like a vice pinned her gun arm to her side and she knew she was hopelessly outnumbered.

'I wouldn't do that, old chap. No way to treat a lady.'

A familiar upper-crust voice, calm and sardonic. Marler. A close colleague of Paula's at the SIS. An arm covered in a cream-coloured sleeve wrapped itself round the ape's throat, cutting off his windpipe. The ape's eyes bulged, his body sagged away from Paula. The voice spoke again.

'I say, Paula, attend to the driver. Get info.'

As she moved round the car Marler suddenly threw the ape forward, crashing him into the hook-nosed attacker. Paula darted to the driver's window, Browning in her hand. The window was down. She aimed her automatic point-blank at the driver, a weasel-faced thug.

'You've got ten seconds to live,' she snapped. 'Turn off the ignition. That's a good boy. Six seconds to live, then I press the trigger. Who is your boss? I'll know if you lie.'

'Assam,' the driver croaked.

The sound of a patrol's car's siren was approaching rapidly. Marler had used the butt of his Walther to eliminate Ape and Hook-Nose. He heaved the two bodies one by one into the back of the car, slammed the door shut, ran to the front, tore open the door where the weasel-faced thug sat terrified under Paula's gun. Leaning inside, he snatched the ignition key out of the lock, used the other hand to hit the driver across the forehead. The head slumped over the wheel.

'We get moving instanter,' Marler called out to Paula.

They crossed the street with the immense spire of the Dom looming on their right. Marler hustled inside the entrance to Do & Co, a fantastic erection of modern architecture with a curved glass front many storeys high. Before Paula knew what was happening they were inside an elevator, Marler had pressed the button for the top-floor restaurant and they were walking into a modernist restaurant with tables by curved windows looking straight across at the Dom. The giant ancient cathedral sheered far above them.

'This place,' Marler explained, 'is trying the experiment of staying open very late.' He ordered drinks. Then listened with close attention as Paula told him what she had seen and experienced. She showed him the fragment of black gauze she had extracted from the stonework, then the pictures which the camera had automatically developed and printed.

'Something diabolically wrong here,' Marler commented. 'This is murder. We'll call Tweed from the Post Office early tomorrow morning.'

8

1

Tweed, Deputy Director of the SIS, was eating a hearty breakfast at Summer Lodge, an outstanding country hotel in Dorset, on the edge of the village of Evershot. His dining companion was Bob Newman, famous international foreign correspondent, who had long ago been fully vetted and helped Tweed on dangerous missions.

'Do you think Willie could be connected with this series of assassinations of top men in Europe?' Tweed asked in a low voice.

Tweed was a man of uncertain age who wore hornrimmed glasses, the type of person you could pass in the street without noticing him – a factor which had helped him many times. Of medium height, he radiated an air of calm and iron self-control in any situation. Clean-shaven, the shrewd eyes behind the lenses missed nothing.

'By Willie you mean Captain William Wellesley Carrington,' Newman replied. 'I've checked him out and, as you know, he owns a bit of land near the village of Shrimpton. He's also an arms dealer on an international scale. We know he's an ex-member of the SAS – but he's adopted the captain title to impress people, although he *was* a lower-ranking officer. What I can't find out is where his money comes from – unless it's from arms. Not inherited – that I do know.'

Newman was in his early forties, five feet nine tall, also clean-shaven and had thick flaxen hair. His features were strong and many women found him attractive, although he rarely responded to their overtures. He had high-level contacts all over the world, which Tweed found useful.

'So there is a question mark over Willie,' Tweed mused. 'Otto Kuhlmann in Germany reported Willie was visiting Stuttgart when one of the assassinations took place one week after his visit. Chief Inspector Loriot told me Willie was in Paris just before the assassination of another of Europe's elite – in Paris. Arthur Beck, head of Federal Police in Berne, told me Willie was in that city a week before the assassination there. Once, twice could be coincidence. Three is once too many. In any case I don't believe in coincidence, as you know. And what about Tina Langley, Willie's girlfriend? They talk about her as though most men would give their eye-teeth to know her – she's so attractive.'

'The glamorous Tina has disappeared. Not seen in the usual pubs and bars she haunts for weeks. Just vanished overnight.'

'I find that a trifle sinister. Then there's Amos Lodge, the eccentric strategist who advises governments. Any news about him?'

'Yes. He's in residence in a small thatched cottage he owns just outside Shrimpton.'

'Shrimpton again. I'd like to visit that village after dark.'

'Only if I come with you,' Newman said firmly.

'Morning paper, sir,' a waitress said to Tweed. 'I'm sorry, but they arrived late today.'

'Thank you.'

He opened the folded newspaper and the banner headlines hit him.

10

'Look at this.' Tweed handed Newman the paper. 'We've got to get moving.'

'Suicide?' Newman's expression was grim. 'Don't believe a word of it. The other seven were classed as suicides.'

'But the police everywhere unofficially – at the moment – call them murders.'

Tweed stopped speaking as the waitress reappeared.

'Excuse me, sir. There's a call for you. The lady's name is Monica.'

'I'll take it in my room.' Tweed was already on his feet. He waited until the waitress had gone. 'I'm sure this isn't the sort of place where whoever's on the switchboard listens in. But go and chat to the operator while I take the call . . .'

'Will do.'

Tweed ran upstairs to his tastefully decorated bed-room, which overlooked the hotel's garden and open countryside beyond. He picked up the phone, knowing that by now Newman would be inside the room with the switchboard.

'Tweed here.'

'I've had an urgent call from your friend, Otto Kuhlmann. Wants you to phone him back within one hour. Then he's leaving on stand-by aircraft for the land of Strauss waltzes. Marler is waiting on another line I'm holding. He's in a post office. Kuhlmann first, I suggest.'

'Thanks. I'm going off the line.'

Tweed had detected a note of anxiety in Monica, for many years his competent, trustworthy assistant at Park Crescent. He put down the phone, lifted it again, pressed the numbers of the private phone of Otto Kuhlmann in

11

Wiesbaden from memory. The German Chief of Criminal Police answered at once in his growly voice. He spoke perfect English.

'Who is this?'

'Tweed. Monica passed on your message.'

'You've heard the news?'

'I just read it in the paper.'

'Suicide? You have to be joking. I'm on my way to Vienna soon as I've finished this call. I know the police chief there – in any case the victim is a German national.'

'Paula and Marler are there.'

'How do I contact them?'

'Both are staying at the Sacher. Otto, don't arrest anyone – just have them followed if you find a suspect.'

'If you say so. Have to fly now. Literally . . .'

The connection was broken. Again Tweed put down the phone, waited a moment, called Monica.

'Marler is still on another line,' she said instantly. 'I'm transferring you to him. Now.'

It was Paula he found himself talking to. He listened while in her concise manner she reported her experiences from the moment she had entered the building on Annagasse. She told him she had extracted the name Assam from the driver. Tweed gripped the phone a little tighter as she described the kidnap attempt.

'Thanks for sending Marler to back me up. I didn't know he was anywhere near this country.'

'You weren't supposed to know. You wouldn't have liked the idea.'

'You're right – I wouldn't. Thank Heaven you did what you did. Bless you.'

'No time for that. I've spoken to Otto. He's flying out there now. I've told him you're both at the Sacher. Both of you wait until he contacts you. That's an order.'

'Which will be obeyed. You have grasped that the

12

sheet of paper I took away has a *full* list of all members of the *Institut de la Défense*?'

'I know what you mean.'

'Any product where you are now? Or maybe I shouldn't ask.'

'You just did,' he pointed out to her. 'Something weird here. Haven't put my finger on it yet. Must go now. Take care. Stay with Marler.'

'I promise.'

Monica, who had been listening in, which was part of her job, came back on the line.

'Any further instructions?'

'Yes. Phone Loriot, then Arthur. Tell them what you heard. Give them a request from me. Don't arrest any suspects – just have them followed. That's it . . .'

'Don't go, Tweed. Howard wants a word with Bob Newman.'

'Hold the line.'

Puzzled, Tweed left the room, locked his door, hurried down the staircase. Howard was the pompous Director of SIS, a chief he often concealed his movements from, but in a crisis Howard had his feet on the ground. He reached the room where Newman was chatting up the girl handling the switchboard.

'Bob, Howard's on the line. Wants to speak to you. Here's the key to my room.'

As Newman left Tweed began talking to the girl, asking her about her holidays, where she went. Upstairs Newman picked up the phone, identified himself.

'Bob . . .' Howard's plummy voice sounded tense. 'I'm making a very strong request to you. I've read the papers and heard from one of my own personal contacts. Could you, please, be sure not to let Tweed out of your sight. I sense danger. Do that for me, be a good chap.'

'Tweed won't like it.'

13

'I know. Don't tell him. If necessary be devious. Can I rely on you?'

'That's a question you shouldn't have asked. You've had enough experience of me. Thanks for the warning.'

'I'll sleep easier now. Bye.'

What on earth is going on? Newman wondered as he slowly made his way back downstairs. He had never before known Howard to express such anxiety. Tweed talked to the girl for a few more minutes, then walked out with Newman.

'Bob, let's go for a wander in their garden.' As they walked out into the courtyard leading to the extensive garden he asked the question Newman knew was coming. 'What did Howard want?'

'To make sure I wouldn't be dashing off on some assignment for *Der Spiegel*. He thinks the situation down here calls for at least two of us to cover the ground.'

'I see,' said Tweed, who saw perfectly. 'Now I have a lot to tell you . . .'

He gave Newman all the details of his phone calls. He included every single detail Paula had provided. Newman listened without saying a word, waited until Tweed had finished. They were wandering round the splendid walled garden of Summer Lodge, which was more like a small estate and beautifully laid out. A curving gravel drive led to the distant entrance and no one else was about. Everything was perfect.

'Why did you warn Arthur Beck, Chief of the Swiss Federal Police, as well as Kuhlmann and Loriot, not to arrest suspects – just to track them?'

'Because I feel a phantom network closing round us – look at the attempt to kidnap Paula, the systematic way they followed her down Kärntnerstrasse, the thug with the mobile who had obviously summoned the kidnap car to be waiting. I am now casting out our own

14

network to locate who is behind these sinister actions – involving eight murders.'

'What is this *Institut de la Défense*?'

'A kind of club of the top brains in Europe – men who know not only that something appallingly menacing is facing Europe but are using all their influence for Europe to rebuild a huge defence system. Before it is too late.'

'Who is the enemy?'

'We don't know. It's not Russia – that much we have established.'

'We? I've heard of the outfit but I didn't know you are a member.'

'We try to maintain a low profile. You are probably one of the few people – with your worldwide contacts – who has heard of us. Apart from myself, they are the elite of the continent. None has official positions – as you know Norbert Engel was not, never has been, a member of the German government. But he was making headway, persuading Bonn it should consider expanding its army, to purchase the most advanced powerful weapons in the world. Now I think we had better investigate that village, Shrimpton. Something odd about it. And I'd like a chat with Willie – and with Amos Lodge.'

'I'll drive you there. I wonder what is happening to Paula and Marler? They're in the firing line.'

On the afternoon of the same day Otto Kuhlmann walked inside the world-famous Hotel Sacher in Vienna. A short, barrel-chested man, he was very like the film star Edward G. Robinson. His head was large, his mouth wide and from it protruded his trademark, a large cigar. His appearance intimidated those who did not know him well. Aggressively he marched up to the reception desk, glared at the man behind the counter. He briefly flashed his identity folder.

'Chief Inspector Kuhlmann of Kriminalpolizei,' he growled. 'Show me the card index of guests arrived during the past seven days,' he said in German.

'You're not Austrian police,' the man behind the counter stammered.

'There's a letter from the chief of Vienna police.' Kuhlmann slammed down an envelope stamped with official insignia. 'Authority to operate here. Don't waste my time while you read it. Give me the index. Then waste your own time reading the damned letter if you must.'

Without further question the receptionist produced a card index, pushed it across the counter. Kuhlmann puffed cigar smoke in the man's face as his nimble fingers riffled through the cards. He found Marler's room number, then Paula's. Shoving the index back across the counter he stared at the receptionist.

'I may report your lack of cooperation. Keep your mouth shut. You could be in big trouble . . .'

On which note he headed for the elevator. There was no reply from Marler's room. He headed for Paula's, hammered on the door.

'Who is it?' a cultured voice demanded.

'Otto Kuhlmann.'

Marler, his Walther in his right hand, opened the door, admitted the German, closed, locked it. Kuhlmann looked at the gun, spoke with mock amusement.

'Going to shoot me?'

'Not at the moment.'

Kuhlmann saw Paula sitting on a couch. Slim, with dark hair neatly trimmed just above her shoulders, she had excellent bone structure, was attractive and had very good legs. She wore a cream blouse and a dark-blue skirt, and her only jewellery was a pendant supporting a green stone round her neck. Kuhlmann grinned, went straight over, bent down and kissed her on the cheek.

'Hear you've had a tough time. Vienna is a tough city.'

'So I'm beginning to find out. How do you know? And you got here quickly.'

'I move.' He sat down on the couch beside her, stubbed out his cigar. 'So do you. Tweed gave me a résumé of your visit to Annagasse, the kidnap business. Since I flew in from Wiesbaden I've been to the scene of the crime, to the morgue where they took Engel's body. Someone pretending to be Engel phoned headquarters here, asked for protection, reported a prowler.'

'What time would that be?' Paula asked quietly.

'Midnight.'

'Then "pretended" is the right word. I found him dead at about eleven. Why the fake phone call?'

'Oh, that's easy.' Kuhlmann waved a large hand. 'They – whoever they are – wanted it to hit today's newspapers. I gathered from Tweed you had the wit to take several flash shots of Engel.'

'Here they are.' She produced the prints from inside her shoulder bag. 'I'm not sure why I did that.'

'Glad you did.' Kuhlmann's voice rose, then he got up and switched on the television. 'If this room is bugged that will scramble our conversation.'

'And why may the room be bugged?' Marler enquired.

Kuhlmann looked at Marler who was leaning against a wall and had lit a king-size. He saw a slim man, five feet eight tall, always well-dressed, clean-shaven with light brown hair; a cool man who was the top marksman in Europe. His tone was sardonic and nothing ever ruffled him. He was wearing a linen jacket and razor-

17

edged creased slacks of the same cream colour. Kuhlmann liked, admired him.

'Because you two have been booked here in separate
rooms for two days. Plenty of time for the opposition to
slip inside while you're out with a master key.'

'And who, may I enquire, is the opposition?'

'Wish to hell I could find that out. No police chief
has the faintest idea, neither have the Intelligence
people. But my bet is this is the start of something pretty
big – eight assassinations so far of the top brains in the
world. Someone is laying the groundwork for a catastrophe of historical dimensions. At least that's my opinion. We may not have much time to identify who is
behind this campaign.'

'Which is Tweed's opinion,' Paula said quietly.

'Then I'm right.' Kuhlmann took the photos Paula
had handed him and spread them over a coffee table.
'You've seen these, of course?' he asked Marler.

'I have.'

'Then take a look at these photographs, both of you.'

He extracted photos from his jacket, spread them out
alongside Paula's. She leaned forward and frowned as
Marler peered over her shoulder. They showed Engel
slumped over his desk – but now his right arm drooped
by his side and the Luger lay on the floor.

'He wasn't like that when I saw him,' Paula commented. 'You can see from my pics. I don't understand.'

'I do,' the German said grimly. 'The killer botched
this job. If Engel had blown the back of his own head off
the Luger wouldn't have landed neatly on the desk. His
gun hand would have sagged by his side and he'd have
dropped the weapon. So my bet is the man you saw
slipping inside the Annagasse building after you'd left
went there to check. He saw the mistake, hauled Engel's
right arm off the desk, then placed the Luger on the

floor. Paula, you were there about eleven at night,' Tweed said.'

'I was.'

'These photos were taken by the police photographer when the scene of the crime team arrived in response to the fake phone call from the man saying he was Engel. They got there about midnight. Suicide? Forget it.'

'I thought it was murder,' Paula said in the same quiet voice.

'Like all the previous seven – where again it was made to look like suicide,' Kuhlmann went on grimly. 'I checked the records. We have cases of suicide by the victim shoving the muzzle of a gun into his mouth, by placing it against one side or the other of his head. But how can anyone be sure of killing themselves by placing the muzzle against the back of the his or her head? I've acted it out myself with an unloaded Luger – the position is too damned awkward. No one would even try it. Then there's your sighting of the veiled woman, the weird business of your seeing the woman dressed normally on Kärntnerstrasse later. I can't make head or tail of what is happening. But we need a lead – just one lead. What are you two doing?' he asked suddenly.

'Tweed has ordered me to stay close to Marler, to stay in this part of the world,' Paula replied.

'Like the first part – not so sure about the second,' Kuhlmann responded. 'There's been a violent prison breakout by those men who tried to kidnap you. Haven't told you about that.'

'Then why not tell us?' Marler suggested.

'Last night the police arrested the three men who attempted to hijack Paula. Tried to interrogate them. None of them would say one word. Had no means of identification on any of the three. Locked them up for the night. In three cells next to each other. Not very

19

clever. Dawn comes. A big man they said looked like King Kong—'

'The Ape,' Paula interjected.

'Fits the description I was given. At dawn the Ape starts kicking up hell, complaining he's ill. He was injured, had trouble walking. The night guards let him out. The other two cell doors are thrown open from the inside – must have been an inside job. A small stocky man produces a machine-pistol, guns down three guards. All are dead. The Ape can't move because of a damaged leg. The small man turns the gun on him. They blast their way out. Outside a car is waiting. They dive inside and they're gone.'

'Trifle ruthless, that,' Marler mused. 'Killing one of their own when he can't make it.'

'I don't know how you two managed to knock them out during the kidnap business,' Kuhlmann commented. 'I know you are both good – but you were up against top professionals.'

'We weren't too polite,' Marler told him.

'I said earlier we needed just one lead. We might just have got it. The stocky one had flushed something down his toilet, but what he tried to destroy got stuck. One of the surviving guards found it, had it disinfected. I persuaded my friend, the chief of police here, to give it to me. Brochure of a hotel. Here it is.'

He handed a creased folder to Marler who looked at it. Then he passed it to Paula.

'That might be our lead. Hotel Burgenland, Eisenstadt. As I'm sure you know, Burgenland is the most easterly province of Austria. Borders on Slovakia to the north, on Hungary to the south and east. Wild, remote territory.'

'We'd better pay it a visit,' Paula said calmly.

'I can't recommend such a trip,' Kuhlmann warned.

'And I'm still mystified that the killer of Engel appears to have been a woman.'

'In this age of equality women can be greater villains than men,' Paula told him.

2

The battered Volvo estate car sped across the vast plain well east of Vienna which was Burgenland. The metal body was crumpled, the windows covered with meaningless graffiti which concealed the occupants. At a fork in the deserted landscape it swung north towards a strange mountain rising three hundred feet above the plain. Along the summit of the great barrow-like eminence stood a large long one-storey building.

Behind the hook-nosed driver sat a woman garbed in a long black robe. The black material extended from the top of her head, her face masked by a veil. Her white hands clenched together nervously. She turned to the stocky man beside her, swarthy and unshaven.

'Where are we going?' she demanded.

'Shut your stupid face. You made the mistake,' he snarled, his deep voice mouthing an accent she couldn't identify.

'You're such a nice polite little fellow,' she told him cheekily.

'Always the politeness,' he replied, mistaking her meaning.

'You smell of cordite,' she taunted him. 'Killed a lot of people this morning, have you?'

The unintended accuracy of her remark enraged him. His hairy fists tightened. He would have loved to smash her face in, to spoil her extraordinary beauty for life. He restrained his fury: Hassan would shoot him if he so much as touched her.

'We speak no more,' he snapped through gritted teeth.

'Oh, I like talking to men. Especially to real men.'

She glanced at her companion – guard – and delighted in the confusion her response had caused. She knew she could play the little thug like a fisherman hauling in his catch. Her natural sauciness had overcome her earlier nervousness. The car slowed down as the driver sneaked it across the frontier from Austria into Slovakia by a lonely side road with no checkpoint.

The woman stared ahead through the clear windscreen to check the route it was taking. The road spiralled up the western end of the isolated mountain, reached the summit and she saw the long single-storey house perched above a quarry where she had originally been trained. Now she knew who she was going to meet.

She realized she had messed up at Annagasse but she'd had the feeling someone was watching her. That was confirmed later by Roka, the stocky man at her side. He had questioned her once the car had picked her up from the quiet hotel in Vienna. He had tried to intimidate her, which had amused her.

'What sort of woman follows you down Kärntnerstrasse?'

'I didn't know anyone was following me.'

'You looked back . . .'

'Of course I did. That was to see if you were protecting me. I saw the signal telling me I should disappear off the main pedestrian street. Since I reacted at once what are you waffling on about, you jerk?'

'What is the waffle? The jerk? You insult Roka?'

'As often as possible . . .'

They stopped talking as the car pulled up at the entrance to the strange house with a shallow sloping roof. The house was constructed of plaster walls painted an acid green colour. Only a few small windows were set into the wall and each had a closed, shabby shutter. The moment Roka pressed the button which released the car's door locks she threw open the one nearest to her, stepped out into the blazing sun, holding her black dress to avoid tripping.

Show no fear, she told herself. In any case she wasn't in the least frightened by Hassan. She was simply wary of his childish tricks. She approached the plain heavy wooden door and it opened. Through the veil she stared at the slim man with brownish skin who scared the wits out of his staff.

'Welcome back,' he said.

'I didn't ask to come here,' she rapped back. 'I was escorted here like a prisoner. I don't like that.'

'A thousand apologies,' he said smoothly and bowed from the waist. 'Because of what happened in Annagasse I thought you needed a little more help. A little more training.'

A little more brainwashing, she thought. She was careful not to express her thought in words.

'Please keep on the robe and the veil,' he continued. 'Now be so very kind as to follow me.'

She knew where she was going, knew what she was about to be subjected to. Nothing in her expression gave away her annoyance at this unnecessary waste of time. Hassan took out a key, led the way across a large hall paved with stone flags, unlocked a door, ushered her inside a small room.

Inset into a wall were three powerful strobe lights. They were positioned at eye level and aimed at a high-backed leather chair in the middle of the room. In the

23

wall behind the chair two cine-cameras were attached to the white surface. On each arm of the chair a handcuff was attached with one cuff dangling.

She had endured this previously. Before Hassan could order her she sat down in the chair. The moment she was seated she felt she had made a mistake in showing such confident indifference. She glanced up at Hassan as he bent over her to attach a handcuff to each wrist. His Eurasian face betrayed no surprise – he had assumed she was inwardly quaking, had submitted without protest because she was trembling with fear. He's not all that smart, she said to herself.

'You know what is going to happen,' he whispered in one ear.

'Y-e-s . . .'

She had managed to fake trepidation.

'Then, my dear, I will leave you for a little while.'

She heard the door close behind her, locked. It was now impossible for her to leave the heavy chair screwed to the floor. Weird psychedelic music began blasting from invisible speakers, deafening wild music. The strobe lights began flashing on and off – a blue one, a red light and a green. Strange pictures appeared on the walls, films of men and women cavorting in tempo to the music. A seductive perfume filled her nostrils, very powerful and head-spinning. She crushed a capsule of strong peppermint she had slipped into her mouth when she had left the car. It countered the mind-bending perfume.

Crude brainwashing, she said to herself. An attempt at total disorientation.

Half-closing her eyes, she concentrated on a walk to the sea she had often taken in Devon. She filled her mind with each twist and turn in the path, saw the ocean waves coming in below the cliffs, the freighter she had seen ploughing its way towards the nearest port.

She blotted out the sound of the music by listening to the crash of the waves below the cliffs, neutralized the mad films gyrating on the walls by concentrating on the progress she had seen the freighter making. She ignored the strobe lights which flashed on and off by seeing the picture of the walk in Devon in her mind.

Everything stopped suddenly. The so-called music. The films on the walls. The flashing strobe lights. The peppermint had countered the perfume. She sat very still as she heard the door being unlocked, as Hassan appeared by her side.

Without saying a word he unlocked each handcuff. She made her arms stay limp along the chair. He stroked her cheeks gently to bring her round. She remained like a waxwork figure. He bent down to whisper in her ear.

'You can stand up now.'

She stood up slowly, as though it was a great effort, shook her head, pretending to be dizzy. His strong fingers grasped her arm and she forced herself to hide her revulsion at his touch. Guiding her to another door, he unlocked it and held her still as he spoke in his oily voice.

'Are you all right, my dear?'

Damn his 'my dear' to hell.

'I'm perfectly OK,' she snapped in a normal tone.

'Do not remove the robe or veil. Take this.'

He handed her a Luger. Her fingers clasped the weapon she had practised with for so many hours at the shooting range. She checked the weapon. Fully loaded.

'You made a bad mistake at Annagasse,' he told her in a grim voice. 'Inside this room there is another dummy figure. You have been in there before. Let me see you handle this in the way you should have dealt with Engel.'

She walked quietly into the room which had been carpeted on the previous occasion. No carpet now and the stone flags were exposed. She rested the Luger on a nearby couch, put on a pair of surgical gloves she extracted from a concealed pocket in the black robe. As she did so she stared at the back of a life-like figure sitting in a chair behind an antique desk. They had reproduced the scene she had looked at in Engel's study.

She picked up the Luger, walked one cautious step at a time as she had done in Annagasse, when she had tested the floor for a creak which might have disturbed her target. Pausing, she glanced swiftly behind her – again as she had in the study in Vienna. Checking to make sure no one else was in the room.

Hassan stood with his back to the door he had quietly shut. His arms were folded and there was a sinister smile on his bland face as he watched her. He raised one hand, gestured for her to continue.

The dummy figure at the desk was motionless. It gave her an eerie feeling – Engel, a man noted for his intense powers of concentration, had sat as motionless as this figure, studying a sheet of paper. He had then suddenly slid the sheet of paper into a drawer, ramming the drawer closed. She had moved swiftly, alarmed that he had heard her.

She moved swiftly now. Holding the tip of the muzzle an inch from the head she pulled the trigger. The special silencer attached to the gun muffled the sound of the shot. The top half of the head exploded, scattering shards of bone, hair and blood all over the desk, spilling on to the floor. The figure slumped forward over the desk, both arms outstretched over its surface. Just like Engel.

In a partial state of shock, she still reacted quickly, knowing Hassan was watching. With her gloved hand she lifted the right arm by the sleeve, dropped it so the arm sagged by the side of the body. Bending down, she

26

grasped the right hand, pressed the fingers round the butt of the gun. Then she placed the weapon on the floor, a short distance from the lifeless fingers.

As she stood up, compelling her trembling knees to stiffen, Hassan came forward. He put an arm round her. She turned to face him and he was still smiling.

'Very good, my dear. You have earned your hundred thousand dollars.'

He handed her a fat sealed package. She gripped it tightly, stared through her veil at his smiling face, the smile now tinged with evil satisfaction.

'I've killed another real man,' she said in a steely voice. 'It was a test of nerve. Who was he?'

'No one of importance, my dear. No one will be missed. He was doped, of course – which is why he didn't move.'

'I killed another live man,' she said in a calm voice.

Then she did something which startled even the cold-blooded Hassan. She giggled.

3

At Summer Lodge in Dorset Tweed had taken a decision. He had talked it over with Newman as they took a second walk in the garden of the country house hotel.

'We'll delay our visit to talk to Willie and Amos Lodge at Shrimpton until the early evening.'

'You have a reason for waiting until then?' Newman asked impatiently.

'Yes. First, people are more relaxed at the end of the day, more likely to let something slip. Especially in this glorious sunny warm weather we're enjoying. I'd like to get there when the locals are in the pubs. We might learn something by chatting to a few of them – about the two men we're visiting.'

'Sounds like a good idea. But I sense there's another reason.'

'You do read my mind. I want to be here during the rest of the day where I can be reached.'

'You're worried about something.'

'I'm worried about Paula and Marler. Kuhlmann, as you know, called me from Vienna. He said the two of them are proposing to follow up a lead. They may have a lead, a place called Eisenstadt in Burgenland . . .'

He explained what the German had told him about the hotel brochure one of the kidnap thugs had tried to dispose of before the murderous breakout from prison.

'They sound a pretty tough bunch,' Newman remarked.

'With people like that involved the opposition we seem to be up against sounds highly professional and totally ruthless. I'm trying to stop Paula and Marler going on their own to that wild area. I've called the Hotel Sacher but they were both out. I'm going inside now to phone again.'

Newman followed him inside the hotel and then went to the bar while Tweed ran upstairs to his bedroom. Ordering a double Scotch, Newman sat on a couch close to the bar. As he sipped his drink he mulled over what he knew so far. Some vital element was missing – if only he could put his finger on it.

In his room Tweed had called the Sacher, then he phoned Monica at Park Crescent. She sounded calm but thankful that he was on the line.

'You'll never guess who has just called me. I can get him back on the phone – a safe one . . .'

'Who is it? I don't like guessing games.'

'Sorry. Philip Cardon phoned me! Philip, of all people. I can get him now and switch the line to you.'

'Get him. I'll be out of the room for thirty seconds.'

Laying the receiver on the bedside table, Tweed raced downstairs, then slowed to a normal walk. As he passed the doorway into the switchboard room he glanced inside. He caught a brief snatch of conversation between the girl manning the board and some potential guest.

'I'm sorry, sir. We're pretty fully booked. But since you're a regular I'll juggle with the reservations. It will take me a few minutes. You'll hold on? Good.'

She was absorbed in her task. Tweed ran back upstairs. He picked up the phone and Monica told him Cardon was on the line.

'I'm short of time, Tweed. I'm calling you from Vienna. Couriers are flying from here via Zurich to Heathrow. Each one carries a load of money. In cash. I was urged to report this to you by an unusual character who is known to you. I refer to Emilio Vitorelli. Must go.'

'Thank you.'

Tweed put down the phone, found Newman esconced in the bar with his Scotch. Tweed kept his voice quiet.

'Developments. Another stroll in the garden. Bring your drink with you . . .'

He told Newman what he had learned over the phone. He had a grim expression which Newman noticed as they walked along paths between trim lawns in blazing sunlight.

'Something bothering you?' Newman enquired.

'I called the Hotel Sacher twice to stop Paula and Marler leaving for Burgenland. First time they couldn't be found, as you know. Second time I was told they had both checked out of the hotel. That means they're heading for that weird plain. I wish I was out there with them. I am taking extreme precautions. Butler and Nield are flying out to that part of the world as back-up.'

'They won't get there in five minutes. They have to fly to Zurich, then disembark and take an Austrian Airlines plane to Schwechat Airport outside Vienna. I have visited Burgenland. Weird is the word for that place. There is a feeling of terrible isolation.'

'I admit to a feeling of foreboding,' Tweed replied.

'Amazing that Philip Cardon has come back into our lives. It must be over two years since he left us after he had avenged the torture and murder of his wife. What can he be up to?'

'I predicted he would roam the world. I think he got fed up with that aimless existence, then stumbled on something which just happened to be connected with what we are now investigating.'

'What is this business about couriers flying money to London – large sums in banknotes?'

'Ah, that is something I have told none of you about. It is why we are down here – one reason, anyway. Before Philip told me I knew money was being infil-trated to this part of the world. A Slovene courier was caught at Heathrow flying in from Zurich with an executive case stuffed with banknotes. Luckily, Jim Corcoran, Security Chief at Heathrow and a close friend of mine, as you know, decided to call me first. I asked him to delay the Slovene's departure, then let him go. The courier had documents – forged, no doubt – which made it look like a genuine commercial transaction. Butler followed the Slovene in his car to Dorchester. Then his quarry turned up the road we used to get to Evershot. Unfortunately Butler lost him. He hadn't turned off to Evershot and Butler pressed his foot down.

No sign of the Slovene after Butler passed the turn-off to Shrimpton.'

'And we've found out that the only two men who were in that area who are well off are Amos Lodge and William Wellesley Carrington – both of whom travel to Europe a lot.'

'So far you're right, but I put Keith Kent, the genius at tracing where people get their money, on to the problem. He's reported to me quickly that he can't trace where either of them obtained their wealth.'

'The big fish must be Amos Lodge or Willie,' Newman ruminated.

'Another intriguing problem is where the money is collected from. Remember you reminded me the air route from Vienna passes through Zurich, where you change flights. Maybe it is Vienna, but it could be picked up in Zurich.'

'So why is this mysterious business so momentous?'

'Because Cord Dillon, Deputy Director of the CIA at Langley, called me. American satellites have picked up enormous concentrations of tank manoeuvres in a certain Muslim state. Not Iraq. The tanks are coming in by the horde, supplied by both China and Russia.'

'That does sound menacing,' Newman said quietly.

'Especially when we add the fact that this particular power has built up a huge stock of bacteriological weapons. Plus an advanced type of gas. One whiff of that and opposing troops are paralysed.'

'So our next move is to visit Shrimpton in the early evening. On top of all this Emilio Vitorelli appears to be involved.'

'I'd like to meet Emilio again. He's a riddle.'

Emilio Vitorelli emerged from the Hotel Hassler, strode along in the direction of the Borghese Gardens high above Rome. As in Dorset, the sun was shining out of a clear blue sky. But here, in June, the heat was torrid in the afternoon.

As he walked beautiful women gazed at him with longing. He ignored them. It was not surprising he attracted their attention. Forty years old, a tall man with a lithe gait, his sunglasses were pushed up over his thick black hair. Beneath a well-shaped forehead thick eyebrows were poised over his strong nose, his full-lipped mouth normally twisted in a cynical smile above a firm jaw. Today there was no smile and the women held no interest for a man once notorious for his many and easy conquests.

He wore a smart pale Armani suit and walked with an easy lope, like a panther. A man of many interests, some of them dubious, he had business connections at the highest levels in Milan, New York, London, Paris and Vienna. It was rumoured he had made his wealth in money laundering for the Mafia. Nothing had ever been proved. He had organized the most high-class escort agency in Europe and there were rumours about this – that he profited from blackmail among high society. Again, his enemies had found no proof. The most elegant and aristocratic of women staffed his agency. He met Mario on the Pincio Terrace, above the square of the same name far below.

'You followed the new courier with the money through to the Englishman?' Vitorelli asked in Italian.

'The money went through safely,' Mario replied. 'There was an anxious moment for the courier at London airport when his executive case was opened. He was taken to the Security Chief, but after a while he was released and drove straight to the Dorset village, Shrimpton. Is that the right name?'

'It is.'

Vitorelli was frowning. He pulled down the sunglasses over his eyes, a pair at the height of fashion.

'Let us hope we are on the right track.'

'Yes, we are.' Mario hesitated, unsure whether to bring up the subject, then plunged in. 'You look so sad these days, Emilio. Nothing is going to bring Gina back. You used to be so joyful and brimming with enjoyment of life.'

Behind the dark sunglasses Vitorelli's eyes glazed over. No one except his closest friend, Mario, his most trusted confidant, would have dared to raise the topic of the tragedy. He sensed his friend's discomfort at bringing up the terrible incident. He put an arm round the man's shoulder.

'You are right, Mario. But it takes time to accept what happened. Give me a little more time.'

'Of course. I only wished to show you that I care.'

'I know you care.'

'I had better go. Understandably, I think you prefer your own company these days.'

'Nonsense. Tomorrow you come to my suite at the Hassler and we will get drunk. After the sun goes down.'

'I will look forward to it with great pleasure . . .'

The small fat man, who always reminded Vitorelli of a teddy bear, walked away. Vitorelli placed his slim brown hands on the balustrade, gazing down at the tiny figures of people walking slowly in the heat without seeing them. His mind travelled back to the tragedy of two months before.

He had been on the verge of marrying Gina, an Italian beauty if ever there was one. His whole life as a woman chaser had changed. He had known he could spend the rest of his time on earth with Gina. Then the hated Englishwoman had come into his life.

Arrogant, accustomed always to getting what she wanted, she had wanted Vitorelli. He had treated her with courtesy, had explained the situation, but she

33

would have none of it. Relentlessly, she had pursued him, confident that she would win. He had told Gina of the problem and she had told him to let the woman down lightly. He could remember her musical voice saying it to him.

'You are an attractive man, to say the least. She has a crush on you. Treat her nicely.'

He had followed Gina's advice, had done everything in his power to discourage the Englishwoman. Nothing had worked. There had come a time when the English-woman became convinced that he would never leave Gina. Her hatred at what she considered rejection – something she had never experienced before – welled over.

When Vitorelli was away on a business trip to Zurich she had called at his villa. Gina had opened the door. The Englishwoman had aimed the special phial she was holding, pressed the button which released the jet. Sulphuric acid had splashed all over Gina's face, ruining her beauty for life.

In desperation Vitorelli had taken her to a plastic surgeon. He had assured Gina a great deal could be done to repair some of the damage.

'*Some* of the damage?' Gina had screeched. 'You mean I will still be scarred for life?'

'No, no!' the surgeon had protested. 'I can do a great job for you . . .'

Gina had persisted and, eventually, the surgeon had found himself forced to admit there would always be scars. The acid had bitten so deep. She had left him without making another appointment, her face so band-aged that when she looked in a mirror she felt she was staring at a mask, a quite different woman whose face had been destroyed.

One night when Vitorelli was fast asleep she had slipped out of bed, put on the clothes she had prepared in advance. Calmly she walked to the Pincio Terrace, and without a moment's hesitation climbed over the balustrade and plunged to her death on the square below.

Vitorelli had been distraught, had felt guilty. Earlier that evening he had drunk too much so he could sleep, hoping to escape the nightmare of trying to reassure Gina. Later there had been an incident which converted his grief into cold fury.

He had received a long-distance phone call, doubtless from some other country. The call had been brief, a satisfied, cold, almost detached voice. The Englishwoman had spoken, then slammed down the phone before he could react.

'I warned you, Emilio. If I can't have you no other woman can. Goodbye . . .'

From that moment the idea of revenge had come to him, the iron had entered his soul as the British sometimes said. So far he had not located her whereabouts but his many underground contacts were supplying him with information. He was working on it. Justice would be done one day. He was working on it in the most devious manner, aware that he was swimming in dangerous waters.

4

In his office inside the strange house in Slovakia perched on the edge of a sheer quarry wall which fell three hundred feet, the man who called himself Hassan walked briskly to a corner. His massive steel safe was located in the corner. Operating the combination, he swung open the door, extracted a file, closed the safe.

He took the file to his desk, which had weird

hieroglyphics engraved in the leather top. Settling down in his chair he opened the file. It contained several typed sheets, the one he was looking at listed the members of the Institut de la Défense.

In a similar manner to what Engel had done on his list Hassan had crossed out the names of seven members who had been assassinated. But on this list there were the initials of three different women, all of them attractive but with very different personalities. The Englishman in Dorset had drawn up the list – and so far his insight as to which of the women would appeal to a certain type of man had proved flawless.

Hassan crossed out the name Norbert Engel. Alongside his name were the initials *T. L.*, the woman he had subjected to the ordeal in the training room.

Hassan had a habit of talking to himself as he worked. 'The next target is Pierre Dumont. Most important. The man is a strategic genius. I see our Dorset friend recommends Simone Carnot. Dumont must be interested in tall redheads. He lives in the outskirts of Zurich. I must contact Simone, give her the data on Dumont . . .'

It was early evening when Newman drove Tweed along the country road close to the village of Shrimpton. The sky above the trees lining each side of the road was cloudless, azure blue. Tweed had not spoken since they had left Summer Lodge. Suddenly he sat up straighter.

'Stop the car, Bob.'

Newman reacted immediately. They had seen no other traffic since starting out. Tweed reached over, turned off the ignition, pressed a button to lower the window on his side of the Mercedes.

'Listen to it,' he said.

'To what? I can't hear anything.'

36

'Precisely. There is an extraordinary silence about this part of Dorset. I noticed it when I went for a walk on my own from our hotel. It's uncanny, almost unnerving.'

'You find it significant?'

'It's an area where anything could be going on and no one would know. We haven't seen a single patrol car since we arrived. It is a district of England hidden away from the world. May seem a bit fanciful, but my sixth sense tells me we've come to the right place. Stop the car again when we reach the outskirts of Shrimpton . . .'

Newman parked in an opening to a field as soon as he saw the first houses. He backed the Mercedes in so they could drive off fast in case of an emergency. Tweed got out, waited while Newman locked the car. The same heavy silence descended on him. They began walking along High Lane, the main street of the village.

Tweed was immediately aware of something very odd about this village. The street was cobbled and on either side huddled together were ancient two-storey houses, joined in terrace fashion. Built of Purbeck stone long ago, each house had a curiously deserted look.

Frayed shabby net curtains were drawn across the windows, making it impossible to see inside. The wooden front doors had not seen a coat of paint in years. But it was the absence of people which disturbed Tweed. There was not a sign of life anywhere. Newman reflected his reaction.

'It must be very dark inside the rooms of these places but I haven't seen a light on inside any house.'

'I had noticed that. Almost as though we are walking through an abandoned village. The atmosphere is quite eerie. There are no TV aerials to be seen either.'

They continued their walk through the brooding silence, which was becoming oppressive, uncomfortable.

There was hardly any street lighting, Tweed noticed, only the odd ancient lantern suspended from a rusty bracket outside one of the houses. They had almost reached the end of the empty street when Newman whistled softly.

'Don't believe it. There's a pub ahead of us, the Dog and Whistle. And it's open – with plenty of lights inside the place.'

'We'll go in,' Tweed decided. 'If any of the locals are in there you do most of the talking while I observe . . .'

As he had expected, the interior of the pub had low-beamed ceilings with large upright oak beams support-ing the structure. Between the uprights he caught sight of the wooden counter of the bar, well polished. A large inglenook brick fireplace occupied the right-hand end wall.

He counted eight men in the pub – some leaning against the bar while others sat round small tables in the corners with their glasses of beer. Not a single woman to be seen. Newman led the way to the bar, smiled at the barman, a jolly, red-faced man who greeted him as though he was a regular.

'So what can I do for you two gentleman? Good evening to both of you.'

'I'll have a pint of mild and bitter,' Newman told him.

'The same for me,' said Tweed. He hated the drink, but it was important to merge with the background. 'Seems quiet in the village tonight.'

'Quiet every night,' the barman replied. 'Quiet as the grave.' He corrected himself quickly. 'Shouldn't have said that. You'll think you've arrived at a cemetery. I will have my little joke,' he went on hastily as he served the drinks.

Tweed looked round the pub. The customers were clearly locals – farm workers, probably. Most wore shirts rolled up at the sleeves, corduroy trousers stained with soil marks; they had the weatherbeaten complexions of men who spent their lives working outdoors. Newman turned to an old boy standing next to him.

'I have a couple of friends round here. Haven't seen them for ages. One is Captain Wellesley Carrington. Has he moved? I hope not.'

'The Cap'n.' It was the barman who answered. 'One of the nobs. Don't get me wrong. He comes in here now and then for his pint. Just like the rest of us. Trouble is, he's abroad a lot. You ask Jed there and he'll tell you more than he should.'

Newman turned to the old boy, white-haired and with a stooped back. He ordered him another glass.

'Go on, Jed.' Newman grinned. 'Spill the beans.'

'Bit of a one for the ladies. Seen some real beauties driving in through those gates of his. Classy stuff – at least that be from the ways they dress. Like those pics you see of models in the papers. I wouldn't mind spendin' an hour or two with one of 'em.'

He gave a lecherous wink and the barman, not wishing to be left out of any conversation, intervened. He shook his head at the old boy.

'Face it, Jed – you're long past it. Just pictures in that wicked old mind of yours.'

'You might be surprised,' Jed responded indignantly.

'Still lives in the same place, does he?' Newman enquired casually.

'Dovecote Manor is still his nest for the birds,' Jed said, still glaring at the barman.

'So long ago I've clean forgotten how to get there,' Newman remarked.

'You've got a car? Good. As you goes out of the pub you turn right, follow the road away from the village 'bout 'alf a mile and gates is on your right. In middle of nowhere.'

39

'I didn't get your name,' the barman said, polishing another glass.

'Dick Archer,' Newman replied quickly. 'I'm in computers.'

'Bet you make a fortune out of them.'

'I earn the odd crust of bread.'

'I have an old friend in this neck of the woods,' Tweed said, speaking for the second time. 'Amos Lodge. Now there's a brain if ever I met one. And as Chief Claims Investigator for an insurance outfit I've met a few. Trouble is I've lost his address.'

He was looking at Jed as he phrased the indirect question. Jed chimed in, ignoring the warning glance the barman gave him.

'He's still at The Minotaur. Used to work for him in the garden. It's a large thatched cottage. Go on past the Cap'n's place, take the first turning to the right. Country lane – only room for one car. The cottage is 'alf a mile down the lane on the left. Can't miss it. No one else lives that way.'

'Amos has been in here once or twice,' the barman interjected, 'and you're right. His mind is so far above mine I can't rightly get what he's saying.'

Tweed realized his tactic had worked. By revealing his fake profession he had reassured the barman. He pressed home the advantage, again staring at Jed as he asked a tricky question.

'Walking down the street to get here we noticed all the houses seemed derelect. No sign that anyone lives in any of them.'

'It's a quiet village . . .' the barman began.

'That tells our friend nothing,' Jed intervened. 'The whole village is owned by a man called Shafto. He rents out the cottages to staff for his place. I live in one of 'em. Can see why you says what you did. Peculiar things go on inside some of those 'ouses.'

40

'Jed . . .' the barman warned, stopping polishing a glass.

By now Newman had bought Jed another pint, noticing how swiftly he had downed his previous glass. The old boy was well away, but still his mind functioned. He had the eyes of a squirrel as he explained to Tweed.

'Couldn't sleep one night because of the 'eat. Got up, put on clothes to go for a walk and went out into the street. From a cottage lower down I saw an Arab woman come out. She walks off to the end of the village, past the Dog and Whistle. Then I hear a car starting up. Drives off the other way.'

'He has nightmares . . .' the barman began.

'What made you think she was an Arab woman?' Tweed persisted.

'Way she was dressed,' Jed continued. 'Has a black thing on. Covered her from head to toe. And she wore a black veil and that thing on her head Arab women wear. I've seen pictures of them. What was she doing in a place like this? That's what I wondered to meself.'

'That's the only Arab woman you've seen here?' Tweed asked.

'The only one. But it was three in the morning. I'm usually in the land of Nod at that hour.'

'Could have been a woman in fancy dress,' Tweed commented.

Making the effort, he swallowed the rest of his pint, then checked his watch. Newman took the hint.

'Better be on our way,' he said. 'Another pint for Jed.'

Slapping money down on the counter, he followed Tweed out. They chatted as they walked back to the parked car.

'We've come to the right place,' Tweed said grimly.

'Looks like it. Which one first?' Newman asked.

41

'Willie – also known as Captain William Wellesley Carrington. En route we come to his place and he's the man I want to talk to first. Let's hope he's not on one of his trips abroad.'

The gold-painted wrought-iron gates were open and a curving drive beyond led to Dovecote Manor, a small Georgian gem of a house. Parked on the tarred turn-round close to the entrance to the house was a new red Porsche. Newman moved at a leisurely pace, stopped just behind the Porsche.

'Reeks of money,' he commented. 'Those gates cost a pretty penny. And Heaven knows what he's got concealed behind the closed doors of that double garage by the side of the house. Probably a Roller.'

Tweed said nothing, leaving the car and marching up the flight of stone steps to a terrace and the freshly varnished front door. He pressed the bell, waited. A couple of minutes later the door opened and Wellesley Carrington gazed at Tweed, then smiled with pleasure.

'This is an unexpected delight. Long time no see. Do come in with your friend. I say, isn't he Robert Newman, the famous foreign correspondent?'

'He is,' Newman said without enthusiasm.

Unusually for him, he took an instant dislike to the man framed in the arched doorway. Wearing a navy blue tracksuit, he was about five feet eleven tall, and in his forties, Newman estimated. Well-built, he exuded an arrogant self-confidence verging on the aggressive. His voice was a good public school, his manner said he knew he belonged to the elite and he had a pug nose. His thick hair was a light brown colour with a pencil-thin moustache of the same colour. His eyes were ice-blue and his thick-lipped, sensuous mouth had a beguiling grin above a hard jaw.

42

A gigolo, Newman said to himself. But a tough one you had to be wary of. A man confident he could dominate anyone, any situation. He gripped Tweed's hand, then shook Newman's. His grip was firm. On the surface he gave the impression he was sociable, glad to have visitors call on him. So why did Newman sense that the timing was bad from his point of view?

'Come in immediately,' he said in an animated tone.

'I hope our arrival isn't inconvenient,' Tweed suggested – which told Newman Tweed also had detected a certain reservation in their host's manner. 'We could always come another time,' Tweed went on, 'but we couldn't get through to you on the phone,' he said smoothly. 'Do say if it's inconvenient, Willie.'

'Damn it! I've just invited both of you in. So come on inside, fellers. We'll have a drink to start with.'

Tweed entered a medium-sized hall with wood-block flooring. In the panelled walls were alcoves with vases of flowers. Closing the door, Willie led them to an open door which led into a drawing room extending from the front to the back of the house.

The room was expensively and tastefully furnished with antiques, a couch as large as a spacious single bed, a scatter of armchairs, a cocktail cabinet with an interior illuminated light, various *objets d'art* on coffee tables which had an Eastern character; the result of his travels, Newman assumed. But what caught his attention was the beautiful brunette lounging on the couch with her legs tucked under her, shapely legs, very much on view. Willie made introductions.

'Gentlemen, this is Celia, my latest girlfriend. Celia, my darling, this is Tweed, and this is Bob Newman.'

'Interesting friends you have, Willie,' Celia commented, staring straight at Newman. 'Such a pity I have to leave now. Another one of those bloody parties I promised to attend in a weak moment. Such a crashing bore but I did accept the invitation.'

She finished the drink in her long-stemmed glass, which Tweed guessed was champagne. Standing up, she straightened her blue, sheathlike dress, which appeared to have been rumpled. She kissed Willie on the cheek, smiled ravishingly at both visitors and with the elegant walk of a model left the room. They heard the Porsche's engine start up and then a scream of tyres as she drove off.

'Girl in a thousand,' Willie commented.

'Bet you always say that,' Newman mocked him.

Willie's expression changed for a millisecond, became venomous, then he replaced the look with his broad smile.

'What's your tipple, both of you?'

'I'll have a double Scotch, please. Neat,' said Newman.

'A glass of white wine for me,' responded Tweed, who rarely drank.

Taking off his glasses, he rubbed them with a clean handkerchief, seated on a corner of the couch Celia had vacated. He put on his glasses and gazed round. A pair of French windows were open at the rear end, looking out onto a large expanse of garden. Inwardly he tensed.

The garden stretched away across a neat lawn and he could see a strange stone arch inscribed with symbols. It had a distinctly Middle Eastern character. Bringing back the drinks on a silver tray, Willie caught the direction of his glance.

'Take you out into the garden later. That arch was shipped to me from Beirut. I take a fancy to things when I'm overseas, try to bring back mementoes. Cheers!'

'Cheers!' said Newman, occupying one of the armchairs. 'I rather liked the look of Celia. What's her second name?'

44

'Ah!' Willie perched on the arm of the couch at the opposite end from Tweed. 'I can recognize a woman chaser when I meet one. Not going to tell you her surname. She's my friend – for the moment. Drink up – then I'll refresh your glass.'

Tweed was amused. He realized Newman had intended tracing Celia if he could – to get information out of her without any amorous intentions.

'You can't stand the competition,' Newman mocked their host.

He had assessed Willie's character. He steam-rollered people when he could get away with it. He only respected men who stood up to his bluff aggressiveness.

'You think so?' Willie sipped at his Grand Marnier. 'Well, I haven't got where I have without smashing some pretty nasty types into the ground – yourself excluded, of course. The world has become a rough place,' he said genially. 'It comes down to survival. That's the bottom line, survival.'

Newman found he was beginning to like Willie. He was out of the ordinary. A man who went his own way regardless of what more convential types thought of him. He had an engaging smile and Newman could easily see why he was attractive to women. His vitality, the I-don't-give-a-damn attitude, would appeal to the opposite sex. He could also get on with men, provided they were of strong character.

'Tell me again, Willie,' Tweed said suddenly, 'what kind of business you're in.'

'Import-Export. Same as before.'

'Doesn't tell me a thing,' Tweed said. 'So what do you handle?'

'What the West wants from the East, I deliver. What the East wants from the West, I deliver. Crates of Scotch, like Newman is drinking, to Muslim countries. At ten times the price I buy them for over here. There are certain things they'd like I won't touch with a bargepole. I make that very clear to them and they respect my view. Now I'll freshen up our drinks and we can take a walk in the garden . . .'

Newman asked for mineral water, explaining that he was driving. Tweed put his hand over his half-empty wineglass. Willie shrugged, refilled his own glass with Grand Marnier, then led the way out. It was cooler outside than it had been when Tweed and Newman had arrived.

Huge banks of rhododendron bushes flanked both sides of the estate-like garden, masking it from the outside world. They followed Willie along a flagstone path set into the lawn, reached the strange arch. Tweed paused beneath it, stared at the symbols inscribed into the stone. Arabic.

'What do these insignia mean?' he asked.

'No idea,' his host said brusquely.

'But don't you understand Arabic – dealing as you do with the Middle East?'

'I taught myself to speak the lingo,' Willie said in a throwaway manner, 'so as to help with the haggling. But written down I don't understand a word. Contracts are always drawn up in English. Come on, lots more to see.'

Indeed there was. They walked along another path curving round a large lake. In its centre stood an island, and perched on the island was an Eastern statue in stone. A man and a woman were the main feature, with a serpent twined round them. It struck Newman as erotic.

The dead silence of this part of Dorset descended on them as they walked on, turning a corner to see another large lake. This also had an island. Newman stopped and stared. An ancient eight-sided temple-like edifice

46

stood on this island, but what caught his attention were the tall windows, all painted black.

'What on earth is that?' Tweed enquired.

'No idea,' Willie replied. 'But I liked it so I had that shipped over here. There's more to see,' he said quickly and hustled ahead of them.

Curious as to why Willie had attempted to hasten them on, Newman dragged his feet. When he looked back he saw one side was open, the interior illuminated by a huge lantern. Under the lantern stood a large double bed with a Persian rug thrown over it. Willie looked back, saw Newman staring.

'Got a boat to take me over there,' he called out. 'It's an ideal place for me to take a nap, think out a problem without being bothered by the phone or fax messages. Call it my hideaway. At times I need privacy.'

'I'm sure you do,' Newman said cynically.

He was thinking of Celia, of Willie's faint discomfiture when they had arrived, of Celia's swift departure. This is not a normal place, he mused as he started walking after Tweed.

They passed through a narrow closed-in avenue – closed in by seven-foot-high box hedges. Emerging into a wilder, more overgrown area, Willie pointed.

'Another lake. I like water.'

Tweed stood stock still and stared. This large stretch of water was curved in a half-moon shape. Again an island stood near the middle of the lake. This island was shaped like a half-moon, reproducing the shape of the lake. A peculiar squat building occupied half the island. Built of great blocks of misshapen stone, it reminded Tweed of paintings he had seen of the ancient civilization of Assyria. What he found especially odd was a huge stone plaque attached to one rock. It carried the design of the Turkish flag of the present day.

'That's just a bit of fun,' said Willie, now standing alongside his two visitors.

'I have noticed that with each lake you have a landing-stage concealed in the reeds at the water's edge,' Tweed said slowly. 'And each one has a large dinghy with an outboard motor – presumably the way you reach each island.

Willie's manner changed. His face became expressionless. When he spoke his tone was abrupt.

'Time to get back to the house. It's getting chilly.'

Saying which, he hurried back the way they had come, keeping up a rapid pace until they reached the drawing room. He went to the cocktail cabinet, refilled his glass, turned to his guests.

'One for the road?'

'Not for me,' said Newman.

'I'll pass,' Tweed replied. 'Thank you, Willie, for your hospitality. We must keep in touch.'

'Great idea,' Willie said without enthusiasm.

Making their farewells, Tweed and Newman returned to their car. Neither said anything as they proceeded down the drive. They were about to pass through the gates when Tweed spoke.

'Turn right. Keep a lookout for that lane which leads to Amos Lodge's place.' He lowered his window. 'I feel like a breath of fresh air.'

'*Dovecote* Manor,' Newman commented. 'A misnomer if ever I came across one. The house struck me as a front. Once in the garden the place reeked of Roman orgies.'

'That's carrying it a bit far,' Tweed said in a dreamy tone. 'But he knows how to impress visitors from the East. You'll find Amos Lodge a very different proposition.'

5

The same day Butler and Nield received the order from Tweed via Monica to fly to Vienna – to back up Paula and Marler – they boarded a flight for Zurich from Heathrow. In Zurich they were lucky – they just managed to catch an Austrian Airlines plane to Vienna.

'Hope we get there in time to link up with them,' Butler remarked.

'We'll link up. No doubt about it,' replied Nield, who sat alongside his team-mate.

They were very different in appearance and temperament. Harry Butler was heavily built, sturdy and a man who worried. In his mid-forties, he took little trouble with his clothes and wore a windcheater and creased grey slacks. He had put his backpack in the luggage compartment above their heads, next to Nield's. They were travelling as though they were tourists.

Pete Nield was slim with a neat moustache, unlike Butler who was clean-shaven and had a strong jaw. Normally Nield, who was in his late thirties, took a pride in his appearance and had attracted the attention of more than one woman. Now, to fit the part, he was clad in a black Adidas tracksuit with white stripes. He looked by a long way the smarter of the two men.

'I think we ought to hit the Hotel Sacher first before we go out to this Burgenland place,' Butler suggested, always looking ahead.

'I agree,' Nield said. 'My hope is that something has taken them back to the Sacher before they took off into the wild blue yonder. Monica has arranged for a hired car to be standing by for us to collect at Schwechat Airport.'

'Monica never misses a trick.'

'She's the best.'

He checked his watch. Although outwardly cool and in control, as always, he also was worried. The kidnap attempt on Paula, plus the murderous prison breakout of the thugs involved, told him they were up against some pretty ruthless characters.

He wanted the plane to move faster but forced himself to relax. As the machine started its long descent he kept his fingers crossed.

As it happened, chance had kept Paula and Marler in Vienna. After checking out of the hotel, Marler determined to keep Paula close to him. They had locked their luggage inside the trunk of a BMW Marler had hired and parked in a nearby garage.

'We're walking down Kärntnerstrasse,' he told her. 'We only have two handguns. We need more than that – and I know a good man who can supply me – for a price, of course.'

'Do you want an Armalite?'

'It's on my list.'

Reaching the Dom, Marler took Paula inside a crowded department store, told her to wait in the lingerie section. He couldn't take her with him to the arms dealer, who insisted on remaining anonymous.

Checking to make sure he had not been followed, Marler entered an art gallery on Graben, a street of old buildings leading off from the Dom and at right-angles to Kärntnerstrasse. He realized this was the same area where the three thugs had attempted to kidnap Paula before he had intervened, so he was very cautious. He had slipped inside the art gallery doorway suddenly and swiftly.

The owner, Alexander Ziegler, stood with his arms

50

folded, watching a woman he knew would never buy a picture. He greeted Marler in English, careful not to use his name.

'Welcome back, sir. It has been too long.'

Ziegler was a big man, well dressed in a dark business suit. Very tall, he had a high forehead and hooded eyes.

'I've come to look at that Monet you phoned me about.'

'It is waiting for you in here. Anna,' he called out, 'look after the gallery for a few minutes.'

As he unlocked a door a slim woman with her dark hair tied back to counter the heat appeared. Ziegler ushered Marler inside, closed and relocked the door. On an easel there was a picture which looked like a Monet, but this was pure stage dressing.

'I'm in a hurry,' Marler said.

He gave Ziegler his shopping list and handed over the large canvas satchel slung over his shoulder. The transaction only took a few minutes. With the weapons and ammo packed inside the satchel Ziegler reappeared from the cellar behind a door he had unlocked.

Marler paid for the armoury he had purchased with a large sum in cash. He was out of the shop and hurrying back to the department store in no time. He found Paula waiting for him, fingering some lingerie.

'Pretty sexy,' Marler whispered.

'Not my style. Where to now?'

'Back up Kärntnerstrasse. I'll walk a few paces behind you. We're heading for the garage.'

Paula left him, feeling safe knowing he was watching her. Halfway up the pedestrian street she sensed she was being followed. She glanced across the other side of the street and saw the small stocky thug, one of the men who had tried to bundle her into the stretch limo. She stopped, gazing into a shop window, not knowing that Marler had already spotted the shadow.

Roka had been flown back from Slovakia by helicopter with strict instructions from Hassan. He had been alarmed by the ferocity with which Hassan had addressed him.

'You have the description of the woman who followed our contact with Engel. Go back and find her. Bring her here if you value your life.'

Roka had started at the Hotel Sacher, had seen Paula leave the hotel with a slim man dressed in a linen suit. He followed them at a distance. He thought his chance had come when she entered the department store, but going inside he realized the place was too crowded.

Later he followed her back up Kärntnerstrasse, determined to kill her with his flick-knife if he couldn't frighten her into accompanying him to his parked car. Hassan wouldn't be able to interrogate her but would be relieved she was out of the way.

Roka was pleased the man with her had disappeared. He had recognized him as the swine who had successfully prevented their kidnap attempt. He was so intent on watching Paula it never occurred to him to worry about the man she had been with.

Marler had dropped back, had crossed over to Roka's side of the street. Just as Roka had earlier recognized him, Marler had now recognized Roka. With the heavy satchel slung securely over his shoulder, Marler unfastened the flap and extracted a Walther automatic. He continued tracking the thug.

Paula stopped briefly to glance in a shop window – in its reflection she saw Roka, and Marler behind him. She resumed her walk, strolling at a slower pace. How on earth was Marler going to deal with the situation? The street had quite a few people ambling along.

Marler was waiting until Roka reached a certain building. Then he moved. He was alongside the thug in seconds, rammed the muzzle into Roka's side under cover of the satchel. His voice was hard.

'Move inside this place. Slowly. One mistake and you get a bullet in you.'

'This is a church!'

'Get inside, you bastard.'

Roka obeyed, scared by the tone of Marler's voice. The two men went inside the Maltese church. The previous day Marler had explored Kärntnerstrasse, had gone inside the same building, curious that anything connected with Malta should exist in Vienna. The place had been empty.

It was empty now, a vaulted cavern of darkness with a faint light filtering in the gloom. Rows of wooden pews stood on either side of an aisle leading to a distant altar. The babble and hustle of Vienna might have been a million miles away.

Once inside, Marler slipped behind Roka, pressed the Walther against his spine. The thug moved with a slow heavy tread, was urged well down the aisle. Marler then grabbed him by one arm, shoved him into one of the pew spaces.

'Kneel down,' he hissed.

Marler was in a rare rage – controlled but still a rage. He recalled how this thug had treated Paula. Roka, even more frightened by the coldness in Marler's voice, squeezed himself into a kneeling position. The muzzle of the Walther was transferred from Roka's back to his head, just above his thick hairy neck.

'This is how they do it, isn't it? Place the gun an inch from the back of the head and then blow it off.'

'Please, sir. Beg you . . .'

'Begging will get scum like you nowhere. So talk fast and don't stop to think. Where is the headquarters of this outfit?'

'You say what, sir?'

'I don't say anything. I'm asking you a question. And you damn well know I am. Answer the bloody question. Where is the headquarters? Answer now or you'll never speak again, filthy scum.'

'I know not.'

'Take your last breath.'

'Please, please, sir . . .'

'You're a dead man.'

'Slovakia . . .'

'Who is the top man?'

'My knee, sir.'

Roka crumpled forward, his right knee giving way. It was a convincing manoeuvre but Roka had under-estimated the man he was dealing with. Forcing himself to swivel round, he held the flick-knife he had extracted from inside his jacket. There was a click, a stiletto-like blade emerged from the carved handle he was holding. He lunged for his opponent's stomach. Marler's movement was so swift a witness would not have seen it. He brought down the barrel of his Walther with ferocious force on the bridge of Roka's fleshy nose.

The thug collapsed, his fall taking him half under the pew. He lay very still. Marler did not wait to check his pulse. This was one of the men who had murdered prison guards in the breakout from an Austrian gaol.

As he walked towards the exit he slipped the Walther inside his satchel, fastened the flap, blinked as he emerged into the blazing sunlight. Paula was shop-window gazing, again using the curved window to watch the Maltese church across the street.

Marler smiled as he crossed the street. He had noticed the expression of anxiety on her face, anxiety for what might have happened to him.

'We walk back up the street to the Sacher,' he told

her. 'I have information for Tweed. It's urgent so maybe we'll try and reclaim our rooms.'

'Why?'

'Because I need a phone to call Tweed. I can code this one. Also I'm not sure now Burgenland is the right place to head for.'

He told her what he had extracted from the thug. She was thoughtful before she replied.

'Shouldn't we get out of Vienna – for your sake? Tell me what happened.'

'I put him out of action.'

'The police may come looking for you.'

'They won't. No one saw us go inside – or observed me coming out. I checked. Let's move it. Got your Browning . . .'

They were able to reclaim their rooms. At Paula's suggestion Marler changed into a polo shirt and a pair of casual slacks, a navy blue and white combination, which transformed his appearance. He went along to Paula's room and she commented on how different he looked. He dumped the heavy satchel behind a chair.

'Goodies,' he explained. 'Here's the Browning and ammo.'

He had just spoken when there was a gentle tapping on the door. Grasping a Walther out of the satchel he went to the door, called out.

'Who is it?'

'Harry Butler, delivering the male. A jerk called Pete Nield.'

Marler let them in, relocked the door. They exchanged the briefest of greetings. There had been so many link-ups like this in the past. Paula felt relieved as each of the new arrivals hugged her. She couldn't rid herself of the feeling that Vienna was a trap.

The Minotaur was exactly as Jed had described to Tweed and Newman. A small gate led to a pebbled pathway between grass and beyond was a large thatched cottage. In the dark purple dusk lights glowed behind the mullion windows. To their right a pebbled drive ran up to a small garage and a Jaguar was parked.

'Willie's place should have been called The Minotaur,' Newman commented. 'And Dovecote would have been more appropriate for this place.'

Tweed pulled the chain which rang a bell inside. There was a pause and the old wooden door swung open. Newman, who had never met Amos Lodge, stared in surprise. He had imagined an aged professorial type.

A six-foot man of large build stood in the doorway with a half-smile on his strong face. Lodge had a squarish head and a short tough nose; his shrewd eyes studied Newman briefly through a pair of steel-rimmed glasses with a double bridge. The lenses were squarish, matching his build. His thick hair was dark and he was clean-shaven. Before he opened his small mouth Newman would have typed him as the boss of a major international corporation.

'Tweed, good to see you. Isn't this Bob Newman? Thought so. Welcome and all that stuff. Come on in.'

None of the effusive greetings they had received from Willie. This was a man who came straight to the point. Newman was impressed by the dynamic energy which radiated from their host.

They entered a neat book-lined hall, passed on through a kitchen-breakfast room with a tiled counter dividing off the kitching from the eating area. Lodge led the way along a short passage into a larger hallway

56

furnished with an oak table, then into a living room with a brick fireplace at one end.

The furniture was comfortable, with a square oak table and four carver chairs round it. Lodge gestured towards the table, asked them what they would drink. Newman opted for a Scotch well watered down. Tweed stayed with a glass of wine. Lodge joined them with his own glass of Scotch as they sat round the table. This was going to be no idle conversation, Newman sensed.

'How much does Newman know?' Lodge demanded, settling himself opposite Tweed.

'He knows about the *Institut de la Défense*,' Tweed replied. 'But maybe you could fill him in on the picture better than I have.'

'Doubt that. But I'll try. Briefly, myself excluded, it's like a club of fifteen men of great talent in their special fields. Men worried, like I am, about the fact that at this time Europe is wide open to attack from the East. Not Russia. We assemble now and again at a mansion near Ouchy on the shores of Lake Geneva, check each other's progress.'

'Progress in what direction?' Newman asked.

'The West is leaderless. We have a bunch of softies at the top: the PM in London, the President in Washington, the Chancellor in Bonn, President of France, and so on. The *Institut* has people with clout, trying to influence our spineless leaders, so-called, to recognize the menace, to do something about it, to rebuild fast the most sophisticated defence systems. So far we're hammering our heads against brick walls. And some organization does fear us – it has wiped out eight members so far. Faking murders as suicides. Eight down and seven to go.'

'Including yourself,' Tweed remarked.

'And including your good self. Then there's the moral issue.'

'Never heard you refer to that before,' Tweed commented.

Their host had refilled his glass with neat Scotch. Tweed had the impression Lodge had knocked back a few before they had arrived. Which surprised him. It was making him more talkative than usual as Lodge explained in his gravelly voice:

'The Roman Empire fell because it became decadent. Every kind of perversion occupied them in the last days. I see the same situation in the West. I believe in equality but women have become the dominant force in the West. They're running the show. The situation shows up in many ways. In fashion you see decadence in the way film stars, society women are dressing – or undressing – in public. "Anything goes" is the motto. Men feel they're a back number. Sure, that's a generalization. I'm not a woman-hater – you know that, Tweed. But the whole fibre of Western civilization is being undermined. In many marriages there is no stability. In the moral behaviour of many people, men and women, all sense of moral values, of decency has collapsed. Our politicians – not all of them – are tarred with the same decadent brush. The same descent into moral chaos applies to America, to Britain, to other key Western countries.'

Amos had spoken with vehemence. Behind the square lenses his eyes glittered with conviction. Tweed asked a question.

'What is your solution to the problem?'

'The assertion of strong leadership in the West. A great deal more discipline, the restoration of stability. No good, I fear, looking to the Church. Few people place any real value in it any more. Take the films people see, the pictures our so-called artists paint. It is a descent into bestiality. Not always, I grant you, but too often, too widespread. As I said earlier, anything goes.'

'Could you be a little more specific?' Newman suggested.

'There is a moral and military vacuum. We are wide open to the imposition of a stronger code of behaviour from the East. I refer to Muslims. Not the Fundamentalists – to more extreme groups who have taken control behind the scenes. They know what they are doing – which is why they are wiping out members of the *Institut de la Défense* one by one. They fear our influence might just reach the top, that the West will rearm. The East is confident it has a moral code it can impose on the West, once we are overwhelmed.'

'Men first, women walking a few paces behind them,' Newman pointed out.

'Exactly. This they believe is the natural order of society. History shows it can be done. Remember Muhammad, the Prophet. His armies started from nothing, swept along the North African shore, crossed the Mediterranean via Gibraltar, which they called Jeb-el-Tarik. They flooded into Spain and then crossed the frontier into France. Only Charles Martel, Charles the Hammer, stopped them at the Battle of Poitiers. That was in mid-France! It will be swifter next time. They have modern weaponry – rockets, tanks, all the equipment for a swift conquest of Europe which, I emphasize, is defenceless under the present pseudo-leadership.'

'Militarily you're thinking of it from a strategic angle,' remarked Tweed. 'That's your forte – strategy.'

'That is correct.' Amos paused, his expression grave. 'Within a few days I am travelling to Zurich to consult Pierre Dumont. He is one of the greatest intellects in the world.'

'He certainly is.' Tweed stood up. 'If you will excuse us I have another appointment.' He smiled. 'Not that we had one with you here – it was very good of you to

59

give us the time you have. I know you never stop working.'

'It is one of my bad habits,' Amos responded amiably. He also stood up as Newman held out his hand. 'And I am glad you have shown the patience to listen to my ramblings, Mr Newman.'

'Hardly ramblings.'

Newman also smiled as they shook hands and he stared hard at their host. Amos's hypnotic eyes were glowing with the intensity of his thoughts.

Tweed remained very still and silent as Newman drove them back towards their hotel. He appeared to be watching the lane ahead, illuminated now night had fallen by the beams of their headlights. Newman was accustomed to these moods of Tweed's when he was mentally wrestling furiously with a major problem. Tweed spoke suddenly.

'When we get back can you pack quickly? I'll be doing the same thing. Also I want to phone Monica. We are returning to London immediately. Park Crescent is our centre of communications and I need to be there urgently.'

'That's easily taken care of. And I'll pay the bill.'

Newman had agreed casually. But he knew that from now on they were facing a grave emergency, that from now on the momentum would build and build until it reached its inevitable climax, whatever that might be.

Hassan put down the phone with a satisfied smile. He had just provided Simone Carnot with the essential data on Pierre Dumont. He was a very well-organized man –

with the list the Englishman had provided him he was able to place the right woman close to her target.

Simone had had a photograph of Dumont in her possession for over a week. Hassan had established her in an apartment in the middle of Zurich off Bahnhofstrasse and now she knew his address, his normal movements. Dumont was a man with a firmly established routine he followed every day.

'He leaves his apartment on Talstrasse at ten o'clock each morning,' Hassan had told Simone. 'He then arrives at ten minutes later at Sprungli, the coffee and cake shop on Bahnhofstrasse. He has a routine like a Swiss watch, being Swiss, I presume. Going to the first floor, he spends precisely thirty minutes eating croissants and drinking coffee. Then he . . .'

He continued, outlining Dumont's day until he went to bed in his apartment. Hassan's watchers were experts – they should be, considering the amount he paid them. Then it was cat's play for the chosen woman to make herself known to the target. And, Hassan reflected, Simone Carnot was a fast worker. The recruiter, the Englishman, had shown great psychological insight in selecting the right women.

6

Simone Carnot wandered through the entrance to the Hotel Baur au Lac in Zurich and paused. Several men stared at her without inhibition. Simone was five feet eight inches tall, slim, a redhead, in her thirties. She ignored the stares as she scanned the terrace to the left of the drive, a place in the open where couples sat drinking.

She recognized Pierre Dumont, who, following his

daily routine, sat at one of the tables which had umbrellas over them. The June evening was hot and she wore a short white sleeveless linen dress which emphasized her figure. A gold-link necklace was clasped round her swanlike neck.

She noticed an empty table next to Dumont's, strolled to it, and down under the yellow umbrella, crossed her long, tanned and well-formed legs. She was half-facing Dumont, who sat writing down his latest conclusions in a leather notebook in a neat script.

A waiter swiftly appeared to serve her. She raised her husky voice slightly as she gave her order.

'You know, I think I'd like a dry Martini.'

Dumont, attracted by the sound of her voice looked up, put down his cigarette. That is a plus point, Simone thought. He also smokes. She casually caught his long glance, her greenish eyes meeting his, then looked away. She knew he had been separated from his wife for over three months, that it was the wife's fault since she had taken a lover and had not been sufficiently discreet. Hassan had supplied a very full report on her prey.

Dumont suddenly found he had lost interest in what he was writing down. This was a very attractive woman and she had no rings on her fingers. He told himself to continue with his work – his speech at the Kongresshaus nearby was less than a week away – but he couldn't concentrate.

Simone timed it after she had received her drink and no other waiter was near. They were all clustered under the yellow awning which splayed out above the serving area. She took out a pack of cigarettes, put one in her mouth, fiddled in her handbag as though searching for a lighter.

Dumont sprang up, walked the few paces which divided his table from her, his gold lighter extended.

She looked up, stared straight at him with the ghost

of a polite smile. She had good bone structure, a chin which expressed determination.

'*Merci, Monsieur.*'

This was another bull point in her favour. She knew that he came from the French-speaking part of Switzerland. He began speaking in French.

'I think the evening is the best part of the day at this time of the year. There is a sensation of peace and serenity you only get now.'

'True. You have a good sense of atmosphere. So many men do not have it. I have been working all day inside my study behind a computer. It is pleasant to be outside, to relax.'

'You prefer to do so by yourself?'

'Not really.'

She tapped the end of her cigarette in an ashtray, which was not really necessary yet. Dumont noticed this, put it down to a slight touch of insecurity.

'Then may I join you, since we are both alone?'

'That would be pleasant. But you were busy with your notebook.'

She had a sophisticated approach. Don't push it, she told herself. Far too early for even a hint of flirtation. He assured her he had had enough of his notebook, fetched his own drink and sat beside her. He pointed to beyond the terrace where the hotel's garden spread away towards the lake, to Zurichsee.

'They have improved the garden enormously in recent years. I can remember when it was neglected. Now it is a park, a park of great beauty. I come here every evening not only for a drink, but so I can watch the shadows spreading over the lawn . . .'

Pierre Dumont was a small tubby man in his midfifties. He had a fuzz of brown hair, a plump face, an easy manner. Since his wife had left him he had been very lonely, although nothing in his manner betrayed

63

this to his many friends. His blue-grey eyes had a dreamy look – his mind was so often focused on the world situation and possible solutions. During the three months on his own he had drowned his disappointments in furious work, sitting behind the desk in his apartment as late as 3 a.m. This way he found he could drop into a deep sleep the moment his head hit the pillow. Now he felt the need for some feminine company.

At Summer Lodge Tweed and Newman packed quickly, paid their bill, started their drive back to London through the night. Again Tweed was silent for a long distance and Newman was careful not to interrupt his thought flow.

Frequently, Newman glanced in his rear-view mirror without making any comment. It was Tweed, who had checked his wing mirror without Newman realizing it, who eventually brought the situation out into the open.

'We have been followed ever since we left Evershot. It is still happening.'

'Want me to lose him?' Newman enquired.

'Certainly not. I'm getting the hang of what is going on. Let them go on following. It helps to bring whoever is behind the assassinations out into the open. Then we can confront them.'

'You think it's either Willie or Amos who has set loose the hounds on us?'

'Could be. Who can tell?'

You could, if you wanted to tell me, Newman thought. But he knew Tweed's methods. He played it close to the chest, revealing his hand to no one until he had discovered the identity of the opposition. They were well inside London, approaching Park Crescent, when Tweed spoke again, his voice vibrant with energy despite lack of sleep.

'I called Monica before we left Summer Lodge. She'll be waiting for us when we arrive.'

'Poor Monica. The hours she works.'

'She wouldn't miss it for the world. She realizes we are now getting somewhere.'

'Are we?'

'Yes. I have to stop Paula, Marler and their escorts making a mistake.'

'Then you can get some shut-eye. It's been a long day.'

'Forget sleep. It's going to be a long night.'

Newman bent over Monica when they entered Tweed's office on the first floor. George, the tough guard on the door, had let them in.

'Everyone except you and Monica have gone home,' Tweed had remarked as they had entered.

'Not on your life, sir. Howard is in his office.'

Tweed had groaned. The last person he wanted to see during the night was the pompous Director. Then he remembered that Howard had warned Newman to take care of him when he had spoken to Bob after their arrival at Summer Lodge.

Newman had kissed Monica on one cheek. She had looked up with surprise and pleasure, then teased him.

'Next thing you'll be inviting me out to dinner.'

'It's a date,' Newman joked.

Monica, Tweed's personal assistant for as long as anyone could remember, was a woman of uncertain age, her grey hair tied back in a bun. Tweed sat behind his desk, called out to her.

'Get me Marler at the Sacher in Vienna.'

'I should know where it is now.'

As she spoke she was pressing buttons, recalling the number from her remarkable memory. She warned him as she asked the switchboard operator to put her through to Marler's room.

'Don't forget he'll probably be woken up. Marler? Yes, I know you can always recognize the lilting tones of my voice. Hold on. Someone is calling you.'

'Marler? Good. I'm back at headquarters. This is a direct order to you. It applies to all of you. You are in charge. You stay where you are until you hear from me. No prowling round the streets looking for attractive ladies.'

'Understood.'

Tweed put down the phone, asked Monica to get Pierre Dumont on the line. Then changed his mind, said he'd get the number himself. A woman's voice answered his call.

'Yes? Who is it?'

'Put me on to Pierre Dumont, please.'

'So sorry, he is not available. Who is this calling?'

There was a trace of a French accent in the husky voice which had spoken in English.

'The milkman,' Tweed said, and he slammed down the phone.

He sat thinking for several minutes. He knew Dumont's wife had left him. It was unlike him to seek comfort elsewhere. But it had been three months since Dumont had been left on his own. He had no way of knowing Dumont was taking a shower, that the woman who had answered was Simone Carnot.

Newman was watching him as Tweed sat upright in his swivel chair, gazing into the distance. It was a moonlit night and beyond the heavy net curtains across the windows he could see in the distance the trees of Regent's Park.

'Trouble?' Newman enquired.

'I hope not. In less than two days Pierre Dumont is giving a major speech at the Kongresshaus in Zurich.

He has let it be known that what he says will contain sensational developments in the world situation. What a target – standing up in front of a large audience. CNN is expected to be there with cameras, as well as the world's press and a distinguished audience. I don't like the sound of it. Monica, please get me Arthur Beck.'

Monica phoned, once more from memory, the private number of the Chief of Federal Police in Berne, Switzerland. He was an old friend of Tweed's. Monica nodded a few minutes later, signalling to Tweed that she had him on the line.

'Tweed here . . .'

'Ah, the great man himself,' Beck replied humorously in his perfect English. 'You have a problem? You always have.'

'I'm at HQ in London. Pierre Dumont is giving an important speech at the Kongresshaus in Zurich two days from now.'

'I know. There has been enough publicity about it.'

'I think he could be the target for the next assassination.'

'We've already had one in Geneva. Not another, please.'

'I think he should be heavily guarded. He'd make a star target while he's speaking. I'm guessing.'

'Your guesses worry me. They usually turn out to hit the bull's-eye.' Beck prided himself on his mastery of English. 'I'll call the Police Chief in Zurich, tell him to get cracking. Any clue as to who is behind these murders? And I may have a bit of news for you. One of my brighter types watching Kloten Airport saw Emilio Vitorelli arrive. Tracked him to the Baur au Lac. Booked into a suite indefinitely.'

'Emilio always does that – then no one knows when he plans to leave.'

'When he arrives anywhere it usually means something's afoot.'

'Have him followed. As to who is running the enemy, it could be a man called Assam. I'll spell that . . .'

'It's a state in India. I don't think this concerns India.'

'Neither do I. Keep in touch.'

Tweed began to doodle on a pad. As he did so he repeated out aloud to himself, 'Assam? Assam? Assam?' Could Paula have misheard what the driver of the kidnap car said to her?

He then told Newman about the arrival of Vitorelli in Zurich. Newman pulled a grim face.

'His reputation for dubious dealings runs all the way from Milan to New York. When he turns up something is rotten in the state of Denmark.'

'Which is Beck's opinion.'

Minutes later he took a call from Beck in Berne. He was reassured by what the efficient Chief of Police told him.

'I have alerted Zurich. No one is going to be able to creep up behind Pierre Dumont and shoot him in the back of the head – not in full view of a large audience. Emilio dined at the Baur au Lac, then went straight to bed.'

'Thanks for keeping me so closely informed.'

Beck's remark was to haunt Tweed in the near future.

Mario Parcelli, who posed as a gigolo, had walked past the police watchers at Kloten, Zurich's airport, without being seen. A dapper little man, neatly dressed in a lightweight blue suit made in Savile Row, London, he was actually Vitorelli's chief lieutenant.

He had been careful to disembark from the plane some distance behind his boss.

Ever cautious, he did not take the first waiting taxi, but hung back until he could climb inside the third cab to pull up. Now he knew he was not being followed. He perched his Louis Vuitton case beside him. Crossing his feet encased in navy blue Ferragamo loafers, he looked out of the rear window. He could not resist the instinct to check again.

Turning to face the front, he glanced down at his loafers. His appearance was all part of his image. His main task for Vitorelli was to control the wide-flung network of informants who kept him in touch with what was going on. So often he had enabled Vitorelli to bring off a business coup. Now he had a more difficult task to perform and he reckoned he had come up with pure gold.

'Take me to the Schweizerhof Hotel in Bahn-hofplatz,' he had told the driver.

Arriving at the hotel opposite the main rail station, he had paid off the driver, waited until he had gone. Then he had walked away from the hotel round the corner into the Bahnhofstrasse, bought a ticket from the machine and boarded the first tram.

'You overdo the precautions,' the casual Vitorelli had once remarked.

'I know my job,' Mario had rapped back.

Alighting from the large blue tram near the end of Bahnhofstrasse before it reached the lake, Mario walked into the Baur au Lac, booked himself a room. He looked at the concierge before heading for the lift.

'You have Emilio Vitorelli staying here. I have an urgent message for him. I need his room number.'

'I can deliver the message if anyone of that name is here,' the concierge replied discreetly. 'Excuse me, sir.'

Fuming with impatience, Mario waited. Vitorelli had stayed at this hotel many times before. The concierge returned quickly with a pleasant smile. Having phoned Vitorelli, describing the new arrival, he gave Mario the room number.

Hurrying to the lift while a porter took his case to his own room, Mario stopped at the correct floor. Vitorelli was standing in his doorway, the raised hand in greeting, ushered him inside, relocked the door.

'I could not approach you on the plane,' Mario began, 'even though I had what might be an important discovery.'

'From one of your informants?'

'Yes.

'The name?'

'I cannot reveal that, even to you. Part of the deal. One to one. Someone in the underworld. They told me there is a strong rumour that the organization which is behind the eight assassinations is called The Sisterhood.'

7

Tweed had stayed inside the SIS building – mostly in his own office – for two days. He had hauled out a camp bed from a cupboard, Monica had made up the bed for him, and he had managed a few hours of sleep.

'Action this day?' Monica had suggested on completing her self-imposed task.

'We are at the difficult stage of a loaded pause,' Tweed had replied.

He was not idle. He had got in touch with Keith Kent, based in the City. Kent could locate the mysterious sources of large sums of money more swiftly than

70

anyone. Tweed's instructions over the phone were simple.

'Keith, there are two people I want investigated – where their money comes from. One is Captain William Wellesley Carrington, lives in Dorset at . . .'

He provided as much data as he could and then mentioned the second name.

'Also an apparently less wealthy man living in the same area. Amos Lodge, the well-known expert on world strategy. He lives at . . . Finally, is the village of Shrimpton owned by one man and, if so, who is it? I need the information yesterday.'

'You always do,' Kent's educated voice replied ironically. 'Do either of these men travel abroad?'

'I was coming to that. Willie – that is Carrington – makes frequent trips to the Middle East. Lodge also travels overseas but I don't know where or how often. I have been told by a friend that couriers bring in large sums in cash to someone in the same area. We know one large consignment was delivered recently – but we don't know where in Dorset it went to, or who was the recipient. It could be a matter of life or death to a number of people. Sorry I have no more data to give you.'

'So I'll get working on it now. It will cost you.'

'It always does,' Tweed replied.

Newman had been listening to the conversation. He knew Kent. When Tweed put down the phone he asked his questions.

'You think one of them – Lodge or Willie – is mixed up in these assassinations?'

'I have no idea. It could be a third party we missed down in Dorset.'

'I was waiting for you to ask Willie about what had happened to Tina Langley, his previous girlfriend. You didn't.'

'Deliberately. I didn't want to make him suspicious

of me. I noticed her picture was on the grand piano in the living room. The photo of a petite auburn-haired woman in her thirties, standing with her arm through Willie's.'

'I noticed that picture. Tina is a very attractive woman. Had a good figure, an inviting smile on her face. A lot of men would fall for a woman like that.'

'What did you say?' asked Tweed, whose thoughts had wandered.

Newman repeated what he had said. Tweed looked thoughtful, gazing out of the window at the distant morning sun in Regent's Park. It was going to be another heatwave day.

'Did I say something?' Newman pressed.

'You repeated what you had said earlier. Monica, try and get Kuhlmann on the phone. He should have left Vienna now and returned to his base at Wiesbaden in Germany.'

He had just spoken when the phone rang. Monica told him that Paula was on the line.

'What is it, Paula?' Tweed asked.

'If necessary, we'll go on doing it – staying holed up here at the Sacher, I mean. But isn't it an appalling waste of manpower? To say nothing of myself.'

Her voice was grim. Tweed realized she was in one of her rebellious moods. Not because she was impatient but because she sensed an imminent crisis. He had great respect for her judgement, took an instant decision.

'Are you packed and ready to go?'

'As ready as we can be under the circumstances.'

'Then all of you are to catch a flight to Zurich. When you—'

'Could you hold on a moment while I speak to Marler?'

'Of course.'

Marler came on the line very quickly. As always his wording was terse and to the point.

'We don't want to catch a plane. I strongly urge that instead we drive in two hired cars the length of Austria, then cross the border into Switzerland. I have my reasons.'

'I agree,' Tweed said. 'Occupy separate rooms at Baur au Lac and the Gotthard. Rooms will be booked for you.'

Marler turned to the others in his room at the Sacher. He told them about Tweed's order. They had heard his preference for going by car.

'Why by car?' Paula demanded.

'What are you carrying in that special pocket inside your shoulder bag? A .32 Browning. What have I given Harry and Pete?' he said, turning to the two men. 'Each has a Walther and plenty of spare ammo. I have my own Walther – plus my Armalite rifle. We can't fly with them.'

'Dump them in the Danube,' said Paula.

'I know a reliable arms dealer in Geneva.' Marler shook his head. 'The one I know in Zurich is tricky. We don't know what we're walking into when we reach Zurich. Using the two cars I can tape my stuff under my car, plus your Browning and Harry and Pete's weapons. Harry can drive you while Pete comes with me. I know a way we can cross the frontier into Switzerland avoiding any checkpoint.'

'It will take ages to drive across Austria,' Paula protested.

'Tweed has sanctioned the idea.'

'Then that's what we must do,' interjected Butler.

'I suppose you're right,' Paula agreed reluctantly. 'But it isn't as though we're going up against a tough mob in Zurich.'

'Don't count on that,' Marler warned.

Newman was present when Tweed took the phone call from Paula. When he had ended the call, Tweed explained what had happened.

'I suppose you can understand them getting a locked-up feeling, being confined to the Sacher,' Newman commented.

'I had to take an instant decision. A sixth sense tells me Zurich could be the next flashpoint. That we'll need plenty of back-up in that city. I'm still worried about Pierre Dumont making that public speech which has been so widely reported in advance.'

'You have warned Beck and he's taking action. I'm going back to my flat – I'm a bit short of sleep. You know you can always get me if anything develops.'

For the rest of the day and late into the evening Tweed worked with Monica on admin, which he hated, but it had to be cleared off his desk. He was just about to take to his camp bed when Howard strolled in. The Director had a habit of intruding at an inconvenient moment. Monica pulled a face behind his back as he settled into an armchair, one leg perched over an arm of the seat.

As usual he was faultlessly dressed in a Chester Barrie suit from Harrods, this time a blue bird's-eye. He adjusted his club tie over a spotless white shirt and looked at Tweed as he spoke in his public school accent.

'Any news from the Dorset front?'

'We met both Willie Carrington and Amos Lodge,'

74

Tweed began. He had decided to give Howard some news to satisfy him after the way he had taken the trouble to warn him to be careful. 'We didn't really get anything vital out of either of them.'

'So we cross them off the list of suspects about the money you told me a courier was carrying to that part of the world?'

'I didn't say that.'

'I'm worried about the way these top brains are being polished off one by one. I knew Norbert Engel. Nice chap.'

'We're all worried. We just have to wait for something to point us in the right direction.'

'See you're sleeping here. You should go home to your flat.' Howard heaved himself out of the chair. 'That's where I'm going. Keep me in touch . . .'

Five minutes later the phone rang. Monica answered, told Tweed Keith Kent was on the line.

'Any luck, Keith?'

'I've spent many hours checking out both Carrington and Lodge. I've used methods and sources I rarely resort to. It's very odd – I've come up with nothing.'

'Unlike you, Keith.'

'There's something funny about where both men get their income from. I can smell it. But I can't penetrate how they live in style. Thought I'd give you this first report. I'm going on digging. I never give up. I'll come back when I do have something solid.'

'Thanks for phoning me. I'll leave it to you.'

He said good night, gazed at Monica, who had been recording the call.

'What do you make of that, Monica?'

'One or both have a secret source of income and have covered their tracks exceptionally well. People don't do that unless they have a great deal to hide.'

'Could be.'

Tweed had a dreamy look which Monica was familiar with. She posed her question tentatively.

'Where is your mind drifting now?'

'Zurich.'

Earlier Hassan had phoned the Englishman, who was the director of the whole operation. The only man more powerful was the head of an Eastern state, who frequently checked on the group of generals who were preparing the massive onslaught on the West.

'Hassan speaking. I have had reports that a certain person on the list is becoming very active – or rather his cohorts are. There has already been an unfortunate incident in the city of Vienna.'

'Then the right person should visit him next. In case she fails, proceed with the next person below him on the list. You understand me, I trust?'

'Perfectly, sir. I will launch the procedures immediately.'

The man he was talking to had not replied, had merely broken off the call. Hassan, in his fortress-like headquarters on top of the low mountain in Slovakia, shivered. It always worried him, talking to this man. The voice was so cold and menacing. He was unnerved for another reason. *In case she fails* . . .

The Englishman had never before suggested such a possibility. The list he had referred to was the names of all the fifteen members of the Institut de la Défense. Hassan could recite the list in sequence from memory. The next person on the list after Pierre Dumont had only a single name. Tweed.

What, Hassan asked himself, was so special about this man, Tweed? He was the first member the Englishman had showed respect for – even fear of.

He unlocked a drawer to check his memory. Yes, after Dumont there was the name. Tweed. Alongside it were the initials. *K. B.* – Karin Berg, a glamorous blonde Swede noted for her intellect. She had studied psychology and world history at the University of Uppsala, north of Stockholm.

Unlike the others she was not in place. So where to move her to? She had once been a member of the Swedish counter-espionage organization. Hassan picked up the phone, pressed numbers which would put him through to her apartment in Stockholm. He had little hope she would be at home.

'Who is it?' her cool voice enquired in English.

'You know who it is calling,' he replied in his slightly lilting voice.

'I do.'

'Your next appointment is with a man called Tweed.'

'So now you give me an extremely difficult one. I shall need to double the fee.'

Double the fee! Two hundred thousand dollars. Hassan was on the verge of exploding, then he remembered the Englishman's direct order, the fact that the Eastern Head of State had a vast fortune at his disposal. But he had to make a protest.

'That's a lot of money.'

'I have already told you,' she said in her arrogant voice, 'this is an extremely difficult one. That is my fee. Or forget it.'

'I accept,' Hassan said quickly.

She was quite capable of slamming the phone down on him. He had to obey the Englishman.

'Where do I locate myself?'

'I'm not sure yet.'

'I am. Zurich. Dumont, the global expert, is giving a speech in the Kongresshaus. It has been reported in all the papers. Tweed will be there. The nearest de luxe hotel is the Baur au Lac. Book me a suite there. I will be flying from Stockholm to Zurich today. Reserve the suite in my name. Leave the rest to me. Goodbye.'

Taken aback, livid that he should be spoken to in this way, Hassan replaced the receiver. Berg was the only one of his three women who did not treat him with the respect he was sure he deserved. He shrugged his slim shoulders, mopped sweat off his forehead.

He called the Baur au Lac, persuaded them to let him have their last suite in Berg's name. Then he called the arms dealer in Zurich who would supply her with a Luger – to be delivered in a Cartier gift box, well wrapped in polystyrene.

He was still puzzled. Why was this man Tweed so dangerous?

In his own suite at the Baur au Lac, Emilio Vitorelli sat watching his trusted assistant, Mario Parcelli. Mario, who avoided alcohol, had just returned after being away for many hours. He was drinking all of a half-bottle of mineral water.

'This heat,' he complained in Italian, 'we don't get it in Italy.'

'Yes, we do. Have you yet found a clue as to where Tina Langley is?'

'Not really. She disappeared from Dorset in England over four weeks ago. I found a local taxi driver who had taken her – with luggage – to London airport. Then she vanished.'

'You checked the aircraft leaving about the time she got there?'

'Of course. Flights were leaving for New York, Zurich and Geneva soon after Tina arrived at the airport. That I checked out.'

'Interesting.' Vitorelli, clad in a cream open-necked

shirt and trousers of the same colour, stirred his Campari with a swizzle stick, moving round the lumps of ice. 'From here you can easily link up with a flight to Vienna.'

'That's significant?' Mario asked.

'There's been an upsurge of trouble in Vienna. Norbert Engel had the back of his head blown off there. Then they found a dead creep in a Maltese church in Vienna, of all places. A clever German Chief of Criminal Police I have evaded by centimetres on several occasions, Otto Kuhlmann, announced today he's sure the corpse is linked with the Engel murder in some way.'

'I don't see the connection,' Mario commented.

'I'm not sure I do. But an idea is forming at the back of my mind. You have people in Vienna. Tell them to check out the Engel murder – that's what Kuhlmann is calling it. They should concentrate on whether a woman is involved.'

'I'll get moving on it now.'

Marler, Paula, Butler and Nield, in their two cars, were approaching the Swiss frontier in the middle of the night. Marler calculated they should reach Zurich some time during the morning of the coming day.

In the first car, driven by Butler, Paula sat by his side. She had dozed off for a few hours but had now woken up fully alert. She asked Butler to stop the car for a few minutes, then ran back along the road to the other vehicle.

'When do we reach Zurich?' she asked.

Marler told her of his estimation, provided they crossed the border without incident. She nodded, stood thinking.

'That means we'll arrive in time for Dumont's big

79

speech at the Kongresshaus. I'd like to attend that. It takes place in the evening.'

'Probably be a crashing great bore, but that's up to you. Go back to your wagon and eat while we're on the move. Good job we brought rations with us.'

Everyone was moving in on Zurich. Amos Lodge had driven up from Dorset, caught an early Swissair flight. The big man refused breakfast on the plane and studied a folder stuffed with papers. He drank strong coffee and never once looked out of the window.

When the machine touched down at Kloten he caught a cab to the Baur au Lac, claimed the room he had booked earlier. He made several phone calls, then went downstairs to have something to eat.

Afterwards he walked out of the wide drive, where a Rolls-Royce was parked alongside a Daimler, and headed for the lake. Several women looked at the imposing figure with steel-rimmed glasses but he hardly noticed them. Outside the large modern block on General Guisan Quai which is Kongresshaus he paused. He was staring at a poster advertising Pierre Dumont's speech that evening.

Nothing in his expression betrayed his reaction but he was noted for never giving away what he was thinking. From the lake there was a hooting of a siren as one of the large boats which plied the lake prepared to leave. At the same time a smaller steamer approached the landing stage, carrying commuters who worked in Zurich and had expensive homes well outside the city.

'A lovely day,' Lodge said to himself as he resumed his walk round the glasslike lake with the sun shining out of a clear blue sky. 'A lovely day for Pierre Dumont's speech.'

He resumed his long strides. Amos Lodge was a man who believed in exercise every day.

Hassan picked up the phone when it started ringing. It was the Englishman. Hassan gazed out of his window while he listened. On the side of the long house facing the quarry there was no need to have shutters. Blazing sun scorched the plain which was Austria.

'I thought over the data from Vienna you gave me. You said one of your men had seen the brunette.' He was referring to Paula Grey without realizing it. 'She left with three men in two cars. Your man followed her, then lost them south of Salzburg. They could be heading for Zurich. Isn't that probable?'

'It is, indeed, sir.'

Hassan didn't follow the reasoning but always agreed with anything the Englishman said. He didn't want to be replaced. Permanently.

'I have taken precautions. The Monceau gang is heading for Zurich via Geneva. I have given Monceau instructions – and your phone number. Do anything he says.'

Again the phone had gone dead. When the Englishman came to the end of giving an order he saw no reason for prolonging the conversation. He had an upper-crust British public school accent.

Hassan swore to himself in Arabic. The Monceau gang. By Allah he didn't like this development. Jules Monceau was notorious for his ruthlessness. His gang had robbed banks, killing people in the process. He engaged in blackmail of top people in France. Any activity which made big money.

* * *

81

The phone rang in Tweed's office early in the morning. It was Beck, calling from Berne.

'His voice sounds very urgent,' Monica informed her chief. She had her hand over the phone. 'I put him through?'

Tweed nodded. He had just finished taking his shower and shaving. He was now fully dressed with the light meal Monica had prepared in front of him on his desk.

'Arthur, Tweed here.'

'Pierre Dumont has had the back of his head blown off. During the night in his apartment. The local police chief has the approaches to the Kongresshaus swarming with armed men in plain clothes, but omitted to have the apartment watched. I have a witness. He saw a veiled woman in a black robe leaving the apartment . . .'

8

No one is going to be able to creep up behind Pierre Dumont and shoot him in the back of the head . . .

Beck's words came back to Tweed with shocking clarity as he put down the phone. He sat still for several minutes, rather like a Buddha. Monica kept silent while she watched him. He clenched his right hand into a fist twice and she knew he was in a rare mood of controlled fury. Tweed in a state of fury was a formidable opponent.

'You heard,' he said eventually.

'It's dreadful. And Paula said a veiled woman in a black robe left Engel's apartment in Vienna before his murder was discovered.'

'So we have a professional female serial killer on the loose. A very skilled woman with her murderous work.'

'It's a horrifying thought.'

She had just spoken when Newman arrived. One look at Tweed's face and he knew there had been a serious development. He listened while Tweed told him the news.

'So we don't sit around here any longer,' Newman suggested.

'No, we don't. Monica, book Bob and me on the first Swissair flight available to Zurich. Then reserve us rooms at the Baur au Lac. Even though it's the season they will find something for us. Give Howard the details after we have left,' he went on, rapping out instructions at top speed, his mind racing. 'Then call Beck, tell him we're coming, the flight data, where we're staying. I've no doubt he's on his way to Zurich now. If so, you can get him at police HQ in Zurich.'

Monica was taking no notes. She had all the instructions in her memory. Tweed looked at Newman.

'Bob, you'd better fetch your packed suitcase from your flat in Beresforde Road.'

'It's already here. Alongside your own case packed for swift departure. I sneaked it in while you were sleeping on that camp bed. I guessed we were close to some real action.'

'Good.' He looked at Monica who was waiting for Heathrow to answer. 'Later, call Amos Lodge. If he answers we'll know he's still in Dorset. Do the same with Willie Carrington.'

'You think one of them is involved?' Newman enquired.

'Somebody in Dorset is – and I think they're in the Shrimpton area. Something about that peculiar village isn't right.'

Ten minutes later, just after Monica had completed a call, the phone rang. She listened, asked the caller to hold on, looked at Tweed.

'It's your friend in Paris, Loriot . . .'

'Tweed,' Loriot began as soon as Tweed had announced he was on the line, 'I have news that might or might not concern your investigation. The Monceau gang, including Jules Monceau himself, has just slipped across the border into Switzerland. In the Geneva area.'

'Inform Beck.'

'I will. He'll pick them up. They always move by car. I'll suggest he watches the airport, too.'

'Thank you.'

Tweed leaned back in his swivel chair, told Newman the news from Loriot. Newman whistled softly.

'We must remember what a tough bunch that lot is – if we have to tangle with them . . .'

'Stop hanging around,' Monica interjected. 'I have seats for you on an early flight. I think you'll miss it.'

The Monceau gang slipped through Beck's grasp. Instead of using cars they arrived at close intervals in taxis. They were deposited at Zurich's rail station, Cornavin.

Separately, they bought tickets for Zurich, boarded the first express, spread through the long train. The express stopped only at Lausanne and Berne and then thundered on to Zurich. On Jules Monceau's instructions they kept well apart as they alighted at the Hauptbahnhof. Each pair knew which small hotel they should put up at, using forged passports.

As soon as he was settled in his own hotel Jules called the number the Englishman had given him. Hassan, nervously, put Jules in the picture.

Tweed and Newman just caught their flight. The waiting hostess ushered them swiftly aboard into their Business

Class seats, the main entrance door was closed, secured. Within minutes the plane was airborne.

'Close-run thing,' Newman commented, sitting in the aisle seat.

'I think there are going to be a lot of close-run things,' Tweed replied. 'I'm not confident Beck will be in time to round up Monceau and his cohorts.'

'Then isn't it a good job Marler, Paula, Butler and Nield are approaching Zurich?'

'Yes, sometimes I get it right.'

'You nearly always get it right – in the end.'

'The end of this could be a long way off. We need to locate, identify, this woman assassin before she can strike again. We need to find out who is running this massive operation. We need to track down their head-quarters. We need to do this before it is too late.'

'I'd say that is a tall order,' Newman remarked.

'There is only a minority of members of the *Institut de la Défense* left.'

'And you are one of that minority,' Newman said grimly.

The first person Tweed and Newman met after they had booked in at the Baur au Lac was Paula. Tweed, relieved at seeing her safe and sound, hugged her. She wore a cool white dress with a blue leather belt round her slim waist and he was surprised how fresh she looked. He complimented her on her appearance.

'Well, Marler and I got here three hours ago,' she explained as they settled in his room. 'Monica is an angel – she had booked each of us a room, using your name I suspect. I was pretty tired, but I had a shower before slipping between the sheets and slept for two hours. I snoozed a bit of the way and Marler was in the lead, keeping up a cracking pace. I had a light breakfast after getting dressed and I'm ready for anything.'

'Marler's in his room here?'

'Yes, sleeping, I guess. It was one hell of a drive across Austria. Butler and Nield are staying at the Gotthard. Once again Monica had done her stuff and the rooms were waiting for them.' She lowered her voice. 'We have weapons. I've got a Browning in that shoulder bag and Marler has a .38 Smith & Wesson with hip holster for Bob.'

'Lucky to get them across the frontier.'

'Marler knew an area where we could slip across unobserved. He would—'

She broke off as the phone rang and Tweed picked it up. It was Beck and he was downstairs. Tweed asked him to come up.

Arthur Beck was a man in his late forties, slim, tall, erect as a British Guardsman. His thick hair was greying round the temples and beneath his strong nose was a trim grey moustache above a firm mouth and jaw. His grey eyes had a steely glint with the hint of a sense of humour. He smiled easily.

He stooped over Paula, grasped her by the shoulders and kissed her on both cheeks. Tweed knew he was very fond of Paula without a touch of amorousness. He refused a drink when Tweed offered him one, sat down in a hard-backed chair, facing them both, seated on a large couch.

'No time for that now. The newspapers are printing new editions, reporting the assassination of Pierre Dumont. It will be hitting the world's media now. Dumont had friends in high places. Monica phoned me that you would be here – I called the concierge to inform me immediately of your arrival. We botched this one up badly.'

'Difficult to foresee,' Tweed said sympathetically.

'Someone moves very quickly, is very dangerous. You said you had a witness?'

Tweed explained briefly to Paula the gist of Beck's urgent phone call which had brought him hurrying with Newman to Zurich. She listened intently.

'I have the witness downstairs guarded by two plainclothes men,' Beck told them. 'He is a bank teller.' He looked at Paula. 'From what you saw it sounds like the same woman assassin who killed Norbert Engel.'

'Reliable witness?' Tweed asked.

'Yes. He worked late at his bank, and left a late-night bar and was walking up Talstrasse when he felt so exhausted he sat down on some shadowed steps – which happened to be opposite the entrance to Dumont's apartment. That's when he saw the veiled woman leave. His description sounds like the woman Paula saw entering and leaving Engel's place in Vienna when he was murdered.'

'Could I talk to him?' Paula asked suddenly.

'Of course. I'll have him brought up now. He's a bit nervous but quite intelligent. Excuse me . . .'

He went to the phone, spoke for a couple of minutes, then resumed his seat. Again he looked at Paula.

'You have an idea?'

'No, I haven't. I just wanted to hear what this witness saw. It will probably correspond with what I saw in Vienna.'

'One witness meeting another,' Beck said with an attempt at cheerfulness.

There was a tapping on the door. Beck jumped up, went to the door, unlocked it, let in a pale-faced man in his thirties, dressed in a dark business suit despite the heat which was already building up. Outside the closing door Paula saw two men in suits, obviously the plainclothes guards.

Beck cleverly led the witness to an armchair facing

Tweed and Paula, a chair where he would be comfortable, relaxed. He introduced the bank teller.

'This is Alfred Horn. He spent a year in London with a bank to broaden his experience. He speaks good English. Alfred, this lady and this gentleman want to ask you a few questions about what you saw early this morning in Talstrasse. You can answer them as freely as you did with me. I repeat, we know you had nothing to do with the unfortunate incident.'

Paula leaned forward, her blue-grey eyes studying Horn as she smiled. The pale face suggested hours spent indoors away from the burning sun. His dark hair was neatly combed and his eyes were held by hers, his hands were tensely clasped together in his lap.

'Mr Horn,' she began quietly, 'I would like you to describe what you saw when you were resting on the steps in Talstrasse.'

'I have already told Chief Inspector Beck everything I know.'

'Mr Horn, you saw a woman leave in the middle of the night. I am a woman and I might just spot something in your story a man wouldn't appreciate. Please, I am a good listener.'

She was still smiling and she noticed the clenched hands loosen their grip on each other. Horn did not even glance at Tweed, who was lolling back at the other end of the couch as though this hardly concerned him.

'I heard no sound of a shot, although I understand poor Mr Dumont was killed with a gun. What I did see was this woman, dressed from head to foot in a black robe, leaving. She had a kind of black cap on her head and this veil which reminded me of how Arab women dress.'

'This is promising, Mr Horn. How tall would you say the woman was?'

'About five feet nine. Something like that. Quite tall and slim.'

Paula concealed her sense of shock. She continued smiling as she went on with her questions.

'We know that, as we all do at times, you had had a certain amount to drink. Could that have dulled your observation?'

'No. By then my mind was perfectly clear. I only stayed seated on the steps a little longer to get the strength back into my legs.'

'The street would be dark,' Paula persisted gently, 'which would not give you a good view of her.'

'It was moonlit. But as she passed under a street lamp the breeze blew her veil away from her face. She quickly held the veil back over her face but she was a redhead.' Horn was speaking more rapidly as what he had seen came back to him vividly. 'Her hair was cut very full – like a flame. She was very attractive.'

'The sort of woman you wouldn't mind taking out to dinner?' Paula asked, smiling more broadly.

'Oh, yes, she was very attractive. Oddly enough, I am sure she was a Western woman, with a good background. The sort I have seen walking down Old Bond Street when I was in London.'

'Do you think she saw you?'

'I am certain she didn't. I was sitting in dark shadow. Before she walked away she looked quickly in both directions. Her glance never paused at the alcove where I was sitting well back.'

'Thank you, Mr Horn. May I suggest you do not mention what you saw to anyone – not even to a close friend or relative.'

'Your life could depend on your keeping your mouth shut,' Beck broke in, much to Paula's annoyance.

'It's just a question of being discreet,' Paula added in

her most gentle tone. 'Thank you for being so coopera-
tive and helpful. One more question. Would you recognize this woman if you saw her again?'

'I doubt it. It all happened so quickly before she was
gone.'

'Thank you again,' said Paula.

She waited until Beck had ushered Horn out, handing him over to the waiting detectives. Then his
expression changed to one of unusual grimness.

'That was a brilliant interrogation,' Beck said when
he came back. 'He didn't tell me she was a redhead, that
he had had a glimpse of her face. Is something wrong?'

'Very wrong,' said Paula. 'The woman with a black
garb and a veil I saw later walking down Kärntnerstrasse was no more than five foot three inches tall. She
had auburn hair.'

'A wig?' Beck suggested.

'No. How could a woman alter her height by five or
six inches? This assassin was someone else.' She looked
at Tweed. 'We are dealing with more than one woman
assassin.'

9

Tweed, after a long discussion in his room, had given
certain orders to Paula and Marler, who he had called to
join them. Saying he would like a breath of fresh air, he
had gone to the door by himself. Behind him Newman's
voice issued the warning.

'I've read the list of members of the *Institut de la
Défense* Paula gave me, the one she found sticking out
of a drawer in Norbet Engel's apartment. Below Pierre
Dumont your name is the next on the list. You're now a
top target.'

'I have a spare Walther you could carry,' Marler suggested.

'You know I hardly ever carry a weapon,' Tweed replied, and he left the room.

Stepping out of the elevator on the ground floor, he walked casually to the main entrance, peered out. The uniformed doorman greeted him, Tweed nodded, his eyes scanning the outside. Another very hot day was in the air and already there were people sitting on the open terrace. Nothing seemed out of the ordinary, but it wouldn't when it came.

Turning back, he wandered into the spacious lounge where a few guests at widely separated tables drank coffee, conversed. She was seated by herself at a corner table. He immediately recognized Karin Berg.

The tall, highly attractive Swedish woman, in her thirties, wore a light-weight green trouser suit with a white cotton round-neck blouse. Her psychology was good – she knew Tweed would not have approved of a display of her long legs, of a low-cut blouse. She raised a hand to catch his eye, not knowing he had already seen her.

Tweed remained standing in the doorway, as though uncertain where to sit. He was thinking of the time when, operating in Scandinavia, he had cooperated with Berg, then employed by Swedish counter-espionage. He had heard she had moved on – no one knew where she had gone.

He pretended to see her for the first time, walked over and shook her extended hand, sat down at a chair facing her, which left an empty chair between them.

'It's been quite a while,' Tweed said with a smile.

'Hasn't it. Too long. We always got on well together.'

'That's true,' Tweed agreed.

Berg had blonde hair trimmed close to her head. Her features were well-formed, her full lips a strong red,

91

contrasting with her flawless pale complexion. Her eyes stared straight at his as she watched him over the glass of iced coffee she drank from. Tweed ordered the same from a hovering waiter.

'I heard you had left your job,' he remarked. 'Why? Where did you go to?'

He had observed she wore no rings on the third finger of her left hand. She put down the glass and smiled warmly.

'Is this an interrogation? You were always good at that.'

'Just questions. Obvious ones, since we once worked together.'

'Well . . .' She paused, still looking at him. 'I left the organization because the money wasn't good enough. Also I had an offer of big money from a security outfit belonging to a major corporation. I'm running the organization.'

'Which major corporation?' he asked sharply.

'There you go again. It's part of my contract that I never reveal whom I'm working for. It's a big hitter, international. I like the things money can buy.'

'A lot of women do.' He waited until the waiter had served his drink and gone away. 'You had two pretty bad affairs. Put you off men, did it?'

'That's rather personal.'

'You talked to me about them when I was in Stockholm. Said I was the only person you'd told about the bad time you'd had.'

'You were. You are.'

She stopped speaking as Newman appeared, his hand on the unoccupied chair. He was smiling broadly as he spoke, glancing at both of them.

'May I join you for a few minutes? Unless I'm intruding – in which case I shall vanish in a cloud of blue smoke.'

92

Tweed made introductions. Karin Berg indicated she would be quite happy with his company. She gazed at him through half-closed eyes, assessing him.

'Robert Newman? The international foreign correspondent? I thought so. You don't write much these days – I used to read your very perceptive articles in *Der Spiegel*. And in different publications.'

'I saved money. And there's nothing much going on in the world to write about these days,' he said easily, placing the drink he had been carrying on the table. 'But I may be writing a big piece on the eight assassinations of prominent men which have taken place. That is,' he went on, watching her, 'the moment I have tracked down the assassin.'

She froze. Only for a millisecond, but Newman caught her reaction before she resumed her interested look.

'Assassinations? I read it was a series of suicides.'

'Don't believe everything you read in the papers.'

Newman grinned. Lifting his glass he swallowed a little more Scotch.

'I recognized you from the photographs which used to appear in the press. You haven't changed a bit. You look, if anything, younger.'

'Flattery will get you somewhere,' Newman assured her.

'I always speak my mind,' she rapped back and the arrogance showed for the first time.

Tweed stroked his right eyebrow with a finger. He was signalling Newman that he would now like to be alone with Berg.

'I'll leave you two to continue your chat,' Newman said getting up. 'Nice meeting you,' he said to Berg before he wandered across the lounge.

'You could call me a career girl for a while,' Berg told Tweed, continuing the conversation where it had left off. 'But what about yourself? It's a long time since your wife ran off with that Greek shipping magnate. Or have you divorced her?'

'No, I haven't. I never hear from her but all the trauma of a divorce seems a waste of time.' He smiled. 'In any case, I'm a career man, as you should know.'

'You ought to relax more. If you like, I'll cook you a meal in my apartment some day.'

'A generous offer. I've got a better one. We'll take a cab to the Ermitage. It's rather a fine restaurant by the lake's edge, outside Zurich, in the Küsnacht district. Say nine tomorrow evening? I'll book a good table. I could pick you up here at eight thirty.'

'I accept with pleasure.'

'Then if you'll excuse me, I'm going out for a walk. I have a problem I want to sort out.'

'I remember this habit of yours . . .'

In case she fails . . .

The warning the Englishman had spoken over the phone when he had ordered Hassan to eliminate Tweed next had panicked him. If Karin Berg did fail in her murderous mission he was sure whose head would be on the block. He decided to take action on his own.

When Jules Monceau phoned him for the second time Hassan was ready with his instructions. Gripping the phone like a man whose life depended on this call, he began speaking to Monceau.

'You have a target in Zurich . . .'

'Which is where I am,' Monceau rasped.

'Excellent! I have had a report – reliable – that the target is staying at the Baur au Lac Hotel. He has to be liquidated. His name is Tweed.'

'Tweed!' Monceau could not keep the surprise and exultation out of his voice. 'Tweed, you said?'

94

'Yes. I will give you his description. We have it on file. It is rather vague—'

'No description needed. Immediate liquidation?'

'Yes. There will be a substantial fee in cash.'

'No fee needed.'

The phone connection was broken off. Hassan was puzzled – could not understand the Frenchman's reaction. He began to bite his nails. Had he done the right thing? He was going strictly against the Englishman's orders, but if Monceau succeeded then surely the Englishman should be pleased – whoever succeeded.

Jules Monceau had made his call early in the morning from a call box in the lobby of the small hotel he was staying in. Tweed! He could not believe his luck. Several years ago, before the Berlin Wall collapsed, Monceau had made the mistake of dabbling in obtaining French military secrets and selling them to the Russians.

It was Tweed, working with French counter-espionage, who had tracked him down. It was Tweed who had interrogated him in a cell at Rue des Saussaies, HQ of French counter-espionage, Tweed who had tripped him into a damaging admission.

During the years Monceau had spent in the Santé prison he had sworn that one day he would kill Tweed. Now the chance for revenge had been handed to him on a platter. Dawn was turning to daylight as he sat on his bed in his tiny bedroom.

Tweed, he knew, liked an early morning walk when he was able to cram it into his day. Within half an hour he had worked out his plan. He phoned three of his men, after returning to the call box in the hall. Two were staying at the same obscure hotel, not half a mile from his own hideaway. The third could get there even more quickly on the motorcycle Monceau had ordered him to buy.

Jules Monceau was a small, portly man, his black hair smoothed greasily above is forehead. His long nose, thick at the nostrils, combined with a wolfish smile had given him the nickname of The Wolf.

When they were all crammed into his room he stood with his back to the wall, smoking a cheroot as he told them what they had to do, the purchases they must make, including a wig, another item Bernard must buy after donning the wig, then the final item.

'Who will detonate it?' Bernard asked anxiously.

He was tall and lean with a sallow skin and thin eyebrows. Once a gymnast, he could move with great agility, altering his body language at will.

'André, of course. He, as you know, is an expert with explosives, with activating a radio-controlled bomb from a distance.'

'Do not worry, Bernard,' André mocked his colleague, his tone sarcastic, speaking in French as the others were doing. 'Worry about the baby, not yourself.'

'Shut your mouths, both of you,' snapped Monceau. 'Yves, you will drive the car as back-up. I will go over the plan once more. As I stand by the tram stop I will signal you when Tweed appears for his morning walk, rubbing my chin like this. I will be wearing a dark business suit like the bankers – even in this weather. I shall wear pince-nez, as I have before, and will be smoking a cigarette. The target associates me with smoking cheroots. The kill takes place this morning if the target appears.'

When his three men had gone Monceau treated himself to a fresh cheroot. He was enjoying that vision of Tweed's corpse being spread all over the road. So he'd follow at a discreet distance.

10

It was several hours later when Tweed strolled out of the Baur au Lac. Reaching Talstrasse, he glanced around. A few tourists trudging about. A portly man standing, smoking a cigarette, wearing a banker's 'uniform' – a dark business suit – and reading a newspaper. Probably checking on stock market figures. The banker type rubbed his chin. Maybe the news wasn't so good.

Tweed continued his stroll down to the lake. Waiting for the brief moment when the lights at a pedestrian crossing were in his favour, he crossed to the promenade alongside the lake. Zurichsee was calm, a brilliant blue. A steamer was coming in to berth as Tweed walked more quickly towards Kongresshaus on the opposite side of the road. Traffic was speeding along General Guisan Quai in both directions.

A woman with dark frizzy hair passed him, going the same way, propelling a push chair with a small doll-like baby swaddled in clothes inside. Tweed admired the pace at which she was moving as she went on into the distance.

Looking out across the large lake he saw at the point where the lake curved round a bend the silhouettes of large mountains backed by a cloudless sky. He caught sight of a mountain he knew well – the volcano-like shape of the Mythen.

One part of his mind took in what was happening around him while another part worried at the deadly problem he was trying to solve. He muttered to himself the strange name the kidnap car driver in Vienna had told Paula.

'Assam? Assam? Assam? Doesn't make sense. I must

ask Paula to explain again what she heard,' he said to himself.

A grey Volvo, moving more slowly than most of the traffic, passed him. The driver wore a peaked, American-style baseball cap and large wrap-around sunglasses. Tweed prepared to throw himself to the ground. The car continued past him. He relaxed, thinking now of the portly banker he had seen near the Baur au Lac. There had been something familiar about the man. Tweed wracked his brains, thought back into different episodes he had been involved in. Just couldn't place him.

Thirty yards or so behind Tweed Monceau kept pace. He was dying for a cheroot but forced himself to take another brief puff at his cigarette. It had to happen soon. His face twisted into a vicious grin as he anticipated the carnage.

Tweed glanced back, as he had done several times, but Monceau had masked himself behind a couple of backpackers. Tweed looked ahead of him. In the distance he saw the frizzy-haired woman with the pushchair coming back towards him. She must have completed her daily walk along the promenade. He recalled how silently the pushchair had moved. Well-oiled wheels.

Out of the lake a steamer approaching the landing stage hooted its siren. Zurich was a beautiful city, Tweed reflected. It had not one but two Altstadts – old quarters, one on either side of the Limmat River which flowed out of the lake under the bridge well to his rear.

He noticed that the woman with the pushchair was walking far more slowly. Tired out by her initial burst of speed, he assumed. Glancing across the street he saw strolling along the far pavement a stoop-shouldered man carrying a golf bag. He wore a check peaked cap, a windcheater and a pair of slacks. He was trailing along as though he had just completed eighteen holes of golf. His eyes were hidden behind sunglasses and he walked staring down at the pavement.

'Assam, Assam,' Tweed repeated to himself.

He could still make no sense of the word. Concentrate on what is going on around you, he reminded himself. Newman would be furious if he had gone off on his own. But he needed the isolation to get his brain fitting the pieces of the jigsaw together.

Looking ahead, he saw the woman with the pushchair dragging her feet. The baby inside the chair must have been asleep when it passed him – it hadn't made a sound. Then he saw the woman stop, brace her arms, hurl the pushchair towards him at top speed. It raced towards him like a projectile. At the same moment he noticed a man behind the woman holding a small box like the instrument used for guiding model planes by radio.

It was too late to avoid the onrushing pushchair. Out of nowhere the grey Volvo driven by the man with the baseball cap appeared on his side of the road. It had found somewhere to turn round. Behind it a motorcycle was screaming towards him with Newman astride the saddle.

The Volvo mounted the pavement, hit the pushchair, sending it hurtling towards a gap in the wall where steps led down to a small landing point. As the pushchair started sliding down the steps with the doll dressed as a baby André pressed the button on his radio-controlled explosive device. The pushchair exploded with a roar, scattered in fragments over the surface of the lake.

The Volvo was still stationary, halfway across the pavement, when a cream BMW raced along the far side of the road towards Tweed, a machine-pistol poked out of the rear window. Newman had already shot the 'woman', who slumped to the ground, the gun 'she' had produced leaving the man's hand, his wig sliding over the edge of the pavement into the street.

Across the street, the man with the golf bag had hauled out an Armalite rifle. Marler, tearing off his sunglasses, aimed the rifle at the driver of the BMW, pressed the trigger. The driver slumped over the wheel. The car slewed across the road, causing an oncoming car to brake to an emergency stop. The BMW hit the lakeside wall, burst into flames. Newman had fired his second shot, killing André, who had operated the radio-control device.

Tweed had now run back, crouched low against the wall, avoiding the fireball which had seconds earlier been a BMW. Marler had thrust the Armalite back inside the golf bag, ran across the front of the stationary traffic, jumped behind Newman on the motorcycle and it raced away towards the bridge over the Limmat.

Tweed stood up, walked rapidly back towards the Baur au Lac. Way ahead of him, Monceau, his face convulsed with manic fury at the fiasco, turned on to the landing stage, bought a ticket, was just in time to board a steamer on the point of departure. He went up to the enclosed top deck, chose a seat at the stern well away from other passengers and fumed.

Another man in Zurich was furious. Beck stormed at Tweed who had returned to his room at the Baur au Lac.

'Why in hell's name did you go out on your own?'

'I wasn't alone,' Tweed said quietly, seated on a couch. 'You know that now.'

'And did you know that?' the Police Chief demanded.

'No,' Tweed admitted. 'But if I'm to destroy the

enemy – whoever that might be – I have to think things out quietly on my own.'

'Well, we know who the enemy was in this case. It was the Monceau gang. The three dead men have been identified – we have the whole gang on file.'

'Monceau isn't the real enemy,' Tweed insisted. 'He must have been brought in as back-up. What we have to concentrate on is the man behind the eight assassinations. And I'm sure you are not sorry to be rid of these three thugs.'

'Monceau has at least seven more men on the loose,' warned Beck. 'He may try again to kill you.'

'Oh, he will. I'm not exactly his best friend. As you know I put him behind bars in France quite a while ago. This was his personal vendetta. Did you find out who wiped out those thugs?'

'I have not found out,' Beck said carefully, 'because it all happened so quickly that no witness can give a description. But I have my suspicions.'

'Good for you, Arthur. I can tell you that the assassins we are looking for – note the plural – are women. Crime has crossed the equality barrier. The one who murdered Dumont is a redhead – Horn told you that.'

'It isn't as though Zurich isn't full of red-haired women,' Beck said ironically. 'But why did you imply there is more than one woman assassin on the streets?'

'Because I know a very different-looking woman killed Norbert Engel. Know it for certain.'

'This is disturbing. Very,' commented Beck, who had quietened down, and stopped pacing round the room. He checked his watch. 'I'd better go – I have to write a discreet report on that mess of corpses on the promenade who are now in the morgue. I want you to promise me something. That you will not go out without at least Newman or Marler by your side.'

'I'll follow that advice when I can.'

'Which means that, as usual, you'll go your own damned way.'

Paula, Marler and Newman came into his room shortly after the police chief had left. Paula looked anxiously at Tweed.

'Are you sure you're all right?'

'I've never felt better. We are beginning to smoke out some of the opposition who obviously brought in Monceau and his nice friends to beef up their power. And thank you, Marler, and you Bob, for saving my life. A feeble appreciation. Again, you went into business on your own – when I had asked you to trace the Monceau mob.'

'Oh,' Newman said casually, 'we know you. So we cooked up a careful defence plan in case you were in danger. Which you were. Rather a diabolical mind planned that bomb in the guise of a baby in its pushchair.'

'That has all the hallmarks of Jules Monceau himself. I'm sure he was somewhere about wanting to see my end. Now,' he said briskly, 'Marler, I want you to explain again in detail the mood when you compelled the thug in the Maltese church in Vienna to name his headquarters.'

'Church was empty,' Marler said tersely. 'I had him on his knees inside a pew. My Walther was aimed point-blank and he thought I was going to pull the trigger – unless he spilt the beans.'

'So you must have really frightened him?'

'Only way to make him talk.'

'Did he answer you clearly?' Tweed persisted.

'Gibbering a bit. Then he came for me with the knife.'

'Gibbering?' Tweed repeated the word thoughtfully. 'So you may not have heard exactly what he did say? By which I mean he was incoherent. Slovakia. That was what you heard?'

'Something close to that.'

'Ah, this is interesting. You realize I'm not criticising you – it was an emergency situation, to say the least.'

'You could say that,' Marler drawled.

'Thank you.' Tweed spoke briskly. 'I told all of you earlier that we're dealing with at least two quite different assassins. Both of them women. Paula gave you her description of the one she saw in Vienna. Beck's witness, Horn, has only been able to provide the flimsiest picture of the woman who probably murdered Pierre Dumont. Of course, in the past women have been used by people like the old KGB to entrap men, but this is something quite different. That's the priority – to track them down. The second priority is to round up what remains of the Monceau gang. I think the two problems are interlinked. The whole city has to be trawled for Monceau's people – Beck says there are at least seven more. He's sending photos of them.'

He had just spoken when there was a knock on the door. Newman unlocked it, opened it a few inches, then took a large sealed envelope from a uniformed policeman, addressed to Tweed.

Opening it, Tweed glanced at the seven glossy prints inside. He spread them out over the table for the others to see.

'There they are. The seven gentlemen I just referred to.'

'Not very nice-looking men,' Paula commented.

'As ugly a bunch as I ever saw,' Newman chimed in. 'This one is Jacques Lemont. Expert knife-thrower. Once worked in a circus before Monceau recruited him. I interviewed him once. At that time Monceau was trying to fool people into thinking he was some kind of crusader – robbing the rich to help the poor. It was a load of rubbish but Monceau was in the room, wearing a mask to cover the upper part of his face.

He smoked one cheroot after another, a short tubby man.'

'That was him,' Tweed said suddenly. 'A short tubby man wearing a banker's outfit. Standing near the Baur au Lac when I set out for my walk. Smoking a cigarette with pince-nez perched on his nose. Thought he was familiar but I couldn't place him.'

'Waiting to see you blown into kingdom come,' Marler remarked.

'Earlier you said this is something quite different,' Paula reminded him. 'Are we dealing with terrorists?'

'Something far more sinister,' Tweed told her.

In the Middle East, well beyond the River Euphrates, a vast black cloud, emitted by numerous machines, hung above the desert. Below it a huge array of fast-moving modern tanks emerged from the underground bunkers where they were hidden.

The cloud, invented by scientists who had emigrated from Russia, was composed of harmless chemicals which made the American satellite crossing the area at intervals unable to photograph what was going on below it.

Under the control of several generals, the tank armada was engaged in more training manoeuvres. Each machine carried a long-range gun. Inside each gun was a shell containing a deadly biological material. The crews manning the tanks were all hooded with a certain advanced type of gas mask which made the wearer immune to the lethal gas.

At one stage the guns were fired. The shells travelled an enormous distance, landing in the desert. Several roaming camels suddenly froze as they inhaled the gas. Then they keeled over, instantly dead. The onslaught on the West was in an advanced state of preparation. All they were waiting for was the signal from the Head of State controlling Hassan. The signal which would tell him the West was now without anyone who could stiffen its leadership.

Newman went into the inside lounge after leaving Tweed and gazed swiftly around. He was convinced the danger was near at hand. Simone Carnot looked at him warily, smoothed down her blaze of red hair.

Normally, after leaving Dumont slumped dead on his couch with half his head missing and 'setting the stage' as Hassan always put it (using gloved hands to press the fingers of his lolling hand on the Luger), she would have caught the first flight out of Zurich. Hassan had again acted on his own initiative, was beginning to enjoy taking a hand in the game.

When Simone phoned to report in a coded manner that she had succeeded in her mission, Hassan had an idea. He told her to remain in Zurich for at least a week. He went on to say that the new target was a man called Tweed and spelt out the highly vague description he had. If the media hadn't reported his assassination by the end of the week she was to eliminate him herself.

'That will earn you the usual fee,' he had told her. 'I want you to call me when you have located him . . .'

Another one hundred thousand dollars. Simone had been more than willing to take the risk for more money. She had no idea that both she and Hassan were breaking the Englishman's golden rule. Once an assassination had taken place the woman responsible had to flee the city involved.

In the lounge she dropped her eyes quickly when Newman caught hers. She had recognized who he was from her extensive reading of the papers and the news magazines. He had an unusually striking appearance and she felt she must maintain a low profile. She had no idea who had been ordered to deal with this new target.

Simone Carnot had been running a public relations agency for top fashion models in Paris when she had been recruited on the basis of her looks and her love of money. She also had the advantage, like certain modern women, of regarding men as marauders, to be exploited at every possible opportunity.

When she realized Newman was approaching her she changed her mind. It would draw attention to herself if she pointedly ignored him. There was always the chance that with his vast knowledge of important people he might just know this Tweed, who had to be important to be singled out as a target.

'Excuse me,' Newman began as she looked up at him, 'but I am always direct. I'm bored and need someone to talk to. You certainly don't look boring. What drink can I order you?'

'A Kir royale,' she said immediately.

He ordered her drink from a waiter and a single Scotch for himself. She was very attractive with her glossy, flame-red hair.

His motive in approaching her was anything but what he had told her. True there were other redheads in the world but her appearance fitted the description Horn had given of the woman who had murdered Dumont. Newman had a vivid imagination and it had struck him that the assassin had to be a woman of great nerve. He would have expected her to get the hell out of town by the first available plane or train. But an astute woman might think it safer to stay put for a few days.

'I'm Bob Newman,' he said as they clinked the glasses the waiter had produced swiftly.

'Simone Carnot. What do you do, Mr Newman – when you are not accosting strange ladies?'

Aggressive, he thought – which again would fit his

image of the murderess. Not that it was likely that he had hit on the right woman.

'I investigate people,' he said provocatively.

'Are you investigating me, then? I wonder why?'

Every word she said fitted in with the portrait of a woman cold-blooded enough to shoot the back of a man's head off. It was too long a shot, he thought – that he could have found the assassin so easily. She had crossed her long legs, exposing them through a slit skirt. He glanced at them, knowing that was what she expected.

'No to both your questions.' He paused. It had occurred to him that Tweed would be the next target for a woman assassin. And she was in the same hotel. 'Are you staying here?' he asked her.

'I wonder what is behind that question, Mr Newman?'

'Which means you are staying here.'

'Possibly. Who can tell?'

'You could,' he said quickly.

'You're very direct. More like an American.'

She was smiling, her firm lips holding the smile. But the eyes which continued staring into his were like ice. He raised his eyebrows, took another sip at his drink.

'I don't know that I regard that as a compliment, but we'll let it pass.'

'How considerate of you,' she retorted, goading him. 'And if you are not investigating me, who are you investigating?'

'The killer of Pierre Dumont.'

He had spoken with great emphasis and didn't look at her as he took a further sip. At that moment Tweed walked into the lounge. He was walking past them when Newman called out.

'Do come and join us. Simone – may I call you that? I just did. This is Tweed. Meet Simone Carnot, Tweed.'

11

A little earlier, before Newman had left the bedroom, Tweed had summoned Butler and Nield from the Hotel Gotthard at the other end of Bahnhofstrasse. While waiting for them Paula and the others, seated, had watched Tweed walking slowly round his suite, hands clasped behind his back, a faraway look in his eyes, a determined look on his face.

No one had spoken. They knew from long experience he needed silence, that he was taking a major decision which would affect them all. Suddenly he stopped, perched himself on the arm of Paula's chair, his arms folded.

'It was Butler who was behind the wheel of the Volvo which hurled the pushchair bomb into the lake, wasn't it?'

'Yes,' said Newman. 'Pete Nield was crouched down in the rear with a gun and a stun grenade. We didn't know what was coming but we planned behind your back for various forms of attack on you—'

He broke off as there was a tapping on the door. He let in to the room Harry Butler and Pete Nield. Tweed greeted them with a grim smile.

'Please sit down, make yourselves comfortable. Harry, I have to thank you for saving me from that bomb.'

'All in a day's work,' replied Butler, who used words as though each one cost him money.

'I've decided we can't play it softly, softly any more,' Tweed began. He explained to the newcomers that there were two women assassins prowling Europe. 'I am now the next target,' he went on. 'Knowing this, that is the ace up our sleeve I am going to play. The technique they're employing is now obvious, cold-blooded, diabolically clever.'

'What technique is that?' asked Nield quietly, fingering his neat moustache.

'To put themselves close to their targets these fiendish women have to first make the acquaintance of their targets. Because they're dealing with sophisticated men, top-class intellects, they have to be very attractive, very experienced at handling men. I suspect someone who knows all the members of the *Institut de la Défense* has analysed each one to decide the sort of woman who would attract him. Someone with a deep insight into a man's psychology. And a lot of money is being sent secretly to Dorset.'

'That fingers Amos Lodge or Willie Carrington,' Newman suggested.

'Possibly. Unless there's a third man in that area who has not yet appeared on the scene . . .'

'Excuse me,' Paula interjected, 'but is either man a member of the *Institut*?'

'Amos Lodge is.'

'And he's still alive. Do we have to look further?'

'We do. His name is below mine on that members' list you brought from Vienna. But before the serial assassinations started we held a party at our headquarters inside a mansion on the shores of Lake Geneva, not far from Ouchy. The subject was the Middle East. We invited a number of people who know the area very well to tell us about it. One man invited was Willie Carrington.'

'His name is not on the list,' she persisted.

'We tried to cover ourselves by announcing this was the last meeting, that the *Institut* was being dissolved. Not my idea – didn't sound convincing. It didn't convince someone. I have worked out our strategy.'

'He said softly, softly was out, a few minutes ago,' Newman whispered to Paula as Tweed stood in the middle of the room. 'Sounds like a thunderbolt is coming.'

'I am now the next target,' Tweed repeated. 'So, knowing their technique, some attractive woman has to approach me, try to persuade me to join her in her apartment or somewhere quiet. All the previous victims have had houses or apartments which the killers could use. I'm in a hotel. This gives them a problem. I want to trap her, whichever woman turns up. Then *we* persuade her to tell us who she is working for.'

'I'll handle that problem when we get there,' Paula said, and there was an undertone of cold anger. 'I told you – in this age of equality certain women can be greater villains than men.'

'How can they do it?' Pete Nield asked. 'Creep up behind a man they've got to know, maybe seduced, then blast the back of his head off?'

'Women, in some ways, are different from men,' Paula explained. 'I'm more likely to penetrate their minds than any man. Take a simple fact. A number of women feel more comfortable talking to their own sex. They have women friends in preference to men – partly because they can talk freely about subjects they'd never dream of discussing with men. And a lot of women are guarded when encountering a new man – for obvious reasons.'

'Give me an obvious reason,' Nield had urged.

'I think it goes back through history – to a time when men were the dominant force. To survive, women had to learn how to handle a man, manipulate him, if you like. Now they have huge freedom those methods are no longer necessary – or desirable in my opinion. But they remain steeped in their old wily ways – so we have an unbalanced situation where some women set out to run the whole show. This bewilders some men, does nothing to make for a stable society. We are on the edge of chaos with some relationships, maybe have gone down into chaos already.'

'I still don't get how a woman can blast a man's head off,' Nield insisted.

'I suspect certain women – a small minority – could do that and enjoy it.'

'That's horrible,' Nield protested.

'It certainly is. Another powerful motive is money. They must be paid a big fee for their filthy work. Tweed has said they must be attractive women. It costs a lot of money for a conceited woman to outgun her rivals in appearance. Cosmetics, clothes, hairdos – later they want facelifts and Lord knows what else. That costs a load of money. They're prowling predators, they want to try to be always desirable to men.'

'You're putting me off ever getting married,' Nield said.

'I'm not trying to do anything of the sort,' Paula said with great emphasis. 'The other side of the coin is there are a majority of women who are decent, honest; who will only marry a man they love – and go on loving. If it's a good match – and there are millions of them – they are content to raise a family, to support their husband always in every way, to live in modest circumstances. They make up the bulk of women in the world, in the West. So don't get me wrong, Pete . . .'

It was shortly after this conversation that Newman left, went into the lounge downstairs, and later introduced Tweed to Simone Carnot. He was following Tweed's strategy – the key to which was that the unknown assassin had to get to know Tweed as an opening gambit.

* * *

When his name was mentioned, Simone stretched out a hand to grasp Tweed's as he sat down. In doing so her hand caught her glass of Kir royale, spilling the contents over the table.

'I'm so sorry,' she said quickly, as a waiter came to mop the table, then brought her a fresh drink. 'That was really very clumsy of me.'

'I've done it myself,' Tweed assured her. 'Think nothing of it.'

Without revealing their reactions both Tweed and Newman were thinking a lot about the incident. It had been the mention of Tweed's name which had thrown Simone temporarily off balance. She could hardly believe her luck – the target was sitting opposite her, conjured up out of the blue. Then she recalled that he was staying at the Baur au Lac, that although she had pretended not to recognize Newman, he was an international foreign correspondent, the type of man Tweed, whoever he was, would mix with, since he had to be important.

'I'll have a glass of orange juice,' Tweed asked the waiter who had brought Simone a fresh drink. He looked at Simone, smiling as he asked the question, and he had noticed her slim legs, that she was very attractive.

'What is your role in life, if I may ask? You could be a successful model.'

She liked that. Her manner towards Tweed was entirely different from her defensive attitude with Newman. This is a fish I can hook, she said to herself. Instead she said something else aloud.

'Thank you. I take that as a great compliment. It is a fact that at one time I ran a fashion agency for models in Paris.' The moment she mentioned the French city she knew she had made a mistake. What was it about this man which caused her to let down her guard? 'Now I am getting over a broken marriage.'

'I'm sorry to hear that. I can't understand how any man could contemplate leaving you.'

He's laying it on with a trowel, Newman was thinking. But it seems to be going down well. When he put himself out Tweed could be charming because there was something which many women found reassuring about his personality.

'It just didn't work,' Simone explained. 'May I ask, are you married?'

'Yes, I am,' replied Tweed, without going into the real circumstances behind that statement. 'For a long time,' he added.

Better and better, Simone thought cynically. Some married men came to a point where they needed a little variety in their lives. This could be an easy mark. So why did a little warning bell sound at the back of her shrewd mind?

'I'm glad,' she replied. 'It's comforting to know that a marriage can work. I'm sure yours does. No sensible woman would dream of leaving someone like you.'

'We seem to be vying with each other to exchange compliments,' Tweed said drily.

'It's a more civilized conversation than I have had with many men. Perhaps we could have a drink together some time? I am staying at this hotel.'

'I shall look forward to that. Please excuse me now. I have a business appointment.'

He left Newman with her, walked to the revolving door leading to the drive, passed through it on to the drive. Out of sight of the lounge he paused. The last man in the world he had expected to see was seated at a table on the terrace. Amos Lodge.

Tweed walked slowly towards the terrace, his eyes scanning everyone seated at the various tables. Butler, better dressed than usual, was drinking from a cup. Further away he saw Pete Nield reading a newspaper. Tweed had no doubt that Marler was somewhere close at hand, then he saw him seated close to the bar, with a glass of iced coffee in front of him.

He strolled towards Marler's table, appeared to stumble, and his outstretched hand knocked over the glass. It was the earlier Kir royale incident which had given him the idea. He apologized, as though speaking to a stranger, and then lowered his voice.

'Tomorrow I'm taking a woman I once knew called Karin Berg to dinner at the Ermitage on the edge of the lake outside Zurich. Leave here at eight thirty.'

'Don't worry about it, sir,' Marler said in a loud voice. 'The waiter's coming to clear it up.'

Tweed changed direction, appeared to see Amos Lodge for the first time. The big man with the square-rimmed glasses he had last met in Dorset was wearing a panama hat which seemed to emphasize his bulk. He looked up as Tweed reached his table.

'Good Lord! Last person I expected to see out here. Sit down. Join me in a glass of cold lager?'

'Thank you. Think I'd prefer coffee. I was thinking the same about you – last person, et cetera. What brings you here, Amos?'

'I came to listen to Dumont's speech at the Kongress-shaus. A bloody awful thing – I read it in the paper – about him committing suicide. Last thing I'd have expected.'

'You're right. It was murder.'

'My God! Why? Who did it?'

'That, Amos, is what I'm here to find out. I'm getting closer to the murderer by the hour.'

'You are? He had a big life insurance policy, I suppose.'

'Well, I am Chief Claims Investigator for an insurance outfit,' Tweed replied, evading a direct answer. 'But what are you going to do now?'

'Give a speech at the Kongresshaus tomorrow night. Officially a kind of memoriam – in fact I'm going to use the occasion to express my views forcefully. The agency who acted for Dumont has informed the audience who had tickets. Posters are going up. It will be a big audience.'

'Isn't that a bit dangerous? You're a member of the *Institut*. So were all the previous so-called suicides.'

'You think that will stop me?' The eyes behind the glasses stared at Tweed with a steely look. 'You'll be there, I hope? I have an invitation card – in fact a batch so you can bring any friends you have in this part of the world.'

Saying which, Amos produced a fat envelope from the breast pocket of his summer jacket. He laid a small pile in front of Tweed, who pocketed them.

'Thank you. You got them printed fast.'

'A Swiss printer. The Swiss are very efficient and can move fast. Here's your coffee. Wish me luck with my speech.'

'I wish you luck – and safety.'

'Safety? Forget it. Half Dorset seems to be in Zurich. I'm waiting for someone you know well. Willie Carrington.'

'Willie is here?'

'Staying at the Dolder Grand, up on the hill behind the city. I'd mentioned to him on the phone I was coming to listen to Dumont. He said he was in Zurich for the same reason. Here he comes – the lady-killer . . .'

Willie was wearing the most extraordinary outfit. Over his head and draped behind it was a white cloth as worn by Arabs. The rest of his clothes were a straightforward

Western suit and he had a pair of wrap-around sunglasses masking his eyes.

'Speak of the devil – I heard what you said,' he greeted Tweed as he sat down. 'I certainly didn't expect to find you here. You've heard about poor Dumont committing suicide? Can't understand what made the feller do it. Nasty shock. He was a guest at my club recently, back in London.'

Willie made it sound as though suicide wasn't the done thing as Dumont had visited the club. 'A brainstorm, I suppose. Waste of a world-class brain. I'll have a double vodka,' he told a waiter, then turned back to Tweed. 'I need it after that.'

'Why the unusual garb?' Tweed enquired, putting down his cup of coffee and refilling it from the pot. 'People will think you're one of those fabulously rich sheiks.'

'Oh, that.' Willie pulled at his moustache and grinned. 'After listening to Amos's speech tomorrow I'm off to the Middle East. They like you to turn up like this. Think it shows respect and all that.'

'Another business trip?'

'I hope so. Can't tell until I've seen them. They like playing cat and mouse. Hoping to get the price down. It won't succeed. If necessary I'll say I'm on the first plane home. Usually brings them to heel.' His drink had arrived. He raised his glass. 'To the memory of Dumont. Nice chap. Down the flaming hatch. And I've just pulled off a huge deal on the phone in the Middle East. A real coup. Supposed to keep it quiet.' He winked. 'Just among friends.'

Tweed realized Carrington was already half drunk. Then he recognized the symptoms from the wording Willie had used. He was power drunk, but still under a strange iron self-control. His eyes gleamed when he stared at Tweed, gleamed with triumph. Why?

Amos had also noticed the phenomenon. Tweed glanced at the big man. The very different eyes gazed at Willie's with a fierce intensity, as though he could read his mind. The atmosphere had become electric.

'You don't give a damn for Dumont,' he began in his gravelly voice. 'All that concerns you is making another pile of money.'

'I say, old chap, that's not a very nice thing to say,' Willie responded in a quiet voice.

'In this world the truth often isn't very nice,' Amos shot back. 'To hell with your deal. What was it? Guns for the Arabs? Missiles?'

Tweed relaxed in his chair, keeping out of it. He studied both men as he sipped his coffee. What most intrigued him was that Willie was not in the least taken aback by Amos's onslaught. If anything, Willie suddenly seemed sober, was watching Amos with calculating eyes. Tweed hadn't realized how strong was Carrington's willpower, how he could handle any situation. The hail-fellow-well-met manner Tweed was accustomed to had been replaced by a man with great force of character. It was a revelation.

'Come off it, Amos,' Willie said coolly, 'Dumont was a close friend of mine. I know the last thing he'd want is a wake, so we'll let bygones be bygones.'

'If you say so,' rasped Amos.

'I do say so. Now I'll leave you two to chat. I feel like a walk in the sun – to recall old times.'

Saying which, he left them. Tweed watched him walking away and Willie's step was firm and steady.

'Never liked him,' Amos said.

'Why?'

'Too much bravado. Never trusted him. If you'll excuse me, I must go. See you later . . .'

He had just disappeared when a tall, bronzed man in a tracksuit strolled up to Tweed's table. Emilio Vitorelli sat down, carrying his drink.

'Something you should know . . .'

'I haven't seen you in a while, Emilio,' Tweed said to the Italian. 'At least three beautiful women have you in their sights.'

'Forget them. I suspect you are here to track down the women assassins who have wiped out eight men like swatting flies.'

'You're guessing.'

'Like you, I'm a good guesser.' Vitorelli stroked a hand over his thick fair hair. 'One of them is my meat.'

'You always talked in hints and riddles. Just for once be a little more specific.'

'You know my fiancée had her faced ruined for life by a woman who threw acid into it. Which caused my fiancée to plunge to her death by jumping from the platform in the Borghese Gardens in Rome straight down into the Pincio Square. That's a long drop. The name of the acid thrower, whom I had done my best to evade, is Tina Langley.'

Vitorelli, his handsome face, expressionless, took a long gulp at his drink. He looks so very athletic, Tweed thought – a man who was bound to attract the attention of women.

'Interesting. Very,' said Tweed.

'You always were cautious in your reactions,' Vitorelli remarked, and gave his engaging smile.

'What makes you say that?'

'Because you know very well, I'm sure, that Tina

Langley is an ex-girlfriend of Captain William Welles-ley Carrington. Willie, as he is known, just left your table.'

'Is this what I should know?'

'What you should know is that Tina Langley is a member of the notorious group of women assassins – The Sisterhood.'

12

Tweed glanced around the terrace while he absorbed the shock of what Vitorelli had said. Marler, Butler and Nield had all disappeared, but Tweed had not been left on his own. Behind him, with her back to the wall, Paula sat drinking coffee, looking past him at the garden. Her shoulder bag hung over her shoulder and he guessed inside the special pocket was her Browning .32, fully loaded.

'The Sisterhood?' he repeated. 'Who are they?'

'At least three very attractive women used to lure their targets to destruction, to a place where the assassin concerned can shoot her victim in the back of the head – and then make it look like suicide,' Vitorelli replied grimly.

'Who controls The Sisterhood?' Tweed asked.

'No idea. Probably someone in your county of Dorset.'

'Hence your message about the courier carrying a large sum of money to that area.'

'It was all I had at that time.'

'How did you find out more?'

'I shouldn't tell you this, Tweed.' Vitorelli emptied his glass and grinned. 'I suspect that as Chief Claims Investigator for some big insurance outfit you have

119

contacts all over the world who supply information on the quiet. I have the same kind of network. The difference, I imagine, is mine operates at a much lower level than yours – deep in the underworld. Money changes hands, nothing is written down, whispers are exchanged. You understand me?'

'So far. But you haven't told me how you found out about the existence of this Sisterhood.'

'By pure chance. I am trying to trace the whereabouts of Tina Langley. The last I heard of her she was in Salzburg recently. Have I touched a nerve?'

Tweed warned himself to be more careful with his expressions. Emilio Vitorelli was clever, a very observant man.

The Italian *had* touched a nerve. Salzburg was not very far from Vienna. Norbert Engel had been murdered in that city – and Paula had caught a glimpse of his assassin.

'No,' he said quickly.

'I was about to depart for Salzburg,' Vitorelli went on. 'I then heard that she had disappeared again. I also heard she was a member of The Sisterhood. As an assassin . . .' he began slowly.

'What did you just say?' Tweed asked.

'As an assassin she fits the role. A woman who could throw acid in another woman's face is capable of anything. She is clever – up to a point – is Tina. She whisks from one place to another. Hence her nickname, The Butterfly.'

'Some butterfly.'

'If you find her, will you promise to let me know?'

'I will do what I can,' replied Tweed evasively.

'Why is it that I supply you with data and get so little in return?'

'The nature of my work.'

As a cover for the HQ of the SIS there was a plate

120

outside the building in Park Crescent. General & Cumbria Assurance. Tweed's pose as a Chief Claims Investigator explained his many trips abroad, his secrecy. The dummy insurance company was supposed to negotiate ransom claims when rich men were kidnapped.

Soon Tweed excused himself and Paula waited a moment, then strolled after him.

As an . . . Those were the words Vitorelli had spoken. Tweed repeated them to himself. *As an . . .* Hassan. Assam. The name of the man controlling The Sisterhood was Hassan, an Arabic name. It fitted perfectly.

'Hassan?' Paula said. 'That's a pretty common name.'

Tweed and Paula had met up inside his room after leaving the terrace. Walking slowly round the furniture, Tweed took his time before replying.

'It's a name,' he said eventually. 'Something we haven't had before.'

'Clever of you to catch on from what Vitorelli happened to say by chance. Assam – Hassan. They sound similar. Understandably, I must have misheard what the car driver said to me after the kidnap attempt.'

'With your gun on him the driver was probably scared stiff and stammering.'

'Marler told me you're having dinner this evening with Karin Berg at some place called the Ermitage. Aren't you taking yet another needless risk?' Paula commented.

'I knew Karin when she was with Swedish counter-espionage. She's no stranger.'

'So what is she doing now?' Paula demanded.

'Said she had a big security job with some international security organization. She's made for the job,' Tweed remarked.

'Which international organization?'

'She couldn't say. Part of her contract is not to reveal the company she's working for.'

'Very convenient,' Paula said vehemently. 'About The Sisterhood Vitorelli told you about. Women who kill cold-bloodedly for money – because you can be sure they get a big fat fee for their dirty work. Why should Karin know anything about them? She's out of the business.'

'She may know something without realizing she knows it. I'm exploring every avenue,' Tweed emphasized.

'Every dangerous avenue.'

'You know a better way?' There was an edge to Tweed's voice. 'I'm listening. Tell me.'

Paula was stumped. Desperately she tried to think of an alternative. Her mind kept coming up against brick walls.

'You're using yourself as bait,' she said eventually.

There was a knock on the door. In a state of tension and anxiety Paula jumped up, the Browning in her right hand. She went to the locked door.

'Who is it?' she called out.

'Message for Mr Tweed.'

'Shove it under the door.'

'I was asked to deliver this personally into his hands.'

'Shove it under the bloody door or I'm calling the Chief of Police.'

There was a pause. Then a white envelope was slid under the door. She picked it up, saw that it was addressed to Tweed, marked Personal. Picking it up she handed it to her chief. He opened it, took out a photograph, looked at it, slid it back inside the envelope.

'Calm down,' Tweed told her. 'Everything is under control.'

'The last time you said that the world nearly blew up in our faces.'

'Which could really happen if we don't neutralize the enemy. I had a phone call. From Beck. He was sending a car with armed guards to pick me up. I went downstairs in double quick time and two of Beck's men I recognized escorted me to an unmarked car. I was driven at top speed down one-way streets the wrong way to police headquarters overlooking the Limmat River. Beck was waiting for me. He'd had an urgent call from Cord Dillon, Deputy Director of the CIA in Langley – to call him on a safe phone. He had alarming news.'

'Alarm me,' she said quietly.

'Dillon reported the presence of a vast black cloud over the Middle Eastern state which is worrying us. The nature of the cloud made it chemically impossible for the sophisticated cameras of the American satellite passing over the desert area to penetrate it. They estimate the dimensions of the cloud were fifteen miles long by twenty miles wide. No wind, so it remained stationary. They suspect huge military manoeuvres were taking place under cover of the cloud. Beyond the edges of the cloud the cameras picked up ten dead camels, lying prostrate on the sand. It makes Washington think bacteriological weapons were being used.'

'Scary.'

'The President has forbidden any action to be taken – says it is a bluff.'

'What do you think?' Paula asked.

'A vast army is preparing to sweep across the Middle East to obliterate Israel. If successful, that would cause several Arab nations to ally themselves with the aggressor – would compel them to take that action. The army would then advance north to pass through Turkey, where Ultra-extremists – far more fanatical than Fundamentalists – are poised to take over the government in Ankara. From Turkey they would move north through the Balkans. First major objective, Vienna. Then on to

Munich. From there a swift advance to the Rhine. Their missiles could annihilate London.'

'You are quite a strategist – like Amos Lodge.'

'Oh, I expect he's worked all this out for himself,' Tweed replied.

'You have alarmed me.'

'Now, do you still think I shouldn't be using all my energy to find out who is behind the prelude – the assassinations?'

'I'll come with you tonight.'

'That would spoil everything. The answer is no,' Tweed told her.

'You expect me to sleep on that?'

'I don't expect you, of all people, to sleep. Now, I think I should show you the photograph which Vitorelli has sent me with a note. Here is the note.'

I have made copies. Here is a photo of Tina Langley.
Yours, E.

Paula stared at the glossy print which had accompanied the note. It was a good colour print and she studied it for two minutes, then looked up at Tweed.

'This is the woman who murdered Norbert Engel.'

'You're sure?'

'She only glanced round once on Kärntnerstrasse but I had a good look at her. I'm quite certain. We have identified one member of The Sisterhood.'

Tina Langley was staying at the Hôtel des Bergues in Geneva. She had registered as Lisa Vane and had been 'sidelined' there by Hassan. She knew the meaning of being 'sidelined' – it was rather like the coaches of a train which had, for the moment, been parked in a siding.

124

With her thick auburn hair, her well-shaped figure and her seductive smile she had already acquired a temporary Swiss man friend, a banker. This had been an easy capture for Tina, who was a beauty with smoky eyes. Her slow-moving eyes were her chief weapon, combined with a long nose and the full red mouth above a determined chin. She simply had to look at a man with those eyes and she had him in the palm of her hand. Only five foot five inches tall, she wore high heels to enhance her height. Her escort spoke English as they walked along the Rhône promenade.

'What part of England do you come from, Lisa?'

'Kent,' she lied immediately. 'Not a million miles from Dover. Which bank are you a director of?' she enquired casually.

He told her and she smiled inwardly. One of the major banks. It might be amusing to see how much she could take him for. Her real motive in striking up the acquaintance was that an attractive woman with a man was less likely to stand out than a woman by herself. Not that she expected the police to be looking for her in Geneva while she waited for Hassan to give her details of her next 'assignment'. It was a long way from Vienna.

She led him down a side street where there was a top-class jewellery store. Her preference was for diamonds and she gazed at a necklace glittering with the jewels. Anton, her new friend, stirred restlessly and she knew it was too early to try for a fabulously priced piece.

'It's nice,' she said, 'but so expensive.'

'You like it?' Anton asked.

He could immediately have bit off his tongue. The necklace was worth a small fortune. She glanced at him sideways, a long, slow look.

'Any woman who wore that would have to go out with guards. It's asking for trouble.'

She moved further along the window and stared at a string of pearls. Also very expensive but a fraction of the cost of the necklace.

'You fancy that?' he enquired.

'It's just the kind of thing which suits me.'

Anton, a tall, good-looking man in his forties, couldn't wait to get into her room. He took her into the shop and the manager, who had unlocked the door for them, then relocked it, took the pearls out of the window, placed them round her slim neck, fastened the clasp. She spent just the right amount of time gazing at herself in a mirror.

'They are me,' she said eventually.

Anton produced his credit card. While he was attending to the purchase with the manager Tina took a scarf out of her Gucci handbag, wrapped it round her auburn hair, concealing it. There was a strong breeze blowing along the Rhône but her main reason for the action was to change her appearance.

'The wind blows my hair,' she remarked, explaining why she had put it on.

'Such attractive hair.'

She made no reply. This was her first visit to Geneva and she thought the city beautiful. To their left flowed the green Rhône, which had flowed out of the lake under the Pont du Rhône. Now it was dividing and there were islands, linked to the shore by an intricate system of footbridges. On the far shore a line of old office buildings rose several storeys high. Beyond them a massive cliff, sheer and more like a mountain.

'Geneva is a very cosmopolitan city,' Anton told her. 'A lot of wealthy foreigners live here, working for big international companies.'

She pricked up her ears. It sounded as though there could be rich pickings here. What puzzled her was why she had been 'sidelined' to Geneva. Was there some unknown significance about the city? Without realizing it she had put her finger on the key.

'That Swiss mountain must have a marvellous view from the top.'

'It has. They call it Salève. But it is not in Switzerland. It is actually in France.'

When the phone rang in Jules Monceau's tiny bedroom he let it ring before picking up the receiver. It was bad tactics to make anyone think he was just waiting for the call.

'Yes,' he answered eventually.

'You know who is speaking,' began Hassan's smooth, oily voice.

'Of course.'

'I have heard that tonight Tweed will be dining with a woman at a restaurant outside Zurich called Ermitage. Ermitage,' he repeated. 'They will have a lakeside table, will arrive about nine in the evening. The rest is up to you.'

There was an evil smile on Monceau's face as he put down the phone. He reached for a map of the city which included the Zurichsee. A telephone book would give him the location. He had a lot of elaborate planning to do. This time Tweed would be killed. He'd be too absorbed by his companion, too full of wine to realize what was happening. Before it was too late.

13

Tina Langley was not known as The Butterfly without reason. Her mood changes, her dislike of staying in one place for long, were notorious. The strong-minded Willie

Carrington would certainly have agreed. Anton, her banker friend, was experiencing the same reaction.

'I want to go to France,' she suddenly announced in her soft, persuasive voice.

'Go to France?' Anton asked in surprise. 'It's a bit late in the day.'

'How long would it take to go to the top of Salève?' she persisted with a moue. 'You said your car was parked nearby.'

They were sitting in the bar of the Hôtel des Bergues, situated on a side street leading off the promenade road. She had been knocking back glasses of champagne as though they were water. Anton was hoping she would soon consent to inviting him up to her room.

'I'm not sure that's a good idea,' he said slowly.

'If I think it's a good idea then it's a wonderful idea,' she shouted at him. 'And if you're not interested then say so now and I'll leave. Who do you think you are? If I want to do something I do it. Right away. Hear me?' she hissed loudly in his ear.

It was embarrassing. There were other couples in the bar and they were all staring, some amused, some indignant at this outburst. Anton was not only embarrassed – he was fascinated by this sudden wild streak in her nature.

'If we go now,' he said, 'we should be there and back before dark, Lisa.'

Her mood changed again. She turned, gave him a flashing smile and kissed him on the cheek.

At the imposing Dolder Grand Hotel, perched on a hill overlooking Zurich, Willie was enjoying himself. He was chatting to a woman who was expensively dressed in the height of fashion. She would be, Willie said to himself – to afford to stay here.

'Might be able to put you on to an unusual assignment which would bring you in piles of money,' he said jovially.

'Really?'

The Spanish beauty, separated from her husband, her glossy hair black as the dead of night, was thinking: This is a new ploy. But I'll go along with it, up to a point, she decided. She was bored and Willie's personality had an exuberant animation which was fascinatimg to many women.

'Tell you what,' he continued, pulling at his moustache and grinning, 'we could have dinner at the Ermitage. Supposed to be one of the "in" places on the lake shore. Concierge here told me about it. Tomorrow night suit you? I'll suss out the place, make sure it's good enough for a lady of your standing. Do that this evening.'

'You're very thorough,' she observed, amused.

'Have to be, in my job.'

'What is that?' Carmen enquired.

'Selling guns, ammunition to Arab sheiks. They pay a mint because I'm known out there. Dine at palaces and all that nonsense. I imagine I've shocked you.'

'I'm not easy to shock, Willie.'

If he was telling the truth she was impressed. It sounded romantic, reminded her of what she had read about the days of the Spanish *plata* galleons, carrying gold plate, fighting the English raiders.

It was, in fact, just the impression of bravado Willie had attempted to create. He had a shrewd insight into what would impress a woman. Didn't matter whether they believed what tale he spun them as long as they liked it. In this case he had told the truth – which he rarely did.

'Tomorrow evening, then,' he said. 'Meet you here at eight – I'll drive us there. If the place is pukka. If not, I know somewhere else in Zurich.' He stood up. 'Excuse me, Carmen, but I have an appointment. Hope to pull off a big deal. Probably it will fall through.'

Clad in a blue tracksuit – which normally the management would not have approved of, but he spent a lot of money – he gave her a smart salute and was gone.

Physically, Amos Lodge was the least active. He was spending a lot of time in his room, drafting out the details of the speech he would be giving the following evening at the Kongresshaus.

His speech would be as terse and controversial and hard-hitting as when he was talking to individuals. A natural orator, he intended to blow the roof off Kongresshaus. He was annoyed when the phone rang. It was Beck.

'Mr Lodge, I'm calling to tell you that tomorrow night the Kongresshaus will be crawling with my armed men.'

'That would be a big turn-on. Uniformed police all over the place. Don't do it.'

'All my men will be in plain clothes. They will mingle with your audience. I have already bought a large number of tickets. You can't stop me doing it.'

'Plain-clothes men make it a bit better. I think you're wasting your manpower.'

'I don't. You could be a target. I have men inside the Baur au Lac now. You will be discreetly escorted to Kongresshaus. No good arguing with me, Mr Lodge.'

'If you say so,' Lodge growled, and slammed down the phone.

Anton was worried as he drove Tina up the spiralling road at the eastern end of the mountain called Salève.

They had passed through the French frontier post and this was a relief for Anton.

'Can't you drive any faster?' Tina demanded in a petulant tone. 'I could drive up here at twice your speed.'

'I'm sure you could.'

Anton relapsed into silence. At the bar in the Hôtel des Bergues he had made the mistake of keeping up with the woman he knew as Lisa Vane. His head was spinning and he refused to increase his speed. Lisa seemed able to consume huge quantities of champagne without it affecting her in the least.

'Travelling like a snail,' she gibed.

Seething inwardly, he maintained his careful pace all the way to the top of the mountain and then began the descent down the other side. He glanced at her several times and she was always staring ahead, expressing her frustration. As they pulled into the drive the Château d'Avignon in the middle of remote countryside her manner changed abruptly.

'Anton, what a beautiful chateau. And I appreciate your driving so safely.'

He realized she was not being sarcastic, that once again her mood had changed. Before getting out of the car she put a hand on his arm, leaned over and planted a brief kiss on his cheek. He was bewildered as she looked at him with distant eyes and gave him the most inviting smile, then jumped out.

The Château d'Avignon was an ancient building which had been carefully renovated. They mounted a flight of steps, walked through a vast hall to a dining room beyond. Two large doors were thrown open on to a terrace where tables were laid and couples sat drinking. Tina gasped at the view.

Below the wide terrace the land fell away in a series of vineyard-like levels. Grassy fields spread out in

131

descending slopes beyond. In the distance a vast panorama of France stretched out with here and there a small range of hills, a brownish colour in the evening light which was casting a luminous glow over the endless landscape. Hamlets were nestled in the valleys between the hills, the houses like toys. To their left a distant lake glittered azure in the setting sun.

'It's like a painting,' Anton remarked.

Tina didn't hear him. She was staring at a handsome tanned man sitting at one of the tables with a woman. He was gazing back at her with considerable interest. Tina felt a thrill – she lived for admiration from good-looking men, and for money.

'The view is pretty marvellous,' the man said. 'Sam West.'

'Nice to meet a fellow countryman,' she purred, soaking up the admiration in his look.

Then West noticed Anton and realized she had an escort. He nodded, averted his gaze from her. The woman with him was amused. She said in a low voice which Anton heard.

'Enjoying yourself, Sam?'

'We're having a great evening,' he assured her with a smile.

There was an empty table next to where West sat. Anton was looking at other empty tables further away. He moved towards one but Tina spoke sharply.

'Anton, let's sit at this table. We get the view to the best advantage.'

'If you prefer it.'

'I do.' She sat down close to West. Waving both arms in the air she called out as the waiter approached. 'We want champagne. Oodles of it.'

Anton groaned inwardly. He asked the waiter to bring a large bottle of sparkling mineral water as well. West had tactfully swivelled his chair so he was not looking at Tina. One bottle of champagne disappeared and Tina asked for another bottle. She had drunk most of the first because Anton was sipping at his glass and drinking a lot of mineral water. I have to drive back, Heaven help me, he was thinking.

Tina changed to another chair, which positioned her so she could face West. Anton leaned forward, whispered to her, making sure his voice didn't carry.

'He has his own girlfriend with him.'

'You don't own me,' she yelled at the top of her voice.

Other couples at their tables turned round to stare at her. It appeared most of them were French and they looked disapproving at the way she had raised her voice. Once again Anton felt embarrassed. Tina was starting on yet another full glass of champagne when Anton spoke to West.

'Excuse me, sir,' he said in his flawless English, 'but do you happen to know who owns this place?'

'It's a bit weird. I understand French and we were here before when the accountant was talking to the manager. I gathered from what I overheard that some company in the Channel Islands bought it. At least it's registered there. But it's really controlled by some Englishman in Dorset.'

Tina choked on her champagne. She spilt some of her glass on the table. Then she gave Anton a warm smile.

'It's the bubbles.'

14

Tweed had found Emilio Vitorelli sunning himself on the terrace. He asked the Italian to come with him to his room. Paula was waiting when they entered.

'You know Emilio,' he said to her.

'We all met quite some time ago in Rome. Good morning, Mr Vitorelli.'

'Emilio, please.'

She didn't reply as Tweed ushered him to a hard-backed seat behind a polished table. Tweed sat down opposite his guest who was eyeing Paula. She stared back with no particular expression, even when he smiled at her with great warmth.

He had always liked Paula on the few occasions they had met. Paula's reaction was not so approving. She regarded him as the typical Latin on the make with women – but she was still astute enough to realize he had a dynamic personality, that he was clever.

'I asked you here to show you something,' Tweed began. 'The photo you were kind enough to send me. This is Tina Langley?'

He produced the glossy print he had concealed on his lap and slid it across the table. Vitorelli stared at it and Paula noticed the change in his expression. It was now grim.

'That is the lady in question,' he replied quietly.

'I can tell you she murdered a man in Vienna. She is the one who killed Norbert Engel. Came up behind him with a Luger, shot him in the back of the head. You could say she's a fully paid-up member of The Sisterhood.'

'I see.'

Vitorelli teetered back in his chair, folded his large hands across his stomach. He glanced at Paula who was once more studying the list of the men belonging to the *Institut de la Défense*.

'For a moment you surprised me,' the Italian commented. 'On thinking about it I imagine a woman capable of hurling acid into another woman's face – as she did to my late fiancée – would not stop at murder if big money were involved.'

'It had to be a very attractive woman to tempt Norbert Engel,' Tweed continued, pursuing his theme relentlessly.

'Tina Langely is an exceptionally attractive woman. She very nearly distracted me from my fiancée with her vibrant personality. But I pulled myself up, knowing my fiancée had so much more to offer – not only in the way of appearance and poise but, very important, in intellect. Had she remained on this earth,' he reflected sombrely, 'we would have been the perfect couple. A very remarkable woman was destroyed by this hideous killer.'

Paula was startled. His voice had changed. He had spoken with terrible venom. His normally laughing eyes had become ice-cold. Tweed tapped the photo.

'Are there other copies of this print, other than the one I am sure you have kept for yourself?'

'Why do you ask?'

'Because I am convinced there are many copies. We both are after the same person.'

'I'm surprised you wish to collaborate with a rogue like me,' Vitorelli replied with a broad smile.

'The position is so serious I would collaborate with the Devil if it came to it.'

'Perhaps you are doing just that. Yes, there are many copies. They are in the hands of my large underground network which is searching Europe for her. No wonder she has been nicknamed The Butterfly. She flits from place to place, never staying anywhere for long. She is a restless creature. Sometimes I think she is a lost soul, seeking some paradise on earth, a paradise she will never find.'

'You paint a vivid picture of her,' Tweed commented.

'Also, my chief lieutenant and confidant is trawling the main cities of Switzerland with a photo, looking for her.'

'Why Switzerland?'

'Because I know how her devious mind works. She was last seen briefly in Salzburg. So she would move on to another country. Now you tell me she was involved in Norbert Engel's murder in Vienna I am even more sure she would pick a neutral state like Switzerland.'

'Also,' Paula spoke for the first time, 'it strikes me it fits in with your description of The Butterfly – temperamentally never able to stay in one place for long.'

'That is clever,' Vitorelli said slowly, looking at Paula with fresh respect. 'It is very good psychology.'

'Merely one woman seeing into the mind of another.'

'Which cities,' Tweed enquired, 'has your deputy visited so far?'

'Zurich, Basle, Lausanne. He is now in Geneva. From scraps of information my network has picked up there is something odd about Geneva, something important.'

'It is the city where the Monceau gang infiltrated Switzerland from France,' Tweed told him. 'Maybe there is a link somewhere.'

'Who knows. I must go now.' The Italian stood up. 'Perhaps we should keep in touch?'

'I think we should,' Tweed agreed.

* * *

Marler arrived soon after Vitorelli had left them. He wore a rather dingy lightweight suit. No creases in his trousers, his clothes crumpled. Paula stared at him.

'What's happened? Normally you're sartorially so elegant and now, if you'll excuse me, you look more like a scarecrow.'

'Not very noticeable?' Marler replied ironically.

'Hardly, to say the least.'

'That's the general idea. I've been snooping round.' He took off the sunglasses, excessively larger than the pair he would normally have chosen. 'I applied for a job as porter at the Dolder Grand. They turned me down. Amazing!'

'Supposing they'd accepted you?'

'I'd have told them the pay wasn't good enough. Then I pulled out a roll of banknotes which made the concierge's eyes pop. Said I was going to the bar. He was so taken aback he didn't try to stop me. Probably thought I was one of those oddball millionaires who don't care how they look, that it was all a practical joke.'

'You found something there?' Tweed enquired.

'I found someone wasn't there. Captain William Wellesley Carrington, who had been staying there, had checked out suddenly. I got on well with the barman.'

'He's disappeared?' Tweed asked.

'Checked out. Next stage of the report. Amos Lodge so far has spent the whole morning locked away in his room. Had his breakfast sent up. Learn anything from that amiable rascal, Emilio Vitorelli?'

Tweed told him everything the Italian had revealed. Marler looked thoughtful. He leant against a wall, lit a king-size.

'So there's something special about Geneva?'

'Possibly,' Tweed said vaguely.

'I'd better trot off, get into some decent tropical gear before the Baur au Lac throws me out.' He paused at the door. 'Oh, by the way, Butler and Nield have also been very active. Won't bore you with the details. And Carrington is staying at the Gotthard at the other end of Bahnhofstrasse.'

'How did you find that out?' Tweed demanded.

'I gave them a description of Carrington. Not easy to miss *him*. Pete Nield saw him booking in with his luggage at the hotel they're staying at. See you.'

When he had gone Paula stood up and restlessly began walking round the spacious room. She was looking out of the window down at the entrance drive when she saw Marler, smartly dressed in a white linen suit, hurrying to the car he had hired. Butler appeared, got into the front passenger seat. Marler drove off. She told Tweed what she had seen.

'Marler is a law unto himself,' Tweed responded. 'He's up to something. Why are you acting like me, pacing round as though you can't keep still? I'm wondering whether to ask you to go to Geneva. You could take this photo with you – I shall certainly recognize Tina Langley if I ever see her.'

'Marler told me to stay here.'

'And I thought I was running this outfit,' Tweed said with a smile.

'You just approved of Marler going his own way. Newman has disappeared too. Why do you think Willie abandoned the Dolder Grand and slipped away to the Gotthard? He could be running scared.'

'Doesn't sound like Willie. He may have another reason.'

'Such as?'

'The Gotthard is closer to both the main rail station and the airport. Just a thought. What I'm wondering is what is Jules Monceau up to?'

* * *

138

Mario Parcelli, Vitorelli's confidant, was footsore. The sun was blazing down on Geneva out of a clear sky and the temperature went on rising. He had enquired at every major hotel in the city and had drawn a blank. His technique had been carefully thought out. He approached the concierge in each hotel.

'I am trying to contact my sister, Tina Langley. She sent me a fax just before flying out here but the name of the hotel was unreadable. I'm talking about Tina Langley. You might like to see my card.'

He had then produced the visiting card swiftly printed in Zurich and had laid it on the counter.

RUTLAND & WARWICKSHIRE BANK
Mark Langley. Director.

He knew that in Switzerland bank directors ranked high in the social league. He also knew that no concierge of a major hotel would dream of revealing to a stranger the name of a guest staying there. But he had a trump card. Before a concierge could react he then placed the photo of Tina Langley on the counter.

'That is my sister.'

Again he anticipated total discretion on the part of a concierge. But Mario was very observant. The moment a concierge looked down at the glossy print he watched him like a hawk, watched for the brief sign of recognition in an otherwise impassive face. So far he was convinced Tina was not staying at any place he had visited.

He had just left the Hôtel des Bergues. It was Mario's bad luck that the concierge he dealt with was new to the job, was standing in for the permanent concierge. No reaction.

He picked up card and photo, walked out into the heat, turned right, glanced into the Pavillon restaurant attached to des Bergues. The windows fronted on to the promenade. No sign of her. He started walking along the promenade, looked down a small side street running alongside the hotel, saw her.

She was gazing into a shop window as he walked slowly along the opposite side of the street to make sure. He glanced down at the photo in his hand – which was a mistake.

Tina saw the man dressed like a banker look down at something in his hand, guessed it was a photo. She stiffened, then strolled slowly further down the street. The enemy was looking for her – probably the people Roka had saved her from back in Vienna.

She strolled on, forcing herself not to hurry. Ahead she saw a large department store she had investigated earlier. She walked straight inside, relieved to see it was crowded with people escaping from the heat. Her mind was racing. She had in the past had plenty of experience in the art of disappearing from men she had exploited. She looked back and saw the small fat man standing at the entrance. She decided to nickname him Teddy Bear.

He was obviously afraid of losing her so he was staying hanging about at the entrance. In the luggage department she bought a cheap suitcase. She then proceeded from one department to another, buying cheap clothes at random, anything to make the suitcase heavy.

When Tina had finished buying her purchases she strolled back towards the entrance. Teddy Bear was waiting on the opposite side of the street. She paused, saw a patrol car moving slowly down the street. The perfect opportunity. Going outside, she hailed one of the numerous taxis crawling past.

'Please take me to Cornavin, the rail station,' she called out in a loud voice.

As her taxi took off Mario hailed another cab, gave the driver the same instructions. Tina was careful not to look back, but in the rear-view mirror she saw Teddy Bear's taxi following hers. She smiled to herself.

Arriving at the station, she paid off the driver, carried her case into the station. There was a queue at the ticket counter but she knew Teddy Bear was behind her with one woman between them. He had probably been careful not to be too close to her. She raised her voice again when she reached the counter.

'One single ticket to Zurich, please. Thank you. When is the next express leaving?'

'In about five minutes. Check the monitor for the platform.'

She hurried down a ramp, climbed the steps to the *quai* – the platform from which the express was leaving. Checking with a station official, she located where the front of the express would stop and hurried along to the right place. Putting down her bag, she took out an expensive lace-bordered handkerchief, mopped the moisture off her forehead.

Teddy Bear had stopped a distance away, close to where the end of the express would halt. She picked up her case when the gleaming express, many coaches long, glided in. Boarding a coach opposite a pillar on the platform near the front, she rested her suitcase in an empty compartment, picked up a copy of the timetable which showed her exactly when the express would arrive and leave at the few stations it stopped at.

It was one advantage of Swiss trains that they arrived precisely at the scheduled time, left exactly on the scheduled time. She picked up the suitcase, parked it in the corridor near the exit door. Then she watched the hands turning on a huge station clock outside the window.

Once she risked a glance out of the window, looking down the platform. No sign of Teddy Bear among a whole crowd of last-minute passengers who were scrambling aboard. Fifteen seconds before the automatic door would close, she descended back on to the platform with her case, hid herself behind the large pillar.

Promptly, the automatic doors closed, the express glided out of the station. When it was gone she took a last look at the rear of the end coach. She giggled.

Mario, starting from the end of the train, had a difficult job. So many passengers had piled aboard just before the express had departed it was a slow job trudging slowly from compartment to compartment, from coach to coach, checking every passenger.

He was only halfway along the train when it stopped at Lausanne. He poked his head out of a window, thinking Tina might get off. No sign of her. The train started moving again and the next stop, Berne, was a long way north. His feet were killing him. He was wearing smart shoes to go with the image of a banker and they pinched his toes.

He had checked the whole length of the express long before it reached Berne. He sat down in an empty compartment, bought three cartons of coffee and two bottles of mineral water from the food and drinks trolley when it eventually reached him.

Exhausted, he got off the train at Berne. Sinking down on a seat he waited for the next express travelling in the opposite direction. Remembering he only had a single ticket, he forced himself to walk the long distance to the ticket office, bought a single back to Geneva.

The heat inside the huge cavern which is Berne station was near unbearable. Mario, having bought his ticket, parked himself on a seat to wait for the express. His shirt was pasted to his back, his collar was damp and shapeless, he could feel sweat trickling down from under his armpits. He'd have given anything to remove his shoes but he daren't – if he did he would never get his feet inside them again. But Mario Parcelli was a determined man.

He was sure Tina Langley was still in Geneva – and he was going to find her.

When the express arrived it was apparent the heat was affecting other people badly. Normally well-behaved, they pushed people aside to secure a seat on the train. Mario found himself lifted up by the crush, literally forced aboard. He had to shove himself to avoid tripping over the high step into the coach. He chose to stand in a corridor rather than join other passengers crammed into seats.

The first thing he was going to do on arriving in Geneva was to find a shop which sold shoes. Then have a brief meal – before he took up the search for Tina Langley in earnest.

After taking a cold shower, which made her feel much better, Tina put on a fresh set of clothes. Earlier she had taken a taxi back to the Hôtel des Bergues. Instead of going into the hotel she had wandered along the river front. The heat had driven most people indoors. At a quiet spot, she had thrown the unwanted suitcase into the Rhône.

She checked her appearance carefully in the mirror after making herself up. Until Hassan contacted her she had decided to call Anton, at the number he had given her. She would accept the invitation to dinner she knew he would suggest – but at a restaurant, not at his apartment. She rehearsed in her head how she would make her move after the wine had flowed.

'This is embarrassing for me, Anton, but some traveller's cheques which should have come to me by Federal Express have not arrived. It's left me very short. Do you think you could loan me twenty thousand francs? As soon as the cheques arrive I'll bring the money back to your apartment . . .'

She would give him her very special smile. He was crazy about her. Strike while the iron is hot before the fire begins to fade, she thought, mixing her metaphors. The phone rang. She knew it would be Anton. She let it ring for several times, then lifted the receiver.

It was Hassan on the line.

'I have to leave this hotel for somewhere else . . .' she began.

'You will stay where you are. On no account are you to move.'

'I don't like people speaking to me in that way—'

'I have had too much of your impertinence. Don't dare to interrupt. You will just listen. You are a highly paid employee of the company,' he went on, phrasing his words carefully. 'We can always find someone else to take your place,' he said arrogantly.

She sucked in her breath. This was a different Hassan from the man she had known so far. His voice was demanding, brooking no arguments. The smooth, oily manner had vanished. In its place was a hard, ruthless voice.

'You will have another assignment to carry out soon. You will obtain tomorrow any references you need for the job from this man at this address . . . He has your description. That is all.'

144

References? She knew he had given her details of where she could obtain a Luger and ammunition. She was about to put down the phone when he spoke again.

'In future, for the moment, you can get me at this number . . .'

This time she did put the phone down. Thinking for a few minutes, she called the concierge, asked him which city had the code number Hassan had given her for his new phone number.

'That is Zurich, madame,' the concierge replied immediately.

In his room at the Baur au Lac Tweed had sat in silence for ten minutes. Paula knew this because she had discreetly timed him. He spoke suddenly.

'I'm checking my memory. You have the list of members of the *Institut de la Défense*. I am next on the list, below me is Amos Lodge. Who is below Lodge?'

'Christopher Kane. Why?'

'We have assumed so far the enemy is working his way down the list. We have overlooked the fact that he may jump one or two names. That would eliminate any chance of the target asking for protection.'

'Who is Christopher Kane?'

'The world's greatest expert on biological warfare – and the antidotes to all its forms. He's moved from London to Geneva.'

'Why?'

'I'm not sure. I knew him in London and asked him the same question. He gave me a curious reply. Said he wanted to move closer to the battlefield.'

'What did that mean?'

'I don't know. I asked Chris the same question and he didn't elaborate. Odd the way Geneva keeps cropping up. Mario Parcelli is in that city, looking for Tina

145

Langley. Monceau and his gang slipped through Beck's clutches passing through Geneva. I sense the net is closing on whoever is behind the murders – and on what I'm convinced are preparations for a great catastrophe so far as Europe is concerned.'

'I keep wondering where Monceau is, what he's doing.'

'So do I.

Hassan had been careful to give members of The Sisterhood the impression he was a middleman, the go-between for someone very much higher up and more powerful. In fact, he was the son of the Head of State of the power which had conducted military manoeuvres under the blanket of the black cloud. The Englishman had great influence with his father, an influence Hassan was jealous of. He had argued with his father to no avail.

'The Englishman understands the psychology of the members of the *Institut de la Défense*,' his father had insisted. 'They must all be destroyed before we can launch our great operation. Even one of them might influence his government to take steps to organize a formidable force at short notice. Do as I say.'

Now Hassan's patience had snapped. He was convinced he could achieve what the Englishman was causing to happen himself. At the moment most of the members of the *Institut* were in Switzerland, or visiting it. Which made sense – their headquarters were at Ouchy on the shores of Lake Geneva.

On the verge of leaving the strange house in Slovakia, he had booked a suite at the Hotel Zum Storchen in Zurich which overlooked the Limmat River and was situated in one of the Old Towns. He had used the name Ashley Wingfield.

Hassan had once been educated in England, had attended the military establishment at Sandhurst, rising to the rank of lieutenant. He would have no difficulty passing himself off as an Englishman and he had a forged passport in the temporary name he had chosen for himself.

The fact that his skin was brownish didn't worry him at all. He knew that half the people walking round Zurich had a suntan due to the ferocious heat.

He drove himself down the spiralling road at one end of the mountain and it took him little over one hour to reach Schwechat Airport, well outside Vienna. Ashley Wingfield's planning was always precise. He arrived in time to board the flight for Zurich on Austrian Airlines. In a little over two hours he was esconced in a suite in Zum Storchen.

He wore a Savile Row suit and the tie of a well-known British regiment. The heat did not bother him – he was used to far higher temperatures back home. Lighting a Havana cigar, he stared down, at Zurich's second Altstadt – Old Town – across the gently flowing Limmat River.

Now he had arrived there would be fireworks in this citadel of the declining West. He wanted the remaining members of the *Institut* wiped out quickly. Who, he was wondering, would kill Tweed first? Karin Berg or that piece of rubbish, Jules Monceau? Hassan was a cultured man.

15

'Curious,' Paula said, as Tweed sat in a chair in his room, his mind roaming, 'that Willie should suddenly move from the Dolder Grand to the Gotthard.'

'Yes, it is. I'm wondering if he's meeting someone secretly. The Dolder Grand would be a rather public rendezvous.'

'Who do you think he could be meeting?'

'Maybe someone who has just arrived in town and doesn't want to be observed.'

'So who could that be?'

'Maybe the mysterious Hassan.'

Paula stared at him. She knew Tweed had these odd flashes of insight. It came from his ferocious concentration on all aspects of a problem. He made mind-leaps which had astounded her in the past.

'What would he be doing in Zurich?'

'If he's running The Sisterhood, as I suspect he is, he may have arrived to hurry up the elimination of the surviving members of the *Institut*.' Tweed frowned. 'If my theory should be correct – and it's only a theory – the danger to the West is even closer than I had thought.'

'An Arab should not be impossible to track down . . .'

'I prefer the word Easterner. Don't forget that many have been educated in the West, particularly in Britain. So he'll speak perfect English, could pass for an Englishman.'

'The colour of his skin would give him away,' Paula objected.

'Look out of the window. The heatwave has lasted long enough for most of the locals to have a strong tan.'

'But we could ask Marler to check the top hotels,' she persisted. 'To find out if anyone new has arrived today. Marler has a way of persuading concierges to talk. I'd start with the Dolder Grand.'

'Why that particular hotel?'

'Because it's the one Willie suddenly checked out of.'

'I don't follow that.'

'Because if Willie was going to meet someone in

secret he'd be bound to move to another location to meet that person.'

'Not a very logical conclusion.'

'Call it a woman's intuition. I know it doesn't always work – but often it does . . .'

There was a knock on the door. Paula jumped up, Browning in her hand, unlocked the door. As if on cue, it was Marler who walked in.

'Everything is arranged,' he announced. 'Think I'll have a catnap in my room. I came along to see if there have been any developments.'

'Unfortunately for you,' Tweed said with a smile, 'Paula has come up with a development. You started this, Paula, so you can tell him.'

Marler leant against a wall while he listened. Just when she thought he had forgotten Marler took out a king-size and lit it, studying her.

'I can check the expensive hotels, but it's a long shot. So what have we go so far, Tweed?'

'We have a series of cold-blooded murders. By The Sisterhood. Only known member Tina Langley – confirmed by Paula and the photo Emilio Vitorelli gave me. We know the Monceau gang is close – Beck reckons with seven thugs left after the abortive attempt to kill me. We have Geneva, which may or may not be a key city. According to Vitorelli, and I believe him, large sums are sent by courier to someone in Dorset. Two prominent citizens from Dorset, Amos Lodge and Willie, are here. The Americans report a certain Eastern state is preparing an attack on Western Europe. We have Hassan, who runs The Sisterhood, whereabouts unknown. That's it.'

'In other words,' Marler summed up, 'we have damn-all.'

'We do have a little more,' Paula said. 'We have penetrated the technique whereby the murders are carried out. We know now that an attractive woman approaches The Sisterhood's target, gains his confidence, then at her first opportunity shoots him in the back of the head with a Luger, followed by an amateurish attempt to make it look like suicide.'

'Why amateurish?' Marler queried.

'I've cracked that one,' Tweed broke in. 'It's deliberately made to look amateurish. These nice people led by Hassan are out to intimidate and terrorize after they have killed a target. To make every remaining member of the *Institut* look over his shoulder, to turn him into a nervous wreck – then he'll be easier prey for The Sisterhood, will welcome some feminine company, will then let his guard down.'

'That's fiendish,' Paula protested.

'It's a ruthless, cold-blooded system which has been worked out well in advance. I've analysed their psychology and the method fits. What complicates everything is the arrival of the Monceau gang – which makes two enemies to deal with.'

'I have a suggestion,' Paula said. 'Why not deal with one problem at a time? Concentrate on cleaning up Monceau and his thugs. Then we can turn our full attention to wiping out The Sisterhood.'

'Which means using Tweed as bait,' Marler drawled.

'God!' Paula was horrified. 'I'd forgotten that angle.'

'I hadn't,' said Tweed. 'I think your tactics are sound. Monceau will undoubtedly try again to eliminate me. That is when we trap him. Now,' he went on briskly, 'I must warn Beck about another target – Christopher Kane, who has moved to Geneva. I'll ask Beck to have him guarded night and day. As the prime expert in the world on bacteriological warfare he has to be a number one target. I'm calling Beck now . . .'

* * *

In his cramped quarters inside his small hotel Jules Monceau had summoned the remaining six members of his gang. On the bed he had spread out a map which he had studied for hours. It was a detailed map which showed the Küsnacht district and the lake beyond. He addressed most of his remarks to Georges Lemont, his explosives expert.

'You've been to the Ermitage?'

'Yes,' Lemont replied in French, the language his chief was using.

Lemont was a tiny figure with a long face tapered to a pointed chin. He was always smiling as though he found life amusing.

'You really know the layout?' Monceau demanded.

'Yes,' replied Lemont, a man of few words.

'You know it thoroughly?'

'Yes.'

Lemont dropped a carefully drawn pencil sketch on the table which indicated a complete plan of the hotel and restaurant. He had even measured the length of its lake frontage by pacing out the distance. His plan showed the jetty projecting out on the Zurich city side of the hotel terrace.

'You have prepared the special weapon?' Monceau went on.

'Yes.'

'Are you sure it will work? This laser-guided rocket from the boat out on the lake?'

'Yes.'

'And you have back-up weaponry in case the rocket does not work? Will you have a fusillade ready to bombard the terrace?'

'Yes.'

'Tweed will arrive there with a woman companion at nine o'clock this evening. You have the timing worked out?'

'Yes.'

Monceau gave up. Georges Lemont was still smiling when he was dismissed from the room with the other five men. Well, he said to himself, you will see tonight what an excellent planner I am. He had no doubt Monceau would be somewhere near but safe – so he could watch the destruction of Tweed.

'Is that you, Tweed?' Beck's cheerful voice enquired over the phone. 'I have news for you. Amos Lodge's speech at the Kongresshaus has been postponed until tomorrow night.'

'Really? Why?'

'We have had an anonymous call warning us a bomb has been placed inside the building. It will take hours to check the whole complex. It may be a hoax, but we can't assume that.'

'How did Amos react to the news?'

'In a storming fury. I told him to arrange for stickers to be printed and plastered across all the posters he's had put up in Zurich. At his own expense, of course.'

'So he's not best pleased?'

'He thundered at me down the phone. I have more news, which you won't like. You asked me to guard Christopher Kane, the bacteriological warfare expert, in Geneva. Kane has refused point-blank to have any protection assigned to him.'

'That sounds like Christopher. He's a very independent and private person.'

'He's going to be even more private if he has the back of his head blown off. All for now. I expect it's enough . . .'

Paula sat very still for several minutes after the phone call which Tweed had told her about. She was staring at her shoes before she expressed her thought.

'I find something sinister about this bomb hoax thing.'

'Really?' Tweed's thoughts were miles away. 'In what way could it be sinister?'

'The trouble is I don't know. Again, call it my woman's intuition, but don't laugh.'

'I'm not laughing. If you'll excuse me it's almost evening and I have to change for my dinner at the Ermitage with Karin Berg.'

Paula's intuition was dangerously correct. Not far from the top of Bahnhofstrasse the Englishman had boarded a tram which took him up to the summit of the Zurichberg, the high forested hill behind the city.

The tram climbed and curved until it had left the suburbs behind and reached its terminus. Even in the sunlight the dark fir forest looked menacing. He found Hassan sitting on a seat at the edge of the forest.

There was no one else about. The heat had kept the locals and the tourists close to the lake. Sitting next to Hassan, the Englishman stared into the distance. He had left a space between them. Anyone observing them from a distance might well assume they were strangers – they were occupying the only seat in sight.

'Tweed is going tonight. For ever,' Hassan said, his lips hardly moving.

'Good show.'

'The killing will take place just outside Zurich. It is important the police force is otherwise occupied.'

'Would help, I suppose.'

'So when you get back to Zurich you make a call to

153

police headquarters, disguising your voice. You tell them a bomb has been placed in Kongresshaus.'

'What on earth good will that do?'

'My psychology is better than yours. They have a certain number of police guarding Kongresshaus. I visited the place late this afternoon. It is enormous. Imagine how many police it will take to search such a vast place for a bomb. It will take them well away from where the next target will be tonight. You had better go now, my friend. A tram is arriving – it will soon be returning to Zurich. Make the call as soon as you can. So, Tweed goes down tonight.'

Tweed, smartly dressed, arrived in the lounge of the Baur au Lac promptly at 8.30 p.m. Karin Berg, dressed all in black, which contrasted well with her blonde hair, was waiting for him.

'Punctuality always was one of your virtues,' he greeted her.

'Probably my only one,' she replied with a smile.

The limousine Tweed had ordered was waiting for them in the drive. The chauffeur opened the rear door and they settled themselves. It was air-conditioned, which was a relief. The heatwave had gone on so long that even at night it was humid and sticky.

Tweed took out a silver cigarette case, a present from his wife in the days when he smoked. He offered one to Karin, knowing she still smoked. He'd seen her stub out a cigarette in the lounge when he appeared. He lit it for her with an old lighter as the car swung out of the drive, proceeded towards the lake.

'I told you it was my only virtue,' she said, giving him her slow smile.

Tweed appeared to have trouble closing the case. He

154

tapped it against the window. As he'd thought, it was armoured glass. Who on earth had arranged that?

Earlier Marler had phoned Beck. The conversation was short, to the point.

'Beck, Tweed is dining with an old woman friend at the Ermitage this evening. He's ordered a car from the concierge, which I have cancelled. Can you provide protection?'

'I can and will,' Beck had replied. 'I will send a car with armoured glass and reinforced bodywork. Unfortunately I can do no more. I can't even send an armed plain-clothes man as driver – most of my men are tied up searching for a bomb at Kongresshaus, the rest are helping with a multiple collision on a road outside Zurich. Alternately, persuade Tweed to cancel his dinner.'

'You know Tweed. He wouldn't do it. Thanks for the car . . .'

Soon Tweed noticed they were driving along Seefeldstrasse. The long street lined with office blocks and later with old villas seemed to go on and on. Küsnacht was further out than he had realized.

'Do you mind if I smoke another cigarette?' Karin asked.

'Of course not.'

She was chain-smoking, lighting one cigarette from another. He remembered from their acquaintance years before it had been a habit of hers when she was either concentrating ferociously on some problem or when she was nervous.

'Something wrong?' he enquired.

'Yes, the heat. Remember, I come from Sweden. On occasion it is very hot in Stockholm but only rarely. I have never experienced such heat going on for so long. Thank Heaven the car is air-conditioned. Do you think it will be cooler where we're going?'

'Let us hope so. The Ermitage is by the lake.'

Secretly he doubted whether there would be any relief there. The heatwave had persisted for long enough to make the nights as sultry and oppressive as the days. Perhaps there would be a breeze off the lake.

'You seem cool enough,' she remarked, discreetly mopping her moist forehead.

'I find I can stand the heat, but that doesn't mean I like it.'

It was a fact that Tweed, although dressed in a dark business suit, was able to endure torrid heat without it affecting his alertness.

Normally, in the past, his social conversations with Karin had always been intriguing. She had talked about serious issues, about the world situation. Now she was indulging in trivia. He sensed the triteness of what she was saying was due to a feeling that she ought to be saying something rather than sitting beside him in silence. It could be the heat, of course, so why did he feel so strongly it had nothing to do with the temperature?

The Ermitage was reached when they had passed a number of very expensive-looking old villas. This was a district for the wealthy. The car eventually turned off the endless road and parked in a drive which was crammed with cars. The manager came out to meet them.

'Mr Tweed, sir? Your friend, Beck, phoned and asked us to look after you. We have reserved one of our best tables at the edge of the lake.'

'Good,' Tweed replied, 'that was what I asked for when I made the reservation myself.'

'You may have an even better table, sir, with Mr Beck calling me. This way, please.'

The Ermitage was a large building standing back a little from the lake. Behind it was a wide terrace with scattered tables overlooking the Zurichsee. Tweed's table was at the very edge of the water with a low stone wall dividing terrace from lake.

'This is a lovely place,' Karin commented, looking round at all the lights illuminating the terrace. 'As in the past, your taste is perfect.'

'Thank you.'

Once they were seated Tweed glanced round at the other tables. All of them were full. At one table further back sat a single man, tall and thin with dark hair draped across his forehead in a way which gave him a faint resemblance to Hitler. He also had a small dark moustache. He was studying the menu and summoned a waiter as soon as Tweed and his companion had sat down. Presumably he had got fed up waiting for his guest.

At another table close to some bushes there was the shadow of a man. He also was alone and sat very still, almost like a statue. At other tables couples and groups were having the time of their lives. There was a lot of noise – the babble of the guests' voices, laughter, mingling with the clink of glasses. The atmosphere on the terrace was one of great party celebrating some great event.

'What would you like to drink?' Tweed asked.

'A dry Martini.'

Tweed also ordered one of his rare aperitifs. He was thinking Karin still liked a strong drink. On her left wrist, exposed below the black cuff of her dress, which did not hug her figure too tightly, she wore a diamond-studded wristwatch. She had glanced at it as they sat down. Now she checked it briefly again.

'We have plenty of time,' Tweed assured her with a smile.

'All the time in the world. Cheers!'

They clinked glasses. Karin drank half hers at one

gulp as Tweed sipped his own. A waiter laid menus before them, a wine list in front of Tweed. He told them there was no hurry, that he would be back later. Tweed was looking at the wristwatch.

'A present from some admirer? You must have plenty of them?'

'Wristwatches?' she joked.

'No, admirers,' he said gallantly.

'As a matter of fact it's a present from myself. I don't mix with men much these days.'

'Why not? You used to. And you're still in your thirties.'

'My job takes up most of my time. If I have a few free hours I usually sleep – ready for the next business onslaught. Security at the top, as you know, requires all your energy. What about yourself? Surely you have the odd girlfriend?'

'My job takes up most of my time,' he replied, repeating what she had said about herself. 'Maybe we should study the menu – I hear it is a good one . . .'

As he held the menu he studied the lake shore and what lay out beyond it. The night was still very hot and humid, had the feel of a pea-soup fog although the view was crystal clear. On the far side of Zurichsee the opposite shore was studded with lights, rather like the diamonds on Karin's watch, which she had just surreptitiously checked again.

The night had a romantic aura. A steamer was passing well out, lit up like a floating Christmas tree. During a brief lull in the babble of voices on the terrace Tweed could hear dance music from the steamer drifting across the water, which was as still as the proverbial millpond.

He would have expected Karin to flirt mildly with him, as she had done in the past. Instead, she sat with her eyes lowered to the menu. He studied her. She really was the most attractive woman with her naturally blonde hair, her perfect complexion, her sympathetic voice when she was in a good mood. And she had the added advantage of a first-rate intellect.

Tweed tore his gaze away from her and again gazed out at the lake. A large launch was approaching, about two hundred yards out. It was moving slowly, had a high foredeck and a luxurious-looking cabin. It was still some distance away, showed up clearly in the moonlight despite the fact that it had nowhere any lights showing – except the warning lights to port and starboard.

Further out a large powerboat was skimming round in circles. It occurred to Tweed that perhaps the owner had a girlfriend aboard and had fixed the wheel to continue its circling motion. Tweed imagined that racing full out it would be able to move at phenomenal speed.

'Have you decided,' he asked Karin, 'or would you like a little longer? No hurry.'

'I have decided,' she said and gave him her quirky smile. 'You were right. It is a very good menu. A surfeit of choice.'

The waiter appeared and they gave their orders. Tweed chose a bottle of wine after consulting Karin. He rather went overboard on the price. She raised her eyebrows when the waiter had gone.

'You really are going over the top with the wine. It happens to be my favourite, but I expect you remembered. You do have the most amazing memory.'

Tweed almost remarked on what a romantic night it was and then stopped himself. Despite the jollification going on all round them an alarm signal was buzzing at the back of his brain. He hadn't been able to identify what had triggered it off.

Except where the moon cast a path across the water the lake now looked like black ice. Not a ripple anywhere. The large launch had stopped, still at least two hundred yards out and less than a quarter of a mile away. The big powerboat was continuing to circle.

The babble was louder now on the terrace, the laughter more pronounced as large quantities of alcohol took effect. Tweed glanced over to where the two single men had been seated at separate tables. 'Hitler' was eating his meal rapidly, as though annoyed his escort had not turned up. The shadow man was still almost motionless, holding a glass near his invisible mouth without drinking from it.

They were now on their main course and Karin was eating with relish. She suddenly became very talkative, speaking rapidly.

'You really should get a girlfriend, Tweed.'

'Now you're lecturing me,' he chided amiably.

'I mean it. You'd probably do your job better if you had a bit of feminine fun.'

'Are you putting yourself forward in the role of helping me to do a better job.'

'That's up to you,' she challenged.

'If I did – notice I said "if" – it would probably be with someone like you. I also like someone worth talking to.'

'Well, don't you think I'm worth talking to?'

Was it the wine? He detected nervousness under the surface of her gaiety. She had never gone so far as this before. It really sounded as though she meant it.

'Let me think it over,' he said evasively. 'I do have a lot on my plate.'

'No, you don't. Like me, you've just cleared your plate. I must say this is the most wonderful meal I've had in ages.'

She dabbed at her lips delicately with a napkin. Her glass was empty. She had consumed most of the bottle, which was unusual for her. Tweed said he would order a fresh bottle and she agreed.

'Have some dessert,' he suggested.

'Yes, please. You don't mind if I have a smoke and wait a few minutes?'

'The night is young, to coin a cliché.'

'You haven't changed. You've given me your full attention – and a woman likes that. You've admired my clothes, my appearance, but I'd bet money you could still describe every guest seated on the terrace.'

'I'm sorry if I've *not* given you my full attention.'

'I'm not. If you couldn't describe everyone round us I would think you were going downhill. If anything, you seem more formidable than ever, if that's possible.'

'Flattery will get you somewhere, to coin another cliché,' Tweed said with a smile.

'That's what I'm hoping for.'

She was positively glowing, her eyes never leaving his. Her blonde hair, caught in one of the nearby lights, had a smooth sheen. One part of Tweed felt more relaxed than he had for ages, another part of his mind still kept sending out danger signals.

Was he getting over-suspicious? he wondered. He dismissed the thought quickly. That route led to complacency. The very thing he hammered home when interviewing a new recruit. He slowly drank a whole glass of water – to counter any effect the wine might have had on him.

An alcoholic haze was drifting over several tables. One man stood up, stumbled, had to grasp hold of the table to keep himself upright. A girl seated close to him shoved his thigh and he very nearly fell full length. She gave a high-pitched laugh. The party spirit was well under way. The man decided his visit to the toilet could wait, sank bank into his chair and reached for his glass of wine.

At another table the guests started singing a French song and people at nearby tables joined in. It was becoming a carousal as wineglasses were raised and in some cases the wine slopped over the rim.

'They're enjoying themselves,' said Karin, who had twisted round in her chair to watch what was going on.

'I hope they have taxis to take them home,' Tweed observed amiably.

Then he remembered the last risk they had to fear was being stopped by the police. All Beck's men would still be searching Kongresshaus for the bomb – unless they had found it. The rest would probably still be somewhere outside Zurich tending to the multiple car crash victims.

Weird, he thought, so peaceful and full of enjoyment here and not so far away there is tragedy. What a strange mix the world is. Better to be here.

'I'm not sure I could face dessert,' Karin decided. 'That was quite some meal. Maybe strong coffee would be the best answer for me. But you have dessert if you feel like it,' she added suddenly.

Nothing had changed out on the lake. True, there were no more illuminated steamers with dance bands. But the large launch was still stationary in the same position. The same powerboat was still circling. Tweed had never seen a craft keep it up for so long. And the two men who sat alone at their individual tables were still there. Men on their own were not always a happy sight.

Once again Karin took a quick glance at her watch as the waiter came to their table. Tweed ordered coffee for both of them, saying they couldn't face any dessert. As he walked away to fetch them coffee Karin pushed her chair back, looked at Tweed.

'If you'll excuse me for the moment, I'll go to the powder room.'

Tweed sat quietly, his head not moving, his eyes everywhere. He sensed imminent danger. But from which direction? The large launch was now moving slowly towards the Ermitage. The circling powerboat was now still, its powerful engine ticking over, its prow pointed towrds the shore.

Tweed glanced towrds the two single men still seated at the tables at the back of the terrace. They were still there. Quietly, he edged his chair further away from the table. He placed both hands on its edges, lifted it slightly. It was a substantial weight but one he could handle.

Aboard the launch Georges Lemont had positioned his laser-guided rocket launcher on the foredeck below the bridge. He had his eye close to the rubber-enclosed crosswires. He saw Tweed clearly in the magnification. There was hardly any motion, but a slight swell on the lake moved the crosswires up and down slowly. He would wait for exactly the right moment.

On the bridge the man behind the wheel kept the vessel moving slowly on target. He was waiting for Lemont, visible below him because his eyes had become accustomed to the dark, to give him the signal. Lemont would raise his left hand and drop it while his right hand remained on the trigger.

A window on the port side of the bridge was open. Crouched behind it was another man, holding a Heckler & Koch machine-pistol. When they were close enough he could spray the whole terrace with a fusillade of bullets. Monceau, inside his car close to the Ermitage, had insisted on plenty of back-up.

A fourth man was standing behind the bridge, holding a more convential rocket launcher. The shell inside was filled with deadly shrapnel. The first man to act would be Lemont. Seconds after he had fired the others would operate their weapons.

They all knew they had the right target. A man sitting with a blonde woman, dressed in black, her hair cut close to her head like a helmet. She had left the table at precisely the agreed time. Eleven o'clock. Her appearance, her timing leaving the table – both these factors confirmed the target.

It would all be over in less than two minutes. There would be other casualties, a lot of them – innocent diners. This had worried Monceau not at all. It was far more certain that a target would be shot down, annihilated, among a crowd. A similar technique had been used before in a big bank raid in France. Eight civilians had died, but they had walked away with a small fortune in untraceable banknotes.

Aboard the stationary powerboat Paula waited tensely behind the wheel. Normally, in such a situation, she would have been ice-cold – but the realization that Tweed was a sitting duck for the killers made her hands clench the wheel more tightly.

An outstanding car driver, she had now mastered the art of steering a powerboat. Taking it round in wide circles for so long had been Marler's ploy to distract the launch's attention from it. But it had also given Paula excellent practice in handling the craft with skill.

'How much longer?' she whispered to Marler.

'Any moment now,' he answered quietly, standing by the hull.

His loaded Armalite rifle was slung over his shoulder. He was peering with great concentration through night-glasses, seeing every movement aboard the launch. He was paying the greatest attention to Lemont, whom he could see clearly with his rocket launcher.

'When I say "full throttle" smash into the side of the launch at top speed.'

On the deck just below the bridge Pete Nield was aiming his own Armalite point-blank at the man aboard the launch gripping an automatic weapon. Before they had left England Marler had treated him like a sergeant major addressing a rookie while Nield practised with the weapon.

Holding the wheel with one hand, Paula used the other to grip the lever which would turn the powerboat into a flying projectile. Marler had even used his engineering knowledge earlier in the day to soup up the engine.

'Not yet,' Marler warned her.

His glasses were now hanging from a strap round his neck and he was holding the Armalite, peering down the sight, which was focused on Lemont. To some extent he had the same problem as Lemont. The powerboat was moving up and down slightly with the faint swell on the lake. It was only a matter of a few inches rise and fall and Marler was not going for a tricky head-shot. He was aiming for Lemont's broad back.

'You're waiting too long,' Paula hissed.

'Patience is a virtue.'

'If we move forward now . . .'

Paula had only started to say they ought to move closer in when Marler uttered the magic words.

'Full throttle!'

As he spoke he pressed the trigger, a fraction of a second before Lemont launched his missile at Tweed. The bullet struck him under the left shoulder blade. He died instantly. But a reflex action tightened his finger on the trigger and the rocket, laden with high explosive, arced into the air.

Because it was the reflex action of a dead man the

165

aim was changed. The rocket soared up, descended, landed on an empty villa next to the Ermitage. At the same moment, hearing Marler's order, Nield had fired at the man holding the Heckler & Koch machine-pistol. Again the dead man, hit in the head, had with a reflex action pulled the trigger. Paula had already pulled the lever and the strong powerboat headed full throttle for the starboard side of the hull of the launch.

On the terrace all hell broke loose. Tweed saw the rocket's shell arcing downwards. He shoved over the table, crouched behind it, using it as a shield. When the rocket shell landed on the empty villa it detonated with a roar, hurling fragments of stonework into the sky. A small piece hit the table top, tore a hole in it, passing over Tweed's shoulder.

'It's good to get lucky,' he said to himself.

Peering through the hole he saw what happened next. Sheer panic among most of the guests. Women were screaming, men were yelling. Everyone was running, colliding into each other, falling down. There was nothing gentlemanly about their behaviour. Men pushed women out of the way as they fled desperately for the exit to the road.

There was a burst of shrapnel from the launch, fired into the air as the thug holding the weapon panicked, then fell dead as the second shot – this time from Nield's Armalite – hit him. Nobody aboard the launch had switched off the engine as Paula, her gloved hands braced for the shock, rammed the launch amidships. It keeled over, less strongly built than the powerboat.

Paula was ice-cold now the action had started. Swiftly, she reversed the powerboat well away from the stricken launch, an instruction which had been ham-

166

mered into her by Marler. He had suspected there would be plenty of ammunition stored aboard the vessel – and he was right.

Fire broke out aboard the launch. It reached the stock of ammunition. Paula had reversed the powerboat a good distance away when the whole launch exploded. There was a gigantic roar which was heard in distant Zurich. The launch vanished in a tower of flames. Above it sections of the craft were hurled high into the air, falling back into the lake with a hiss. There was a sudden eerie silence.

Tweed nimbly extricated himself from between the legs of the table, stood up. He was brushing himself off when he looked to his right. 'Hitler' was advancing towards him, holding Newman's favourite weapon, a Smith & Wesson .38, aimed at him. For once Tweed wished he had carried a gun himself.

The gunman was leering with sadistic satisfaction as he stopped, taking his time over aiming the gun at Tweed's chest. His target stood quite still, knowing that any movement on his part would activate the pressing of the trigger. There was nowhere to hide, nowhere to run to on the terrace which was now a shambles of overturned tables, smashed glasses.

Strangely enough, beside the gunman one table stood upright. Even stranger, a bottle of unopened red wine stood upright on the same table. The heat had never seemed more intense to Tweed. He thought of talking to the killer but that might also cause him to press the trigger. He remained very quiet, very still. It was suddenly very silent. Not a sound anywhere. It reminded Tweed of the silence he had experienced in Dorset.

A shot rang out. Tweed stiffened, waiting for the impact of the bullet which would end his life. The gunman's face showed an expression of disbelief. He collapsed sideways on to the table. Blood from the hole in his back mingled with the redness of the wine bottle his corpse had smashed. The shadow man came into the open. Newman lowered his own Smith & Wesson, grinned at Tweed.

'You do take chances.'

He bent over the body slumped across the table, checked the neck pulse. He glanced up at Tweed.

'Dead as a dodo . . .'

The manager, ashen-faced, came from inside the Ermitage, looked round at the carnage which had been his restaurant on the terrace, at the slumped body.

At that moment Karin Berg emerged from inside the building. She looked dazed as she stumbled towards Tweed. She tripped over debris, was about to fall, when Tweed grasped her round her slim waist. Newman had disappeared.

'What happened?' she gasped out.

'Some gentlemen who don't like me too much were rather active. We'll go to the car, back to the Baur au Lac.'

'What happened?' the manager asked, also looking dazed.

'I think it's probably a matter for the police. Why don't you call Beck?' Tweed suggested, guiding Karin towards the parked car.

16

It was early in the morning of the following day, not long after midnight, when Tweed assembled his team in his room at the Baur au Lac. After thanking Newman

168

for saving his life, an expression of gratitude which Newman brushed aside, he then told the others of his admiration for the way they had protected him by destroying the launch.

'All in a day's work,' Marler replied.

'It must have been a long day's work,' Tweed told him.

'I simply thought like the enemy after surveying the Ermitage,' Marler said off-handedly. 'I used a detailed map, decided the attack would come from the lake. Newman was back-up close to you. Very simple, really.'

'If you say so.' Tweed paused. 'The incident exposed another member of The Sisterhood. Karin Berg.'

'How on earth do you come to that conclusion?' Paula asked.

Tweed described the constant attention Berg had paid to the time by her watch. He described how she had gone to the powder room just before the onslaught had been launched, her nervousness.

'In the car on the way back,' he went on, 'she invited me to her apartment off Pelikanstrasse for a drink. She tried to become amorous, but I said I was tired. I have the exact address on this piece of paper.'

'Let me visit her,' Paula said grimly. 'I'll get the truth out of her.'

'I need you for something else later. I phoned Beck and he has plain-clothes men watching her apartment round the clock. He is going to phone me the moment she attempts to leave the city – probably by air.'

'He should arrest and interrogate her,' Paula broke in.

'No, we'll play a long game. She may lead us to The Sisterhood's headquarters or base. I'm giving this job to Harry Butler and Pete Nield. The two of you should buy clothes in the morning as soon as the shops open – holidaymakers' clothes and equipment, maybe backpacks. I leave it to you. You all have plenty of money for any emergency.'

'I'll go out and buy what we need,' Nield volunteered. 'That will leave Harry here to take any message from Beck.'

'Maybe I ought to draw a sketch so you can identify her,' Tweed suggested.

'Not necessary,' Nield said promptly. 'I saw the blonde you were dining with on the terrace clearly when Marler loaned me his night glasses. That, I presume was Karin Berg.'

'It was, is. Follow her halfway across the world if you need to. Keep in touch with me.'

'Will do,' replied the taciturn Butler.

'Isn't that suspicious in itself?' Paula remarked. 'She has a room at this hotel – and an apartment in Zurich.'

'That had occurred to me,' Tweed agreed. 'Beck also told me that they found no bomb in Kongresshaus. It was a ruse to tie up a large part of the Zurich police so they would be nowhere near the Ermitage. We won't let on to Amos Lodge what happened. He has a quick fuse.'

'Will you go to listen to the speech he's now making this evening at Kongresshaus?' enquired Paula.

'Yes, I'm rather looking forward to it. He's a first-rate orator and won't mince his words.'

'In that case,' Newman said firmly, 'Marler and I will come with you. Don't try to argue.'

'I always do as I'm told. Thank you. By all means come with me. One other thing – Beck has sent out a large force onto the lake to try and identify the bodies of the men aboard that launch. Let's hope there are seven – including Jules Monceau himself. Since he has photos of the gang he may get lucky.'

'What if Karin Berg does a moonlight flit?' Newman asked.

'Beck will warn me. He has installed a fake road

170

gang to use drills all night long outside her apartment. That was a clever notion.'

'What's his idea?' Paula queried.

'To keep her awake all night. To help break down her nerve. Then if she does take flight, she won't be so alert for anyone following her.'

'Should help,' Butler said.

'Another thing I'm going to do, a precaution which must be taken,' Tweed continued, 'is to phone all the surviving members of the *Institut* to warn them of the nature of the danger. I'll start with Christopher Kane in Geneva.'

'You'll wake everybody up at this hour,' Newman commented. 'I'm sure they'll be asleep.'

'Better to be woken up alive rather than dead,' Paula observed.

'Talking of sleep, I think you'd all better get some,' Tweed told them. 'Tomorrow will be a busy day.'

'What's sleep?' enquired Nield before he followed the others out.

Karin Berg had the jitters, an unusual reaction. Even though the double-glazed windows muffled the road-drill bombardment a little the noise preyed on her mind. She decided to call Hassan at the new number he had given her before leaving Slovakia.

'Could I please be put through to Ashley Wingfield?' she requested the night operator at the Hotel Zum Storchen.

He had given her his pseudonym when he had informed her of the phone number. In his room Hassan was studying his list of members of the *Institut*.

'Yes?'

'Karin here. It was a bust. Our objective survived. And now he's very suspicious of me – he has to be

171

under the circumstances. He's no fool. I don't think I can take him. He'll end up taking me – putting me away for a long, long time.'

'Who do you suggest among the Sisters might do the job?'

'Neither of them. But I do have an audacious idea. He has an assistant, trusts her completely, she's always by his side.'

'They're lovers?'

For Hassan it was the obvious explanation. He could imagine no other sort of relationship.

'They are not,' Karin said coldly. 'But if you doubled the fee, I think she might just go for it. God knows she's eliminated several men – in the line of duty. She's a wizard with a gun. And . . .'

'Be careful what you say,' Hassan snapped, aware that whoever was on the hotel switchboard might be listening in. 'No mention of the names of our competitor. What is the name of this person who might pull off the deal?'

'Paula Grey . . .'

Tweed was very busy in the morning and had asked not to be disturbed. The call from Beck was unsettling, complicated his plan of action.

'If my voice is hoarse, Tweed, it's because I've been up all night with my teams scouring the lake off the Ermitage.'

'You came up with anything?'

'Far more than I'd ever hoped for. Not a task to undertake just after eating a heavy meal. We were fishing bits of the Monceau gang out of the lake. A leg here, a foot there, some beheaded torsos.'

'You wouldn't, I assume, be able to identify everyone.'

Actually, we did. Two were reasonably intact. Then, by trawling and dredging endlessly, we fished up five heads in nets. All seven of the Monceau gang were wiped out by someone – I'm not guessing who.' Beck paused and Tweed realized he knew who had been responsible. 'But we found no trace of a certain Jules Monceau. Didn't expect to.'

'Why not?'

'Work it out for yourself. He'd be watching from a safe distance, preparing to enjoying your destruction.'

'So you think he's still at large?'

'I'm sure of it. He's likely to decide to come after you himself. Don't forget he's good at disguises. Nothing crude like a false wig or moustache. In Paris the police call him The Chameleon. He's a master at blending in with his background, altering his whole personality. Rather like a Dr Jekyll and Mr Hyde. Except he's always Mr Hyde.'

'Trying to put the wind up me, Arthur?' Tweed joked.

'Now look here, Tweed' – Beck sounded exasperated – 'I am very serious. You underestimate this man at your peril. The whole French police force have been after him for years – and have not once laid a hand on him.'

'I appreciate your concern.'

'Then for the Lord's sake, watch your step.'

'You should know by now I never underestimate an enemy. And I know Monceau's motive is strictly personal. That's why he agreed to help The Sisterhood organization.'

'Changing the subject, no move yet by Karin Berg. She's still hibernating in her apartment. If she books a flight I'll know within minutes. I have friends high up at the airport.'

'I have two men standing by,' Tweed told him.

'I'd love to bring her in for questioning.'

'Don't do it,' Tweed said urgently. 'She's possibly our one lead to where this insidious organization is operating from.'

'As you wish.' Beck sighed. 'Sometimes I wonder who is running this police force. Guard your back . . .'

He rang off before Tweed could reply.

The mysterious call came through to Paula midmorning. She picked up the phone, expecting it to be Tweed.

'Miss Paula Grey?' a cultured English voice enquired.

'Yes. Who is this?'

'My name is Ashley Wingfield. You have been rec-ommended to me my a mutual friend who must remain anonymous.'

'Mutual friend? Charles Dickens?'

'I told you I couldn't reveal his name.'

It was at this point that Paula's suspicions were aroused. She didn't expect every educated Englishman to have read the novel – but she did expect him to have heard of it. She listened more carefully to the accent as the conversation proceeded.

'What is the point of this call?' she asked sharply.

'Two hundred thousand dollars. For yourself.'

'And how do I earn this sum?'

She had been astute enough not to appear impressed by such a huge amount. And the English was just a little too perfectly enunciated. She had heard literate Arabs speak with this calculated precision.

'My dear lady' – inwardly Paula winced as she listened – 'I can't explain what is involved over the phone. Such a large business deal.'

'Well, when and where can you explain it?' Paula demanded.

'May I suggest we meet at noon at the top of the Zurichberg? You take a tram—'

'I know how to get up there, so don't waste your breath.'

'I will be waiting on a seat midway between the tram stop and the restaurant where you can obtain refreshments. It is very important that you come alone. If I see any sign that you are accompanied by anyone I shall vanish . . .'

'In a cloud of blue smoke.'

'I beg your pardon.'

'Never mind. How shall I know it is you? Anyone might take it into their head to sit on a public seat.'

'I was coming to that, Miss Grey. I shall be wearing a panama hat and dark glasses.'

'And clothes, I hope?'

'But of course. I don't think you should have said that.'

'I don't give a damn. I'll meet you at noon on Zurichberg. Goodbye.'

Paula sat down to think. She checked her watch. 11 a.m. She had plenty of time before she decided whether to accept this weird invitation. Normally she would have consulted Tweed before doing anything, but she knew he was busy and a very strange idea was forming at the back of her mind. She dismissed it as outlandish.

After a few minutes' thought she went into her bathroom and took trouble over changing and tending to her hairstyle. She tied back her hair – a natural way of wearing it in this heat. She also spent more time than usual over her make-up, applying a generous but tasteful amount of lipstick.

Afterwards, she would have been hard to explain why she acted like this. If pressed, she would have said sixth sense. She then put on a pale blue trouser suit. The jacket had a secret pocket in the inside on her left. Then she took out a large pair of sunglasses.

She hid the glasses in her shoulder bag, tucked her Browning inside the special pocket. Then she went to see Marler, hoping he was in his room. He opened the door, ushered her inside.

'You brought in quite an armoury from Vienna,' she recalled. 'I wonder if you have a Beretta?'

'As a matter of fact, I have. But you don't usually carry that automatic.'

'No, I don't, do I?' she said with a smile.

'None of my business?' He smiled back. 'I'll get it and you might need spare ammo. Tweed knows about this?'

'Of course.'

She disliked telling an untruth but it was necessary. Marler opened a cupboard, pulled aside some clothes and brought out the satchel they had concealed. He handed her the automatic and spare ammo. She thanked him and left quickly.

Hassan had had his doubts about Berg's idea of recruiting Paula Grey for this one assignment. He had even hesitated before he phoned her. If he was doubtful after talking to her he'd simply go nowhere near Zurichberg.

Paula's aggressive attitude had changed all his doubts. He had disliked the way she had talked back to him but he'd had the same trouble with the other three members of The Sisterhood. To do the job they had to be tough nuts, hard as nails. Above all they had to have greed for big money.

On all points Paula had scored ten out of ten. She had not even sounded impressed by his mention of two hundred thousand dollars. Yet in a second call to Berg he had been told that Paula must earn a mere pittance compared with such a sum. This, above all else, had convinced Hassan that Berg's idea might work. There was one other factor which weighed heavily in his decision.

If it fails ... The Englishman's warning kept echoing in his mind. He was certain the phrase had been originally uttered by his father, the Head of State, whom he feared. His father had a swift and deadly way of dealing with failure – and his son was worried he would suffer the same fate. After all, he had younger brothers, any of whom could be substituted for himself. And Berg *had* failed. Not that this meant he would not use her again. Her initials were on the list alongside certain remaining members of the *Institut*.

Paula boarded the tram for the Zurichberg, still with mixed feelings. Tweed would go ballistic if he found out what she was doing without back-up. The heat inside the tram was appalling. Other passengers were removing jackets, ties. One woman never stopped mopping the back of her neck with a handkerchief.

When the tram reached its terminus and she left it the temperature had dropped because of the height. She walked a few paces, then stopped. If she was being observed it would be obvious she was alone.

She saw a road curving upwards and realized she was not yet at the top of Zurichberg. The view was spectacular down over the many church spires of Zurich with a hint of the blue lake beyond. Reaching the top of the hill she saw a man sitting by himself on a seat.

He was wearing a panama hat and dark glasses which concealed most of his face. Slimly built, he wore a cream linen suit similar to the one Marler had in his wardrobe. It was an expensive item. So were his hand-made shoes. His skin was brownish, but it could have

177

been tanned by the sun. She sat on the same seat, leaving space between them.

'So far you have obeyed instructions,' he commented.

'Who are you?' she asked aggressively.

'You know who I am from the way I am dressed. From the fact that I am here.'

'I want a name or I'm catching the next tram back to Zurich.'

'Ashley Wingfield. I believe I have the honour of meeting Miss Paula Grey.'

He knew he was. Berg had given him a detailed description of Paula Grey. Only one detail was different.

'You have changed your hairstyle.'

'None of your damned business. It's a hot day.'

'Are you interested in earning two hundred thousand dollars? In cash. Forget the taxman.'

'Depends what I have to do for the money.'

'We are fencing,' he complained.

'Get to the point. I can't sit here all day.'

'Excuse me.'

He moved closer, gently removed her bag from her shoulder. She glared but let him get away with it. She had left her SIS identity card in the hotel safe. Nothing else in the bag showed the organization she belonged to. He found the Browning, raised his thin eyebrows, removed the magazine, hurled it over his shoulder into the undergrowth behind the seat, did the same with the gun.

'You came armed,' he said.

'Of course I did. I didn't know who you were, what you might try to do.'

'You can use firearms?'

'I belong to a shooting club back in England. I'm not popular with the men. I'm the club's crack marksman.'

'Can you use a Luger?'

Inwardly she froze. She had come to the right place.

178

She stared at the invisible eyes behind the dark glasses. She was wearing her own sunglasses which she had put on as soon as she had boarded the tram.

'I've practised with it. Get to the point, for God's sake.'

'For two hundred thousand dollars could you shoot Tweed?'

She didn't answer at once. First because she sensed it would be a mistake not to appear to think it over. Second, the question was not totally unexpected but spoken in cold blood it enraged her. She stared out at the view, considering her reply. Eventually she replied.

'It will be difficult.'

Inwardly, Hassan's heart sank. She had used almost the same words Karin Berg had used when he had first mentioned Tweed's name. What made this man so important?

'Why will it be difficult?' he asked after a pause.

'Because he is so heavily guarded,' she replied promptly.

'But I understand you have been his personal assistant for a long time. There must be times when you are alone with him.'

Karin Berg, Paula thought. That's the bitch who has given this piece of work the idea of trying to employ me. All this flashed through her mind and again she replied quickly.

'Yes, there are, but a guard is never far away.'

'Use your sex appeal to isolate him.'

'That might just work.'

'So there is no problem.'

'Yes, there is. I want fifty thousand dollars in advance. To be specific – now.'

'You don't want much.'

'Then forget it,' she said, wrenching her shoulder bag from his grasp.

'I can give you something . . .'

'Fifty thousand or I'm leaving and you'll never see me again.'

'I have twenty thousand in this envelope.'

She grabbed the envelope, which was very thick, glanced inside it, riffled through a number of hundred-dollar bills, shoved the envelope inside a compartment of her bag, zipped it up. Her hand rested in her lap. She was on the verge of producing the Beretta and escorting him back to Tweed when he said something else.

'You'll have to fly to my headquarters for a brief training exercise. The flight leaves later this afternoon. You'll get the other thirty thousand the moment we arrive. Now, I want to see your eyes. Remove your glasses.'

'And I want to see yours, or the deal is off.'

She had changed her mind. This was a unique opportunity to locate where they were operating from.

'Take your glasses off,' he snapped.

'Take yours off at the same time or I'm leaving. I like to see who I'm dealing with.'

Reluctantly, Hassan removed his glasses as Paula took off hers. They stared at each other. His eyes were pale, without a trace of human feeling. She had no trouble in making her stare hard. She loathed this man.

'You have a tough look,' he said as he put his glasses on again. 'I think you could do the job. We'll stay together until we board the flight. I have a return Business Class ticket in your name in my pocket.'

You're well organized, she was thinking. Which makes you that much more dangerous. Don't give in to this thug on any point.

'I need clothes, certain personal things,' she said. 'I won't travel without them.'

'So we'll go shopping together. Don't go to any ladies' room. You can attend to that on the plane.'

180

17

Hassan was a good planner. On the off chance that Paula Grey would prove suitable, would take up his offer, he had checked out of the Zum Storchen, had deposited his case in a left-luggage locker at the main station. He was not surprised when Paula eventually accepted his offer – in Hassan's mind all that Western women were interested in was money, the more the better. It was the way his brain worked.

He had arranged for Karin Berg to travel on an earlier flight to Vienna. He hadn't wanted to risk Paula seeing the blonde on the same plane. While she was shopping for clothes and essentials Paula kicked up.

'I can't have you peering over my shoulder while I purchase certain personal items,' she told him savagely.

They were in the beauty shop of a department store and Paula found herself hoping against hope that someone like Newman would see her. No such luck.

'I'll stand back a few yards but you have to remain in view,' Hassan had snapped.

'Get lost.'

As she contemplated the items for sale she was trying to work out some way of leaving a message for Tweed. It proved to be impossible. She bought an expensive suitcase, knowing that Hassan would expect her to start spending the twenty thousand dollars he had given her.

Then she rammed inside the case the carriers containing the expensive clothes she had bought. Not her usual method of packing, but it would have to do. All the time she looked for a phone she could use, but Hassan was always at her heels.

Later, he escorted her to the Hauptbahnhof, collected

his own case and hailed a taxi outside. He gave Paula
her air ticket. She examined it. Destination: Vienna.
She had her passport inside her shoulder bag which
gave her profession as Business Consultant.

'The airport,' Hassan told the driver.

Earlier, Tweed had received an urgent phone call from
Beck. The policeman's tone had been grim.

'I've heard from the airport that Karin Berg is catching the next flight to Vienna. Now what is it to be? I
have a strong urge to arrest her, detain her and interrogate her. She marked you out at the Ermitage. We can
lay our hands on a member of The Sisterhood at last –
I'm convinced that's what she is.'

'Let her go. I'll warn two of my men. They are ready
to leave for the airport now. I've booked seats for them
on all flights to Vienna. Business Class. Is that how Berg
is travelling?'

'Of course.'

'Then I'd better get off the line. How long have they
got to reach Kloten in time to make that flight?'

'Three-quarters of an hour.'

'Call you later . . .'

Tweed had run to Butler's room where Pete Nield
was waiting with him. They had left immediately.
Tweed had had a taxi standing by for most of the
morning.

Arriving at the airport, they mingled with the other
passengers in the final departure lounge. Both of them
had spotted Karin Berg. Nield had given her description
to Butler earlier. Both men carried backpacks which
contained all they needed. In this way they could take
their belongings aboard the plane.

It was, of course, impossible to carry weapons. Nield
had consulted Marler, who had given him the name and

182

address of the arms dealer in Vienna who had supplied Marler with the armoury he had smuggled over the border.

They were careful to board the Austrian Airlines aircraft after Berg had taken her seat near the front. The machine was barely half-full and they had chosen two seats alongside each other well back from her. Nobody occupied the seats behind them, in front of them or across the aisle. They were able to talk in quiet voices as the plane became airborne.

'I think I ought to send a radio message ahead to book a hire car,' Nield suggested. 'If she has a car waiting for her at Schwechat Airport we'll lose her without transport.'

'Good idea,' agreed Butler.

Nield signalled to one of the stewardesses after writing out the message. He told her the matter was confidential. Taking the message with her, the steward-ess disappeared inside the control cabin. Nield sat back, relieved he had taken action.

'That's that,' he said.

'Just so long as we don't lose her at the airport,' Butler warned.

So far Berg had not even looked back once. She appeared not to suspect that she might have been followed. Sitting with her head turned towards the window, she was watching the scenery below her, a vista of green and brown fields without a town in sight. Occasionally she glanced to her right where, through the starboard windows, she could see the snowless savage peaks of the Austrian Alps. But never a look backwards.

'I don't think she has any idea that she might have been followed,' Nield remarked.

'Why should she?'

'Because she's a professional – an ex-member of the

Swedish counter-espionage, which is how Tweed came to know her.'

'Maybe she's worried about something,' Butler replied with a flash of insight.

He was right. Karin Berg was wondering what was waiting for her when she reached the strange house in Slovakia.

Boarding the later Austrian Airlines flight for Vienna, Paula insisted on occupying the aisle seat. Hassan tried to compel her to take the window seat, which gave him control over the situation. It almost erupted into a public row. A stewardess arrived to find out why the aisle was being blocked by the two passengers.

'My friend is being kind and wants me to sit by the window,' Paula explained with a smile. 'I don't like flying and I do not sit in window seats.'

'The plane is about to depart,' the stewardess said firmly, staring at Hassan.

Reluctantly, he took the window seat. For Paula it was a small victory in two ways. The aisle seat gave her greater access. Also she had outmanoeuvred Hassan, had showed him he couldn't get it all his own way.

The aircraft had few passengers in Business Class. There was no one near them so she felt she could converse in a quiet voice.

'Why is this trip necessary? I'm quite capable of using a Luger.'

'Let us say it is a psychological test you must undergo.'

'Sounds a bloody waste of time to me.'

'Don't talk to me like that,' he said indignantly.

'Why not? I'm not your servant.'

'You are getting two hundred thousand dollars,' he whispered.

'Of which so far I have only seen twenty.'

'We shouldn't be discussing this in a public place.'

'Haven't you realized there is no one near us? That not a soul can hear what we're saying? Do be more observant. I want to know what happens when we reach Vienna – otherwise I'll catch the first flight back to Zurich.'

Hassan was in a dilemma. He didn't want to tell her too much. On the other hand her aggressive attitude confirmed that Berg had chosen the right woman. He was becoming more and more convinced that Grey could do the job.

If she fails . . .

Hassan was still haunted by what the Englishman had said. Tweed had to be killed. Hassan knew that in an emergency the Englishman had a direct line of communication to the Head of State, his father, who had no patience with anyone who let him down – even his own kith and kin. The Eastern penalties for failure were drastic. They included beheading.

'We don't go to Vienna,' Hassan eventually said. 'A limo will be waiting to take us to the training house.'

'Where is that?'

'I don't know,' Hassan lied quickly, foreseeing the question. 'It is moved from one area to another – for security reasons. Only the driver knows where to take us, the driver of the limo.'

Paula decided to give up for the moment. She didn't believe him but she had sensed fear in Hassan's voice. Who was he afraid of?

It was evening, still hot and muggy, when Beck phoned Tweed in his room. He had just phoned Newman in his room enquiring as to the whereabouts of Paula. Newman had said he had no idea, had told Tweed he was coming to his room. Beck called at the moment Tweed let him in.

'You won't like this, Tweed.'

'These days, when you talk to me I usually don't like it,' Tweed joked.

'I'm very serious. Prepare yourself for a shock. One of my men at Kloten checking passengers spotted someone he knew boarding a later flight. The heat had got him so he went to the security chief's office for a drink of water. Then he promptly fell asleep on a couch. He has apologized for the lapse and has just told me.'

'Told you what?'

Tweed was becoming alarmed. It was something so serious that Beck was having trouble coming to the point.

'He saw Paula Grey boarding a later flight to Vienna. In the company of another passenger, now identified as a Mr Ashley Wingfield . . .'

'Stop the plane in mid-flight,' Tweed said urgently. 'Order the pilot to return to Zurich at once.'

'I would have done just that – after consulting you. But it's too late. The plane landed a while ago. All passengers have disembarked.'

'I want to interrogate your man who saw her board the plane.'

'I've already done that myself.'

'Did it appear she had to go aboard under duress? This is my first news that Paula has gone to Vienna.'

'No duress. How could there be? Wingfield would need a gun. You know all passengers go through a metal detector. The odd thing is she appeared to leave of her own free will . . .'

'Check with the Schwechat Airport police.'

'I have already done that too. They couldn't help. Although there weren't many passengers aboard Paula's flight, another plane landed at the same time. You know how passengers mingle when more than one flight comes in. I regret to say she has vanished without trace. I'm very sorry – you sound worried.'

'I am. Thank you, Arthur. I may call you back . . .'

Tweed told Newman what had happened. After listening, Newman said he would take over, that he was going to phone the Sacher, the hotel she had stayed at with Marler, Butler and Nield.

Tweed paced the room, unable to keep still while Newman made the call. After a few minutes he put the phone down, turned to Tweed.

'The Sacher has no booking for a Paula Grey.'

'I see.' Tweed continued pacing, hands clasped behind his back, then he spoke. 'Get Beck for me, please.'

It seemed to take an eternity before Newman handed him the phone, said Beck was on the line.

'Arthur, have you got a description of this Ashley Wingfield?'

'I called the man who saw her board the plane. He was at home, asleep. He describes him as wearing a panama hat and dark glasses, above five feet eight tall, his complexion very brown, clean-shaven, carrying a suitcase. Paula was also carrying a case, a Louis Vuitton.'

'Louis Vuitton? She doesn't go in for expensive items like that. Are you sure?'

'The man I woke up is very reliable, has the eyes of a hawk.'

'Thank you.'

Tweed gave Newman the additional information, began pacing the room once more. Newman sat on a couch and lit a cigarette. He was careful not to say anything. He knew Tweed's mind was racing, despite his deep anxiety. Suddenly Tweed stopped.

'We've both forgotten something. Nield and Butler are heading for the same destination, following Berg. I must find out from Beck—'

He never completed his sentence. The phone started ringing. Tweed darted for it before Newman could pick it up.

'Yes?'

'Pete Nield here. We've just arrived at Schwechat. Our plane had to return to Zurich – engine trouble. Butler is watching the Berg. She seems to be waiting for transport.'

Tweed swiftly told him about Paula. He gave Nield every detail Beck had provided. When he had finished Nield's cool reaction was typical.

'Harry and I will have to do something about that. It is just possible that Paula's destination is the same as Berg's. I find it significant that Paula isn't at the Sacher. That suggests to me she isn't going anywhere near Vienna. We'll keep in touch. Paula is now our top priority . . .'

'So now,' Newman commented after Tweed told him about Nield, 'we have two good men in the area. No point in my going out there. Yet.'

Tweed resumed pacing. He felt he couldn't keep still. Had he done all he could to locate and protect Paula? Should he adopt Newman's suggestion – or send him out to Vienna?

'Why would she do a thing like that?' he asked aloud.

'Perhaps she stumbled on an important lead. Decided to follow it up. May have had no time to contact you.'

'She's gone over the top this time.'

'That's worry speaking. Don't forget that last year you sent her to California on her own,' Newman reminded him.

'That's true,' Tweed admitted. 'Bob, phone Howard and ask him to check with the passport people whether there's a British passport in the name of Ashley Wingfield . . .'

Racked as he was with anxiety, Tweed had not forgotten there were other aspects of the problem. When Newman had made his call he phoned Christopher Kane in Geneva. He was relieved to hear the very upper-crust Scots voice on the line.

'Well, dear boy, what is bothering you? I always know when you call me something is worrying that dynamo you term a brain.'

'I hope you heeded my earlier warning.'

'To be on the lookout for being approached by attractive women.' Kane chuckled. 'I should be so lucky. The technique you described they use is quite ingenious. Rest your active mind. And thank you for calling . . .'

In his apartment in Geneva, Kane put down the phone and was amused. He doubted whether Tweed would have been amused if he had told him of his recent encounter with the glamorous auburn-haired woman Lisa Vane.

He had seen her in the bar of the Richemond, where it was his daily habit to have one drink. She had made eye contact and Kane had responded.

Now they were going to have dinner at Les Armures, a fine restaurant at the top of the Old City on the far side of the Rhône. He had told her he lived in an apartment but had fended off her question for his address.

Christopher Kane was six foot one tall, quite thin, with black hair and a long face tapering to a determined chin. Speaking with a drawl, it was sometimes difficult to catch what he said. His manners were faultless and he had a charm which women of different ages found very attractive. He was still a bachelor although in his early forties. At random intervals he played the field as a contrast to the intense mental concentration his work involved.

Unlike many scientists or boffins, Christopher did not have tunnel vision, nor did he focus on his work to such an extent he was out of touch with the world outside. On the contrary, he was very shrewd.

Taking a taxi, he deliberately arrived late at Les Armures. Tina Langley, still posing as Lisa Vane, had received fresh instructions from Hassan. Since the fee involved was so much larger than what she had managed to extract from her banker friend, Anton, she had left Anton on the shelf. When she needed more spending money she would contact him again.

'You're late,' she snapped as Christopher was shown to the table in the first room off the entrance.

'It happens,' he agreed, refusing to apologize, and let her score a point in the opening round of the game. 'We'll have two Kir royales,' he told the waiter.

'I like to be consulted,' Tina fumed.

'My dear,' said Christopher calmly, leaning over to pat her hand, 'I know this place. They have the best Kir royales in the world. Just leave everything to me.'

'It would be nice if you allowed me to choose from the menu later,' she said, changing her mood, giving him a ravishing smile which would have hypnotized most men.

'No. I'm a gourmet. If you chose you'd miss the best they have to offer. Just relax and you'll have the meal of your life. I repeat, leave everything to Christopher.'

Tina was confused. By now she would have most men eating out of her hand. What was it with this long streak of a Scot? For the first time she felt out of her depth. It will be a pleasure to blow the back of this

bastard's head off, she was thinking. Instead she gave
him her smile again, leaned forward so he would get a
whiff of her perfume.

'We're going to have a wonderful evening. The two
of us,' she said.

'I'm enjoying myself now. There are some interesting
characters at the other tables.'

What about this table? she said to herself. He hasn't
paid me one single compliment – on my appearance, my
clothes, on anything. Yet he kept looking her straight in
the eye and had a pleasant smile. She had the uncomfortable feeling he could see inside her head. This was very
different from her experience with Norbert Engel in
Vienna. He had been a pushover. She expected most
men interested in women to be pushovers when they
were with her.

She let him choose the wine and the the meal.
Perhaps his weak point was his vanity, his confidence
that he knew everything. Maybe she ought to play on
that.

'You have a remarkable brain,' she said, halfway
through the main course.

'Other people have said that. Not an original
remark.'

'What exactly do you do? I'd love to hear more about
you and your work.'

'What work?'

Tina was taken aback. She noticed he had drunk a
lot of the wine. She refilled his glass. He ordered a fresh
bottle. She began drinking heavily herself – she knew
she could outdrink any man. Alcohol could be her main
weapon.

'I see you have a large briefcase,' Christopher
remarked.

'Papers in connection with my job,' she said quickly.

'And what job is that?'

191

'Personal assistant to a Swiss banker,' she replied, thinking of Anton, making it up as she went along.

'So you speak fluent French? You'd have to.'

'I get by. Cheers!'

She raised her glass and drank half of it to divert his dangerous questions. He smiled. Christopher smiled a lot.

'You speak fluent French,' he repeated. *'Peut-être?'*

She had no idea what he had said. Her mood changed immediately to throw him off balance. Her warm smile vanished. She glared at him, her eyes like bullets.

'For God's sake, I speak the bloody language all day long. I do it but I'm sick of it. Talk in English or I'll stop speaking to you,' she said at the top of her voice.

It had always worked before. Her swift changes of mood fascinated men. They usually did their best to warm her up again, fearing the night would end there instead of elsewhere.

'I'd talk a little louder if I were you,' Christopher observed. 'Then they'll hear you the other side of the Rhône.'

He drank more wine and she hastened to refill his glass. His reaction had been one of complete indifference. Tina was nonplussed. What did it take to get inside this man?

By the end of the meal Christopher had drunk a great deal of the excellent wine. He passed a hand across his high forehead, blinked. He pulled his chair closer to the table as though for support. She smiled inwardly. When coffee had been served with liqueurs she gave him a certain look.

'Why don't we finish off the fresh bottle of wine in your apartment.'

'Great . . . idea.'

He seemed to have difficulty saying the words.

Paying the bill, he fumbled with the banknotes in his wallet. He gave the waiter such a large tip Tina was convinced he wasn't aware of how much he had left inside the folder with the bill.

Inside the taxi which took them to his apartment she hugged the briefcase with her left hand and rested her right hand on his knee. He responded by putting his arm round her slim waist, leaning against her.

His apartment was in an old building near the river. Tina let him lead the way as he stumbled from step to step, holding on to the wooden rail. He had trouble inserting his key into the lock, so she removed it gently from his fingers and unlocked the door herself. He held out his hand for the key and she dropped it into his palm.

'What a lovely apartment,' she enthused. 'Beautiful furniture. They're antiques, aren't they? Oh, what a grand desk. Now, you sit in your comfortable swivel chair. I've got a map of the city in my briefcase. Can you drive up that mountain on the other side of the river?'

'If . . . you wanna go to . . . France.'

'I'd love to. Perhaps you would take me there sometime.'

'Great . . . idea.'

'Which is the bedroom?'

'Through that . . . door.'

'Maybe you'd show me it.'

'What's map for?'

She had spread out a map of Geneva and the surrounding areas on his desk as he sagged in the chair. On the far wall was a collection of pictures. One frame held a mirror which had a curtain slung at both sides, so it was hardly visible to anyone visiting the apartment for the first time.

Standing behind him with the open briefcase from which she had extracted the map, Tina slipped her hand inside it again. Christopher saw the action in the mirror he had been watching. Swinging round in his swivel chair, he jumped up, was by her side before she realized what was happening. She had her hand on the Luger. His hand grasped her wrist, twisted it with great strength. She yelled, let go of the gun, scraped her foot down his shin. He let go of her and she ran, opened the door, fled down the staircase, dropping the briefcase she was still holding. Christopher, suddenly sober, ran down after her, slipped on the briefcase, fell forward. He would have smashed his skull on the stone steps but he grabbed hold of the rail, saved himself. The entrance door to the block of apartments banged shut. He reached it, flung it open and was just in time to see Tina vanishing down an alleyway. He stepped into the street, closed the apartment door behind him and strode to where his car was parked.

Christopher knew Geneva inside out and he drove a certain route which would take him into the street the alleyway led to. His long legs had enabled him to reach his car quickly and as he swung into the street where the alley emerged he was again just in time to see Tina get into a parked Renault.

He didn't think for a moment she would suspect she was being followed. In this he was right. Tina was suppressing a state of panic. She drove off in the car she had hired in the name of Lisa Vane, using false papers supplied by Hassan. Crossing the Pont du Rhône she drove along the same route Anton, the banker, had taken her.

Night had long since fallen but there was a certain amount of traffic. This enabled Christopher to keep her in view without getting too close. He had once been a racing driver and he soon had the opinion that Lisa Vane was a good driver. He passed the checkpoint into France without being stopped – as had Tina.

Half an hour or so later, having passed the summit of Salève, the mountain overlooking Geneva, Tina pulled in to the parking place in front of the Château d'Avignon. She had just entered the hotel, carrying a suitcase, when Christopher drove slowly past, continued on to drive back to Geneva by the western descent from the mountain.

'Think I'd better call Tweed,' he said to himself. 'He'll be amused by my little experience.'

18

Earlier that evening Tweed had attended the Kongresshaus to hear Amos Lodge's speech. The place was packed as Amos thundered from an elevated platform behind a lectern. Behind Tweed sat Marler while Newman stood near the end of the row of seats, next to one of Beck's men in plain clothes.

'Our Western civilization has become decadent . . .' Amos roared.

'You either lead a decent life or indulge yourself, regardless. There is no middle way.

'The once stable relationships between men and women have broken down. Certain women have adopted the American way. They have become dominant, aggressive, and men allow themselves to be beaten down, shoved aside – in politics, in business.

'Once men no longer have confidence in themselves then society collapses into chaos!

'The Roman Empire fell when it became decadent,

when it spent its energy in orgies. Western society has reached the same low level. Filthy films, filthy telvision, filthy books, filthy behaviour between the sexes . . .

'Absorbed by orgies Rome was overwhelmed by stronger forces from the East, destroyed by its own decadence . . . The West faces the same fate!

'There are more disciplined religions, more disciplined societies, therefore stronger powers in the East today. The West is leaderless, its so-called leaders are pathetic dummies concerned only with hanging on to power.

'They have reduced the West to a defenceless state. There is a power vacuum, morally and militarily.

'Equality between men and women is a sound basis for a stable society. Now we have a mushrooming superiority of certain women. Unless the situation is corrected the West faces total disaster – will be taken over by the East.

'Haul our present mock-leaders down . . . put stronger men with the right moral attitudes in their place!' Amos thundered.

'Powerful and controversial stuff,' Newman commented to Tweed as they left. 'You may not agree with him, but for a strategist he must be one of the world's great orators.'

'The ovation lasted ten minutes,' Tweed observed. 'Look who we have here.'

Willie had appeared at their side. They were swept along with the crowd emerging, which was excited and talking nonstop about what they had heard. Willie, more red-faced than ever, tapped Tweed's arm.

'Amos certainly carries you along with him. The audience was almost in a state of hysteria. Adulation might be a better word.'

'Where did you pop up from?' Tweed enquired. 'Still enjoying yourself in Zurich?'

'I moved from the Dolder Grand to the Gotthard. Needed somewhere less public to meet a client. Pulled off a big deal. Now I'm going back to the Dolder Grand.'

'Staying on in Zurich?' Tweed enquired.

'Never can tell what my next move will be. I'm a globe-trotter. Tell you what, why don't I come to the Baur au Lac tomorrow morning, buy you both a few drinks? At the Pavillon. Noon suit you?'

'Thank you. I'll be there,' said Tweed.

'Me too,' Newman agreed.

'Got to fly, chaps, make a phone call. No peace for the wicked.'

Unlike most of the audience, Willie was dressed in a green tracksuit which looked expensive. Round his neck he wore a silk cravat. Yet his appearance was smart and dressy.

'Well, at least there was no attempt to assassinate Amos,' Newman remarked.

'I was thinking about that,' Tweed replied. 'Reminds me of the Sherlock Holmes story. The dog that didn't bark in the night. Something like that.'

They were approaching Newman's parked car, hired by him in Zurich, when a solid body of men pushed their way through the crowd. Beck was in the lead, looking everywhere. Behind him walked Amos Lodge, an expression of disgust on his squarish face. Men in plain clothes walked alongside him and behind him.

Beck walked forward rapidly. He took Tweed by the arm and his voice was firm.

'Amos Lodge is going back to the Baur au Lac in a special unmarked police car. You will travel with him. Both of you are targets.'

'I can drive back by myself,' Newman said.

'Thank you,' Tweed responded to Beck. 'I'll take advantage of your kind offer.'

He had decided it would be a good opportunity to talk to Amos. Tweed was particularly interested in the fact that Willie was lingering in Zurich. Entering the back of the large limo with Amos, he suspected it was the same car which had transported him to the Ermitage. He tapped the window. Armoured glass.

The plain-clothes driver was separated from them by a glass partition which was closed. Amos settled his bulk in his seat as he made the remark.

'Lot of bloody fuss.'

'Beck is simply taking care of you. Remember what happened to Dumont. Incidentally, Willie is still in Zurich, staying at the Dolder Grand. The best is always good enough for him.'

'You can say that again.' Amos grunted as the car began to move off. 'He's Eastern mad.'

'Naturally, that's where his income comes from.'

'I wasn't thinking of that,' the big man commented. 'You've seen his peculiar Oriental garden outside Shrimpton? He's shown me all over the place. Gives me the creeps. Like transferring an Eastern state to Dorset. Of all places. Funny chap. But we seem to get on.'

'You've been to the East?'

'I've travelled everywhere. I'm a good listener. The Arabs like to talk. Sometimes they give away too much.'

'You're talking about military matters? About strategy?'

'I'm talking about strategy.'

Amos lapsed into silence for the rest of the journey. When they reached the Baur au Lac he said good night and went up to his room. Tweed had deliberately not mentioned to Amos the speech he had made. He knew he wouldn't want to talk about it.

Tweed was not amused when Christopher Kane phoned him and related his experience. Newman, who had joined him in his room, saw his expression become grim.

'You were a damned fool to take such a risk.'

'It turned out all right, dear boy. And climbing back up the staircase I picked up – using a handkerchief, fingerprints, you know – the briefcase the murderous lady had dropped with the Luger still inside. Give me credit – it could be valuable evidence.'

'It could be,' Tweed agreed. 'I'll ask Beck, Chief of Federal Police in Berne, to send a courier to collect it.'

'I know Beck. We've played bridge together. Tell him to call me.'

'Can you describe this girl, Lisa Vane?'

Christopher promptly gave a concise picture of what she looked like, how she spoke, the fact that she didn't speak French, although she pretended to.

'You're the first target to avoid being killed by a member of The Sisterhood,' Tweed warned.

'I'm the first at a lot of things. What is The Sisterhood?'

Tweed explained the meaning of the word in grisly detail. He recalled the murder of Norbert Engel in Vienna, that surviving members of the *Institut* were all at risk.

'So that includes yourself,' Christopher reminded him amiably.

'Yes, it does. But I'm asking you to be more careful from now on.'

'Then I won't meet any more beautiful assassins. I've

a good mind to come to Zurich, find out what all the uproar is about.'

'I can't advise that.'

'Don't recall asking for your advice. Toodle-pip . . .'

Newman listened while Tweed relayed the contents of his conversation. He lit a cigarette, blew smoke rings, watched them disperse before he reacted.

'I think you were a bit hard on Christopher. He can look after himself. He was a very good rugger player. I was at school with him.'

'What's that got to do with it?'

'It means he doesn't miss much, that his reflexes are excellent. What about the description he gave of Lisa Vane?'

'It matches perfectly the description Paula gave us of the woman she saw walking down Kärntnerstrasse in Vienna after Norbert Engel had his head blown off.'

'So Tina Langley gets around. If Christopher does turn up here it might be interesting to show him the photo Vitorelli gave us of her.'

'Agreed. What is more interesting is this Château d'Avignon where Tina took refuge. The fact that it is in France, not far from Geneva. That city keeps cropping up.'

'And what did you and Amos talk about, riding like kings in the limo to get back here?'

Tweed recalled the conversation. He was able, despite being very tired, to remember every word that had been said. Newman was frowning as he finished.

'It sounds as though Willie takes a great interest in Eastern objects. And he called Willie Eastern mad. Intriguing remark.'

'I thought so . . .'

He stopped speaking as the phone rang. It was

Monica, still at SIS headquarters in Park Crescent at that late hour.

'You know that fragment of cloth Paula found at the entrance to Norbert Engel's apartment – the bit you sent me by courier for analysis?'

'Yes. I don't expect they came up with much.'

'But they did – the boffins in the basement. They know a man who is an expert on cloths all over the world. Guess what he said it is.'

'Tell me.'

'It's quite definitely a fragment from the long black dresses or robes worn by Arab women.'

'You're sure?'

'I'm not sure,' she said peevishly. 'The expert is sure. It is obviously used as a disguise, from what you've told me. The interesting thing is the nature of the garment used to disguise The Sisterhood.'

'It suggests to me an extreme sect – far more extreme than the Fundamentalists. They are showing how Western women will be dressed – treated – once they have conquered the West.'

'You think the women who wear this disguise to kill our top intellects are aware of this?'

'I'm sure they aren't. They just think it's an excellent way of concealing themselves. The only thing they think about is money. Thank you, Monica. Keep in touch . . .'

'It is an Arab state, then?' queried Newman.

'Possibly. No word from Paula. No word from Nield and Butler.'

When they had arrived at Schwechat Airport Hassan had flown into a rage. Escorting Paula outside, he had been appalled to find no vehicle waiting for him. Well outside the Austrian capital, the airport was surrounded by flat countryside.

Trying to use his mobile, Hassan found he could make no contact. He shook the thing angrily.

'That won't help,' Paula goaded him. 'A tower must be down.'

'Tower? What the hell do you mean?'

'Obviously,' she said with a smile, 'you don't know much about the system. The radio signal is transmitted via the nearest tower. When you can't get through it means the tower which should connect you is down. *Kaput!*'

'I can't wait here all day,' Hassan blazed.

'I can – if you tell me where we're going.'

'I told you I don't know.'

'So you say!'

They went back inside to escape the blazing sun. Even Hassan seemed affected by the humid heat. He took off his glasses to wipe his streaming forehead. Again she looked into pallid, soulless eyes. Nasty piece of work, she said to herself.

'My car is waiting outside,' he said.

'So why don't we use that?'

'Because you have one destination, I have another.'

'Who will be taking me where I'm supposed to be going?'

'Don't you ever run out of questions?' he snapped.

'Not often.' She sensed she was wearing him down. 'Where are you going?'

'To a secret rendezvous.'

'Lots of secrets. You could get into your car now and leave me here to wait.'

'You think I would do that?'

'Why not? I'm hardly likely to run away from two hundred thousand dollars.'

'We have to follow the arrangement.'

'What arrangement?'

'Give your mouth a rest, for God's sake . . .'

* * *

They had to wait so long other flights began to arrive. One was from Zurich.

Harry Butler, disembarking from his delayed flight with Pete Nield, walked alongside his partner, both with their packs on their backs. They wore linen shorts and open-necked shirts, looking like a score of other holidaymakers.

Butler grabbed Nield by the arm as they were about to emerge into the blinding sunlight. He pointed.

Paula was being escorted to a Volvo estate car by a man wearing a panama hat and dark glasses. Nield ran to the car-hire desk, went swiftly through the formalities, was shown by the desk girl to their waiting Ford. In the distance Paula was being driven away while Panama Hat entered another car, an Alfa Romeo.

'Nothing but the top cars for some people,' Nield commented as Butler started the engine, after they had slung the backpacks into the car. 'Don't lose that Volvo. Thank Heaven she was still here. Wonder why?'

'Main thing is she was. I can still see her. This country is as flat as a billiard table.'

'Not Vienna,' Nield remarked, as they turned at a fork away from the city. 'Out into the wild blue yonder.'

He little knew how right he was in his description.

Paula had been escorted into the rear of the Volvo by Hassan. He had left immediately without a word, perhaps fearing more questions. The driver had centrally locked all the doors so she was trapped in the back.

Shortly after leaving the airport an Alfa Romeo flashed by at speed. She didn't recognize the driver as Hassan. He had removed his hat and wore a shaggy grey wig. Soon the swift dart vanished from sight ahead of them.

Her driver was a squat, muscular man with a thick neck and a brutal face like some boxers. He had taken her case and parked it on the seat beside him. Presumably another security precaution.

'What's your name?' she asked after a while.

'Me Valja.'

'Sounds as though you're from what used to be Yugoslavia.'

'Me Valja.'

'Is that your first or second name?' she persisted politely.

'Me Valja. Must drive.'

Which Paula interpreted as 'Shut up.' She decided she was not going to be able to needle him as she had with Hassan. For a short time she looked at the countryside. This soon palled. It was all the same. An endless plain stretching away for ever. Cultivated fields on both sides of a road without fences or borders of any kind.

From the direction of the sun she could tell they were travelling roughly south-east. Heading further and further away from Vienna. She felt pretty sure they were in Burgenland, Austria's most easterly province, bordering on the Slovak Republic – or Slovakia – and Hungary.

It was lonely countryside with only the occasional isolated and small village which Valja passed through at speed. This was not difficult as there seemed to be no other traffic, although the road was well surfaced.

'Where are we going, Valja?' she asked after an endless drive.

'Me Valja.'

Hassan had arranged in advance for his own car which he could drive himself. He wanted to reach the base in Slovakia well ahead of the arrival of Paula Grey.

First, he could check out the situation there. Second, he could arrange to have the training room set up for

Paula. A live target who would be injected with drugs to keep him still before the trial kill.

Racing along in the Alfa he arrived at the remote crossing point from Austria into Slovakia where there was no checkpoint. He had the flat-topped mountain and the long house above him before he turned up the winding road at the western end of the moutain. He had a bad shock as soon as he parked the car in a barn at the far end of the house and returned to the main entrance. The door was opened by his brother, Ahmed, second offspring of the large family.

'What the hell are you doing here?' Hassan demanded.

He brushed past him into the coolness of the house. Behind him Ahmed followed at his heels.

'The Head of State ordered me to come here as your assistant.'

None of the sons ever referred to their begetter as 'Father'. He insisted on being called Head of State. His discipline was unbending and ferocious.

'I don't need an assistant,' Hassan raged over his shoulder.

'We all have to obey the Head of State. I am here to help you.'

'To spy on me,' Hassan said to himself.

His worst fears were confirmed by Ahmed's next remark, spoken with a hint of pleasure and malice.

'The Englishman has phoned the Head of State. You appear to have altered the agreed plan, to have acted on your own.'

'I have to get the job done – and quickly,' Hassan shouted back. 'When the situation changes the plan has to be adapted to the new circumstances.'

'The Head of State will require a full explanation after you have completed your mission. Assuming you do complete your mission.'

'If you don't keep out of my way any failure will be your fault for interfering without understanding what you are doing.'

Hassan felt better having said that. It might give him an excuse for anything which went wrong. The trouble was several things had gone wrong. Tweed was still alive. Tina had called him from the chateau in France with a story as to why Kane was still alive – a story he did not believe.

He entered the training room, slamming the door in Ahmed's face. The innocent peasant who would be the live target for Paula Grey was tied with ropes to the chair in front of the desk, which had been cleared of blood. Hassan went to the cupboard, took out a syringe containing the drug. It would render the victim motionless, but still very much alive. The peasant had been kidnapped working alone in the fields many miles from the house on top of the mountain, perched on the edge of the abandoned quarry.

Karin Berg was nervous. Arriving on the same flight as Nield and Butler at Schwechat Airport, she had mixed with the few passengers disembarking. Nield and Butler had been following her when Pete had spotted Paula. All thought of tracking Berg had left their minds – Paula's safety was their priority.

Berg had waited near the exit and only when all the other passengers had gone did a swarthy man hold up a piece of cardboard with her name on it. Without a word he took her to a waiting BMW, opened the rear door, shut it, got into the driver's seat and locked all the doors.

As he took off Berg smoothed down her blonde hair and smiled at the driver in the rear-view mirror. All men responded to her smile. The driver simply glared, looked away, concentrated on his driving.

Remembering her previous journey to the training house Berg soon realized again she was being taken on a roundabout route – which would make it difficult for her to identify where they were. Realizing she would get nowhere with the driver, she lit a cigarette and closed her eyes.

Vaguely she had heard a helicopter take off as soon as the car left the airport. Inside the control cabin of the Sikorsky Emilio Vitorelli sat in the co-pilot's seat, holding a powerful pair of field glasses. Occasionally, as they tracked the car from a distance, he focused the glasses. Berg's blonde head came up clearly inside the lenses.

'Keep her in sight. Don't lose her. But don't let the driver think we are following him,' he told the pilot.

'In other words,' the pilot answered in Italian, 'perform a miracle.'

'That's what you are paid to do.'

It had been Tweed who had warned Vitorelli that he suspected Berg was a member of The Sisterhood. It was his way of repaying the favour when the Italian had given him a photo of Tina Langley. Tweed had had no idea of how Vitorelli would handle the information but the Italian had acted quickly.

Obtaining a description of the striking woman, he had posted men to watch for her at the airport, at the main station, in areas overlooking the main road exits from Zurich. A small army of his men normally engaged in activities which were not always strictly legal had been flown in to the Swiss city.

He had taken a shrewd gamble in flying in his Sikorsky to Schwechat – because Tweed had told him about the murder of Norbert Engel and the subsequent attempt to kidnap Paula in a car. Knowing the Austrian capital had an incredible mix of nationalities he suspected the base of The Sisterhood might well be in the deserted hinterland outside Vienna.

Inside the Sikorsky, Vitorelli also began to think the driver was deliberately taking a devious route to his destination, wherever that might be. Naturally volatile, the Italian could exert endless patience once he had made up his mind. So he settled back and waited as they kept away from the tiny car moving through the deserted countryside.

'You have the friends?' Valja suddenly asked.

'What are you talking about?' Paula demanded.

'I see Ford car long way behind.'

'What are you talking about?' Paula repeated.

'You have the friends?'

'I have no friends out here. I don't know where we are. So where are we?'

'Me Valja.'

Paula gave it up. She concentrated on trying to see a signpost but there were very few of them. Surreptitiously she had taken a map of Austria out of her shoulder bag. She spread it out on her lap so Valja could not see it.

They had been travelling for a long time when they passed a signpost. EISENSTADT. She recalled the brochure of a hotel in that town which a policeman in Vienna had scooped out of a toilet in a cell during the prison breakout. What was the name of the hotel? Burgenland. Same name as the province on the eastern borders of Austria.

Paula stopped looking for signposts as she considered what lay ahead of her. Aboard the aircraft when she had needled Hassan into talking he had made a reference to 'the training house'. What kind of hideous ordeal had he planned for her? Then she was distracted from her thoughts by Valja picking up a mobile phone and talking rapidly in a language she couldn't identify. It sounded as though he was giving orders.

Her left hand crept stealthily towards her make-up bag, then she withdrew the hand. Whatever happened she had to find out the location of the base of The Sisterhood.

19

Butler was behind the wheel of the Ford. Beside him Nield was studying a map of Burgenland and surrounding areas he had grabbed from a display holder in the airport. Even travelling a good distance behind her they had kept Paula's Volvo in sight, with no other traffic and the countryside so level.

'Driver of the Volvo slowed down for a few minutes,' Butler reported. 'I wonder why, when you have an open road and no other cars to bother about?'

'Maybe using a mobile phone,' Nield suggested.

'You think he's spotted us?'

'I'd be surprised if he hadn't. For miles there have been two cars going the same way – his and ours.'

'Could mean trouble,' Butler observed calmly.

'My very thought. Keep your eyes peeled.'

They came to a fork and Butler took the left turning. Nield was looking south. In the far distance a helicopter was flying steadily on a course parallel to the road they had just left behind.

'Could be that chopper,' Butler mused.

'Don't think so. He'd have come closer to get a better look at us. And since Charlie used his mobile the chopper hasn't altered its course.'

'Charlie?'

'The driver taking Paula. I've got to call him something.'

'Charlie has speeded up, is moving faster than he has since he left the airport.'

'Could be a danger signal. Something Charlie doesn't want to be near when it happens. To us.'

Paula was very alert. She could hardly believe what she was seeing. Rising up from the level plain was a long hill. Perched on top was a weird long single-storey house. The roof, of wood like the walls, sloped up and then rose vertically. It was a large house and she had never seen anything like it before.

They had now turned on to a track, hidden from the house up above them. She saw where the track spiralled up at the left-hand end of this strange hill. In the rear-view mirror Valja caught her eye, grinned wolfishly.

'We go there.'

He took one hand off the wheel to point up to where the house was perched. His evil grin suggested he was anticipating what was in store for her. She extracted the metal nail file from her make-up bag, then leaned forward and while the car was moving slowly pressed the sharp pointed end into his thick neck.

'Valja. Stop the car – or I'll ram this knife right through you.'

His change of expression in the rear-view mirror was dramatic. The grin disappeared and fear showed as he stared back at the hard look in his passenger's eyes. She pushed the point deeper into his neck.

'Lady, please—'

'I've had enough of your bloody nonsense,' she told him, her teeth gritted. 'Make a U-turn. You can do it driving over the grass.'

She could tell he didn't understand, that he was scared witless. She used her left hand to indicate a U-turn. Now he understood her order. Swinging the wheel slowly, he turned the Volvo round on the arid burnt grass and stopped, facing the way he had come.

'Valja!' She snapped out the name with all the venom she could muster. Her expression was not pleasant. 'Airport. Go back to the airport. Move, you bastard.'

He had slipped back on his seat and this caused the nail file to dig more deeply into his fleshy neck. He began driving back the way they had come at a moderate pace. Paula was worried that someone inside the house would soon notice that the plan was going wrong. They were likely to send cars after her.

'Valja!' she screamed deliberately. 'Speed! Faster! More speed! Or I'll kill you.'

He understood enough of what she had said to press his foot down. Soon they were racing along the open road. She kept the nail file pressed into his neck. A few minutes later, looking back, she saw another car appear behind them in the distance. Someone had reacted quickly.

'Faster!' she shouted.

Valja obeyed. Looking back again for a second she saw that the black car coming up behind was closing the gap.

Butler had increased speed, seeing Paula's Volvo disappearing as it turned a corner, then reappearing. Nield was the first one to notice the giant yellow excavator digging up the road in the distance. He focused a small pair of field glasses he had extracted from his backpack.

The driver of the hulking piece of machinery was elevating an evil-looking scoop with huge metal teeth. The scoop descended, tore up a large piece of the surface of the road, dropped it into the field on the verge. Butler shrugged.

'It's the same even out here. Just like back home. They dig holes in the road, then fill 'em up. Just to keep the workforce in a job.'

'I'm not so sure,' Nield replied. 'Slow down. Crawl.'

'OK. But why?'

'Because the driver inside his cabin keeps swinging the arm supporting that huge scoop out over the road where we'll have to pass it.'

'You think he's going to . . .'

'My bet is he has a mobile phone. Watch it, Harry.'

'I'm watching. My damned hands are slippery on the wheel. It's as hot as Hades out here.'

'And very lonely. They could bury us in one of those fields, using the scoop to dig a hole. Who would ever find us?'

'Archaeologists digging for dinosaur bones a hundred years from now. Trouble is we have no weapons.'

'Remember our training course at that mansion down in Surrey. The instructor said there's always a weapon you can use.'

'Surrey seems a helluva long way from here . . .'

Nield's only expression of tension was to light one of his rare cigarettes. He had taken the pack and lighter from one of his pockets. He smoked without inhaling as they came closer and closer to the excavator, travelling at a slow pace. He was studying the terrain alongside the road. Grass and reeds had grown tall, stretching away across the fields. It must have grown during an earlier rainy season.

Now grass and reeds were brown and dead. The fiery sun, day after day, week after week, had burned the life out of the vegetation. It was tinder dry. Butler was concentrating on approaching the excavator, a truly massive machine on caterpillar tracks.

'I may take off suddenly,' Nield warned. 'You save the car.'

'You seem sure it will need saving.'

'I'm dead certain. Emphasis on dead.'

'Time somebody cracked a joke.'

'Maybe he's digging for gold. Best I can manage just at this moment.'

'Ha-ha,' Butler responded with a mock laugh.

'Here we go . . .'

Butler drove slowly forward, now very close to the excavator on the right-hand side of the road. Automatically, he had tested the car's reactions in different situations soon after leaving the airport. He knew what he could do with it.

'I'm leaving you,' Nield said.

He opened his door on the verge side of the slow-moving car, dived out, slammed the door shut behind him. He walked a short way into the field beyond the verge, grabbing up handfuls of long grass and reeds. The driver in the cab of the excavator had seen Nield get out but was concentrating on the Ford approaching him.

To pass the machine, parked on the right-hand side of the road, Butler had to swing over to the left. Not that this mattered since there was no other traffic as far as the eye could see. As he did so the excavator's driver, inside his glass-walled cabin, elevated the massive arm, hauling the scoop with its murderous, steel-fanged teeth high up in the air. He held it there for a moment, suspended above the cavernous hole he had gouged out of the highway.

Butler continued to drive slowly forward, watching the man inside the cab closely. He saw him suddenly start moving levers just before the Ford passed the machine. The arm supporting the scoop swivelled out over the road, began to descend at great speed.

Butler reversed quickly, backing a distance away from the machine. Where his Ford had been moments before the scoop crashed down. It was operated with such force its dragon's teeth slammed deep into the road. Had Butler not reversed so swiftly the immense weight of the scoop would have smashed through the roof of the car reducing him to a spiked corpse, skewered to his seat.

While this lethal assault was taking place Nield had collected several sheaths of burnt dry grass and reeds, using some of the reeds to wrap round the sheaths. He ran forward to the side of the cabin as the driver, seeing him coming, flung open his door on the verge side.

The man inside the cab was fumbling with a machine-pistol when Nield, using his lighter, set fire to the first sheaf, hurled it inside the glass cab. Setting fire to a second sheaf, he threw the burning brand after the first. Flames enveloped the driver, who dropped his machine-pistol into the road. Darting forward, Nield picked up the weapon, ran back a few paces, waved to Butler to reverse further back. The Ford shot back, Nield lit the third sheaf tucked under his arm, cast it under the excavator beneath the fuel tank. Then he ran like hell back up the road towards where Butler was waiting.

The third sheaf ignited the fuel tank. There was a thunderous roar, like a bomb going off. Nield dropped flat in the road alongside the Ford. The excavator exploded, vanished in a sheet of flame. Huge fragments of its disintegrated metal soared into the sky, crashed down in the fields. One large piece, lethal in size, landed alongside the Ford, on the far side away from where Nield crouched, holding the machine-pistol.

There was a sudden silence after the deafening blast.

Nield climbed back into the front passenger seat of the Ford. He brushed dirt off his clothes. Butler was staring beyond where the excavator had once stood.

'A car coming – like a bat out of hell. Another one behind it . . .'

Nield snatched up his field glasses, focused, then lowered them. His tone was grim.

'The first car is the grey Volvo with Paula in the back, a driver in front. The black Mercedes coming up behind her like a bullet from a gun has four men inside it.'

Paula still had the nail file pressed hard against Valja's neck. She no longer had to glance back. She could see the black Mercedes coming in the rear-view mirror.

'They kill me,' Valja gasped.

'I kill you. Keep driving,' Paula rasped.

She had heard the huge explosion, had seen the column of fire, had no idea what it meant. In a supreme emergency she was ice-cold. She threw the question at Valja, banking on his state of terror to answer without thinking.

'*Where is the house on the mountain?*'

'Slovakia,' Valja croaked.

It was only when they had raced past the flattened wreckage of what remained of the bulldozer that she recognized the figure standing near the rear of the Ford and outside the vehicle. Harry Butler. She nearly cried with relief. But she kept her nerve.

'Stop behind that car,' she yelled at Valja.

He braked suddenly, almost turned the Volvo off the road into the fields. But he obeyed her, parking behind the Ford. Her nail file was still pressed against his neck when she gave her next order.

'Get out! Crouch – get down – behind the Ford!'

215

Valja jumped out, took cover behind the stationary car. She jumped out herself, was grabbed by the arm as Butler forced her to take cover on the verge side of the Ford. He joined her as the black Mercedes arrived, moving slowly now. All its windows were open and the barrels of guns protruded. She waited for the fusillade.

Before any of the four men could open fire a hail of bullets raked the open windows. Lying in the grass of the field near the Ford, Nield was operating the machine-pistol with deadly precision. Only the driver ducked in time, threw his door open and, holding a machine-pistol, started to run into the grass of the field opposite.

Nield, now near the rear of the Ford, peered round, aimed his weapon. He shot the driver in the back who fell into the grass. Valja, who had not moved from the rear of the Ford, lay on the ground, killed by one shot from a thug inside the Mercedes before he slumped out of sight.

20

Tweed and Newman were sitting at a table in the open-air Pavillon attached to the Baur au Lac when they were joined by Willie.

'Hello there, chaps. Another super day. Hope this heatwave goes on for ever. Drinks are on me.'

'I have one,' Tweed said, pointing to his orange juice.

'I'll have another Scotch,' Newman replied.

'We'll make that a double. Waiter! Over here, my good man.'

Willie was dressed in a smart white jacket and white trousers with a razor-edged crease. Round his neck he wore a yellow cravat. Several attractive women had eyed him thoughtfully as he had walked with a springy step to Tweed's table. His face was red as a beetroot. He sat down in a spare chair, crossed his ankles.

'I hope this heatwave breaks tomorrow,' Tweed told him.

'You're not as accustomed to the heat as I am, old boy. I've spent so much time in the Middle East I love it. You'll get used to it if it lasts long enough.'

'I don't wish to get used to it,' Tweed remarked. He paused as the waiter brought the drinks Willie had ordered. 'I was talking with Amos last night. I gathered he admires your Oriental garden at Dovecote Manor.'

'He should. He supplied most of the statuary and so on from the East. Gave it to me since I have the space for the stuff. He has a key to the place and looks after it when I'm absent abroad. Cheers!'

'Cheers!'

Tweed went silent as he absorbed the statement Willie had just made. The two men were telling totally different stories about the weird sculptures.

'Must cost a packet to transport such large items from the Middle East,' he remarked.

'It has to,' Willie agreed. 'More than I'd fork out. I spend my ill-gotten gains on entertaining sheiks.' He grinned. 'To say nothing of entertaining a bevy of attractive ladies.'

He winked, ran a finger over his light brown, pencil-thin moustache. His expression suggested satisfaction at the memory of some interesting interludes with girlfriends. He does like himself, Newman was thinking.

'I don't suppose Amos meets any of your attractive ladies?' Tweed enquired.

'Oh yes, he does. When I'm going off some filly I phone him up, invite him round for a drink. Amos has a way with the ladies. At times he takes them back to his place to show them his cottage. At least that's his story.' He winked again. 'I wouldn't be surprised if they ended up spending the night there.'

'You don't know that,' Newman said mildly. 'Surely that is a guess on your part?'

'Boys will be boys. What's wrong? Amos is a bachelor.'

'Nothing's wrong,' Tweed intervened. 'Incidentally, do you happen to know whether Tina Langley knew Amos?'

'Yes, she did. They got on well together when he met her at my place.'

'Did she later go round to The Minotaur, Amos's cottage?'

'She might have done. Can't be sure. They both left at the same time. That I do recall.'

'Tina Langley has gone missing.'

'Probably sunning herself on some tycoon's yacht in the Med. She was quite a looker. I found her too expensive. There is a limit.'

'Why would she be on a tycoon's yacht in the Mediterranean?'

'Plenty of fun – at someone else's expense – was her way of life. Time we had a refresher. Told you I'd pulled off a big deal.'

'Not for me. Willie, I'm afraid we'll have to go. An urgent appointment.'

Tweed hurried to the lift with Newman. The two men went to Tweed's room. Newman waited on a couch and was relieved when Tweed sat down instead of pacing like a caged tiger.

'What appointment?' he asked.

'With Beck. He'll be here soon. I've got certain jobs I'm hoping he'll take on. We're overstretched. That was a very strange conversation with Willie. I told you last night what Amos said to me in the limo.'

'Doesn't add up.'

'It most certainly doesn't. First, Amos gives me the idea that all the artefacts – weird objects – in Willie's large garden were brought back by Willie from the Middle East. Now Willie tells us it is Amos who imported them, gave them to Willie because he has the space. He also mentions that Amos has a key to Dovecote Manor.'

'One of them is lying.'

'Yes, but which one? And why?'

'Because,' Newman suggested, 'the man who brought them in has a lot of money – sufficient to have them transported all the way from the Middle East to here. And transporting that lot must have cost one of them a small fortune . . .'

There was a knock on the door. Newman jumped up, opened it cautiously. Beck, wearing a grey business suit, stood outside, was ushered in by Newman. Tweed offered him a comfortable chair.

'I'm going to be asked to do you an impossible favour,' Beck said with a smile.

'You are, if you will.'

'Tell me the worst.'

'I'm short of manpower. I want Amos Lodge and Captain Wellesley Carrington watched round the clock. Amos is staying here while Willie is at the Dolder Grand. I need to know if they make any phone calls from public booths, if so the time they make the call, how long they take to make the call, where they return to afterwards.'

'You don't want much. That will tie up Heaven knows how many plain-clothes men to do the job properly. You do require a twenty-four-hour surveillance?' Beck asked ironically.

'Round the clock. Also anyone they meet, how long they are with them and a description.'

'You have yourself, Newman and Marler. To say nothing of the two who flew to Vienna – Butler and Nield . . .'

'They're looking for Paula,' Tweed said grimly. 'You know she has gone missing.'

'I'm as sorry and worried about that as you are, if possible.' Beck stood up. 'I'll arrange the surveillance of those two men within the hour. But what are you planning on doing?'

'Flying to Vienna . . .'

Tweed was packing his bag. Newman had booked seats for three people aboard the next Austrian Airlines flight to Vienna when the call came through.

'Pete Nield here. Paula is safe. I'm calling from the Sacher. The three of us are staying here. Tried to call you yesterday evening, but you were out. Decided not to leave you a message. We don't know who is OK and who isn't in Zurich.'

'Thank you, Pete,' Tweed said in a subdued voice. 'Could I have a word with Paula?'

'She's still fast asleep. We thought it best to let her recover. She's OK, but there was a bit of a bust-up. Nothing to write home about. Paula has discovered the base, if you understand me.'

'I do.'

'I won't name the location. This phone may not be safe.'

'That's all right. Give Paula my congratulations. When you are all back to normal catch the first flight back to Zurich.'

'Paula thinks we ought to stay here.'

'Tell her that's a direct order.'

'What about us?'

'You escort her back here. That's another direct order. Call me with details of the flight when you know them. You'll be met at Kloten.'

'You're the boss.'

'Remind Paula of that . . .'

Putting down the phone, Tweed sagged on to the couch next to Newman, told him the news. His expression was one of great relief.

'Paula is safe,' he repeated. 'Thank the Lord for that.'

'You need a drink,' Newman suggested.

'A double brandy. No water.'

'Are you sure?'

'Do get it brought up here now.'

When the drink arrived Tweed swallowed half of it slowly as Newman watched him. He then drank the rest. Newman expected Tweed, who rarely used alcohol, to show signs of wooziness. Instead, he sat forward, very alert and obviously thinking hard.

'We have to distribute our forces carefully,' he said.

'Why bring back the team already in Vienna?'

'I need to cover every contingency. When they get back we will hold a battle conference.'

Inside his office in the house in Slovakia, Hassan was in a rage. All the guards who looked after his safety kept out of his way. The cause? The day before, when Berg had eventually arrived, a Sikorsky helicopter had flown several times over the house.

Hassan had no way of knowing that Vitorelli was on board the chopper. Using a powerful German camera with a telephoto lens he had recorded the structure of the building from every angle. Earlier, through his glasses, he had seen the blonde Berg get out of the car and disappear inside the front entrance.

'We have dug up pure gold,' he told the pilot, Mario Parcelli.

'Gold?' Mario enquired as he circled the house.

'This has to be the base of The Sisterhood. Observe it well, my friend.'

'It looks most peculiar,' Mario replied in Italian, the language they were conversing in. 'Someone has run out of the house to observe us with field glasses.'

'He won't see much, will he?'

The perspex-enclosed cabin had a faint amber tint which made it impossible to see who was inside. Vitorelli's camera was aimed through a narrow slit he had opened in the window on his side.

It was Hassan who had rushed out with binoculars. Determined to identify the intruder, he wrote down details of the markings on its fuselage. Then, realizing he might be being photographed, he ran back inside, slammed the front door shut.

Hassan had to wait until the following day to phone a friend in the aviation world, a friend who would expect a large payment for his trouble. The later conversation with Hassan had not gone well.

'I cannot identify the helicopter,' he told Hassan on the phone.

'Why not?' screamed Hassan. 'I gave you the markings.'

'It will do you no good to yell at me,' his informant replied indignantly. 'I have checked with the Records Authority for helicopters. They contacted every country in Europe. No one knows the markings you gave me.'

'I am not paying you for no information,' Hassan shouted.

'I can tell you the same helicopter landed at Schwechat Airport where it refuelled and took off again.'

'Bribe someone in the control tower. They must know where the helicopter was going to.'

'I have no contact in the control tower. Any attempt to pay a bribe to one of their staff would get me arrested.'

'All you think of is your own skin.'

'Someone has to think of it,' his informant rapped back.

'You are useless. A piece of nothing.'

'The fee will be a thousand pounds. Sterling.'

'Send me a bill!'

Hassan had slammed the phone down. He couldn't understand what had happened. Who could have been aboard the chopper? It was very worrying.

What he didn't know was that when the refuelled helicopter had landed at Kloten it had asked to be guided to a remote part of the airfield. There Vitorelli had helped Mario to remove the thick sheet with false markings, exposing the machine's real markings.

Mario, whom Vitorelli had ordered back urgently from Geneva, had then taken the film to an apartment his chief rented in Zurich under a different name. Once closeted in the secret hideaway, Mario produced a set of prints of all the shots Vitorelli had taken in Slovakia. He had worked through the night and delivered them to his chief the following morning.

While Tweed was drinking his brandy and talking to Newman, Vitorelli was studying the photos under a high-powered glass in his room. He grunted with satisfaction and eventually placed them back inside the envelope Mario had brought him. He looked at his assistant.

'Well done, Mario. Order drinks to be sent up so we can celebrate. Our next task is to locate Tina Langley.'

Unknown to Vitorelli, Tweed was engaged on the same mission. He had taken out the photo of Tina that

Vitorelli had given him on an earlier occasion. Showing it again to Newman, he asked his question.

'Photos are deceptive. But what is your impression of this lady from a single photo?'

'First, I suspect it is a good one, showing her character – or, rather, her lack of it. I'd say this woman spends her life living off her looks.'

'I'm waiting for Paula to arrive. I want her to look at the photo again. Then I'm going to ask Beck to have a huge number of prints produced from it.'

'What's the idea?'

'You'll hear when Paula has seen the picture . . .'

'I hear an engine revving up.'

'Engine?'

'Your engine, Tweed. You're so relieved Paula is safe your normal dynamic energy has returned. I sense we are going to get cracking soon. I can't wait for the battle conference.'

'We are going to have to take action swiftly. The clock is ticking. I sense we haven't much time left.'

The Englishman phoned Hassan soon after the call which told him the helicopter could not be identified. With an effort Hassan remained calm when he realized who was phoning him. It would be very dangerous to upset the Englishman.

'I am here,' he said, his hand clammy on the receiver.

'You have not carried out any of the recent instructions.'

'We have had bad luck.'

'You have been incompetent. Tweed and Kane are still alive.'

'Neither of them responded to the women you allocated to them.'

'I hear that Karin Berg is with you. Why?'

'With me?' Hassan was stupefied that the Englishman had this information. 'We withdrew her because she panicked.'

'*You* withdrew her because *you* panicked. Send her back on the first flight to Zurich. She stays at the Dolder Grand. A room is booked for her. Her target is Christopher Kane.'

'Kane is in Geneva.'

'Kane has arrived in Zurich. Baur au Lac. Send Tina Langley back from Geneva to Zurich. Her target is Tweed. Again at Baur au Lac.'

'Preparation will be necessary.'

'You have three days to complete the assignments. Zurich will be the killing ground. I have another call to make.'

The line went dead. Hassan, sweat streaming off his brow, wondered how long it would be before he was dead. He was most worried by the Englishman's last remark. Was he calling the Head of State? How could he know so much?

Then Hassan remembered that when he had returned to the long house he had been greeted at the entrance by Ahmed, his hated brother and chief rival. Hassan rose slowly from his chair behind the desk, strolled across to the door, locked it.

Only three people knew the combination to the massive safe in a corner – the Head of State, who knew everything, himself and Ahmed. Inside the safe was a book where Hassan noted down all developments in the master plan, however minor, so he could send regular reports to the Head of State, a man who insisted on meticulous records. The book contained all the details of the accomplishments and movements of The Sisterhood.

Bending down, Hassan examined the circular combination lock. It was not quite in the same position as he had left it. So Ahmed had checked the records. It was Ahmed who had informed the Englishman about his failures.

A Persian rug covered most of the tiled floor but there was a margin round it where the exotic tiles were exposed. Picking up a valuable Eastern vase, Hassan, his face convulsed with fury, smashed it down on to the tiles where it broke into a score of pieces. He felt better now, ready to deal with Ahmed.

He found his brother in one of the many living rooms overlooking Austria. Ahmed was holding a bottle of whisky as he poured himself a fresh glass. His hand trembled and he kept tapping the bottle against the rim of the glass. He was unaware of Hassan's silent entry.

Alcohol was forbidden by the Head of State. Ahmed enjoyed his visits to the long house. He could indulge his liking for drink – and on secret trips to Vienna his appetite for a certain type of woman.

'I have had an important message from the Head of State,' Hassan informed him smoothly. 'It is so secret I think I had better tell you outside on the terrace.'

As he spoke he opened the door leading to the terrace, a narrow paved area adjoining the house. Beyond it there was an area of arid sandy ground with rocks protruding at intervals.

Hassan led the way on to the terrace. Ahmed, still holding the bottle, staggered after him, almost tripped as he came out. Hassan saved him by gripping one arm. He guided him to the edge of the terrace. Ahmed, a small heavily built man with a fat face lined from his frequent experiences with the bottle and his trips to Vienna, mumbled, 'What's this all about?'

'Have you yet reported your findings to the Head of State?'

'Not yet. You in big trouble, brother.'

'I'm sure you'll help me out of it.'

226

'Tell me – why should I do that, *brother*?'

There was a sneer as he pronounced the last word. Ahmed lifted the bottle, drank, spilling part of the contents down his suit. He staggered again and Hassan grasped his arm again, guiding him off the terrace.

'We are being watched,' Hassan whispered. 'There are people at the bottom of the quarry with listening devices. Right below us. Look for yourself . . .'

Hassan was now a couple of steps behind Ahmed, had let go of his arm. His brother shook his head, as though to clear it. He was only taking in half what his brother had said.

'Spies . . . you mean? Let's kill them . . .'

Hassan clenched both fists, punched Ahmed in the back, shoved him forward a couple of paces. Perched on the edge of the rim Ahmed fell forward over the edge of the sheer drop. He had dropped the bottle a few paces back. He screamed in terror as he plunged down the sheer wall of the quarry. The scream faded as his body hit the ground three hundred feet down.

Hassan felt the ground shifting under his own feet. He jumped back just in time as a huge boulder went over the drop, followed by a cascade of smaller rocks. Sweating all over, Hassan peered over the edge from the stable terrace. The boulders had buried Ahmed, clouds of dry dust rising. Hassan ran back to waken the servants who were taking a siesta in rooms at the cooler front of the house.

21

The timing was unfortunate by five minutes. The Englishman who had made the call to Hassan from Zurich had left the public phone box, had returned to his hotel

227

before the two plain-clothes watchers sent by Beck arrived. Two other men took up positions where they could watch the hotel where the second Englishman was staying.

'Both your suspects are now under twenty-four-hour surveillance and will be relieved in due course by more of my men,' Beck reported to Tweed over the phone.

'Any movement so far?' Tweed asked.

'None at all. The one in your hotel is in his room. Probably having a sleep in this heat.'

'Amos will be working.'

'The other one is in the hotel lounge of his place, chatting up an attractive lady.'

'How attractive?' Tweed wanted to know.

'A stunner is the correct description, I believe,' said Beck, who was proud of his command of colloquial English.

'Thank you, Arthur.'

Tweed told Newman what Beck had said. Newman grinned as he put down his drink of mineral water. The heat seemed, if anything, to be getting worse. He had decided to switch to water to avoid dehydration.

'Don't know how Willie keeps it up. He has the energy of the Devil,' Newman commented.

'Perhaps he is the Devil. Or are you just envious?'

'I must get to the airport. Paula's flight is due soon.'

'I'll come with you. I think she'd appreciate a reception committee. Let's take your car. Then we can talk in privacy on the way back here.' He unlocked a drawer, took out the photo of Tina Langley. 'I want to call in on Beck on the return trip from the airport. He's set up his HQ at the Zurich Police Chief's place overlooking the Limmat and the University across the river. Let's go.'

Paula was the first to appear at the airport, followed closely by Butler and Nield. She flew into the arms of Tweed, who hugged her affectionately.

'Glad to be back?' he asked as he escorted her to Newman's car, carrying her bag.

'You could say that,' she said as she settled herself in the rear between Tweed and Nield. Butler, parking his backpack on his lap, sat next to Newman and the car took off.

'Slovakia,' Paula started, 'that's where The Sisterhood base is. I've marked the exact location on my map.'

'As far east as that,' Tweed mused. 'Yes, it fits in with the other pieces of the jigsaw I'm building up. Now I'll just listen. Unless you don't feel like talking.'

'I'll talk my head off . . .'

Concisely, she related all the events which had taken place since boarding the plane for Schwechat with Ashley Wingfield. To Tweed's relief she sounded very fresh and alert. Later, Nield gave a brief summary of the encounter with the excavator. Then they pulled in at police headquarters.

Beck greeted Paula in his office with a warm hug. He had always had a soft spot for Paula. Tweed then placed the photo of Tina Langley on his desk.

'Could you reproduce at least fifty prints from this at top speed?'

'Yes,' Beck replied. 'Why?'

'I want them distributed to the police forces in all the major Swiss cities – with special emphasis on Geneva. We have to warn them about the lady – if that's the right word – before she kills someone else as she did Norbert Engel. She attempted to shoot the back of the head off Christopher Kane in Geneva, but he was too smart for her.'

'Christopher Kane? The expert on bacteriological warfare? Is that what we may be facing?'

'Yes.'

'I must alert the Army chiefs – they have advanced equipment to protect troops against such an attack.'

'I'd do that, if I were you. You can guess which Eastern power is behind all this. I suspect China, which has supplied them with modern equipment, is using them as an advance guard.'

'What makes you think that?'

'China is making too much fuss about overtaking America. I think it's a smokescreen to cover her real objective. Europe.'

'We live in grim times,' Beck said as he escorted them to the door.

'And few in the West realize the terrible menace hanging over us. But it was the same with Rome – as Amos pointed out in his speech. Rome in ancient times had little inkling that the barbarians were coming from the East.'

'Photos of Tina Langley will flood Switzerland,' Beck promised.

On their way back in the car Paula was silent for a while. She is tired, Tweed decided. He was wrong.

'You know what I would do if I was running The Sisterhood?' she said suddenly.

'What would you do?' Tweed asked.

'Bring them all back to Zurich. The targets are here.'

'Kane said he was coming to Zurich from Geneva.'

'There you are.'

'I meant to ask you if you're sure that photo of Tina Langley *is* the woman you saw walking down Kärntnerstrasse after Norbert Engel was murdered.'

'I'm not sure – I'm absolutely certain.'

The first person they met as they walked into the Baur au Lac was Christopher Kane. Smartly dressed in a light grey suit and a pink shirt, he looked pleased to see Paula.

'Always a great pleasure to meet this delightful lady. She has looks, personality – and brains. A most unusual combination. To have everything.'

'You really do go over the top,' she teased him.

He kissed her on both cheeks, gripping her shoulders in his strong hands. His eyes met hers and he seemed genuinely pleased to see her. He presented her with a floral bouquet he had laid on a nearby table.

'Thank you so much, Chris.'

'Merely a tribute to a brave, resourceful lady.'

'I think,' Tweed broke in, 'that the brave lady would like to go to her room to freshen up. I'm sure you will see her later.'

'I shall hope and pray,' Christopher replied, still smiling.

Newman escorted her to her room and left when he heard her lock the door. Downstairs Tweed turned his attention to Nield and Butler.

'Your rooms are here now. I cancelled the Gotthard. We are concentrating our resources. Marler is here.'

'I'll pop in and see him first,' Nield decided.

As the two men headed for the lift after being handed folders with their room numbers, Tweed smiled to himself. He guessed they hoped to obtain fresh weapons from Marler. It was a marvel they had coped with the excavator's driver without weapons – until Nield had got hold of the machine-pistol the driver had been holding.

'Let's go into the lounge for a drink,' Tweed suggested, 'unless you'd sooner go to your room first.'

'Had a shower before I left. Slept on the train. A drink is called for. Waiter, service, please. What are you having, Tweed?'

'Mineral water. Non-sparkling.'

'A dry Martini,' Christopher ordered as they sat down in a corner of the deserted lounge.

'Why have you come here?' Tweed wanted to know when they were alone.

'Like to be in at the end of the game. In rugger you don't sit around waiting for the other chap to get you – you go after him. Same applies if the aggressor is a woman. Lisa Vane tried to clonk me for good. This seems to be the centre of the action so that's why I'm here.'

'You're a major target,' Tweed warned quietly. 'And there are at least two different women assassins. Lisa Vane and Karin Berg. We think we know who murdered Dumont, but we can't prove it. Berg's slim, tallish, has blonde hair cut short like a helmet, just in case you meet her.'

He stopped talking, aware that someone had come up behind him, had placed a gentle hand on his neck. He looked up. It was Simone Carnot, the desirable redhead he had last met in this very lounge when she was talking to Newman.

'Hello, Mr Tweed,' Simone said with a devastating smile which Christopher appreciated. 'I'm not going to interrupt, but I just wanted you to know I was still around.'

'Please join us for a drink,' Tweed said immediately.

'Are you sure?'

'We're certain,' Christopher said jovially. 'That vacant chair was just waiting for you.'

'How nice to be invited to join two gentlemen with such good manners,' Simone responded with a quirky smile. 'I think I'll have a Kir royale,' she requested, after eyeing Christopher's drink.

'This is Simone Carnot,' Tweed introduced. 'Miss Carnot . . .'

'Simone, please.'

'Simone, this is Christopher Kane.'

'Delighted to meet such a beauty,' Christopher said gallantly. 'And I'm Christopher. My friends call me Chris.'

'I'm glad to meet you, Chris. You look as though your conversation will be interesting.'

As the waiter brought the drink Kane had ordered Simone was thinking: Thank Heaven I stayed on here. I am talking to both targets. I'm looking at two potential corpses who would earn me two hundred thousand dollars.

Hassan had been very direct when he phoned her. He had told her to kill the two men at the first opportunity, not to bother about faking them as suicides, and had given her the name and address of a man in Zurich who could supply her with a Luger and ammunition. Hassan had been in a hurry.

'You live in Zurich, Chris?' Simone enquired.

'No, in Geneva.' He was watching her closely. 'This is not the best Kir royale in the world, although it's very good. To get the best you go to Les Armures in Geneva. Expect you know the place.'

'I'm afraid I don't.'

'You've never been to Geneva?' he asked amiably.

'Not so far.'

Both men noticed the tiny pause before she had replied to the question. Simone was wearing a form-fitting green sheath. It exposed one shapely bare shoulder. Simone worked on the basis of 'show them a little flesh and they'll want to see more'.

'You're from the French-speaking part of Switzerland?'

'No, I'm from France.'

'The best French in the world,' Christopher went on, 'is spoken in Geneva.'

'Parisians would not agree with you.'

'So you're from Paris?'

'I didn't say so. You do it well, Chris, but you almost sound like a detective questioning a witness.'

'I'm just interested in you.'

'So I should be interested in you, which I am. What is your profession?'

'I'm the world's expert on bacteriological warfare.'

Christopher was never backward in broadcasting his importance, thought Tweed, who was deliberately keeping silent while he studied Simone. He knew she thought he was taking a more than gentlemanly interest in her from the sidelong glances which occasionally came his way.

'What a horrible thing to be involved in,' Simone protested.

'It's bound to happen sooner or later,' Christopher said cheerfully. 'The thing to do is to be prepared for it when it comes. Anyone working for the Eastern state concerned should be shot. Stone-cold dead.'

Both men saw Simone blink. She recovered her poise almost immediately, sipped the last of her drink, put down her glass. Checking her watch, a Rolex, she stood up.

'I have enjoyed our conversation. Possibly we could continue it over dinner one evening. My treat.'

'You would be my guest,' Tweed insisted. 'We'll fix something up in the near future. You are staying at this hotel?'

'I have a room here, yes. Sometimes I have to travel for a few days.'

'I will find you sooner or later,' Tweed said in an odd tone.

'What do you think, Christopher?' Tweed asked when she had gone.

'From the technique you described they use on the phone I'd say we could well have been talking to a third member of The Sisterhood.'

'I agree. They're getting desperate, or their controller is.'

'I'm not saying so positively,' Christopher said carefully. 'In Scotland we have a jury verdict "not proven". That would be my verdict on the very sinuous Simone Carnot.'

'Well, I got in first with my invitation.'

'You certainly did, you old dog. I was about to make the same suggestion to her. What is happening?'

'The enemy is panicking. They're working to a timetable and running out of time. So are we.'

A man in civilian clothes came into the lounge, saw Tweed and presented him with an envelope. 'From Chief Inspector Beck,' he whispered.

'Thank you.'

'Who was that?' Christopher asked.

'A plain-clothes policeman I recognized. Ah, Beck has returned the photo I gave him. Recognize this lady?'

'It's Lisa Vane,' Christopher said.

'Otherwise known as Tina Langley. The woman who murdered Norbert Engel in Vienna – and the woman who nearly killed you in Geneva.'

'Then I've left her behind.'

'I wouldn't bank on that. I think they're all coming here. I think an Englishman from Dorset is controlling the whole operation to wipe out all members of the *Institut*. I mean either Amos Lodge or Willie.'

'That's a trifle fantastic even for you, Tweed. When did you come to that astonishing conclusion?'

'Just now. They've been working their way down the list of members in sequence. Only someone with the list could work that out.'

'Willie isn't a member,' Christopher objected.

'You'll recall he once attended a session we held at the HQ of the *Institut* near Ouchy on Lake Geneva. He gave us a very informative lecture on conditions in the Middle East. While he was there Dumont foolishly showed him a list of the members.'

'You think he'd remember them in exact sequence?'

'He could have done. Willie, I happen to know, has a photographic memory. I once joked with him about it, tested him. I gave him a page of Somerset Maugham's novel *The Painted Veil*. He read the page once, then recited it back to me word for word.'

'So it could be either of them,' Christopher said.

'Exactly. And both of them keep hanging about in Zurich.'

At that moment Newman came into the lounge and Tweed beckoned to him to join them. He then told Newman what he had been discussing with Christopher.

'Makes sense,' Newman agreed. 'And both of them right under our noses. So which one is it?'

'I have no idea,' Tweed replied. 'But I'm certain whoever it is plans on Zurich being the killing ground. Adrian Manders, the specialist on ballistic missiles, is next on that list. He came here for a holiday and to listen to Dumont's speech. When Amos took over Manders was in the audience.'

'Where is he staying?' Newman asked.

'At the Dolder Grand. Both Amos and Willie must have seen him. Manders had a front-row seat, was the first to stand up and leave during the ovation.'

'Zurich is getting more dangerous,' Newman observed.

'That's why we're going to take drastic action, to move on to the offensive. Today.'

'Tell me, first, about this chateau you traced Tina Langley to,' Tweed asked Christopher.

'Isn't this a public place for us to talk?' Newman intervened.

'Yes,' said Tweed. 'Chosen deliberately. We are the only ones here. Everyone else is getting a sunbath out on the Pavillon. Also, my room may be bugged – and we haven't the equipment to check it.' He turned to Christopher. 'That chateau?'

'I'll go over it again, even though I told you on the phone, so Bob is in the picture. Called the Château d'Avignon. A few miles further down the road is the very beautiful Château des Avenières, which is pukka. Run by a nice couple who are renovating it. They advertise it – hand you a brochure if you ask for one. *La Missive du Château!*'

'You said pukka,' Tweed said. 'You mean there's something odd about the Château d'Avignon?'

'Very odd. No one knows who owns the place. Went there for a drink once. The waiters were more like guards. Bad when it came to serving – as though they hadn't been trained for the job. Watched me like a hawk all the time I was there. On the way out I caught one of them noting down the registration number of my car. A mysterious place.'

'And that's where Tina Langley walked inside with her case?' Tweed queried.

'Yes.'

'Monceau and his gang came from France – and you said the chateau is in France.'

'It is. Top of Mount Salève,' Christopher confirmed.

'The great cliff facing Geneva which most people think is in Switzerland?'

'That's it. Eleven hundred metres high. Over three thousand feet.'

'We simply mustn't forget Monceau,' Newman emphasized.

'I'm aware he won't forget me,' Tweed agreed. 'And he's good at disguise. I've warned everyone about that. We're all leaving Zurich,' he announced casually.

'Where for?' Newman wanted to know.

'I've tossed up between Vienna and Geneva. Zurich is a death trap because of its size and complexity.'

'So could be Vienna,' Newman warned. 'Look what nearly happened to Paula.'

'I've thought of that.'

'Geneva could be the same,' Christopher commented. 'Remember my interlude with Tina Langley.'

'So I've decided to get us all out of cities.'

'Where the heck are we going?' Newman asked.

'Somewhere to throw the enemy off balance. We go there openly. Then our opponents will see us. We are checking out of here in one hour. Christopher, I need you to come with us. I'll warn Manders to fly back to Britain immediately. Who knows? We may have the company of three attractive ladies. The three members of The Sisterhood.'

'Where are we going?' persisted Newman.

'To the Château des Avenières on Mount Salève. Book rooms on the phone for all of us, Bob. Except for Butler and Nield. They'll stay at this weird Château d'Avignon. They're good at taking care of themselves.'

His decision startled Newman, even though he was hardened by Tweed's sudden decisions in the past.

* * *

238

In the park opposite a road leading directly from the drive to the Baur au Lac a man in the uniform of a Swiss private soldier waited. His peaked cap was pulled well down over his face and he was wearing contact lenses. Nearby, against a thick hedge, stood a motorcycle.

He was so intent on watching the exit from the hotel he failed to notice there were two other watchers. One, a Swiss pickpocket, sat in his car a few yards up Talstrasse, pretending to study a road map. The third man, Mario Parcelli, was more skilled in his surveillance. He had lifted the bonnet of his parked car and appeared to be having trouble with the engine.

Mario had been positioned by Vitorelli, who had realized Tweed was avoiding him. He wondered why. Could Tweed be on the verge of leaving for a new destination? He might even lead Mario to Tina Langley. Vitorelli had great respect for Tweed and his bloodhound personality.

Several taxis entered the drive to the Baur au Lac at almost the same moment. Tweed and Paula, rearmed with a Browning .32 supplied by Marler, entered the first taxi. Tweed told the driver to wait. In the taxi behind them Newman, carrying a .38 Smith & Wesson, also supplied by Marler, got into the back with Marler. Keeping to Tweed's strict instructions, they waited while Butler and Nield boarded the third taxi. Only then did Tweed's taxi move off, with the other two vehicles close behind him.

It was a deliberately noticeable cavalcade which proceeded from the Baur au Lac. Tweed's audacious plan was for the enemy to see them. As they headed for the Hauptbahnhof Tweed soon saw Mario's grey Fiat following them. He smiled to himself – the plan was working.

What he failed to observe was the soldier on the motorcycle keeping pace behind the Fiat. Nor did he notice for a few minutes the pickpocket trailing after them in a white Renault.

'Anything happening?' whispered Paula.

'A grey Fiat is following us. Also a white Renault, so far as I can tell.'

'We seem to be popular,' she replied. 'Did you expect two of them?'

'No, I didn't. One of them has to belong to The Sisterhood. The second one is anyone's guess. The trouble is I can't see the driver of either vehicle. The sun keeps reflecting off the windscreens. The Sisterhood's organization may be using two cars – in case one of them loses us. Relax.'

'Never felt more relaxed in my life,' she said ironically.

The three taxis pulled up in front of the main rail station one behind the other. Tweed had hardly paid the fare before Newman and Marler were by their sides.

'We're being followed,' Tweed said.

'We know,' Marler replied. 'A grey Fiat and a white Renault. Here they come.'

'Get inside the station. I'll buy the tickets.'

He joined the queue already formed in front of the window. Tucked behind a woman next to Newman, Mario listened carefully. The motorcyclist abandoned his machine at the kerb, joined the queue, was close enough to hear Tweed, who was deliberately speaking in a loud voice.

'Six first-class return tickets to Geneva, please.'

They left the queue and hurried to the platform where an express was waiting for them. Mario got back inside his Fiat, headed for the nearest telephone, which he knew was near Talstrasse. The soldier bought a first-class single for Geneva.

* * * *

240

After settling himself in a first-class coach, Tweed took out a book to read. Paula sat alongside him. Marler sat in a corner seat on the other side of the aisle, diagonally opposite to Tweed. Newman sat facing him as Marler closed his eyes, head back against the rest.

Butler chose a seat at one entrance to the coach while Nield sat at the other end. They had all placed their suitcases on the rack above them to give themselves room for manoeuvre, if an emergency arose.

'Wake me up when we're approaching Geneva,' Tweed asked Paula.

'I'll do that. I'm very alert.'

Looking out of the window two minutes before the train was due to leave she saw a Swiss Army soldier hurrying past. He is obviously afraid of missing the train, she thought. Looking across at Marler she saw his eyes open briefly. He wasn't asleep at all and she knew he wouldn't be before they reached Geneva.

As the express began to glide out of the cavern and into the blazing sunlight she wondered why she felt uneasy. It must be those two cars who were following us, she decided. I wonder who was inside them?

'Mario here,' the Italian said inside the phone booth.

'What is it?' asked Vitorelli from his hotel room.

'Tweed and his whole team have just boarded an express for Geneva. It has probably just left . . .'

'Drive to the airport. Get the helicopter ready for instant departure. I'm driving to the airport now. We might arrive before the train does.'

'I doubt it.'

'Get to the bloody airport.'

Vitorelli put down the phone. He called the concierge, told him he was leaving, perhaps for a few days, that he wanted the room kept for his return. Five minutes later he was driving through Zurich, heading for Kloten.

What was the significance of Geneva? he kept asking himself. Why would Tweed be taking his whole team with him? There had to be some important development which had caused him to leave so suddenly. Something, he suspected, to do with The Sisterhood.

The Englishman, who had been informed by the Swiss pickpocket he had hired as a watcher, called Hassan as soon as he heard what was happening. In the long house in Slovakia Hassan had just reported to the Head of State about the 'accident' which had resulted in the death of Ahmed. His nerves were still tingling from the effort he had put into telling a convincing story.

'Yes?' he snapped into the receiver.

'You know who this is. Tweed has just left Zurich for Geneva. Tina is still at the chateau? Good. Tell her to stay there, that her main target is still Tweed. Also tell Karin Berg and Simone Carnot to go to Geneva immediately. One of them must find Tweed. Kill him immediately. Then kill Christopher Kane. Move, man, move . . .'

Hassan was left holding a phone where the line had gone dead. He swore foully, then began to make phone calls.

Tweed was still asleep when the train stopped at Berne. His companions were all alert and watchful. Nothing happened and the express was still nearly empty. They were the only passengers in their first-class coach.

Few passengers boarded the train at Berne. Marler had opened a window, peered out. He saw nothing unusual about those who had come onto the train at the Swiss capital. Paula watched him as he closed the window. She was still feeling nervous and unsuccessfully tried to work out what was worrying her. At least the train was air-conditioned so they had a respite from the fatiguing heat.

She watched Marler, as the train moved away from Berne, using his mobile phone. Probably reporting their progress to Beck, informing him of their new destination. She also wondered whether the strain was telling on Tweed.

The only reason Tweed was sleeping was that he had been up most of the night, pacing round his room. In his mind he had reviewed a whole kaleidoscope of events. The curious experience in Dorset when they had visited Willie's garden with its weird statuary on islands in the lakes. The contradictory versions Amos and Willie had given him in Zurich as to who had purchased the statuary. The fact that Willie had, at one time, known Tina Langley. The mysterious long house in Slovakia, which was on the way to the East.

Christopher Kane had politely declined Tweed's offer to go by train with them to Geneva. He had driven to Zurich in his Porsche, and packing and paying his bill in five minutes, he had driven out of Zurich.

Once a racing driver, Christopher was confident he could beat any express – which had several stops en route – to Cornavin, Geneva's main rail station. As he sped along the motorway, he tried to work out how he could uncover who owned the Château d'Avignon.

No good approaching one of his banker friends – they had mouths like steel traps. He needed someone who knew about property. Then he remembered a friend he had done a favour for and who happened to be a top-class estate agent. He might be the key to unlock the mystery.

He was also keeping an eye on his rear-view mirror. It seemed unlikely he was being followed, but he had grasped from Tweed the octopus-like spread of The Sisterhood. Knowing what he was doing, he began to talk to himself, his lips moving without any sound emerging.

'One blonde, the Swede, Karin Berg. One red-head, Simone Carnot. One auburn-haired lovely – who called herself Lisa Vane, but whose real name is Tina Langley. Well, poppet, I'll know you if we meet again. Come to that, I'll recognize Simone Carnot equally well. The Sisterhood is coming out of its murderous shell.'

Then he saw a blonde coming up behind him at the wheel of a Ferrari. The trouble was she had long flowing hair. As she passed him she made a wave with her hand, a 'Come on, Buster, catch me if you can,' gesture. He let her go. He was determined to beat the express to Cornavin.

'Wake up, we're close to Geneva,' said Paula, giving Tweed a gentle nudge.

'I am awake. Have been for the last half-hour.'

'Then you're a fake. I feel safer now we've left Zurich behind.'

'Nowhere is safe. Don't forget two cars followed us to the main station. Who knows who might be aboard this express.'

'You're trying to make me nervous,' she grumbled.

'I'm trying to make sure you're as on the alert here as you were back in Zurich – or in Vienna, for that matter. We cannot relax anywhere until we have destroyed the enemy – The Sisterhood.'

The express moved into Cornavin station, the automatic doors were opened. Passengers began to alight. One of the first to leave from the front coach was the uniformed soldier. Lifting his pack onto his shoulder, he moved across to the opposite platform, as though waiting for another train.

Marler was first off the train. On the platform he scanned its very long stretch, saw only a handful of passengers trudging away, a Swiss Army soldier waiting on the opposite platform. Paula lowered herself down the long drop, like Marler carrying her case in her left hand. She kept her right hand free in case she had to use her Browning.

Tweed joined them, followed by Newman, Butler and Nield. As he walked towards the exit his team gathered in front, behind and alongside him. He grunted before he made the remark.

'Stop crowding me. I'm not the King of Siam. Or Thailand, as it is these days, and it hasn't got a king.'

'Just for once leave it to us,' Paula reprimanded him. 'You never know when there could be danger – even on this platform.'

'You phoned ahead from the hotel for hired cars?' Tweed asked Newman.

'They will be waiting for us. Marler will deal with the paperwork – that's why he's now going ahead of us.'

Marler walked briskly, glanced at the soldier on the other platform. You saw them all over the place – soldiers returning from manoeuvres, or setting out to take part in them. They had hired two cars and he had the necessary papers inside his pocket.

'This must be the longest station platform in the world,' Tweed commented.

They were approaching the point where the soldier waited and Butler dropped back a few paces behind Tweed, also carrying his case in his left hand. They were all right-handed. As soon as they had left the platform the soldier moved. He followed them at a discreet distance, then paused when he saw them waiting for a moment at the car-hire office.

The moment they moved off he ran to the office, produced his own papers, asked for the Citroën he had hired by phone. Before leaving Zurich he had also called another firm and hired a car to be waiting for him at the airport, not knowing which form of transport might be used.

He was at the wheel of the Citroën, the engine started, when Tweed's two cars left the station.

Prior to entering one of the cars in the front passenger seat, Tweed had been startled to see Christopher Kane, hands on hips, standing by a red Porsche. He came forward with a grin.

'Even Swiss trains are slow, you know. I've driven here from Zurich while your lot was tanking up in the dining car.'

'Not one drink has passed our lips,' Tweed informed him. 'I want to get away from Geneva quickly. We're heading for the Château d'Avignon. Maybe you'll be able to keep up with us . . .'

Paula drove a cream Renault with Tweed next to her. The rear seats were occupied by Newman and Marler. In the blue Ford behind them Butler had the wheel with Nield alongside him. Christopher's Porsche started by following Butler.

Earlier, back in Zurich, Paula had studied a map of the area, and Christopher had marked the position of the chateau just before he dashed off to his Porsche. She had a clear picture of the map in her head. Passing through the checkpoint for Customs and Passport Control into France, she was soon speeding up the lower slopes of Mount Salève.

As she climbed higher Geneva began to spread out below them and they had a glimpse of the famous sixty-foot-high fountain in the lake which is Geneva's trademark. Moving fast, she went on climbing, climbing. Suddenly she was overtaken by the red Porsche. Christopher gave a wave of his hand. She read the wave as a message, 'Come on, girl, catch me if you can.'

'Chris really slams his foot down,' Tweed commented.

'He does have a Porsche.'

'So what? Can't we go any faster? We're crawling.'

Paula stared briefly at Tweed in amazement. She had never known him to make such a statement. His blue-grey eyes glanced back at hers. He appeared to be enjoying a great surge of energy, and then she understood. They were on the move, taking action, performing a manoeuvre which might well totally confuse and alarm the enemy. Imbued with his sense of purpose, she pressed her foot down.

There was no other traffic on the road and the intense heat they had experienced on getting out of the air-conditioned train had been left behind as they moved into a higher elevation. Soon, she saw Christopher's Porsche ahead of them. Choosing a straight stretch, she overtook him, waved her hand.

'Heavens above!' Christopher said to himself. 'She's going like a rocket.'

He made no attempt to pass her, contenting himself with keeping her in sight as the spiralling road climbed ever higher. Behind Christopher, Butler, driving his Ford, had raised his thick eyebrows and maintained an even distance behind the Porsche.

'I don't suppose we have company?' Nield queried. 'There's a blue Citroën which joined us in Geneva and it's still a little way behind us. Can't see the driver.'

'Let's see if he's still with us when we reach the Château d'Avignon,' Butler suggested. Mustn't forget that's where we have rooms booked. The others are going on to the Château des Avenières. Christopher is going to flag us down when we are close to it.'

23

The Butterfly was appalled when Hassan ordered her over the phone to remain at the Château d'Avignon. Tina Langley never liked to stay in one place for long – partly due to her volatile temperament and partly because she felt it was unsafe not to keep moving.

'I want to go back to Switzerland,' she protested.

'What you want is irrelevant,' Hassan had snapped. 'What is relevant is that you wipe off the face of the earth Christopher Kane and Tweed. Do it any way you can. No more stage-setting – kill them on the street if you can. A Luger with ammunition is on the way to you by courier. In a gift-wrapped Cartier box.'

'I don't like it here.'

'But you do like the prospect of earning another one hundred thousand dollars in cash. Maybe two hundred if you manage to get them both.'

'They both know me. At least, Kane does . . .'

'Why should Tweed know you? I have other calls to make.'

'A man in the street in Geneva was watching me – he looked at a photo in his hand, then tried to follow me.' Her voice lifted, had a tone of domineering confidence. 'But I was too smart for him – I lured him onto a train going to Zurich and I was still on the platform when the train departed.'

'Then be smart is what I've told you to do.'

The line went dead while she was still holding the receiver. She heard a click. She froze. Someone had been listening in. She didn't like the Château d'Avignon – the staff were peculiar, the whole atmosphere of the place was peculiar. She simply couldn't put her finger on what was wrong.

When worried she always sat down in front of a dressing table when she could. In her room she did that now. The top was littered with every type of cosmetic to make a woman look her most attractive. She began to apply lipstick.

'You are catching the first flight from Schwechat to Zurich,' Hassan told Karin Berg in his office in the long house. 'I have booked your return ticket, Business Class.'

'I don't want to go back to Zurich.'

'From Zurich you will catch a connecting flight to Geneva. I have booked a room for you at the Hôtel des Bergues. You have two targets. Christopher Kane and Tweed.'

'You're bloody crazy. Tweed knows me well.'

'Shut your arrogant trap. There's two hundred thousand dollars in this for you. Again, in cash. You've always been paid promptly before,' Hassan raved on. 'Don't you want the money? The fact that you know Tweed is a huge advantage.'

'Tweed suspects me.'

'How does he suspect you? Tell me that.'

'Because I took him to the Ermitage. Monceau told me when the attack would take place. I went to the powder room just before they did attack. Tweed is no fool.'

'Can he prove anything?'

'I suppose not . . .'

'Can he be sure you were involved?'

'I suppose not.'

Berg was weighing up the odds. Money meant everything to her. No, they couldn't be sure she was involved, she decided. Hassan was obviously desperate to eliminate both men.

'My fee will be three hundred thousand dollars.'

'Three hundred thousand! That's absurd.'

'Forget it, then.' She stood up. 'I'm flying back to Sweden. If anything happens to me my lawyer in Stockholm has a document he will send to the newspapers and the police.' She gave her quirky smile. 'You could call it my insurance policy.'

'For both men?' Hassan asked after a long pause.

'Yes. Two hundred thousand if I only get one of them. Where are they?'

'They took the train to Geneva today. I had a man on a motorcycle watching Cornavin station in Geneva. He followed them to the French border but was stopped for questioning by the French Customs. He thinks they were heading for Mount Salève.'

'Big help. When do I leave?'

'Now. I told you to keep a case packed.'

'Which I did, to go back to Sweden.'

'You'll be a rich woman. Here are the tickets in this envelope. And your hotel reservation.'

When the car had left, taking her to the airport, Hassan called Simone Carnot at her apartment. He put the same proposition to her. To his surprise she didn't argue, but she had one objection.

'So long as Tweed or the police haven't linked me to the Dumont episode,' she said cold-bloodedly.

'Has anyone questioned you about it?'

'No!'

'Then here are your instructions. You're flying to Geneva . . .'

When he put down the phone Hassan was weary and worried. He was throwing the entire Sisterhood into this operation. No one would be left to deal with the surviving members of the *Institut*.

Hassan had just finished a glass of brandy when the phone rang again. Cursing, he picked it up. He badly needed some sleep. It was the Englishman.

'Have you carried out my instructions?'

'Yes. All three women are on their way to Geneva. How they are going to trace their targets I don't know.'

'I personally chose them because they are resourceful.'

'But it leaves no one to deal with the other members of the *Institut* who are still alive.'

'It doesn't matter. Once those two men are underground we have dealt with the most dangerous ones. And time is running out.'

'You have been in touch with—'

'Yes. He agrees with me.'

Once more the Englishman slammed down the phone. Hassan felt relieved. He had been going to ask whether his caller had been in touch with the Head of State. Obviously he had, so Hassan felt covered. And what was a few hundred thousand dollars? The Head of State had billions under his control.

When the phone rang again Hassan, sprawled out on a couch, wanted to throw it out of the window over the cliff. With a sigh he got up, answered the call.

'Monceau here. I've decided it should be worth something to you when I kill Tweed.'

Hassan immediately named a large sum. The Frenchman accepted the deal immediately. He would need extra money to recruit a fresh gang in France.

'You can really do the job? You know where he is? Where are you?'

'Zurich,' Monceau lied.

'Tweed is in Geneva. Last reported heading for France via Mount Salève.'

'Really? I can get there fast.'

'Wait a minute.'

'I haven't got a minute.'

Hassan had had an idea. If any of The Sisterhood were arrested he was sure they would try to make an arrangement to provide information in return for lenient treatment. This had worried him when the Englishman had given him the original order – but the Englishman was not a man to argue with.

'Monceau, there are three women I'm concerned about. But only if one of them is arrested. It would be best if they were eliminated if that happened. I'm not sure how you could do it once they were in police custody.'

'A large enough bomb left in a car parked outside the police station where they were held. Or where one of them was held.'

'I'll give you names, descriptions and where they are staying.'

'I have two minutes. Give me the details. I'm on a mobile phone.'

Christopher's Porsche cruised past Paula's Renault as they reached the summit. He waved for the following cars to follow him and parked with a few other cars at the viewing point. Getting out of his car he walked with long strides to Tweed's car which had also parked, followed by Butler and Nield's vehicle.

'The panorama from here is rather splendid. As you can see all Geneva is spread out three thousand feet below us.'

'Tweed's not leaving this car,' Newman said grimly.

'Doesn't have to. You can see the view from the window.'

'We've seen it,' Newman said impatiently.

'Humour Christopher,' Tweed said as the tall man walked nearer to the view. 'He may have given us invaluable information concerning this Château d'Avignon. I've had a feeling for some time that Geneva is a key city.'

'Why would it be?'

'Because, as you've just seen, it is so very close to France. Anyone wishing to escape – or avoid – Beck's eagle eye can be in another country, where he has no jurisdiction, within a few minutes.'

Marler had left the car as soon as it stopped. With his jacket hanging loosely, so he could reach his Walther quickly, he strolled around the small plateau. He was checking on everyone who had stopped to admire the view.

At the edge of the plateau Geneva seemed far away. Marler could pick out individual streets of a city he knew well and to the east the famous fountain was hurling its enormous jet towards the cloudless sky. It was late afternoon and in the clear light he could see every detail of the ancient city, spread out like a map.

Nield had left his car, walked to the roadside at the point where cars entered the viewing plateau. He looked back. The road they had come up quickly turned a sharp bend and went out of sight. He walked back to the car.

'Restless?' enquired Butler.

'Just checking. No sign of that blue Citroën – although I couldn't see far because the road bends where it starts to go downhill.'

'Probably turned off further down. Looks as though we're off again.'

Christopher led the way in his Porsche. Paula followed and Butler's car brought up the rear. Driving along the summit of Salève the character of the countryside was very different. Whereas before, the ascending road had provided glimpses of the lake and distant mountains they were now hemmed in on both sides by dense forest, a mix of pines and firs like a palisade. Tweed was staring out of the window with great concentration.

'Something interests you?' Paula enquired.

'The Château d'Avignon intrigues me. There could be trouble up here. I'm studying the terrain.'

'That chopper is somewhere above us,' she observed. 'I first heard it when we were leaving Cornavin station. I thought it was a traffic helicopter. Now I'm not so sure.'

'The world is full of helicopters,' Tweed said offhandedly, more interested in the forest.

With Mario at the controls of the chopper, Vitorelli sat beside him, gazing through his field glasses down at the convoy of cars passing through the forest of Salève.

Before they had taken off from Kloten Mario had phoned the Hauptbahnhof to find out the arrival time of the express to Geneva. Flying across country as direct as possible, they had arrived at Cointrin Airport, Geneva, in time to refuel.

They had then timed their fresh take-off to coincide with the express pulling in to Geneva's rail station.

Through his glasses Vitorelli had seen Tweed and the others entering the hired cars. They tried to keep a discreet distance but had to keep the cars in sight. Which was why Paula had become aware of the chopper's presence.

'It's odd,' Vitorelli commented, 'but that blue Citroën driven by a Swiss soldier appears to be following them. I wonder who he could be?'

'Probably Tweed's rearguard disguised as a soldier. That would be clever.'

'I suppose you could be right,' Vitorelli replied.

The forest was even more dense as they drove along the well-made road. Here and there were gaps to their left. Through them they caught brief views of a vast landscape receding into the distance.

'France is a lovely country,' Tweed commented. 'Incidentally, I took the precaution of phoning Loriot in Paris. He was very interested when I mentioned the name Monceau. He may be flying down to see us. He could provide massive back-up.'

'Exactly why are we coming to this isolated part of the world?' Newman asked.

'As you will have realized, I advertised our departure. Did everything except take out a TV ad. I want to draw the enemy out of dangerous places like complex cities, as I believe I mentioned earlier. Out here we have to see them coming. It is a much more dangerous battleground – for the enemy. We have to destroy our opponents quickly. I sense we have very little time left.'

'That chopper is still high up but overhead,' Paula commented.

'Good. That might mean . . .'

He never finished his sentence as Christopher slowed

to a crawl. Out of his open window he waved his hand up and down. Paula made the same signal to Butler and Nield behind them.

'We must be close to the Château d'Avignon,' she said.

A minute later they crept past the entrance to a chateau with a fantastic number of turrets. An ugly building, it looked old and decrepit with a creeper covering most of the stonework, a creeper which reminded Paula of a green octopus extending its strangling tentacles. By the open gates she saw a uniformed guard. In her rear-view mirror she saw Butler and Nield's car turn in, then stop.

'I wonder what sort of a reception they will get there,' she mused. 'Eerie-looking place.'

24

A few miles further on Christopher waved his hand again out of his window. Paula slowed down and turned slowly off the road to her left, following the Porsche. At the Château des Avenières there were no gates and the building was standing a short distance back from the road. Paula let out a whistle as she parked.

'What a difference. It's quite beautiful. My idea of what a French chateau should look like at its best.'

Tweed got out, holding his case, while Christopher locked his Porsche. There was no uniformed guard here. Instead, as Tweed walked up the steps a handsome woman came out of the open door.

'Mr Tweed?' she said in perfect English. 'Welcome to the Château des Avenières. We are always pleased to welcome new visitors. A porter will take your case.'

256

She greeted Paula, Newman and Marler with the same warmth and ushered them inside. Tweed immediately felt at home as he gazed round at the splendid decor. It was rich and tasteful without being overdone. Porters had relieved them of their cases when she made a suggestion.

'I know you must be travel weary after your long journey from Zurich. May we offer you a glass of champagne on the terrace?'

'Yes, please,' called out Christopher, who had just arrived.

They crossed a large room which was also furnished with quiet luxury. Beyond it large doors were open to a long wide terrace where several couples sat having a drink at tables. Tweed chose a large table at the edge of the terrace because it was on its own. Sitting down, after pulling out a chair for Paula, he gazed at the view.

'Never seen anything like it,' he said.

Below was an even larger terrace with an oval swimming pool. Beyond that the ground fell away to fields sloping even further down. But it was the distant view which fascinated him. In the luminous evening light was a series of ranges of hills, one behind the other. To his right, a long way off, a blue sheet glittered in the setting sun. Christopher pointed to it.

'That's Lake Annecy. You can just see part of the old town.'

'It's heaven,' said Tweed. 'I could spend a holiday here.'

Paula gazed at him as he sipped his champagne. She had never before heard Tweed refer with longing to a holiday. The place had a magic atmosphere. Like something out of a Turner painting. The couples at other tables were chatting quietly.

'This is peace,' Tweed decided.

'I wonder how Nield and Butler are getting on,' Paula remarked.

Arriving at the Château d'Avignon was rather a different experience. Butler, compelled by Tweed to wear a well-cut linen suit, was stopped by the uniformed guard.

'You can't come in here without an advance reservation.'

The guard was six foot tall, heavily built, and his English accent reminded Butler of the less well-patronized part of the East End of London. He wore a leather belt and from it dangled a holster with the butt of a revolver protruding.

'Really?' Butler paused, staring at the guard. 'Is that how they train you to greet a guest who *has* a reservation?'

'Names?'

'Don't you mean,' Nield intervened, '"Could I please have your names?"'

'If you have reservations it's OK.'

'What is this?' Nield continued. 'A hotel or San Quentin? Why do you need that gun? Overrun with rabbits round here, are we?'

'It's very lonely up here,' the guard informed him.

'I had noticed that,' Butler told him. 'Nield and Butler. Rooms reserved from Zurich. Make with the feet. Go inside and check. We'll come with you.'

'And you can carry our bags,' Nield snapped.

Reluctantly, the guard carried a bag in each of his prizefighter's hands. They reached the reception desk. Behind it a weasel-faced man looked up suspiciously.

'Yes, Ben.'

'Big Ben,' Butler said in a loud voice.

'Nield and Butler. Say they have reservations. From Zurich.'

'They do, Ben.' Weasel became oily, smirking as he pushed forward the register for them to fill in. 'Welcome to the best hotel in France,' he went on.

'Heaven help France, then,' Butler snapped.

He scribbled his name illegibly together with all the other details required. Nield followed suit, staring at Weasel as he scrawled, then shoved the register back across the counter.

Weasel had a French accent despite his good English. He took keys from a board behind him, smirked again. Nield had an idea it was his way of being pleasant.

Both had rooms overlooking the drive and the road they had come along. Neither thought it worthwhile to ask for rooms overlooking the view at the back. After a wash they met in the gloomy corridor and went down in search of food.

There were few people in the restaurant, which did have a panoramic view. The head waiter, who looked down his nose at them as though he was doing them a favour to let them in, escorted them to a table behind a pillar. Butler did not sit down.

'We'll have that table over there.'

'I fear it is reserved.'

'Of course it is. Reserved for us.'

Butler, with Nield following, marched over to the table with a view, sat down. The head waiter rushed after them. He was not pleased.

'The people who reserved this table will be upset.'

'From Birmingham, aren't you?' Butler replied. 'Bring us the wine list, two bottles of mineral water. Sparkling – and we'd appreciate some quick service.'

'Our service is always quick. Sir.'

'Prove it.'

259

When the waiter had gone Butler glanced round the almost empty restaurant. Most of the guests appeared to be French. At one corner table sat a very attractive woman with auburn hair. She caught his glance, held his eye, then looked away. She began to slow down drinking her coffee. It struck her the sturdily built man could be a wealthy industrialist.

'Don't look now,' Butler whispered to Nield. 'The siren at the corner window table on the far side of the room. We've found Tina Langley.'

'I know,' Nield agreed. 'I studied her photo – as we all did. Maybe we have come to the right place.

The driver behind the wheel of the blue Citroën had caught up with the convoy just in time to see Butler and Nield turn into the Château d'Avignon. He drove on until he saw the car containing Tweed turn in later to the Château des Avenières. Slowing down, he cruised past, saw Tweed being greeted on the steps by his hostess.

He drove a little further, then executed a U-turn. Driving back at a leisurely pace, he checked his rear-view mirror to make sure no traffic was coming behind him. The road was empty. He swung his wheel over to the right, drove slowly up a track deep into the forest.

He parked the car in a deserted glade, got out. Listening for several minutes he heard nothing, not even birdsong. It took him only a few minutes to erect a tent. Taking a pack containing rations, the soldier in Swiss Army uniform began to eat.

After finishing their dinner – the excellence of the food had surprised them – Butler suggested Nield should come to his room. It was several doors from Nield's bedroom on the first floor.

'I've got something to show you. You were a cat burglar once, weren't you?'

'I was not – and you know it.'

'You're going to be one now.'

Butler unlocked his door, looked up and down the empty corridor, switched the key to the inside of the lock, walked in without switching on the light. Puzzled, Nield followed him. Butler relocked the door, closed a sliding bolt.

'The window,' Butler whispered. 'The moon gives us enough light. Follow me. There's no furniture in the way. You have got a gun, I hope.'

'Of course.'

Butler had left the curtain over the window pulled back and the moon illuminated the interior. As his eyes accustomed themselves to the dark Nield saw it was a very spacious room with a king-size bed. Even larger than his own room.

'Something funny about this place,' Butler whispered.

'I had already got that impression.'

Reaching the mullioned window, Butler opened the casement very quietly, peered out. No sign of the guard. The gates were shut. Grasping Nield by the arm, Butler guided him to look out. Butler bent down, pulled two pairs of strong gloves from under the curtain draped to the floor where he had concealed them. He handed one pair to Nield, who put them on, still mystified by what his partner was doing.

'It was daylight when I looked out,' Butler whispered. 'You know I don't miss much.'

'On occasion.'

'This room is under one of the large turrets at the front we saw when we arrived. Look what's under this.'

261

Leaning out, Butler used his gloved hand to pull a piece of the creeper away from the wall. By his side Nield saw a very thick cable ascending upwards towards the turret. He knew enough about communications to recognize it as a section of fibre-optic cable.

'What have they got above us?' whispered Butler.

'Could be a highly sophisticated communications centre. Why would a hotel need that?'

'I'm climbing up there to see. I've tested the creeper. It is as thick and strong as a rope. We'll have to leave our shoes behind. I can loan you an extra pair of socks to give extra grip . . .'

Nield found that although he had smaller feet the extra pair fitted well over the socks he was already wearing. Checking to make sure his Walther was secure inside his hip holster, he straddled the window ledge.

Butler was already hauling himself up the creeper rapidly, but exercising due care. Before he climbed higher he tested the strength of the creeper above him. Nield looked down, saw there was no sign of life below, began his own climb.

At the training mansion in Surrey they had practised scaling the wall of the large house using ropes. This seemed no different – except if Big Ben emerged and looked up Nield had no doubt he woud use them for target practice. The large man would enjoy that.

When Butler reached the second storey he edged his way round a darkened window, then continued his ascent. The fact that they were wearing socks helped them to keep a good grip. Arriving at the second storey Butler again had to edge his way round another darkened window. He had to perform the same manoeuvre at the third storey. Then, close to the turret which had a light shining from a window, he felt Nield tugging gently at his ankle. He froze, looked down.

Big Ben had appeared, was patrolling the drive below.

Butler pressed himself slowly closer to the wall, then stayed motionless. Below him Nield did not dare reach for his Walther. The slightest movement could attract Big Ben's attention. He watched as the guard lumbered unsteadily towards the gate and Nield realized he was drunk. This was confirmed when Ben stopped, raised a wine bottle he had held by his side, drank from it.

Arriving at the gate, he seemed to check that it was locked. The tricky part would be when he returned to the entrance – so he could easily glance upwards. The fact that he was drunk wouldn't help, Nield was thinking. He had no doubt there were other armed guards Ben would alert.

Staggering, the big man left the gate, made his shambling way back to the entrance. Nield clearly heard the door shut and let out a sigh of relief. He looked up at Butler, gave him a thumbs-up sign. Butler resumed his climb.

He waited by the side of the turret's open window and Nield joined him, choosing the other side. The reason the window was open, Nield assumed, was the heat, which was still uncomfortable even at this altitude. The earth was giving up the heat it had absorbed during the day. Nield peered round the edge of the window.

The cable ran inside the illuminated room which had six sides. He heard a whirring sound, glanced up in time to see an aerial elevating automatically. The aerial, a complicated affair with a spider's web of wires, had emerged from the summit of the peaked turret.

Inside the room Weasel sat in front of a large transmitter with his back to the window. He wore earphones and spoke into a microphone in English.

263

'Two possible intruders. Harry Butler and Pete Nield. A reservation for each was received from Hotel Baur au Lac, Zurich. Please confirm what action, if any, should be taken. Yes, they could easily disappear for ever out here. You will confirm after checking identities? I await your confirmation, Dove . . .'

Nield signalled Butler to commence his descent. If anything, they took even more care going down than they had coming up. He kept looking up now, praying Weasel would not feel the need for fresh air and peer out of the window. Both men also had to fight the impulse to return to the safety of Butler's room as swiftly as possible. They were close to the open window when a piece of creeper Butler was holding on to came loose.

Nield watched, his pulse rate rising. Coolly, Butler let go of the dangling creeper, grasped another section. He then tucked the section which had broken loose back inside the rest of the creeper. He wanted no evidence left that someone had climbed up to the turret.

Looking up just before he heaved himself inside his room, the turret reminded him of an evil witch with a hat. Nield joined him, relief flooding through him as his feet felt the firm floor under him. Butler closed the window, pulled the curtains across it, felt his way across the room and switched on the light.

Neither man spoke until they had washed the sweat off their hands, foreheads and necks. Leaving the bathroom, Butler opened a bottle of champagne he had brought up to the bedroom.

'Bit of a snarler, that,' he observed.

'The things we do for England,' Nield replied. 'This place is much more than a hotel. We have to let Tweed know as soon as possible about that communications room.'

'Well, we can't tonight. The gate is locked. If we asked to be let out we'd arouse more suspicion. So, drink up. Cheers!'

Nield remained worried. Butler, on the contrary, accepted they would have to wait. The difference in attitudes highlighted the difference in the temperaments of the two men.

Hundreds of miles away to the east an identical advanced aerial had been elevated above the long house in Slovakia. It was Hassan who had received the information the Weasel had transmitted.

The communication had worried him. The Château d'Avignon was one of the three keys to passing information across Europe and then on to the Head of State even further east. Sitting in his office he had the curtains closed – it was a very black night outside and clouds obscured even a glimpse of the moon.

He was still pondering the communication he had received when the phone rang. In a bad mood, he picked up the receiver.

'Who is this?'

'You know who it is from my voice,' the Englishman replied.

'I am glad you have called. I have just heard from the Château they have two intruders.'

'The exact wording of the message?'

'"Two possible intruders."'

'"Possible"! They sound absurdly nervous at the Château. You know they take ordinary guests to make the place look like a normal hotel.'

'That is true . . .'

'You sound absurdly nervous yourself. Is there any news of the killing of Tweed or Kane? Preferably of both.'

'No, not so far.'

'Wake up, for God's sake. That is the top priority. The Sisterhood should have located their targets by now. Time is getting very short!'

The phone went dead. The autocratic Englishman had again slammed down the phone on him. Hassan sat and simmered with frustration.

Tina Langley was frustrated. The sturdily built man whose eye she had caught had left the restaurant with his male companion. She knew she had caught his eye – and Butler had reacted so quickly she didn't realize he had recognized her. From the way he had been dressed and the meal they had ordered she felt sure she smelt money. Normally her instincts in this direction were right.

She had decided to have coffee in the lounge. At the doorway she looked around. No sign of him. A French couple who had noticed she was on her own looked up. The fashionably dressed woman spoke in English.

'Excuse me, but are you on your own? Such a pity. I have been in that position myself.'

'But not any more,' her husband said with a smile as he clasped her hand. 'We would be happy for you to join us. We like Britain. I spent two years in London.'

'That is very kind of you. I am feeling a little lonely.'

She sat down in the chair the Frenchman pulled out for her. Her main motive in accepting the invitation was she had seen the size of the diamond engagement ring on the wife's finger next to her wedding ring. The Frenchman was good-looking, in his forties, was wearing an Armani suit. There was certainly money here.

The fact that she thought she should succeed in luring this married man away from his wife bothered her not at all. Men liked variety. She might even be able to extract blackmail after she had compromised him. They began conversing after coffee had been served.

'I am Louis Marin,' the man introduced himself. 'This is my wife, Yvette.'

'I'm Lisa Vane. This is very kind of you. Do you often stay at this hotel?'

'Do you?' Marin had lowered his voice. 'It is our first visit.'

'It's my first time here too,' she answered with a seductive smile.

'You know the owners?' asked Yvette.

'No. I don't know anyone here.'

'We made a mistake,' Yvette explained. 'The staff here are not what one expects at a five-star hotel. Please excuse my saying this, but some are English and not pleasant types. We know because we stayed at some wonderful hotels in Britain.'

'How did you make a mistake?' enquired Tina, who was curious.

'We got the wrong place. Since arriving we have phoned friends in Paris. They say we should have stayed at the Château des Avenières, a real five-star hotel.'

'It is a mile or two further along the road,' interjected her husband, who was having difficulty taking his eyes off Tina's crossed legs. She tapped him on his knee and he started drinking more coffee.

'When you go out of the drive here,' Yvette continued, 'you turn left. Our friends said the Château des Avenières has a better view, has superb food, wonderful service. It is run by a very pleasant couple, apparently, on extremely professional lines.'

'Are you thinking of moving, then?'

Tina tried to catch Louis Marin's eye but he was

267

carefully looking across the room. Scared stiff of his wife, thought Tina contemptuously. If I got him on his own I bet he'd be much more uninhibited. Particularly in a bedroom.

She chatted to them for a while, then pretended to suppress a yawn. She glanced at her watch.

'It has been so nice talking to you both.' She made a point of smiling at Yvette. 'I hope you'll excuse me but I have had a long day . . .'

In her room she became very busy. The members of The Sisterhood were normally provided with all the data they needed to find their target. But they were also trained to locate the target. Tina had purchased a guidebook in Geneva which also gave the details of top hotels in the city. She began calling each hotel. Her technique was always the same.

'A serious emergency has arisen in London. Mr Tweed will want to know about it immediately. It's a crisis situation . . .'

In each case she was informed that no one of that name was staying at the hotel. She persisted. She rang every leading hotel in the city. Every time she drew a blank. No one of that name was staying at the hotel she phoned.

She sat in front of her dressing table mirror, brushed her auburn hair, applied various cosmetics. In the past this had often given her an idea. In any case, she might just meet Louis Marin alone in the corridor. Then she remembered their conversation.

Reaching for the directory with hotel numbers in France she pressed buttons for the Château des Avenières. Again she gave the same story. Her lips tightened as the night porter replied, 'I think he is still in the lounge. I will get him . . . Hello! Hello . . .!'

The connection had been broken. Perched on her bed, Tina was smiling unpleasantly. A million-to-one shot had come off. Tweed, her target, was within a few miles of her. Hassan had provided a very detailed description of Mr Tweed.

25

Marler would have been interested. The soldier, after eating his meal outside his tent, was practising with his Armalite rifle. Equipped with a telescopic sight, he aimed the weapon at a bird sitting motionless high up in a tree. In the crosshairs the bird came up so close he could see its eyes. The weapon was unloaded but as he pressed the trigger it made a small click. The bird took off.

The soldier smiled and continued taking aim at different 'targets'. A leaf near the top of a tall tree, a withered cone attached to a pine, a very small rock he could see by a shaft of moonlight a distance away.

When he was satisfied that he had not lost his skill, he walked back along the track, turned left and began to route march along the deserted road. Since it would be difficult to conceal the Armalite he had hidden it under a pile of branches.

He continued his route march. One, two, three, four . . . one, two, three, four . . . He had taken off his jacket to consume his rations, but now the chill of night had descended on the silent forest and he was wearing the jacket for warmth.

He was close to the entrance to the Château des Avenières when he heard a car coming in the opposite direction. Before he could react the car's headlights came round a bend and illuminated him. He had stopped route marching and was strolling along as though taking a walk in the fresh night air.

Well after the rest of the team had retired to their rooms at the Château des Avenières, Marler, who was an owl and needed only four hours' sleep, had taken a decision. He would drive back to the Château d'Avignon in the hope that he could make contact with Butler and Nield.

He was driving at a moderate pace, studying the terrain, when he turned a bend and in his headlights saw a uniformed soldier walking along the opposite side of the road towards him. He drove slowly past, trying to recall where he had seen a soldier earlier.

Then he remembered. As they had walked down the long station platform after arriving at Geneva a soldier with a pack had been waiting on the opposite platform. It was probably a coincidence, but Marler recalled that Tweed didn't believe in coincidences. He was driving on slowly when he took a sudden decision. In his rear-view mirror the shadow of the soldier had disappeared round the bend.

Marler extracted the Walther from his hip holster, laid it on the seat beside him. He executed a perfect U-turn, managing it the first time. Slowly, he began driving back the way he had come.

'I think I'll have a word with you, mate,' he said to himself.

The language problem didn't worry Marler. He spoke French fluently enough to pass as a Frenchman. In fact, he had once had to do so. He drove with one hand as he turned round the bend, his right hand gripping the Walther by his side. Beyond the bend was a straight stretch.

Marler turned his headlights full on. The road was empty. No sign of the lone soldier. Was that peculiar?

Then he recalled that one British Army technique to test a man's ability to survive on his own was to drop him off at some isolated location and see if he could find his way to an agreed destination. Perhaps the Swiss Army used a similar method – in this case marooning him in France.

Marler had noticed there were a number of tracks leading into the depths of the forest. The soldier had probably used one of these to cut across country. He performed a fresh U-turn, headed for his original objective.

He was driving very slowly, with his lights dimmed, when he reached the entrance to the Château d'Avignon. The tall wooden gates were closed, barring entry to the drive. Odd, he thought. Since there was no possibility of contacting Butler and Nield he drove back the way he had come, turning into the open drive to des Avenières.

A short distance from the bend in the road the soldier had darted up one of the tracks leading into the forest. He had then settled down to wait behind the trunk of a huge tree. He heard and saw the car return, shortly afterwards driving back along the original route it had been taking.

He was puzzled. Were people in the car looking for him? It did not seem likely. He continued to wait. He had endless patience. When the car returned later, driving back the way it had come, he thought he knew the explanation. Blinded by the glare of the headlights, he had not been able to see originally who was in the car. Now he thought he had solved the mystery.

Some man had his girlfriend with him. They had just had time to do together what the soldier would have done. But first they had returned to make sure the soldier had not sneaked back to watch their amorous activities. He waited for half an hour before resuming his route march along the road.

When he saw lights he knew he had reached the Château des Avenières, where Tweed was spending the night with his bodyguards. He took time checking the trees which faced the exit from the hotel. He found one large fir near the edge of the road. He began to climb from branch to branch.

Not too high up he found the perfect place. He could straddle a heavy branch, resting his back against the trunk. He had a clear view of the exit from the hotel. He raised both arms as though he was holding the Armalite. From here he could kill Tweed when he emerged from the drive inside a car.

Behind him was thick undergrowth, a jungle of bracken and bushes. It would provide an ideal escape route. If anyone came after him he would with ease ambush them. He climbed down the tree swiftly and agilely. Then he began the walk back to his tent. When he reached it he loaded the Armalite before going to sleep.

Before sunset Vitorelli, from his helicopter, had seen Tweed's convoy turn into the chateau. He had smiled. He gave a fresh order to Mario as he watched Tweed enter the hotel through his field glasses.

'Now we know where he is we can return and land at Geneva's airport. In the morning we'll hire a car and drive up Mount Salève so I can have a word with my friend.'

'Why do we do that?'

'Knowing Tweed, I think he is conducting some devious manoeuvre. His departure from Zurich was so very public. I suspect he may know where Tina Langley is hiding. I'm convinced that his strategy is to lure The Sisterhood into the open.'

'He told you there were several of them.'

'We are one jump ahead of Tweed,' Vitorelli said with a grim smile. 'We know their base is that isolated house in Slovakia.'

'How do we know Tina Langley is not hiding there?'

'Because *you* saw her in Geneva. Then she tricks you by not getting on the train you were aboard. Which means she did not want to leave Geneva. Why? Because it is only a half-hour drive to that chateau in France. Which takes her safely – she hopes – out of Switzerland. And there may be another obvious reason.'

'What is that?' Mario asked as he guided the chopper over the top of Salève and headed for Geneva's airport.

'Tweed is her next target.'

In the lounge at the Château des Avenières Tweed was lingering over coffee with Paula and Newman. Despite the day's exertions his brain was alert as he stirred a fresh cup. Paula asked her question with a note of anxiety.

'What has happened to Marler? He slipped away without saying a word.'

'I wouldn't worry about Marler. He can look after himself. He is checking the surrounding countryside in case we experience a firefight here. I hope so, otherwise our stage-managed departure from Zurich has failed.'

'So again you're using yourself as a target,' Paula snapped.

'Let's say I'm a magnet to attract the iron filings – which are the enemy – to an isolated area where there are unlikely to be innocent casualties.'

They were alone in the lounge so able to converse

without fear of being overheard. Tweed paused as the night porter approached them. The porter stopped to speak quietly.

'Excuse me, Mr Tweed, but I had an odd message over the phone. Someone said there was an emergency in London, then the connection was broken. The caller did not come back. They asked specifically for you.'

'How long ago did this happen?'

'A few minutes ago. I waited to see if the caller would ring back before I came to let you know.'

'Was the caller a man or a woman?'

'A woman, sir. She had a soft voice. I would say she was English.'

'Did you detect the slightest trace of a foreign – that is, a non-English accent?'

'No, sir.'

'Thank you. If she calls back I will take the call.' Tweed waited until the night porter had gone. 'Of course, she won't call back. That was Tina Langley, tracking me in a clever way.'

'How do you know it was Tina?' Newman asked.

'Because,' Tweed said grimly, 'I can always catch just a trace of accent with Karin Berg. Even more so with Simone Carnot.'

'You're a sitting duck,' Paula commented vehemently.

'My plan has worked.' Tweed smiled. 'The Sisterhood is emerging from underground. They are walking into my trap. Paula, we can use their own tactics against them. You can obtain the telephone numbers of the top hotels in Geneva?'

'Yes, I can. I know the names of the leading hotels very well.'

'Then phone the concierge at each hotel. Tell them you have to speak urgently to Karin Berg or Simone

Carnot. That there is a grave emergency in Stockholm, a matter of life and death. With a bit of luck a concierge will let slip the fact that one of them is staying at the hotel you are phoning. Then break the connection.'

'You're turning their own guns on them. And it is a matter of life and death. Look how many members of the *Institut* have died.'

'It may not work,' Tweed warned, 'but it worked for Tina.'

'Then I'll make it work for me. I meant to raise another subject. There was a helicopter overhead when we drove across Mount Salève. I think it was following us.'

'Aboard it, I am sure, would be my old partner in crime, Emilio Vitorelli. He is hoping I will lead him to Tina Langley. He is determined to kill her for causing the death of his fiancée, Gina.'

'Yes, but I've never mentioned that when I was being taken to the base of The Sisterhood, that bizarre house in Slovakia, there was a helicopter in the distance. Perhaps it was a coincidence.'

'You know I don't believe in coincidences.' Tweed thought for a moment. 'I wonder how he located that place? Can you make those phone calls before you go to bed.'

'I'll go to my room and start now.'

'We'll wait here and see if you get lucky . . .'

After enjoying a first-rate dinner with Tweed and the others Christopher Kane had excused himself. He had refused Tweed's offer to join them for coffee in the lounge.

'Must get my beauty sleep,' he said to Paula. 'Otherwise I shall find all the attractive ladies ignoring me.'

'I rather doubt that,' replied Paula, amused.

'Christopher didn't look tired,' she had commented later when they were first settled in the lounge.

'He isn't,' Tweed had told her. 'He's gone off to work. Like me, he finds he can concentrate in the early hours. He'll be working on some theory he's created to counter bacteriological warfare.'

As soon as he reached his bedroom Christopher locked the door and took off his jacket. He then perched himself on the bed, lifted the phone, pressed numbers for a long-distance call. The person he had hoped to contact answered immediately.

'Christopher here. I need a lot of information which only you can give me. So make yourself comfortable, old boy. This is going to be a long session . . .'

He was on the phone for a quarter of an hour. He asked questions. He made suggestions, gave instructions. He emphasized the extreme urgency of the situation. Christopher was very relieved when the person he had called agreed with him. He thanked the person and again stressed the supreme urgency of what he had requested.

Putting down the receiver, he opened a bottle of champagne he had collected from the bar on his way to his room. Then he opened a notebook and began to work on formulae and calculations. As he did so he voiced his thoughts aloud, his lips hardly moving.

'Tweed would give anything to have listened in but I think he'd understand. He knows I'm a loner. And the fate of the Western world could hinge on that conversation . . .'

When Paula had left them to make her phone calls, Tweed became even more alert, if that were possible.

Newman, who had plenty of stamina, relaxed, sensing Tweed had had an idea.

'I'm going to make a couple of phone calls myself.'

'At this hour? Who to?'

'First to Amos Lodge. I'm going to ask him to fly to Geneva first thing in the morning. If he agrees, we can have a car at the airport waiting to bring him here.'

'You said a couple of calls. Who is the other one to?'

'Willie at the Dolder Grand. I'm going to make the same request to him.'

'You never forget Dorset, do you?'

'It would be a great mistake to forget Dorset. Don't forget that Vitorelli told me he had traced a courier carrying a large sum of money to someone in Dorset.'

'So you're certain the money was for Lodge or Willie?'

'I'm not certain of anything yet. If you like, you can wait here while I go up and make the calls. Then I'll come back and let you know how each man reacted . . .'

Newman had lit a cigarette, was drinking more coffee, when Marler strolled into the lounge. He sat down beside Newman and told him about the incident of the Swiss soldier, about the curious fact that the gates outside the Château d'Avignon had been closed for the night.

'I don't like the sound of that Swiss soldier,' Newman responded. 'There was one waiting on the opposite platform when we got off the train from Zurich.'

'It could be a Swiss Army training exercise,' Marler replied, and outlined his theory.

'In France? I don't believe it. If a French patrol car saw him they'd question him immediately, probably put him inside.'

'Exactly. That would make the exercise more

gruelling. Would make him far more alert. I told you how he disappeared into thin air when I went back to look for him.'

'I suppose you could be right. But I don't like the sound of the Château d'Avignon. Butler and Nield could be trapped inside.'

'Have you ever heard of Butler and Nield being trapped by anybody? Look how they handled that experience with the excavator in Austria near the Slovak border. And neither of them were armed – until Nield got hold of the machine-pistol.'

'I suppose you're right. But if they don't turn up in the morning I'm off to march into that chateau.'

'I'll come with you. Has Tweed gone to bed early? Early for him, I mean.'

Newman explained why Tweed had gone to his room. He told Marler about the two men he was phoning, inviting them to the Château des Avenières. Marler frowned.

'What's he up to? He's like a spider attracting all the dangerous – lethal – flies into his web here.'

'Which is exactly what I think he's planning.'

He had just finished speaking when Paula briskly returned to the lounge. She had just sat down when Tweed reappeared. He sat down and Newman poured more coffee from the fresh pot the waiter had recently brought to the table for both of them.

'Ladies first,' Tweed said, then sipped coffee.

'After a lot of phoning it worked. We have both Karin Berg and Simone Carnot on our doorstep, so to speak. Berg is staying at the Hôtel des Bergues overlooking the Rhône. Simone Carnot is at the Richemond. I think you'd better be very careful, Tweed.'

'I'm always careful. Now my bit of news. Paula, after you'd gone I decided to call Amos Lodge and Willie –

inviting both of them to fly to Geneva and then come on here.'

'You don't forget Dorset, do you?'

'Which is what Bob said. No, I don't. Amos said he had a lot to attend to but he would catch a mid-afternoon flight to Geneva. Willie was apologetic, said he couldn't make it – he has a very big deal he hopes to conclude, that a fortune might be involved.'

'Two very different reactions,' Paula observed.

'Which I find very significant.'

He didn't explain what he had found significant.

26

In her room at the Château d'Avignon Tina Langley sat in front of her dressing table, gazing at herself in the mirrors, attending to her make-up. Then she began brushing her thick auburn hair, paying a lot of attention to perfecting the curls. Her complexion was white, which contrasted with her carmine lipstick. She smiled invitingly, the smile which entranced men. And they loved to run their fingers through her hair.

Full-bodied where it counted, she was slim and had kicked off the high-heeled shoes under the dressing table. They helped to enhance her small stature. She was enjoying herself as she thought of Anton, the banker. She had already spent the twenty thousand francs she had 'borrowed' from him.

It satisfied her self-conceit that she now had two men at the end of a string. She was sure that Louis Marin, husband of the couple she had chatted to in the lounge, was more than interested. When she returned to the lounge she had no doubt Marin would have made some excuse to his wife to dally there while his wife went to bed. She needed more money. She always needed more money. Her tastes were extravagant. Only couturier clothes were good enough for Tina. She swore foully when the phone rang.

'You know who is calling,' Hassan's familiar voice said.

'I should by now.'

'It is vital that you cultivate the acquaintance of Tweed and Kane. If you succeed with both the fee is three hundred thousand dollars. Payable in cash, of course. Have you located either of them?'

'I'm working on it.'

'Work harder. You have received the present?'

'Yes. It arrived during dinner.'

'Then what are you waiting for?'

The phone went dead. She swore foully again. Hassan was a pig, had no manners at all. But he had phrased what he meant cleverly. 'Cultivate the acquaintance' meant kill them. Going to a cupboard she had locked, she again took out the Cartier box she had received earlier, delivered by special courier. Hassan had responded quickly to her earlier call informing him where she was staying. The box was full of flowers. Wrapped in tissue beneath them was a Luger with ammunition. She had already loaded the gun.

Next, she unlocked a case, took out a black Arab garb with a veil. She didn't like wearing this garment, but it was a good disguise in case she was seen leaving a building after an assignment. She was trying to decide how to 'handle' Tweed and Kane. Hassan, the bastard, had told her in his earlier conversation that she had competition – that both Karin Berg and Simone Carnot had been given the same task. This had infuriated her, although she had concealed her reaction.

Hassan had organized a race to kill to speed up the outcome.

'I'll go downstairs and see if I can hook Marin,' she decided. 'Then tomorrow I'll visit the Château des Avenières. After all, there is no danger that Tweed will recognize me.'

'Your room is ready, madame,' the concierge at the Hôtel des Bergues informed the elegant blonde woman.

'I'll go straight up to it. I've had a tiring day travelling,' Karin Berg replied.

'Oh, a package from Cartier arrived for you. The porter could take it up for you.'

'I'll take it up myself. Thank you. The porter can deal with my luggage . . .'

Once alone inside her room, Karin took the wrappings off the package. The usual 9 mm Luger was concealed inside tissue, together with a magazine containing eight rounds. She concealed the automatic pistol, unloaded, with the magazine, under the extra pillow on the double bed.

After taking a bath, she looked at herself in a full-length mirror before putting on pyjamas and a dressing gown. She still had a beautiful body which drove men wild, but she was under no illusions.

'This won't last for ever,' she said to herself. 'And despite all the silicon treatments and other nonsense available men go for someone young. I think I've been wise.'

Born of a Swedish father and a Serb mother, Karin had acquired her looks from her father, who had been a very handsome man. It was the way he had experimented with many women so long after his marriage that had influenced her opinion of – and attitude towards – men. She despised them, marvelled at the ease with which she could play with them.

Her serious, almost severe, side, had made her take a very different view of money from Tina. Karin had a good wardrobe of clothes, but she had selected them carefully. The bulk of the large sums she had received from Hassan had been stashed away in different safety deposits.

She had already killed three men – members of the *Institut* – but she had decided this would be her last assignment. Then she would vanish, assume a new identity – something her experience with Swedish counter-espionage had taught her how to do expertly. She would go to Rome and settle there. She spoke fluent Italian. And taxes in Sweden were very high.

Her only hesitation was concerned with her mission to kill Tweed. She knew about his unfortunate marriage, how his wife had left him for a Greek shipping millionaire. Tweed, she knew, never played around with women. He seemed to have dedicated himself to his work.

'I'll have to steel myself,' she said aloud as she slipped into her dressing gown. 'Three hundred thousand dollars is a lot of money. But if he looks me in the eye, as he will, when I point the gun at him, will I be able to pull the trigger?'

Simone Carnot, only having to fly from Zurich to Geneva, had arrived in the city hours earlier than Karin Berg. Simone, who liked to live it up at night, slept a lot during the day. Now in her room at the Hôtel Richemond she had just returned from a walk and an early dinner in the fine restaurant.

She checked her main asset, her hair as red as flame, in a wall mirror. During her walk along the banks of the

Rhône several men had eyed her hopefully. Used to this attention, she had ignored them. Businesslike – she had run her agency in Paris so it made a good profit – she concentrated her mind on her difficult new mission. How to locate Tweed and Christopher Kane?

Her life had changed when she had tried to increase the profits of her model agency by evading paying taxes. She was on the verge of being investigated when an Englishman who had visited her agency 'in search of a really attractive woman willing to earn thousands of dollars' had asked her to accompany him to Dorset in England.

This had given her the chance to escape from France. After a while she had been flown to Slovakia. When she realized what she would have to do she had accepted the strange offer at once. Simone needed money – a lot of it. A year before she had become involved with a man she knew was married. The liaison had not bothered her at all.

'After all,' she confided to a girlfriend, 'he is rich, generous and you know men – they like variety.'

It had all gone wrong when, after a few months, her lover had told her it was over, that he was going back to his wife. Simone was livid. Had she thrown him over that would have been different, but one night she spent an evening in a bar. For a long time she drank heavily.

Later, she realized she knew what she was going to do. To cover her red hair she had worn a dark wig before entering the bar which had a dubious reputation. It was rumoured you could buy almost any type of gun from the barman.

Still clear-headed, despite the amount of different wines she had drunk, she waited until the place was almost empty and casually asked the barman, 'I'm in need of protection. Can you supply me with a gun and some ammunition?'

Clutched in her well-shaped hand she held a sheaf of banknotes. The barman continued polishing glasses while he studied her. She stared him straight in the eye, wily enough to say nothing else.

'You need a Beretta,' he replied eventually. 'Perch your hand over the counter and drop the money on my side.'

She walked out with a loaded Beretta which the barman had shown her how to use as they were now alone in the bar. He had chosen a 6.35 mm Beretta because it was the perfect weapon for a woman. Weighing only ten ounces empty, it was only a little over four and a half inches long. It easily slipped into her handbag.

It was late at night when she waited at the bottom of basement steps close to his apartment. Her lover had also borrowed money off her which he had not returned, a great deal of money. When he eventually appeared she saw he was with another woman who was not his wife. Up to this point she had experienced hesitation about what she had planned.

Any doubts disappeared when the couple paused above the steps she was crouched under. The good night embrace was passionate. Her lover's hands were all over the new woman in his life. He hailed a passing taxi, saw the woman inside. Simone waited until the taxi had gone and Paul was climbing the steps to his apartment. She ran up the basement steps.

'Paul,' she had whispered, 'I thought we ought to say goodbye.'

'Goodbye, Simone,' he had answered with a leer.

Her rubber-soled shoes made no sound as she followed him up the steps. He was fumbling with his keys when she pressed the muzzle of the Beretta against the back of his head, pressed the trigger. As he fell against the door she continued to fire, emptying the gun of its bullets, then ran back into the street.

No one was about as she walked away, shoving the gun inside her handbag. Reaching her apartment, she poured herself a drink, then another. What had surprised her was how easy it had been. She felt no reaction except one of satisfaction.

There was never any danger of her being caught. Because of his wife, Paul had met her at discreet cafés in another district where no one knew either of them. They had used his car for amorous activities, after driving out into the countryside. No suspicion was ever attached to her.

She found it equally easy at the training room in the long house in Slovakia. She realized the 'dummy' sitting with his back to her in a chair was alive. She detected slight movement. As instructed, she walked up behind the peasant, aimed the Luger at the back of his head, and blew it off. It had been easy. And it had netted her an advance of twenty thousand dollars.

Before murdering Pierre Dumont in Zurich she had killed one other member of the *Institut*. In neither case had she had any reaction of shock. Both victims had been married, so she reasoned that they deserved to die since they were scum.

She had been surprised on her arrival at the hotel to find that a Cartier package had arrived. Inside she found a Luger with ammunition. She realized Hassan must be in a frantic hurry since he had originally given her the name and address of a dealer in arms in Geneva.

She stayed in her room, using a list of Geneva's top hotels to phone their concierges. Her method of approach was similar to the one used by Tina Langley, but her wording was different.

'I need to speak to Mr Tweed. His wife is dangerously ill back in England. If he's not available his friend, Christopher Kane, will take a message . . .'

In every case she drew a blank. Her next move was

to take out a map of Geneva and the surrounding areas and draw a circle round them. She noticed that included inside the circle was France, with the border very close. She went down to have a quick meal and noted the night concierge had not yet come on duty. She preferred to chat to him since they were usually bored with very little happening.

It was very late in the evening when she emerged from the Pavillon restaurant, which recalled to her the outdoor restaurant at the Baur au Lac. She smiled slowly as she went up to the night concierge's desk.

'I have reserved my room for two nights. A close friend of mine is staying at a hotel in France but I have forgotten the name. He said it wasn't far across the border. It's a five-star hotel. Have you any idea of which hotel he could be staying at?'

'Well, madame, let me show you somthing. Please come with me to the front door.

'You see that mountain rising up in the moonlight? It is called Salève. I have heard good reports of the Château des Avenières. You reach it by driving up the mountain. Then you are in France. You have a car?'

'I do,' Simone replied.

'I will show you on a map how to get there. Remember you are looking for the Château des Avenières. There is another hotel you will drive past first, the Château d'Avignon. That is not quite in the same class.'

With not much hope, when she returned to her room Simone obtained the number of the hotel the concierge had suggested. She had her story ready when she called the Château des Avenières and the night concierge answered.

'I have to speak very urgently to Mr Tweed. His wife is seriously ill in London.'

'Did you call earlier?'

'Yes,' Simone replied with a flash of inspiration.

'You went off the line. Your voice sounds different.'

'I have a cold. Please put me through to Mr Tweed. He is needed desperately urgently.'

'One moment and I will inform him . . .'

Simone put down the phone, hardly able to credit her good luck. Then she poured herself a drink, sat down in a chair and began to think hard.

Both Tweed and Christopher Kane – if he happened to be staying with Tweed – would recognize her. Did it matter? If the police in Zurich had been able to connect her with the murder of Pierre Dumont she would have been arrested. No one had come near her.

She had hired a car immediately on her arrival in Geneva. She was also disturbed that the concierge had mistaken her for another woman. Had another member of The Sisterhood also located Tweed? Simone thought, decided quickly when she had a problem. She would drive to the Château des Avenières through the night – on the off chance that they'd have a room for her.

27

There were other men in the world who were owls, who had succeeded because they worked while the rest of mankind slept. One of these was Captain William Wellesley Carrington. In his room at the Dolder Grand – where he had taken the earlier phone call from Tweed and declined his invitation – the phone rang as he was studying different estimates for the purchase of machine-pistols.

'Yes? Who is it?'

'You should be able to recognize me by now,' said Hassan.

'No names, no pack drill.'

'Pardon?'

'Just an old Army expression, my dear chap. What keeps you up in the early hours?'

'An enormous deal for you. If the price is right – and you can deliver.'

'I'll decide if the price is right and, once agreed, I always deliver. You should know that by now.'

'You have to fly here. My father has loaned me a Gulfstream jet. It will transport you from Kloten at nine o'clock in the morning.'

'No, it won't,' Willie snapped. 'It will transport you here. I will expect you at the Dolder Grand by ten in the morning.'

'You can't talk to me like that,' Hassan raged.

'I thought I just did, my dear chap. Take it or leave it. I'm too busy to leave Zurich. What is the nature of this so-called enormous deal?'

'You will make millions.'

'I can't wait. But I will. Wait for you here. Unless you decide not to bother coming. And I need a clue. I may have to stay up the rest of the night phoning contacts.'

'I cannot tell you over the phone. The size of the consignment is gigantic. And we need instant delivery at the usual destination in the Middle East.'

'Give me a clue or forget it.'

There was a long pause. Over the phone Willie could almost hear Hassan hesitating. To wear him down Willie kept silent, resumed working on calculating the differing prices in the estimates he had in front of him. He heard Hassan take a deep breath.

'Can you hear me?' he whispered.

'Quite clearly.'

'A bacillus,' Hassan whispered.

'Gigantic quantities, you said?'

'Yes.'

'Be here at ten this morning prompt,' Willie said and put down the phone.

Bacillus? Bacteriological warfare. Willie sat twiddling a pen in his fingers. By providing Hassan with a whole variety of services he had made a load of money out of the Middle East. *You will make millions.* Dollars or pounds? Willie wondered.

Tweed seemed fresher than ever as he ordered more coffee in the lounge of the Château des Avenières. Newman stifled a yawn but Marler and Paula seemed as alert as Tweed.

The waiter had just left them to bring a fresh pot of coffee when the night porter appeared. He approached Tweed again and lowered his voice.

'I've had another strange call for you – again from a woman. She said your wife is seriously ill in London.'

'What?'

For a few seconds Tweed was shaken, then his mind functioned. He knew this was not possible – his wife had left him years ago. He had never heard a word from her since. Even if she had been taken ill in London he was the last person she would bother to inform. Also, she'd have had no idea where to find him – Tweed had not yet informed Monica at SIS HQ of his latest movements.

'Did this sound the same woman who called earlier and then the connection was broken?' he asked.

'No, it didn't. I asked if she'd called earlier. She said yes and I commented that her voice sounded different. She said she had a cold. I'm sure it was a different woman.'

'I seem to be popular tonight,' Tweed joked. 'I haven't got a wife. Did she say anything else?'

'She asked to be put through to you and I said I

289

would inform you. Then the connection was broken again.'

'Tell me if she calls again,' Tweed said.

'What's going on?' asked Paula, who had heard every word.

'A second member of The Sisterhood has somehow traced me to this hotel.' He smiled. 'My plan is working better than I expected.'

'And,' Paula pointed out, 'only three people know you are here. Christopher, Amos, and Willie. One of them has to be linked with The Sisterhood.'

'Not Christopher, for Heaven's sake,' Newman protested.

'I don't trust anyone,' said Paula. She stood up. 'I'm going to ask the porter when that second call came through.'

'She's getting paranoid,' Newman commented after Paula had left the lounge. 'She doesn't trust anyone.'

'In this situation safety lies in being paranoid,' Tweed replied. 'I should have asked the porter that question myself.'

'This is interesting,' Paula said when she returned. 'The porter was apologetic. Just after he received the call he had another one from the chief supplier to this hotel. He had to give him a whole list of provisions they require urgently. The call from that woman was made over an hour ago.'

'This is getting interesting,' said Tweed as he stretched out his legs and crossed them at the ankles. 'I think we're in for one of our long nights.'

'Then I'm going to have some more black coffee,' Newman responded.

'I only need four hours' sleep anyway,' announced Marler.

'I'm suddenly alert,' Paula remarked.

Tweed began to review the entire situation. Verbally,

he played with pieces of the jigsaw he was building up, suggesting various positive actions they might take. He was still talking when he looked up as a woman entered the room. She wore a white form-fitting sheath dress with one enticing bare shoulder exposed.

'We have company,' Tweed said with a broad smile. 'What a nice surprise to see you in this part of the world. I'm not sure everyone knows Simone Carnot.'

A few minutes earlier Simone had parked her car in the drive and, carrying a suitcase, had walked into the reception area. She had asked the night porter for a suite and he had accompanied her upstairs.

Once alone, with the door locked, she had opened her case and taken out the Cartier gift box containing the Luger. She placed this on the floor of a wardrobe together with a carrier holding the black dress and veil. Very quick in her movements, she unpacked, using her hanging clothes to conceal carrier and box before locking the wardrobe and dropping the key into her handbag.

She left out the white sheath dress, stripped off the suit she was wearing, spent only a few minutes in the bathroom before putting on the white dress. Then she went downstairs and into the lounge where she had heard Tweed's voice on her arrival.

'Do sit down and join the happy throng,' Tweed invited her.

Simone chose to sit at the opposite end of the couch from Paula, smiling briefly and watching her like a hawk. Paula had shifted her position slightly so her right hand could dive inside her shoulder bag for the Browning.

'Now what would you like to drink?' Tweed asked. 'This is a great hotel. You can stay up all night and still there is the perfect service.'

'If Christopher were here I'd ask for a Kir royale,' Simone said now that Tweed had made introductions.

'A Kir royale for our guest,' Tweed requested from the waiter who had appeared out of nowhere.

'I think I'll have one too,' Marler decided.

Both Newman and Marler were deliberately gazing at Simone's bare shoulder, knowing that was what she would expect. Simone's eyes slowly switched from one man to the other. She felt sure they were avid to stroke her shoulder with one hand while the other strayed.

Paula read her mind. She forced herself to conceal her loathing of the creature. Tweed was playing some game so she joined in the charade. Smiling, she twisted round so she could stare directly at their guest.

'I do like your dress. It's not only fashionable but it suits you.'

'Thank you, Paula,' Simone replied. 'I've had quite a journey so I thought I'd change into something different. It's good for my morale.'

'Did you say morals?' Paula enquired politely.

'No. *Morale.*'

For a brief second her expression changed and she flashed a look of venom at Paula, then changed it into a seductive smile as she returned her attention to Newman and Marler.

'Cheers!' she said and sipped the Kir royale the waiter had already served. 'Aren't you drinking, Mr Newman?'

'Yes. I'm addicted to coffee at this hour. A long journey, you said. Where have you come from today, then?'

'I flew from Zurich to Geneva very late this afternoon. Then I came by car to this hotel a friend had recommended to me. Zurich was getting on my nerves after that horrific murder of Dumont.'

You really are an audacious bitch, Paula was think-

292

ing. I can see why you belong to The Sisterhood. If you do, she added to herself. After all, we can't be certain. Simone had sat more erect. In doing so she had opened the slit in her dress, revealing her superb legs.

'I'm surprised you didn't linger to taste the delights of Geneva,' Newman probed.

'I find Geneva such a crashing bore.' She looked at Paula. 'Is that the correct English phrase?'

'Spot on,' Paula assured her.

'It's not really a Swiss city at all,' Simone continued. 'There are so many international companies based there it's swarming with foreigners.' She made a moue. 'Coming from me that must sound odd. I'm French, from Paris.'

She's clever, Tweed thought. She's sticking to the same story about her background. He was deliberately keeping quiet and he noticed her conversation was directed towards anyone but himself. Yes, he mused, she's very clever, this one. She bears watching.

'The world seems to be going crazy,' Simone went on. 'People are getting shot every day. Read the newspapers.'

'Often with a Luger,' Marler said jovially.

'What's a Luger?' Simone enquired innocently.

'It's a German automatic pistol. Nine-millimetre calibre. It has a magazine capacity of eight rounds – bullets. Very effective.'

'Sounds quite horrid. You seem to know a lot about weapons, Mr Marler.'

'Me? I couldn't hit a barn door at a range of ten feet.'

Paula smiled to herself. Simone had no idea she was talking to the top marksman in Western Europe. In one way Paula was fascinated by Simone. She had met a number of daring and extremely confident women but Simone was something else again. And she had walked into the lion's den with coolness and poise.

'How long do you expect to stay here?' Marler enquired.

'As long as the place amuses me. Maybe you and I could have a few drinks in the bar tomorrow?'

'Today, you mean,' Marler corrected her with a grin.

'Then we haven't long to wait.'

Paula stiffened inside. There seemed to be no limit to Simone's pursuit of men. Could Amos have recruited her in Dorset? Then again, would Willie be her cup of tea? She couldn't make up her mind – assuming that either of the two men had persuaded her to join The Sisterhood. Assuming she *was* a member of that hideous outfit.

'It has been lovely talking to you all,' Simone said. 'But if you will excuse me I do need my beauty sleep. I'm afraid I have rather left you out of the conversation, Mr Tweed.'

'I've had my enjoyment simply watching you. Really you need not worry about sleep – you already have beauty.'

'How very gallant.' Simone stood up, extended her slim hand to each of them in turn. Paula noticed she had a very strong grip. She gave a little wave and then glided from the room. Marler accompanied her to the door, watched her walking up the staircase. At the top she threw him a kiss. He returned to the lounge, sat down, lowered his voice.

'You know something? I have a plan. It's a bit complex. I will explain it in the morning. I need Pete Nield and Harry Butler to help me carry it out. Especially Nield.'

'Can't you give us a hint?' Paula whispered.

'Dead men tell no tales . . .'

* * *

Tweed went to his room but did not go to bed. His mind was too active. He decided it was time to inform Monica where he was in case there had been any developments. When she answered his call she sounded relieved and tense at the same time.

'Thank heavens you called. Yes, I've got your number and where you're staying. Howard is deperately anxious to speak to you. He's been prowling the building like a caged tiger, wanting to talk to you. Oh, here he is now.'

Howard was usually pompous, even speaking on the phone. Tweed knew that when he dropped his normal affected air something very serious had happened.

'Tweed, have you identified our friends?'

Monica had obviously warned him he was speaking on a hotel line which might not be safe. 'Our friends' meant 'our enemies'.

'Not for certain yet, but I'm getting close. Can't say more at the moment. You sound edgy.'

'There is a crisis. Car bombs of enormous destructive power have been exploded near key power stations. All the stations in London and a number in the industrial North and the Thames Valley where there are stations serving our version of Silicon Valley.'

'IRA?'

'Definitely not. One bomb didn't detonate and I've just had a secret report after the Bomb Squad laddies dismantled it. The mechanism was far more advanced than anything available to the IRA. Incredibly sophisticated.'

'You said "near key power stations". Have any stations been put out of action?'

'No, that's the strange factor – I find it alarming. That's why the perpetrators have not been found. They placed the cars just outside the guarded areas. Doesn't make sense – and that I find disturbing. The country is in an uproar, near to panic. It all happened this evening. And it was a highly sophisticated operation – every car bomb detonated at exactly ten o'clock tonight, that is last night. A few hours ago.'

'Has anyone claimed responsibility?'

'No one.'

'Any casualties?'

'Fifty people killed. Mostly men and women coming out from a night club. The Government is close to panic, although trying to hide it.'

'From what you said earlier it was brilliantly organized. All the bombs detonating at the same moment.'

'You're right. The people who planned this are professionals of the highest order. But to what purpose? No car was near enough to any of the power stations to cause any damage. Could this have anything to do with what you are working on, Tweed?'

'Not obviously.'

'What does that mean? For God's sake don't go cryptic on me.'

'I know as much – as little – as you do. I'll keep in touch.'

Tweed ordered two large bottles of mineral water from room service. When they had arrived he had a shower, put on his pyjamas to relax, and slowly paced his room. It was four in the morning when, going back over the whole series of events which had taken place since he had visited Dorset, he remembered a certain incident and understood.

It meant zero hour was even closer than he had feared.

28

Tweed was about to get ready to go to bed when there was a gentle tapping on his door. He recognized Paula's way of telling him who was there but he picked up a glass of brandy room service had sent up at his request. Paula slipped inside when the door opened and sat in a chair as he relocked it.

'Not like you to drink brandy,' she remarked.

'I'm not drinking it. But if you had been the wrong person a glass of brandy in the eyes can be off-putting.'

'I think you ought to take greater precautions. That's why I'm here. With Simone in this hotel – and Tina Langley at the other chateau only two miles away – you're in great danger.'

'I think you exaggerate.'

'Either woman might get hold of a master key while you're sleeping. Marler or Newman could sleep in the other bed.'

'They would disturb my thinking. What really concerns me is a factor we haven't considered. Clearly we are confronted with a professional and skilled organization. They will need more than one major communications centre. Slovakia is a long way east. And they already have teams operating in Britain.'

He told her of his conversation with Howard. He emphasized that the large number of car bombs hadn't been close enough to wipe out, or even damage, a single key power station. Paula frowned.

'Why do you link this up with The Sisterhood outfit?'

'It's a diversion, to distract the security forces at home from some other target. By now every important power station inside Britain will be guarded by our top security forces. They have played this trick before. It's a hoax.'

'When did they do that?'

'When they lured most of Beck's police force to guard the Kongresshaus on the night Dumont was supposed to make his speech. That was to keep them away from the Ermitage out at Küsnacht where I had dinner with Karin Berg.'

'But that was the Monceau gang who attacked you.'

'I haven't forgotten that. But the ingenious, complex planning had all the hallmarks of the Englishman who, I am convinced, is the mastermind behind The Sisterhood.'

'So we're back to Amos and Willie.'

'I always have both men in the forefront of my mind. Remember the courier Vitorelli told us about, the courier who took a large sum of money secretly to someone in Doreset.'

'And Amos arrives here some time later today.'

'I'll be glad to see him. But it's the major communications centre they must have I want to locate.'

At the Château d'Avignon in the morning Butler and Nield had a quick breakfast. Nield, who liked a full English breakfast, made do with six croissants coated with lashings of butter. As they were walking out to their car Big Ben appeared, looming over them with his huge bulk.

'Will you be staying a few days longer?' he demanded.

'We will,' Nield replied genially. 'The food and the service are first-rate at this hotel. We've been working pretty well nonstop – running a courier service in London. We need the rest. And you make us so welcome.'

'You piled it on a bit, didn't you?' Butler suggested as they settled inside the car with Butler behind the wheel.

'Well, he's such a charming fellow, don't you think?'

'No, I don't,' growled Butler as he drove out of the exit now the gates were open, turned left towards the Château des Avenières.

Even in daylight the road was gloomy, almost sinister, hemmed in by the wall of evergreen giants on both sides. Butler checked his rear-view mirror but no one was following them. As he turned into the drive to the hotel Nield glanced to his right.

'That's a monster of a tree overlooking the drive on the opposite side of the road.'

'Looks like a Douglas fir, although I doubt if they have them out here.'

The soldier in Swiss Army uniform had risen very early. After eating some of his rations and drinking from a flask of tepid coffee he had walked the two miles along the deserted road with his dismantled Armalite concealed inside his clothes.

Climbing the giant tree, he had perched himself on the chosen branch, had carefully assembled the Armalite, then had loaded it. He had heard Butler's car approaching and had hidden himself on the far side of the massive trunk. Then he settled down to wait. He doubted whether anyone inside the hotel had started breakfast when he had first arrived.

Before Butler and Nield appeared he had again practised with his weapon. In the crosshairs he caught the driver of a large provisions truck as he turned slowly into the drive. The face of the driver came up so close in his sight that the soldier felt he could reach out and touch him.

He kept the crosshairs positioned on the man's forehead as he continued his turn. He could have shot him dead three times. He smiled unpleasantly as he lowered the weapon.

'Come on, Mr Tweed. Hope you had a good breakfast. It will be your last,' he said to himself.

'I've phoned Paris again,' Tweed told his team as they walked on the terrace. I wanted to speak to Loriot, Chief of the Direction de la Surveillance du Territoire.'

'You think what we're investigating concerns French counter-intelligence, then?' asked Paula.

'I'm sure it does. If I'm right about a planned invasion of Western Europe the key targets will be France, Germany and Britain. My main worry at the moment is to locate the enemy's communications centre, which I'm convinced must exist.'

'Château d'Avignon,' Butler said tersely.

Nield, the more voluble of the two men, explained how they had both climbed up the ivy creeper and what they had seen inside the turret room. Tweed listened but it was Newman who reacted.

'We could destroy it today. We have enough men.'

'No, we won't do that yet,' Tweed replied. 'Discovering where it is gives us a tremendous advantage over our opponents. Let me think about it.'

'And Tina Langley is staying at the Château d'Avignon,' Nield told him.

'We have two members of the hideous Sisterhood on our doorstep,' Paula said grimly.

'Two members?'

Paula described how Simone Carnot had arrived the previous night, how, bold as brass, she had walked into the lounge and talked to them. Butler's reaction was typically blunt.

'Then let's grab them both.'

'Not yet,' Tweed warned. 'We can be on our guard but it's the big picture which is important. In due course they may lead us to the headquarters of this fiendish organization.'

'Unless one of them kills you first,' Paula snapped.

'I said we can now be on our guard,' Tweed responded. 'Pieces of a massive jigsaw are falling into our lap. We'll wait for a while longer. But I think I would like to meet Tina Langley and have a chat with her. Some of us could drive over to the Château d'Avignon. Not too many of us.'

'You'll enjoy meeting the staff,' Nield remarked.

He then described the peculiar make-up of the people running the Château d'Avignon. Tweed was particularly interested when he described the tough English types who made up the majority of the staff. Nield also recalled how they had not been made welcome when they arrived. He conjured up vividly the atmosphere of hostility under the surface.

'Paula, you remember what I said about those hoax car bombs which were detonated in Britain last night?'

'Yes, is there a connection?'

Tweed first put Butler and Nield and the others into the picture about the outrages. He again drew a parallel with the incident in Zurich when most of Beck's police force had been diverted away from the Ermitage by the threat of a bomb being placed inside the Kongresshaus.

They were wandering on the terrace while they conversed. Marler seemed restless, keeping away from Tweed, Paula and Newman, who walked with Butler and Nield. The morning was a perfect summer's day. Dazzling sun shone down out of a clear azure sky and everyone except Tweed and Paula wore dark glasses.

Paula kept glancing at the fabulous view of France stretching away towards the glittering Lake Annecy which was like a mirror of mercury. Such a wonderful peaceful morning, she thought – so far away from the horrors of Zurich they had experienced. She realized Marler was keeping watch, his eyes everywhere.

'Paula asked you if there was a connection,' Newman recalled as Tweed became silent.

'I'm sure the car bombs in Britain were planted by British killers. Now we hear from Nield and Butler about the toughs at the Château d'Avignon – and they're British. I've told you before that I'm sure the master-mind behind The Sisterhood has to be English. The grim women involved in the assassinations were recruited there, I'm sure.'

'And Amos Lodge is arriving here this afternoon,' Paula repeated.

'Exactly. But there we have mystery. Willie, appar-ently, has the type of personality which attracts beautiful women. But we also found out that some of them later went off with Amos.'

'So it could be either of them?' Newman suggested.

'It would appear so.'

'What makes you think the car bombs would be planted by British killers? Isn't that a bit of an assump-tion?' Newman probed.

'The mastermind behind The Sisterhood is a perfec-tionist,' Tweed explained. 'Look how successful he's been. He's known the right sort of woman who would attract different members of the *Institut*. He wouldn't make the mistake of using foreigners to plant those car bombs. A foreigner might attract the attention of the police.'

'So we're up against a brilliant opponent,' Newman concluded.

'We are.' Tweed took one last look at the view. 'Now I would like to be driven to the Château d'Avignon. I think a few words with Tina Langley, if she's still there, might be intriguing.'

'We'll all go,' said Marler, who had not missed a word.

'Too many of us would arouse suspicion. I think Nield should drive me – then he can say he wanted to show his friends round the place. Butler, you could travel in the back of my car with Marler.'

'I'm coming too, in the other car,' Paula said firmly. 'Try and stop me.'

'It's not worth the effort, so I give in.'

They walked up the steps, into the hotel, and continued to the drive where the cars were parked. Tweed sat in the front as Nield climbed in next to him behind the wheel.

At the Dolder Grand Willie checked his watch after a phone call had told him Ashley Wingfield had arrived. He wondered just what Hassan was going to ask him to procure this time.

'Can we talk in the garden?' Hassan suggested when Willie met him in the hall. 'What I have to talk about is supremely confidential.'

'It always is, old boy. All right, we'll waffle about in the garden.'

'Waffle?'

'Forget it. You look very smart in your panama hat.'

'Three women – most attractive – have given me the eye since I got here.'

'Better when they give you both eyes.'

'Pardon?'

Hassan always had the uncomfortable feeling that Willie did not give him the respect which was his due. He never caught on that this was a deliberate tactic to strengthen Willie's hand when it came to the haggling over price.

'Forget it. Let's sit here. No one else is about. Now, I have a number of other deals in the pipeline, so what makes this so very special?'

'The nature of the substance, the method of packing it, the size of the order. Look at these.'

Hassan produced a sheaf of typed papers from the leather executive case he carried. Despite the mounting heat he handed them to Willie wearing white gloves. No fingerprints on the sheets. Willie read them rapidly. Nothing in his expression betrayed his amazement at what he was being asked to supply.

'Delivery in one week from now. At the usual destination,' Hassan snapped. 'Immediately the consignments are received twenty million dollars will be deposited in your Cayman Islands bank account.'

'This is enough bacteria to wipe out half Western Europe. I need to know how it will be distributed.'

'Why?'

'Because that will decide the type of containers which will be used.'

'I don't know that I can tell you that.'

'Then take these papers back. I have another appointment.'

'Let me think,' Hassan pleaded.

'Think fast.'

'Twenty million dollars, I said.'

'Heard you the first time.'

'There are other suppliers . . .'

'Go talk to them. You're wasting my time.'

Hassan removed his panama hat, mopped his smooth brown forehead with a silk handkerchief. He was sweating profusely. He carefully replaced the hat on his head.

'The bacteria, which are, of course, lethal, will be inserted into all major reservoirs for drinking water in Britain, France and Germany. At exactly the same moment. We have spent months reconnoitring every key reservoir, with special attention to military installations in those three key countries. No tank's engine will ever start, no war plane will leave the ground.'

'Then your armies roll West.'

'I cannot comment on that. But once you have made delivery I would advise you immediately to board a plane for the Cayman Islands.'

'Delivery in one week, you said. You need containers which will dissolve immediately on contact with water. They exist. So do the contents. You will, of course, wire five million dollars to the Cayman Islands today, as an advance payment.'

'We have to trust you, then.'

'How long have we been doing business? I resent that remark.'

'I withdraw it. Can you do it?'

'Yes, if you get the hell out of Zurich now. Don't forget the five million advance.'

'That can be wired before I leave Zurich.'

'Then why are you still here?'

Tweed was looking forward to meeting Tina Langley. He wanted to see what kind of woman had cold-bloodedly blown off the back of Norbert Engel's head in Vienna. The car began to move forward towards the exit from the Château des Avenières and on to the road leading to the other chateau.

Paula, with the key to the other car she had obtained from Butler, was walking rapidly to her vehicle. The sun, blazing behind her, warmed the back of her neck.

She had a feeling it was going to be the hottest day yet – as hot even as what she had experienced in Valja's car when he had driven her towards Slovakia.

'There are some strange kind of women about nowadays,' Tweed remarked. 'They recall to me certain aspects of Amos's speech.'

Perched on the branch of the large tree opposite the drive the soldier gripped his Armalite. In the crosshairs Tweed's face behind the windscreen came up close. The car was nosing its way out of the drive. Nield looked both ways along the road – he expected what he saw, a deserted stretch in both directions. But this was how accidents happened – you assumed there would be a clear road and some macho fool could come round a corner, also assuming he had a clear way ahead.

In the crosshairs Tweed's face came up so close the soldier could see his eyes behind his horn-rimmed glasses. The car was still moving slowly, would very shortly turn. The soldier's finger began to sqeeze the trigger. He couldn't miss at this range.

Paula reached her car, looked up. She caught the glint of the sun reflecting off something which had to be glass. Up a tree? Her left hand dropped the car key, her right hand had already withdrawn the Browning from her shoulder bag. She was gripping the gun in both hands. Her instinct controlled her reflexes which were so swift there was only a flash of movement.

She fired. Once. Twice. Three times. The shots were so close that afterwards Marler, an expert, thought he'd only heard two shots. A body toppled slowly off the branch, then fell to the ground and lay still, the Armalite a few feet away from the slumped body.

Tweed was out of the car first. He ran forward. The soldier's cap was still on his head, crumpled by the fall. Tweed bent down, carefully lifted the cap from the head. The body had twisted over on its back as it had fallen. He checked the neck pulse. Nothing. The soldier was dead. There were three gaping red bullet holes in the forehead. He stared down at the visible face as the others arrived in a rush.

'Jules Monceau,' he said quietly.

A convoy of four cars arrived a few minutes later. Out of the front car jumped a small man, clean-shaven, in his fifties, with dark hair brushed back over his dome-like forehead. He wore a dark blue business suit and rushed towards Tweed, hand extended.

'You've arrived quickly, Loriot,' Tweed greeted his old friend. 'Your timing is remarkable. That body at the foot of a tree over there is Jules Monceau. He was going to assassinate me. Paula here, whom you know, saved me.'

'Good for you, my dear,' Loriot said in his excellent English.

He hugged her, kissed her on both cheeks. She smiled with pleasure at seeing him. Most of the top Intelligence and police chiefs in Europe liked her, Tweed reflected. They appreciated her tact, competence and strong character.

While Loriot went to examine the corpse personally Tweed took her by the arm and led her back on to the terrace of the hotel. She sagged into a chair.

'That was a damned near run thing, as the Duke of Wellington said after Waterloo. Something like that. I caught sight of a glint of sun reflecting off something and reacted automatically.'

'Thank you, which sounds feeble,' Tweed replied as he sat down beside her. 'What would you like to drink? Brandy or coffee.'

'Coffee. Black as sin.'

'Talking about sin,' Tweed said after ordering the

coffee, 'I'm going to postpone my visit to the Château d'Avignon until this afternoon. There will be formalities Loriot will want me to deal with. He must be very happy with you. He's been trying to trap Monceau for years since he escaped from the Santé prison. No one is sure how many people Monceau killed during those two years. Can I help you?' he asked as the concierge appeared.

'There is a call for you, sir. A Mr Carrington.'

'I'll take it in my room.'

Tweed was away for quite some time and Paula had begun to worry when he suddenly reappeared. He waved his hands.

'Willie is always talkative. He wanted to tell me he had to go away to attend to some urgent business. He said another deal had fallen into his lap. I wonder what he's supplying and to whom this time.'

'He didn't give you a clue?' asked Paula.

'He always plays his cards close to his chest. And Christopher has left the hotel. I was handed this note by the concierge. You might like to read it, Paula. If you can read his writing, which is always atrocious.'

Tweed. Something urgent has cropped up. Will be away for two days. See you when I get back.
Christopher.

'Rather mysterious, isn't it?' Paula commented as she gave the note back.

'Christopher lives a life of his own. He's always been like that. He disappears, Heaven knows where, then pops up when you least expect him.'

'Loriot is coming,' she warned.

'Not a word about that communications centre at the Château d'Avignon. And don't say anything about Tina Langley.'

'Christopher isn't the only one who keeps things to himself,' she retorted.

'I have my reasons . . .'

29

Tweed had completed the formalities with Loriot in his room. He had provided a detailed statement of the events leading up to the shooting of Jules Monceau, sparing Paula the ordeal. When the statement was ready he had asked Paula to come to his room to sign the document underneath his own signature.

'You have done France a great service,' Loriot told her, bowing.

'She has done the world a great service,' Tweed commented. He smiled at Paula. 'Now I need to use the communications system Loriot has in his car – that was how I was able to contact him earlier when he was well on his way here from Paris.'

The neat, compact Loriot led the way downstairs and outside to his large car, which stood apart from the other two vehicles. Curious, Paula accompanied Tweed to the front door. She had not forgotten that Simone Carnot was still in the hotel.

Standing at the exit as the two men hurried to the car, she gazed round. At a distance – where they could not possibly hear what was said – stood several plain-clothes men and even more uniformed French police, each man armed with a machine-pistol. She was satisfied that Tweed was well guarded.

Loriot ushered Tweed into the front passenger seat of the empty car. He pointed to a black box attached to the dashboard. It had a number of dials and switches. Loriot leaned across Tweed, pressed a switch. A large

309

aerial automatically elevated from the rear of the vehicle.

'This,' he explained, 'is one of the most sophisticated communication systems in the world. It cannot be intercepted or listened in to.'

'Are conversations recorded?'

Loriot pressed down a switch. 'Not now. I was about to cut out the recorder. You have complete privacy.'

'I may be making several calls which will take some time.'

'You are my guest.'

Paula sat on the terrace staring at the view by herself. She wanted to think. Also she was experiencing a reaction to the killing of Monceau. She felt no regrets. The shock came from realizing how close Tweed had come to being shot dead. It had all hinged on a fraction of a second. She could so easily have missed seeing the sun glinting off the lens of his Armalite.

Tweed was absent for about half an hour. When he joined her at the table she detected a bouncy spring in his step. He sat down and a waiter appeared.

'I think I'll have a Kir royale,' he said.

'More strong coffee for me, please,' Paula ordered. 'You're starting to drink,' she chaffed him.

'Only for the moment. I feel like celebrating. We now at last have a chance of a major reaction from the people who count. If they move in time.'

'May I ask who are the people who count?'

'I had a long talk with the PM. This time he listened to me. And he's going to speak to the President of France and the Chancellor of Germany later.'

'You must have been very persuasive.'

'If only he acts quickly. If only it is not already too late. We could be the key to the outcome. What I plan we do is very dangerous. And I have conducted a devious manoeuvre.'

'I won't ask you what it is.'

'I wouldn't tell you. This afternoon we'll investigate that Château d'Avignon. And some time today Amos Lodge will visit us.'

'Amos is here,' a gravelly voice said behind them.

'Talk of the devil,' Tweed joked.

Vitorelli was enjoying himself behind the wheel of the Alfa Romeo as he drove it up the curving road on Mount Salève. Beside him Mario was clutching both sides of his seat, wanting to close his eyes but not daring to do so. Vitorelli, who had once been a racing driver, loved speed.

'What made you suddenly buy this car?' Mario asked.

'I do many things on a whim, my friend. You should know that by now. You're not nervous, are you?'

'Of course not. I'm enjoying the ride,' Mario lied.

He knew that if he admitted his anxiety Vitorelli would press his foot down further. Not out of cruelty, but because the Italian loved to thrill people, as he imagined he could do. Before meeting his fiancée he had had many successes with beautiful women by taking them for a spin in one of his fleet of expensive cars. He had found it made them extremely amenable.

'I'm not certain why we are going to meet Tweed,' Mario remarked.

'Because I know the old fox. You can bet on it he will be in at the kill. And I want to be there.'

'You're thinking of Tina Langley?'

'I never think of anyone else,' Vitorelli said.

He wore wrap-around dark glasses, which emphasized his handsome face. He spun round another bend and Mario dug his fingers into the seat, then saw they had reached the summit. Mario felt he needed a break from the ferocious drive.

'They say the view from here is magnificent. You could pull in for a moment.'

'I could, but I'm not going to. You know me. When I get an idea I go for it. I want to find out what Tweed is planning next.'

'He won't tell you,' said the shrewd Mario.

'You've arrived early – to catch me on the wrong foot,' said Tweed as he invited Amos to join them.

'That will be the day,' Amos replied.

Paula watched him as Amos eased his bulk into a chair. He wore a smart cream linen suit, a cream shirt and a wild tie decorated with a riot of large flowers. His squarish head seemed larger than ever and he studied Paula from behind his square-rimmed glasses as though trying to read her mind. Then he smiled and she felt attracted by his dynamism. The powerhouse of a brain she detected in the eyes was hypnotic.

'What are you having to drink?' Tweed asked as a waiter hovered.

'Double Scotch. I saw Newman in the hall and I guess that will be his drink when he joins us. You realize, Tweed, we are all close to annihilation? I refer to the whole of Western Europe.'

'You've made my day,' said Paula who liked Clint Eastwood's later films.

'No good burying our heads in the sand. We're not ostriches.'

'Trust you to cheer up the party on such a beautiful day,' said Newman, who had come up quietly behind them. 'Look at the view.'

'The view?'

Paula realized Amos had not even noticed the magnificent panorama spread out before him. With the exception of Tweed, she had never met a man like Amos, whose concentration on strategy was total from the moment he woke. He probably dreamt it.

'Don't you ever enjoy yourself?' Paula enquired.

'All the time. With my work. Mind you, I have my moments.' He smiled again at her. 'Maybe we could have dinner together when it is convenient to you. Unless Tweed objects.'

'Tweed doesn't object,' Tweed said. 'Why should he?'

'Have you got anywhere?' Amos asked Tweed. 'I mean as to who is behind the assassinations? Don't forget, I am also a target.'

'Then don't go around with any exceptionally attractive women.'

'But I have just invited one to join me for dinner.'

'So you have.'

'Amos,' broke in Newman, who had occupied a fourth chair. 'Just come with me, for Heaven's sake.'

Taking his drink with him, after excusing himself to Paula, Amos walked with Newman to the wall of the terrace a distance away. He was pointing out the different features of the view to Amos.

'Don't mention Tina Langley or any aspect of the Château d'Avignon to Amos,' Tweed whispered. 'The same applies to Willie, if he turns up here.'

'You think Willie will arrive out of the blue? He said he was too busy to come.'

'That's what he said.'

'Does Loriot know any of this?'

'No. He'd have raided the place, closed down the communications centre – which I want left open for the moment. And he'd have arrested Tina Langley, if she's still there. I want to leave the situation fluid.'

'You're playing with fire.'

'According to Amos we're playing with an inferno. And I'm certain Amos is right.'

He stopped speaking as Newman returned with his companion. Amos was talking rapidly, continued to do so as he resumed his seat at the table.

'I don't seem able to convince the powers-that-be that with the collapse of morals – and morale – in the West, we are wide open to attack from a certain Eastern power. The whole family fabric of Europe is dissolving into chaos. "I want it, and I want it now" seems to be the attitude of so many people. Often perversity is involved – just as it was in ancient Rome before the barbarians, again from the East, overwhelmed them. Only a stable, self-disciplined society can survive. Now all we hear about are rights. Hardly anyone ever mentions responsibility, the keystone of a strong civilization able to defend itself.'

Sitting facing the entrance to the terrace Newman saw Simone Carnot appear at the top of the steps. She wore a pale green dress which ended above her knees. It had full-length sleeves and a high neck. The colour emphasized the sunset red of her well-coiffured hair. Standing with her right hand clasped against her hip she looked like a dream.

Walking slowly down the steps, she chose a table as far away as possible from Tweed's. She crossed her legs after sitting down, waved to Newman, then beckoned to him to join her.

'Might as well,' he said to himself. 'See what she's up to.'

He wasn't sure whether this really was his motive. She looked so attractive as she folded her hands in her lap and gave him a warm smile as he arrived, sat down opposite her.

'I suppose this was the idea?' he remarked in a neutral tone.

314

'This was the idea,' she agreed. 'I know you're going to ask me what I'd like to drink. I'm going all the way. I'll have a Kir royale. You'll think I'm addicted to champagne, asking for one at this time of day. Well, I am.'

'Anything to please a beautiful lady,' he said with a smile and ordered two Kir royales from the waiter who had appeared.

'Thank you, kind sir,' she said. 'Who is that large man with the square-rimmed glasses? He just stared at me for a few seconds.'

'I don't know. Friend of Tweed's, I suppose.'

'He gets around. I saw him at the Baur au Lac.'

'We all do. You were there.'

'One of the staff told me the police had been here, that a man had been shot dead. How awful. That man with Tweed has just glanced at me again.'

'He has something to stare at. Cheers!' He lifted one of the glasses which the waiter had just placed on the table. 'You drink champagne all day long?'

'Heavens, no! This is an exception.'

'Are you free for dinner tonight? We could make another exception. I'm thinking we could dine here. The food and service are out of this world. Or would you prefer somewhere in Geneva?' he said, testing her.

'No, I think here would be perfect. Would eight thirty suit you? Give me time to get ready.'

'Call it a date.'

Newman's mind was in a whirl. Simone kept looking at him with her magnetic eyes. One part of his brain toyed with what a wonderful experience it might be to have her as a girlfriend. The other part knew she was going all out to bring him under her spell. She was devious, calculating, the most wily woman he had ever met. Her real objective, he was certain, was to use him to get closer to Tweed. A very wily, cold-blooded woman indeed.

He was smiling broadly to conceal his real assessment of her as she stood up after finishing her drink. She gave him a sensuous half-smile as she spoke.

'That was very pleasant, Bob. I look forward to carrying on this evening from where we left off. If you'll excuse me now, I want to write some letters.'

She leaned forward and her lips brushed his cheek, her hand grasped his briefly and then she was walking slowly away towards the exit.

30

They chose the early afternoon to visit the Château d'Avignon. At Tweed's suggestion Butler and Nield had returned earlier to have lunch there. It was important that there should appear to be no connection between the two men and the rest of Tweed's team.

Tweed was behind the wheel of the car with Paula next to him. In the back sat Marler and Newman. With the exception of Tweed they were all armed. Tweed had decided that four people were not too many to arrive at the chateau, not knowing what reception they might receive. He was driving along the deserted road under the tunnel of trees when Newman spoke.

'I'm having dinner with Simone Carnot tonight at des Avenières.'

'Be careful – that woman is very clever. I noticed how she was playing up to you on the terrace this morning.'

'I thought Amos was the only one who took any notice.'

'That was my intention. Simone did not realize I was observing her from a distance.'

'How is the forceful Amos spending his afternoon?' enquired Marler.

'In his room, of course. Studying strategic ideas. He never stops working.'

'Marler, before Nield left he described to you the exact location of their communications room in the turret at the Château d'Avignon. If it had to be destroyed, could one man, namely Butler, do it in due course?'

'It sounded a tough place to reach, but Butler is tough. Yes, I have explosives and timers in my satchel. I could provide him with a time bomb which would blow the turret to pieces – subject to my seeing it this afternoon.'

'Then take a good look at that turret from their terrace while we're there.'

'If they let us in,' Newman pointed out.

'They will let me in.'

Tweed slowed down as they approached the chateau. The huge heavy gates were open as he turned into the courtyard. Paula looked up and thought this chateau seemed even more ugly than when they had passed it the night before. As Tweed parked the car a giant of a man hurried towards them out of the hotel.

'This must be Ding-Dong, Big Ben,' Marler drawled.

'Don't think we 'ave room for you lot,' Big Ben informed them in his semi-civilized English.

'We're just visiting,' Tweed said pleasantly after jumping out of the car. He looked up at the giant. 'Chief Inspector Loriot of French Internal Security wants a holiday in about a couple of months from now. He'd heard this was the ideal place to have a peaceful rest.'

'You're police?'

'Me? No. I run a security organization in England. If you're interested I could check your security.'

'It's watertight.'

'Then you won't be worried about floods.'

'Floods?'

Big Ben was clearly taken aback, having no sense of humour. He stared as Paula left the car, his eyes glued to her legs. She smiled at him. He started to lick his lips, then stopped when he realized what he was doing.

'At least we can have a drink in the bar,' Tweed persisted. 'Or maybe on the wonderful terrace we heard you have.'

'Don't suppose there's any 'arm in that.'

'Well, this is listed as a hotel. Who owns it, by the way?'

'I'll show you the way to the bar.'

They were passing the reception counter when a man behind the counter Tweed recognized as the character Nield had nicknamed Weasel stood up. From behind half-moon glasses eyes like those of a turtle studied the new arrivals. Then he gave an oily smile as Big Ben explained.

'This feller is a friend of the boss of French Internal Security.'

'Oh, really, how extremely interesting.' The remark came after a significant pause. 'Very interesting, I am sure.'

'What's 'is name . . .'

'Loriot,' Tweed repeated.

'Lawriot is comin' for a bit of peace and quiet about two months from now.'

'We'll be most pleased to welcome such a distinguished guest. I am Frederick Brown. Perhaps you'd be kind enough to ask him to mention my name.'

'We'd like a drink on the terrace,' Tweed said abruptly.

He had noticed through an open doorway Butler and Nield seated at a table on the terrace. Walking through with the others he stepped down and forced himself not to pause. At another table, sitting by herself, was Tina Langley.

Tweed led the way to a table close to the woman whose photo was circulating throughout Switzerland. He realized the photo had been a striking portrait of her. The table was quite a distance from where Butler and Nield were sitting.

'Do you mind if we sit here?' he asked. 'It provides a perfect place to look at the view.'

'I could do with some company. Preferably English. Those two men over there are British and very stand-offish.'

'I'm Tweed.'

He was watching her closely. Her ice-blue eyes blinked. The hand holding her glass of Campari and soda gripped it tightly. She recovered quickly. Her left hand smoothed her thick glossy auburn hair. Her high-coloured face flushed and the eyes switched from Newman to Marler and back again. Paula, whom she had ignored, could almost hear the wheels going round. Which of the two men would be easier to hook?

Tweed made introductions and Paula chose a chair facing her. It was like a direct confrontation. Tweed was thinking she was superficially very attractive. The recruiter of The Sisterhood in Dorset had been very skilled. He had selected very different women, all of them exceptionally desirable – doubtless knowing that men had varying tastes.

'I'm Lisa Vane,' she said in a quiet, seductive voice.

'You're here on your own?' Newman asked with his infectious smile.

'I was until you came along.' She was looking straight at Marler. 'A long-term relationship I had got smashed up. You could say I'm here to drown my sorrows.'

'You've finished your drink,' Newman said. 'Have another.'

'A good strong one.'

Unlike the service at the Château des Avenières, Newman had to go and find a waiter, who reacted sullenly to his request. He had been sitting looking at a girlie magazine.

'Bring them to you soon.'

'Make it now – not soon. I'll be timing you.'

'Didn't realize His Lordship had arrived.'

'Well, he has. I don't want to complain to the manager..'

'Fred doesn't like complaints.'

'Albert, serve the gentleman.' It was Brown, who had overheard the conversation. 'Make with the feet, you lout.'

'You've been here long?' Tweed asked Tina.

'I never stay anywhere long. It gets boring. I enjoyed shopping in Geneva. And doing my job.' She giggled.

'What job is that?' Tweed enquired.

'I'm a model. For high-class TV commercials.'

'They pay well, I hope?'

'They pay very well. If they didn't, I wouldn't do them.'

Tweed had had a mild shock. He suddenly realized that, unlike Karin and Simone, Tina was totally lacking in any kind of intellect. She was, he suspected, a woman with only one object in life – obtaining money by any means and then spending it lavishly. The dark blue outfit she was wearing must have cost a small fortune. At her feet was a Gucci handbag.

She was also concentrating on attracting the attention

of the three men at her table. Every now and again, carefully timed, she gave Tweed a certain look. It promised a very interesting experience. A lot of men, he felt certain, would go crazy over her.

She had a snub nose and was skilfully made up. Paula recognized she must spend hours in front of a dressing table. It would pay good dividends. She was the kind of woman many men would expect to have a lot of fun with, and would not be disappointed – so long as they spent plenty of money on her. She was just the kind Paula despised. And there was no doubt this was the woman she had seen ahead of her in Kärntnerstrasse in Vienna, the woman who had shot Norbert Engel.

'What part of the world do you come from?' Paula asked.

'Hampshire,' Tina said after a brief pause.

'I know it well. From some interesting old village?'

'I hate old villages. They're so boring.'

'You like travel?' Marler interjected.

'I simply love it. I never stay in one place for long,' Tina said, repeating what she had said earlier. 'It's boring.'

The Butterfly, Tweed thought. A perfect name for her. She was easily bored because she had no inner resources. Tina asked for another drink. Her third in five minutes. The alcohol seemed to have no effect on her. When the fresh glass came she drank half the contents.

'What is your aim in life?' Tweed asked jovially.

'Aim?'

'What would you like to achieve? What are your ambitions?'

'To enjoy myself.' She drank the rest of her glass. 'Nothing lasts for ever.'

'Not even human life,' Tweed said casually. 'Not if it's brought to an abrupt end. People get shot.'

'I don't see what you mean.'

'They get murdered in cold blood.'

'Now you're spoiling a beautiful day.'

She had one ability, Tweed was thinking. She responded swiftly. She could probably out-talk most men. From having a great deal of experience in talking to them, in manoeuvring them. She had had enough of Tweed and turned her attention to Newman.

'What job do you do?'

'I'm a foreign correspondent.'

'Really? That must involve a lot of exciting travel.'

'Up to a point.'

Tweed realized she'd never heard of Newman. But he felt sure she never read the type of serious newspapers and international magazines where so many of his articles had appeared. Not her cup of tea. Earlier she had removed from one of the chairs a copy of a magazine which specialized in scandals. He stood up.

'Excuse me, I have a spot of work to do. Soon we shall be departing for Vienna. It has been most interesting meeting you.'

'Vienna?' She had jumped up and followed him as he left the table alone. Taking hold of his arm, she asked her question. 'I was hoping we could be friends. When do you expect to go to Vienna? I hear it's a fascinating city.'

Her determination to be asked to accompany him was obvious. He crossed the terrace, being careful never to glance up at the turret once. Big Ben was watching them from the top of the steps.

'I'm not sure. First I have to go to Ouchy in Switzerland. To attend a meeting of certain of the top brains in the world – that is, the few who are left. I'll probably go there in a couple of days. Now I'm going back to my hotel, two miles down the road.'

'Which hotel is that? I thought this was the only one.'

'The Château des Avenières. Frankly, it's much more luxurious than this place.'

'I'm used to luxury. Maybe I'll move. Could you book me a very nice room? A suite, if possible? I could move today.'

'I'm sure they have accommodation available. I'll tell the proprietor you're coming . . .'

'You must be stark raving mad,' Paula burst out as Tweed drove them back to their hotel. 'Giving all that information to that tart.'

'I gather you don't like her. She's reasonably well-educated, you have to admit.'

'Which makes the way she lives worse. She's a murderous predator. And her education was wasted, considering her level of intelligence – that is, except when it comes to attracting men and looting them.'

'I had a reason for giving her that information. And we shall soon be moving on to Ouchy, where the *Institut* headquarters is located, as you know.'

'Sometimes I can't fathom you.'

'Then other people won't be able to, which encourages me. Marler, did you get a chance to tell Butler and Nield to have dinner tonight at des Avenières?'

'I did. And I can quickly design for Butler a bomb which will sort out that communications centre in the turret. Will he have Nield to help him?'

'I'm afraid not,' said Tweed, driving slowly, checking the forest on either side. 'We're going to need as large a team as we can muster. I'm going to arrange with Butler to fake a twisted ankle – which will be his excuse for staying on there alone.'

'I had the chance of a quick chat with Butler alone in the loo before we left,' Marler continued. 'I put him in the picture. He's asked me to drive him to Geneva this afternoon so he can purchase a motorbike for his getaway when he's done the job.'

'Poor Harry, I don't envy him,' Paula remarked. 'He'll be lucky to survive.'

'So will all of us,' Tweed told her. 'But the job has to be done. Even if we all end up dead.'

31

The decision Tweed announced as he drove Paula, Marler and Newman back to the Château des Avenières astounded them. He spoke quite calmly but they detected in his tone the iron will he was noted for in an emergency.

'We are leaving des Avenières this evening. Butler is hoofing it with Nield up the road somewhere behind us. Marler, you will produce the bomb Harry needs in the shortest possible time – together with the timer device and so on. I will arrange to call him with a code word when the vital moment occurs. You can drive Harry to Geneva to purchase his motorcycle before we leave late in the evening.'

'Where are we going to?' Paula asked.

'We will be driving to Ouchy on the shores of Lake Geneva – to the headquarters of the Institute. I told Tina that's where we are going, before we move on to Vienna. Undoubtedly she will inform the Englishman we are on our way there.'

'Why, for Heaven's sake?' Newman demanded.

'Because it is the next stage of my plan. All I will say is I noticed at the Château d'Avignon there is a large staff of English thugs of the worst kind. It takes me back years ago to when I was with the Homicide Division at Scotland Yard.'

'The youngest superintendent in its history,' Paula recalled.

'Ancient history,' Tweed said dismissively. 'In those days I met some pretty ugly customers. But they were nothing compared with today's villains, who do not hesitate to use knives and guns. So pack your bags . . .'

There was silence inside the car from that moment until Tweed turned into the drive of the Château des Avenières. He made one more remark before hurrying away to his room. With his hand on the door of the stationary car he looked back at Newman.

'Have your dinner with Simone. During the conversation I'd like you to inform her casually that we are bound for Ouchy – and later for Vienna.'

Saying which, he slammed the door shut, and left the others dazed inside the car. Here they could react undisturbed.

'I'd better love you and leave you,' said Marler. 'I have a job to do. See you for dinner – if we're back from Geneva in time.'

Newman and Paula knew what he was in such a hurry for. He had to prepare the bomb for Harry before Butler and Nield arrived. Then he'd have to drive Harry to Geneva and back after purchasing the motorcycle.

'Tweed has surprised me before,' Newman said, 'but this takes the cake. What can he be up to?'

'I'm trying to work that out myself,' Paula mused. 'Surely he's not going to risk assembling the surviving members of the *Institut* at Ouchy? They'd make the biggest target yet for The Sisterhood organization.'

'I've never heard him sound more determined, more urgent.'

'He must have a plan – the way he's deliberately informed two of those vile women who are key figures in The Sisterhood. He's taking one hell of a chance.'

'I think he knows he's working against a deadline.'

'Let's hope the emphasis isn't on *dead*,' Paula said.

'Well, he did say earlier the job had to be done even if we all ended up dead. I get the impression he thinks the odds are against him.'

'Then he's at his most effective, his most dangerous – to his opponents. Don't forget that. Look, Amos is leaving.'

The strategist had appeared at the exit, run down the steps, flung his bag into the back of his car and, as they watched, driven past them without a glance in their direction. In the rear-view mirror Paula watched him turn on to the road. She heard him ram down his foot on the accelerator and he vanished.

'He's heading back for Geneva,' she told Newman. 'And he seems to be in a great hurry.'

'Perhaps Tweed had a word with him.'

'There's a car creeping into the drive behind us.'

Newman had his .38 Smith & Wesson in his hand almost before she had finished speaking. From the back seat he pressed his left hand on her shoulder to push her down onto the floor.

'It's all right,' she told him. 'Harry and Pete didn't hoof it as Tweed suggested. They've come in the car which originally they drove to the Château d'Avignon.'

'I'll have a word with them,' replied Newman and climbed out.

It was still daylight but Harry had his headlights on. It must have been darker inside the forest than it was when Tweed had driven back. Newman walked over to their car as the two men climbed out. They spoke in little more than whispers and Harry was carrying a satchel over his shoulder. Nield had emerged with his suitcase.

'Tweed phoned us, spoke in coded language,' Nield explained. 'He told me what to do. I told charming Fred I wanted to keep my room and paid in advance for it. Said I had to attend to some business in Geneva, that I'd be back. I won't be.'

'Marler's room number,' Harry said in his terse way.

Newman told him and Harry disappeared inside the hotel. Nield looked at Paula as he asked what was going on.

'We're driving to Ouchy tonight,' Paula informed him. 'After dinner, so you'd better join us. It's going to be a tight squeeze in one car.'

'No, it isn't,' Nield assured her. 'Harry is route marching it back to the Château d'Avignon, after Marler drops him close to the place when they return from Geneva.'

'What about the motorcycle?'

'Harry is insisting on hiding it in the forest on their way back. I'm sure he knows what he's doing. I don't understand the idea of our going to Ouchy.'

'I've just worked it out,' said Paula. 'It's going to turn out to be a battlefield.'

At the reception desk Newman paused to make an enquiry. A well-dressed French girl looked pleased to see him.

'I wanted a word with another guest,' Newman explained. 'Amos Lodge. But I think I saw him just leave.'

'You are quite right, sir. Mr Lodge made a phone call. Then he called down asking me to have his bill ready because he had to check out. Some urgent business had compelled him to leave unexpectedly.'

'Thank you. What about Mr Tweed?'

'He's been on the phone ever since he dashed into the hotel. I think he's off the line now.'

'Your English is perfect.'

'Thank you, sir.' She blushed. 'I spent two years in London with a big hotel. If you're going up to see him perhaps you could tell him a Mr Emilio Vitorelli has arrived. He asked for Mr Tweed. He's out on the terrace having a drink with a man who came with him.'

'I'll tell him.'

Paula left to have a shower, preferably a bath if there was time before dinner. Leaving Nield in the bar, Newman went up to Tweed's room. When the door opened he found Tweed dressing in a dark business suit for dinner.

'The receptionist told me you'd been on the phone,' Newman remarked as Tweed brushed his jacket.

'I have. Time I had a word with Monica. Nothing to report – except Howard is worked up about the hoax bombs planted in the vicinity of key power stations. They haven't picked up anyone who was involved yet. I advised them to concentrate on the East End of London.'

'Why?'

'Because of the character of the staff at the Château d'Avignon. They all come from that part of London, from the way they talk. On my way out I noticed a small slim man who Big Ben called Stan. That type never changes. Wears a permanent sneer on his smooth face. I once arrested someone just like him. He went down for fifteen years for attempted murder with a knife. I think the Englishman has hidden away a powerful reserve of deadly thugs at that chateau.'

'Talking of the Englishman, Amos Lodge received a phone call, according to the receptionist. He reacted by checking out and driving off towards Geneva.'

'Amos is a law unto himself. He's probably gone to

meet one of his secret contacts. And you're having dinner with The Butterfly. The receptionist also told me Emilio Vitorelli has just arrived. He's out on the terrace. Supposing he sees Tina? Anything could happen.'

'I'll go down and see Emilio now. We don't want any more complications in this part of the world . . .'

Tweed found Vitorelli sitting with Mario at a table on the terrace. As soon as Mario saw Tweed approaching he got up and left the terrace, nodding to Tweed as he passed him.

'What brings you to this neck of the woods?' Tweed asked as he sat down facing the rear of the hotel.

'You do, you old bloodhound.'

'I'll take that as a compliment. It doesn't explain why you are here when I'm on the verge of leaving tonight.'

'It would be stupid of me . . .' Vitorelli paused and gave an engaging smile, '. . . to ask where you're off to now?'

'If I said London you wouldn't believe me.'

'I might.' Vitorelli smiled again, ran a hand through his thick hair. 'You're a master of the double bluff.'

'If you say so.'

From where he sat Tweed could see the bedroom windows overlooking the terrace. Tina Langley was peering down at them from a window. She closed the curtain as Tweed spotted her. She now knew that Vitorelli was on the premises. Tweed didn't expect her to have dinner with him.

'I passed this hotel earlier this afternoon,' the Italian said and sipped at the last of his drink. 'I asked for you but they said you were away.'

'I was.'

'If you're leaving there can't be what you're looking for here.'

'If you must know, he has left the hotel.'

'That sounds like either Willie or Amos Lodge. Both

live in Dorset. I gave you a big tip about the courier who travelled there with a case full of money. You owe me.'

'I'll remember that.'

'Sounds as though you really are about to leave. I'm still on the lookout for Tina Langley.'

'You have been for a long time.'

'See you, Tweed. Don't do anything I wouldn't do.'

'There are a lot of things you do I wouldn't dream of doing.'

'Getting chilly out here. I don't think it's the evening air.'

Saying which, Vitorelli gave a little salute and left. On the way out he stopped at reception. He gave the girl behind the desk a great big smile to soften her up.

'I came here hoping to meet my old friend Amos Lodge.'

'Mr Lodge left the hotel suddenly. Do you want to leave me a message in case he comes back?'

'He won't come back.'

Satisfied that Tweed had told him the truth, Vitorelli went outside. If his reference to Amos hadn't worked he'd have asked about Captain Wellesley Carrington. Mario was waiting in the second car they had borrowed from a contact in a distant village earlier in the afternoon.

'Mario,' Vitorelli said quietly. 'Tweed is leaving this hotel soon – or so he says. I'm driving back to Geneva airport to the chopper. You wait here out of sight. Follow Tweed if he does leave.'

'Out of sight? Where?' Mario asked indignantly.

'You'll find somewhere.'

Vitorelli got behind the wheel of his Alfa Romeo, which he had parked behind a large van. He drove off, tyres screaming as he turned the bend from the drive into the road.

He had missed seeing Tweed watching him from behind one of the open doors leading to the terrace. Guessing that the Italian had checked up on him, he felt a wave of relief. The last man he wanted in his vicinity during the next twenty-four hours was Emilio Vitorelli.

Returning from Geneva, Marler had stopped his car a few hundred yards from the Château d'Avignon. He had helped Butler lift the motorcycle from the rack on top of the car. Butler had then wheeled the machine down a narrow track leading into the forest. He had hidden the machine under a dense mass of undergrowth behind a tall fir.

Going back to the car where Marler waited behind the wheel, he climbed in beside him. Marler drove at medium speed past the Château d'Avignon and Butler was relieved to see the gates were still open. He pulled up again beyond a bend and Butler stepped into the road. Marler called out in a low voice.

'Good luck. Don't take any chances. Remember, once you activate the timer the bomb detonates five minutes later.'

'Maybe I'll check my wristwatch,' Butler replied. 'See you.'

He waited for a while so anyone who had heard a car at Château d'Avignon wouldn't associate it with him. Then he shouldered the satchel which contained the bomb and strolled back to the entrance. Big Ben met him as he climbed the steps.

'You've been away a helluva time.'

'I'm a hiker. Like walking.'

'Mug's game. And they're servin' dinner.'

'Wouldn't care to join me, I suppose?'

Butler, who didn't give a damn for the hulking brute, went on upstairs before the other man could reply. He had kept the key to his room in his pocket. Once inside, he relocked the door and went to his suitcase. Bending down he checked for one of his hairs he had inserted when closing the case and before locking it. The hair was gone. His own key didn't work as smoothly as it had before. So there was a man who picked locks on the premises.

Going to the tall heavy and ancient wardrobe where he had stored his clothes, he reached up, ran his finger along the rim. It came away covered with dust. No one had thought to check the top.

From his satchel he extracted the circular bomb about the size of a small dinner plate. It was wrapped in strong blue paper. The timer and certain other small devices were separately and neatly wrapped in tissue. He tugged two hairs from his head, inserted one in each package, then slid the packages well back on top of the wardrobe.

'Don't reckon you'll find those, matey,' he said to himself.

As he got ready for dinner he contemplated what lay before him, a prospect that would have daunted many men. He had to stay in this hotel full of hostile thugs by himself for an unknown period. Until, in fact, Tweed phoned the code word to him.

Being on his own worried Butler not at all. He had the patience of Job. His only regret was he would be missing whatever fireworks Tweed was planning at Ouchy. Knowing Tweed as well as he did, Butler had sensed the time for continuing and mounting action had arrived. Ouchy was going to be an explosion of fireworks.

32

At the Château des Avenières Tina, who had driven there with her luggage and accepted a room overlooking the terrace, had made a phone call soon after arriving. A long way east in Slovakia Hassan answered immediately.

'I have vital news for you,' Tina said.

'I will decide whether it is vital. What is it?'

'Tweed, together with a team of men, is leaving here this evening. He is going to attend a meeting of the surviving members of the *Institut* at Ouchy on Lake Geneva. That should be worth a good fee.'

'You are sure he leaves this evening?'

'I want to know what my fee is,' she demanded.

'You know what happens to people who try to intimidate me?'

'Well, I think it is worth something,' she said in a much more conciliatory tone.

'Answer my question, damn you.'

'Yes,' she said quickly, 'I am certain.'

'Ten thousand dollars.'

Hassan slammed down the phone. He thought for several minutes. Which group was nearest to Ouchy? It was necessary to move very quickly. Then he realized the solution was obvious. He called the Château d'Avignon. Fred Brown came on the line.

'Frederick,' Hassan began in his most persuasive voice, 'I have some urgent and important instructions for you . . .'

When the phone call was finished Fred began to search out certain members of his staff. He took each one aside and spoke to them individually and away from the few guests staying at the hotel. Sitting on the terrace with a drink, Butler noticed some of this activity.

Later, curious, he strolled into the bar, ordered another drink as camouflage, then carried it as he strolled back into the main hall. He was in time to see three cars appear from the side of the chateau where, presumably, they had been parked out of sight.

He sipped his drink, observed that Big Ben was behind the wheel of the leading car. They crawled quietly out of the exit between the open gates and turned in the direction of Geneva. Aware that someone had crept up behind him, he turned and saw Stan standing close to him.

'Feeling restless, Mr Butler?' Stan enquired with a smirk.

'Getting a breath of fresh air.'

'Dinner is being served on the terrace. Don't want to go hungry, do we? Some of the staff are being given a party elsewhere. An expression of appreciation by Mr Brown for their support.'

'You giving me an explanation?'

Stan's smirk vanished. It was replaced by a sneer and he walked away. Butler watched him. Stan had a peculiar walk, reminding him of the slither of a crocodile. Not the sort of chap he'd invite to have a beer with him.

Ignoring the broad hint to go immediately on to the terrace for dinner, Butler went upstairs. Inside his room he called the Château des Avenières and gave a coded message to the receptionist.

'If my friend Pete Nield turns up there for a drink please tell him Harry Butler called. It's gone very quiet here now so I'd appreciate his company. Thank you.'

He put the phone down before the receptionist could say a word. It took him ages to have his dinner that

334

night. There were long gaps between courses because of the shortage of waiters.

Tweed had just joined Paula, Newman and Marler for dinner at the Château des Avenières when the receptionist delivered Harry's message. Nield looked puzzled but Tweed was smiling. He remarked that Harry was not only reliable but also very clever at delivering disguised messages.

'I don't understand,' said Paula.

'That means the receptionist didn't. Harry is good.'

'I thought you were dining with Tina Langley,' Paula said, keeping her voice down.

'She sent me a note, saying she wouldn't be able to join me. She has a headache. I think seeing Vitorelli here scared her.'

'She gives me a headache,' Paula snapped.

'I've been let down too,' said Newman and mocking himself pulled a long face. 'Simone called me, said she was exhausted.'

'So exhausted,' Tweed told them, 'that I spotted her leaving with her bags. I remarked on it to the receptionist and she said the lady received a phone call, then called down to check out.'

'I suppose I'll survive without her,' Newman remarked with a sigh.

'You're more likely to survive without her than with her,' Paula said. 'Remember what she did to poor Pierre Dumont.'

'Tweed, why did you change your instructions and tell me not to mention Ouchy or Vienna to Simone?'

'One is enough.'

They ate their dinner in silence as Tweed was clearly in a hurry. Also, Paula noticed, he had a faraway look

335

as though he was concentrating on his next moves. At the end of the meal she looked at Marler.

'We have to cross the French border to get back into Switzerland. Are you dumping your armoury beforehand?'

'Absolutely not. Everything will be taped under the chassis of my car. The explosive is harmless, of course, separated from the timers. Which brings me to something important I was going to suggest. I think it's safer if Tweed, Nield, Paula and Newman travel in one car. I'll bring up the rear in the other car – just in case I'm caught with the goods.'

'Agreed,' said Tweed.

'Then,' Marler went on, 'in case I lose you in the Geneva traffic I suggest we meet up outside the main rail station.'

'Agreed.'

It was dark on the terrace when they had finished their dinner. Illuminated by lamps, it had an incredible atmosphere of peace and serenity. Paula was trying to forget the attempt on Tweed's life when he stood up, took her by the arm.

'Let's take one last look.'

While the others went up to their rooms to collect their cases Tweed and Paula walked to the edge of the terrace. The moon was hidden behind the only cloud in the sky and France spread out before them. Between the shadowed silhouettes of the hills here and there were tiny islands of light like pockets of diamonds – the hamlets huddled between the ridges. Then the moon came out and bathed the whole landscape in a soft light.

'It's like something out of a dream,' Paula said quietly.

'When I can manage it maybe I'll give you time to come back here,' Tweed suggested.

'Maybe you could come with me.'
'It would be my first holiday in twenty years.'

Hassan had second thoughts after calling Fred Brown at d'Avignon. He drank some water to counter the humid air which persisted in Slovakia even after dusk. *Water*. The ultimate weapon of war. He phoned Tina Langley a second time.

'I want you to drive to Ouchy tonight. I'll book you a room at the Beau Rivage – not far from the *Institut* headquarters along the lake front. I think Tweed and the other members will not last tomorrow night.'

'Why tomorrow night?'

'I've heard from Ouchy the meeting takes place tomorrow night. I don't think you'll be needed to do the job.'

'What about my fee, then?' Tina demanded indignantly.

'You'll get some sort of fee.'

Then he was gone. Tina slammed down the phone in a fury. Then she thought about what Hassan had said. With a bit of luck Tweed would survive so she could earn the small fortune he had earlier offered.

Hassan then called Simone Carnot, gave her the same instruction. Unlike Tina, she took the news calmly. In any case, she had saved enough to last her for many years. She was not the type who lived extravagantly – and like Karin Berg, she saved money.

They drove away from the Château des Avenières in convoy, with Paula behind the wheel of the first car and Marler following on her tail. As they came close to the point where they would pass the Château d'Avignon

Marler dropped back. Tweed had said they would not risk being observed by anyone who might be in the drive of that chateau.

'Poor Harry,' Paula said as she drove past the entrance. 'The gates are closed – he must feel he's in prison.'

'Harry is always content to operate on his own,' replied Tweed, sitting beside her.

'He'll have gone to bed,' Nield called out from the back, 'with a chair propped up under the handle of the door. He never takes any chances.'

'Better him than me,' commented Newman, seated next to Nield.

'I think the thugs there have other things on their so-called minds,' Tweed remarked.

'What other things?' Paula asked.

'I like driving at night,' he said. 'It's soothing. Can you see Marler? I can't.'

'No, he's dropped back. I'm sure he'll catch us up. Yes, here he comes . . .'

Marler had a problem, or felt fairly sure he had. A Peugeot had appeared and, although not close, seemed to be keeping pace with him. He would decide later if he was right. Marler never worried about problems which might be a figment of his imagination.

Paula drove at a cautious speed past the summit of Mount Salève. It was late but even at this hour several cars were parked at the viewing point. She presumed some people liked to look down on the dazzle of lights far below which was Geneva. She maintained her careful driving as she descended the spiral of curves leading to the city.

Now well behind her, Marler was convinced he had a problem. The Peugeot had come closer as he also descended. He suspected that it was someone from the Château d'Avignon who was tailing Tweed and himself. He slowed down, as though inviting the other car to overtake. The Peugeot slowed down. Not normal behaviour. The other car was always keeping him in sight as Marler drove round the series of endless bends.

Inside the Peugeot Mario felt pleased with himself. He would get a pat on the back from Vitorelli when he told him where Tweed had headed for. Marler was operating so skilfully that it never occurred to Mario that he had been rumbled. Mario was anxious not to lose sight of the two cars when they entered the complexities of the Swiss city.

He was nervous when they approached the checkpoint on the border. Supposing the car in front of him was waved on and he was stopped? He little knew that Marler had played with the idea of using the checkpoint in some way to lose his tail. He had rejected the idea almost immediately. With what he had taped under the chassis he wanted to pass straight through.

'Marler is acting in a peculiar manner,' Paula commented as they reached level ground and she saw the checkpoint ahead.

'Marler always knows what he's doing,' Tweed reminded her.

She slowed down, prepared to stop as the checkpoint loomed in front of her. The officer on duty waved her on. Marler gave a sigh of relief as the officer also waved him on. In his rear-view mirror he saw that the Peugeot had received the same wave. Marler really began to concentrate.

In his mind's eye he saw the route ahead, the route he knew that Paula would take. She would drive across the great bridge over the river, the Pont du Rhône, and then she would be in the main and complex part of Geneva. From the bridge it was only a short distance to the rendezvous point, the rail station.

'I've got to mess you up, chum,' he said to himself, thinking of the Peugeot's driver.

He deliberately drove quite slowly. Other cars, emerging from different routes, overtook him. One driver honked his horn. Marler was careful not to look at him. We can do without road rage tonight, he thought. There were traffic lights close to the entrance to the bridge. He drove on very slowly.

He timed it so the lights turned red when he arrived. Behind him a car honked, annoyed that it had missed the lights. Now the Peugeot was one car behind him. Not because Mario had wanted that to happen, but an impatient driver had cut in on him. Paula's car was already halfway across the bridge.

Marler kept stopping and starting his engine, knowing from past experience that the lights would stay red for a while. He then raised the bonnet, got out and pretended to peer inside the engine. The driver of the car behind him climbed out and addressed him in French.

'If you've broken down I'll help you move the blasted thing to the side of the road. I haven't got all night while you fool about.'

'I don't speak the lingo,' Marler lied.

The driver cursed in French, returned to his car. The lights had turned green. Marler, sitting behind the wheel, played with starting and stopping again. He had checked swiftly to make sure there were no patrol cars about. On his right, waiting to enter the bridge when it could, was a juggernaut.

Marler watched the green light, ignoring the chorus of blaring horns behind him. He had created a major traffic jam. The lights changed to red against him. He rammed his foot down, shot forward as the juggernaut rumbled forward, its driver pressing his horn which sounded like a large cruise ship's foghorn. Then

Marler was on the bridge, racing across it. Soon after reaching the far end he turned down a side street, followed a devious route which would take him to the rail station.

In his frustration, Mario hammered his clenched fist down on the horn. The irate French driver in front of him reversed his car, slammed it with not too much force into the front of the Peugeot. It was nobody's night. Except Marler's.

Arriving at the station he found Paula parked and waiting for him. Jumping out, he ran to the window Tweed had lowered.

'Sorry about that. Slight problem with a tail. Lost him.'

'Then on to Ouchy. To the Beau Rivage,' said Tweed.

In only a few minutes Paula was enjoying herself driving along the motorway which ran parallel to Lake Geneva, mostly some distance away to their right. There was very little traffic and she drove fast, keeping just within the speed limit.

'This is relaxing,' she said.

'And Marler is behind us,' called out Newman.

'So all is well,' Paula enthused.

'I suspect all is not well at all,' Tweed interjected.

33

One hour earlier a cavalcade of three black cars had proceeded along the same motorway. The front car was driven by Big Ben, who drove fast, but also kept just inside the speed limit. Beside him sat Jeff, a large man whose body was all muscle. His face wore a permanent menacing expression. His head was almost bald and he had the eyes of a lizard.

Years before, Jeff had built up an enviable reputation in the East End of London as The Extortioner. His methods of persuading reluctant shopkeepers and club owners to pay up were legendary and horrific. He had left behind a number of victims crippled for life. Faced with a murder charge, he had broken out of a police station, badly injuring three policemen in the process.

The two men in the rear of the car, and the four men in each of the following cars, had also fled Britain to avoid the risk of long prison sentences. Several of them had recently taken on the Mafia in Germany. The Mafia was still reeling from the onslaught and at least ten mutilated bodies had been dragged out of the Rhine.

They were, in fact, what Tweed would have termed 'the *crème de la crème* of people better never to have been born'. These were men who were the living proof of another of Tweed's maxims, 'There is such a thing as pure evil.'

'Well, we got the bomb past the bloody *flics*,' Jeff recalled as they continued their drive.

'So how does it feel, sitting on it – when it's gutsy enough to blow Buckingham Palace sky high?' asked Big Ben and he chuckled.

'Comfortable,' replied Jeff. 'Bloody comfortable.'

The car they were travelling in had been skilfully adapted in a French workshop in a remote barn in the countryside. The brilliant mechanic who had done all the work himself had been promised a million francs if he succeeded. He had succeeded, hollowing out part of the chassis, believing it would contain a huge drug consignment. Instead, it was carrying the bomb with a radio-controlled device which would detonate it from a distance.

The French mechanic had never seen his million francs. He was now buried in a deep hole under his own barn. Fred Brown, carrying out the orders Hassan had given him, had arranged with Big Ben to 'dispose of the body once the job is done'.

Originally, Hassan's target had been the French President. Then the bomb would have been driven by remote-controlled car without a driver into the court-yard of the Elysée at the very moment when the gates were open for the Presidential car to leave the building, which was the official residence of the President.

Hassan had changed the plan at the last moment. He had realized he had in his possession the means of totally destroying all the surviving members of the *Institut* when they assembled at their headquarters in Ouchy. His instructions to Fred Brown had been precise and these instructions had been passed on to Big Ben.

'I feel like a fag,' Jeff said, his ugly hand reaching for his pocket.

'Light that and I'll smash your face in,' Big Ben said in a normal voice.

Big Ben abhorred smoking. As a youngster his father had forced him to smoke a large Havana cigar until it was no more than a stub. Big Ben had been ill for days. He considered that his only virtue was a sense of humour. Before the corpse of the French mechanic had disappeared down the deep hole he had pinned a note to the Frenchman's blood-stained chest. *IOU.*

'Don't get this business about a boat on the friggin' lake,' Jeff said, removing his hand reluctantly from his pocket.

'Orders. We hijack a big launch from the 'arbour at Ouchy. One man who swims well takes it out opposite the place where these nutcases are meetin' and punts about. With what we 'as in the car, behind us we make up dummies to look like real men. That's it.'

'Don't get it.'

'You don't get a lot of things. Your job is do as you're told and don't ask too many questions. Got it?'

343

'I got it.'

Big Ben never missed an opportunity to show who was boss. This was how he had become the top man in one of Hassan's key groups of killers. As he drove on he went over again in his mind the plan Hassan had outlined to him for Ouchy.

Hassan, despite his self-conceit, had a good brain and was a first-rate planner. He would never have admitted it but some of the key ideas had come from the Englishman. Hassan presumed he had picked up some of his more brilliant plans from his travels in the Middle East.

He had not forgotten Karin Berg, who had been placed in the Hôtel des Bergues. He had decided he needed a reserve. Just in case everything went wrong. The fact that Tweed was still alive was worrying him. He had called Berg.

'Karin, there has been a change in the situation.'

'What change?'

'Don't keep asking questions. Pack your bags and leave Geneva by the first flight in the morning.'

'Where the hell am I going now?'

'Watch how you talk to me!'

'And you mind your manners when you're talking to me. So where do I fly to?'

'You board a flight for Zurich. You don't leave the airport. You then catch a flight for Vienna – for Schwechat airport. A car will be waiting to pick you up.'

'To take me back to that boring headquarters?'

'You want a bonus of ten thousand dollars to start with, don't you?'

'Make it thirty thousand.'

'You think I'm made of money?'

'I know your father is. Do I get it?'

'You do—'

344

Hassan cursed. She had slammed down the phone on him again. He sat back in his chair and imagined strangling her slowly.

The three black cars, with Big Ben still in the lead, passed the marina on their right after they had entered Ouchy. A forest of masts swayed slowly in a light breeze. As arranged before it had left the Château d'Avignon, the rear car parked, then the car behind Big Ben overtook him, drove past the harbour and parked a few hundred yards along the lake front.

'We don't want a crowd of us drawing attention,' Big Ben had explained when he had briefed them at the chateau.

He parked his own car in a side road leading up to the Beau Rivage hotel. Like all his men, he wore a tracksuit. In June there were always joggers running at all hours. Before getting out of the car he stared at the Café Beau Rivage, where well-dressed and beautiful women were dining with their escorts both inside and out on the pavement.

He licked his lips as he studied some of the women. They were class, not the sort of companions he had spent his time with. He was due for a huge bonus when the operation was completed. I'll have to smarten up my wardrobe, he thought. He felt sure some of those women would like something different.

'Shouldn't I check the 'arbour?' Jeff suggested cautiously.

'We'll check it together. You two in the back keep your eyes peeled for patrol cars. Use the horn once to warn us if any local *flics* arrive. Ignore them if they drive past. If they check you you're waiting for friends to join you for a jog. Keep your friggin' eyes peeled.'

He climbed out with Jeff and they strolled down to

345

the small oyster-shaped harbour which was full of sailing craft and powerboats. No one else was about and the lake was not too close to the hotel.

They had nearly reached the end of the rows of boats when Big Ben grabbed Jeff's arm and stopped. A bald-headed man was on the deck of a large launch, painting a door to a cabin. Even his working clothes were fashionable and expensive. There was no sign of anyone else aboard.

'That's just what we need,' Big Ben whispered. 'Guy looks like the owner. You've got your gear.'

Jeff was carrying a cloth bag. Inside were several pots of paint and a number of brushes, together with an instrument for scraping off paint. The Englishman had passed very precise instructions to Hassan who, in his turn, had relayed them to Big Ben.

'Nobody about,' Jeff whispered back.

'Then get on with it . . .'

Jeff went closer to the launch. He noticed several items on the deck – a marlinspike, a loop of chain, a pile of cleaning cloths. It was as though the owner had known what was required. Making no sound with his rubber-soled shoes, Jeff stepped off the pavement onto the deck. His weight caused the bald-headed man to stop painting. When he turned round Jeff had picked up the marlinspike and, holding it behind his back, was close.

'Lost me way,' said Jeff. 'Tryin' to get to Vevey.'

'Really?' The bald-headed man was not happy about the ugly face staring at him. 'Well, you simply—'

He never finished his explanation. Jeff brought the marlinspike down with all his considerable strength on the bald pate. The skull was cracked as he sagged. Jeff had dropped the weapon, had gripped the dead man under the armpits, dragging him along the deck to the prow under the small bridge. The corpse was out of sight as he glanced around. On the pavement Big Ben gave him a thumbs-up sign.

Jeff went up into the wheelhouse. He'd had considerable experience stealing expensive boats on the Hamble in Hampshire back in England. The trouble was that starting up the engine would easily attract attention onshore.

Meanwhile Big Ben had waved his arms, signalling to the car parked outside the Beau Rivage café. One of the men who had been in the rear was waiting behind the wheel. He started up the car, drove slowly past the diners on the pavement, turned down to the harbour and executed a U-turn close to where Big Ben was now standing at the stern of the launch. The boot of the car was now hidden from anyone dining who might glance in their direction.

Big Ben helped the two men haul out large sacks from inside the boot. They heaved the sacks onto the deck of the launch at the stern. They had just completed the job when Jeff had a bit of luck.

A posse of motorcyclists arrived opposite the hotel. To annoy the diners they stopped, revving up their engines. Jeff started up the launch's engine under cover of the racket. Big Ben had slipped the towrope, which was looped round a bollard. Jeff guided the launch slowly out into the darkness of the lake and was gone.

'That's the worst part done,' Big Ben said as he slipped behind the vacated wheel of the car.

'Les,' he said to the man who had driven the car and was now sitting behind him, 'is there someone from the car parked near the marina close by?'

'Gave him the go-ahead, as I drove over.'

Les was a tall wiry man with a broken nose. His speciality was as a knife-thrower. He had learned his trade working for a circus – until in a rage he skewered a poor girl through the throat for not agreeing to his suggestion. He had escaped before the police had arrived and Big Ben had met him holed up in the East End of London.

As they drove slowly along the wide road with the lake beyond a wall on their right the third black car appeared behind them. Big Ben grinned, showing his bad teeth. He had given his gang the impression the plan was his own. You took every chance to build up your authority. As he crawled along he glanced out across the lake. The launch had disappeared.

'A job well done,' he said with evident satisfaction.

'He has to do a lot more,' said Les.

Once well away from the shore, Jeff stopped the launch, let it drift as he did a lot more. First, he stripped the owner naked. Using an axe he found among the launch's tools, he chopped off each hand at the wrist. No fingerprints for swift identification. Then, wearing rubber gloves, he put each hand inside a small bag weighted with lead which he'd extracted from the large cloth bag also containing paint and brushes. What he did with the face to make it unrecognizable is best not described.

After binding up the corpse with the chains and loop of rope he had found on the deck, he then heaved the body inside a large sack. He carefully tied up the neck. Stripping off his rubber gloves, covered with blood, he shoved them inside another small sack.

After washing his hands in the galley he went back to the wheelhouse, looked round carefully, started up the engine and headed into the middle of the lake. He was anxious to finish this part of the job before the moon rose. He stopped the launch briefly in the middle of the lake. He did this three times.

At one point he heaved overboard the sack containing the body. On the second occasion when he stopped he threw over one of the sacks containing a hand. On the third occasion he threw overboard the second hand. He allowed himself a sigh of relief as he started up the engine again.

Later, he stopped again. With the aid of a torch and the paint and brushes he had brought with him he painted a green line round the squat funnel. The moon was rising as he covered up the original name of the vessel with sheets of special paper he extracted from his sack and unrolled. The paper carried the name *Starcrest V*. His next task was easy – he removed the Swiss flag flying from the stern and replaced it with a French flag. It wasn't a perfect transformation but the launch would only lie off Vevey for a day before it played its key role in the destruction of the remaining members of the *Institut*.

Tweed, reaching Ouchy, drove to the Beau Rivage's front entrance, which faced away from the lake. Handing the car keys to a porter he went inside the vast and palatial hotel to reception. Paula was beside him while Newman and Nield followed them.

A few minutes later Marler drove up as though an independent visitor. On Tweed's instructions he had reserved his own room by phone before leaving the Château des Avenières.

'Welcome back, Mr Tweed,' the smartly dressed girl behind the counter greeted him. 'We have again reserved you a room overlooking the lake.'

'Thank you. I'm sure my friends could do with a drink in the bar . . .'

After registration he led the way. Paula stared up at the very high vaulted ceiling decorated in excellent taste. She liked the atmosphere of the whole place.

Instead of being handed one of those horrible computer keys she was carrying a traditional key.

As they walked down the long, wide and deserted corridor she continued to admire the decor. The bar was a large room on the left with comfortable chairs and a spacious feel. A Dutch girl sat behind a grand piano singing romantic songs while the few guests inside the bar listened.

'This is civilization,' Paula commented as she sank into a chair which seemed to wrap itself gently round her.

'What is everyone going to have to drink?' Tweed enquired. 'I expect, Paula, you'd sooner have gone straight up to your room but after the drive I thought a drink would help.'

'A glass of wine. And it will help. At least we can relax here.'

'We can't relax anywhere,' Tweed said sharply. 'Not until we have destroyed our opponents or they have destroyed us.'

He smiled after ordering drinks to take the edge off the grimness of what he had said. Paula thought she had never known him show quite such iron determination and ferocious energy. Tweed had reverted to ordering orange juice for himself. When they were refreshed he made his request.

'Paula, Bob, I'd like us to stroll along the lake front to take a look at the Institut building. We can unpack later.'

'We'll come, too,' said Marler who had joined them, glancing at Nield, who nodded agreement.

'Fair enough, but keep well behind us as though you're strangers.'

Tweed knew a short cut to the lake front. They descended in a lift to the ground floor, walked along a corridor and out onto the pavement where people still sat at tables.

Striding out, Tweed walked down the side road alongside the gates which led to the extensive gardens of the hotel. Then, crossing the road, he headed along the pavement by the lake in the direction of Vevey. The moon was up and Paula gazed across the sheen of the lake to the huge mountains of Haute-Savoie in France on the far side. The sight filled her with awe.

After a walk of several minutes Tweed pointed to a large mansion on their left, standing on an eminence above the road. There was something sinister about the ancient dark pile towering above them. It stood well back with a green lawn sloping down to the road. Double wrought-iron gates were closed, barring off a curving drive. A few yards further along a noticeboard was illuminated in front of the railed wall which preserved its privacy. Paula read the notice, which was in English and French.

A meeting of all members will be held at 22.00 hours tomorrow.

'I presume all surviving members have been informed,' she said.

'What sort of meeting would it be without members?' Tweed asked in the same grim tone he had used in the bar. 'There's a side entrance.'

Walking several yards further, he stopped in front of a small railed gate behind which climbed a flight of stone steps. He tested the padlock, which was closed. Nothing about its appearance told him the lock had recently been expertly picked and opened.

'No lights on inside the mansion,' Paula remarked.

'Why should there be?' Tweed's tone softened. 'I

think we'll go back now before the Café Beau Rivage closes. You must be hungry.'

'My tummy is rumbling,' Paula admitted.

They had crossed the deserted road to look at the HQ of the *Institut*. Marler and Nield waited on the opposite side, leaning on the wall, apparently staring at the lake and the view beyond in the distance. Both men had observed the mansion closely.

No one had noticed as they were approaching the mansion the rear of a black car disappearing round a bend towards Vevey. The Englishman who had studied the layout during a visit had given very careful instructions to Hassan. He, in his turn, had passed on the details to Big Ben. The large bomb was now in place.

34

They ate an excellent meal at an isolated table inside the Café Beau Rivage. Paula had decided food was more important than a trip to her room to change. Marler had not joined them, to keep up the appearance that he had nothing to do with them. He sat at a table outside, enjoying the view of a number of very beautiful women.

'Do you think there's anything to choose between the three members of The Sisterhood?' Paula asked Tweed over coffee. 'I mean they are all prepared to murder for money, but are they as bad as each other?'

'My choice for the most evil one would be Tina Langley.'

'Why?'

'From certain enquiries Monica has made it's obvious that Tina has only one god. Money. Human emotions mean nothing to her. She's never had any desire to work for her living. From an early age she's concentrated on exploiting men, then throwing them over when she's drained them of money.'

'Anything else?' Newman asked.

'Yes. At least Simone tried to earn her living running an agency in Paris. Before that she was personal assistant to the managing director of a big company – and good at the job. As for Karin Berg, we all know that for years she worked high up for Swedish counter-espionage. I know how well she operated. It was only later in life that they went bad, tempted by big money.'

'And Tina?' Paula persisted.

'Has never had any job of any kind all her life. Doesn't have the brains – or the inclination – to earn her living like other people. As I said, I can only think of exploiting wealthy men. Pure evil.'

'I'm inclined to agree with you,' said Paula. 'Contemptible is the word I would use. Now I'm looking forward to sleep.'

'I won't get any,' said Tweed. 'I'm not complaining. It goes with the territory, as I believe the Americans say. I have to meet someone in another part of the hotel.'

'I'll come with you,' Newman said quickly.

'No one will come with me.'

'You may just need protection,' Newman insisted.

'I can assure you all that I certainly don't need protection.'

When they left the table Tweed expressed the desire to have some fresh air. He led them out onto the pavement and then up a side street. A cool breeze was now blowing off the lake. Near the top he paused, listening to a weather forecast in French coming through an open window.

'You heard that?' asked Paula. 'They expect major thunderstorms tomorrow night.'

'Tonight,' said Tweed, 'it's just after midnight.'

Turning right at the top of the road led them to the

main entrance to their hotel. They were standing waiting for the lift when Paula glanced up. The hall had an immensely high ceiling and it was possible for someone on any floor to gaze over a rail down into the hall. She nudged Tweed and he looked up.

Leaning over the rail on the second floor, gazing down at him, was the auburn-haired Tina Langley.

The three black cars drove slowly into Vevey, the next important town on the edge of the lake from Ouchy. Big Ben knew Vevey well. He had once worked as a packer in a pharmaceutical plant there. His main income had come from drugs he stole and then sold elsewhere. He never took drugs himself, just as he never smoked. His main indulgences were drink and ladies of the night. Since he had a large capacity for alcohol he'd found the two went together rather well.

'Signal to that hotel,' he ordered Les, seated next to him.

The knife-thrower waved a hand out of the window he had opened. The car behind them parked outside the hotel. This technique was repeated a few minutes later and the third car parked outside another small hotel. Big Ben sighed with satisfaction.

'It's goin' good,' he said.

'What's the idea?' asked Les.

The tall thin man with the broken nose stretched his legs, which were becoming cramped. He was always the one who asked questions, and Big Ben would have got rid of him but he was too good at his work to lose. He decided to humour his awkward associate.

'There are twelve of us. Use that thing in the top of your 'ead. It's the tourist season – but twelve of us shacking up in one 'otel could make people talk. Stuck in three different 'otels we won't be noticed. They're all booked in for three nights. So, with it paid for in advance, no manager is goin' to worry when they stay in their rooms all day.'

'And,' Les said brightly, 'we all then meets up at the agreed place outside this Vevey after dark tonight. We 'as the guns and we gives the others theirs when we meet up. Then we drives back in the dark to that big 'ouse in Ouchy. Any guys who gets out after the bomb goes off we shoots down.'

'Les, if you goes on like that you'll be an Einstein.'

'Who's he? Another helper?'

'You're slippin' again.'

'What about Jeff? Be bloody cold out on the lake.'

'Jeff's a wiz with a watch. Timin' to you. He stays with the launch off the 'arbour 'ere. When it gets dark he fixes it up. At the right time he takes it back opposite that big 'ouse at Ouchy. Part of the plan, matey. There's our 'otel . . .'

In his room half an hour later Tweed had had a bath and dressed again, this time in casual clothes – a polo-necked sweater and slacks. The room, almost a suite, was spacious and comfortable. He was just settling himself down at a desk and reaching for the phone when he heard someone tapping on his door.

Going to the door, he stood against the wall opposite the hinge side, opened it. Paula stood outside. She had changed her clothes and was dressed in a smart blue suit. She nodded approval when she saw he was holding a canister of hairspray.

'I can't sleep. Do you mind if I stay with you for a while?' He noticed she was carrying her shoulder bag and smiled as he ushered her inside, relocking the door.

'You've appointed yourself my personal guard.'

'Well, I was worried all the time in the bath. I was remembering Tina peering down at us from a balcony.'

'There's a fresh pot of coffee just delivered by room service. They must have assumed I wouldn't be alone – hence the two cups.'

'I'll pour. I'm not in the way, am I?'

'Not at all. You're company in the wee small hours. I have to make some phone calls. It's all right, you can hear what I say. That couch over there is comfortable. My first call is to the Baur au Lac.'

He returned to the desk, sat down and pressed numbers.

'Baur au Lac. Could I speak to the concierge? Tweed speaking. Is that the concierge? I'm trying to contact my old friend, Amos Lodge.'

'He's not in the hotel, sir,' the concierge informed him. 'He left earlier. He has kept his room on hold. Said he expected to be back in a few days.'

'Did he leave a number where he could be contacted?'

'No, sir . . .'

'Amos has disappeared,' Tweed told Paula after putting down the phone.

'Did you expect that?'

'I rather did. Interesting.'

He had just spoken when there was a light tapping on the door. Before Tweed could move Paula was on her feet. She had extracted the Browning from her shoulder bag and held it openly by her side. Unlocking the door she found Tina Langley standing outside.

Tina was wearing a nightgown, low-cut, exposing cleavage. She was carrying a large canvas bag out of which the neck of a wine bottle protruded. The two women stared at each other. Paula thought their visitor had eyes like slate.

'I had some information for Mr Tweed,' Tina said stiffly. 'I didn't realize he'd have company. I expect it will be like that all night long.'

'Like what?' snapped Paula.

'Isn't that a gun you're holding?'

'You should be able to recognize a gun by now.'

'Horrid things. I didn't expect to be interrupting Mr Tweed's tête-à-tête,' she said with a suggestive smile.

'I'd say you're an interruption, an unwanted one, wherever you turn up.'

Paula closed the door in Tina's face, her lips tight. Tweed was still sitting at the desk when she turned round. He looked amused.

'I'd like to have put a bullet through her,' Paula said viciously. 'You got a good look. Would you have been tempted?'

'Silly question. She's rubbish. Thank you for seeing her off. Drink some coffee – you look furious. I'm calling the Dolder Grand now to have a word with Willie.'

After a brief conversation he again put down the phone. Drinking some of the coffee Paula had poured, he turned round.

'Willie has also gone missing. He checked out of the Dolder Grand earlier today – or yesterday. Left no forwarding address. Gave no indication he'd be returning. Interesting, very interesting, what I've learned from two phone calls.'

Paula knew better than to ask him what he found so interesting. If he wanted to tell her he would do so. He turned back to the phone after checking his watch.

'Now I have to call someone inside this hotel.' He pressed numbers, waited for only a short time. 'You know who this is,' he began. 'We're all here – except for Butler. I left him behind in France to do a job when the time comes. How is everything going? Too early to say?

357

They've got a very tough job. Can I come along to see you now? Good.'

After completing the call, Tweed drank more coffee from the cup Paula had again refilled. Then he stood up, glanced at a large map he had spread out on the bed.

'As I told you, I have to visit someone in the hotel. I'm afraid it's highly confidential.'

'You're not wandering round by yourself. Not with *that* woman in the place.' Paula spoke firmly, standing up. 'I'll accompany you, then leave you once you reach wherever you're going. No argument.'

'Then I'd better not argue. Why not go to bed, get some sleep?'

'Because I'll be coming back here if you loan me the key again. Then you call me when you're ready to come back. I'll collect you. Call me fussy, but I'm sure Tina stands to earn a load of money for shooting you in the back. And you once told me that in the case of all the murders no one had heard a shot fired.'

'That's true. They have obviously designed an effective silencer for the Luger. So let's stroll along where I have to go together . . .'

Tweed would have preferred to go on his own, confident of his ability to deal with any situation. But he would not risk disappointing Paula – such loyalty was very rare. They started a long walk through the wide corridors. They met no one on the way. Nowhere is as silent as a great and ancient hotel in the middle of the night.

'Don't forget to call me when you're finished,' said Paula as they stopped in front of a certain door. 'Wait until you hear me tap out our tattoo before you come out.'

She waited while Tweed knocked on the door. He had one finger to his lips as someone opened the door and he vanished inside. Paula was walking back, well away from where she had left Tweed, when she encountered Tina coming towards her.

No longer in her night things, Tina wore a pale blue dress and had clearly spent time perfecting her make-up to match her outfit. Paula smiled as they came close before passing each other.

'All tarted up?' she said. 'Hunting for fresh prey, are we?'

Tina gave her a venomous look, walked past without a single word. She was even more infuriated because Paula had hit the nail on the head. Tina was hoping to bump into a man who had returned late to the hotel by himself. A brief episode might earn her some pin money.

Tweed was absent for an hour. Paula kept wondering what could have kept him so long. Where was Amos? Where was Willie? What could they be doing? Questions without answers. She was greatly relieved when Tweed called, said he was ready to come back.

'Another phone call to make,' he said as Paula relocked the door to his room. 'This one will surprise you. I'm calling Chief Inspector Roy Buchanan of the CID back home.'

'At this hour?'

'I hope you weren't bored while I was away. There are plenty of magazines you could have looked at.'

'I'm not Tina. I've been reading a serious novel I brought with me.'

Tweed didn't hear her answer. He was too busy calling his old sparring partner. He was surprised how quickly Buchanan, at his home number, reacted.

'Who is it now?'

'Roy, this is Tweed. Calling from Switzerland. Sorry if I have woken you up.'

'Of course you've woken me up. I'm in bed at this

hour. It has to be important, I hope. I'll send you some sleeping pills.'

'There's a village in Dorset called Shrimpton. North-west of Dorchester. It's a weird place. Apparently most of the ancient cottages are rented out. No idea who owns them. They may house some dangerous criminals. Can I suggest you go down there, find out who does own them, who does occupy them? There's a pub at one end of the village. You might find something out from local gossip. This is very urgent. Concerns an inter-national menace which could threaten Britain in the near future.'

'Sounds serious, but I'm in a dilemma. The Com-missioner needs my advice tomorrow.'

'I've just had an idea. Send Sergeant Warden. He'll fit into the local landscape better than you would.'

'Why, may I ask?'

'I can only put it one way. You come over as a bit of a toff. I think the locals might clam up. Warden has the sort of wooden personality they'd chat to.'

'I'll tell Warden that.'

'You can phrase it more diplomatically. There's something very strange going on at Shrimpton.'

'I could call Warden in the morning . . .'

'I'd feel happier if you called him now. Then he can drive down and put up at a hotel in Dorchester. That would give him time to take a look at Shrimpton in daylight. I suggest he pretends to be a property sales-man – after buying local properties.'

'That's a clever idea. I just need convincing this is serious enough to avoid the Commissioner's request.'

'I don't want to sound pompous, Roy, but this involves the Defence of the Realm. I'm talking about the biggest menace since Adolf Hitler.'

'You can be so blasted persuasive, Tweed. I may go myself with Warden.'

'While you're there check discreetly whether two bigwigs have arrived back suddenly. They both live on the outskirts of the village. One is Amos Lodge, the other Captain William Wellesley Carrington.'

'How high up does this go?'

'To the PM. That's between the two of us.'

'All right, Tweed. I'll do my best. Where do I contact you?'

'At the Hotel Beau Rivage, Ouchy. Here is the number . . . If I move on I'll inform your assistant at the Yard where I am.'

'One question. Do you ever sleep?'

'Only when I can. A thousand thanks, Roy.'

'Jump off a cliff . . .'

'More coffee?' Paula offered when Tweed had dropped the receiver.

'Not now. My head is beginning to buzz.'

'You're really spreading a vast net this time.' Paula walked over to the map spread over the double bed. 'All the way from Dorset to Slovakia. I see you've marked the Château d'Avignon with a cross. Then another cross at that strange house way east in Slovakia. I presume they indicate the main communications centres.'

'They do.'

'Does this business really go up to the Prime Minister?'

'No comment.'

The phone rang as Tweed pulled down the top of his polo-neck, which felt too tight round his throat. He went back to the desk from where he had been studying the map with Paula. A familiar upper-crust voice spoke.

'That you, Tweed? Keith Kent here. I had the devil of a job persuading Monica to tell me where you were. You needed to know who owns the village of Shrimpton in Dorset and surrounding land. It wasn't easy – hence the delay.'

'You mean you've found out?' Tweed asked calmly.

'A man called Conway.'

'Conway?'

'You sound puzzled. I can understand it. He owns a company in the Channel Islands. But it gets complex.'

'I thought it might.'

'The Channel Islands company, which is difficult to penetrate, has a connection with the Cayman Islands. I suspect money – large sums – sent to the Channel Islands is then routed on to the Cayman Islands in the Caribbean. Infiltrating a bank account in the Caymans is next to impossible.'

'You've achieved the impossible before.'

'I think I can do it. I have a very good contact out there – but it will take time.'

'I haven't got time,' Tweed commented.

'I knew you were going to say that.'

'Keith, I need a photocopy of Conway's balance sheet because it will give his real name. I need it tomorrow. No – today.'

'You're a hard taskmaster. I'll drop everything to get you what you want.'

'It's appreciated, Keith.'

'My fee for this won't be appreciated.'

Tweed gave him the same message he had given to Buchanan. He would leave at the Beau Rivage a number where he could be found if he left Ouchy.

'You'll move on from Ouchy. I know you . . .'

'Who is Conway?' asked Paula as Tweed stood up from the desk. 'I'd forgotten that you'd asked Keith Kent to find out who owned Shrimpton. It was a while ago,' she said.

'One of those two Dorset men – Amos or Willie – once mentioned they'd visited the Cayman Islands. The trouble is I can't recall which one. It was a long time ago. When we know who Conway is we'll know who is masterminding this vast operation.'

35

The events which took place on that June night became known as the Battle of Ouchy.

The day started quietly on the surface. Despite being up for the whole night Tweed appeared for breakfast fresh and spruce. He had an almost jaunty air as his team settled down in the Café Beau Rivage for their meal. He had arranged for a table at the end of the restaurant in a corner where they would not be overheard. In any case, the only other occupants while the other tables were being prepared for lunch were the early drinkers at the bar at the far end.

'You look optimistic,' remarked Newman before he tackled a plate of bacon and eggs.

'Let it be clear to everyone,' Tweed replied, 'that complacency is our main enemy. Our opponents are powerful, resourceful, cunning and ruthless.'

'Then we'll have to fight dirty,' responded Nield.

'Any method will be used,' Tweed agreed. 'You'll all have seen that Marler is absent. He had an early breakfast and is now in his room. He is, shall I say, cleaning his equipment. Some of that will be distributed to you late in the day.'

'I can guess where the war will take place,' Paula said. 'At that big mansion along the lake front which we visited last night.'

'In that area, yes. Also a number of red berets were handed to me in a case. You will all wear one when the time comes. That red beret may save your lives.'

'That's right, be mysterious up to the last moment,' Nield commented.

'I suggest,' Tweed went on, 'that after breakfast we separate. Each of us at intervals will take a stroll along the lakeside promenade. This will enable you to study by daylight the HQ of the *Institut* and its surroundings.'

'Don't forget the lake,' Paula warned. 'Remember what happened at the Ermitage on Lake Zurich when you came under attack.'

There were brief pauses in their conversation when a waitress came to serve more coffee. Paula waited for her opportunity to issue her edict.

'This business of walking individually along the front does not apply to Tweed. I will accompany him. Not long ago I saw Tina Langley in the bar knocking back drinks. She had a bottle on the table so I think she must have ordered a generous supply to be sent to her room last night.'

'Reluctantly Tweed agrees,' said Tweed. 'Otherwise he knows that Paula will simply trail close behind him, even if I said no.'

'Well, that saves an argument you wouldn't win,' Paula told him.

Tweed told his fellow diners about phoning Willie and Amos and finding they had disappeared. He didn't mention his hour-long night visit to someone inside the hotel. Nor did he tell them about the unknown Conway. He always keeps something up his sleeve, Paula mused. I wonder what he's kept up his sleeve that he hasn't told me?

'Exercise this morning,' Tweed went on. 'Then use the afternoon to rest inside the hotel. You will need all your wits about you this evening. At 9 p.m. everyone assembles in my room and all will be revealed. Also, I will hand out your red berets. That includes you, Paula.'

'I always fancied myself in a red beret,' she joked,

trying to introduce a lighter note into the conversation. 'And isn't it a lovely day?'

The tall glass doors leading to the pavement tables had been opened and they had a view over a small park to the harbour beyond. Out on the lake, reflecting a duck-egg blue sky, small white triangles moved slowly towards France. They were yachts which sailing enthusiasts had taken out earlier. It was like a vision of paradise, Paula thought. A few miles across the lake the massive giants of the French mountains provided a dramatic background. There was no snow on the summits. The long heatwave had melted the last remnants which had clung to the savage peaks.

'A day to remember,' Tweed observed.

'I'm going to enjoy our stroll along the lakeside.'

'But,' Tweed warned, 'I predict it will also be a night to remember.'

Vitorelli picked up the phone in his room at the Baur au Lac. He was in a bad temper.

'Who is it?'

'Mario. You told me you were returning to Zurich. You flew the chopper there?'

'Of course. It's waiting at Kloten here. Where the hell are you calling from?'

'Geneva.' Mario took a deep breath. 'When I called you on the mobile I was following them down Mount Salève . . .'

'Don't tell me you lost them. I've been waiting all night for you to call.'

'It was the traffic in Geneva. Terrible. I've spent all night touring the city, looking for their parked cars.'

'You could have saved yourself the trouble by reading a newspaper.'

'I could?'

'Yes, dumbhead. The Swiss papers are making it a lead story. I will read the headlines in the one I have here. "Survivors of Mass Murders Risk Assassination. Meeting tonight at Ouchy."'

Vitorelli went on to read the details. They even gave the time of the meeting at the Ouchy headquarters at the mansion on the lakeside: 10 p.m. Mario was sweating as he listened in a café and his eyes wandered to a copy of the *Journal de Genève* a man was reading at a nearby table. A similar headline glared at him.

'I haven't seen a paper,' Mario lied as Vitorelli finished reading the report to him.

'I thought you were grown up,' Vitorelli thundered down the phone. 'Get yourself back into the car. If you haven't had breakfast you'll have to go hungry. Might sharpen up your wits. Drive now to Ouchy, put yourself up in a small hotel, then report to me this evening what happens at 10 p.m. in Ouchy. Shall I spell it out more slowly?' he asked as though dealing with a ten-year-old.

'No. I heard you. I will leave now.'

Mario had not had breakfast. He had been going to order a large meal at the café. Instead he ran to his car. Why, he was wondering, had his boss returned to Zurich and left the chopper at the airport?

In Slovakia Hassan was talking to the Englishman, who had called him. Their conversation was not warm.

'You've heard about the Ouchy meeting?' the voice snapped with military precision.

'Yes. A contact – it was Tina Langley – called me yesterday from the Château des Avenières. It gave me time to make certain arrangements. No one will survive.'

'Including Tweed?'

Tweed, Hassan thought. Always it was Tweed. He

seemed to live a charmed life. And he was everywhere. It was difficult to keep up with his swift movements. Always to – or near – sensitive places. He was developing a hatred of this strange man, who seemed invincible.

'Yes, including Tweed,' he replied. 'Tina said he would attend the meeting.'

'You have time then to fly there.'

'You can't fly to Ouchy—'

'Heaven give me strength. You leave immediately. Catch a plane to Zurich, then another to Geneva. I will have a Daimler with a chauffeur waiting at Geneva's airport. Call me back at this number with the ETA of the Geneva flight.'

'The Daimler—' Hassan began, puzzled.

'Bang your head against a wall. Wake up! The Daimler will drive you to Ouchy.'

The rasping voice of the Englishman sounded like a sergeant major addressing a particularly stupid recruit.

'I see . . .'

'Do you? Wonderful! I need a witness to tell me Tweed is dead. You're the bloody witness. Afterwards the Daimler drives you back to Geneva where you board the first flight for Zurich and, when you can, another flight to Schwechat Airport.'

'I'll have to dress the part . . .'

'He's catching on! The Daimler will be noticed – but it will be assumed it's carrying an important man.'

'It will be.'

'Look in the mirror sometime. Now, get *moving*!'

Strolling along the lakeside with Tweed after breakfast Paula studied the large mansion where the *Institut* held its meetings. A lot of details she had missed in the dark became clear. The first danger point struck her immediately.

'When those large gates are opened,' she said, 'anyone going up to that place, even by car, is terribly exposed.'

'Not if they're concealed behind that railed wall protecting the mansion from the road.'

'But they won't be able to attend the meeting then,' Paula objected.

'Wait until I give everyone my briefing in my room tonight.'

'It would be much safer,' she persisted, 'if they entered by that side gate where you checked the padlock. The stone steps leading up are shielded by a solid wall about man-high.'

'You are reading my mind.'

'I can't see anywhere else safe.'

'Look to your right at the gap in the lake wall. Steps lead down to a landing stage,' Tweed pointed out.

'You don't miss a thing. I read in the paper this morning before I came down that TV crews are expected to film the event. That could be dangerous – with all their lighting.'

'I have thought of that.'

'You're going quiet on me. All right, I'll change the subject. It occurred to me when I couldn't sleep last night that you've had no contact with Christopher Kane recently.'

'I tried to phone him after you'd gone back to your room. No answer,' Tweed told her.

'So three key men have vanished off the face of the earth.'

'Interesting, isn't it?' Tweed said with a smile.

'You are the most exasperating man I've ever known at times. I wonder why I work for you.'

'Because you like the work. A City job behind a desk would drive you round the bend.'

'That's true. At least you said interesting, instead of significant ...'

In the evening Paula watched the brilliant red sun sinking in the west like a blood-red coin. Fatalistically, she was wondering how many of them would be alive in the morning. From Tweed's mood which she had sensed during their morning stroll she knew he felt he was carrying a heavy responsibility. He was a man who cared.

As instructed, she had dressed herself in a trouser suit for ease of swift movement. Her Browning fitted invisibly behind the elasticized top of her trousers. She could reach it in a second and her shoulder bag would have restricted her. She sat down and read a book until 9 p.m. arrived. Everyone had had a quick light meal sent up to their rooms. Marler had not been seen for most of the day and she was curious where he had been.

Promptly at 9 p.m. she knocked on the door of Tweed's room. When she was admitted she saw the others had already arrived. Nield, Newman and Marler were seated in chairs. She noticed Marler had a number of large cloth bags perched against the side of his chair.

Tweed sat behind the desk, having removed the chair to the far side so he faced everyone. It was the fifth man who startled her. Arthur Beck, Chief of Federal Police, was seated on a wide couch. He stood when Tweed ushered her inside, came forward and gave her a hug.

'Welcome to the war conference.'

'You were the man Tweed visited secretly in a room here,' she whispered.

'He was,' said Tweed, who had overheard her.

'Come and sit with me,' the handsome greying police chief invited Paula.

Each man in the room had a sheet of paper on which was drawn a plan. Tweed handed her an identical sheet. One glance told her it was a plan of the mansion. She studied it quickly as she joined Beck on the couch.

'Marler has worked out the main tactics,' Tweed announced, seated behind his desk. 'In conjunction with myself and with the full agreement of Arthur Beck, who suggested some changes. I won't beat about the bush. No, I think Arthur might like to open the proceedings.'

'Tweed suspected that a large bomb had been planted under the mansion,' Beck said, standing. 'He was right. I had the Bomb Squad brought here. Some brave men worked in the night, checking the mansion. They discovered a huge bomb hidden in the cleaning store under the building. We are sure from certain aspects of it that it was to be detonated by remote radio control. It has been made harmless but we dare not remove it from the building in case the mansion was under surveillance.'

'Could it still detonate?' Paula asked quietly.

'Our top man in charge of the Bomb Squad would give you a reply which differs from mine. He would say that with high-explosive you never can be certain. I say no – in its present state, it is safe. When we can, we will put it aboard a dredger, take it out into the middle of the lake, lower it to the bed of the lake and detonate it there. The top man will not risk transporting a bomb of that size through the streets. Now, the main objective. Tweed will explain . . .'

Taking up the position he had handed over to Beck, Tweed stood behind the desk. He polished his glasses with his handkerchief before speaking. The brief interval was to make sure his audience gave maximum concentration to what he had to say.

'Chief Inspector Beck has given us full cooperation. Just before we left the Château des Avenières Nield received a second brief call from Butler at the other chateau. Butler said, I quote, "I'll take you on with that horse race bet. Odds twelve to one."'

'What did that mean?' Newman enquired.

'It was a coded message telling Nield that twelve of the so-called staff, twelve of the toughest thugs in the world, were on their way somewhere. I guessed it was to here. One of Beck's men, dressed like a tourist, counted twelve men passing along the lake-front road in three black cars. Twelve of the most dangerous men in the world.'

'It takes twelve men to plant a bomb?' Marler called out sceptically.

'No. They're back-up. Partly, I suspect, in case the bomb doesn't work. Partly to gun down any member of the *Institut* who escaped. When the bomb doesn't detonate they'll move in.'

'What is *your* real objective?' asked Paula.

'Paula knows me too well.' Tweed smiled briefly. 'This has to be one of the core groups in the main operation which even Washington now suspects will be launched from the East.'

'How do you know that?' persisted Paula.

'Because I have been in touch with Cord Dillon, Deputy Director of the CIA.'

'The West is then, at long last, waking up?'

'Let's say it's stirring from its long slumber. Can't reveal any details. Marler, hand out those red berets Beck provided us with.'

'It's a fancy dress ball,' Nield said, notorious for joking at moments of high tension.'

'It's to save your lives,' snapped Beck. 'A lot of my men are in position, some in plain clothes, some in uniform. When the shooting starts they'll know anyone wearing a red beret is a friend.'

'If it's a shoot-out the public could be in danger,' warned Marler.

'They will be,' Beck said grimly. 'Which is why I've had the lakeside road closed at either end. Not a lot of traffic at zero hours, fortunately. If the three black cars appear—'

'*When* they appear,' Tweed interjected.

'The easily moveable barriers will disappear to let them through,' Beck continued. 'From Tweed's description of the type of thug we'll be up against it would be best to exterminate the lot. That's off the record.'

'Are you risking the *Institut* members arriving?' asked Paula.

'No!' Beck shook his head. 'I am providing plain-clothes men to impersonate them. We're sure they will be observed – probably from the lake. And that's where the main attack may come from.'

'I don't think so,' Tweed contradicted. 'Arthur Beck and I disagree on that . . .'

Beck then took Tweed's place and outlined in detail the plan the two men had worked out together in the early hours. It involved close cooperation between Tweed's team and Beck's large force. At one stage Beck handed out certificates to Tweed's group, permitting the use of firearms. Marler had earlier handed more weapons to Newman, Paula and Nield. In addition to her Browning Paula was equipped with stun and shrapnel grenades and a small pair of high-powered binoculars. Her shoulder bag was bulging, despite her removing all her personal effects.

'You all know the positions you have to occupy,' Beck concluded. 'It's getting close to zero hour.'

36

Three black cars drove slowly along the lakeside road from the direction of Vevey. They were well spaced out. Inside the boot of the rearmost car was a motorcycle and the lid of the boot was partly raised to accommodate the machine inside. Big Ben sat in the front passenger seat of the third car beside the driver, Les.

Ever observant, Big Ben had caught a glimpse of the barrier across the road being wheeled out of sight. His thick lips twisted into a smile as Les kept his distance from the car in front.

'They had a checkpoint. Kinda nice of them to move it out of our way.'

'Means they know we're comin'. That ain't too good,' Les replied.

'If it's across the road when we're comin' back we smash it to bits, gun down anyone who gets in our way.'

'What's the motorbike for?'

'Me.' Big Ben grinned. 'I go ahead when we leave to check out what's goin' on.'

In his lap Big Ben was holding a dark box with an aerial he could extend at the press of a switch. There was another switch – the one which, when pressed, would detonate the bomb. His plan was simple. The men in the cars ahead would lay down a field of fire if there was any opposition. Every man was armed with a machine-pistol. The combined fusillade could annihilate an army platoon.

'I see Jeff's launch out on the water,' Les remarked. 'What's his job? You don't tell us nothin' about that big launch.'

'You'll see, you'll see. We're gettin' close to where

we blow that mansion to a thousand pieces. All I needs is a signal from the front car that the big heads of the Institute have arrived. Then – *boom*!'

Tweed and Paula were crouched down on the steps in the gap in the wall leading down to a landing stage. Like everyone else they were holding specially designed scrambler mobile phones. It would be impossible for anyone to overhear their conversations. Beck, holding his own mobile, was crouched beside them.

'A man is entering the drive to the mansion,' Paula commented. 'Now another man has appeared – he's also going up the drive.'

She had pushed up her red beret slightly to give her a clear view. The two large wrought-iron gates had earlier been opened. More men arrived, turned up the drive. She counted seven entering the mansion which was a blaze of lights behind the tall windows, the lights of chandeliers. Beck was listening on his mobile. He replied, '*Bon*.'

'Three black cars have passed the checkpoint,' he told them. 'They are well spaced out. Coming from the direction of Vevey. Just a minute – look out on the lake. That big launch some distance out. It's moving in this way.'

'Ignore it,' said Tweed.

'I can't do that. I have powerful patrol boats coming in from the French side.'

He began to speak rapidly in French over the mobile. Paula was able to catch the drift of his orders. He was warning everyone the main attack could be launched from the lake, that the three black cars could be a diversion.'

'Ignore the damned launch,' snapped Tweed, who

had also understood his orders. 'The launch is the diversion. This was organized, I am sure, by the Englishman with military precision. He's trying to fool us. Make it look like a repeat performance of the attack on me at the Ermitage on Lake Zurich. That's why you are looking in the wrong direction.'

'And you think the right direction is?'

'Those three black cars approaching from Vevey. Arthur, I'll stake my reputation I'm telling you the truth.'

'Never heard you say that before.' Beck paused, then began issuing quite different instructions over the mobile which, Paula realized, were being relayed also to Beck's men surrounding the mansion – and to the whole of Tweed's team. Beck had just countermanded his previous orders, warning his men to concentrate on three black cars approaching along the lakeside road. That was when she heard the first clap of thunder.

She had been aware that the atmosphere had changed suddenly – the temperature had dropped and a strong wind was shaking the trees lining the promenade. The first clap was a mere overture. It was followed by giant rolls of thunder which continued nonstop. Forked lightning slashed down over the mountains of France and then spread over the lake itself. This was going to be a storm to remember.

'Thank the Lord we're dressed for it,' she said to Tweed.

'Let's hope so. This is going to complicate matters.'

Like the police and the other members of Tweed's team they were all wearing waterproof windcheaters. Paula buttoned hers up to the neck as large drops splashed down, then the heavens opened up. A Niagara-like cascade of rain hammered down, bouncing back off the road. The thunder increased in intensity. The forked lightning was so brilliant it illuminated the mansion like a stage set, dulling the lights inside the building.

'This is going to be a night out of hell,' said Tweed.

Just before the storm broke Les saw the driver of the first car, now in sight of the mansion, wave a hand out of his window up and down twice. He had seen seven men in business suits enter the mansion and had stopped his car.

'This is it,' said Big Ben.

He pressed down one switch, the aerial elevated. He pressed down the master switch, waited for the sound of a tremendous explosion. Nothing. No explosion. Nothing. Frantically he pressed the switch down several times. Nothing. He swore foully.

'Signal to the two cars to launch a total attack,' he yelled. 'I'm going to get on the motorbike. I can see what's happening better from it. Soon as I get it out drive forward, join the attack.'

Leaving the car, he flung open the boot, heaved out the motorcycle. Big Ben had also listened to the weather forecast and was clad in an oilskin. Dragging the machine onto the pavement, he sat astride the saddle and, for the sake of appearances, started it and rode on the pavement alongside the car, which was already moving.

The storm was now blasting down on Ouchy. As his men jumped out of the cars a stun grenade landed in front of each of the front two cars, smashing their headlights. Big Ben slowed down, stopped. There were too many figures who were not his men darting about. The men from the front car opened up with their automatic weapons. A hail of return fire flailed both cars. They had walked into a massive ambush.

Big Ben turned his machine round, sped back along

the pavement the way they had come. Both hands gripped the machine but in his left hand he held a live shrapnel grenade. Ahead of him he saw the barrier had been re-erected across the road, but it did not extend over the pavement.

His machine flew along. For a fraction of a second his left hand released his grip on the machine and he hurled the grenade at uniformed police. In the driving rain he saw figures collapsing as the grenade exploded. Then he had driven past the barrier and was heading at top speed for Vevey.

Many of Beck's men were crouched behind the wall at the side entrance to the mansion. They laid down a fusillade from their own automatic weapons at the figures which had emerged from the cars and were firing at random. Marler, always going his own way, had earlier climbed a tree lining the pavement, gripping his Armalite. He remembered the incident in France when Monceau had chosen a tree as his firing point.

'The launch is closing in on us,' shouted Beck. 'It has a lot of men on board with weapons!'

'They're all dummies,' Paula yelled back at him. She had seen the launch coming in fast. Through her binoculars, the lenses streaked with water, she had seen that none of the 'men' aboard moved, that they held their weapons in the same position, like waxwork figures.

'Look out,' roared Tweed.

One of the gang had slithered along the other side of the wall on his stomach. He had spotted the group on the steps above the landing stage. He had reached the gap, had half-stood up, was aiming his machine-pistol at them. Paula swung round, hurled her binoculars. They caught the thug on the bridge of his nose. He staggered, shook his head, then raised the machine-pistol, which had drooped. Paula shot him twice with her Browning. His hair, soaked with rain, was plastered to his skull. He reeled backwards, fell into the gutter which was a river of running water.

The crash of the thunder, never-ending, drowned the sound of continuous gunfire, so to Paula the weird scene resembled some wild chaotic ballet of men running, aiming, falling as Beck's men on the steps of the side entrance went on firing.

Perched high up in his tree, Marler was watching a cunning thug who was making his way up the opposite side of the wall, separating him from Beck's men on the other side. He saw him reach the top, reaching a high point above all Beck's concealed men. The thug stood up, gripping his machine-pistol, aiming it down at the men below him, entirely unaware of his presence. Marler already had his Armalite aimed; in the crosshairs loomed the man's chest. He pressed the trigger. The thug, about to massacre Beck's men, jerked. His machine-pistol elevated skywards for a second, then he dropped in a lifeless heap on his side of the wall.

The front black car burst into flames. The driver had forgotten to switch off his engine. By the glare of the flames Paula realized there was now no movement anywhere. The rain thrashed down on bodies lying in the road. Beck's men were moving out of the side entrance, running along the road as they checked each corpse. The Battle of Ouchy was over.

Wearily, with Tweed holding her arm, Paula trudged back to the hotel. As they passed under a street lamp a Daimler, driven by a chauffeur with a man dressed in a business suit beside him, slowly moved away in the direction of Geneva. Hassan saw Tweed and Paula, closed his eyes.

The Daimler drove at a stately pace towards the checkpoint by the marina. It was allowed to proceed as Hassan shook his head to express his horror. Paula squeezed Tweed's arm when she saw the Daimler begin to move away.

'Some bigwig has decided he doesn't like Ouchy any more . . .'

Another car, a Peugeot, had quietly driven up the side street leading to the Beau Rivage. Mario, seated behind the wheel as the rain hammered his roof, had also seen Tweed and Paula pass under the street lamp. He had been deafened by the crescendo of the storm, had been shaken by the number of bodies he had seen on the lake front. Earlier, he had passed through the marina checkpoint by saying he had a reservation at the Beau Rivage. The police had confirmed this by phoning the hotel's reservation desk. From Geneva he had called the hotel for a reservation, as had Ashley Wingfield, also known as Hassan.

'I'm soaked,' said Paula. 'All I want is a hot shower. I'll not sleep tonight.'

Over an hour later she emerged from the shower in her room, and dressed herself in day clothes after ordering coffee from room service. Looking out of her window, she saw a large dredger moving out towards the centre of the lake. She recalled that Beck had said they would remove the huge bomb by this means. She heard a familiar tapping on her door. It was Tweed, also fully dressed in day clothes after taking a long hot bath. She poured him coffee.

'Come and look out of the window,' she suggested. 'I'll turn off the lights and then we can see more clearly.'

They had stood by the window for a while, neither

of them saying anything, both of them surprisingly alert. The dredger, with its dreadful cargo, had moved further away until it was in the middle of the lake.

They had watched through Tweed's binoculars until it got well clear. The historic thunderstorm had abated and it was strangely quiet in the early hours of the morning. Paula poured more coffee and they both drank in silence.

'I won't expect you up very early in the morning – this morning,' said Tweed.

'I think I'll suddenly cave in. What's happening?'

'I expect Beck's explosives expert has rigged up his own radio-control device to explode the bomb. You realize they have lowered it into the lake.'

'No. It must have been while I was pouring more coffee.'

She had hardly spoken when there was a tremendous eruption in the lake. They heard a muffled thump. This was followed by a gigantic upheaval. A portion of the lake climbed vertically into the night, a huge billowing fountain which, by Tweed's estimate, far exceeded the famous sixty-foot-high fountain off the shore of Geneva. It mounted higher and higher as tons of water were lifted to an incredible height. Then the elevated man-made fountain, like a colossal geyser, began to fall. They stood still as it generated giant waves which rolled majestically towards the shore and then crashed against the lake wall, hurling more water into the road.

'That was some bomb,' said Tweed.

'Tina Langley is in this hotel at this moment.'

Beck gave the news to Tweed after knocking on his door the day after the carnage. It was eight o'clock in the morning and when Tweed opened the door to the police chief he was fully dressed and his eyes behind his horn-rims gleamed with alertness and energy. A couple of minutes earlier Paula had arrived.

'How do you know?' Tweed asked in an off-hand manner.

'Because one of my men carrying her photo saw her hurrying back to her room. Presumably her curiosity had overcome her caution since she appeared to have returned from a walk along the lake front. I propose to arrest her and interrogate her until she breaks.'

'*Don't do that, Arthur.*' Tweed's tone had changed, had become determined. 'Instead, if she leaves here have her followed by some of your best men.'

'Sorry, Paula.' Beck remembered his manners, turning to talk to her. 'I hope you are recovering from last night.'

'This morning's experience? My brain won't settle, is racing at top speed. Thank you for the enquiry.'

'I don't like it,' Beck snapped, swinging on his heel to face Tweed. 'She's a murderess.'

'She's also a key player in the worldwide drama which is unfolding. She may well lead me to the heart of this enormous conspiracy which threatens the West.' Tweed's voice rose as he hammered at the police chief. 'You've had elite men in our civilization assassinated in Switzerland. You've had an orgy of violence not a quarter of a mile from where you're standing. Don't spoil a major victory.'

'Victory?' queried Beck in a puzzled tone.

'You wiped out one of the hardest cores of the opposition. Those men in the black cars were, I am certain, intended to take part in a much more dangerous operation. So leave Tina Langley alone, but don't let her out of your sight when she moves on, as I know she will. They don't call her The Butterfly for nothing.'

'Reluctantly I'll agree. Now, do you want the bad news?'

'You're so reassuring,' Paula half-joked. 'I think I'm going to need more strong coffee for breakfast.'

'Tell me,' Tweed said quietly.

'Pete Nield gave me a clear description of Big Ben. You told me, Tweed, that he was likely to be the top man.'

'What about him?'

'We have examined all the corpses – now in the morgue – and not one of them bears the slightest resemblance to him. Big Ben somehow escaped last night.'

'The worst of the lot. Well, I suppose at some later stage we will meet the gentleman in question again.'

'I've thought about Tina Langley,' Beck said slowly. 'You are usually right in your decisions. I will put my best trackers on her. If she moves on I'll call you. We need a code word for her. I suggest Jungfrau, which in German means young lady.'

'I know it does.'

'Hardly appropriate,' said Beck with a dry smile. 'Now I must get back to work . . .'

'At least he showed a certain sense of humour,' Paula commented when he'd gone. 'Jungfrau indeed.'

Marler, never a man to indulge in wastefulness, had spent half the night carrying a satchel he had fetched from his room. He wore his red beret as he had quietly mixed with the police who were collecting bodies. When unobserved he had picked up some of the weapons lying everywhere, especially automatic weapons which he had secreted in his satchel.

The fact that a number of the weapons would be marked with fingerprints normally used in evidence bothered him not at all. Who would need evidence when Big Ben's gang were all corpses soon to be on their way to the morgue?

His task was made easier because many of the police realized he had saved their lives by shooting the member of the gang who had made his way to the top of the wall enclosing the entrance at the side. His last trip was to follow the route the thug had taken up the side of the wall. The body had been taken away and there were no police about as he shielded the beam of a small torch to search the ground. Behind a rock he found a collection of magazines which the thug had dropped ready to reload his weapon. Marler scooped them up, added them to the collection inside his satchel.

He walked back to the hotel with an unlit king-size between his lips. Once inside his room he repacked his new armoury. He then took a long hot shower after casting off his sodden clothes.

'There'll be another time, another place, another gang,' he'd said to himself.

Paula, after eating a much larger breakfast than she'd thought she could manage, had told Tweed she was going to sit in the hotel gardens by herself reading her book. She didn't tell him she was suffering from a reaction to what had happened or that she felt a desperate need for sleep.

She found it soothing to wander in the grounds,

which resembled a vast park with many different levels of lawns and flower beds. She had deliberately left behind in the lobby the newspaper which carried banner headlines.

Sitting on a secluded seat, she ran her fingers through her hair, stifled a yawn. She was dozing off, the book in her lap, when a gentle hand grasped her shoulder. She knew it was Tweed before she opened her eyes. He sat down beside her.

'I imagine your bag is packed for instant departure? I told everyone else to be ready to leave at a moment's notice.'

'My case is packed. Except for toilet things. I imagine that nothing is going to happen today.'

'I'm afraid it has happened already. Are you very short of sleep?'

'I was. Now I've had a snooze in the sun I feel much better. So what has happened?'

'Beck called me. He said Jungfrau has left the hotel. While she was having breakfast in the main dining room Beck sent a man to her room to tap her phone. He thought the management wouldn't appreciate anyone listening in on a guest's calls.'

'So she did call someone?'

'She has ordered a hotel limo to drive her to Cointrin Airport in Geneva. She has booked a Business Class ticket on a flight to Zurich. A man who gave no name phoned her, told her to reach Zurich as soon as she could. Then she had to phone him again from Zurich airport. His English was just a little too upper crust. He was obviously disguising his voice.'

'We're moving on, then?'

'Yes. But we'll be travelling in the hired cars to Zurich. Marler apparently is carrying enough weapons to start a small war. So he drives there alone in the other car. I will drive with you, Bob and Nield as passengers. Are you sure you're all right?'

'Quite sure. I told you – I had a snooze. You know if I have a nap I can keep going for hours. Stop worrying about me,' she said with a hint of irritation.

'We'll leave by the front entrance thirty minutes from now. I tried to get Amos and Willie on the phone, thinking maybe Willie'd returned to the Dolder Grand. Neither of them appear to be in Zurich.'

'Just don't say it's significant. I keep thinking about Christopher Kane.'

'So do I. He didn't answer my call either.'

'It's strange that all three men have vanished into the blue at the same time.'

'It's very strange . . .'

It was another gloriously sunny day as Tweed drove his three companions to Zurich. There was little conversation because they realized that Tweed was deep in thought as he handled the car expertly. Beside him, Paula had closed her eyes again but she was still awake. She was marvelling at Tweed's stamina; she had lost track of how little sleep he had enjoyed. It did not surprise her. On other occasions she had known Tweed summon up endless reserves of energy in an emergency. And it told her that there was a grave emergency facing them.

'I had a phone call from Harry this morning,' Nield whispered to Newman. 'Again he coded his message, which was brief. The gist was that most of the remaining staff at the Château d'Avignon had disappeared early this morning. Just enough left to keep the place barely going, I gathered.'

'Big Ben is assembling a second hard core of thugs,' called out Tweed, who had heard every word. 'I'd very much like to know where Big Ben is now.'

'Probably scuttering off back to Britain,' Nield suggested.

'I don't think so,' Tweed replied.

'We're staying at the Baur au Lac again, I presume,' said Newman.

'You presume wrong. I want to lie low, out of sight this time. We'll be staying at the Zum Storchen, a good hotel in the Old Town on the banks of the River Limmat.'

He then lapsed into silence and no one else spoke. Paula had taken in this information and wondered what Tweed was up to now. She had no doubt he had a clear plan for the next move but she couldn't work out what it might be. She sagged against the headrest and suddenly fell fast asleep.

At the Château d'Avignon Harry Butler was again displaying the patience of Job. He had no one to talk to – the few remaining guests were all French. Harry could understand what was being said but his command of the language was not sufficient for him to carry on a proper conversation.

He spent part of his time in his room reading a new manual on high explosives and how to handle the latest inventions. At breakfast he had noticed how few staff were left, but he had already covered this development by his brief call to Pete Nield at des Avenières the previous evening.

After lunch he went for a brisk walk. As he passed reception Fred Brown leaned over the counter. He gave Butler his oily smile.

'Taking the exercise, are we?'

'Stretching the legs. I had an accident I'm recovering from,' Butler lied.

It gave a reason for staying on by himself, he thought, as he checked his watch and walked along the deserted road in the direction of Geneva. It was cooler under the tunnel of trees overhead. When he reached his objective – the track leading into the forest where he had concealed a motorcycle – he walked straight past, but checked his watch.

Five minutes from the d'Avignon. Running, he reckoned he could cut that down to two minutes. Harry had not spun a yarn when he'd told Oily Fred he was stretching his legs. He was also keeping in trim for the mad dash he foresaw when he had planted Marler's bomb.

Returning to the hotel, he slowed to a walk before passing between the open gates. He had run all the way back, again checking his watch as he ran past the track from the opposite direction. He glanced at the watch as he sat down by himself on the terrace. Just over two minutes.

One thing Harry was careful not to do during all the time he spent on the terrace was so much as glance up at the turret containing the communications equipment.

Tina Langley disembarked from her flight which had taken her from Geneva to Kloten Airport, Zurich. She now had to find a phone to call Hassan at the Dolder Grand. She had no idea that Hassan had arrived in Zurich on the flight before the one she had taken.

Wearing a rather daring Versace number she put down her Louis Vuitton case, took out a mirror from her handbag and started to apply lipstick. Her eyes were scanning the airport concourse and she noticed a well-dressed man looking at her. He'd had something in his hand which she felt sure was a photograph.

Helmut Keller was one of Beck's senior detectives assigned to check passengers coming off this flight. He had made the mistake of glancing at the photo because

Tina also wore a stylish hat with a turned-down brim. Keller had also been momentarily distracted by her good figure. The expensive suit had been loaned to him by Beck to perfect his cover.

Saucily, Tina walked up to him, carrying her case. She passed close enough to him so he caught a faint whiff of her perfume. The photo was held in the hand behind his back. She snatched it from him, stared at it. Startled, he swung round. She gave him a seductive smile.

'Have you seen this woman?' she asked. 'It's my twin sister and she phoned me to say she was having a problem.'

'Twin sister?'

Keller was confused. He was dazzled by her. This was the last development he had expected. Had there been some frightful mistake?

'Twin sister, I said,' Tina continued, pursuing her advantage as she sensed his confused state. 'Rosemary.'

'Rosemarie?'

'She's English. What are you doing with her photograph? Now you have *me* worried.'

'We wish to interview her.'

'So who is "we"?'

'A private investigation agency,' said Keller, recovering his wits.

'Oh, my Lord. She hasn't passed another dud cheque, has she?'

'Dud cheque?'

'Maybe that's why she ran out on me from the Hôtel des Bergues in Geneva. I knew she was up to something. Poor Rosemary. She sometimes uses the name Tina. Now I'm really worried. And I have an appointment with a director at the Zurcher Kredit Bank.'

'Your sister is still in Geneva?'

'She must be. On top of that she's having an affair with a Swiss banker. You can keep the photo. I must run.'

Keller's head was reeling. He had been so struck by this woman he'd been wondering whether he dare ask her out to dinner. Then duty asserted itself. He decided he'd better call Beck who had arrived in Zurich by car.

Out of sight of Keller, Tina had got into a taxi and told the driver to take her to the Eden au Lac, the only other good hotel she could think of on the spur of the moment. She must avoid the Baur au Lac at all costs.

Tina was a little disappointed. Keller had been a handsome man and his clothes suggested money. She had read his mind and guessed he had been wondering whether to invite her out. Bloody Hassan could have waited if she'd found she had hooked a big fish. But now she knew they were looking for her all over Switzerland. She had not forgotten the tail in Geneva she had recently lured aboard an express train.

'Mario, now you've had some sleep tell me again in full detail about this outrage in Ouchy.'

In his room at the Baur au Lac Emilio Vitorelli was sipping a drink while his subordinate sat down and reached for the bottle on the table. Vitorelli shook his head.

'No alcohol until you have given me the full story. There is a long report in a late edition of the newspaper. But you were there. Tell me about the bomb.'

'Bomb? I don't know anything about a bomb. When the shooting stopped I went straight to my room at the Beau Rivage—'

'Your windows faced the lake?'

'No, the front of the hotel where you arrive.'

389

'Pity. I am very interested in that bomb.'

'And then I left the hotel in the early morning when you called me, told me to come here.'

'Just tell me what you did see.'

Mario repeated in greater detail what he had seen. When, dog-tired, he had arrived at the Baur au Lac he had given his boss a briefer version of the night's events. Vitorelli had then told him to get some sleep and they would talk later. Mario eventually came to the point where he had seen Tweed passing under a lamp with an attractive woman.

'*Stop!*' Vitorelli stroked his shaggy hair, leaned forward to listen more intently. 'You're sure it was Tweed?'

'Yes, you pointed him out to me when I was last at this hotel.'

'Tweed. I see everything now. In the paper it reports that a huge bomb placed under the mansion where the *Institut* meets was immobilized. After the killing was over – doubtless the attack was the work of The Sisterhood – they transported the bomb aboard a dredger into the middle of the lake. There it was lowered to a great depth, then detonated. A police photographer has supplied this picture of the bomb exploding.'

He passed to Mario the newspaper. Under the glaring headline was the picture of the immense fountain of water the bomb's detonation had created. Mario lifted his eyebrows.

'That must have been a great bomb.'

'You could create such a bomb?'

'With the right materials – including a radio-control device and plenty of advance warning.'

'And several thermite bombs?'

'Fire bombs would be easier still.'

'Tweed,' said Vitorelli, changing the subject. 'Tweed,' he repeated. 'I understand now. He planned an elaborate trap for The Sisterhood's gang. He worked in cooperation with the police. Doubtless with the top man, Beck. Tell your network to locate Tweed. Then you prepare the bombs.'

'The target? I need to know the target.'

'I have no idea. Yet. Use your imagination.'

'You're not saying you've lost her?'

Beck's voice was steely over the phone as he sat in his office at police headquarters in Zurich. He could hardly believe what Helmut Keller was reporting from the airport.

'She talked about this twin sister. So I thought—'

'No, you didn't think! You were so dazzled by Tina Langley you couldn't do your duty. Twin sister, indeed. How was she dressed?'

Beck's expression became cynical as Keller gave a highly detailed description of the glamorous outfit Tina had been wearing. He realized now how easy it must have been for her to deceive Norbert Engel and then blow off the back of his head in Vienna. This was a siren of sirens.

'All right, Keller. I'm sending two men to replace you. Now. They'll arrive in about fifteen minutes. Hand over the photo to them. Clever of you to get it back from her,' he said with withering sarcasm. 'When the two replacements arrive you go home. Where do you think she went?'

'She probably headed for the taxi rank . . .'

'We can check that, find out where she went. But it will take time. Of course, you didn't ask to see her passport?'

'No. Your instructions were not to intercept her. Just to keep her under surveillance, check her movements.'

'You got one thing right, then. When the replacements arrive you go home, as I said before. You're suspended.'

Beck stood up, crossed to the window, stared down at the River Limmat and the University on the far bank. He was uncertain what to do next. When his phone rang he was relieved to hear Tweed's voice.

'We're back in Zurich. Staying this time at the Zum Storchen. Thank you again for your cooperation in Ouchy.'

'Forget it. Tina Langley is floating round Zurich again. I had a call from the airport.'

He told Tweed about the call from Keller. When he had given him all the details of the incident he exploded. 'What is it with this woman? Does she hypnotize men?'

'Quite often she does exactly that. I'm sure she's had a lot of experience in that field of activity. That was a good idea to send two different men to the airport. If she leaves here I'm sure she'll fly out. She'll probably move further east. That suits me – just so long as she's followed. I suggest one of your two men checks passengers arriving for departure and the other one stays in the background, ready to board the same flight she eventually takes.'

'I'm sure you're still her main target,' Beck warned.

'I'm going monastic – avoiding all attractive women.'

Arriving at the Eden au Lac, The Butterfly booked a suite in the name Lisa Vane. Once she was alone in the suite she called Ashley Wingfield at the Dolder Grand. Hassan came on the line immediately.

'I've arrived in Zurich,' she said quickly. 'Staying at the Eden au Lac. I think they're looking for me at the airport,' she lied. 'I saw a man in a business suit checking a photo. Fortunately I was dressed very differently and I was wearing a floppy hat to conceal my hair.'

'You're sure you were not recognized?'

'Quite sure.' The Butterfly made a suggestion typical of the way her mind worked. 'I think I should move from here.'

'Change your clothes first. Tell reception you've just had an urgent call to return to London . . .'

'That's where I'm going?' she asked eagerly.

'No. You come to the Dolder Grand. Get one taxi to take you to Parade-Platz in the centre of the city. Wait until it has gone. Then get another taxi to bring you here. If you see me in a public room ignore me. Sooner or later I'll come to your room. Register as Lisa Vane. If you want food—'

'I need a drink.'

'Get drunk, then, but do it in your room. Now, *move!*'

Hassan, from his suite in the Dolder Grand, shouted the last words down the phone. He slammed the phone down with such force he almost broke it. Jumping up, he began prowling round the room, wishing he could smash some of the ornaments. His face was contorted into an expression of ferocity.

He was known – and feared – back east in his home state for these unpredictable and dangerous outbursts. He had once clubbed to death a colonel who had answered him back. His father, the Head of State, had felt compelled to cover up the murder. He had arranged for the body of the colonel to be taken out into the desert aboard a tank. The colonel's corpse had then been laid out on the sand and the tank's caterpillar tracks had rolled back and forth over it to account for the savagery of the blows the body had endured. The colonel had been a popular man in the military and his death was reported as a tragic accident while on manoeuvres.

It was the huge fiasco in Ouchy which had gradually built up Hassan's inhuman rage. With his own eyes he had seen Tweed walking back to the hotel. Tweed. Always it was Tweed who had upset the Englishman's carefully laid plans transmitted to Hassan.

'May he rot in hell,' he growled as he moved round the suite.

He had ordered Tina to come to the Dolder Grand with the idea that she might be able to locate Tweed, to blow his head to smithereens. A large vase perched on a table grazed his elbow as he continued prowling. With a shriek of rage he grasped the heavy vase, hurled it against a wall where it burst into fragments.

In his imagination he had pictured the giant bomb lifting the mansion into the air, scattering it far and wide, annihilating the remaining members of the *Institut*. Including Tweed. Now he had read in the newspaper that no members of the *Institut* still alive had travelled anywhere near Ouchy. He suspected – and he was right – that Tweed had phoned each member and told them to leave Switzerland immediately.

His large hands clenched and unclenched, as though he was in the act of strangling Tweed with his bare hands. For the moment Hassan had gone berserk – as he had when he clubbed the colonel to death.

At the Zum Storchen Tweed sat on a balcony overlooking the Limmat flowing past below with Paula seated at the same table. At that hour in the scorching afternoon only one other person sat on the balcony at a table at the other end. The ever-watchful Marler.

'You are carrying out a plan, I'm sure,' said Paula.

'Yes, I am. I'm waging psychological warfare. My aim is to demoralize and destabilize the enemy. I want to throw him off balance, to break his nerve by pounding him with blow after blow. Then his judgement and self-control will snap.'

'And we are now succeeding.'

'Yes. To start with he was doing well. Key members of the *Institut* were being assassinated by The Sisterhood. Eight of them were killed. Suddenly the balance swings the other way. The Sisterhood is on the run, which is what I intended. Then a hard core of what, I'm sure, were his top thugs was sent to Ouchy. With the exception of Big Ben all of them are now dead. And his attempt to destroy the rest of the *Institut* with the bomb has failed.'

'What is our next move?'

'We are systematically driving surviving members of The Sisterhood further east. It would not surprise me if Karin Berg and Simone Carnot were now in Vienna. It may be more tricky to break the Englishman's nerve – the key figure in all their planning, I am sure.'

'Which means Amos or Willie. Or possibly Christopher.'

'Or someone we know nothing about yet, but someone who lives in Dorset,' Tweed replied.

'Well, Christopher doesn't.'

'Christopher rents a small cottage north of Dorchester. I heard this from Monica when I spoke to her while we were in France.'

'You have a good idea who it is?' she suggested.

'The field remains wide open.'

'So what do we do now? Apart from enjoying a wonderful rest in this super hotel?'

'It has the great advantage of being tucked away in the Altstadt. The Old City is a maze of streets.'

'But I think you are waiting for something to happen.'

'I am waiting for The Butterfly to take wing again.'

38

In her suite at the Eden au Lac Tina changed into a less glamorous outfit. For once she didn't want to be noticed. Checking her appearance in the bathroom, she swallowed the contents of a miniature cognac, drinking from the bottle. She had pinched it from the minibar in her room at the Hôtel des Bergues in Geneva. She had told reception at that hotel that she hadn't used the minibar. Always prepared to spend a small fortune on a couturier dress, she was mean when it came to paying for something she could have for nothing.

'I'm sorry, but I've had an urgent message to return to London,' she told reception over the phone.

'We understand. There will be no charge for the suite.'

'Most kind of you. Could you call me a taxi?'

As she was leaving she failed to notice a small plump man who sat reading a newspaper. Detective Windlin casually followed her out as she climbed into a waiting taxi. An unmarked police car pulled in at the kerb and Windlin jumped in beside the driver.

'Don't lose that taxi. Beck would not be pleased . . .'

Beck had moved with great speed after hearing of the arrival of Tina Langley. With her photograph in front of him he phoned in quick succession the Baur au Lac, the Baur en Ville, the Dolder Grand, the Eden au

Lac. In each case he gave the concierge a brief description of Tina, emphasizing she would have arrived within the hour if she was staying there. He struck gold at the Eden au Lac.

'Yes, sir,' the concierge informed him in a low voice, 'a lady of that description has just arrived. She has gone up to her suite.'

Beck instantly dispatched Detective Windlin to the hotel. Like many plump men Windlin was surprisingly swift on his feet. When the taxi they were following reached Parade-Platz and Tina paid it off he was out of his car in seconds. He stood at a tram stop, watching Tina, who bought a magazine off a bookstall until her taxi had disappeared. She then hailed another and as she climbed inside Windlin was already seated again next to his driver.

'Tricky, this one,' Windlin commented. 'Beck is clever. You know who we are following?'

'No idea.'

'Tina Langley. I have her photo in my pocket. Half the force in Switzerland is looking for her.'

'We arrest the lady?'

'We do nothing of the sort. We track her, then report back to Beck over the radio.'

In his room at Zum Storchen Tweed hurried to answer the phone. He liked the hotel – it had a certain atmosphere remote from the powerhouse of Zurich with its crowds, its rumbling trams and dense traffic.

'Yes?'

'Beck here. The Butterfly had just moved from the Eden au Lac and has arrived at the Dolder Grand.'

'So she obviously feels she still has unfinished business here.'

'You, would be my guess,' Beck said grimly.

'I think I rather fancy a visit to the Dolder Grand. It's a unique hotel. Where all the bankers dine.'

'I suppose if I asked you not to go I'd be wasting my breath.'

'Politely put, yes you would. I'll be going there shortly. And thank you for the information.'

'I should never have told you . . .'

Tweed was just about to leave his room when Paula arrived. As he opened the door to her she stared hard at him. When she was inside she folded her arms and tackled him.

'I know that expression. You're up to something.'

'Beck has just phoned to tell me Tina has moved into the Dolder Grand. I'm going up there to have a chat with her. I want to get her moving again.'

'You don't think you're going by yourself? Promise me you'll wait here until I get back. I'm just going to my room.'

'You do bully me.'

'Only way to make you see sense.'

When she reappeared she was not alone. Both Newman and Marler were with her. Tweed frowned and lifted his hands in protest.

'I don't need a delegation.'

'You're getting one,' Paula told him. 'Marler will be acting as chauffeur. You had enough driving getting us here from Ouchy. Bob has never seen the Dolder Grand. He's just coming along for the ride.'

'If I believed that I'd believe anything!'

As they left the hotel Paula looked round, appreciating the character of the Old Town. The buildings were ancient, built of stone quarried hundreds of years ago. The streets, narrow and twisting, were paved with worn cobbles. To her right the River Limmat flowed between the banks of the two Old Towns of Zurich, the other being across the water. It was a scene of stability and history with hardly anyone about. Beneath the hotel was a covered walk alongside the river. I must explore that, she thought, as Marler drove up with the car. She was very quiet as she got into the back with Tweed.

As Marler drove them away she had a weird feeling that something extraordinary was about to happen. She had no idea what it might be, but the feeling persisted after they had crossed the Limmat and started to climb up the lower slopes of the Zurichberg, the high and dominating hill which overlooks Zurich. Soon the houses were spread out further from each other, had become massive old villas behind railed walls. Then they were travelling through a fir forest with here and there an exceptionally large villa perched higher and well back from the curving, climbing road.

Below she began to get glimpses of the aged buildings and church spires of Zurich, all jammed together. There were other glimpses – of the lake, a sparkling blue under the sun searing down. Tweed nudged her.

'We're coming to the bottom of the funicular. You can use that to get up to the Dolder Grand.'

'What's the point? Coming down you'd find yourself halfway up the Zurichberg.'

'I've often thought of that myself . . .'

They climbed higher and the white stone palace of the Dolder Grand came into view. It had turrets with strange stiletto-shaped spires. Paula's feeling that they were approaching something ominous intensified.

Tweed led the way into a huge lounge furnished with antiques and deep-pile carpet. Several chairs and couches were occupied by distinguished-looking men and women. When they spoke their voices were little more than whispers.

A man had entered the lounge at the same moment as Tweed. Of medium height, his clean-shaven complexion was very brown and smooth. He was wearing an Armani suit and suddenly he saw Tweed. He stood stock-still and gazed across the room as though he could hardly believe what he was looking at. Tweed kept his voice low as he spoke to a middle-aged waiter.

'I think I know that gentleman over there. His name escapes me for the moment.'

'Mr Ashley Wingfield. He stays with us occasionally. A most courteous man.'

Tweed was also standing stock-still, hands inside his jacket pockets. His eyes never left the strange pallid eyes staring back at him like a man hypnotized. There was expression in those eyes – disbelief, then hatred, then blankness. The man called Ashley Wingfield had a plumpish face but there was a hint of strong cheekbones which suggested to Tweed the Middle East. Years before at Scotland Yard Tweed had been known for his flashes of insight. He was experiencing just such a flash now. This was the barbaric man behind The Sisterhood. Tweed went forward.

Paula was so disturbed she moved to one side, her right hand inside her shoulder bag, gripping the Browning. Newman moved in the other direction, so at a distance they flanked the two men. Marler leant against a wall, an unlit king-size between his lips.

'Mr Ashley Wingfield, I believe,' said Tweed. 'I am Tweed.'

Hassan, still recovering from the episode in his room when he had gone berserk, smashing the vase against a wall, could hardly speak. Their eyes were still locked.

'I am pleased to meet you, sir,' said Hassan in a choked voice. 'You strike me as an important man, but I regret I have so far not heard of you.'

'Or of what I do?'

'Please tell me.'

It can't be, Paula was thinking. He looks so dapper in his smart suit. She noticed the man had thrust his very dark brown hands inside his jacket pockets. Tweed, she thought, looks so poised, so in command of himself. Wingfield looked as though he might recently have had a fit. The hands which were now out of sight had been trembling. With rage. Why do I think that?

'I don't like any kind of dramatic language,' Tweed went on. 'But perhaps you should call me Nemesis. That is what I do – I destroy evil men.'

'You . . . what?'

Hassan's eyes were blinking as though he had a nervous twitch. He was struggling to control his manic fury. Something about Tweed's personality made him feel at a disadvantage, a unique experience for a man accustomed to unquestioning obedience and servility from all those around him. He had an overwhelming desire to dominate this man, but he felt incapable of exerting the necessary force of will. He controlled the blinking but he was growing more and more nervous of the expression in the eyes staring into his.

'You expect to stay in Zurich long?' he managed to say.

'Further and further east,' Tweed told him softly.

'I beg your pardon, sir?'

'You will retreat – further and further east. Massive forces in the West are stirring. You are too late.'

'I do not understand.'

'I think you do.'

Tweed turned on his heel, walked slowly towards the exit from the lounge. Hassan remained like a man carved out of stone, still standing quite still, the blankness remaining on his incredibly smooth face. Paula remained where she was, as did Newman and Marler. They were guarding Tweed's back.

The guests in the lounge had stopped talking. Like Hassan they were like figures carved out of stone. They had not heard a word of the confrontation, but the large room was full of an electric tension which everyone could sense. It was like the moment when people see a bomb falling from a plane and freeze.

Hassan suddenly came to life, left the lounge by the distant door he had entered by. Newman nodded to Paula to follow Tweed, which she did quickly. He walked slowly after her as Marler lit his cigarette, bowed to the guests, then made his way to the car.

39

Leaving the lounge, Hassan hurried to Tina Langley's room. He was on the verge of hammering his clenched fist against the door when he paused. He had to get control of himself. Taking a deep breath, he tapped lightly.

'Oh, it's you . . .'

He pushed her aside without ceremony, slammed the door shut behind him. He took another deep breath and rushed round the room. His expression was vicious. He had his back to her and forced himself to look calm.

'You're shaking,' Tina said. 'What's wrong?'

'Where is the Luger I gave you? Tweed is downstairs. He is just leaving the hotel. Where is the bloody Luger?'

'In that drawer you are leaning against. Beneath some of my underclothes.'

She stopped speaking. Hassan had hauled open the drawer. He was hauling out her underclothes, hurling them onto the floor. She opened her mouth to protest, then decided against saying a word. Hassan had found the Luger, checked quickly to make sure it was loaded.

He had wrapped a silk vest round his hand to hold the gun. He ran over to her, shoved the Luger at her.

'Take it! Tweed will be getting into his car. He must have come by car. Go down now and shoot him. What's the matter with you?'

Tina had stepped backwards away from him. She leant against the bathroom door. She was on the verge of hysteria. Her expression was a mixture of fear and anger.

'You've gone over the top. The hotel is full of staff and guests. How the hell could I get away if I did manage to shoot him? Don't you realize you would be involved? The police would question everybody in the hotel. Look at my hand. It's trembling. I couldn't even aim the gun, quite apart from pull the trigger. You always take care to be nowhere near an assassination.'

Hassan's mood changed. She had experienced this before. At one moment he was in a titanic rage, then he was calm and so cool. He smiled at her, then he grinned and went on grinning.

'It was a good joke, was it not?'

'Joke?' Her saucy nature asserted itself. 'One thing is for sure. You would never earn your living as a comic.'

'You think I am comic?' he asked indignantly.

'Sometimes you are. Hassan—'

'Ashley.'

'OK. Ashley, you are a man of many talents. You have such a powerful personality.' She smiled seductively. 'That is why you are who you are. A great man.'

'I hope to be. Now, let us be practical. You must unload the Luger, then get rid of the gun and the bullets.'

'I put them in the rubbish bin?' she asked with mock innocence, knowing she now had the upper hand.

'There is forest all around us. Take them for a walk. Dump them under some bushes. Just get rid of them.'

'Thank you so much. I'll do what I can.'

'Tweed has been here,' he said seriously. 'Zurich is no longer safe. It is time you left this city.'

'I can't wait to get out of the place. And you have spoilt my best underclothes. They cost a lot of money.'

She began gathering up the clothes he had hurled onto the floor. Folding them neatly, she put them back into the drawer. He watched her and then realized perspiration was pouring off his forehead and into his eyes. Taking out a large embroidered silk handkerchief, he mopped his forehead and face.

'You did say it was time I left Zurich,' she prodded him.

'I think you should leave as soon as possible. Today would be best. Yes, today. I will book you a seat on the next flight.'

'Where to?'

'Vienna. You will be met by a driver and car at Schwechat airport. A room will be reserved for you at the Sacher.'

'Vienna?' she repeated nervously. 'That's where Norbert Engel died . . .'

'Where you killed him,' Hassan said viciously. 'You will not stay in Vienna for long. You will be moved to a safer place. Now, get on with your packing. I will contact you again very shortly.'

'That was one of the most gripping experiences of my life,' said Paula as Marler began driving back down to Zurich. 'The way you looked at that man. He was terrified.'

'That man,' Tweed said slowly, 'is the enemy. I recognized him from photographs I've seen in our files. His name is Hassan, the eldest son of the Head of

State of one of the most dangerous powers in the world now.'

'I heard you say "further and further east",' commented Newman. 'You repeated the phrase. What are you planning?'

'A double trap. I think I unnerved him sufficiently for him to leave Zurich and fly east. That is exactly what I want him to do. He knows I will come after him so, when he thinks it over, he will believe he has a chance to lure me into *his* trap. East is where he feels at home, has Heaven knows how many men at his disposal who will kill at a word from him. Also he'll become nervous at the presence of Tina Langley in the same hotel. I expect him to send her east. When we reach police headquarters . . .'

'Now I know where I'm going,' Marler called out cynically.

'I was about to tell you. When we reach our destination I'll ask Beck to have his men at the airport check on any flight reservations made from the Dolder Grand. Also they must keep a close lookout for Tina Langley. And I'll give Beck a description of Ashley Wingfield, also known as Hassan.'

'Why not have him arrested and interrogated?' Paula wanted to know.

'Because we have no evidence against him. Also, arresting him would cause a diplomatic incident. But the main reason is I need him on the loose to see what he's up to.'

'That scene in the lounge at the Dolder Grand was very tense,' Paula recalled. 'The guests couldn't hear what was said but they were affected by the atmosphere. They all fell silent.'

'So let us hope Hassan was equally affected . . .'

* * *

Big Ben had to make an effort to phone the Englishman at the telephone and room numbers he had been given. The intention had been for him to report his success at Ouchy.

'Yes,' the Englishman replied to his call. 'I recognize your voice. Where are you?'

'I've taken a room at the Bellevue Palace in Berne. I had to get here during the night on a motorcycle. It didn't go well . . .'

'It did not. I read the newspapers. Who survived?'

'Well, I did. And Les, the knife-thrower, is here in another room. He hijacked a—'

'Shut up! You seem to have kept your nerve. What about Les?'

'He's OK.'

'This is what you do. Later you will take charge of another unit. Buy some good clothes, a decent suitcase. You have plenty of money?'

'I raided the safe at d'Avignon before we left to—'

'Stop gabbling. When you both have bought clothes you board an express from Berne station, a nonstop to Zurich. Come out of the main station, cross the road and book rooms at the Schweizerhof Hotel opposite. I'll contact you there.'

'Everything here is Switzer . . .'

'Schweizerhof, idiot. I'll spell it.'

Big Ben put down the phone and drank some more beer from a bottle he had taken from the minibar. He had a room which had windows overlooking the river Aare below. In the distance a panorama only seen in the best of weather stretched west and east – the majestic peaks of the Bernese Oberland, one of the great sights of Europe.

Big Ben hadn't even noticed it. Views were not his cup of tea, unless they were of ladies' legs. His talents lay in running a gang of killers. He burped, and went along to another room to give Les his orders.

Simone Carnot had disobeyed the order she had received over the phone from Hassan while at the Château des Avenières. When he had instructed her to move to the Beau Rivage at Ouchy she had had her doubts.

Unlike The Butterfly she disliked always being on the move and she was anxious to get out of France. She could never forget that in Paris she had left behind an unsolved murder – the murder of her married lover. Without informing Hassan she drove her hired car to Geneva's airport. There she handed in the car and flew to Zurich.

She had phoned the Baur au Lac from the airport and a room was waiting for her when she arrived at the hotel. She was brushing her flame of red hair, which so attracted men, when she decided to risk trying to contact Hassan. After all, he didn't own her. She had simply carried out 'assignments' for him – successfully killing two members of the *Institut*. He had paid her the large sums owing to her and this gave her a feeling of independence. On the off-chance she called the Dolder Grand.

She was checking her appearance in the dressing-table mirror when, to her surprise, Hassan came on the line when she asked for Mr Ashley Wingfield.

'Simone, where have you been?' he snapped.

She didn't know she was contacting him only an hour or so after his confrontation with Tweed, followed by the argument with Tina. His emotions were still a mixture of rage and doubt.

'I'm at the Baur au Lac . . .'

407

'What?'

'If you're in a bad mood I'll call you back,' she said quietly.

'Stay on the line!' Hassan forced himself to calm down. 'I've been up all night. Tell me what has happened.'

'I've only been here a short while. Reading the papers, it's a good job I didn't go to Ouchy. It sounds horrific.'

'We won't talk about that,' he said persuasively. 'Thank you for calling me. I was worried about you. Give me a moment to think.'

A jumble of thoughts passed through Hassan's disturbed mind and then he began to think clearly. The news that another member of The Sisterhood was in Zurich – at the same time as Tweed – was dangerous. His mind cleared and he took a decision.

'Simone, it is going to be safer for you if you do not spend too much time in Zurich. I have my reasons for saying that. I want you to fly to Vienna. I will send you your ticket and flight details by courier. A car will be waiting for you at the other end. A room will be booked for you at the Sacher.'

'You have another assignment for me?' she asked.

'I may have, but it will be up to you whether you accept it or not. In any case you will receive a generous fee.'

He had to wait for her to reply. Simone had once visited Vienna on a business trip. It had struck her as a city where you could easily get lost from the world. And Hassan had given her the option as to whether she undertook another assignment or not. She applied lipstick while she decided whether leaving Zurich would be sensible. At the other end of the line Hassan was forcing himself to control his natural impatience. Instinctively he felt it would be unwise to upset her.

'I'll fly to Vienna,' she said eventually. 'So send me the ticket.'

'In the meantime may I suggest you stay in your room? You can use room service for meals.'

'I'll do that,' she agreed, having no intention of carrying out his suggestion.

In his suite at the Dolder Grand Hassan mopped his forehead after ending the conversation. He was sweating a lot there days, despite the fact he was accustomed to far higher temperatures in his own country.

He left his suite and met Tina coming up the stairs, carrying a large expensive bag. She did not look in the best of tempers. Ignoring him, she walked to her room while he followed her. Once inside she continued to ignore him as he sat down on a couch. She flung the bag on the floor.

'What is it?' he enquired gently.

'I've got rid of the bloody Luger – and the bullets. And for your information it wasn't easy. The garden was full of geriatric guests and I had to find a path where no one was about before I could dump the stuff. You never do your own dirty work.'

She was working herself up into a rage. Standing with her hands on her hips she glared down at him. He would have liked to hit her but he knew that would be a very bad mistake. He congratulated her but that only seemed to fire her up. She picked up an envelope, waved it under his nose.

'The air ticket arrived. I always travel First – or Business if First isn't on the flight. This ticket is Economy. I don't like travelling with the peasants who travel Economy.'

'We are on the same flight,' he said quietly. 'It would not be wise if we were seen together.'

409

'Oh, I see. There are only two seats in Business, are there?'

'Tweed has turned up. He was in this hotel not very long ago. He had members of his team with him. If you had stayed he might have decided to have you arrested. I look after my own.'

'I see.' She calmed down suddenly. 'I'll just have to put up with the indignity, then.'

'You will have a suite at the Sacher.'

'I should damn well hope so.'

Hassan got up and left the room. He heard her slam the door shut before she locked it. Hurrying back to his suite where he had his bags packed he had no idea that he was doing just what Tweed had hoped he would do. He was moving further east.

In the outskirts of a Midlands city in Britain Willie was standing inside what the company called the laboratory. The factory was hidden in a large underground complex. Admission could only be obtained through steel doors with combination locks rather like those on a bank vault.

'Those containers will immediately dissolve on contact with cold water?' Willie asked.

'That is what we have perfected and produced on a huge scale,' Joseph Harbin, the dwarflike director, explained. 'Bacteria inside one of those containers are quite safe. You have to add a few drops of the substance inside one of these bottles, which are made of armoured glass. You note that the nozzle on each of the containers is divided into compartments. When the substance in the bottles contacts the liquid in the compartment nearest the water in the container the bacteria are released. A further turn of the plastic screw on the nozzle makes the water active.'

'How long from pouring the substance from the bottle into the nozzle and turning the nozzle does it take for the water inside the container to become active bacteria?'

'Ten seconds.'

'How can you demonstrate that this works?'

'I was expecting you to ask that. Come with me to the tank of water over here.'

Willie tried to guess the age of the chemist and found it impossible. The dwarf's face, long and pinched, was lined. He could have been anything between forty and eighty. Walking with a shuffle to the tank, he carried one of the ellipsoid containers made of a special plastic.

The huge laboratory with its tunnel-shaped ceiling had tables everywhere, each with an enamel surface, each supporting a fantastic collection of weird chemical apparatus. To Willie it looked like something out of a horror film where Frankenstein worked on creating his monster.

'Now watch carefully,' Harbin cautioned. 'This is a bottle of blue ink. I am going to put a few drops of this highly concentrated ink into the nozzle of a container.'

It was silent inside the underground laboratory, due to its depth below the surface of the dummy factory above them. Harbin added a few drops of ink into the nozzle of a container, then took off his watch, pointed to it, turned the nozzle three times. The ink dropped to the lowest level and Harbin turned it once more. Inside the container full of tap water the liquid turned a strong blue. Harbin handed the container to Willie.

'You do it. Throw it into the tank.'

Holding the container in both hands, Willie dropped it gently into the large tank of tap water. The entire contents of the tank turned a wild blue as the container immediately dissolved and disappeared. Harbin opened

411

both hands in a gesture of satisfaction. Then he shrugged and shuffled back to his desk in a distant corner as Willie followed.

'I noticed the container had a glutinous substance inside,' Willie said sharply. 'Have all the containers been filled with the substance I supplied?'

'Look at them on the rows of shelves all around you. Every container has been treated with that substance. I don't understand why we need that or what it is.'

'Another chemist produced it. That substance strengthens the containers until they are immersed in water. You saw for yourself how quickly the container dissolved into nothing, releasing its contents immediately. You have on that sheet I gave you the different addresses a specific supply of containers and bottles must be delivered to when I phone you the code word. You are quite clear on that instruction?'

'I am a precise man, like yourself.'

Harbin chuckled and his strange face twisted into an expression which reminded Willie of a devil's mask. Obviously he had at some time in his life suffered a severe accident. He spread out a document on the large desk, produced a pen.

'I need you to sign this as a form of insurance for myself.'

Willie read every word quickly. Its main theme was that he had acted under the instructions of Captain William Wellesley Carrington and took no responsibility. Willie took out his own pen and scrawled his signature. He stared hard at Harbin.

'This is a waste of time. Everyone will be dead.'

'I like to take precautions.'

'The only precaution you have to take is to leave the country as soon as you have displatched the consignments. Someone suggested the Cayman Islands. And don't drink any water before you leave. You will also, I

412

assume, make delivery to the cargo planes flying abroad with their consignments?'

By 'abroad' Willie meant to certain obscure airfields inside France and Germany. At each delivery point in Britain and the other three key countries trained men would be waiting to distribute the containers to reservoirs. The deposit of the containers into the reservoirs of the three countries would all take place at exactly the same time.

'I presume you have brought my cheque,' Harbin said and chuckled again.

'Here is a certified cheque for you to present to your bank in this city. You hand it to a man called Arnold. He will then wire it to your personal bank account abroad within minutes.'

'Thank you.' Harbin frowned. 'It is dated today but the date has brackets round it.'

'That is because it only becomes viable when I have heard from you that you have made all the dispatches.'

'I expected more.'

'Can't you count the zeroes? When you do you will be happy. Now give me the active container.'

'You must be very careful. So very careful. It has a special protective wrapping to make it safe. It is active. Let us hope your plane doesn't crash.'

'I've taken care of that.'

Willie had indeed taken care of that. It was quite understandable that Hassan had asked for a sample to test in his own country.

Big Ben was a man who moved fast. As soon as they had paid the bill at the Bellevue Place in Berne they had caught a taxi to the station. After buying tickets they were lucky. Running, they were just in time to board an express for Zurich. Arriving at the main station, they were soon installed in rooms at the Hotel Schweizerhof facing the station. Big Ben called Hassan immediately.

'We're here,' he informed his boss.

'Are you equipped?'

'We're always armed.'

'Be careful what you say. Tweed is your objective. He is in town. I have a feeling he may soon leave for Vienna. Both of you go to the airport.'

'We need to buy more clothes.'

'Be quick then. Hire a car. Les drives. He stays in the car while you check the airport.'

'We're on our way.'

Big Ben knew he was noticeable. He favoured black – for a suit, for jogging gear, for a polo-necked sweater in cold weather. Collecting Les from his room, he left the hotel, avoided the expensive shops in Bahnhofstrasse, found what he wanted in the big department store Globus.

He changed inside a locked cubicle in the toilet. Emerging, he wore a grey business suit, a wide-brimmed black hat. Les came out of another cubicle, wearing a smart suit. He stared at Big Ben, startled by the transformation. From the chemist's section at Globus Big Ben had bought a white surgical collar which was now supporting his neck. In his left hand he carried a prayer book he had also bought at Globus. Big Ben now looked like a clergyman.

'Wouldn't 'ave known it was you,' Les whispered.

'Let's get crackin' – the airport!'

The only other item they had to deal with was a hired car. They quickly found a firm in Bahnhofstrasse. Les used a credit card in another name, but which was backed by substantial credit. He had the other documents required in the same name. A Citroën was placed at their disposal within five minutes.

'I'll guide you to the airport,' Big Ben told Les as they drove off. 'I've worked this city before. Crawls with the filthy rich. You go over the bridge here, then turn left. Twenty minutes and we're at the airport. Watch your speed – the Swiss are fussy old women.'

Tweed sat in the car outside police headquarters where he had spent fifteen minutes talking to Beck alone in his office. Marler sat behind the wheel, patiently awaiting instructions, while Newman, beside him, discreetly checked his .38 Smith & Wesson.

'Expecting to use that piece of old iron?' Marler enquired.

'At any time, the situation being what it is. Zurich is a time bomb. We have Hassan here and Tina Langley.'

'I think one of them at least is due to depart for Vienna,' said Tweed from the rear seat, speaking suddenly.

'How can you be sure of that?' asked Paula seated next to him.

'First, because of the confrontation at the Dolder Grand. But don't forget, at des Avenières I casually mentioned to Tina that we were moving on to Ouchy – and Vienna.'

415

'The further east we go the more hostile the territory,' warned Newman. 'Remember what happened to Paula when she flew to Austria and Roka – wasn't that his name – drove her into Slovakia? Then Butler and Nield had to cope with the excavator driver. That's Hassan's home ground.'

'Where, sooner or later, we must take him on,' Tweed told him.

'It's Hassan's familiar territory,' Newman insisted. 'So he holds all the cards. Even Vienna could be dangerous. Again, Paula was in great danger – damnit, she was almost kidnapped in broad daylight.'

'Paula can look after herself,' said Paula, annoyed.

'If you two would keep quiet for a moment maybe I could think,' said Tweed. 'We are at a crossroads. Which route we take may decide everything. And I have decided. Marler, drive us to the airport. I want to see whether Tina does board a flight for Vienna. Beck told me his detective – name of Windlin, I believe – reported seeing Tina leave the Dolder Grand. As she was getting into a taxi she was stuffing an air ticket into her handbag. Get us there as fast as you can, Marler.'

Willie had reached Folkestone in his car and traffic was boarding the Shuttle ready to cross the Channel by the tunnel to Calais. There was a queue of cars and he had purposely not joined it as he watched what was happening.

He parked the car in a waiting area, made sure it was locked before he went in search of a phone. He was not sure where Hassan would be by now but he first called the Dolder Grand. He had guessed right but he soon realized the volatile Hassan was in a furious temper.

'Where are you now?' Hassan demanded. 'Why waste time calling me?'

'I won't bother if you talk to me like that. Instead I will return to London. There are other deals I can be attending to.'

'London?' Hassan sounded taken aback. 'I thought you would be on the Continent with the sample. So, if you please, I would appreciate it if you tell me what is happening.'

'I am waiting at Folkestone.'

'May I ask why you are waiting?' Hassan enquired politely.

'Because there is a hold-up.' Willie phrased his next words carefully. 'There is a long delay in getting on to the Shuttle. I have heard that Customs are searching for a large drug consignment.'

'I understand. It will not delay your arrival in Vienna, I hope?'

'Not for very long, I would say.'

'Please keep me informed of your progress. Timing is so very important. If you can't get me here try the Hotel Sacher in Vienna.'

'I'll do that. I have decided to drive via Switzerland.'

'You are going to come here across Germany. It would be much quicker.'

'I just told you. Via Switzerland. Think for a moment. I've heard rumours from secret contacts on the Continent. I will not repeat them over the phone. Goodbye.'

Willie put down the phone inside the public booth before Hassan could ask him about the rumours. Then he returned to his car and sat inside it calmly, watching the progress of the cars boarding the Shuttle at a snail's pace.

* * *

Marler pulled in to the airport at a place where he could park. Tweed jumped out of the car and hurried into the concourse, followed by Paula and Newman. There were more passengers waiting to board flights than he had expected. After checking in, they were patronizing cafés and food stalls.

Paula was close to him as he stood scanning the crowd. Then his head stopped and she looked in the same direction. Tina was seated at a table, sipping coffee, her boarding pass clutched in one hand.

She was chatting to a well-dressed man in his forties. From his expression he was entranced by Tina. She is dressed to kill – an unfortunate phrase Paula thought. And even here she is plying her wares in the hope that she had found a minor gold mine. Paula was not worried that she might be recognized by Tina. During the swift journey to the airport in the car she had tied back her glossy hair and was wearing a fake pair of horn-rimmed glasses she always carried. These two changes had transformed her appearance into that of a schoolmistress.

Beck appeared at Tweed's side out of nowhere. He stood as though waiting for a passenger off a flight. When he spoke he was rubbing his hand slowly over his mouth. Paula heard clearly what he said to Tweed.

'Tina Langley is boarding the next flight to Vienna. I waited until she had left the check-in counter and then questioned the girl who had dealt with her. She's definitely off to Vienna.'

'Where we may lose her,' Tweed replied.

'No, we won't. I foresaw this might happen after what you told me at headquarters. One of my men will be aboard the same flight. I have already spoken to the Chief of Police in Vienna. He will have two men there to contact my man. They will have strict instructions to follow her unseen.'

'That was a good bit of organization.'

'I'll leave you now . . .'

Paula's eyes travelled round the concourse. Near the exit, but only yards away from them, stood a very tall clergyman. He appeared to be reading to himself from something he held in his hand, which she guessed was a prayer book. His lips were moving as he read.

'We'll just wait until we actually see Tina heading for the final departure lounge,' said Tweed. 'She's very tricky and might just not board her plane at the last moment. The Butterfly takes various forms of flight.'

'It doesn't look as though Hassan is taking off for Vienna,' she said.

'That's another reason for waiting here. He could turn up at the last moment. He's another very tricky character and I'm sure I put the wind up him. People are starting to move.'

Paula's eyes were still scanning the concourse. She wasn't sure why. Before they had been part of the crowd. Now they stood as an isolated group. Tweed was checking every person as they disappeared from sight. He didn't expect Hassan to adopt a disguise – he was too arrogant for that – but he wasn't taking any chances.

Paula glanced across at the clergyman again. He was putting the prayer book inside a pocket. Perhaps the passenger he had come to meet hadn't turned up, but there had been no new arrivals coming out. She was about to look somewhere else when she saw his hand come out of the pocket – holding a Colt automatic. He gripped it in both hands and aimed it point-blank at Tweed. She had no time to reach for her Browning. With her left hand she gave Tweed a great shove. The Colt had been aimed at his back. Tweed stumbled sideways. The bullet passed over his shoulder and the report echoed through the concourse. The bullet hit a partition, shattering the glass. Several women started to scream.

Her shove had been so forceful Tweed nearly fell over, but his great agility saved him. He stood upright, swung round. Newman had his Smith & Wesson in his hand but the clergyman was disappearing out of the exit. Beck again appeared from nowhere, shouting orders to men who, like their chief, came out of nowhere.

'Stop that man! Shoot him if you have to!' Beck shouted.

Newman was running to the exit, followed by Tweed and Paula. Beck reached the exit first. Outside Big Ben had dived into the waiting car. Les had thrown open the door for him. He drove off at speed, heading back for Zurich. Beck waved to a patrol car to follow the fleeing vehicle. The patrol car was held up by a taxi just pulling out. With siren screaming and lights flashing it manoeuvred round the now stationary taxi.

Les, who had been chosen for his driving skills, overtook one car after another, going well over the speed limit. He made good progress but the patrol car was gaining on him. After a few minutes he entered the curving tunnel which leads into the city. He pressed his horn, warning cars ahead to keep out of his way. The tunnel seemed to go on for ever. Behind him the patrol car had to brake to an emergency stop to avoid a collision. Les was now well ahead. Beside him Big Ben kept glancing back to see how much leeway they had. He gave the order before they reached the end of the tunnel.

'Slow down now. Keep up the maximum speed permitted but when we leave the tunnel we soon pass the Europa Hotel. Turn in there.'

After the tunnel, emerging into the blazing sun was a shock. Les was moving at the speed of other cars now. Big Ben pointed to the Europa. Les slowed a little more, moving at a reasonable speed. The traffic in front and behind him had no idea there was anything wrong. Sedately, he turned and parked in a slot among other cars. They sat and said nothing.

They heard the siren of the patrol car approaching. Traffic was getting out of its way. The patrol car flashed past and descended into Zurich. Very soon it had to crawl despite its siren and flashing lights.

On the pavement outside the airport Beck was listening on his mobile. Paula saw him purse his lips, then speak rapidly. He shrugged as he tucked away the mobile.

'They lost him. He's somewhere in the city traffic. At this time of the year you can hardly move with all the tourists about. Are you all right, Tweed? I should have asked before now.'

'Alive and kicking, thanks to Paula.'

'I should have seen him,' said Newman.

'So should I,' agreed Marler.

'It was a clever disguise,' Paula commented. 'He looked just like a clergyman.'

'It's a reminder that the enemy is formidable,' Tweed replied. 'You'll track him down, Arthur.'

'I'm not so sure about that,' Beck said grimly. 'There are so many ways he could have gone. We'll do our best. Where are you off to now?'

'The Zum Storchen. I want to phone someone. Well, at least you will pick up Tina again at Vienna airport.'

'You can take that as already dealt with. I must get back to headquarters now. Call me at once when you need me . . .'

Inside the car on their way back, sitting next to Tweed, Paula clenched her hands against her thighs. The bullet had passed so close to Tweed. Her emotions were a mixture of relief and fear for the future. He sensed her reaction and squeezed her arm. She smiled wanly.

'The trouble is we won't recognize that bastard if we see him again. He won't be dressed as a clergyman.'

'He was stooped and hobbled a little on his right foot as he ran,' said Marler.

'Part of the disguise,' Newman snapped. 'He was at least six foot tall, thin build and the hobble was probably a fake.'

'Who are you going to call?' Paula asked. 'Or maybe it's a secret. I'm talking too much.'

'No, you're not. I'm going to try and contact Amos. He may have returned to the Baur au Lac.'

When he reached his room Tweed was not able to put in his call immediately. The phone was ringing. He grabbed it.

'Tweed speaking.'

'Monica here. I've been trying to contact you for over an hour. Have you been busy?'

'You could say that. What is it?'

'I'm getting rumours from contacts abroad. Something is up. First it was our man in Singapore. Rumours that the US Fifth Fleet has entered the Indian Ocean. Then Delhi reported the same thing. Nothing in the newspapers. The contacts said what they told me was highly confidential. Should I check with Cord Dillon at Langley?'

'No, don't do anything. Just keep me fully informed. I'll always let you know where I am.'

'It would help if you did. You've been flitting about all over the Continent.'

'Like The Butterfly.'

'Pardon?'

'Just a bad joke. It might be wise if you slept at the office from now on.'

'Slept at the office?' Monica's tone expressed great

indignation. 'What do you think I've been doing for the past week? I brought my own sheets and blankets and used your camp bed.'

'Sorry. Knowing you I should have guessed. I'm grateful.'

'You're forgiven.'

Paula had been sitting in a chair in his room. As the call ended she looked at him with a smile.

'You haven't been upsetting Monica, I hope?'

'I'm afraid so. She's a brick. I must increase her salary when we get back – if we get back. Now I want to try and get Amos.'

Calling the Baur au Lac, he was put straight through to Amos. His voice sounded more like gravel going down a metal chute than usual.

'Who is this calling, may I ask?'

'You may. Tweed here. Have you heard any rumours?'

'No. What kind of rumours?'

'The US Fifth Fleet is heading into the Indian Ocean. That's a big fleet. At least one aircraft carrier, could be more. And they'll be armed with nuclear weapons. I'm telling you because you're a strategist on a global scale.'

'Changes the whole picture. I'll have to rethink my forecast. Thanks for letting me know.'

'Who gets your forecasts? Or shouldn't I ask?'

'One favour deserves another,' said Amos, his tone now amiable. 'Washington, London, Paris and Bonn get my forecasts. They pay well, especially Washington. Just as well. I need the money. Switzerland is expensive.'

'Let's keep in touch.'

'Where are you, then?'

'Just about to move on. I'll call you from my new destination.'

'Amos is good, isn't he?' asked Paula when Tweed left the phone.

'First rate. One of the best strategists in the world. Let's go for a walk along the riverside.'

'Don't you think you ought to stay indoors, particularly after what happened at the airport?'

'No one is going to keep me locked up like a fugitive.'

'I'll just freshen up. I'll be exactly five minutes. Time me.'

Alone, Tweed stood to one side of his window overlooking the Limmat. At the far end of the covered walk below him he saw a man coming down the steps leading to the walkway. He watched as the man glanced up at the windows of the hotel, pausing as he did so. Then he disappeared along the walkway.

Tweed frowned. Hassan, he felt sure, had a vast organization. It was possible he had men out checking the hotels. Tweed picked up the phone, told the concierge that if anyone asked if he was staying there he should say no one of that name was a guest. The concierge replied that he wouldn't even say that – he'd just send any noseyparker packing.

Paula returned in exactly the five minutes she had promised, ready for her walk. The phone rang and she cast her eyes upwards.

'Keith Kent is on the line,' he told her.

'I spoke to Beck,' said Kent. 'I gather you'd told him to give me your number if I called.'

'I did. Have you dug up something else?' he asked Kent.

'Yes. Within the past five minutes. A contact I have in the Channel Islands has told me Conway, whoever he is, has instructed his bank out there to move all his assets to the Cayman Islands by electronic means. Before you ask me, I'm no closer to identifying Conway. For the moment, that's it . . .'

Tweed then told Paula what Keith Kent had said. She stared at him with a puzzled look.

'Is that significant?'

'Yes.'

He had to pick up the phone again as it started ringing. Paula sat down, convinced their walk was off.

'Tweed? Beck here. Ashley Wingfield has just phoned the airport and booked a seat, Business Class, on the next flight to Vienna. You'll have to hurry if you want to catch it. I can book seats. You want me to, then? How many?'

'Five in Economy. Me, Paula, Newman, Marler and Nield.'

'Consider it done.'

'We're off to Vienna,' Tweed informed Paula. 'I hope everyone has kept their bags packed, as I asked.'

'They have.' Paula was on her feet. 'Hadn't you better inform Monica?'

'I'll do that while you let the rest know. The cars can be handed in at the airport.'

'What's happening?' she asked, on the verge of leaving.

'The battlefield is moving further east.'

41

Aboard her flight to Vienna Tina sat fuming in her Economy seat. The flight was midway between Zurich and Vienna. Once it was airborne she had left her seat and walked down the aisle to peer through at the Business section.

There were very few passengers in Business although Economy was full. She saw that Hassan was not on the plane. She swore foully to herself and returned to her seat, squeezing past the man sitting next to her. She could have killed Hassan.

'Here I am stuck with the rabble,' she said to herself. 'And Hassan is not on board. Plus the fact there are plenty of seats available in Business. What does he think I am? A peasant?'

She debated whether to call the stewardess, to insist that she was transferred to Business. Reluctantly she decided against taking any action. It would draw attention to herself. He'll pay for this, she raged inwardly – in more cash. Then she was irritated by the man next to her who tried to strike up a conversation with her. One glance at his suit told her he was not in the money. And he was travelling Economy.

'You get a marvellous view of the Austrian mountains on a day like this,' he had said.

'I'm not interested. I don't want to talk. I have a migraine.'

'I have some tablets.'

'Keep them.'

She turned her head away and stared out of the window. The mountains were to be seen on the starboard side as the plane curved, beginning its long descent to the airport.

Two rows behind her Detective Windlin, wearing a civilian suit, had been amused as he had watched her peering into Business Class. The Butterfly was becoming notorious among the Swiss police force. Her liking for wealthy men had percolated through to them.

She pushed past other passengers after the flight had landed.

Back in Geneva she had purchased a small suitcase, one she could carry aboard a plane and stow in the luggage compartment above the seats. It saved time waiting at the carousel. Behind her Detective Windlin saw an Austrian plain-clothes man he had cooperated with in the past. Windlin nodded towards Tina's back.

The Austrian hurried over to a man clad as a motorcyclist who was holding his crash helmet in his hands. The Austrian had a brief word with his colleague who was walking towards Tina as he put on his helmet. Tina noticed nothing – she was scanning the waiting drivers. One held a board with the name *L. Vane*.

'I'm in a hurry to get to the Sacher,' she said with a smile.

'Consider we are at the Sacher.'

Tina was pleased when he opened the rear door of a de luxe limo. It was the only way to travel. They had left the airport, were travelling over flatlands with fields on either side which she found boring. But she thought the driver was rather handsome and in tune with the car.

'What is your name?' she called out. 'You are from the Sacher? I may need a car while I'm in Vienna.'

'After we reach Sacher I go off duty,' the driver said quickly.

The motorcyclist drew alongside them after they had covered a certain distance. He stared at her through his goggles, waved his hand at her, then made a gesture as though drinking. She looked away.

'Bloody sauce,' she said to herself. 'A motorcyclist.'

The man in the crash helmet zoomed ahead and out of sight. As he swept round a bend he raised one hand. The signal was picked up by two plain-clothes men waiting in a Volvo hidden in a side road. They began to follow the limo as it entered the outer suburbs of Vienna.

At Zurich's airport Tweed and his companions appeared scattered. In fact Paula and the four men with her were waiting in tactical positions chosen by Marler. They were covering Tweed from every angle. Beck stood next to Tweed.

'Hassan has passed through Security and is waiting in the final departure lounge,' Beck remarked.

'Could you arrange it so we go aboard at the last moment? They usually let Business Class on to the plane after Economy.'

'Already arranged. No danger of him seeing you.'

'Marler won't be coming with us. He has a job to do for me in Zurich. He insisted on coming with me as protection.'

'Understood.'

What Beck did not understand was that Marler had decided he had to drive to Vienna – to take his armoury across the border into Austria at a remote point, as he had done when he had driven from Vienna after Paula's grim experiences near Slovakia. Marler had also given Newman a note for and the name and address of an arms dealer in Vienna he had dealt with on his earlier trip. As though reading his mind, Beck suddenly said: 'None of your people have weapons, I hope? The metal detector.'

'Dumped them in the Limmat,' said Tweed.

When, at the last moment, they boarded the flight they had seats near the front of Economy. One passenger at the back had a shock when he saw Tweed. Big Ben, slumped in his seat, appeared to be a man of medium height. He was clad in a jogging outfit and his cadaverous face was changed by the large-lensed *pince-nez* perched on the bridge of his nose. He had in his lap a scientific magazine of which he didn't understand a word. But he now had the appearance of a professor, and there were plenty of them in Austria.

He glanced across at Les, occupying the aisle seat opposite. From Les's expression he could tell he had also observed Tweed's arrival. Big Ben wished he had his Colt automatic. At Vienna's airport there was bound to be crowds and confusion. He could have hit Tweed. But Big Ben *had* dumped his Colt in the Limmat.

Paula, seated next to Tweed, who had the window seat, glanced round at the other passengers. The professorial-looking type pretending to read his magazine as the aircraft took off meant nothing to her.

'Look at those mountains,' Tweed said to her later. 'Really you should have had the window seat.'

'You always give it to me. I can see anyway,' she replied, leaning over him.

In the glaring sunlight sabre-toothed peaks seemed to pass just under the plane's fuselage. She stared down, fascinated by the grimness of the view.

'I wouldn't like to be climbing one of those,' she remarked.

'People do. They must have different minds from us.'

Newman and Nield, seated immediately behind Tweed and Paula, were also gazing down at the awe-inspiring view. Therefore they did not see the curtains closing them off from Business Class part. Hassan gazed at the passengers, nervously checking on who else was aboard. Suddenly his eyes met those of Tweed, who had caught the curtain's movement. For seconds their eyes were again locked, then Hassan closed the curtain.

Returning to his set, Hassan thought rapidly. It was a situation he had not foreseen. He checked his watch. In just over half an hour they would be landing. He bit his fingernails, not seeing the view below him. Eventually, he took out a pad and wrote a message addressed to a man called Vogel. Summoning a stewardess he gave her the sheet he had torn off the pad.

Bring a party to meet me at Schwechat Airport. Some of our best friends. Ashley.

He had been so busy working out what to say he had failed to notice a stewardess from Economy had earlier taken another message to the pilot's cabin. This one also had to be radioed urgently. But whereas Hassan's message was sent to a village halfway between the airport and Vienna, Tweed's had been sent to Zurich. To Arthur Beck.

Expect reception group to await us at Vienna's airport. Can you counter them. Tweed.

Ashley Wingfield, a passenger well known to Austrian Airlines, was the first to leave the plane on landing. He carried no luggage, hurried through Security and Passport Control. Vogel, in his forties, of medium height, built like a boxer, had a bald head and squinted through pouched eyes. He hurried to greet Hassan on the crowded concourse of Schwechat.

A large group of Croats, singing a national song and waving flags, were gathered together. Some were dancing while other compatriots clapped. It appeared to be some kind of celebration. Vogel bowed his head, to show respect, then whispered, 'They are over there – the Croats singing and dancing. Every man has a concealed knife. How many to kill? It will look as though the targets have collapsed from the heat. Knives are silent.'

'I will point them out to you and then hurry to my car. It is waiting outside?'

'Yes. Your limo and your driver.'

Hassan turned round, took a few paces forward to get a better view of the disembarking passengers. It seemed to take for ever as the people off the flight slowly appeared, carrying their luggage. No sign of Tweed and his friends. Hassan began to worry. Surely they must have left the aircraft.

Then he saw Tweed with the girl. They were chatting, walking very slowly. Behind them trailed Newman and Nield. They were moving at such a weary pace all the other passengers off the flight had headed for the exit. Hassan began biting his fingernails at how long it was taking. He heard Vogel's voice behind him.

'Cars are ready to drive off with the Croats once they have down their work.'

'I should hope so.'

Now the first of passengers disembarked from another flight were hurrying forward. They overtook Tweed and his team as the Croats continued singing and dancing, waiting for the signal from Vogel. Hassan fretted some more. Then a dribble of passengers overtook Tweed and once again he was alone with his three companions.

Detective Windlin was now talking to his opposite number from Vienna. Verbally, he identified Tweed. As he watched, the last passenger to leave the plane appeared. A short plump-faced man, he carried a small case. Mario looked around at the concourse. Besides the Croat singers and dancers a number of men were gathered in groups, talking to each other.

'I think it's time now,' Hassan said.

Vogel turned to give the signal for the Croats to attack, about to point out their targets. A man came running up to him, spoke rapidly in German. Vogel froze for a moment, then touched Hassan's arm.

'What is it?'

'Bad news. The concourse is crawling with a heavy detachment of Austrian police in plain clothes. It would be madness to launch an onslaught now.'

'Damn it to hell.'

Hassan almost reeled physically from the report. He clenched both hands, took one last look at Tweed and then stormed out to find his limo. Vogel had already sent his messenger back to the chief of the Croats, ordering them to leave the airport at once.

As he was doing so Nield, who had noticed several Croats looking towards his group, took out a small pocket camera and took three pictures of them in quick succession. There were no flashes as he pressed the button. The camera had been designed by the boffins in the cellars under SIS HQ in Park Crescent. It took perfect pictures even in the dark and there was never a flash of light.

The Croats stopped singing and dancing suddenly. Several of the detectives in groups had their hands inside their jackets, gripping automatics. They watched with grim satisfaction as the Croats hurried towards the exit and silence descended on the concourse.

'What is happening?' Tweed asked as Windlin hurried up to him. 'And who are you?'

'Detective Windlin from Zurich. Chief Inspector Beck told me to fly here.' He produced a folder. 'My identification.'

'So what *is* happening?' Tweed asked after glancing at the folder.

'The concourse is full of plain-clothes men from police headquarters in Vienna. Those Croat singers and dancers you saw were going to assassinate you. Beck apparently contacted the Chief of Police in Vienna.

'I rate him as among the best police chiefs in Europe. Give him my thanks. Now have we cars waiting for us?'

'Yes. Two cars. I will take you to them.'

Mario watched them talking from a distance. Standing by a food stall he sipped orange juice. On Vitorelli's instructions he had waited for a long time at Zurich's airport. He had also booked a seat on every flight leaving for Vienna.

'Why Vienna?' he had asked Vitorelli hours before in the Italian's suite at the Baur au Lac.

'Because Tweed has a sixth sense about where the operational centre of The Sisterhood will be. You remember when we were flying near Slovakia?'

'Yes, you took photographs from every angle of that strange house on top of a hill which is almost a mountain. I see you have them on that table.

'At one moment,' Vitorelli continued, 'I saw a car driving along the road leading to that house. You know how powerful my field glasses are. I focused on that vehicle. In the front was a Balkan-looking driver. His passenger in the back was Tweed's assistant and confidante, Paula Grey. So Tweed knows about that house. I think Tina will end up there.'

'Why should she?'

'From the newspapers I know The Sisterhood organization made an attempt to destroy all surviving members of the *Institut* with a huge bomb. The Sisterhood is no longer being used to carry out assassinations. Tina knows too much for the man running that organization for him to risk her being picked up and making a deal with the police. I am sure she will be taken to that house in Slovakia,' Vitorelli had said confidently.

'I'd better get to the airport here,' Mario said.

'Just before you leave. Is the equipment aboard my helicopter at the airport?'

'Yes,' Mario replied and rubbed his hands as though drying perspiration off them. 'It was a job. I spent hours inside the basement of that secret flat you rent off Rennweg . . .'

He recalled this conversation as he discreetly followed Tweed's party. He made a careful note of the registration numbers of the two hire cars which were waiting for them. Then he settled down to wait after buying two litre bottles of mineral water.

Vitorelli's chopper would take some time to reach Schwechat as it had taken off just ahead of Tweed's flight. Mario had used his mobile to report that Tweed *was* leaving for Vienna.

42

At the Château d'Avignon Butler, who had gone for a walk, hobbled back, dragging his right leg painfully. Fred Brown, who had helped himself to a few drinks, peered over the counter.

'What's the matter with your bloody leg?'

'Fell down the stairs, didn't I.'

'Drunk again,' Brown responded unsympathetically.

'Means I've got to stay on a bit longer. Don't know how long it will take to heal.'

'That's more money in the till,' Brown said gleefully.

'Don't you ever think of anything except lolly?'

'Yes, women. They go together. Women and lolly. Haven't you found that out yet?'

'I'll know where to come if I'm feeling depressed.'

'Go break a leg,' said Brown and chortled.

As Butler made his way slowly up the stairs to his room, holding on to the banister rail for support, Brown reached for the cognac bottle hidden under the counter, upended it and swallowed another large drink. His head began to swim. He didn't worry. He was used to cognac – he knew his head would clear within the hour.

Once inside his room, Butler removed the large bandage wrapped round his right leg which helped to make the hobble look convincing. He had needed a plausible reason for staying on longer without arousing suspicion that a single man should remain so long.

He was just about to take a shower when the phone started to ring. He lifted it cautiously.

'Yes? Harry here.'

'You know me,' said Tweed's voice. 'Not yet. The code you need for the drug consignment when it arrives is ...' He gave the number of the Sacher with the code for Austria, adding on his room number. He had reversed all the numbers. 'We're going backwards, I think,' he went on, informing Butler of what he had done. 'Ask for Pete if I'm not here. You're all right? This is Tweed.'

'I'm OK. Understood ...'

In the deserted lobby Brown was listening in. Befuddled, he still managed to note down the string of numbers and the name. With an effort he found the piece of paper which gave the hotel numbers Hassan had phoned, saying where he could be found if anyone called Butler. He gave the name Ashley Wingfield, a name Brown knew as he had received calls from him before – and a generous supply of banknotes sent by courier. Hassan was always anxious about the key communications centre in the turret, linked to the house in Slovakia.

With a greater effort Brown called the first number, which was the Zum Storchen. The concierge was brief.

'Mr Wingfield is not staying with us. We don't know the name.'

Cursing, Brown called the second number, which was the Sacher. Still befuddled, he noticed no similarity in the number he was calling and the reverse numbers Tweed had given him.

'Mr Wingfield? Brown here at d'Avignon. Guest staying here had a call from man called Tweed...'

'Tweed? Did you say Tweed?'

'Sounded like it. Said things were going backwards.'

'Going wrong, you mean?'

'Suppose he meant that. Things going wrong. That's what it sounded like.'

'Excellent. Who is the guest he called?'

'Man name of Butler.'

The name meant nothing to Hassan. But although he was delighted to hear that it appeared Tweed was in trouble he didn't like the idea of anyone Tweed knew staying at d'Avignon. He pressed for details.

'I should keep an eye on this guest, Butler.'

'He can't do no 'arm. Got a busted leg. That's why 'e's stayin' on a bit longer. Thought you ought to know.'

'Thank you, Brown. Just keep an eye on this Butler.'

Keep an eye on 'im? What the flaming hell for, thought Brown. 'E's as useless as a chicken with one leg. I'm not wastin' me time botherin' about 'im.

Hassan, seated on a couch in his luxurious suite, took a different view. The phone call worried him more the more he thought about it. And the few staff left to keep the Château d'Avignon going were no good. Six of the professional thugs he had ordered to head for Zurich fast were a different proposition. They were killers. Rudge, the leader of the group on its way, had left the East End of London years ago after strangling a girl. Hassan had left a message at the Zum Storchen that when Rudge called they were to give him the phone number of the Sacher. Big Ben would, of course, take command of the group.

When the flight from Zurich landed at Schwechat Big Ben and Les left the aircraft quickly, well ahead of Tweed. Reaching the concourse they collected the car Big Ben had hired before leaving Zurich. Then, with Big Ben behind the wheel, they waited.

On their way out they had passed the chanting Croats. Ben had glanced at them contemptuously. No discipline. Just a mob. He made his remark to Les, the knife-thrower, as they waited for Tweed to appear.

'What a load of trash that lot were.'

Well, you're not exactly Winston Churchill, thought Les. He was careful to keep the thought to himself. The heat was getting to him already. He glanced at Ben.

'Mind if I smoke 'alf a cigarette?'

'Not so long as you get out of the car.'

'It's like a bloody fire out there.'

'Give you a suntan. Keep a lookout for Tweed.'

Les stepped out into the torrid temperature. He took off his jacket, threw it into the car. His knives were concealed inside what appeared to be a money belt. He lit a cigarette as Ben peered into his rear-view mirror.

'Get back. Here they come.'

'I've only just lit my puff!'

'I said get back into the car,' Ben snarled.

He hunched down in his seat. Several other vehicles, mostly taxis picking up passengers, were leaving as Tweed's car drove off towards Vienna. They had left the second car as a reserve for Marler when he arrived. Ben was able to follow Tweed's car without risk of being spotted – other vehicles masked him. He drove all the way to the Sacher, watched while Tweed and his companions alighted and entered the hotel, then drove to a small hotel close by, where Hassan had booked two rooms.

His first action on entering his small room was to phone Hassan to report his arrival. Hassan put down the phone and rubbed his damp hands with satisfaction. Tweed had made the mistake of following him onto his home ground. Adding the Croats – murderous fighters – to Ben and Les and the six men under Rudge on their way from Zurich, he had a large enough force to wipe out anything Tweed could summon up. Rudge had just called him from Zurich.

'We're at the airport, Chief. Thought you might want us to fly on elsewhere.'

'Clever of you. Board the first flight for Vienna. Cars will be waiting to take you to a small hotel near the Sacher. You report to Big Ben. He's in charge.'

'Right . . .'

Rudge, a man of few words, was very fat. He sported a large bushy moustache, brown like his thick untidy hair. He always smiled and was popular with the ladies because he joked a lot. People noticed Rudge. On the surface he was an amiable man who enjoyed life. Only someone like Newman would have seen the hard look in his eyes.

His five colleagues were less well dressed. Which was why Rudge booked Economy tickets. Personally he would have preferred to travel Business. You met a better class of passenger.

'Are you surviving?' Tweed asked Paula after she had let him inside her room at the Sacher. 'You were very quiet on the way here.'

'Two reasons. One, did you notice the wave of heat that hit us as we left the concourse? I'll get used to it. Two, it seemed weird landing at Schwechat again. I was recalling what happened when Valja, the driver, took me close to Slovakia and I had to ram a nail file into his neck to get him to turn back.'

'We'll see that there isn't a repeat performance of that.'

'When I was in your room I was surprised when you phoned Harry and mentioned your name. Someone could have listened in to your call.'

'I'm sure they did. Then they would report it to Hassan as soon as they could. That will have disturbed him. Which is the way I want Hassan. Disturbed men make mistakes.'

'What is our next move?'

'We wait here until Marler arrives with his armoury. I don't like the idea of Bob visiting that arms dealer here. He may also deal with Hassan. I estimate it gives us twenty-four hours here. Time to recharge our batteries, to coin a cliché.'

'We stay in the hotel meantime?'

'Definitely. I've given orders to that effect to Newman and Nield. Meanwhile Hassan will be assembling his forces to deal with us. He'll probably have more troops than we can muster, so we'll outmanoeuvre him. I had a call from Marler – he's well on his way. Should arrive in the morning. Only then do we walk into Hassan's trap, which will close on him.'

'Let's go downstairs. I could do with a drink,' said Paula, a rare remark for her.

With Tweed behind her, she stepped out of the lift on the ground floor and bumped into a glamorous woman with auburn hair. Tina turned round, stood stock-still, staring at Paula.

'I'm not used to people following me,' she snapped.

'Unless they're men,' Paula said pleasantly.

'You want to mind your manners.'

'Then I won't copy you,' Paula replied, again pleasantly.

Tina's eyes glared with a ferocity which startled Tweed. She walked away into the bar, her body language expressing fury. Tweed whispered to Paula.

'Keep it up. Go after her into the bar.'

As they entered the well-appointed and spacious bar Paula saw Tina sitting down at an empty corner table with her elegant legs crossed. Paula led the way to the next table and sat so she was facing Tina. Tweed joined her. The tables were close and he gave Tina a little wave. She had just ordered a large Martini and she focused her attention on Tweed.

'At least it's nice to see *you* here. Staying long? I'm on my own.'

'We can't have that,' Tweed replied, smiling. 'Maybe you'd like to join us for dinner.'

'Both of you?'

'I can hardly leave Paula out in the cold. I'm sure you would not want me to do that.'

'In that case I think maybe I would prefer to dine on my own. Nothing personal. I feel I have been flying all over Europe nonstop.'

'Perhaps you have,' Tweed said with a smile.

Tina stared at him, confused. She finished her drink, ordered a second large Martini. Inwardly, she felt rage building up. Paula kept gazing at her as though she was some strange specimen. Tweed had relaxed in his chair, holding a glass of orange juice as he looked slowly round the room, studying the extraordinary variety of guests. He reckoned there must be at least eight different nationalities in the room, some probably from the Balkans. This was Vienna.

Paula, with a glass of wine she sipped at occasionally, continued to gaze at Tina. Drinking half the fresh glass which had been put before her, Tina had an almost overwhelming desire to get out a mirror to check her appearance. Had she a smut on her nose? She resisted the impulse, signalled to the waiter again.

'Please book me a table for dinner in the Rote Bar.'

She gave him her room number. Tweed was bound to pick up that item of information but she had reached the stage where she didn't give a damn. She sat back, giving the impression she hadn't a care in the world. Then she couldn't stand it any longer. Signing the bill, she omitted to leave a tip in her haste to get away from Paula. The moment she was gone Tweed summoned the waiter.

'Could you book us a table for dinner in the Rote Bar? Place us at a table next to the one our friend – the lady who was sitting over there.'

'You're getting on her nerves,' Paula whispered.

'Which, as you may have guessed, is the idea.'

They got up and walked along the corridor to the Rote Bar, which was a restaurant. The head waiter escorted them to a table by the window and next to where Tina sat alone. Paula chose a chair where she would be directly facing her. As she sat down she smiled at Tina.

'This is a wonderful hotel, don't you think? So luxurious.'

'Is there any other way to live?' Tina responded in a tight voice.

'Some people have to struggle to exist,' Paula said.

'That's their problem.'

'Yours, of course, is where the next twenty thousand pounds is coming from. Maybe you could go in for some more target practice.'

For a moment Tweed thought Tina was going to pick up something from the table to hurl it. Paula still sat very still, her expression bleak as she stared down Tina.

After eating only half her main course, Tina stood up, gazed round to see if people at other tables could have heard, but the exchange between the two women had been in low voices. Before she left Tina gave Tweed an inviting smile, bent down and brushed her lips across his face. She glanced at Paula, whose expression was now one of amusement. With exaggerated elegance she strolled out. Several men watched her with longing.

'Bit of a hellcat, isn't she,' Paula commented.

'You handled that beautifully. She's in a towering

441

fury. She'll probably go to Hassan – Nield found out he's in the hotel under the name Ashley Wingfield. Pressure. That's what I want – more and more pressure imposed on the enemy. I'm going all out to destabilize Mr Hassan.'

'I won't stay in this place another night!' Tina shouted.

'Keep your voice down,' Hassan snapped. 'They'll hear you in Salzburg.'

Tina had hammered on his door a minute earlier. The moment she entered Hassan realized he had a female thunderstorm on his hands. She was out of control.

'I don't care if they do. I want out.'

'May I ask what has caused this outbreak of annoyance?'

'Tweed and Paula Grey. First in the bar, then they sit close to me at dinner in the Rote Bar.'

'Well,' he said genially, 'Rote is the German for red. You make it sound as though there was blood.'

'I'd like to blow off the back of Paula Grey's head.'

'I'd prefer you to do that to Tweed. Calm down.'

'I'm not calming down. I want to get out of this place tonight.'

'Sit down. Have a drink.' Hassan poured wine in a glass almost to the brim. 'We have to stay here tonight. A car will take you out of Vienna in the morning.'

'Thank God for that.'

Tina had sat down. She lifted the glass without spilling a drop, took a long drink. Hassan was clever enough to say nothing for the moment. Tina took another long drink, put the glass down. He refilled it.

'I need money,' she said aggressively.

'I haven't any at the moment. I'll give you some

when you're in the car in the morning. Order what you want from room service and put it on my bill.'

'How very generous.'

'I can be generous in the morning.'

'I'm going back to my room. I've had enough of people tonight.'

'Make sure you're packed and ready to leave early.'

'It can't be early enough for me . . .'

When she had gone Hassan sat thinking for a moment. Then he picked up the phone and called another room in the hotel. His tone was brusque.

'Carl, you know Tina Langley's room number. Keep an eye on her. Don't let her leave tonight. Your head's on the block.'

Hassan kept tapping his thick fingers on the glass table top. He was very disturbed. If Tina went over the top she might take it into her head to contact the police, the mood she was in. At least Carl would keep her under his thumb until the morning. He needed the time to contact Big Ben, to explain to him the large force he was placing under his control, details of the trap he was planning for Tweed.

Hassan cursed aloud. Tweed. It was always Tweed who got in his way. Tweed was becoming an obsession with him, upsetting his judgement. He picked up the phone again, this time to call Big Ben in the small hotel nearby.

Hassan was not the only one to worry about Tina. In the Rote Bar several tables had emptied near Paula and Tweed, so they had privacy. Paula finished her first and only glass of wine before she spoke.

'I think Tina could walk out of the Sacher tonight.'

'If she does she'll be followed. Nield is waiting outside in a car. He has her photo. Newman is sharing shifts with him throughout the night.'

'I'm worrying about nothing.'

'Don't agree. Tomorrow could bring anything – and probably will. We must all be ready to leave at dawn.'

43

A few hours before, Vitorelli had landed in his chopper at a remote part of Schwechat. Mario had paid a big tip to the driver of a buggy which carried him out to the helicopter. Despite his long flight, Vitorelli was in a cheerful mood and very fresh.

'Tell me the news, friend,' he said after Mario had asked the buggy driver to wait a distance away.

'They're all at the Sacher. Why is the Sacher the hotel they so often choose?'

'Because it is the finest hotel. Also it is strategically located in the centre of Vienna. Now, the news.'

'I phoned my contact there. Tina Langley is staying there. So is Tweed and his assistant, Paula Grey. There was a scene at the airport . . .'

Mario described the presence of the Croats, their rush to leave, the fact that the concourse appeared to be flooded with plain-clothes police. Standing by the chopper, his helmet in his hand, Vitorelli listened. He smiled grimly when Mario repeated the details of the arrival and departure of Tina by car.

'You have transport, Mario?'

'Yes. I hired a car. The equipment travelled safely aboard your chopper?'

'Yes, thanks to you. We leave it where it is. Now, drive us to the Sacher. When we arrive you go in first. Make sure Tina is not about, then I will come in with you. I need food, and I'm sure you do. I prefer the main restaurant to the Rote Bar. Check it out for me. Let's go now . . .'

They had just sat down in the restaurant when Tweed peered in to see who was inside. Vitorelli saw him, beckoned for him to join them. Paula followed Tweed and Vitorelli greeted her courteously, even enthusiastically.

'I feel the need of some intelligent female company. Talking with you is always a pleasure.'

'Thank you. What are you doing in Vienna?' Paula asked.

'Business. You both know Mario. Please join us.'

'I know Mario,' said Tweed. 'I saw him travelling on the same flight as we did. If you'll excuse us, we've had a long day.'

'And maybe tomorrow will be the longest day,' Vitorelli replied with a quizzical smile.

'If you say so,' Tweed agreed. 'Good night to both of you.'

'What did he mean by that last remark?' Paula asked in the lift.

'We'll find out tomorrow. Now, go and get as much sleep as you can.'

Tweed was woken before dawn by a gentle tapping on his door. Putting on a dressing gown he approached the door cautiously. He stood to one side before he spoke.

'Who is it?'

'This is your favourite aide-de-camp. Would you like tea, sir?' a familiar voice replied.

'Marler!' Tweed greeted him after unlocking the door. 'How on earth did you get here so quickly?'

'I made use of the autobahn from Munich to Salzburg. No speed limit. I'd better wake everyone else up and distribute the goodies,' Marler drawled.

'You'll be popular, but I think that is a good precaution. I have a feeling we may have to leave early. You must need some sleep.'

'Waste of time. Saw Newman outside slacking in a car. He gave me news. When he relieved Nield, Pete told him he'd seen Big Ben coming out of a small hotel to meet Hassan. They went for a walk in the middle of the night. Nield told Bob that Big Ben was a formidable thug he last saw at the Château d'Avignon. Hassan appeared to be giving Ben instructions. Looks as though I've got here in time for bit of a blow-up.'

'I'll order you coffee.'

'Tea would be better. Meantime I'll act as a human alarm clock. Tell me where everyone is.'

Tweed sat down at a desk, scribbled names and room numbers. He handed it to Marler. When he had entered the room Marler had been carrying a bulging satchel which was now propped against a wall. Tweed nodded towards it.

'What have you got inside there?'

'Machine-pistols, stun and shrapnel grenades, smoke bombs, handguns and ammo. We'll be well equipped to deal with Big Ben and the mob I'm sure he'll be commanding.'

'Sounds like you're ready for a small replay of the Gulf War.'

'We'll be well dressed. Incidentally, Newman had some really interesting news. Before he went to bed prior to relieving Nield in the middle of the night he saw two taxis arriving separately. He said the scenery was good. First, a luscious blonde who happens to be called Karin Berg. Then a ravishing redhead by the name of Simone Carnot. Bob said he thought Hassan was greedy.'

'That is interesting. We're approaching a real climax.'

'I'll be back for a cuppa tea.'

Wide awake now, Tweed had a shower, and was dressed when Marler returned. His visitor was grinning and the satchel he dropped on the floor no longer bulged. Tweed insisted he drank some tea before saying a word.

'That's better,' Marler said after two cups. 'And I was so popular, waking up people. Except for Paula. She was already up, fresh as a daisy. I tried to persuade her to accept a machine-pistol but all she would take was a .32 Browning.'

'It is her favourite weapon. What about Newman and Nield?'

'Like me, they're walking warriors. When I arrived I booked myself a room. I won't use the bed. I needed somewhere to dump my own equipment. Any more tea left?'

'I ordered a large pot. Help yourself.'

Marler was reaching for the pot when someone tapped on the door. In seconds Marler, a Walther in his hand, was by the door. He called out.

'Identify yourself.'

'It's me. Paula.'

She came in, and after relocking the door Marler poured her tea. She showed no signs of strain, her shoulder bag over her arm and carrying her packed case. Thanking Marler, she looked at Tweed.

'Any news?'

'Yes.'

He told her about the arrival of both Karin Berg and Simone Carnot. Sitting on a couch, she sipped tea with a puzzled frown. She said nothing until she had finished drinking the whole cup, which Marler promptly refilled.

'That's strange. Tina's here. Now they turn up. It sounds to me as though we have the whole Sisterhood under the same roof. Why?'

'I think Hassan is withdrawing them from the reach

of Beck,' Tweed told her. 'At this stage he doesn't want to risk any of them breaking down under Beck's interrogation. This fact alone convinces me we are on the verge of a major climax.'

'What are we waiting for, then?'

'For Pete Nield to report that Hassan is leaving.'

Tweed had been right about the arrival of Karin Berg and Simone Carnot. Earlier in the afternoon Hassan had phoned each of them, had told them they were in danger from being arrested. He had told them to take the last flight – the only one available – from Zurich to Vienna. He had advised Berg to travel Economy and Carnot to buy a Business Class ticket. In this way he had kept them separated from each other. Simone had agreed without argument. Karin was a different proposition.

'I'm not sure I want to fly to Vienna,' she had said firmly. 'I think I'd sooner go elsewhere,' she went on, thinking of Rome.

'Beck is closing in,' Hassan had warned her. 'You need to be hidden and protected for a week or two. You have done a good job,' he added persuasively. 'So you are really independent, I propose to hand you thirty thousand pounds. I did say pounds – not dollars.'

Berg had killed three members of the *Institut*. She felt pretty sure she had outgunned, so to speak, the other members of the Sisterhood. Another thirty thousand and she wouldn't have to worry about money for the rest of her life, being prudent in her spending. She had agreed to take the flight to Vienna.

Relieved, Hassan had given two of his special drivers orders to meet the two women at Schwechat. He had described them carefully, had told them to use the name Ashley Wingfield.

That night he had had little sleep. Meeting Big Ben,

448

he had taken him to an all-night café which was almost empty, had described the plan. With a map of Burgenland open he had drawn a route, had marked a certain village.

'You leave with your men soon,' he had ordered. 'Rudge will be your second-in-command in case you are injured. A woman,' he had continued, thinking of Tina, 'will be the bait leading them to the ambush points. They have to be close to Slovakia so Tweed is not suspicious. Recently, a woman called Paula was near my headquarters. I saw her in a car through powerful field glasses. That means Tweed knows. You meet the Croats here. They may wipe out Tweed and his men on their own. Now, I will go over the plan again.'

Eventually he had returned to the Sacher. On his way in he noticed the same car, parked with a man behind the wheel who appeared to be fast asleep. He smiled wearily to himself. When he returned to his room the phone was ringing. He picked it up cautiously.

'Yes?'

'Mr Ashley Wingfield, I presume?' an upper-crust English voice had said.

'Willie? Where are you now? Time is running short.'

'I'm well east of Paris, old boy. Thought you'd like a progress report.'

'Progress!' Hassan had screeched. 'Why aren't you much closer?'

'Trouble, this time at jolly Calais. The Customs chappies again. Looking for a big drug consignment. Caused one hell of a hold-up.'

'The sample?'

'Intact, of course. I can step on the gas now.'

'You'd better not be late arriving.'

'I'm never late. Sounds as though you need a spot of shut-eye. Bye.'

Hassan started to worry again. He decided not to

report to the Head of State until he reached Slovakia. By then, he hoped, Willie would be close to his headquarters on the mountain. He looked at his bed longingly, checked his watch, decided he'd better just stay up. He ordered more coffee from room service.

When she arrived in her room Simone Carnot decided she was too washed-out to eat. She took a quick shower, got into her night clothes and flopped into bed. She didn't bother to call Hassan. That could wait until morning. She just remembered to switch off the bedside light before falling into a deep sleep.

Karin Berg had more stamina. After taking a shower, she phoned down and ordered an early breakfast to be sent up at once. Spread out on a couch, she considered her present position. She needed to get the thirty thousand out of Hassan as soon as possible.

Unlike the other women, while she was being 'trained' at the house in Slovakia she had gone for walks. Starting out from the front entrance, after telling the guard to go to hell, she had wandered to the eastern edge of the hill. Out of sight of the house she had found a sunken path leading down in the direction of Austria.

'I'm not hanging around there for two weeks,' she said to herself. 'If necessary, once I've extracted the money from Hassan, I'll slip away on foot. Once in Austria I should find transport back to Vienna. From there I'll fly to Rome.'

With this comforting thought in mind, she tackled the generous breakfast with enthusiasm when it arrived. Feeling better, she set her mental alarm clock, climbed into bed, closed her eyes, fell fast asleep.

* * *

Sitting in the lounge after a large dinner, Vitorelli nursed a drink and gave Mario his instructions.

'I'm going to leave you the car. You have a mobile so you can call me when anything happens I should know about. Because something is going to happen during the next few hours.'

'You are going somewhere, then?' Mario asked.

'I am taking a taxi back to the airport. I'll get a bit of sleep in the chopper. With what it has on board I think it best I watch over it.'

'What do I do after I've reported to you?'

'Main thing to report is if Tweed leaves – that is, *when* Tweed leaves. Then you can drive to join me at the airport. If I'm right the whole operation will get under way early in the morning. The fact that Tweed is here with Paula tells me something major is about to explode.'

'You have a plan, Emilio?'

'A flexible one. What I need is a diversion. I think Tweed and his team will provide exactly that.'

'You are leaving now, then?'

'Just a moment. Let me think.' Vitorelli ran his muscular hand through the back of his shaggy hair. 'We must get this right. Tweed has a car parked near the exit from this hotel. After paying a visit to the cloakroom I wandered outside. I recognized Newman sitting in that car, pretending to be asleep. If that car takes off to follow another one call me on the mobile, then wait. I'm sure Tina will be leaving early by car. You follow her, see what direction she is taking, call me on the mobile, then drive like hell to the airport. I'll wait for you in the chopper. That's it. I'm off now.'

Much later in the night, close to early morning, Tweed had also changed his mind. He had a detailed map of

451

Burgenland which he had taken from a display case when he was leaving Schwechat Airport on arrival. It was spread out on a large table and, as Paula watched, he had pored over it. When Marler, who had left to go to his room for a few minutes, returned, he began speaking rapidly.

'Marler, Paula has given me a perfect description of what it is like in Burgenland. It's flat, just flat. So it's like a gigantic chessboard and we must move our pieces across it carefully.'

'The trouble will be,' Marler observed, 'that we shall have no cover.'

'Agreed, but that works both ways. The enemy will also have no cover. We have three cars. Newman will drive one with Paula and me inside it. Nield will drive a second car. The third car will be driven by you.'

'In convoy? A perfect target for the enemy to destroy us at one go.'

'No, not in convoy. The three cars will be well spaced out. To start with, Nield, who is outside now, will take the lead. I leave you to judge the right moment, Marler, when you overtake Nield and Nield drops behind my car. That will put me in the centre of the spaced out cars.'

Tweed was using a walking stick someone had left behind in his room, wielding it as a pointer. Paula thought he looked like a general planning the final campaign in a war. The intensity of his concentration created an atmosphere of tension.

'I see you have put a couple of mobile phones on that desk,' Tweed remarked.

'I know you don't like them because messages over mobiles can be intercepted. I think we need them on this expedition.'

'I agree. We will code-name Hassan as Argus.'

'Good,' Marler said with relief. 'We will all have a scrambler mobile.'

'There will be an ambush on the way,' Tweed warned. 'Once we get anywhere near Hassan's headquarters, the strange house on that hill or mountain in Slovakia.'

'There may be more than one ambush.'

'Like any battle, we have to make it up as we go along. The ultimate objective will be that strange house. Is Nield still outside in the car?'

'He is.'

'Ask Newman to take his place for a few minutes and send Pete to me. Then Pete can go back to the car and Bob can come up here.'

Tweed explained his strategy to Nield when he arrived, then he repeated it to Newman when Nield had returned to his watching post in the car. Newman listened before he commented.

'I agreed. The trouble is there are only five of us. Butler would have been a great asset.'

'Oh, I have arranged communication at the right moment with Butler,' Tweed explained. 'Detective Windlin has stayed here in the hotel. I have given him the phone number of the Château d'Avignon and a coded message to pass on to Butler when the time comes. I can reach Windlin by mobile – I wouldn't contact Harry by mobile from Burgenland.'

'You seem to have thought of everything,' said Paula.

'What worries me is that I may have missed something . . .'

Minutes later everyone was in position. Nield was outside the hotel, waiting and watching from his car. Newman and Paula, with Marler, his satchel bulging again, were in Tweed's room. Newman had paid all their bills so they could leave instantly. Tweed decided it was time he rang Monica.

'I was just about to call you,' she said. 'More news from our secret contacts abroad. The US Fifth Fleet, moving steadily north in the Indian Ocean, has been joined by a second aircraft carrier group. We're there too. A British nuclear submarine surfaced in the same area. It fired one dummy missile a huge distance south towards the Antarctic. Enemy aircraft were patrolling and must have seen it.'

'Any of this in the newspaper?'

'Yes. A brief reference to what they call a rumour in the *International Herald Tribune*. The story also reports another rumour – that British aircraft from our base at Akotiri in Cyprus were seen taking off and heading east. I think soon the world press will be splashing the story.'

'That's very interesting. The West is now waking up, at the eleventh hour – as usual. I may be difficult to reach during the next few hours. I'll call you when I can.'

'What *is* happening?' Paula asked when he relayed the news.

'Pressure will be mounting on a certain Head of State.'

'I don't suppose it means anything,' Newman remarked, 'but I saw Vitorelli leaving the hotel. Mario appeared to be staying behind here.'

'No idea where he went, I suppose?' queried Tweed.

'I followed him to the exit. He jumped into a taxi and the cab rocketed off.'

'Vitorelli is a very tough and determined character. I'm sure he has something in mind. Maybe in due course we'll find out what it is.'

He grabbed the phone before it could ring a third time. Nield was on the line.

'Tina and Argus are just leaving. Big limo. Has an escort car with it. They're moving. Just a minute. Another limo's pulled in. Chauffeur opening door for two women. Blonde is getting in front, redhead in back. They're moving, following Argus. I'm off.'

'It has started,' said Tweed.

44

At that hour, before dawn had broken, Vienna was at its most impressive – and oppressive. Newman, taking instructions about the route from Nield on the mobile, had him in view. Behind them Marler followed. Paula, seated in the back with Tweed, gazed out. The massive stone buildings of Vienna loomed up on both sides, relics of the great days of the Austro-Hungarian Empire before the First World War.

'It must have taken a fortune to build this city,' she commented.

'Built on money extracted from the satellites which made up the Empire of long ago,' Tweed explained. 'The Czechs were especially resentful of the money earned by them which found its way here. The Hungarians too.'

They drove on and on through the wide quiet streets. To Paula Vienna seemed to go on and on for ever. A vast monument to something which had not existed for over ninety years. She noticed that on the seat beside him Newman had two machine-pistols. At the last moment before leaving the hotel Marler had persuaded her to accept several grenades.

'These are stun, these shrapnel, these are smoke bombs . . .'

It had been such a rush leaving the Sacher she hadn't

refused them. Now they nestled in her shoulder bag, which bulged in the way Marler's satchel had. Newman drove with one hand on the wheel, the other holding his mobile as he kept in constant touch with Nield and Marler. They were leaving behind the palatial buildings when Newman spoke again.

'Pete reports he's just passed a signpost. Burgenland.'

'I thought so,' said Tweed. 'So far, so good.'

Some time later Vienna was only a memory and they were crossing a vast plain which, in the first light of dawn, stretched away into the distance. No sign of life anywhere. For Paula this was familiar territory, recalling her drive from the airport with the thuggish Valja. Newman spoke briefly.

'Pete reports the limos have outdistanced him. They must have supercharged engines. But he can still see their lights.'

'Tell him to keep them in sight as long as he can,' Tweed ordered.

'Marler's on,' Newman reported. 'Says Mario dived into a car as he left the Sacher. Tailed him a distance, then turned off to a road signposted *Flughafen*. The airport.'

'Makes sense,' Tweed replied.

'Why?' asked Paula.

'We may see Vitorelli again. In the sky.'

'He must like me,' said Paula, attempting a joke.

'I'm sure he does. But he dislikes another woman.'

The luminous light of dawn had grown stronger, revealing the incredible endlessness of the flat plain, sprawling away to the east. The road surface was good but nothing fenced it off from the level fields running away to the horizon on both sides. In the fields stumpy foot-high vegetation was growing, arranged in straight rows.

'Vineyards,' said Tweed. 'Imagine how the sun beats down on them during the day.'

'I did bring bottles of mineral water,' Paula told him, 'remembering my last trip this way. We just passed a signpost. *Bruck*.'

'We're heading in the right direction,' Tweed confirmed.

'Look, a village. They're weird. There are only a few of them with a long distance between them.'

They passed along a street with one-storey houses huddled close together. No one about. It was still very early in the morning. Tweed imagined the inhabitants were already inside, getting ready for another hard day's toil in the fields. Without warning, Marler overtook them, raced ahead. Shortly afterwards Pete Nield's car appeared, moving more slowly. Newman overtook him. They were now sandwiched between Nield behind and Marler somewhere ahead of them.

Daylight came suddenly and the vastness of the plain was exposed dramatically. They were in the middle of nowhere, on Tweed's chessboard. They could clearly see Marler's car now. A signpost appeared by the roadside. *Morzach*. Tweed leaned forward, seeing a much larger village ahead of them. He tensed.

It was larger but of the same weird character as the smaller village they had passed through earlier. A single line of one-storey houses, again huddled together, bordered both sides of the long street. The houses had shallow roofs and the plaster walls of each dwelling were painted a pastel colour, one green, another pink, another yellow, another blue. Paula assumed the colours were an attempt to cheer up the bleak surroundings.

'Slow down!' Tweed ordered. 'Then stop in the middle of this village. Recall Marler urgently. Tell Nield to drive like the wind until he reaches us.'

'What on earth—' began Paula.

Tweed's sharp eyes had seen the sun glinting off a pile of junk in the road ahead. The junk was a mixture of brutal, star-shaped pieces of iron and glass. It would have ripped their tyres to pieces, marooned them. He threw open his door, told Paula to open hers. Then he got out, looked around, listened.

A dreadful silence descended on him. Not a sound anywhere. It reminded him of the strange village of Shrimpton in Dorset – where he had been similarly struck by silence and the complete absence of people. Like a deserted village, abandoned by the one-time inhabitants. There was something sinister in the heavy silence. Then it was broken by the sound of Marler returning at top speed, followed by the arrival of Nield. Standing close to his car, Tweed waved both hands and arms in an encircling gesture, the signal for danger.

'What's wrong?' Paula asked standing by her open door as ordered.

'It's an ambush!' Tweed shouted, his voice reaching Marler and Nield.

He had hardly spoken when from inside hidden alleys between the houses a crowd of Croats appeared, screaming their guts out and brandishing long knives as they rushed forward. Nield, who had studied the photos taken by his self-developing camera when they had arrived at the airport yelled out.

'It's the Croats from the airport . . .'

One of them, his expression of vicious glee on his high cheekboned face, rushed at Tweed, his knife high above his head to strike. Paula, who had moved to the rear of the car, shot him in the chest. He gurgled, fell over backwards in a tumble of his strange robe-like clothes. As more of the mob came forward cautiously, Marler's voice rang out in a strident shout.

'Get behind the bloody car!'

Tweed dived back into the car, slamming the door

shut behind him, slipped out of the far side where Paula now crouched beside her boss. The Croats, yelling like dervishes, swarmed towards the car. There was a sudden murderous chatter of machine-pistols. The Croats were caught in a triple crossfire. Marler firing from near the front of the car, Newman firing across the bonnet crouched behind the vehicle, Nield firing from the rear. A hail of bullets hit the mob in the massive fusillade. Bodies sagged in the road, followed by more bodies as the second wave of Croats had no time to flee.

Then Morzach was enveloped by the awful silence again. Marler called out to Newman to stay where he was while he checked the houses. Nield joined Marler. The two men disappeared for what was only a short time but which seemed like eternity to Paula. When Marler reappeared, followed by Nield, she thought she had never seen him with such a grave expression.

'They massacred all the villagers to use their houses for the ambush.'

'Oh, my God! How horrible,' Paula said in a subdued voice.

Newman had already hauled out a sheet of canvas from the boot. He used it as a makeshift brush, sweeping the iron stars and the glass to the side of the road. Shaking it, to get rid of any glass, he flung it back into the boot.

'I think we ought to get moving. We have a job to do,' he said.

'Agreed,' replied Tweed. 'We can call the police anonymously later. What's in the road can't just be left here. To say nothing of the poor devils inside the houses. It's barbaric.'

As the cars started moving Paula deliberately avoided looking at the pile of bodies on one side of the road. Tweed put an arm round her and hugged her. He was careful to say nothing, guessing she was in shock.

His determination to finish the job was reinforced. Hassan was a man who would stop at nothing.

They were several miles away from the village and the billiard-table like plain was extending away for ever. At Tweed's order they had resumed their same places. Marler was some distance ahead of them and Nield had dropped back when Newman began contacting both cars on his mobile. He spoke to Nield first, then Marler. He stiffened during the second brief contact.

'Marler says he can see the hill with the long house on its summit,' he reported to Tweed. 'Says we'll see it in a minute.'

Tweed leaned forward, hands gripping the empty seat back in front of him. The sun was now scorching down on them even at this early hour. The temperature inside the cars was rising. Opening the windows, they found torrid heat pouring in, so they closed them again. Then Tweed saw it.

In the distance a long low hill reared up from the level plain. Perched on its summit was the long house which was Hassan's headquarters. It stood out against the glowing azure sky.

'That's it,' said Paula.

Inside the first limo, sitting by herself in the back, Tina had gazed resentfully up at the house before it disappeared from view as the chauffeur drove it across the border, along the track which took them into Slovakia. She had decided she did not want to come here at all. She had been rushed out of the Sacher into the car.

Her resentment increased as the driver negotiated the steep curving road which took them up one side of the mountain. Arriving at the top, the driver swung their limo right and up to the entrance at the front, facing away from Austria. As he pulled up Hassan, seated in front, jumped out to open the rear door for her. They had not exchanged one word during the whole journey. Hassan bowed.

'Welcome home.'

'I hate this bloody place,' she snapped. 'It's like a morgue. I'm not staying here long.'

'Come inside. Have a drink.'

'There should have been drinks on the way. Some limo you have.'

'It cost a fortune.'

'They must have seen you coming.'

He escorted her inside, followed by the chauffeur with her case. She heard the door being closed and locked. The sound did not soothe her temper.

'I'll have my drink on the terrace,' she said.

'First, let me show you your suite.'

Leading the way through the deep-pile carpeted hall, he opened a door to a suite overlooking Austria. It was luxuriously furnished in an Eastern style which Tina detested. Her case was deposited in a dressing room and the chauffeur left as Hassan moved back towards the door.

'These windows don't open,' she fumed after trying to open the French doors to the terrace. 'They did last time.'

'We are air-conditioned,' Hassan replied smoothly.

'How long – how many days – do you expect me to stay in this crazy house?' she demanded.

'Drinks are on the table.'

'I asked you a question. Haven't you any manners at all? If a lady asks a question she expects an answer.'

'We shall do everything possible to make you comfortable.'

'Stuff that. This is like being in Siberia. Answer me or I'm leaving right away.'

Hassan closed the door from the other side and she heard him lock it. She swore foully. Studying the array of bottles she poured herself a glass of red wine, drank, swore again.

It had taken Hassan an effort to retain his composure when Tina had started playing up. He knew that the second limo would soon arrive. When he opened the front door it was just pulling in. He ran to open the front passenger door where Karin Berg sat beside the chauffeur. He glanced at the woman in the back.

'I will be with you in no time. Give me a minute.' He turned his attention to the Swedish woman, opening the door, bowing. 'Very good to have you as a guest again. One of the superior suites is waiting for you.'

'Where is my thirty thousand?' Berg asked over her shoulder as she entered the hall. 'Payment on delivery. I'm delivered.'

'Let me show you the way. Money is such a sordid subject when you have just arrived.'

'I became sordid long ago.'

Her tone was crisp. Hassan led her down a corridor, opened a door to a suite. She walked in as the chauffeur arrived with her case. The room was spacious, the furniture expensive but the arched windows were very small. Karin was tall enough to peer through one without going up on her toes. Outside the wilderness of Slovakia spread away.

'The view is charming,' she said. 'I prefer the other side looking down on Austria.'

She heard a click, looked round. Hassan had gone, had closed the door and she heard it being locked from the outside. She shrugged. She would hammer away at him until he gave her the money. Looking out of the window again she saw to her right a pile of rocks. It was beyond them that the pathway led down the hill until it crossed into Austria.

Hassan had hurried back to the limo. Opening the rear door, he bowed. Simone Carnot stared back at him with an expression of resignation. She was thinking she ought never to have come. She should have taken her chances with the police. Then she recalled the description someone had once given her of Swiss prisons. No brutality, but no comforts of any sort either. Perhaps this prison was preferable – at least for a short time.

'You have the best suite in my headquarters,' he said unctuously.

'If you say so . . .'

Once he had locked Simone in her own suite, Hassan hurried to his office, sat behind his huge desk. He felt relieved. Now he had The Sisterhood under his personal control. The relief gave way to worry as he remembered he hadn't had another progress report from Willie.

Then he realized, knowing Willie, that he would be hurtling across Europe to deliver the bacillus sample. He wouldn't waste any more time phoning. Anxiety returned as he glanced through the copy of the *International Herald Tribune* the concierge had handed him as he had rushed out of the Sacher.

His pallid eyes were riveted to the story about rumours of the US Fifth Fleet entering the Indian Ocean. Hassan reached under his desk, pulled a lever. Above the roof of the house a system of aerials was elevated, the key to an advanced and complex communications device. He had to call the Head of State.

* * *

Leaning forward in his car, Tweed stared at the aerials and dishes which had suddenly appeared. He recognized them and their purpose. He spoke sharply.

'Bob, hand me the mobile, quick.'

Dialling Sacher, he asked to be put through to Detective Windlin urgently. Windlin came on the line almost immediately. Tweed told him to call Butler to transmit the coded message to him at the Château d'Avignon.

At the chateau Butler, an early riser, already showered and dressed, simply said one word.

'Understood.'

He limped down the stairs. Fred Brown watched him with amusement from behind his reception desk. He enjoyed other people's troubles. Stan, the thin sneering porter, joined his colleague in the fun. He called out as Butler limped towards the front entrance.

'Got a bunion have we, old boy? Hope it doesn't hurt. Much.'

Butler could have smashed his face in. Instead he forced himself to smile as he replied, close to the entrance.

'Need a bit of fresh air.'

Once out of their sight he moved. He hadn't bothered to put on the bandage – it would hamper his agility. The previous day he had transferred the satchel containing the bomb, timer and a few of his clothes from the top of his wardrobe to behind a thick shrub in the front of the chateau.

Hoisting it onto his shoulder, he began climbing the network of ivy below the turret. This time he climbed much faster, his gloved hands clutching the ivy. Then he was level with the turret. The deep window had been left partly open, presumably to counter the heat which built up inside it. The eight-sided room was empty, a swivel chair placed in front of the communications system which looked like the control panel aboard a Jumbo jet. He stepped over the window ledge and was inside.

It took him two minutes to extract the pancake-shaped bomb, which had metallic clamps attached to one side. He clamped it over the control panel. Setting the timer for five minutes, he linked it to the bomb. Then, without hesitation, he turned the switch which made it active. Now if anyone came in and tried to remove it the bomb would detonate prematurely. He went to the window, looked down, sucked in his breath.

Below in the courtyard, Stan had decided he needed a spot of fresh air. On his way out Butler had noticed a bulge under the sneering thug's armpit. Stan was carrying some kind of gun in a shoulder holster. Butler checked his watch.

Four minutes to detonation.

Stan was smoking a cigarette, had opened the gates, was gazing along the road.

Three minutes to detonation.

Fred Brown had appeared now. He strolled over to Stan. They were chatting. Butler's hands inside his gloves were sweating. He ran to the door, turned the handle. It was locked. He ran back to the window. Stan was stubbing out his cigarette with his foot. He continued chatting with Fred.

Two minutes to detonation.

The phone rang in the reception area. Both men went back inside. Butler climbed out, half-slithered down the ancient wall, a long piece of ivy came loose in his left hand, he held on with his right hand, grasped some more ivy with his left, slithering down and down, never losing his grip. His feet hit the ground. With the satchel over his shoulder he ran for the exit, not caring that his pounding feet made a noise on the gravel.

'Hey, you! Stop! I said stop . . .!'

Stan the Snake's voice. Butler ran out between the open gates, covering the ground along the road like a marathon runner. *Boom!* He heard the detonation. Much louder than he'd expected. The whole turret exploded outwards, hurling chunks of shattered masonry everywhere. Some of it landed in the road behind Butler. He risked a quick look back. Through a gap in the trees he saw relics of stone like jagged teeth where the turret had reared up.

He was nearing the point where the track led off into the forest when bullets hit the road. Rounding a bend, he dived up the track inside the forest. He could hear feet pounding on the road, coming closer. He thought as he ran. There would be no time to drag his motorcycle out of the undergrowth before his pursuers arrived. Breathing heavily, he slipped behind the massive trunk of a tall tree, his hand feeling inside his satchel. He grabbed a shrapnel grenade, released the safety mechanism.

He could hear feet thumping nearer along the crumpled bracken on the path. He waited, timing his movement carefully. When he peered round the trunk Stan, holding a handgun, was near. Immediately behind him Fred was running towards him, holding a machine-pistol which he was handling clumsily. Stan stopped in surprise as he saw Butler's head. Fred bumped into him.

Butler lobbed the grenade. His aim was perfect. It landed at Stan's feet, exploded. Butler stared. Stan jumped off the ground, jerked his arms in the air. Butler had never seen anything like it. Stan's corpse fell face forward on to the path. Behind him Fred's right arm was hanging down, covered in blood. Fred staggered, turned away, stumbled back along the path towards the chateau. He was still on his feet when Butler last saw him, dragging his way back along the road.

Butler used gloves to drag his motorcycle out of the

prickly undergrowth. He wheeled the machine back to the road, over the machine-pistol Fred had dropped. Sitting astride the saddle, Butler was glad as he switched on the engine that no guests had been hurt when the turret had exploded – he had been the only guest left. His fake limping leg had saved him from suspicion.

The vital communications link between Slovakia and certain other transmitting stations in France, Germany and Britain had been destroyed. Butler raced off, headed down the curving road descending from Mount Salève to Geneva. He was making for the airport, following Tweed's instructions.

45

Hassan had reluctantly decided to let his three guests out of their rooms to enjoy drinks on the terrace looking out over Austria. He had been forced to take this decision because he couldn't stand the pressure. Tina had started the upheaval. Picking up a small stone statuette she had used it to hammer nonstop on the locked door, and the noise had echoed along the corridor to the other suites.

'Let me out of this bloody prison or I'll smash every window,' she had screamed at the top of her voice, beside herself with rage.

When Hassan unlocked the door, opened it, she threw the statuette at him. He just caught it before it hit him and smashed to pieces on the wood-block floor which, unlike the entrance hall, had no carpet. He stared at her, appalled.

'Do you know how much this statuette is worth? It was dug up out of the desert and is thousands of years old.'

'I don't give a damn for the silly thing. I'm going out on to the terrace,' she shouted. 'I hate this flaming log cabin you call a house. Get out of my way.'

Picking up a bottle of wine she had perched next to the wall she pushed past him. She was shouting insults at him as she went past the doors to the other suites on her left. Karin Berg heard her and began hammering on her own locked door with her clenched fist. Sighing, Hassan put the statuette on a side table in the corridor and unlocked Karin's door.

'If you'd just waited I was coming to get you,' he said as she came out.

'Well, you've come, so everyone is happy,' she said calmly, 'I'd like to go for a walk – that means letting me out of the front entrance.'

'You can join my other guests on the terrace. You'll have the view I understood you wanted. Josip will bring you a selection of drinks.'

'Is he still here? Last time he couldn't understand one word of any European language. What is he? An Uzbek?'

Without waiting for a reply she followed Tina out onto the terrace. In one respect Hassan had understood his 'guests'. Intending to let them out onto the terrace later, he had had three tables placed well apart. Tina, holding her bottle, grabbed a glass off a tray Josip was bringing and stalked out. She chose a remote table to the left, sat down, poured herself a drink. She took no notice whatsoever of the panoramic view.

Karin, on the contrary, immediately walked down the steps to the narrow lower level. Gazing into Austria, shading her eyes against the blazing sun, she then looked down. She was on the edge of the ancient quarry and its rock wall fell vertically below her three hundred feet. Not suffering from vertigo, she looked at the litter of huge boulders far below.

'It's like a desert,' she said to herself. 'Now how can I persuade Hassan to let me out of the front entrance? To hell with the thirty thousand if he won't pay up.'

Shielding her eyes again, she searched the sky. She had heard the steady beat of a helicopter somewhere. Unable to locate it, she walked back, sat down at the table as far away as possible from Tina.

Hassan had decided he might as well release Simone Carnot. She said nothing when he unlocked her door and invited her to visit the terrace. When she saw the two women already seated outside she took out a mirror from her handbag, used her hand to adjust her flaming red hair. With no other option, she sat down at the centre table, thankful it was well apart from the other two women.

Hassan had gone back to his office. He felt it vital to pass on the reports in the newspaper to the Head of State. He sat before the communications console after placing earphones over his head. His temper was not lessened by his reception.

'The Head of State is in conference with his generals. He is not to be disturbed.'

'This is I, Hassan. I have urgent news. Put me through to my father at once.'

'The Head of State is not to be disturbed—'

'I'll have your head on a plate!'

In a frenzy, Hassan broke the connection. He had recognized the voice of a man who called himself Secretary-General. He fawned over the Head of State at every opportunity, hoping for more power. In desperation Hassan worked at the console, calling up the centre at the Château d'Avignon. There was no reply. The line seemed to be down. Frustrated almost beyond endurance, he returned to his seat behind his desk and crashed down both clenched fists on its surface.

'I think Tweed is in one of those cars,' said Vitorelli while he looked through his field glasses. 'We are at the right place at the right time.'

Inside the helicopter Mario was at the controls while Vitorelli sat beside him, scanning the bleakness of Burgenland through the binoculars. As they came closer he swivelled his focus on to the terrace of the house on the mountain. Mario heard him suck in his breath.

'What is it, Chief?'

'I can—'

Vitorelli broke off what he was saying as though unable to say any more. Mario glanced at him and saw he was sitting rigidly as though made of concrete.

'Is something wrong?' Mario pressed.

'On that terrace I can clearly see Tina sitting with two other women. I do believe The Sisterhood is there – all of them. And after all this time I have tracked Tina.'

His tone was ice-cold. He was still sitting in the same rigid position. Mario thought he had never seen Emilio, always so full of life and restless, stay so still for so long.

'Carry out the plan,' Vitorelli eventually said, so quietly that Mario, listening through his earphones, had to ask Vitorelli to repeat what he'd said into the microphone. Changing course, it was Mario who spotted something odd in an area between Tweed's three cars and the border of Slovakia.

'There is something strange in that field of vineyards. They look like men sprawled flat on the ground between the rows near the road.'

Vitorelli focused his glasses, stared intently through the lenses. Then he lowered the binoculars and sucked in one of his deep breaths.

470

'They *are* men. Lying flat on the soil. And by their sides they have weapons. Tweed has led me to my objective – without realizing it. One good turn deserves another . . .'

He gave Mario a fresh instruction and again the chopper changed course.

The three cars were, at that moment, well spaced out. In the lead car Marler was behind the wheel. Inside Tweed's car Paula was gazing up at the distant chopper which was coming closer now.

'This is a repeat performance of what I experienced when Valja drove me out here,' she said. 'As I told you, there was this helicopter in the sky further south.'

'Vitorelli,' Tweed replied. 'I rather expected he'd put in an appearance.'

'But what is he doing? Look at the machine.'

Some distance ahead of the car Marler was driving, the chopper was hovering over a field. Then it began behaving in an odd manner. The helicopter, staying over the same piece of ground, climbed a hundred or so feet, then dropped again. It repeated the manoeuvre three times. Then it gained greater altitude and flew towards Slovakia.

'What on earth?' exclaimed Paula.

Marler had caught on to what the pilot of the chopper was trying to tell him. He rammed his foot down, raced at high speed past the marked field, glancing to his right. Several of the stumpy vines quivered, yet there was not a hint of a breeze. Rather the sun was beating down on the plain, turning it into a furnace. Marler slowed down, spoke into his mobile.

'Enemy ambush. I'm turning back. Laager! Laager! Laager!'

They had practised this manoeuvre, had used it in

the past in action. It was based on the tactics of the Boer War when the enemy had formed its wagons into a circle, creating a small fortress, difficult to attack.

'You heard that, Pete,' Newman said urgently into his mobile.

'I'm coming.' Nield replied.

Marler had performed a swift U-turn, was hurtling back towards them. A few hundred yards away he stopped, slanting his car at an angle. Newman rushed towards him, braked only feet from Marler's car, swivelled his car to form the second side of the laager. Nield came up behind them, positioned his vehicle to close the third side.

Everyone left their cars, crouched down inside the protected triangle created by the three cars. A dozen yards or so from the verge of the road men were rising up out of the field like something out of a legend, holding machine-pistols. Marler shouted the order.

'Use smoke bombs! A lot of them! Here we go!'

As he'd started to speak Paula grabbed a smoke bomb from her shoulder bag, handed it to Tweed. She was grasping another bomb when Tweed stood up, arm and hand over his right shoulder like the bowler in cricket he had once been. His bomb landed just in front of Big Ben, exploded. Acrid, choking dark smoke burst in all directions. Ben couldn't see, couldn't breathe. Paula hurled her bomb. At the same time the others were throwing more bombs. They aimed them in different directions, covering the group of advancing killers.

'We'll take them as they come out of the smoke,' shouted Newman.

He had already left the laager, a knuckleduster over the fingers of his left hand, his right holding the Smith & Wesson. Behind him Tweed rushed across the field at astonishing speed, heading for another edge of the black cloud. Paula and Nield spread out while Marler ran round the far side of the cloud.

A tall stumbling figure emerged from the smoke near Newman. It was Big Ben, his machine-pistol clutched under his arm. Seeing Newman, he managed a croaking bellow.

'Rudge . . . here . . . they are . . .'

Newman hit him on the bridge of the nose with the knuckleduster. Ben, face covered in blood, sagged to the ground. Paula saw Newman bending over the body, checked the neck pulse, realized the man was dead. Paula ran towards Newman, Browning in her hand. She had seen Rudge *crawling* out of the smoke, a handkerchief he had spat into covering his nose. Blinking, he stood up behind Newman, lifting his machine-pistol. Paula hammered the muzzle of her gun down on the back of Rudge's head with such force it bounced off his skull. The large fat man dropped his weapon. He fell forward, hitting the ground hard. Paula felt his pulse. He was dead.

A thug stumbled out of the smoke within feet of Tweed. His eyes were streaming as he fumbled with his weapon, waving it about futilely. Tweed kicked him in the groin. The thug bent forward, choking. Standing behind him, both hands clasped together, Tweed brought them down on the back of his neck. The thug collapsed.

At the far side of the cloud, leaderless, two more men came out of the cloud. One tried to aim his machine-pistol when he saw Marler. Stooping, Marler used the barrel of his Armalite like a club, smashing it against his opponent's kneecaps. The other man moved as though drunk. Marler brought the barrel down on his head. The thug curled up on the ground, lay very still. Swinging round, Marler saw the first thug lying on the soil, trying to aim his weapon. Marler jumped on his hands. Releasing his weapon, the thug yelled with pain, opened his mouth and took in more smoke. He rolled his eyes, closed them, lay lifeless. The last man, a handkerchief tied round his face, walked out, his machine-pistol held steady. He looked to his left. The wrong way. He had almost walked into Nield to his right. Nield hit him hard on the side of the neck with his stiffened hand. It was like striking a man with an iron bar. He fell, his head twisted in a grotesque position.

Stepping back from the smoke cloud, Tweed's team stood and waited. Gradually the smoke settled, became a thin transparent smear. It was obvious they had dealt with the whole gang. Tweed waved for his men to return to the cars. He spoke when they had all come back. Paula, who had accompanied him, stood by his side.

'Not a shot fired. That's very good.'

It was one of Tweed's key maxims, one he had dinned into his team on many previous occasions. 'Don't shoot unless you have to.'

Tweed stood in the road with Paula. He waited until Marler had manoeuvred his car and driven off ahead. At the same time Nield steered his car until it was pointed towards the east, then sat still. Paula pointed, her voice full of anxiety.

'Oh, Lord. Look at the chopper. It's on fire.'

Heading close to Slovakia, the helicopter was trailing smoke from its tail. It wobbled, then disappeared behind and beyond the mountain where the strange house stood like a toy building. Tweed shook his head before getting into the car which had Newman already behind the wheel.

'No, it isn't crashing. We still have a way to go before we're close to our objective. Let's get moving.' He nodded towards the field they had just left. 'That rates another anonymous call to the police.'

46

'What the hell is happening?' Tina demanded. 'Is that field on fire? Not that it matters – just a few mouldy old vines.'

It mattered to Hassan, who stood near the edge of the lower level below the terrace. He had been watching through field glasses for several minutes. He had sprung his trap. Now he was struggling to keep his nerve.

To the naked eye the three cars stationary on the road were like miniatures. Seen through his field glasses they were only too real. In disbelief, he continued watching as the smoke cloud cleared. He had his greatest shock when he saw clearly Tweed standing in the road next to Paula. He lowered the binoculars, hardly able to stop his hands trembling. Tweed was now close to his headquarters.

'Oh, look,' trilled Tina, 'that helicopter is on fire. And it is coming this way. It's not going to crash on this house, is it?'

'No, it's veering away,' Hassan said in a strangled voice.

'Could be exciting if we saw it crash in the fields.'

'Shut your mouth.'

'People don't talk to me like that.'

'I told you to shut your face.'

'I'm leaving here.'

'Sit down before I shove you off the cliff.'

Tina was taken aback. She had never heard Hassan speak with such ferocity. She sat down, watched the helicopter, which was still fairly high up. More smoke billowed out and now it was wobbling. Everyone was silent as the machine flew beyond the house, lost altitude and disappeared behind the ridge of the mountain, diving into Slovakia.

'I'd like another drink,' said Tina, expecting Hassan to refill her glass.

'The bottle is on the table,' Hassan said quietly.

He went back inside the house and summoned the chief of the elite force of eight guards who stayed out of sight. Hassan had had the house built as his headquarters. He had specified it must have the character of a house in Slovakia, so undue attention would not be drawn to it.

'Tell your men to be on the alert,' he ordered. 'If anyone tries to break in, shoot them down without mercy. Take no prisoners. All the guards must remain inside the house in their normal tactical positions.'

Tweed had been right when he said the helicopter was not crashing. Once out of sight of the long house behind a ridge, Mario landed the machine where it was invisible to any watchers. Vitorelli had photographed the landing point when he had last flown over the area on the day when Paula had been driven by Valja.

They left the machine when they had loaded the backpacks they had brought with them. With Vitorelli in the lead, they made their way to the sunken path climbing the mountain near the eastern end of the house. This was the path Karin Berg had discovered on her training visit.

The heat was intense as the sun glared down on the path but they climbed it rapidly. Reaching the top, Vitorelli crouched down behind a boulder. The photographs he had taken earlier from every angle, which he had studied so carefully, had shown him accurately the curious construction of the headquarters.

Due to a backward slope at the top of the mountain the men from the east who had built the house had erected the front on short squat stilts. The necessity to do this had left apertures under the building at the eastern end. Vitorelli studied the apertures quickly through his binoculars.

'We can crawl along the ground on our bellies,' he told Mario. 'In no time we will be under the house. We must work quickly. We must keep our bodies flat on the ground so they seem part of that ground. We must move from boulder to boulder.

'You have told me this before,' Mario grumbled in a whisper.

'I tell you again. We shall only get one chance. And on the way back we do the same thing. There will be an impulse to hurry. We do not hurry.'

'You repeat yourself again.'

'Because it is so important.'

'I had realized that!'

'Keep your voice down.'

The last remark was a sign of the tension Vitorelli was labouring under. They had carried on the conversation in whispers. Dragging their backpacks alongside them – perched on their backs the packs would have made them more visible – they slithered like snakes over the arid ground. Here and there boulders were scattered. With Mario following, Vitorelli slithered from one boulder to another, forcing himself to move slowly when he was exposed in the open.

The sun scorched them with blowtorch intensity. Accustomed as they were to the heat in Italy neither man had ever experienced such high temperatures. Their bodies were covered with sweat. Their clothes were already sodden. Then it happened when they were halfway from the top of the path to the house.

They heard the heavy, steel-lined front door being unlocked and opened. Vitorelli lay still behind a boulder he had reached. He hoped Mario was not in the open but dared not look back. He felt sure guards were coming out to patrol.

There were guards, carrying machine-pistols. Two of them had opened the door and stood in the entrance surveying the arid desert. A wall of heat flooded over them. The head guard grimaced and shook his head. Despite Hassan's orders he had intended checking the front of the house. He spoke to the other guard.

'It is too hot to go out there. No one is about. It would be pointless to search for nothing.'

Behind his boulder Vitorelli heard the voices clearly but he did not understand a word. The guard had spoken in a strange language. He held himself absolutely still, although he had cramp in his left leg. The pain was agonizing but he refused to move. Then he heard the door close, several locks being turned. He waited for the crunch of feet on the stony ground, then realized they had returned inside. He stretched his left leg several times, reached back and rubbed his calf with his hand. The cramp disappeared.

Mario had watched all this through a slit between two boulders close together. He began to slither forward again as he saw Vitorelli moving. They had to move very slowly because they made a noise passing over the stony ground. It was a nerve-racking progress, so slow while the sun continued to roast them.

Vitorelli was careful not to move any faster when he left the last boulder behind. Now he had to move across open ground between the boulder and the house. He could hardly believe it when he slipped through one of the apertures between stilts supporting this end of the house. Mario joined him sooner than he had expected.

They lay still for a short time, recovering. It was hot under the house but seemed incredibly cool now the sun could no longer get at them. They communicated with mimes and gestures.

'We lay the bombs well apart,' Vitorelli indicated, waving a hand, pointing to one location and then another.

All the bombs, some high explosive, some thermite, were linked together with a thin cable. The first job Vitorelli had to do was to link up one of his bombs to one of Mario's. It was a tricky undertaking and he first took out a comparatively dry handkerchief to wipe his streaming hands dry. It was dark under the house but gradually their eyes became accustomed to being out of the sun and they could see clearly.

Vitorelli worked partly by feel. It took longer than he had expected to complete the connection but then all the bombs were linked up. He sighed, the first time he had expressed any kind of emotion. Then he froze. Footsteps echoed above their heads. People were walking about inside the house, possibly guards.

'We shall have to be very quiet. If we can hear their footsteps down here then they may hear us slithering about on all these loose stones under the house.'

Vitorelli indicated this message by pointing upwards with his two index fingers, then cupping hands to his ears, then spreading his hands to emphasize the rubble they would have to slither across. Mario kept nodding his head to show not only that he understood but also would Vitorelli please shut up so they could get on with the job. His boss grinned, nodded back. They began their work.

Each man, watching the cable carefully, placed a

bomb under a different part of the house. Slimmer than Mario, Vitorelli carried bombs to the other end of the house. It was difficult. The slope which had caused the builders to erect the eastern section on squat stilts ended close to the front door. There was now less space to slither along and the house was pressing down on him. He had placed the last bomb when he realized he couldn't work his way back. The floor was pressing down on his shoulder blades. He waved a hand, hoping Mario would realize he was trapped.

The next thing he knew was Mario's strong hands had grasped each of his ankles, was gently hauling him backwards. Vitorelli expected that at the least he would suffer bruised shoulder blades but Mario had been slow and careful. Reaching the eastern end Vitorelli stretched himself. No damage.

The last – vital – thing he had to do was to place the transmitter linked to the bombs. Holding the square box, he poked his head out, saw no one, placed it at the eastern corner and elevated the aerial which would receive the signal and detonate the bombs. It was no accident that the prominent aerial, extended outside the house, was the same colour as the house's wall.

They now had to return the way they had come. As Vitorelli, taking the lead, emerged into the open the sun's heat hit him like a blow after the apparent coolness under the house. Gritting his teeth, he headed back for the first boulder.

It seemed to take them twice as long to cover the ground as it had coming. Vitorelli had to strain every nerve of his willpower not to hurry. The ground itself was almost too hot to touch and by now both men were close to exhaustion. With Mario behind him Vitorelli forced his aching body to keep moving. His sodden clothes were caked with dust and he had a pounding headache.

Unexpectedly, he found himself on the edge of the sunken path. He rolled down into it, lay still for a few minutes revitalizing himself until Mario arrived. They said nothing to each other for a short time. Then Vitorelli laughed and spoke.

'Come on. Don't go to sleep. Back to the chopper.'

Still aching, they made their way back down the path, reached the bottom, turned left away from the house to where the chopper was standing. Vitorelli opened a door to the control cabin, climbed up, sat in the co-pilot's seat. From beneath the seat he lifted out a black control box and elevated the aerial. When he pressed a switch it would send a signal to the receiver next to the house, a signal which would transmit simultaneously to every bomb and detonate it.

'Take her up high,' he ordered Mario, already seated at the controls.

The main rotor started to turn, whizzed round faster and faster in conjunction with the tail rotor which guided the machine. The Sikorsky began to climb, climb, climb.

47

The three cars moved steadily along the road, drawing closer and closer to Slovakia. In the middle car Tweed sat next to Paula, who was now driving. In a rear seat Newman, Smith & Wesson in his hand, kept gazing at the fields on either side for any sign of a fresh attack.

'I don't think anything else will happen, Bob,' Tweed called back, guessing what was in Newman's mind. 'Hassan has shot his bolt.'

'Be prepared. The Boy Scout's motto,' Newman

retorted. 'It's always dangerous to make assumptions where safety is concerned.'

'You are right,' Tweed admitted.

Looking ahead, seeing Marler's car in the distance, Paula was blinking at the shimmering heat haze sizzling over the plain in the far distance. She had the car's visor pulled down to shield her eyes against the dazzling light.

'I think it's hotter than when I was last here,' she said. 'And it's incredible the way this plain goes on for ever.'

'Well, this is one of the areas Genghis Khan and his hordes of men on small shaggy horses swept across towards Europe,' Tweed commented. 'Or rather, it was his successor, Ogdai, who reached Liegnitz in Germany, only two hundred and fifty miles from the Channel. There he was at long last defeated by a mixed European army. What happened before could happen again – and this time succeed.'

'You give me the shivers,' Paula told him. 'I wonder what Hassan is doing at this moment?'

As she spoke Hassan was inside his office desperately trying to communicate the news he had heard to the Head of State. And again the Secretary-General was blocking him off.

'The Head of State cannot be disturbed. He is in a meeting with his generals.'

Hassan called him a filthy name and broke the connection. He need not have worried. Enemy aircraft patrolling in the sky above the Indian Ocean had seen the vast array of the US Fifth Fleet, now backed by a second massive aircraft carrier group, moving north at top speed. They had seen a British nuclear submarine surface and fire a trial missile without a warhead to the south. They had reported this menacing development to their home base. Which was why the Head of State was conferring with his nervous generals endlessly.

Frustrated, in a ferocious rage, Hassan had stormed out of his office. To calm down, he had walked slowly along the corridor and out onto the terrace. The three members of The Sisterhood were still sitting at separate tables, hardly exchanging a word with each other.

'There are three cars coming towards us,' said Tina.

Hassan snatched up a drink which she had just poured for herself and swallowed it. Then he grabbed a pair of field glasses off her table.

'For your information,' she protested, 'that was my drink – and I was just going to use those binoculars.'

Hassan ignored her. He screwed the glasses to his eyes and scanned each car. The vehicles were close enough now for him to see who was inside each of them. He slammed the binoculars down on Tina's table. For a moment he couldn't get the words out.

'Tweed is in that middle car. He's coming to attack the house. He will end up stone cold dead.'

'Can I watch it happen, then?' Tina enquired.

'Don't be so grisly, dear,' said Karin, speaking for the first time.

'I was talking to Hassan, not you,' Tina snapped.

'We're all guilty,' Simone said quietly.

'Speak for yourself,' Tina snapped back.

'I'm speaking for all of us,' Simone replied in the same quiet tone.

'You'd do better to keep your mouth shut,' Tina retorted.

She stood up and walked down to the lower level to get away from the other women. Hassan followed her, passed her, stood close to the edge, raised his glasses again. He was hypnotized by the fact that Tweed was still alive.

What had happened to the Croats in Morzach? he wondered. What had happened to Big Ben and his experienced killers? The Sisterhood on the terrace had seen the smoke cloud but it had been so far away they hadn't been able to make out what was going on. As he stood, glaring through his glasses, Hassan suddenly felt movement under his feet. He stepped back quickly as a small part of the cliff gave way. Frightened, he returned to the terrace where Tina, seeing what had occurred, had run to.

'What's that noise?' she said. Turning to the east she giggled. 'Look, that helicopter didn't crash. It's coming back.'

'Probably tourists,' Hassan said in a bored tone. 'We get a few occasionally. A travel outfit in Vienna charges a fortune for the trip.'

'When do I get my binoculars back?' Tina demanded. 'Now!'

He shoved them at her. He was angry, confused, indecisive. He planned to make sure the Secretary-General had an accident – a fatal one – when he got back home. The arrival of Tweed, even though still a distance away, seemed a bad omen. The rock fall from the cliff edge worried him.

When he had had his headquarters built, disguising it as typical Slovakian architecture, he had flown in builders from his home state. They had worked much faster than Europeans would have done. But he had also brought the surveyors who had checked the site from home and now he had the vague fear they had not known their job.

Tina remained standing at the edge of the terrace, close to the lower level. She wanted to be away from the women, away from Hassan who had no manners at all. She was furious that he had taken her drink – and then her binoculars – without asking her permission.

Something was happening to the three spaced-out cars. Puzzled, she watched them, wishing she had picked up the binoculars from her table. Glancing back, she saw Hassan standing near to her. She had no intention of asking him for the binoculars. She did not even want to go near him.

Inside the middle car Tweed was staring upward into the sky. He was about to ask for the mobile when Paula spoke, her tone one of surprise and disbelief.

'That helicopter's reappeared. It must have been all right. And it's climbing to quite a height.'

'Hand me the mobile, please,' said Tweed. He called Marler first. 'I'm waiting here. Come back quickly.' He then called Nield. 'Close up on me. Now!' He then spoke to Paula. 'Stop here.'

As soon as the car was stationary he got out. Standing in the road, a pair of binoculars looped round his neck, he waited as Marler returned, got out of his car, followed by Nield from behind them. Paula had run round the front to join him.

'What's wrong?' she asked.

'Something dreadful is about to occur.'

'What do you mean?'

Without replying he raised the binoculars and focused them on the house at the top of the mountain. Newman, who also had binoculars, followed suit.

'Will someone tell me what is going on?' demanded Paula, exasperated.

'You will see,' Tweed replied in a blank voice.

She stared at the house. Then she switched her gaze to the helicopter which had started to fly away. Aboard the machine Vitorelli was staring down at the house. Without looking, he pressed down the switch which transmitted the radio signal. The result was instantaneous. All the high-explosive bombs and the thermite bombs detonated together.

485

There was a deafening roar which echoed across the plain. A wall of flame enveloped the rear of the house. The high explosive lifted the roof which fell forward. The entire house from one end to the other toppled like a stage set towards the terrace. The unstable ground was shifted by the force of the explosion. It began to give way, a gigantic slab of rock carried the terrace to the edge of the quarry face. Through his glasses Tweed caught sight of The Sisterhood and Hassan, still on the terrace, caught up in the massive landslide. Several men carrying weapons had run out onto the terrace. Guards, Tweed presumed. In the chaos of flames and terrifying movement of the ground The Sisterhood and Hassan vanished.

Then they witnessed an awesome sight. A portion of the mountain a hundred yards wide, which had supported house and terrace, slid forward like a moving platform. It crashed down the three-hundred-foot drop, hit the base of the quarry like an immense clap of thunder. A vast cloud of dust rose into the air as huge chunks of rock were hurled in all directions. For the third time Paula asked Tweed to give her the binoculars.

'No!'

He thought he had seen one of the women, clothes on fire, flailing her arms as she dropped like a marionette when the slab had plunged downwards. It was so terrible he didn't want Paula to see it. Newman, like Tweed, still stood with his glasses glued to his eyes.

They all stood watching it, not moving. It took some time for the dense cloud of dust to settle, to expose what had been hidden behind it. Only then did Tweed hand the glasses to Paula. At the base of the quarry an incredibly high mass of debris had appeared. Tweed was sure all the bodies would be deep under the pile. The whole shape of the quarry wall had been altered. A great curve of rock face was now indented into what had been a sheer straight face. There was no trace of the house left, the terrace had vanished. It was as though there had never been a long strange building perched at the summit.

'I don't believe it,' said Paula. 'It's all gone.'

'And now we must go,' Tweed told everyone. He had glanced to the south and the helicopter was no more than a diminishing dot in the sky. 'Get back into the cars, everyone.'

'Where are we going to?' asked Paula.

'I had a call from Monica just before I left the Sacher. We fly to London, then we drive straight down to Dorset.'

'Dorset?'

'There are two men near Shrimpton I want to interview.'

48

In the late afternoon Newman was driving Tweed and Paula down to Dorset. After returning from the collapsed cliff in Slovakia they had avoided Vienna, motoring direct to Schwechat Airport. From there they had caught a flight to Zurich where they had changed planes and flown on to Heathrow.

Tweed had spent a short time with the Director, Howard, then he had left for Dorset. Butler had earlier arrived at Park Crescent, as instructed by Tweed after destroying the communications turret at the Château d'Avignon. Marler and Newman, who had flown back with Tweed, had gone home to get some sleep.

'How do you know both Willie and Amos are back in Dorset?' asked Paula.

'Because at Park Crescent I called Chief Inspector

Buchanan. You may remember I arranged for Roy to go down with his side-kick, Sergeant Warden, to investigate the strange village of Shrimpton.'

'I do remember. Seems ages ago. Did they find anything?'

'Yes. Patrol cars had to be called in urgently from all over the county – many with armed men inside them. Buchanan had discovered those silent houses in the village were the hiding place of saboteurs – trained thugs from London and the North. They were waiting to travel to a certain Midlands town where they'd have collected containers of deadly bacillus to distribute to reservoirs all over Britain.'

'Bacillus!' Paula exclaimed. 'How horrific.'

'Roy Buchanan had them all rounded up in Shrimpton and carted off for intensive questioning. Some of them broke. Their controller was a man called Conway.'

'Who *is* Conway?'

'That's what we're going to Dorset to find out. Both Amos and Willie are back in their homes. Roy checked that out.'

'Is Conway that important?'

'I think,' Tweed said grimly, 'he is the mastermind behind the whole vast operation which was planned to be launched from the East.'

'I can't see either Amos or Willie being Conway,' Paula replied.

'It could be a third party,' said Tweed. 'Not something I want to speculate on any more.'

Well, it is a glorious day, Paula thought. The sun was shining in a clear blue sky. It was very warm for Britain, but the heat was nothing like what they had endured on the plain on their way to Slovakia.

'You are both armed?' Tweed asked suddenly.

'A Smith & Wesson in my hip holster,' Newman assured him.

'And I picked up a Browning while we were at Park Crescent,' said Paula.

'Good.'

Sitting in the back next to Tweed, Paula was as surprised as Newman. It was rare for Tweed to put such a question when they were on what they both assumed would be a peaceful visit.

'It could be very dangerous,' Tweed remarked.

'Well, we've experienced plenty of danger already abroad,' Paula pointed out.

'So,' Tweed hammered home, 'it would be easy to be complacent on home ground.'

'I'm so glad to be on home ground. Dorset is a beautiful county. It's such a relief to be back among gently rolling hills with here and there a clump of trees. I'm feeling less tense already.'

Tweed grunted, gave her a look. She decided she'd better be more careful what she said. It was early evening as they entered the old town of Dorchester, driving through the narrow main street lined with buildings which had been built centuries before. As he reached the far outskirts Newman turned north on the road to Yeovil. Soon he was looking for the turning on his left. He had passed the road to Evershot and later he saw the signpost. *Shrimpton.*

Tweed's warning remarks had gradually sunk in to both Newman and Paula. There was an edgy silence inside the car as he drove down the tree-lined lane. There was no other traffic and Paula had the odd sense of entering a secret world. They could see the first houses in the distance, the beginning of High Lane, the main street Tweed and Newman had walked down during their earlier visit before heading into Europe. Tweed leaned forward.

'Bob, can you pull into that field as you did before? I'd like to walk down the street, again as we did before. We'll call in at that pub, the Dog and Whistle.'

When Newman had backed his Mercedes into the field they all got out. The cobbled street was so narrow the sun no longer shone on them. It was close to dusk. Paula was struck by the heavy silence of the atmosphere as she walked alongside Tweed. He glanced at her, seemed to read her mind.

'Just like the silence of Morzach before the Croats attacked us.'

'There's no one about. It's eerie. And look at the cottages. They don't look occupied.'

'They are empty now. Buchanan cleared out the saboteurs. It seemed like this when we last here. Remember, Bob?'

'Yes, I certainly do. And to think these places were full of saboteurs. They must have kept very quiet.'

'Look at the frayed net curtains,' Paula commented in a quiet voice. It was a place where you naturally whispered. 'I'd have said no one had lived here for years.'

'Which was the impression we were supposed to get,' said Tweed. 'Mr Conway thought of almost everything. Here's the pub.'

They went inside and the men sitting behind benches were again farm-workers, chatting in subdued tones. The same barman was behind the counter.

'Back again, sir,' he said cheerfully. 'I never forget a face.'

'I'll have a mild and bitter,' said Tweed to merge into the atmosphere. 'What about you two?'

Paula ordered an orange juice while Newman plumped for a Scotch. Tweed stayed by the bar after paying, continued talking to the barman as he sipped the drink.

'I believe my friends are back. Wellesley Carrington for one.'

'The Cap'n. Yes, he's at home again in Dovecote

Manor. Funny thing is he hasn't been in here. Usually comes here when he gets back from abroad.'

'I seem to recall you said he was a bit of a one for the ladies,' Newman reminded him. 'Probably got a girl-friend or two he's entertaining.'

'Don't think so.' The barman was polishing a glass. 'The postman was in here when he came off duty. He'd delivered one of those registered envelopes, a thick one. Said the Cap'n was on his own. In a bit of a mood, the postman said.'

'Then there's my other friend, Amos Lodge,' Tweed remarked.

'Oh, he's back, too. Got back after the Cap'n. Imagine he'd been abroad too. Brown as a berry. Haven't seen him since he returned to The Minotaur.'

'It struck me the names ought to be reversed,' Tweed said casually. 'The Minotaur would be a better name for Dovecote Manor with all that weird statuary and lakes Carrington has in his large garden.'

'Funny you should say that.' The barman leaned on the counter, lowered his voice. 'You remember Jed, who was here last time you were here? He used to do the garden for Amos. He tried to get the Cap'n to give him some work, saw round the crazy garden. The Cap'n wouldn't take him on, said he preferred to look after the place himself. Likes his privacy.'

'Well, I think we'd better be going,' said Tweed after checking his watch. 'Sorry to leave the drink, but I had one in another pub and I'm driving.'

'You're wise. We hadn't see the police for years. Then recently in the middle of the night they raided all the cottages. No idea why.'

'Oh, there was one more thing,' Tweed added. 'Last time you said the whole village was owned by a man called Shafto, that he rented out the cottages. Ever heard the name Conway?'

'Never. Drive carefully.'

Keeping up with Paula, who was striding out, they hurried back up High Lane. To Paula, watching her footing on the cobbles, High Lane seemed to go on for ever. The only sound was that of their footfalls.

'You're stepping it out,' Newman remarked.

'I don't like this place,' said Paula. 'Gives me the creeps.'

'Ghosts from long ago,' suggested Tweed.

'I can do without any more remarks like that,' she retorted. 'I have the feeling something awful happened here long ago.'

'Shafto. Conway,' mused Newman. 'Why the different names?'

'Because Mr Conway is a devious and secretive man,' Tweed told them. 'Here's the car. Do you want to drive, Paula?'

'I'd sooner Bob went on driving.'

'We'll go and see Willie first. While he's still here,' said Tweed as he settled himself in the back with Paula.

Newman drove through the village and past the pub at a moderate speed. He remembered the way to Dovecote Manor and they had left the village behind as he approached the entrance. Again the gold-painted wrought-iron gates were open and beyond them the curving drive led up to the Georgian house.

Glare lights attached to the whole of the front of the house were on. Tweed couldn't remember seeing them when he had last visited Willie so they must have been installed recently. He wondered why. Again a new red Porsche was parked on the tarred turn-round close to the entrance. There were lights on inside the house.

'So, we come full circle,' Newman commented as he parked behind the Porsche. 'This is where it all started.'

'No, it isn't,' contradicted Paula. 'It started when I was in Vienna, standing in a courtyard in Annagasse,

watching the woman in a black robe and veil entering
and leaving Norbert Engel's building.'

As the three of them got out of the car Tweed issued
a fresh warning.

'Be ready for anything.'

49

History does repeat itself, Tweed thought. He pressed
the bell, waited and when the door was opened Willie
stood framed in the entrance, wearing a navy blue
tracksuit. He smiled warmly at his visitors and ushered
them inside.

'Welcome to my humble home.'

'I don't think I have to make introductions,' replied
Tweed.

'Of course not. I do have someone with me but you
are still most welcome.'

He *has* got a girlfriend with him, Newman thought.
He was wrong. Willie closed the door to the panelled
hall, led Paula to an open door and into the spacious
drawing room. As she entered Amos Lodge stood up
from a large couch and began plumping up a cushion in
one corner.

'A long way from Zurich,' Amos said in his gravelly
voice. 'I expect, like me, you are all glad to be back in
England.'

'When did you fly back?' Tweed asked, sitting in a
carver chair.

'Yesterday.' Amos beckoned to Paula. 'Please do
come and join me. You really are a most attractive lady.'

'Thank you.'

Paula thought it would be more comfortable to sit in
the opposite corner of the couch. Like Amos, she shifted

a cushion so she could relax. Newman occupied another carver chair close to Tweed. From where he sat he could see through the open French windows at the back into the extensive garden as far as the strange stone arch inscribed with peculiar symbols. It was a warm evening and the open French windows freshened up the room.

'Drinks for everyone,' Willie said buoyantly. 'Paula?'

'A glass of dry white wine would go down well.'

Tweed asked for orange juice while Newman, expecting to drive, also requested orange juice. Amos had a drink he didn't recognize. Looking at her companion at the other end of the couch Paula thought he looked more square than ever. His large bulk was held erect and his eyes flashed from behind the square-rimmed glasses.

'Well, you survived,' Willie said jovially as he placed Tweed's drink on a coffee table.

'Yes, no thanks to someone,' Tweed replied.

There was an awkward silence as Willie fetched more drinks and then sprawled in an armchair, long legs stretched out and crossed at his ankles. He raised his glass.

'Here's to survival.'

'Of the good,' Tweed added.

'Odd remark that, old chap,' Willie responded. 'Don't get it.'

'Someone does,' Tweed went on, staring straight at him.

'Things looked pretty grim – maybe still do,' said Amos.

'The international crisis is over,' Tweed told him. 'I don't think the media have got hold of it yet, but I heard at Park Crescent that the Head of State has been removed from power. His generals were so alarmed at the arrival of so much naval power in the Indian Ocean they staged a coup.'

'That didn't come into my strategic calculations. But it is always the unexpected which turns the tide. I understand why the Americans reacted so quickly. What persuaded the British to send a submarine?'

'I did.'

The door bell rang and Willie excused himself. When he came back he escorted Christopher Kane into the room. Paula was astonished. Christopher caught her expression, came forward, bowed and kissed her hand. Straightening up, he looked round, chose an armchair, settled himself in it and adopted the same posture Willie had. He stretched out his long legs and crossed them at the ankles.

'*You* did?' said Amos with almost a growl.

'Did what?' Willie asked in an offhand way.

He poured Christopher a glass of red wine, knowing what his new guest liked. This time Willie sat very erect in a carver chair. He studied Tweed as he sipped his drink.

'I'm going to sound egotistical, but I can't help that,' Tweed began. 'While I was at the Château des Avenières in France I spent a long time on the phone. First, I contacted Christopher and eventually asked him to catch the first flight to London. Then I phoned the Prime Minister and explained certain developments. I had to go on at him, threatening to get in touch with CNN and the press to tell them that I had told him. To give him credit, he agreed to phone first the President in Washington, then the President of France and the Chancellor of Germany. It was fortunate that the US Fifth Fleet was in a position to sail into the Indian Ocean immediately. The PM sent a nuclear submarine to support the Fifth Fleet. It fired a trial missile from the same area. Also, a spoke was put in the wheel of a fiendish operation to poison the reservoirs in the West.'

'Poison?' Willie enquired with obvious interest.

'Bacilli.'

'What on earth have bacilli to do with it?' asked Amos.

'That was what the enemy had arranged to be put into our drinking water. The same with France and Germany. The agents who would have laced our reservoirs with bacilli were lodged in Shrimpton. The villain is a local man called Conway.'

'Conway?' queried Willie. 'Never heard of him.'

'Neither has the barman at the Dog and Whistle. Which is very curious. Barmen usually know everything that's going on locally. He doesn't know of any Conway.'

'Not surprised,' Willie said. 'I'd have heard of him.'

'Would you?' Tweed asked with a smile.

'Of course I would. I go into that pub for a drink.'

'But you don't take any of your glamorous girlfriends there.'

'Of course I don't. Hardly the thing to do, old chap.'

'You knew at various times Tina Langley, Karin Berg and Simone Carnot?'

'Over a period of time, yes.'

'And where did each of these three women go when they left here?'

'With Amos. He likes women too.'

'This is nonsense,' growled Amos. 'I've never heard of any of these women.'

'Of course you have,' Willie protested angrily. 'You invited each of them back to The Minotaur to have a drink. What's the matter with you?'

'You made a mistake a few minutes ago, Amos,' Tweed interjected. 'I made a reference to naval power in the Indian Ocean. The American deployment has been widely reported, yet you said, "What persuaded the British to send a submarine?" So how do you know? Incidentally, Hassan was captured and he's trying to save his skin by telling everything. He's implicated you up to the hilt – Mr Conway.'

Amos's right hand disappeared under the cushion he had plumped up. His movement was so quick it was a blur until his hand reappeared holding a Mauser – aimed point-blank at Paula. He stood up.

'I'd hate to shoot a woman . . .'

'Then don't,' rasped Newman.

He was holding his Smith & Wesson, the muzzle pointing at Amos's chest. He remained seated as Paula stared at Amos, her eyes never leaving his. Amos moved slowly back to the open French windows. He began speaking as though orating at the Kongresshaus in Zurich.

'The West is decadent, enfeebled. It has no moral code. It is going down like the Roman Empire did when that organization gave itself over to sexual orgies, and society collapsed, as it has in the West.'

'Pull that trigger and you're a dead man,' Newman warned.

For a large man, Amos moved with great speed, vanishing out of the open French windows into the garden. Newman aimed, then lowered his gun. Amos was a shadow, zigzagging as he ran deeper into the garden, passing under the weird arch. Newman went after him followed by Paula and Tweed. As he left the room Tweed glanced back, saw Willie grab hold of a long thick walking stick.

'That's no use,' he shouted.

He ran after the others. Behind him in the drawing room Willie opened a panel in the wall, pressed down switches. Outside in the maze-like garden lights came on and illuminated the garden islands. Willie followed Tweed, holding his walking stick like a club.

'He's gone under the arch,' Paula shouted back to Tweed.

She ran under it and saw Newman ahead of her. No sign of Amos. They heard the sound of an outboard motor starting up. One of the dinghies was speeding towards the island where a weird statue of a man and woman with a serpent twined round them stood. Newman had stopped, was aiming his gun.

'He's not in the dinghy,' Paula shouted. 'He set it going to fool us!'

Newman started running again, crouching as he ran. Arriving at the second lake, with perched on another island an eight-sided temple, the windows painted black, he paused, stood in a shadow, listened. Paula heard pounding feet running at top speed behind her. It was Willie, holding his stick as though on a hike.

'Amos was out here when I got back!' he shouted. 'I think he concealed weapons.'

He charged past her after Newman, who was again running. To Paula everything seemed bizarre – the statuary, the temple illuminated by spotlights. A nightmare. Ahead of Willie, Newman reached the third lake after passing through the avenue of box hedge. At the end of the avenue he had paused again, gun gripped in both hands. He swivelled it to his left and then his right, suspecting Amos was waiting in ambush. No Amos. He ran on despite a warning shout from Willie.

'You're going into a wilderness!'

Newman slowed down, then began to creep forward through a mass of undergrowth. To his right was the third lake with another island. Perched on it was the squat Assyrian-type building and the stone plaque with the Turkish flag engraved into it. The shore of the lake was bordered by trees with thick trunks. Dense banks of reeds stretched out into the lake, seen by a searchlight projecting from the island.

As he passed one tree Amos, crouching low, appeared behind him holding a machine-pistol. He took aim at Newman's back. Paula opened her mouth to shout a warning she knew would be too late. Willie appeared behind Amos, brought down his clublike stick on Amos's shoulder. Amos dropped his weapon, started to stand up. Willie brought down the stick on his head. The large man staggered back, fell into the lake among the reeds.

Paula saw his arms struggling, waving the reeds. The arms sank. His hands struggled, disappeared below the reeds. Newman, who had turned, seen what had happened, began to strip off his jacket to go in after him. Willie gripped his arm.

'No good. You'd drown too. The reeds strangle you. I had a German shepherd dog. Went in after a swan. Just vanished. Never seen since. Amos has gone for good.'

'We can't do a thing, then?' asked Tweed, who had caught up.

'Not a thing,' said Willie. 'We'll have the lake dragged. It may take weeks to find him, if ever we do. We never found the dog.'

Epilogue

At Tweed's suggestion they were driving back to the country hotel, Summer Lodge, at Evershot, to spend the night. They had left behind Christopher, who was alert and wanted to talk to Willie. Paula felt exhausted, but her mind was still racing as Newman drove through the night.

'Did you always suspect Amos?' she asked Tweed.

'Yes and no. I was bluffing, of course, when I said Hassan was spilling the beans. We had no proof against Amos so I had to provoke him into giving himself away.'

'You didn't suspect him earlier but you did when we arrived at Willie's house?'

'The massive operation which was planned, including the killing of the men from the *Institut* – who might have eventually alerted their governments – was clearly the work of a master strategist. Which was Amos's genius. Also his attitude towards the West – especially his brilliant speech at the Kongresshaus in Zurich – suggested to me he could be the mastermind. Mind you, there are people who would agree with a lot of what he said. It was his solution – being taken over by the East – which was flawed, evil.'

'You showed great perception.'

'I can't take too much credit. Willie is an arms dealer, but also a patriot. When he discovered that bacilli were

500

to be used he reported it to Christoper who in turn reported to me. Fortunately Christopher had discovered the antidote to the bacilli. All the containers produced by a man called Harbin were lined with the antidote on Christopher's instructions. Harbin didn't know what the substance was doing, that it had eliminated the bacilli in the containers. At my suggestion over the phone from Europe, Willie pretended to be driving to Slovakia with the "sample". He called Hassan, telling him where he had reached on his trip. Actually, all the calls were made from Folkestone – in case Hassan had him watched. Customs faked a search for drugs to make Willie's story convincing. Another man, dressed like Willie, eventually drove via Le Shuttle to a place east of Paris. Harbin, by the way, is under arrest by Special Branch. His chemical plant has been sealed off.'

'So we have to thank you, Christoper and Willie.'

'Let's not forget Emilio Vitorelli. He destroyed Hassan – and in doing so also eliminated The Sisterhood.'

'I feel sorry for Vitorelli. I think he's a very unhappy man.'

'And likely to remain so for the rest of his life.'

In Rome it was dark when Mario watched as Vitorelli walked slowly along the edge of the Borghese Gardens. He walked like a man in a dream. Several attractive women looked at him but he did not see them. He continued walking with plodding steps.

Reaching the balcony which overlooks the Pincio Terrace he stopped at the exact place where he had seen his fiancée, Gina, her face bandaged from the horrific acid scars, climb on to the balcony. Too far away, he had called out to her.

She had not turned her head as she sat poised on the

balcony, then plunged to her death on the iron-hard stone of the piazza. Placing both hands on the balcony, he stared down. He was looking at the exact spot where she had hit the stone so far down. There were tears in his eyes.

He had had to identify her body before it was moved. It was a moment he would never forget. Now he had done what he had to do. He had destroyed the woman who had destroyed Gina's face. No amount of plastic surgery would have repaired the damage, a top surgeon had told her.

He gave a deep sigh. Then he began to walk slowly back to where Mario was anxiously waiting. It was the last time he ever went to the balcony. For the rest of his life he would never walk or drive through the piazza again.